MISSION WITH MOUNTBATTEN

When originally published in 1951, this book was the first full-length inside story of one of the greatest world developments of our time—the transfer of power in India by partition and consent—the reconciliation of East and West, of ruler and ruled. This *tour de force* was primarily the achievement of Lord Mountbatten's dynamic diplomacy by discussion, allied to the statesmanship of the Indian leaders. To assist him, Lord Mountbatten gathered a high-powered Staff team headed by Lord Ismay, which included Alan Campbell-Johnson as Press Attaché.

From January 1947 until June 1948, Alan Campbell-Johnson kept daily notes of his experiences. He was in the privileged position of being able to write not just from the material of others but from history of which he was a part. The result is a vivid account of the highest historical importance which records the interplay of great personalities at the hour of decision: Gandhi, saint and seer; Jinnah, the creator of Pakistan; Nehru, world figure and Prime Minister; Liaquat Ali Khan, Prime Minister of Pakistan; Vallabhbhai Patel, India's Deputy Prime Minister; Rajagopalachari, philosopher and elder statesman; and, from day to day, the indefatigable Mountbattens themselves. It is an essential book for any historian of the period.

Alan Campbell-Johnson CIE, OBE, Legion of Merit (USA), was educated at Westminster and Oxford. Between 1937 and 1940 he was political secretary to Sir Archibald Sinclair, Liberal Leader, and wrote biographies of Anthony Eden and Lord Halifax. His war service in the RAF included four years on the Headquarters Staff of Lord Mountbatten at Combined Operations and South-east Asia Command. One of the pioneers of Public Relations work in Britain, he is a former President of the Institute of Public Relations, and founder and Chairman of a firm of Public Relations Consultants in London.

HAMISH HAMILTON PAPERBACKS

In preparation
J. Christopher Herold
MISTRESS TO AN AGE
THE LIFE OF MADAME DE STAËL

Robert Rhodes James
LORD RANDOLPH CHURCHILL

Priscilla Napier
A LATE BEGINNER

Constance Babington Smith
JOHN MASEFIELD

A. J. P. Taylor
BISMARCK

Emlyn Williams
GEORGE

Cecil Woodham-Smith
THE GREAT HUNGER

*For a complete list of available
titles see the end of this book*

MISSION WITH MOUNTBATTEN

by

ALAN CAMPBELL-JOHNSON

C.I.E., O.B.E.

With a Foreword by
ADMIRAL OF THE FLEET
THE EARL MOUNTBATTEN OF BURMA,
K.G., P.C., O.M., G.C.S.I., G.C.I.E.

A HAMISH HAMILTON PAPERBACK
London

First published in Great Britain 1951
by Robert Hale & Company
First published in this edition 1985
by Hamish Hamilton Ltd
Garden House 57–59 Long Acre London WC2E 9JZ

Copyright © 1951, 1972 and 1985 by Alan Campbell-Johnson

ISBN 0-241-11536-1

Printed and bound in Finland
by Werner Söderström Oy

CONTENTS

ILLUSTRATIONS

FOREWORD
by Admiral of the Fleet
the Earl Mountbatten of Burma,
K.G., P.C., O.M., G.C.S.I., G.C.I.E.

Before agreeing to go to India as the last Viceroy I asked for three conditions to be met. The first was plenipotentiary powers in handling complex and decisive discussions with the Indian leaders. The second was a fixed time limit for the transfer of power from British to Indian hands. The third was that I should bring out additional staff of my own choice to supplement the staff I would take over from my predecessor, Lord Wavell.

Alan Campbell-Johnson was one of this hand-picked group, which was headed by Lord Ismay. His task was to be the first, last and only Press Attache to a Viceroy. Though neither of us could have foreseen that the Indians would ask me to stay on as their first constitutional Governor-General after their Independence, when they did so I kept on a few key people to help me in my new role. Alan Campbell-Johnson had proved his worth so thoroughly by then that he was one of the few I asked to stay on.

He had been on my staff in my two previous jobs, as Chief of Combined Operations in London and Supreme Allied Commander in South East Asia, so we knew each other well, and this was a real help.

We both learned a lot from my post surrender tasks when we came face to face with nationalist movements all over South East Asia. So the problems we met in India were not new to us. It was indeed a "baptism by total immersion" for the mission that was to lie ahead of me.

Alan Campbell-Johnson's day-to-day record of his experiences and impressions was first published only three years after the momentous events it described. It was the first authoritative full length account and it had the immediacy and impact of a news story. It was at once recognised as a primary source and nearly every subsequent account of those fifteen crowded crucial months has quoted from it or relied upon it to some extent.

While it is no longer news and has ripened into history his diary narrative of the events of 25 years ago remains as "gripping and vivid" as it did when Nehru so described it at the time of its original publication.

Re-reading this historic document has brought back to me the vivid memory of the excitement and almost unbelievable pressure under which we all worked. But it has also brought back astonishingly happy memories of friendship and trust in the midst of crises and calamities.

I would have liked to have had more time but time was not on our side. My successor as Governor General summed it all up when he said to me in March 1948 "If you had not transferred power when you did, there would have been no power to transfer".

I am glad that this book will now be available to a new generation who were not even born when these events occurred. Through this book they will have the chance of sharing in the living experience of a turning point in history.

June 1972

Mountbatten of Burma

PREFACE

This diary narrative was first published in 1951 just three years after I had originally set it down. It was reprinted on its 21st anniversary with the addition of Lord Mountbatten's Foreword. I noted in the accompanying Preface "the Transfer of Power in India is widely recognised as perhaps the greatest single development in world affairs since the Second World War; it is an irony of history, however, that the larger the scale of the event the greater the danger of its being lost in legend or blurred by controversy. Already the fogs of propaganda and political invective are helping to obscure the view of Lord Mountbatten's momentous mission to India."

With the book's first appearance thirty years later as a paperback in the Hamish Hamilton series it will now be read in the more critical perspective of history and the company of a whole library of literature covering the Transfer of Power. The spectrum ranges from the three massive volumes published by the British Government taking some 2,800 pages to cover the 145 days' transaction to a host of biographies of the Indian leaders and other special studies; from H. V. Hodson's authoritative *Great Divide* to the popular reconstruction of Lapierre's and Collins' *Freedom at Midnight* and from the recollections of such key figures in the Viceroy's team as Lord Ismay and V. P. Menon to Philip Ziegler's definitive and closely researched biography of Mountbatten himself. As for Mountbatten, although he steadfastly refused to authorise a biography to be written in his lifetime, he did allow himself to be seen and heard on television and to register his views and personality in the ambitious 13 part series of his Life and Times on Thames TV in 1969—one part being devoted to the Viceroyalty. Posthumously the TV searchlight plays even more intensely on the transfer of power in the Brent Walker production entitled *Mountbatten—the Last Viceroy*. In both these series I have been privileged to play a small part, and to have the satisfaction of learning that my narrative within its self-imposed limitations of an eye witness report was of some help to the script writers in their search for the physical facts and first-hand impressions.

Against this background of an ever growing volume of commentaries and re-evaluations *Mission with Mountbatten* still is and remains inevitably a primary source. Indeed I have collected over the years more than 50 books the authors of which have drawn on and quoted from it as such. Accordingly I have avoided any temptation to abridge or amend the text of the diary or to seek to be wiser after the events than I was at the time. For Epilogue I continue to rely substantially—with only minor modifications—on the text of a speech I delivered to The Royal

Institute of International Affairs a few months after my return from India, and as such linked to my original perceptions.

Across the ever widening chasm of the years, the dominating reality which abides and which I hope emerges from reading my narrative is the imperative imposed by available time on great events. The words of Henry Kissinger, historian and man of action, and well placed to know what he was talking about, carry particular conviction when applied to Mountbatten's mission to India in 1947. For, said Kissinger, "if one wants to have a realistic—if not compassionate—understanding of policy choices one has to know how the alternatives presented themselves, and not only what the best solution might have been, and one must understand the time span that was available for dealing with the issues. In so many of the *ex post facto* investigations they take individual documents in a seminar type discussion having all the facts that one knows afterwards. But that is rarely the case; usually decisions are made in a very brief time with enormous pressure and uncertain knowledge". And so it is that if this is a hurried, breathless narrative, that is because we all worked at the highest pressure and with an acute sense of urgency. If it appears disjointed, that is because *ad hoc* problems demanding immediate solution cut across the continuity to become our daily routine.

Lord Mountbatten's methods of using a large high-powered staff under these conditions of stress and strain were original and ingenious. For every hour of discussion with the Indian leaders he allowed a quarter of an hour for dictation before seeing the next visitor. Copies of his interview notes were distributed to all the key members of his Staff. He obtained our advice and did his thinking aloud at the daily Staff Meetings, which we all attended already knowing every word that had passed at his private and informal interviews the day before. This is how it will be found that on occasion I have no difficulty in quoting what Lord Mountbatten said and thought at any given time when I was not necessarily there myself.

In spite of the pace, the setbacks and distractions, the transfer of power by Partition was steadily evolved according to schedule. Within seventy-three days of our arrival the Partition Plan had been announced; a further seventy-two days after that, and the Viceroyalty itself was at an end. Throughout Mountbatten's ten months as Governor-General the tempo never substantially slackened. All this immense and self-sustaining concentration of effort is, I believe, better brought out by maintaining as far as possible the original chronological sequence, rather than in the selection and separation of special themes. I have therefore simply divided the book into its two natural parts: the periods before and after the 15th August—Independence Day. Within that framework the narrative is, as I have already said, a day-to-day record.

I am indebted to Mr. V. P. Menon and Vice-Admiral Sir Ronald Brockman, R.N., both former colleagues on Lord Mountbatten's staff in India, and to Mr. A. H. Joyce, Officer in Charge of Information at the Commonwealth Relations Office, for reading through my diary narrative in typescript, also to Mr. K. St. Pavlowitch for checking references, and last but not least to my wife for her accuracy during the long and often late hours of dictation, typing and proof-reading.

Alan Campbell-Johnson

Westminster, 1985

Part I

THE LAST VICEROY

CHAPTER ONE

VICEROY DESIGNATE

LONDON, *Thursday, 19th December, 1946*

I CALLED EARLY on Mountbatten at his home in Chester Street, and arrived in time for the customary Mountbatten breakfast—last-minute dictation, toast and tea all competing for the services of his mouth. As usual, the meal came off second best. He had asked me to go round and see him about his South-east Asia Command Despatches. As erstwhile Recorder and keeper of his War Diaries throughout his tour of duty as Supreme Commander, I retain an almost *ex officio*, now no more than honorary, interest in these Despatches. There are many teething troubles in their production, not the least of which is to fit them into his crowded agenda. As our business was not finished and time pressed, there was, as usual, no alternative but to accompany him to his next appointment—a sitting for an official portrait Oswald Birley is painting of him.

When we got into the car he pulled up all the windows, swore me to the utmost secrecy and whispered that what he was about to tell me was known to no one outside his own family. Mr. Attlee, he said, had called for him the previous evening and invited him to succeed Lord Wavell as Viceroy of India. Although I had become accustomed to associate him with surprises, I was wholly unprepared for this *dénouement*. All was fairly set for him to fulfil his long-thwarted personal ambition of resuming his career in the Navy. His refresher course was in full swing. He was to be Rear-Admiral commanding the First Cruiser Squadron with effect from April 1947. Moreover, the recent conference in London between the Indian Leaders, Lord Wavell and the British Government, while giving no grounds for any easy optimism, seemed to imply that the Cabinet Mission Plan was still in being.

From what I now heard, the Prime Minister had put a very different complexion both on India's and Mountbatten's future. Mr. Attlee had begun the interview by asking Mountbatten whether his heart was really set on going to sea. He replied that it certainly was. By being put back into circulation with his own Service, his whole Naval career was being saved. He added that he had been both surprised and touched at the number of letters he had received from his friends in the Navy expressing their pleasure that he was going back to sea again.

Attlee then switched the conversation to the Indian crisis. Wavell, he said, had come back with nothing more constructive than a military evacuation plan. The Government was most unfavourably impressed with the political trends affecting both the Congress and the Moslem League. If we were not very careful, we might well find ourselves handing India over not simply to civil war, but to political movements of a definitely totalitarian character. Urgent action was needed to break the deadlock, and the principal members of the Cabinet had reached the conclusion that a new personal approach was perhaps the only hope. They had looked round in every direction for a suitable man to make it, and had unanimously agreed that it was Mountbatten alone who had the personality and qualifications required.

At this point Mountbatten intervened to say he must at once make it clear, from what he had seen of the Indian situation when he was Supreme Commander and from his many talks with Wavell, that he had entirely agreed with Wavell's policy up to his last talk in Delhi in June. There was nothing that Wavell had done throughout that time which he would not have done himself. Attlee agreed that fundamentally it was not Wavell's general policy in the past that was in question, but its implementation to-day. The hard fact was that in spite of his unremitting efforts it had largely broken down, and Attlee reiterated that in this new situation the problem was now more one of personality. The need for closer personal contacts with the Indian Leaders was paramount.

Mountbatten told me that he put up a stiff fight against the Prime Minister's pressure and blandishments, stressing his extreme tiredness, and the folly of wearing him out too young and of diverting him from his Service career, where perhaps his most likely usefulness to the State lay. Were there no other names? What about Auchinleck, who was immensely popular in India? The interview ended, it seems, on a note of indecision. Mountbatten wished to know just what Government policy he would be required to implement, and he told me that before making any answer he must in any case consult the King, since a Viceroy was not only theoretically his servant and nominee, but, as far as the Indian Princes were concerned, his Representative.

He asked what my reaction was to this bombshell. I could only reply that the Prime Minister, for his part, had shown considerable psychological insight and made a sound appraisal of his personal qualifications; but that he on his side could not reasonably be asked to take on such an explosive commitment without the clearest directive. Mountbatten then said it was quite clear to him that there would have to be the earliest time limit for the transfer of power if his mission was not to be hopelessly compromised with Indian opinion from the outset. As for the British reaction, he felt that if he agreed to go there would be considerable public sympathy for him in taking on the job at all, and popular support would probably back him up in whatever measures he saw fit to take. He was ready to run any risk, but did not in fact think that the traditional risk of his being made the scapegoat was excessive.

I am afraid that when we got to Birley's studio, and the time came to study the forceful but unfinished portrait, my mind was on other things.

LONDON, *Friday, 20th December, 1946*

My wife and I attended the British Government's Reception at Lancaster House in honour of Pridi Panomyong, the Senior Statesman of Siam, who had combined the roles of Regent and resistance leader during the war. My last meeting with him had been when he had entertained Mountbatten and his party during the Anglo-Siamese peace celebrations in Bangkok last January.

Mountbatten arrived at the party rather late. On seeing me there he signalled me into a quiet corner and showed me his reply to the Prime Minister's offer. It was quite brief; but, while appreciating the honour, he had begged to be excused unless he was able to go at the express invitation of the Indian Leaders. I must say I think it is extremely unlikely that Attlee will be able or willing to comply with this condition, so this may well be the last we shall hear of the whole proposal. He said he was going straight from the party to Downing Street.

LONDON, *Wednesday, 15th January, 1947*

Mountbatten's acceptance of the Viceroyalty is at last firm. His early talks with the Prime Minister were inconclusive. Government policy accepted the principle of a time limit, but havered over the exact date. The second half of 1948 was suggested, but Mountbatten's conviction hardened that political success was bound up with the Government's readiness to accept the earliest possible date of British departure from India, and he at once bid for " second half " to mean June rather than December. With the Christmas week at hand, final decisions were held over, and Mountbatten took himself and his family away for a brief holiday at Davos. He had not been there forty-eight hours when he was urgently summoned to London, and a special aircraft sent to bring him back. This move was calculated to arouse considerable Press speculation, but its meaning was missed. Frank Owen, the Editor of the *Daily Mail*, for instance, told me his own guess was that the destination would be Palestine.

Mountbatten was recalled because the news from India was increasingly serious. The communal deadlock and violence persisted. The Government wished to announce a new policy and a new Viceroy as quickly as possible. After close consideration of the terms of this draft announcement, and in particular the incorporation of a phrase to indicate that his Naval career will not be prejudiced, Mountbatten has finally agreed in principle to take on the job. He went so far, he told me, as to insist that the First Lord and First Sea Lord should associate themselves with the Prime Minister in guaranteeing his return to the Navy. The knowledge that the King was strongly in favour of his undertaking the task helped to confirm his decision. In his discussions with the Government he warned them of the danger of giving any impression that his appointment was designed to perpetuate the Viceregal system or to impose British arbitration. This was his reason for making his acceptance in the first instance conditional upon his receiving an open invitation from the Indian parties to go in a capacity defined by themselves. Mr. Attlee explained in detail, however, that this last condition was not feasible, but he fully accepted the principle of terminating the British Raj by a specific date regardless of agreement or earlier than the time limit if the Indian parties were able beforehand to agree on a constitution and form a Government.

His Majesty's Government has shown itself prepared to go to very great lengths to secure Mountbatten's acceptance. Sir Stafford Cripps offered to provide the necessary liaison in advance between the Indian Leaders and the new Viceroy, and to do his utmost to ensure that the appointment was in fact acceptable to them before it was officially announced. Cripps went so far as to offer to serve in any capacity, even to the point of accompanying Mountbatten to India. This offer was not unnaturally shelved, as Cripps' status and experience in Indian affairs would have prejudiced Mountbatten's position and made it virtually impossible for a new Viceroy to carry on negotiations with the necessary authority or prestige.

LONDON, *Monday*, *17th February*, *1947*

In addition to the Naval proviso, Mountbatten insisted on being allowed to supplement the normal Viceregal staff. He argued that this was a special mission called upon to take unprecedented political and military decisions in what was at most a quarter of the time allotted to previous Viceregal terms of office. It would be asking too much of Lord Wavell's regular Indian Civil Service secretariat, brilliant and experienced men though they are, to carry on without reinforcement. Mr. Attlee at once pledged the Government's support for the appointment of any additional staff Mountbatten wanted; and with this assurance he has immediately gone to work.

He is creating four new posts never before known in Viceroy's House: a Chief of Staff to the Viceroy, a Principal Secretary, a Conference Secretary and a Press Attaché, to which he is adding his personal secretariat, headed by two senior Naval officers. By dint of his persuasive enthusiasm—one of the most potent ingredients in his personality—he has prevailed upon two old friends of his to sacrifice their own personal preoccupations and add their formidable experience to his team. So it is that Lord Ismay has agreed to come out of his retirement, which he has been allowed to enjoy for exactly three weeks, and to serve as Chief of Staff, and Sir Eric Miéville to put aside important business commitments in the City to become the Principal Secretary.

Between 1931 and 1933 Ismay and Miéville served together as Military and Private Secretaries respectively to the then Viceroy, Lord Willingdon. Ismay's subsequent career as Secretary to the Defence Committee of the Cabinet and primarily as Mr. Churchill's personal military adviser and liaison officer with the Combined Chiefs of Staff throughout the war gives him a unique status in the sphere of Allied military diplomacy. Mountbatten and Ismay were, of course, war-time colleagues, Mountbatten as Chief of Combined Operations, and Ismay as Chief of Staff to Churchill, both being members of the Chiefs of Staff Committee. Miéville, who before entering the City had been for several years Assistant Private Secretary to the King, is equally well-equipped to exert informal influence and to help in the moulding of Viceregal policy.

Of the other members of the special party, Captain Ronald Brockman, R.N., Commander George Nicholls, R.N., Lieutenant-Colonel Vernon Erskine Crum, Scots Guards, and myself have all served under Mountbatten either at Combined Operations or in South-east Asia Command, or both. We are all under forty. Brockman, as his Naval Secretary since 1943, is wholly indispensable in whatever capacity Mountbatten may be serving. He is one of the youngest but most experienced Captains (S) in the Navy, having served as Secretary to Admiral of the Fleet Sir Dudley Pound, First Sea Lord, right up to the time of his death in 1943. Thus even before joining Mountbatten he had become closely acquainted with affairs at the highest level. George Nicholls, another highly competent Naval officer, has been invited to come out as Brockman's Deputy. He was Mountbatten's Naval Secretary at Combined Operations Headquarters, staying on there under General Laycock until 1946. Both Brockman and Nicholls, apart from their administrative efficiency, are of a steady and equable temperament and well-adapted to support Mountbatten's dæmonic energy. Vernon Erskine Crum is to be given the job of Conference Secretary. He is already well versed in this particular task from covering Mountbatten's conferences in South-east Asia Command. For Mountbatten is a great believer in diplomacy by discussion, and with him the talk provides the paper rather than the paper the talk.

When Mountbatten first asked me in January to join the team I was not sure whether it would be possible for me to go. I have only recently been demobilised from Wing Commander, after some four years on his staff, both at Combined Operations and South-east Asia Command Headquarters, and I am heavily engaged in catching up with my normal civilian life. Mountbatten's idea then was that I should be " without portfolio ". Now, however, on further consideration, he thinks it would be best if my primary responsibility covered the field of Public Relations, and liaison with the large and influential Press population known to be based on Delhi. So far, it seems, no one on the Viceroy's staff has been available to maintain contact with them save on a low priority and part-time basis; with the result that Viceroy's House has come to be regarded as a " closed shop " for authoritative guidance to the Indian and Foreign Press generally, and the initiative for most of the inspired speculation and comment has automatically passed to other " well-informed quarters ". Mountbatten feels there is a lot to be said for the last Viceroy being accompanied by the first Press Attaché.

LONDON, *Thursday, 20th February, 1947*

I once more called on Mountbatten at Chester Street, this time to see him about India and give a firm and final " yes " to his invitation to join his staff. Once again in order to complete the business I found myself forced to accompany him to the next appointment. This time it was to be driven down by him in his new Riley to Latimer House, where the recently formed Joint Services Staff College has been established under command of Rear-Admiral Douglas-Pennant, who had been an Assistant Deputy Chief of Staff to him in S.E.A.C. He was due to fulfil a long-standing promise to give a lecture there on the strategy and Command set-up in South-east Asia.

As we sped along the frosty roads into Buckinghamshire on this raw February afternoon, his mood was detached, and if he had any emotion at the thought that in a few hours' time his appointment would be flashed across the world, he gave no sign of it. He said that Churchill, before learning the news, had come up to him at the Royal Navy Club Dinner declaring that it was shameful that the Labour Government should be wasting him, and at Mary Churchill's wedding, after he had been informed, although still shaking his head, was full of good wishes. But it seems that to others Churchill was complaining that it was scandalous that the Socialists should try to cover up their own failure behind Mountbatten's reputation.

On arrival at Latimer House, Douglas-Pennant expressed delight none the less genuine for its Naval reserve. In the circumstances Mountbatten's lecture, which was delivered with very little reliance upon notes and lasted for just over an hour, was a remarkable performance. At the end, as a tail-piece to the usual vote of thanks, Douglas-Pennant looked carefully at his watch and said that at this moment Mr. Attlee was telling the House of Commons that Lord Mountbatten was to be the new Viceroy of India. There was a terrific burst of clapping from the audience of two hundred or so senior staff officers on the course. Mountbatten acknowledged it with the comment, " It is not a matter for applause, I assure you."

On the journey home we discussed in detail some aspects of the job he wanted me to do, and he asked a number of searching questions about the desirability or otherwise of Press conferences. On our return to town we heard that Attlee's statement had been the occasion of a lively scene in the House, and that Churchill seemed bent on making political capital out of Mountbatten's appointment and the policy underlying it.

The new Viceroy was given a very wide mandate. If there was no likelihood of a unitary constitution emerging from a fully representative Constituent Assembly by June 1948, then, said Mr. Attlee, the British Government would " have to consider to whom the powers of the central Government in British India should be handed over, on the due date, whether as a whole to some form of central Government for British India, or in some areas to the existing Provincial Governments, or in such other way as may seem most reasonable and in the best interests of the Indian people ". As for the Princely States, the Prime Minister made it clear that the Government did not intend to hand over their powers and obligations under Paramountcy to any successor Government of British India. While Paramountcy was to be retained until power was actually transferred, " it is contemplated that for the intervening period the relations of the Crown with individual States may be adjusted by agreement ".

Churchill at once jumped up to ask a number of barbed questions about the reasons for Wavell's removal. It must be confessed that Attlee's reference to Wavell had been sufficiently cold and perfunctory to provide Churchill with this particular opening. The time limit also came as a considerable emotional jolt to the Conservative Opposition.

What threatened to be a major show-down, however, petered out through the House of Commons' time-honoured technique of passing on to other business.

LONDON, *Friday, 21st February, 1947*

The Press reaction to-day is generally favourable to the new appointment. There had, in fact, been a major leakage in the American Press twenty-four hours in advance of the Prime Minister's statement, but this did not seriously affect the impact of the official news upon world opinion. The American comment was particularly interesting, in so far as the British Raj was almost as traditional a target for American criticism as George III himself! American opinion underwent an emotional jolt of its own. The *New York Times* aptly symbolised the new mood with a leading article headed " Ultimatum to India ". It contained applause and foreboding in equal measure. " This declaration," it stated, " which matches the American grant of Independence to the Philippines, and as such has few parallels in history, marks the decisive step in Britain's self-imposed task to complete self-government. . . . At the same time the declaration is also an ultimatum, though of a kind never before issued by a Power so often accused of being Imperialistic. It is an ultimatum to the Indian leaders to end their quarrel." The *Washington Star* went so far as to ask whether Britain, in the event of the time limit producing no agreement, would, " as a humane nation, feel compelled to stick to her promise if the only clear prospect for India is a vacuum of fratricidal war? "

This afternoon Mountbatten and the members of his special staff foregathered at the temporary offices provided for us at the India Office. This is a more than usually sombre Government department, and civil servants over many years have been called upon to operate in the funereal atmosphere of a rather musty museum. Workmen are to be seen wandering in and out of the tall, dingy rooms on meaningless errands. Fading pictures of Indian scenes and heroes fail altogether to evoke the spirit of the Mutiny, but recall only the " vasty halls of death ". Ismay was full of fury over the place, which he clearly felt was a primary source of our present troubles in India! General satisfaction was expressed with the first reactions in *Dawn*, the mouthpiece of Jinnah and the Moslem League. Ismay said he was seeing Churchill, but had no great hopes of calming him down. He felt there was a danger of an issue being made of Mountbatten's selection as a pro-Hindu and anti-Moslem League appointment.

I listened during the evening to the Editors of our five leading weeklies, who were making their interesting collective broadcast while the fuel crisis deprived them of their papers. Jon Kimche of *Tribune* paid a high tribute to Mountbatten's Burma record. All stressed the time-limit danger, but none made the point that the new Viceroy would have been likely to insist upon it as a condition of taking on the job at all.

CARLISLE, *Saturday, 22nd February, 1947*

Late last night I set out on a train journey with Clement Davies for Carlisle, where we were due to address a big Liberal Rally the following afternoon.   This was to be positively my last political appearance prior to translation into temporary civil service.

Naturally I informed Clement Davies of this, and told him that I had been asked by Mountbatten to go out with him, and that I had decided to accept.   He at once said this was a very great honour, and he realised that the work I would have to undertake was one of heavy responsibility and that I should be taking part in one of the most momentous acts of modern times and present at the making of history.

He then told me he had been asked to attend a meeting with Attlee and Churchill, and that he had then been informed of the Prime Minister's intention to appoint Mountbatten.   He, Clement Davies, considered that this was a stroke of genius, and that it was Attlee alone who had thought of Mountbatten and offered him the appointment.

He added that he felt Attlee was handling the situation with tact and firmness, and that he was sincerely anxious that the people of India should be in complete control of their own affairs.   I gathered, of course, that Clement Davies thoroughly approved.   He, too, was anxious about the situation, and fervently hoped that an agreement could be made which would be satisfactory both to Nehru and to Jinnah.

CHAPTER TWO

DEBATES AND BRIEFINGS

LONDON, *Wednesday, 26th February, 1947*

THE GREAT TWO-DAY Debate in the House of Lords has ended with Lord Templewood withdrawing his motion of virtual censure on the Government for its announcement of 20th February. This was one of the occasions when the opinions of the House of Lords were not unjustifiably regarded by many as carrying greater political weight than those of the Commons. In the first place, in as far as the Lords were discussing the new situation in advance of the forthcoming Commons Debate, it was appreciated that the final attitude of the Conservative Opposition might well depend upon the tone set by their Lordships. Moreover, they were debating not so much in their hereditary capacity, as in the role of elder statesmen, specialists and experts.

A galaxy of names famous in the annals of Indian administration for over a quarter of a century addressed themselves to Lord Templewood's stern declaration that the time limit was a breach of faith imperilling the peace and prosperity of India. Coming from Lord Templewood, who, as Secretary of State while still known as Sir Samuel Hoare, had spent the better part of seven years in steering through the great Government of India Act of 1935 against the most violent and sustained opposition of Mr. Churchill and the Conservative right wing, this motion was indeed a formidable challenge to the Government, and if widely supported calculated to render a united national approach to Indian Independence impossible. By the time Lord Listowel had wound up the first day's Debate for the Government there seemed very little prospect of avoiding a division and a defeat.

This danger loomed larger to-day, when Lord Simon, of Simon Commission fame, resumed for the Opposition. He spoke for just over an hour. It was an essay in closely reasoned negation and foreboding. The accumulated burden of the Government's problems was enough to break down the deliberate considerations of any man or body of men. " However, I am bound to say," he concluded, " that I sadly fear that the end of this business is not going to be the establishment of peace in India, but rather that it is going to degrade the British name."

After yet another highly critical speech, this time by Lord Trenchard, Lord Halifax—the only ex-Viceroy taking part in the Debate—rose to make his last great decisive intervention in Indian affairs. Reaching out far beyond the confines of party faith or discipline, he declared :—

" With such knowledge as I have, I am not prepared to say that whatever else may be right or wrong, this step must on all counts certainly be judged to be wrong . . . for the truth is that for India to-day there is no solution that is not fraught with the gravest objection, with the gravest danger. And the conclusion that I reach—with all that can be said against it—is that I am not prepared to condemn what His Majesty's Government are doing unless I can honestly and confidently recommend a better solution. . . . I should be sorry if the only message from the House to India at this moment was one of condemnation, based on what I must fully recognise are very natural feelings of failure, frustration and foreboding."

Lord Samuel told me afterwards that it was the most persuasive speech he had ever heard delivered in the House of Lords, and that its impact was such that many Conservative Peers who, before he rose, had firmly decided to vote against the Government, changed their minds while he was speaking and fell in with his appeal to Templewood " to spare the House the necessity of going to a Division ". The rest of the Debate was an anti-climax. The tide of opinion had turned, and Templewood, while maintaining his criticisms, duly withdrew his motion. The only comparable Parliamentary occasion Lord Samuel could recall in his lifetime was when the Revised Prayer Book was thrown out by the House of Commons through the moral fervour of a single back-bench speech. He went on to say that the opportunity rarely arises for such a *tour de force*, and that in any case the usual purpose of Parliamentary debate is not so much to change the minds of supporters or opponents in the House as to present a case for the ultimate judgement of the electorate.

LONDON, *Wednesday, 5th March, 1947*

Although the opening of the two-day Debate in the House of Commons was obviously a great Parliamentary occasion, I could not help feeling, when I saw Cripps rise to expound the Government's case with his accustomed poise and lucidity, that the key battle for the new policy had already been won in the Lords. Cripps' speeches are always so closely reasoned and beautifully arranged that the emotional temperature almost immediately drops when he speaks. He would never dream of appealing to your heart without first trying to persuade your mind. But on this occasion I detected a deeper note of passionate conviction than usual.

Already Cripps' contribution to India's forthcoming Independence was assured of its place in history. As Lord Halifax had pointed out, the Cripps' Mission of 1942 was the decisive act from which there could be no turning back. In 1946 he was the dominating figure of the Cabinet Mission. In both negotiations he had been on the verge of complete agreement and unqualified success, only to see his efforts thwarted at the last minute. In proposing the Government's new approach, he must have known that he was in fact confirming the effective eclipse of his own elaborate master plan to transfer power to a united India.

He was at pains to stress that it was administratively and militarily out of the question to stay on beyond 1948. Otherwise he laid no special emphasis on the time limit, and he made no reference whatever to Lord

Wavell. This last omission was undoubtedly a pity, as it tended to confirm the ill-disposed gossip about serious differences of opinion between the Government and the returning Viceroy. Cripps throughout did his utmost to leave the door open for a revised Cabinet Mission Plan. " Now is the time," he said in his final peroration, " when the wider good of all India, throughout which both communities are widely dispersed, must take precedence over the narrower claims of single communities or single parts of that great continental area."

Sir John Anderson moved a detailed amendment on behalf of the Conservative Opposition, which he supported with a ponderous oration. The formula was in effect an elaborate attempt on Sir John's part to reconcile what Lord Halifax had said last week with what Mr. Churchill was likely to say to-morrow. But this was a formidable task even for one of Anderson's drafting calibre. As was perhaps to be expected, he largely confined himself to an exhaustive condemnation of the Government's time-limit proposal. Under cover of a dense dialectical smoke-screen he worked his way towards a position of proposing a final date for an agreed central authority, failing which the Government should resume freedom of action to transfer power to convenient separate authorities " as speedily as possible ". Anderson is a disappointing Parliamentarian. This aspect of his career has been superimposed upon too many other distinctions too late in life. The result is a pomposity of manner and a heaviness of expression which weaken both his arguments and influence in the House.

The more persuasive performances to-day came from back-benchers speaking from their own experience, sometimes against the party line. Perhaps the most original suggestion under this heading was put forward by the Socialist " rebel " Zilliacus, who saw India as the classic problem of national minorities who are distrustful at being left to the tender mercies of the majority. In this instance, however, the Moslem community was more than a national minority, but somewhat less than an independent nation. He cited the example of the U.S.S.R. to suggest that India should enjoy multi-national membership of the United Nations, which would enable the Moslems to have the same status as the Ukraine and become a separate member.

LONDON, *Thursday, 6th March, 1947*

When Churchill resumed the Debate to-day we were regaled with the long-awaited firework display. Over the years Churchill has remained very loyal to his pet aversions, and what may perhaps best be termed his Indian invective proclaims probably the most rigid and unbending of all his opinions upon the public issues of our time.

He started off by taking his stand on the Cripps' Mission of 1942. Although the offer had not been accepted at the time, both sides of the House were still bound by it. He denounced the present plan as involving grave departures from the " scope and integrity " of its principles. There was at last a reference in this debate to Wavell, but it was far from cordial. " The Viceroy, Lord Wavell, has been dismissed. I hold no

brief for Lord Wavell.   He has been the willing or unwilling agent of the
Government in all the errors and mistakes into which they have been led."
But he continued to assert that he did not know why Wavell had been
cast aside at this juncture, and to press for a personal statement from him
on his return.

As for the new Viceroy, " Is he to make a new effort to restore the
situation, or is it merely Operation Scuttle on which he and other
distinguished officers have been despatched? . . . I am bound to say
the whole thing wears the aspect of an attempt by the Government to
make use of brilliant war figures in order to cover up a melancholy and
disastrous transaction."

He then entered the field of prophecy.   " India is to be subjected not
merely to partition, but to fragmentation and to haphazard fragmentation."
The time limit, far from bringing the Indian parties to their senses, was
calculated to make them step up their demands.   These parties' claims to
represent the Indian masses were fictitious :   " In handing over the
Government of India to these so-called political classes, we are handing
over to men of straw of whom in a few years no trace will remain.
This Government by their latest action, this fifteen months' limitation,
cripple the new Viceroy and destroy the prospect of even going through
the business on the agenda which has to be settled."

He found wholly incomprehensible the time limit for India but the
lack of it for Palestine.   Could the House believe that there were three or
four times as many British troops in little petty Palestine as in mighty
India at the present time?   He could find no sense in this distribution of
our forces.   His only positive proposals were that this ratio should be
reversed and—a typical Churchillian surprise—that Zilliacus' suggestion
should be taken up and the problem of the Moslem minority submitted
to the United Nations.   And so to the funereal conclusion.   " Many
have defended Britain against her foes, none can defend her against
herself. . . . But, at least, let us not add—by shameful flight, by a
premature hurried scuttle—at least, let us not add to the pangs of sorrow
so many of us feel, the taint and smear of shame."

When Attlee rose at last from the Treasury Bench there was an air of
expectancy which had somehow been missing before.   Indeed, one of the
things which surprised me while Cripps was speaking yesterday was the
thinness of the Labour ranks.   After Question Time they had trooped
out, not to return again en bloc until the Prime Minister brought the
Debate to a close the following evening.   He certainly did not disappoint
them.   Although I have often listened to Attlee on various themes,
this is the first time I have heard him on India, which is undoubtedly his
special subject.   His two years service as a member of the Simon Commission was clearly one of the most formative experiences of his life,
and historically speaking probably the most important thing about the
Simon Commission.   Those who are interested in working out the contrast between Churchill and Attlee should not overlook the Indian motif.

On this occasion Attlee brought to bear on his famous adversary a
debating armament of a calibre which I for one had no idea he possessed.
He put aside his notes, spoke straight from the heart, and the result was a

genuine eloquence.   His style did not change, but he simply ceased to be commonplace.   This man burns with a hidden fire and is sustained by a certain spiritual integrity which enables him to scale the heights when the great occasion demands.   Churchill was raked with delicate irony. It was close in-fighting, which is sometimes lost upon the general public, but which scores points with the judges and wins bouts in the Parliamentary ring.

Attlee firmly rebutted the doctrine that Wavell was under some necessity to make a personal statement on his return; " to put it colloquially, if a change of bowling is desired it is not always necessary that there should be an elaborate explanation ".   As for the attack on the admission of the Indian politicians into the Government and the desire to continue with the caretaker administration—" the essence of the Indian problem is to get Indian statesmen to understand what are the real problems they have to face. . . . A very grave fault of the reforms that we have carried out over these years is that we have taught irresponsibility instead of responsibility.   All Indian politicians were permanently in opposition, and speaking with long experience, it is not good to be always in opposition."

He then turned to our responsibilities to the minorities.   Here he made the shrewd point that in so far as the existence of the scheduled castes (Untouchables) and their position was part of the whole Hindu social system, the British Raj had lacked not the will but the power to raise these people.   With one or two special exceptions, our policy had been to accept the social and economic system we had found.   " Why are we told now," he asked, " at the very end of our rule, that we must clear up all these things before we go, otherwise we shall betray our trust?   If that trust is there, it ought to have been fulfilled long ago."   Essentially the dangers of delay, the dangers of hanging on, were as great as the dangers of going forward.   He concluded by saying he was sure the whole House would wish " Godspeed " to the new Viceroy in his great mission.   " It is a mission, not, as has been suggested, of betrayal on our part, it is a mission of fulfilment."

The Prime Minister's speech, and in particular his peroration, roused his back-bench supporters, who normally display a somewhat parochial and passive attitude towards India, to a high pitch of enthusiasm.   When the House divided, the vote was three hundred and thirty-seven in favour of the Government's policy and our mission, and one hundred and eighty-five against.   Although Mr. Attlee's appeal that there should be a united message of good-will from the House to the Indian Leaders and people had failed to prevent a Division on strictly Party lines, one could not help coming away from this historic Debate with the sense that the gulf between Government and Opposition was far narrower than some of Mr. Churchill's more sombre polemics might suggest.

LONDON, *Monday, 10th March, 1947*

In general, it can be said that Mountbatten, in briefing himself for the political task that lies ahead of him, is starting from scratch.   But he has, of course, visited India before, first as an A.D.C. to the Prince of Wales on his tour in 1921. Then, between October 1943 and April 1944, New Delhi was his headquarters as Supreme Allied Commander, but this post had been formed for the express purpose of separating the responsibility for the prosecution of the war in South-east Asia from that of the internal defence and security of India and its administration as a base. Moreover, although the scope of his duties ranged beyond strictly military operations, his para-political interests did not include India. He used to see a lot of Lord Wavell, and officially the Viceroy's relationship to him as Supreme Commander was that of Minister of State appointed with a special directive to advise and represent the Government, the exact equivalent post established in the Middle East theatre of war.

Towards the end of his time in South-east Asia Command, Mountbatten had his first meeting with Jawaharlal Nehru, on the occasion of Nehru's visit to Malaya, at the suggestion of Lord Wavell, to see the large Indian minority there. It was a most successful and happy encounter. I was present on the occasion of it, and it was quite clear that the two men made a deep personal impression upon each other.

From the moment his appointment was announced, Mountbatten has been caught up in a hectic sequence of meetings and interviews. He has seen the King, whose constitutional position is vitally affected, and has been in almost regular session with the India–Burma Committee of the Cabinet, which includes Attlee, Cripps, Alexander and Pethick-Lawrence and is concerned with the detailed elaboration and control of the Government's Indian policy. There have also been detailed discussions with the Chiefs of Staff and India Office experts. They have ranged over the whole field, from the terms of the Government's directive to the Viceroy, to compensation for the Indian Civil Service, from the movement of British civilians from India, with its effect on world shipping capacity, to the future of the Gurkhas and the strategic defence of the Indian Ocean.

First and foremost has been the consideration given to the amendment of the so-called " Governor-General's Instrument of Instructions ", the official standing directive which it is his duty to try to implement. Mountbatten has had an important part to play in the issue of new instructions to himself. The existing Instrument is in effect the execution and fulfilment of the intentions of Parliament as embodied in the great Act of 1935, and although its provisions do not directly conflict with His Majesty's Government's new policy, they are not by now fully consistent with it. Strictly there should be a new Instrument, but as there will be no direct inconsistency until new legislation for the actual transfer of power is passed, the Government agreed to let it slide. Mountbatten, however, has insisted on a directive of some sort to amplify the Instrument, feeling it is essential that the object of his appointment should be clearly set out by the Prime Minister. He has asked for it in the form of a letter to himself from Mr. Attlee.

Once this was approved he had a lot to do in the drafting of the text, which contains the following major points of policy for his guidance :—

(1) The definite objective of the British Government is to obtain a unitary Government for British India and the Indian States, if possible within the British Commonwealth, through the medium of a Constituent Assembly set up and run in accordance with the Cabinet Mission Plan. He was instructed to do the utmost in his power to persuade all Parties to work together towards this end. The insertion of the phrase " if possible within the British Commonwealth " is at the special request of Mountbatten, who feels that he must strive for a solution which leaves such good feeling that the Indian Parties will want to remain within the Commonwealth.

(2) Since, however, the Cabinet Mission Plan can become operative in respect of British India only by agreement between the two major Parties, there can be no question of compelling either Party to accept it. If by the 1st October Mountbatten considers there is no prospect of reaching a settlement on the basis of unitary Government, he is to report to the British Government on the steps he considers should be taken for the hand-over of power on the due date.

(3) For guidance in his relations with the States, Mr. Attlee laid down that he was to do his best to persuade Rulers of States in which political progress had been slow to go forward rapidly towards the introduction of some form of more democratic government in their States, and towards the formulation of fair and just arrangements with the leaders of British India as to their future relationships.

(4) As far as his administration of British India was concerned, the keynote of this was to be the closest co-operation with Indians.

(5) Transfer of power was to be in accordance with Indian Defence requirements, and he was to impress upon the Indian leaders the importance of avoiding a break in the continuity of the Indian Army and to point out the need for continued collaboration in the security of the Indian Ocean.

Attlee's letter certainly embodies the most formidable terms of reference ever given by a Government to a Viceroy.

LONDON, *Tuesday, 11th March, 1947*

In the welter of engagements Mountbatten has been careful to include the Opposition leaders. Some of these discussions have been quite private and informal. To-night he came round to my flat for the first meeting he has ever had with Lord Samuel. Lord Samuel arrived a few minutes early, and Mountbatten on time. It came as quite a jolt to see the Admiral in civvies—teddy-bear coat and bowler hat perched on the top of his head. I understand the Admiralty Fleet Orders describe his latest appointment as " Rear-Admiral etc., seconded temporary duty Viceroy "!

He was at pains to stress that as far as he was concerned his appointment had the cordial approval of the King, who had personally appealed to him, on grounds of national duty, to accept it. Attlee had observed all the proprieties, and the Opposition were quite wrong in saying that it was simply the Prime Minister's appointment. He could not see what alternative there was to a time limit. June 1948 might not be long enough, but Wavell himself had advised this date on the grounds that the administrative services would have run down by then. Speaking from the purely personal view-point, he said it was probably better to take over when the situation was at its lowest ebb. Bihar and Bengal had been in a sense inoculated after their recent outbreaks, but he felt the present Punjab crisis was inevitable. The situation in the Punjab had been very tense for some time. The Moslem Coalition Prime Minister had for the past five months been compelled to move from house to house each night to avoid the threat of assassination at the hands of the Moslem League. Mountbatten felt there would probably also be trouble from the north in the North-west Frontier Province.

He recalled the warning he had given to Sir Hubert Rance before Rance left to become Governor of Burma. It was, that he should wait until the situation was at its worst; but he had gone out, from a sense of duty, a bit too quickly, and instead of arriving while the big Rangoon strike was on, did so a few days before it began, thereby incurring some of the blame for it. Mountbatten felt that in his own case it would not be possible for anyone to hold him responsible for the present troubles in India, and that this in itself would be a great advantage n the negotiations ahead of him. He asked for advice on the lines he should pursue. Answering his own question and thinking aloud, he said he favoured a week's private talk with the key leaders in Simla. This should supply occasion for a completely frank and uninhibited exchange of views. Samuel was content to do most of the listening, but stressed the need for maintaining the constitutional link with the Crown after the transfer of power, perhaps even through the retention of the Vice-regal title.

I was very glad to have been able to arrange this meeting, as, in spite of obvious disparities of age and outlook, the two men have much in common. Samuel's influence in the Lords is very great, and his good-will in the coming months may be of value out of all proportion to the Liberal voting strength.

LONDON, *Thursday, 13th March, 1947*

I am doing my best to brief myself with political background information during the few days left to us before our departure. I dined this evening with Sir George and Lady Schuster at the Savoy. Schuster, who had been Finance Member of the Viceroy's Executive Council during Lord Halifax's Viceroyalty, was very happy about Mountbatten's staff set-up. He felt that the tragedy was the lack of first-class Moslem leadership. He recalled that Jinnah had been a complete failure at the Round Table Conference in 1930—so much so, that he did not see fit to return to India for some time afterwards, but instead lived in semi-retirement in Scotland with his sister, where Schuster recalls encountering them on more than one occasion. The Punjab was also a tragedy. Fifty years of reform and communal co-operation had been sacrificed on the altar of Moslem League fanaticism.

Perhaps the most troublesome of Mountbatten's preliminary problems has been to achieve an agreed policy, in advance of his departure for India, on the compensation of the Indian Civil and Military Services, known as the Secretary of State's Services. On this matter he has throughout expressed himself with characteristic energy and decision. To-day the solution upon which he has been insisting has been finally agreed.

As far as the Secretary of State's Services were concerned, three specific promises had originally been made to them. First, with the termination of their appointments, due to constitutional changes, they were to receive lump-sum payments at rates not less favourable than war-service candidates, which meant a lump-sum payment substantially larger than would have been admissible on a voluntary retirement. Secondly, whether or not they wanted to continue with the new Indian Government, their contracts with the Secretary of State would be terminated. So either way they would all be eligible for the compensation. Thirdly, there was to be no compulsion to induce them to serve under the new conditions, and every attempt by the Indian Government to fix low rates with this in view was to be resisted. In all this there was to be no differentiation between European and Indian recruits.

Sardar Vallabhbhai Patel, who held India's Home Portfolio, soon made it clear that he objected to the whole concept of compensation in principle and in detail. The new Government, he said, could not be bound by the pledges of its predecessor under the control of the British Parliament and Secretary of State, and if the " not less favourable " rate was insisted on, the British Exchequer should foot the bill. Arthur Henderson, Parliamentary Under-Secretary for India, went out to Delhi in January in a vain effort to persuade Patel to modify his view and accept the proposal. But this setback did not cause Mountbatten to change his views. He urged in particular that any compromise would be regarded as a breach of faith by all members of the Services on whom he would be heavily relying for a special last effort. After prolonged discussions last week, he declared it was impossible to exaggerate the importance of having authority to announce definite and equitable terms to British officials and officers immediately on his arrival in India. He urged most strongly that the original scheme should stand subject to the proviso that it should apply only to British nationals. If the Indian Government will not foot the bill, then he should be authorised to say that His Majesty's Government was prepared to guarantee the terms. He left those in authority here under no illusion that he was making their adherence to the original terms of compensation a major issue of principle and his view has prevailed. There will be no modifications, civilian or military. It was made clear, however, that if His Majesty's Government is left to bear the burden, the expenditure would have to be taken into account in negotiations for the settlement of the Indian Sterling Balances.

LONDON, *Monday, 17th March, 1947*

A crowded day. In the morning I saw Lady Mountbatten at Chester Street, who is extremely kind and cordial about my joining the party. I mentioned that at dinner last night with the Laytons, Lady Layton had referred to the great influence in Sardar Patel's household of his daughter Maniben, who was reported to be very suspicious of British intentions. Lady Mountbatten agreed, adding that Jinnah's sister, no less influential, was also reported to hold strong views and to be a formidable factor in the situation. Mountbatten, I know, has asked her to establish early contact with the women who matter in India and who have hitherto had no relations with Viceroy's House.

Social diplomacy will be a vital sector of the Mountbattens' goodwill campaign, and I can imagine no better ambassadress to carry out the pioneer work so urgently required in this neglected field. They are taking their younger daughter Pamela away from school to be with them. She is not yet eighteen, but is all set to take her part in the family effort, and in particular to identify herself with Youth movements.

I went on to 10 Downing Street, where I had a most helpful talk with Francis Williams, the Prime Minister's Public Relations Officer. He has given me a number of useful introductions and has shown himself keenly alive to the scale of the Public Relations problems confronting me. I leave fortified by the knowledge of his firm support. I have also received invaluable help from A. H. Joyce, the able and experienced Officer in charge of Information at the India Office, who is most co-operative and full of sound doctrine.

In the evening to India House for a reception given by the High Commissioner, Sir Samuel Runganadhan. From the Press point of view it was a veritable bear-garden, and a most useful commentary on the paper I have just put in warning Mountbatten against large-scale Press conferences in India. We had no idea that the Press was going to be let loose on him at this particular gathering. The whole place was floodlit for a newsreel interview, and Mountbatten was waylaid by about a dozen London correspondents of Indian papers, who buzzed round him like a swarm of bees working overtime. No attempt was made by the host to rescue him. One particularly persistent reporter asked him if he had ever read Karl Marx, and a little later assured him that he approved his appointment, as it would no doubt be best for an Admiral to deal with the British evacuation by sea! I left the party with Mountbatten, who was, I think, much chastened by his experience. His only comment was, " We live and learn."

LONDON, *Tuesday, 18th March, 1947*

I spent most of the morning packing, but dropped in at the India Office, where I told Ismay about last night's bun-fight. He recalled Churchill's motto on his relations with the Press during the war; " No publicity until Victory ".

I had lunch in Fleet Street with an editor who spoke bitterly about some of India's business magnates, "Men with no principles save the acquisition of money, men without taste or culture, who eat bad food in ugly houses". Their outlook, he added, was in striking contrast to the idealism of the political leaders they were backing.

In the evening we attended the big farewell party given by the Mountbattens at the Royal Automobile Club, of which he is President. It was a tremendous crush. The seven hundred guests seemed to include every celebrity in London. The Duke of Gloucester, just off the boat from Australia, and looking very bronzed, and the Duchess of Kent, were both there. Surprised to find Mr. Attlee standing alone and talking to no one, I took the opportunity to introduce myself to him. The name Campbell-Johnson raised an echo in his memory, but we agreed it could not have been my father he had in mind. He spoke about my particular job, and was good enough to say that he considered it a very important one.

I exchanged a few words with Noel Coward. He deplored Mountbatten being landed with such a tremendous task. "The position having become impossible, they call on Dickie." A young Tory M.P. who was standing nearby saw fit to add his word against the Government, but Coward at once retorted, "You're no better. Nicer manners, perhaps, but no more talent." The Mountbattens were at their best, saying just the right word to everyone. Altogether a most encouraging send-off.

MALTA, *Wednesday, 19th March, 1947*

It has been arranged for Mountbatten and his staff to fly out to India in the two York aircraft *MW101* and *MW102*, which were allotted respectively to the King, and to Mountbatten as Supreme Commander South-east Asia, during the war. Mountbatten, Lady Mountbatten and Pamela, with Ronnie Brockman and Peter Howes,*.do not leave until to-morrow. They will be flying rather more ruthlessly than ourselves, and when we reach Delhi they will be only two hours flying time behind us. Fortunately I am in Ismay's plane, who made it clear that he proposes to travel to a comfortable schedule, arriving at the various staging points at civilised hours.

After being obliged to shed some of our luggage, we took off at 11.30 a.m., about half an hour late. The first leg of the journey was uneventful and the route difficult to follow. We passed over Perpignan and Perigeux, and then made a wide sweep, taking the course of a following wind along the North African coast. We came finally to Malta from the south by way of Cape Bon—dark purple in the sunset. On arrival at Luqa, Ismay and Miéville drove off to dine with the mighty,

---

* Lieutenant-Commander Peter Howes, D.S.C., R.N., previously nominated as Lord Mountbatten's Flag Lieutenant on the First Cruiser Squadron, and now to become his senior A.D.C. in India. He included among his A.D.C.'s three Indian serving officers, one from each Service, appointed on a full-time basis and the first to hold such posts.

while the rest of us were graded as V.I.P. 2, which, as Martin Gilliat, Mountbatten's new Deputy Military Secretary, wryly observed, meant that we were low life, mere parasites of the great; it also meant bare beds in bare rooms.

After dinner one member of our party became very learned on Maltese culture, customs and history—their stone-masonry, their goat economy, etc. He explained that some British official, in his wisdom, had laid down a hundred years ago that all ships had to pay their harbour dues by bringing in earth. This ruling, which would seem sufficiently creative and unorthodox to have earned instant dismissal for its perpetrator, has in fact helped to give an arable top dressing to an otherwise bare rock. Ended the day with some good Naval rum to counteract the frosty air.

FAYID, *Thursday, 20th March, 1947*

We were up an hour earlier than necessary in some confusion as between Greenwich Mean, British Summer and Maltese time—in fact, no change was involved. After porridge, bacon-and-egg breakfast, off at nine. Admiral Willis, Commander-in-Chief Mediterranean, was at the airfield to see our party off. The weather was bright and clear, and as we circled over Valletta at about three thousand feet the sea was aquamarine; cruisers, destroyers and an aircraft-carrier looked, indeed, like painted ships upon a painted ocean.

We arrived at Fayid by about tea-time, and I must say it looked the kind of place the Germans would have provided for us if they had won at Alamein. We drove out to an officers' club overlooking the Great Bitter Lake. After the savage English winter it was strange to be taking off one's waistcoat and looking for shade from the heat of the sun. It was good to see once again the magic colour-change from blue to purple as the night loomed up out of the deserts of Arabia. In the evening John Lascelles,* who is coming out as Ismay's Personal Assistant, introduced a friend of his who had been an Intelligence officer in these parts for some ten years. We had a very interesting talk on many things to the accompaniment of the best Cognac I have tasted in years and the lilting rhythm of a German band, raised from among the seventy thousand German prisoners-of-war still left in Egypt. They played " The Blue Danube " and, at our request, " Lili Marlene ", which conjured up visions of Vienna and the lamplights by the banks of Suez.

KARACHI, *Friday, 21st March, 1947*

We arrived at Karachi after ten exhausting hours in the air. The whole of this erstwhile squalid airport has at last been modernised, but the improvements—including an imposing reception office—are at least three years too long in coming. The traffic is now only a trickle compared with the war-time flow. It is infuriating to think of the

* Captain J. F. Lascelles, Grenadier Guards, and son of Sir Alan Lascelles, Private Secretary to the King.

needless discomfort we all suffered here throughout the war. Strangely enough, the first sound I heard on leaving the aircraft was a record of Bing Crosby crooning " Moonlight Becomes You ", which was virtually a signature tune when I first touched down in India in October 1943 to take part in the setting up of S.E.A.C. Headquarters.

CHAPTER THREE

THE FIRST WEEK

VICEROY'S HOUSE, NEW DELHI, *Saturday, 22nd March, 1947*

LEFT KARACHI PROMPTLY at 9.15 a.m., after some fitful sleep on a very hard Indian bed, for the last eight hundred miles of our journey over the deserts of Sind and Rajputana to Delhi. This was my seventh flight between England and India, and the abiding impression is desert, four thousand miles of it, without an appreciable break from the sands of Tunis to the foothills of the Himalayas. We touched down at Palam airfield exactly to schedule at 12.30 p.m. We were met by the Commander-in-Chief, Field-Marshal Auchinleck—a very nice gesture on his part, as two hours later he was due back to join the much larger party receiving Mountbatten's aircraft. We were whisked away without luggage worries in Viceregal cars, and the year's high living had begun.

Immediately on arrival at Viceroy's House we were told that we were due to lunch with the Wavells. It was to be their last lunch-party as Viceroy and Vicereine. It was served on the terrace of the Moghul gardens under the shadow of the south-west wing of Lutyen's vast imperial palace. While waiting for Their Excellencies to arrive, Ismay engaged in a friendly chat with some of the senior *kitmutgars* who remembered him when he was here as Willingdon's Military Secretary.

I found myself placed next to the Viceroy. I had been warned he probably might not have much to say to me, but before long conversation was in full flow. After some inquiries about the nature of my job and career, he began talking about publishing, and, as an author himself, showed a lively interest in the technical difficulties which publishers have been facing since the war. This led him to discuss the publication of military despatches in the light of Mountbatten's Report on the South-east Asia Command campaign, now, after months of hard labour, almost ready for submission to the Combined Chiefs of Staff. Wavell said that he did not take a great deal of trouble over his own. He felt the whole object of despatches had undergone a complete change since Wellington had sat down in the evening after Waterloo to write out his report of the battle. In those days a despatch was simply the first news, official or otherwise, that a battle had taken place. Even Haig's despatch had been completed before the end of the First World War; and he told of one general who was so busy on a despatch that he forgot to follow up the enemy he had just beaten, with most unfortunate results! Nowadays commanders were able to sit back and find explanations long afterwards for their actions that would not have occurred to them at the time of the battle.

He said he understood that General Edmonds, who was a very old friend of his, was still engaged on his mammoth history of the 1914–18 War, having two or three more volumes yet to write. He had to cover up as well. He recalled his comment on one particular narrative, a most elaborate apologia. It was: "of course the whole damned lot ran away". Wavell said that he himself had been asked to take charge of the official history of this War. He rather felt two histories were needed, one for the public, and one that would tell the unvarnished truth.

While on the subject of eye-witness history, I mentioned Hugh Trevor-Roper's new book, "The Last Days of Hitler", a brilliant example of contemporary research and reconstruction. This led Wavell to suggest that the Nuremberg trials and Hitler's violent end would not really discourage future tyrants. The Nazis had had twelve years of the power and the glory, which was far more than they could have expected. Theirs was really only another version of the story of Faust.

Wavell, who looked very bronzed and fit, was most affable. The A.D.C.'s seemed relieved to find him so talkative. Usually to be next to him is to be placed in a silent corner beside a non-conductor; not so to-day. It was difficult to believe that the Wavells would actually be leaving first thing to-morrow morning. Curiously enough, I had first arrived in Delhi on the 19th October, 1943, the day after Wavell had taken over from Linlithgow. It seemed incredible that I should have returned here in such different circumstances, but still with Mountbatten.

A whole era has passed since then, and on the eve of his departure I cannot help reflecting on the scale of the transformation brought about since the outset of his term of office. Then we had the Japanese armies on the borders of Assam, the whole Congress High Command imprisoned. Militarily the atmosphere was one of undetermined danger and politically of indefinite deadlock. I can recall sitting in on Southeast Asia Command planning discussions at the end of 1943 which envisaged us inching our way up the China coast and gave no guarantee that the war would be over by 1947. There were errors, no doubt, as Wavell has once again freely admitted in his farewell address—perhaps too freely, for far too many unthinking people take you at your word in politics if you overdo the apologies, and Wavell may well be the victim of his own modesty. Few men could have seen India so safely and far along the road to self-government.

During the afternoon there was much preparation and bustle in the main courtyard and up the steps leading to the great Durbar Hall of Viceroy's House. At 3.45 p.m. the Mountbattens duly arrived in the open landau with the Governor-General's escort and outriders. They were conducted up the long flight of steps—red-carpeted for the occasion—by Colonel Douglas Currie, the Military Secretary, and an A.D.C. At the top they were received by the Wavells. Lady Mountbatten curtsied and Mountbatten bowed his head to the Viceroy for the first and last time on this mission. They stood talking for quite a while, long enough for the ubiquitous camera-men to take some pleasant shots of them.

Vernon Erskine Crum tells me that European sentiment here is definitely anti-Mountbatten on four grounds ;—

(1) that he knows nothing about India;

(2) that he is bringing a staff who know nothing about India and who are doing good men out of good jobs;

(3) that he is a play-boy;

(4) that Wavell has been treated abominably and there is no good reason for his removal.

Mountbatten can be trusted to deal by his presence and actions with (1) and (3) within a matter of days. (2) clearly cannot refer to Ismay or Miéville—so that leaves the rest of us! We are not, of course, doing any-one out of jobs, but are merely additional to the normal Viceregal set-up. But we shall have to tread carefully and avoid tender corns. (4) is primarily the responsibility of Attlee, who has failed to say the generous word.

All this may be the view of the British about us, but on our side it is all too easy to start off with the feeling that Mountbatten has been called in after the situation has become hopeless, and that the Government has propounded a transfer of power without knowing how it can be effected. We have inherited *inter alia* communal rioting, which is spreading as though by chain reaction; the key Province of the Punjab, with its threefold Hindu, Moslem and Sikh Communal problem, governed by emergency decree; a Viceregal plan which is nothing more nor less than a phased military evacuation; a Congress formula for an Independent Sovereign Republic with a Direct Action campaign by the Moslem League to resist it; Paramountcy which returns to the Indian Princes but contains no machinery for direct negotiation to provide a new relation-ship with our successors in British India or, indeed, with anyone else.

So, in short, we have the people rioting, the Princes falling out among themselves, the entire Indian Civil Service and Police running down, and the British, who are left sceptical and full of foreboding. I detect in Mountbatten, however, just the same incurable optimism that uplifted us all when we arrived here in Delhi some three and a half years ago on the then " impossible " task of creating South-east Asia Command out of the ashes of defeat and depression.

I hear that the Press side of things was badly handled at the airfield. One distinguished European correspondent described himself as seized by the scruff of the neck and herded into a Press pen which was so far removed from the aircraft that he was unable to distinguish any of the *dramatis personæ*! Indian Press correspondents and photographers were equally indignant. Clearly there is a Public Relations job to do here.

Wavell and Mountbatten have been in conference both before and after dinner. They have been discussing what George Abell, Private Secretary to the Viceroy,* calls " diplomacy ", with Mountbatten freely

* In the interests of continuity, and because of the heavy administrative load involved in the speed-up of the transfer of power, Lord Mountbatten asked the existing Viceroy's staff to carry on. In addition to George Abell, they comprised, John Christie, Ian Scott and Peter Scott, Joint, Deputy and Assistant Private Secre-taries to the Viceroy respectively. Among the members of the personal Staff whom Mountbatten asked to remain were Colonel D. H. Currie and Lieutenant-Colonel A. C. Taylor, Military Secretary and Surgeon to the Viceroy respectively. The Indian Civil Service members duly left on 15th August, but most of the personal staff stayed on with Lord Mountbatten during his term as Governor-General.

and frankly picking Wavell's brains and extracting all possible background information in the very few hours at his disposal for doing so. Hitherto the custom has been for the incoming and outgoing Viceroys to cross without any such opportunity occurring.

Mountbatten has wasted no time whatever in sending off two simple and straightforward letters to Gandhi and Jinnah expressing the hope that it will be possible for them to come and see him soon. In Gandhi's case he appreciates his preoccupations in Bihar, where he is carrying out his "repentance tours" through the areas of the worst communal disturbance. Incidentally Gandhi is so preoccupied that it is still doubtful whether he will attend the great Pan Asian Conference which is due to be held under the shadow of the Red Fort on Monday. Mountbatten's immediate approach to Gandhi and Jinnah in this way, even before Wavell has left, is typical of the man and his methods.

VICEROY'S HOUSE, NEW DELHI, *Sunday, 23rd March, 1947*

The Wavells left promptly at 8.15 in the morning. It has certainly been no day of rest for us. There has been much administrative panic in connection with the publicity for to-morrow's Swearing-in Ceremony. It has never before been photographed or filmed, and now is the last chance. I went round to Mountbatten's suite and had a discussion with the Viceroy designate, clad in his underpants and vest, on the implications of letting in all the local news-reel and camera-men, twenty-two altogether, or leaving some out. He proposed that a large platform should be built for them at triforium level near the circular dome, which I am quite sure will not be acceptable to any of the interested parties. He showed me this morning's masterpiece on the front page of *Dawn*. It is a photograph of Ronnie Brockman and Elizabeth Ward, Lady Mountbatten's private secretary, in which they are, of course, described as "Lord and Lady Louis arriving"! *

The reaction of the Indian Press to Mountbatten on his arrival is satisfactory. He is pleased at the tributes paid to Wavell, and says he would have hated to be written up at Wavell's expense. In any case, he prefers to start off on a low note.

He has decided on another innovation—a brief address as part of the Swearing-in Ceremony. He read out George Abell's first draft to me. I think the speech is well conceived and well timed, for he must seize the initiative quickly, and this calls for imaginative and unusual action. During dinner a draft revised by Mountbatten himself was handed to me. It contained one sentence which worried me. After commenting on the British Government's resolve to effect the transfer of power by June 1948, he proposes to add "in fact a solution must be reached within the next six months if there is to be adequate time for it to be implemented". I felt this wording was likely to be misinterpreted, and even taken to imply an escape clause from the Government's hitherto unqualified time limit. Mountbatten's first reaction is that he has the

* As they were Lord and Lady Louis Mountbatten before he received his Viscounty for war services, they are still colloquially called Lord and Lady Louis.

Government's authority to report progress by October, so why not say so now? But this is his specially chosen first bow. If he starts off by unwittingly throwing doubt on the Government's time-limit pledge, I can imagine nothing more disastrous.

It is just after 1 a.m., and an A.D.C. has come through to say that His Excellency has revised his speech, and what is he to do about giving it to the Press? The ambiguous sentence, I am relieved to say, is out.

I saw Lady Mountbatten late this evening, and told her that H.E. had suggested that it might be a good idea if I were to test out the triforium platform for the camera-men, to see if it is safe. She said it was a good thing my wife hadn't yet arrived to hear of this plan!

VICEROY'S HOUSE, NEW DELHI, *Monday, 24th March, 1947*

Up betimes for the Swearing-in Ceremony. It was similar in form to Wavell's first investiture, which I had attended in the Durbar Hall in 1943: the same trumpets from the roof acting as a shattering prelude; then the A.D.C.'s in stiff procession leading Their Excellencies towards the thrones. In all this royal splendour the Mountbattens indeed showed themselves to be to the manner born. Mountbatten himself looked superb with the dark-blue ribbon of Knight of the Garter and the overwhelming array of orders and decorations across his chest. In addition to the Garter they were headed by no fewer than three Grand Crosses, the K.C.B. and D.S.O.

Lady Mountbatten, for her part, was the epitome of grace, with her new order of the Crown of India, besides all her war medals and other decorations, on her dress of ivory brocade. The red-and-gold thrones were set in bold relief by the lighting concealed in the rich red velvet hangings. Arc lights played down upon the scene as Sir Patrick Spens, the Lord Chief Justice of India, administered the oath and Mountbatten repeated it after him, never faltering with his formidable string of christian names.

The film cameras whirred and the flash-bulbs went off for the first time in the confines of the Durbar Hall. I remained on guard with the photographers to ensure that there were no ugly rushes, but they all behaved admirably. Mountbatten's responses and his address, although delivered with great emphasis, were almost inaudible at the back of the hall: the acoustics were abominable; even quite near to him it was most difficult to catch what he was saying.

The whole ceremony was completed in exactly a quarter of an hour, the address taking four minutes. On each side of the thrones were flanked the Leaders of the new India, upon whom will rest such terrifying responsibility in the coming weeks. I noticed both Nehru and Liaquat Ali Khan listened with the utmost attention to the speech, which of course came as a complete surprise to them. Immediate Press reaction to the move was most favourable. Eric Britter of *The Times* came up afterwards to ask me whether it was all right for him to say that it was Mountbatten's own idea. I replied that there was no objection, as it was certainly the truth. Britter said it was an excellent initiative and would get him off to a good start.

There were two important, and as far as I know unexplained, absentees —the Nawab of Bhopal and the Maharaja of Bikaner. George Abell darted up just before ten past ten to see if Bhopal had taken his place, but he had not, and the seat was removed. Considering that both Bhopal and Bikaner are Mountbatten's two oldest personal friends in India, and the importance attached by the Princes to ceremonial etiquette in general and the Viceregal connection in particular, their failure to be present to-day is a good indication of disunity and crisis in their ranks.

In the afternoon I made my first escape since my arrival from the marble halls of Viceroy's House to do some shopping. Lady Mountbatten remarked to me that she always suspected, and now knows, just how easy it is to get engulfed in this labyrinthine palace and live self-centred and cut off from the outside world.

Mountbatten had three hours with Nehru and two with Liaquat this afternoon. They discussed Liaquat's Budget, the immediate bone of contention between the two Parties. Wavell has warned Mountbatten that he will find this a very awkward opening problem to tackle when he presides over his first Executive Council. Liaquat, as Finance Minister in the Interim Government, by proposing heavy taxes on all large incomes, has put the Congress into the invidious position of being called upon to protect its big business supporters and of seeking relief for them apparently at the expense of its own progressive and equalitarian declarations. The feeling is that some compromise will be found, for there is a limit beyond which neither the Moslem League nor the Congress can go in taxing wealthy subscribers.

VICEROY'S HOUSE, NEW DELHI, *Tuesday, 25th March, 1947*

I attended Mountbatten's first Staff Meeting, which took place in his dark, air-cooled study, and consisted of Ismay, Miéville, George Abell, Brockman, Erskine Crum and myself. It is Mountbatten's intention that these informal round-table moots should be held on a day-to-day basis, enabling him to think aloud without any mental reservations. They are to be a direct continuation, in a far more intimate form, of the staff techniques he instituted at Combined Operations and developed in South-east Asia Command. Mountbatten started off with a lively account of yesterday's interviews with Nehru and Liaquat, as well as with Bikaner and Bhopal, who both came round to explain their absence from the Swearing-in Ceremony. At the end of all these sessions, six hours in all, he confessed that he felt like a " boiled egg ".

The Bhopal and Bikaner interviews revealed the full scale of the split among the Princes. This is a great grief to Bhopal, who feels that Bikaner and the other " dissidents ", by allowing themselves to take part in the Constituent Assembly, are becoming the tools of Congress and undermining the whole bargaining position of the States—hitherto they had succeeded in standing on their own outside the communal fury. Bhopal thought the time limit was quite impossible, and if enforced must involve bloodshed and chaos. He asked Mountbatten earnestly whether there was any possible escape from it. Mountbatten said there was of course one, and only one, way out, and that was an invitation from all the Indian parties to us to remain—a most unlikely contingency. But Bhopal was not so sure that as the time drew on such an offer might not be made.

Bikaner, whom Mountbatten questioned on this point, was not so sanguine. He argued for the so-called " dissident " Princes, and while agreeing that the split was most unfortunate, stressed that it was Bhopal who, by his attitude to the Interim Government, had caused the communal issue to be raised among them. The " dissidents ", by taking part in the Constituent Assembly, would immeasurably strengthen the new central régime, and help to ensure that it was not in fact a purely Congress set-up.

Mountbatten's first interview with Nehru was illuminating. In expansive mood Nehru ran through his interpretation of the major developments from the period of the Cabinet Mission onwards. Mountbatten considered it was substantially accurate and tallied with information he had gathered in London. In Nehru's view, Wavell had made one serious blunder in inviting the Moslem League to come into the Interim Government, instead of waiting a little longer for them to ask to be brought in. He spoke of a private Moslem League meeting at which Jinnah had in fact already capitulated on this issue.

Mountbatten asked Nehru to give him his own estimate of Jinnah. Nehru recalled that he had done so in his recent book, but this did not prevent him from giving a further penetrating impression. Nehru said the essential thing to realise about Jinnah is that he is a man to whom success has come very late in life—at over sixty. Before that he had not been a major figure in Indian politics. He was a successful lawyer, but not an especially good one, and Nehru stressed the necessity of making this particular distinction in Jinnah's case. The secret of his success— and it had been tremendous, if only for its emotional intensity—was in his capacity to take up a permanently negative attitude. This he had done with complete singleness of purpose ever since 1935. He knew that Pakistan could never stand up to constructive criticism, and he had ensured that it should never be subjected to it.

Mountbatten next asked what Nehru thought was the biggest single problem facing India to-day, and he replied at once, the economic one. Thereupon Mountbatten asked him whether he was satisfied with the way the Interim Government was tackling it. Nehru said he was not, but the position was made impossible by the League, who were determined to sabotage any economic planning from the centre. Such planning, if it succeeded, would *ipso facto* undermine the case for Pakistan with regard to the Punjab. Nehru put forward a proposal he has made before of a tripartite administration of the Province divided up on communal lines, with a central authority to deal with certain major non-communal subjects. He was convinced this was the only way to break the intolerable deadlock of Government under Section 93,* which Wavell had had to impose at the beginning of this month.

The vexed question of compensation for the Indian Civil Service on the transfer of power was raised at this interview. Nehru thought we were crazy to want to compensate civil servants to whom the offer of remaining on in their jobs was open. The new Government would pledge itself to offer them the same conditions of contract as they had previously enjoyed. Mountbatten said there could be no question of the British Government going back on its word, and he could not think Nehru was suggesting that it should. Nehru admitted that as far as the British were concerned it was, of course, purely the British Government's affair. But even so, why compensate them on such a lavish scale? This could only encourage them to leave their posts. And what about the Indians? Here it was a question of their continuing in the service of their own countrymen. The proposals really were crazy as they stood. Mountbatten, however, firmly asked for his support on them. He thought Nehru had misunderstood British psychology. The more lavish and clear-cut the compensation, the greater was the likelihood of the British civil servants remaining on.

In Mountbatten's view, Nehru was extremely frank and fair, and astounded him by actually suggesting at one point an Anglo-Indian union involving nothing less than common citizenship—in effect, a far closer bond than Commonwealth status, which Nehru felt was psychologically and emotionally unacceptable.

At the end of the interview, as Nehru was about to take his leave, Mountbatten said to him, " Mr. Nehru, I want you to regard me not as the last Viceroy winding up the British Raj, but as the first to lead the way to the new India." Nehru turned, looked intensely moved, smiled and then said, " Now I know what they mean when they speak of your charm being so dangerous."

During his talk Liaquat asked a leading question about Mountbatten's Swearing-in speech. He wanted to know who was responsible for the idea. Mountbatten said he could answer that at once. It was entirely his own, and produced at nobody's request. Indeed, some of his own staff had been against it. " I am pleased to hear that," said Liaquat, " for no fewer than three highly placed and well-informed sources had assured me that you had made the speech at the request of Congress." This little incident is a good example of the prevailing communal suspicion, and no time has been lost by either side in pressing home all possible points it can against the other.

Perhaps the most significant commentary on Nehru's Punjab proposals was a telegram from Sir Evan Jenkins, the Governor of the Punjab, to which Miéville drew attention at the Staff Meeting. Jenkins reported that Giani Kartar Singh, an influential Sikh leader, had stated that in the absence of an agreement between Congress and the League acceptable to the Sikhs, the Sikhs must insist on the partition of the Punjab and

* A reference to Section 93 of the Government of India Act of 1935, which under conditions of civil disturbance enabled the Viceroy and Governors of the Indian Provinces to invoke reserve powers and govern by decree.

would resist with all their resources any endeavour to set up a Moslem League Ministry there in the meanwhile. This speech has additional authority in that the Sikhs have already persuaded Congress to put up a resolution—accepted, incidentally, by Wavell only a week before Mountbatten arrived—in favour of partitioning the Punjab.

VICEROY'S HOUSE, NEW DELHI, *Wednesday, 26th March, 1947*

Mountbatten began this morning's Staff Meeting with another vivid *résumé* of yesterday's interviews. Quite apart from keeping notes, he has a photographic memory and the journalist's perception of human detail. Yesterday he saw Dr. John Matthai, Minister for Railways, Sir Conrad Corfield, Secretary to the Political Department, and, last but not least, Vallabhbhai Patel. Matthai, who is a Christian and in no sense a Party man, gave, in Mountbatten's estimate, a first-class appreciation, in every way balanced and reasonable. Matthai stressed that a horrifying feature of the situation was that all those who were trying to steer an honourable straight course were gradually losing their influence and becoming increasingly disliked and distrusted by both sides. Matthai said that he had done his best, for instance, to back Liaquat's Budget, only to find himself subjected to bitter attack by *Dawn*.

Corfield, who is constitutionally adviser to the Viceroy in his capacity as Crown Representative * on all matters affecting the Indian States, argued with some bitterness that Bikaner, by taking his place in the Constituent Assembly, had seriously weakened the bargaining power of the Princes. Corfield is clearly on Bhopal's side in this controversy, and seems to see the Princes as a potential " Third Force " in the transfer of power.

Mountbatten had been somewhat apprehensive about his first meeting with Patel, who has the reputation of being the strong man in the Congress High Command, but he very quickly detected a twinkle in the Sardar's eye. His approach to the whole problem was clear and decisive. India must get rid of the Moslem League. The League was actually boasting about the developments in the Punjab. They must be mad.

* The term Viceroy comprised the dual but separate functions of Governor-General of British India with its eleven Provinces (Bombay, Madras, Bengal, United Provinces, Punjab, Central Provinces, Bihar, Orissa, Assam, Sind and North-west Frontier Province), and Crown Representative to some five hundred and sixty-five States (the largest of which are Hyderabad, Kashmir and Mysore). The relationship between the Crown Representative and the Indian States was governed by treaties which established Great Britain as the Paramount Power and deprived the States of full sovereignty. The Paramount Power, for instance, reserved control over such central subjects as defence, communications and foreign policy, as well as disciplinary authority over the Princes in the event of misrule. The Princes, whose territories comprise roughly a third of India's territory and a quarter of her population, were given precedence under Paramountcy in terms of the gun salutes accorded to them. Thus they were described in order of seniority as Twenty-one-, Nineteen-, Seventeen-, Fifteen-gun Princes, and so on down the scale. The Crown Representative's relations with the Indian States were administered up to the transfer of power by the Political Department, of which Sir Conrad Corfield was the last Secretary.

All was serene until they touched on compensation. At this point Patel raised his hand and vowed that if any Indian accepted compensation he would never be employed again.

In the evening I dined with Maurice Zinkin, a very clever young Indian Civil Service man whom I first met in Delhi in 1943. He is now working as an assistant secretary in the Finance Department, and as an official has been fairly closely involved in the framing of Liaquat's controversial budget, which soaks the Hindu rich and is calculated to widen the breach between the millionaire and four-anna subscribers to Congress. Maurice had also invited K. M. Panikkar, whom I was particularly anxious to meet. Panikkar sports a small imperial beard. He is an historian, politician and journalist, a man of prodigious learning and profound judgement and no mean practitioner in the dying art of good conversation.

I gave him a clear run by asking, " What would you do if you were in Mountbatten's place?" He replied at once that Mountbatten, as a Naval strategist, must realise that British interest was best served by the creation of a solid centralised State based on India's seaboard, on more than three hundred millions of the people and on geographical and religious unity. Hindustan is the elephant, he said, and Pakistan the two ears. The elephant can live without the ears. He admitted frankly that Jinnah could make an essentially reasonable case. In a four-roomed house he asks for only one room, but he wants that room to be his own. He is unwilling to entrust local Moslem majorities to a strong Hindu-controlled central government. Panikkar's thesis was in effect that we should not try to impose a larger unity than India was fundamentally seeking. Nehru's tripartite proposals for the Punjab were the first sign of Congress acceptance of the Hindustan–Pakistan division. Jinnah's experience with the Sikhs must have made him realise that the unity of the Punjab was physically impossible.

Historically speaking, Panikkar asserted, the Punjab is a British myth, and no more the special home of a fighting race than anywhere else in India. Over the centuries the historical greatness of India was never identified with a strong Punjab. The British should beware of the Punjab myth and of the larger " Central Asia" myth which had dominated so much of their thought and policy in the past. It was necessary to think in post-war terms.

He then turned to the problem of the Princes. As Bikaner's Dewan, or Prime Minister, and principal adviser, Panikkar * occupies a key position. He and Sir V. T. Krishnamachari, Dewan to the Maharaja of Jaipur, have seized the initiative on behalf of the Rajputana Princes. Panikkar admits that Bhopal, the present Chancellor of the Chamber of Princes, is in a difficult position as a Moslem Prince of a Hindu State. But as Chancellor he is really enunciating—although he may not fully realise it—a new doctrine of Paramountcy, by asserting that no action should be taken by States individually, but only collectively and by agreement with the Chancellor. Panikkar said that his concept of

* Some of Panikkar's most constructive and far-seeing ideas are to be found in his monograph " The Basis of an Indo-British Treaty " (Oxford University Press, 1945).

Paramountcy allowed it to be no business of the Chancellor as to whether or no individual Princes opted to have representation in the Constituent Assembly. This was a matter as between each individual State and Britain, and only a direct instruction from the Crown Representative would affect his action.

Some ten of the sixteen big States had taken their places in the Constituent Assembly. Post-war thinking in the case of the Princes was also necessary on Britain's part. As long as they were instruments in a British "Divide and Rule" régime they were powerful factors in the maintenance of the Raj, but once British rule is relaxed, the Princes' power is automatically in decline, and they must seek security within the framework of the dominant political structure which is likely to take its place. The position of the northern group of Princes—Jodhpur, Jaipur, Baroda, Patiala and Bikaner—was particularly difficult. Patiala was only a hundred and forty miles from Delhi.

Although Nehru during his seven days' negotiations with the Princes in February had stressed no fewer than five times the voluntary nature of any agreement with the Congress, and Congress's refusal to coerce any unwilling partner, the decision facing the Princes was none the less to join in or perish. The Nizam of Hyderabad was a special case, and while it was highly desirable to bring him into the fold and to handle him firmly, Panikkar recommended no actual coercion. Hyderabad, the Premier Indian State, with its Moslem ruler, was in the heart of Hindustan, and had eighty-six per cent of its total population of seventeen million, Hindus. It would be impossible for her to remain out. The largest State of all in area, Kashmir, was in a difficult position, and the Maharaja would no doubt be tempted to throw in his lot with Jinnah. Panikkar said that a key motive for the Princes to join the Constituent Assembly is to provide a reinforcement of the right wing of Congress and a counter-weight to Jai Prakash Narain and his Socialist group, who have made considerable headway in Bengal.

Finally I asked Panikkar about the social structure of the two Parties, and he confirmed the view, to which Mountbatten subscribes, that the Congress was in due course likely to split. The Moslem League, he felt, was more closely integrated, lacking as it did the extremes of industrial wealth and poverty. The few Moslem magnates were mainly landowners, and the exploitation of Moslem poverty was mostly at the hands of Hindu capitalists.

VICEROY'S HOUSE, NEW DELHI, *Friday, 28th March, 1947*

During his first week as Viceroy, Mountbatten has set the tempo he proposes to maintain. By the time March is out he will have held comprehensive individual interviews with every member of the Cabinet, as the Viceroy's Executive Council is now colloquially called, with Auchinleck and the other Service Commanders-in-Chief, with the key Princes and Dewans and with the leaders of the British community and Scheduled Castes. He approaches each of these conversations with a completely open mind and handles them without any formality. The objective is to establish personal relationships where none have existed before. All this is extremely hard work. The interviews are of rarely less than a half-hour's duration.

As he is seeing the Leaders in such close sequence, the volume of opinion and information which he is absorbing is very heavy. So he has established a procedure that as soon as a Leader leaves the room there is a fifteen minutes' interval before the next appointment while he dictates to his stenographer a *résumé* of his last conversation. These interview notes are given reference numbers and are circulated immediately to his staff, enabling us to follow every move he makes.

An opportunity to introduce himself to a wider circle has been presented by the great Asian Relations Conference, which has been meeting near the Red Fort in Old Delhi all this week. This evening the Mountbattens gave their first garden-party for all the delegates, members of the Legislative Assembly and senior officials in Delhi, numbering in all some seven hundred guests. The Moghul gardens and the State rooms were crowded with a great number of Congress and other leaders, who were seeing the inside of Viceroy's House literally for the first time. This was psychologically a very important party. In the first place, it was a clear token of the new Viceroy's good-will towards Nehru's most ambitious move to assert Indian status in Asian affairs. But, beyond that, it enabled the Mountbattens to reveal from the outset their splendid social sense and invoke the Indian gift for friendship. As I mingled among the guests I gained no sense of hostility, but only of reserve struggling to suppress curiosity. The Mountbattens did much to-night to break down that reserve.

Afterwards Lady Mountbatten and Pamela and a party from Viceroy's House went on to an " At Home " in the garden of Nehru's house at 17, York Road, where we saw an exquisite display by the famous Chhau or Masque dancers of Seraikella, a small State dedicated for centuries to the service of the dance.

CHAPTER FOUR

GANDHI AND JINNAH

VICEROY'S HOUSE, NEW DELHI, *Monday, 31st March, 1947*

I LEFT EARLY for breakfast with the Nehru household. There was an informal atmosphere, and we sat down to a European breakfast of eggs and tomatoes, tea and coffee, toast and marmalade. Mrs. Pandit, Nehru's charming and brilliant sister, with one of her daughters, had just arrived from the United Nations session in New York. Krishna Menon, of India League fame, one of Nehru's closest friends, to whom he has given a roving commission at this critical time, was there, aquiline and intense. There was another friend present—a Mr. Patel, a tractor manufacturer, who was pleading with Nehru to open a new factory of his in Bombay. Nehru was weighing in his mind whether he could combine such a materialistic ceremony with his principal duty during his next Bombay visit—namely, the handing over of some Buddhist relics. Nehru is very quiet-spoken, and all his reactions in his own home seem to be *pianissimo*.

There has been a terrific story published to-day of his alleged deal with the British Government and his acceptance of Dominion Status for Hindustan, etc. The source of this " revelation " was *The People*, which has in fact no correspondent of its own here. Nehru asked me some questions about the paper, and was surprised to learn that, like the *Daily Herald*, it was owned by Odhams. Nehru said the whole thing would be a two days' wonder and no more.

After breakfast I had an earnest talk with Krishna Menon, who stressed:—

(*a*) The Indian desire for common citizenship but not Dominion Status. He wants what he calls reciprocity. Such are the suspicions about Churchill that if he is prepared to accept Dominion Status, it cannot mean real freedom.

(*b*) The limit of Nehru's patience with the present situation in the Cabinet. The persistent refusal of the Moslem League members to accept him as leader was intolerable.

(*c*) Prevalent criticism of the Viceroy's I.C.S. staff, and in particular of George Abell. I spoke strongly in favour of Abell's high calibre and patent objectivity. Menon admitted that the attacks against him were probably unjustified, but must be recognised by Mountbatten as a political reality.

He said Mountbatten started with an advantage *vis-à-vis* Gandhi, who regarded him as an honest man, but he gave warning that a conversation with the Mahatma was always unpredictable. There was always the danger that it might be side-tracked through Gandhi involving himself in some special subject.

By the time this conversation was over, the day's routine had already seized hold of Nehru, and in the general hubbub of visitors arriving unannounced and generally taking possession of the place, I left without the opportunity of giving thanks to any member of the Nehru family for their hospitality!

I arrived back just in time for the ten o'clock Staff Meeting, where plans for Mountbatten's first interview with Gandhi this afternoon were fully discussed. Press interest in the meeting is naturally immense. When the Mahatma duly arrived at three o'clock I must have had every accredited camera-man in the sub-continent waiting with me in the Moghul gardens outside the Viceroy's study.

After the initial greetings were over the Mountbattens conducted him out to face this battery. He underwent the ordeal with great good humour, joking with the Mountbattens and generally doing his best to meet the conflicting requests of the camera-men, all trying to secure the perfect shot. As it happens, this was achieved by Max Desfor, the brilliant Associated Press of America photographer, who waited until the frenzied scramble for the posed shots was over, and then, with the perception of the artist, saw that Gandhi, on turning to go back into the cool study, had placed his hand on Lady Mountbatten's shoulder. The picture was his. Gandhi by his action was doing no more and no less than treating Lady Mountbatten in the same manner as his own grand-daughters on his way to his Prayer Meetings. Every gesture he makes has consciously or otherwise symbolic meaning, and this afternoon it was spontaneous friendship.

To-day's talk lasted for two and a quarter hours. At the end of it Mountbatten called me in, introduced me to Gandhi, to discuss the immediate issue of a Press communiqué. Gandhi, who spoke with a very soft voice and a slight lisp, said he would be happy to leave the wording to the Viceroy. As soon as he had left, Mountbatten told me that the whole interview had been deliberately taken up with re-miniscence, the first hour and a quarter with Lady Mountbatten present to help produce the air of friendliness, and the last hour on their own. He had deliberately avoided all reference to the immediate political situation, to allow time for them to progress along the path of under-standing and friendship. Gandhi had gone back to his early life in England and South Africa and to his meetings with former Viceroys. Mountbatten told me that the talks are likely to go on for the remainder of Gandhi's week's stay in Delhi. He is quite determined not to hustle him. All this is admirable in itself, but not so easy to explain to the Press, who will find it difficult to believe that momentous discussions have not in fact taken place.

I hammered out a text with all speed, secured Mountbatten's approval, and then went out into the courtyard, where a large crowd of corre-spondents were waiting to take it down. I started to read, " Their Excellencies met Mr. Gandhi at Viceroy's House this evening, and they had a most friendly talk with him lasting for seventy-five minutes ". Before I could take breath an eager correspondent protested that this could not be true. He knew that the Mahatma had been there for over two hours. There was a murmur in the ranks. But when I continued with, "Thereafter His Excellency and Mr. Gandhi had an hour's talk alone in the same cordial vein", it was generally acknowledged that the statement might, after all, bear some relation to the truth!

VICEROY'S HOUSE, NEW DELHI, *Tuesday, 1st April, 1947*

Mountbatten has had his second talk with Gandhi. It lasted for two hours, only a quarter of an hour of which was taken up with solid business. There was a further long excursion into the Mahatma's life-story, and then an astonishing proposal by him to solve the whole problem. It was nothing less than to dismiss the present Cabinet and call on Jinnah to appoint an all-Moslem administration. Mountbatten asked, " What will Jinnah's reaction be?" Gandhi replied, "Jinnah will say, ' Ah, it is the wily Gandhi again '." Mountbatten asked with a smile, " And won't he be right?" " No," Gandhi replied; " I am being absolutely sincere." He told Mountbatten that he had got to be firm and face the consequences of the sins of his predecessors. The British system of " Divide and Rule " had created a situation in which the only alternatives were a continuation of British rule to keep law and order or an Indian blood-bath. The blood-bath must be faced and accepted.

Wavell had been irritated by the time consumed in these interviews, but Mountbatten said he is ready to give ten hours to him, if necessary. He is deeply impressed with him, and thinks he is still of the first importance.

To-day Mountbatten called me in to act as an unofficial *rapporteur* at a very tense and difficult meeting involving the final liquidation of the vexed Indian National Army question. A number of former I.N.A. men were still in prison for war crimes—that is, for specific brutalities, as against purely political offences. The Government was being subjected to considerable pressure to release them, but Auchinleck, as Commander-in-Chief, was adamant that these sentences were to be served if discipline was to be maintained. In Bengal the I.N.A. were widely regarded as heroic liberators, largely because they had been commanded by Subhas Chandra Bose, who had once successfully defied Gandhi's opposition to become President of the Congress, and who carried his enmity of the British Raj to the point of linking up with the Axis and providing the Japanese with the Indian National Army as an auxiliary force for their offensive on India.

By the time Mountbatten arrived on the scene there was a widespread feeling that this issue should be disposed of; but in so far as it touched the Nationalist nerve, and had not been too happily handled in the past, a reasonable solution became more difficult to obtain as each day passed. Wavell had actually used his Viceregal authority to veto discussion of the matter, and had handed it over as one of the outstanding conundrums.

Mountbatten decided to have it out in a completely frank conference with Nehru, Liaquat, Baldev Singh and Auchinleck. The meeting, my first direct experience of the prevailing political climate at the highest level, is not likely to be in character with most of the crises which

Mountbatten will have to face. For once Congress and the Moslem League are on the same side of the fence. One or two of the I.N.A. men in question were Moslems. Although the Moslem League had been careful to avoid identifying itself with the Congress Civil Disobedience policy of 1942 or any direct challenge to the Allied war effort, it was significant that as soon as there was any suggestion that the issue was one involving national aspirations, their differences with the Congress vanished at once.

Nehru was clearly anxious to be rid of the whole problem, but was naturally worried at the possible strength of the Legislative Assembly's reaction. Liaquat, on the other hand, developed arguments which were, I felt, calculated to draw heavily on Auchinleck's limited reserves of temper and provoke a breach between the Government and the Commander-in-Chief. None the less, underneath the surface tension it was clear that there was a tremendous respect for Auchinleck and genuine dismay at the threat of his resignation, which had brought the actual crisis to a head. After three hours of intense discussion, a formula was found. Auchinleck was prevailed upon to write it out himself. It invoked the Federal Court as an adviser on the merits of each particular outstanding case.

VICEROY'S HOUSE, NEW DELHI, *Wednesday, 2nd April, 1947*

At our morning Staff Meeting Mountbatten was busy hammering out the I.N.A. formula. The snag now centres round the status of the Federal Court, which apparently is not in a position to render reports to the Commander-in-Chief.

On Mountbatten's instructions, I attended the Legislative Assembly, sitting discreetly in the Governor-General's box to listen to the I.N.A. debate. A Moslem back-bencher moved the resolution demanding the release of the I.N.A. men and started breathing fire and slaughter. His oration then suddenly tailed away. It looked as though the Congress Whips had given him some friendly advice half-way through his speech.

Then Nehru replied. His speech was a splendid effort. He backed Auchinleck to the hilt, as he promised he would. The speech required great moral courage before a potentially hostile House. The I.N.A., he argued, was subjected to different pulls. There was the pull of loyalty to the Army, there was the pull of a larger loyalty to what one imagined was the good of the country; when loyalty is in conflict the result is an inner conflict in the individual. "When this happens, the best man suffers, the lesser man is insensitive." Not all the I.N.A. men were patriots; as with everyone else, there were some good, some bad and some in the middle. The resolution was ultimately withdrawn. The outcome of this dangerous incident is Mountbatten's first success at mediation and an encouraging example of Nehru's steadfastness.

I had lunch with Sir Akbar and Lady Hydari. Hydari has just been appointed Governor of Assam in succession to Sir Andrew Clow, and they are due to leave for Shillong next month. He follows Sir Chandulal Trivedi in Orissa, as the second Indian to become a Provincial Governor.

It is a well-deserved honour, for Hydari has behind him a brilliant administrative record in the I.C.S. He and his wife, who is a Swede of great charm and vivacity, gave me my first taste of Indian hospitality when I arrived in Delhi in October 1943 as a stranger in the land. Hydari says that we should stand firm for Union and for the Federal solution, invoking the second part of the great 1935 Act to provide the machinery for this purpose. He points out that if we do this seven of the eleven Provinces would come in at once.

VICEROY'S HOUSE, NEW DELHI, *Thursday, 3rd April, 1947*

At the Staff Meeting Mountbatten reported on yesterday's interviews. He had seen P. J. Griffiths, the European leader in the Assembly, who had spoken in very unfavourable terms of the Cabinet Mission's general approach to the European community in their Plan. Their proposal for eight seats in the Assembly was wholly unrealistic, in so far as there were only seventy thousand Europeans and only one seat allotted per million of the inhabitants. Gandhi had naturally gone up in smoke at this suggestion, but in Griffiths' view if three seats had been asked for in the first instance this would have been acceptable.

He then saw J. J. Singh, an influential Sikh with powerful American connections, who has returned from the U.S.A. He stressed that his first impression on arrival in India was the growth of anti-British feeling, and said no one believes that we are going. He was the first to speak of the possibility of revolution. We shall see repeated, he said, in India the new situation producing new leaders.

He also saw Gandhi again, who said he had been remonstrating with Mrs. Asaf Ali, one of the Indian Socialist leaders, for being so aggressively anti-British. He is anxious that she should meet Lady Mountbatten. He has returned to the theme that Jinnah should be called upon to form a government.

VICEROY'S HOUSE, NEW DELHI, *Friday, 4th April, 1947*

The newspaper limelight continues to be on the North-west Frontier. Ismay spoke at to-day's Meeting of what he called " the bastard situation " there—ninety-seven per cent Moslems with a Congress Ministry.

The question arose of Travancore, which is in the far South, and the only Indian State with a sizeable sea-board. Uranium deposits have been found there, so the lapse of Paramountcy now assumes new strategic significance.

There was a full and frank discussion of ways and means of evacuating Europeans should this be necessary. A register is to be prepared of those who wish to leave by June 1948. Passenger-ship shortage is such that any fleet of ships, however modest, will be out of the question. Mountbatten's directive is that shipping losses as a result of the war should be stressed to all concerned, and that in all planning any impression of panic movement must at all costs be avoided.

Dinner with the Zinkins. Maurice spoke of Nehru as Gandhi's

Western face. He also developed at length the thesis that Pakistan was economically viable and that it was all too readily assumed that it would have no economic survival value. I asked him to prepare a memorandum on this, as I think it would be of considerable interest to Mountbatten. In the general frenzy of day-to-day activity the decisive longer-term considerations are all too easily passed over. The Maharaja of Dungapur's younger brother, a very intelligent and charming man who has made the I.C.S. his career, was the other guest. He feels, like Hydari, that one more effort should be made to revive Part II of the 1935 Act.

Maurice tells me that one possible reason for Nehru's and Congress's support for Auchinleck is the fear that if he resigned he would be succeeded by Slim,* who is—rightly or wrongly—regarded as more pro-Moslem. This, of course, would also be an explanation of Liaquat's and the Moslem League's readiness to provoke Auchinleck into leaving. Maurice also told me a pretty story of Nehru at the last session of the Asian Relations Conference, when he walked down the aisle and shook delegates who were talking and drinking during the proceedings. " What are you, a mango tree, that you need so much water?", he said to one hapless representative.

VICEROY'S HOUSE, NEW DELHI, *Saturday, 5th April, 1947*

Gandhi's master plan was discussed, and was described as an old kite flown without disguise. Mountbatten, however, had been the first person sufficiently intelligent to pay attention to it. The vital point was that Mountbatten should not allow himself to be drawn into negotiation with the Mahatma, but should only listen to advice.

Now, at the end of the first fortnight, the main strategy of Mountbatten's plan, together with its tactical application, has already taken shape. He has had to start from scratch, but no time has been lost. His primary aim is to achieve a solution which inspires sufficient good feeling to enable the Indian parties to remain within the Commonwealth structure from the outset. He is bending every effort to keep the Cabinet Mission Plan alive, but on the assumption that Jinnah's power and purpose are sustained, the facilities for partition will have to be allowed for. He appreciates that the logic of partitioning the centre involves similar treatment for those Provinces where the two communities are evenly balanced.

Whatever shape the Plan takes, Mountbatten has been convinced from the outset that the need for the political solution is much more pressing than was apparent when we were in London, and that the June 1948 time limit, far from being not long enough, is already too remote a deadline. He senses the danger of political collapse; the various contending factions—Congress, Moslem League and Sikhs—being strong enough to stake their respective claims, but unable, unless an agreement is reached at once, to prevent the Chinese situation being repeated in

★ Field-Marshal Lord Slim, Commander of 14th Army in the Burma campaign, who succeeded Field-Marshal Lord Montgomery as Chief of the Imperial General Staff in October 1948.

India. The quick political solution carries with it the proviso that its difficult administrative implications should be met during an agreed interim period afterwards.

In preparing the way for the acceptable plan, Mountbatten is resolved to take all the leaders along with him step by step, but he proposes to do so separately on a personal basis, and not by formal and forbidding conclaves. Mountbatten hopes that the diplomacy of discussion will have the effect of playing down the communal tension which the committee method, as can be seen at the Cabinet meetings of the Interim Government, undoubtedly stimulates. In the meanwhile at our Staff Meetings all possible concepts are examined.

This morning the possibility of achieving a solution which leaves something at the centre was considered. Mountbatten mentioned as alternative concepts an alliance on the lines of the League of Nations, autonomy within the U.S.S.R., and the federal structure at Washington. The argument was thrown into the arena that the only chance of a unitary solution would be for a decision to be taken as soon as all data was available, if possible within two months. It would have to be in the form of a decision, and not an agreement—unilateral, from which there was no appeal. The approval of His Majesty's Government would be needed at once, together with the earliest possible legislation and implementation, so that the scheme could be completed before the end of 1947. This would be the most honest approach, and could be presented as the best means of getting out by June 1948. If a scheme was required without a centre, then clearly we could not go so quickly.

The whole of this discussion was a form of mental exercise in preparation for Mountbatten's first vital encounter with Jinnah to-day.

The morning Meeting went on up to Jinnah's arrival. There were not quite so many photographers as for the first Gandhi interview, and Jinnah was obviously far more formal and reserved in his attitude to the Press. Immediately after the meeting was over I got in to see Mountbatten to have my communiqué approved. There was only one minor alteration.

Jinnah and his sister are dining at Viceroy's House to-morrow evening, instead of to-night. The reason is simply that Mountbatten felt he could not sustain another session with him to-day. Jinnah, as he left, said he would put himself entirely at Mountbatten's disposal. Mountbatten's first reaction was, " My God, he was cold. It took most of the interview to unfreeze him."

I went straight in to lunch, where the guests were Nehru and his daughter Indira, and Sjahrir, the Indonesian Premier, with his buxom, blonde Dutch wife. Sjahrir must be the smallest statesman since Dollfuss, the Austrian pocket Premier. Mr. and Mrs. Winkelmann, the Dutch Attaché and his wife, were there also. I sat next to Indira. She told me she was in some of the worst blitzes in London and still has an air-raid warden's hat which was lent her one evening while she was trying to put out incendiaries in Piccadilly. She has kept the helmet ever since as a trophy. She is just off to Simla to a house with the most incongruous title of " Cosy Nook ".

After lunch Krishna Menon and Ismay, at Mountbatten's request, had a prolonged talk about Gandhi's proposals. It was agreed to-day that it was essential to make it clear to Nehru, before Gandhi got to work too hard on the Congress, that Mountbatten was far from committed to the Gandhi plan, and that it would need careful scrutiny. As Mountbatten said at the morning Meeting, Gandhi has come out definitely for inviting Jinnah to form an administration and pledged himself to get Congress support for it. Mountbatten thinks Gandhi's proposals and outlook similar to those of the phenomenal Mr. Pyke, once a scientist at Combined Operations, and author of Habakkuk, the floating self-propelled airfield made of ice—far-fetched but potentially feasible.

At a tea-party to-day at Western Court I was entertained by Sir Usha Nath Sen, President of the Indian Correspondents' Association, Associated Press of India's special correspondent and a more than usually well-informed source. He introduced me to some twenty leading Indian correspondents, who for about an hour and a half gave me a fairly intensive grilling. I got off to a good start by introducing myself as a member of the Liberal Party on temporary leave from party politics and as one who therefore understood the meaning of minority problems. Considerable interest was shown in Mountbatten's personal hobbies. There was a happy, almost child-like, belief among them all that a solution will be found within the next fortnight, and it was difficult to divert them from that.

In the evening I dined with the Mountbattens alone, and heard details of the remarkable interview with Jinnah, who started off the conversation quite blankly—" I will enter into discussion on one condition only." Mountbatten said, " I interrupted him before he could finish his sentence : ' Mr. Jinnah, I am not prepared to discuss conditions or, indeed, the present situation until I have had the chance of making your acquaintance and knowing more about you yourself '." Jinnah was completely taken aback by Mountbatten's attitude, and for some while did not respond, remaining reserved, haughty and aloof. But in the end his mood softened and he duly succumbed to Mountbatten's desire to hear him recount the story of the Moslem League's rise to power in terms of his own career.

VICEROY'S HOUSE, NEW DELHI, *Monday, 7th April, 1947*

The Jinnahs dined with the Mountbattens last night. Jinnah harped on Moslem massacres and described the horrors at length. A quick decision was called for—" It would have to be a surgical operation." Mountbatten replied, " An anæsthetic is required before the operation." Mountbatten emerged from this second encounter reasonably confident. " Jinnah can negotiate with me, but my decision goes." Jinnah stressed that Gandhi's position was mischievous because it entailed authority without responsibility. To prove this point he went through the history of negotiations with Gandhi, ending with the rejection of the Cripps' Plan and the launching of civil disobedience in 1942, which he described as the Mahatma's " Himalayan blunder ". " The Congress want to inherit everything, they would even accept Dominion Status to deprive me of Pakistan."

Mountbatten is using his Staff Meetings to exercise half-considered ideas. He hammers out his thoughts on the anvil of discussion. It is most exciting to be a part of this creative process. Ismay read out Gandhi's latest letter, which contains the germs of a " Gandhi–Mountbatten Pact" conjured up out of nothing more than Mountbatten's sympathetic interest in Gandhi's proposal to let Jinnah form a Government. Mountbatten feels that Jinnah must be brought into the Government, but is not clear how it is to be done.

Apparently while the Mountbattens and Jinnah were being photographed before the first interview, Jinnah, in an effort to be gallant to Lady Mountbatten, spoke of "a rose between two thorns". Unfortunately, it turned out that he was in the middle himself! Walt Mason, of Associated Press of America, came round to see me, and wants me to be quotable as " an official source", which frightens me a bit in this whispering gallery.

This evening, at the end of their latest meeting, Mountbatten called me in to meet Jinnah, who stared at me with eyes like gimlets and said nothing. However, at Mountbatten's prompting he told me he would be very pleased for me to call on him and discuss Press problems. After he had gone Mountbatten indicated that they would be having a difficult talk to-morrow.

VICEROY'S HOUSE, NEW DELHI, *Tuesday, 8th April, 1947*

At to-day's Staff Meeting a letter from Liaquat was read which alleged the inadequate representation of Moslems in the Armed Forces. He wanted these reorganised forthwith so that they could be more readily split up between Pakistan and Hindustan at the proper time. Ismay stressed that to take any action on Liaquat's letter would be to prejudice the political issue. Until and unless the Viceroy reported otherwise to His Majesty's Government, the Cabinet Mission Plan held the field, and that Plan envisaged one National Army.

Mountbatten agreed that there could be no splitting of the Indian Army before the withdrawal of the British, for two reasons. " The mechanics won't permit it, and I won't." He said he was resolved to tell Jinnah that he must maintain law and order, and would not help the Parties at the expense of either. Even if it was decided to demit power to individual Provinces, it would still be essential to keep central control of Defence. Ismay said the British Army stays until Command passes. The 1935 Constitution remains in force. Mountbatten spoke on Nehru's view of Gandhi's plan—they should not let go a strong Centre until there was something to hand over to. Abell said the key question was: Is the Cabinet Mission Plan dead? Tell Jinnah what he will get if he refuses it. He won't be reasonable until this has been clarified.

VICEROY'S HOUSE, NEW DELHI, *Wednesday, 9th April, 1947*

At to-day's Meeting Mountbatten said that he raised yesterday with Jinnah the question of an appeal by both of the major Parties for a truce in the communal disturbances, and had bluntly asked Jinnah whether he really wanted these disturbances to be stopped, or whether the issue of such an appeal would put the Moslem League at a political disadvantage. Jinnah had ultimately agreed to join in.

I was asked to give the Press a background warning that, since the Viceroy was examining a large number of different plans for the future of India, the Press should be on their guard against assuming that the plan known and believed to be under discussion on any day was the one most likely to be decided on. The plan which was receiving most careful examination was, of course, the Cabinet Mission Plan.

We had another policy discussion. Ismay spoke of a talk he had had with Jinnah. He shows himself wholly unaware of the administrative implications of his policy. The British were liquidators. All would be well if Pakistan was conceded, but Jinnah spoke of his fear that all he would get would be a " moth-eaten Pakistan ".

After the Staff Meeting I went round and saw Jinnah at his home. His house at 10 Aurangzeb Road looks rather like a mosque, and is full of red and black inlay. On his mantelpiece was a silver map of India on an oak plaque. Pakistan was marked in green. He was much more cordial than on the first encounter. We discussed the Press situation. The All-India Editors' Conference, he said, was entirely Hindu. Of the Moslem papers there was only *Dawn*, which was under his proprietorship. " Although you may not believe it, I have never exercised direct influence over its policy, and have always regarded that as the Editor's job and within his competence." " The Editor," he added, without a smile, " has always been in agreement with my views." He spoke at length on the completely false reports of the Noakhali killings of Hindus by Moslems. These were first described as a massacre of many thousands, but he claimed they turned out to be little more than a hundred killed and a hundred wounded. Background talks with the Press in India were almost impossible. He spoke of his experience in London, where his off-the-record remarks were completely respected.

In a note of the interview for Mountbatten I wrote as follows :—

" In view of the inaccurate and inflammatory nature of some recent Press comment, I said that I had in mind to recommend that you should send a message to the All-India Editors' Conference urging the need for restraint, etc. I wanted to see what his reaction would be : It was not particularly favourable. 'If I may presume to advise,' he said, 'His Excellency should press on with his work, reach a decision quickly, and avoid exhortations. It is above all his sacred duty to uphold law and order.' The interview was helpful in so far as it will enable me to make contact with the Moslem Press under favourable auspices, but discouraging as indicating that the chances of any working arrangement between the Hindu and the Moslem Press are very small indeed.'"

I had tea this afternoon with the Nehru household. Indira and Krishna Menon recalled the origins of the Moslem League and its leadership—pointing out that Jinnah himself was a Hindu by birth. The League, Krishna said, only began to mean something when Congress became a Direct Action movement. It grew, he alleged, under British encouragement. Krishna wants me to go to the States Conference at Gwalior, where Nehru is handing over the Presidency to Sheikh Abdullah, the Moslem Congress leader in Kashmir, who is at present in gaol there. It is not only the political temperature that is rising. The thermometer reached over 100° F. yesterday. As Nehru aptly remarked to me, " The trouble is we get hot by thinking about the heat."

In the evening we had a big State dinner for the British Residents in the Indian States, who have been called to Delhi for consultation with Mountbatten in his capacity as Crown Representative. The State rooms were opened up and the cobwebs dusted off Lady Willingdon's Persian ceiling. Eighty-four guests sat down to dinner, and the silver plate was brought out, which somehow did not improve the flavour of the food. Portraits of former Viceroys—Minto, Mayo, Halifax and Reading—look down upon the swelling scene. The string band plays a strange blend of Gilbert and Sullivan and Indian rhythms.

VICEROY'S HOUSE, NEW DELHI, *Friday, 11th April, 1947*

In a general discussion at to-day's Staff Meeting Mountbatten observed that Jinnah's original objection to the Cabinet Mission Plan had been that certain Provinces could not opt out of, but could only transfer to another Group. Congress now agreed to opting out, but wanted to hold on to the Cabinet Mission concept of a Union of India. Ian Scott, Deputy Private Secretary to the Viceroy, pointed out that the core of the Cabinet Plan was Union of Groups. Among Mountbatten's thoughts for to-day was that the form of the announcement should be such as to indicate that as far as possible the choice of hand-over was being left to the Indian people. The Indian people were being allowed to make up their minds for Partition or otherwise.

VICEROY'S HOUSE, NEW DELHI, *Saturday, 12th April, 1947*

Mountbatten reported on his latest meeting with Jinnah, who was apparently much shaken when Mountbatten failed to react in any way to his offer, dramatically presented, to bring Pakistan into the Commonwealth. In our general discussion to-day the alternatives of " Plan Balkan " versus " Plan Union " were frankly and fully discussed. Mountbatten went to the root of the dilemma, and put the proposition that he should try to get Congress to accept the Cabinet Mission Plan in full, and then confront Jinnah with coming in or accepting a truncated Pakistan. George Abell was sceptical of Congress changing its policy. It had already forced the Moslem League to retreat by the pressure it had exerted on the northern Groups.

Gandhi has written to Mountbatten that his own plan is not acceptable to Congress, and that he is personally handing over all future negotiations to the Working Committee. Mountbatten says he will try to get Gandhi to stay on and exert his influence in favour of full Congress acceptance of the Cabinet Mission Plan. He feels that, deep down, desire for union still exerts a powerful pull on Congress.

Incidentally there was a charming postscript to Gandhi's proposal that Mrs. Asaf Ali should meet Lady Mountbatten. Lady Mountbatten at once wrote off an invitation, which Mrs. Asaf Ali duly declined. The next day when Gandhi came for a meeting with the Viceroy Mrs. Asaf Ali was with him. "I hear she refused," he said, "so I have brought her with me."

VICEROY'S HOUSE, NEW DELHI, *Monday, 14th April, 1947*

The Press speculators have been busy. An article in the *Hindustan Times* this morning has forecast the issue of the "Peace Appeal" on which Mountbatten has been working. It indicates that it will shortly be issued over the signatures of Gandhi, Jinnah and Kripalani, as the President of Congress. One of the big points at issue is Congress's insistence on including Kripalani, and Jinnah's unwillingness to do so. Ismay and Miéville consider that the *Hindustan Times* article may well have wrecked the chances of persuading Jinnah to sign the document which has been prepared. Mountbatten gave strict instructions to me to point out that the article had of course been published without his knowledge and had caused him great annoyance, as indeed it has. He is also writing to Nehru to find out how the leak occurred.

After many spasms of uncertainty Mountbatten's patience and will-power have prevailed, and this afternoon I have been able to take round to the Ministry of Information the original document over Gandhi's and Jinnah's joint signatures. Jinnah has gained his point over Kripalani, who has not been invited to sign. Actually Gandhi wrote his name twice, once in English and once in Urdu.

The tone and timing of this Appeal are a great personal triumph for Mountbatten and give impetus to his whole effort to produce an acceptable political plan. It enhances his prestige and it exploits to the maximum the initial good-will surrounding him. It is designed to create a *détente* without which no political solution will be worth a pin's fee. It is the first victory for his open diplomacy.

The message is couched in stern and forceful terms, which are urgently needed. The call for avoidance, both in speech and writing, of any incitement to acts of violence and disorder is particularly timely. As each day passes certain of the more communally minded Press commentators become increasingly provocative in their language, stirring up hatreds they cannot control and heroics they are never likely to perform. At Mountbatten's request I have gone very carefully into the Ministry of Information's proposals for disseminating the Appeal. The engine of All India Radio will be at full throttle, and at my suggestion to-night's release will include a photostat copy. Ambitious plans are in hand to show it at cinemas and to distribute it by leaflet from the air over the disturbed areas.

The planned pattern of events now centres round a Simla house-party early in May—the probable guests to be Nehru, Jinnah, Patel, Liaquat, Kripalani, Baldev Singh, and the possibles Gandhi, Bhopal and Bikaner.

To-morrow the Governor's Conference is due to take place, following closely upon a useful session with the Residents. Mountbatten is not likely to put his Plan into final shape until he has heard the Governors' full and frank views on the draft which he has already sent for their consideration. On the eve of the Conference the broad principles of Mountbatten's Plan are:

(1) that the responsibility for Partition, if it comes, is to rest fairly upon the Indians themselves;

(2) the Provinces, generally speaking, shall have the right to determine their own future.

(3) Bengal and the Punjab are to be notionally partitioned for voting purposes;

(4) the predominantly Moslem Sylhet district in Assam is to be given the option of joining the Moslem Province created by a partitioned Bengal;

(5) General Elections are to be held in the North-west Frontier Province.

Some of the Governors have arrived at Viceroy's House, and Mountbatten has already had talks with Sir Frederick Bourne (Central Provinces), Sir John Colville (Bombay), and Sir Archibald Nye (Madras). By the time they are all here the Mountbattens will be entertaining under one roof eleven Governors, their wives, private secretaries and A.D.C.'s— a formidable gathering even for Viceroy's House, with its three hundred and forty rooms and one and a half miles of corridors, to hold.

Sir Mirza Ismail, the Prime Minister of Hyderabad, was called in for the talk with Bourne when they discussed the very tricky question of the status of Berar. This is part of the Nizam of Hyderabad's hereditary domains—indeed, his heir is entitled the Prince of Berar—but is administered by the Central Provinces. Congress will certainly lay claim to Berar as part of the Central Provinces, while the Nizam will certainly want Berar back. Mirza Ismail intimated that the Nizam may shortly be seeing Jinnah. As for himself, he says that he is rapidly losing the Nizam's confidence and does not expect to be in office much longer.

I sat next to Ismail at the Mountbattens' lunch-party. He is a Moslem of moderate opinion, sober judgement and high intellect, who is therefore in a somewhat isolated position. He spoke quite freely to me about the uneasy role of Premier to the Nizam. The maximum period of power one could hope for was about four years. The only exception to this had been old Sir Akbar Hydari, who had clung on for nearly fourteen years. The Nizam's statecraft consisted largely of weaving complex conspiracies against his own Prime Ministers and ultimately depriving them of the power he had wrested for them. It was, by Ismail's account, a depressing cycle of self-defeating intrigue. Also at the lunch was

Compton Mackenzie, who is covering the world's battle-fronts to produce an official account of the Indian Army's contribution to the war.

Colville, it seems, began by offering to resign, but has been prevailed upon to stay on a little longer. Mountbatten said that Colville was likely to be both wrong and right in his objections to the present policy. Wrong, because only short notice and a time limit could make the Indian leaders face up to reality and right because there was not enough time to launch a new constitution.

CHAPTER FIVE

THE GOVERNORS AND THE PLAN

THE GOVERNOR'S CONFERENCE opened to-day with the boost of encouragement provided by the banner headlines announcing the Gandhi–Jinnah Appeal. I attended the first session, which took place in the sombre, panelled Council Chamber. It was an impressive spectacle, with the eleven Governors seated in anti-clockwise order of precedence round the large oval table. Mountbatten's opening speech was a very fluent and persuasive appeal for loyalty both to the letter and spirit of the British Government's decision. He stressed, just in case there was any doubting Thomas in his midst, that June 1948 was a firm departure date.

There was full and frank discussion on the evacuation of Europeans. Colville and Nye, Governors of the two Senior Presidencies, were both robust on this issue, but Sir Evan Jenkins, the very brilliant Governor of the Punjab—George Abell's predecessor as P.S.V. to Wavell—said he felt bound to draw attention to the seriousness of the situation in the Punjab. Sir Hugh Dow, Governor of Bihar, said there were only fifty European officials in his State, covering a population of forty million. So it was not surprising, perhaps, that there was little law or order in his part of the world. Sir Andrew Clow, the retiring Governor of Assam, spoke about the planters, and said there were more young wives than ever before enjoying the sunshine, food and servants.

J. D. Tyson, Secretary to the Governor of Bengal, Sir Frederick Burrows (who was ill and unable to be at the Conference), reported that there were twenty thousand Europeans in Bengal and that he was seriously worried about the five thousand in the outlying districts. He felt that the chances of maintaining law and order in the Province were very slim. Communist agitation—stronger here than anywhere else—was definitely anti-European, and he believed that the Europeans were not looking ahead.

Mountbatten stressed that there was little chance of any support from the British Cabinet for any legislation to prevent people coming to India. The final vote on this delicate subject was in favour of using persuasion with regard to the movement of Europeans, with the Punjab asking for enforcement powers later.

There followed detailed consideration of the vexed question of compensation. Mountbatten gave the history of the negotiations to date. Colville—" George, the automatic pilot ", as he called himself, to cover the various occasions he has served as acting Viceroy—confirmed what Mountbatten had to say about the difficulty of getting compensation for Indians past the Interim Government. Trivedi and Hydari both felt

Indians would, on purely patriotic grounds, wish to remain on and let compensation go. Mountbatten had some interesting things to say about the ambiguities and uncertainties of the Commonwealth link, referring in particular to Eire. Sir John Maffey had told him that the Letter of Credence of the Irish representative to Hitler during the war was actually signed " George R.I.".

In the afternoon session discussion was broken down to allow for reports by Governors on their individual Provinces. Sir Olaf Caroe, speaking about the North-west Frontier, which at the moment seems to be the point of most acute political crisis, wants an election. Dr. Khan Sahib, the Premier who, with his more famous brother Abdul Ghaffar Khan, " the Frontier Gandhi ", leads the pro-Congress Red Shirt group, does not. All the pro-Moslem League Moslems who would stand to gain most from an election are in gaol. Mountbatten's advice is " hold your hand, if possible ", but Caroe looks tense and tired, and is clearly weighed down by his heavy responsibilities.

Jenkins gave a lucid analysis of the implications of Punjab partition, showing just how the Moslem versus non-Moslem issue was complicated by Sikh and Hindu Jat claims. Tyson similarly examined the prospects for Bengal, if under partition. East Bengal, he felt, would become a rural slum. There were some twenty-five million Hindus in Bengal— forty-five per cent of the population—and they all wanted to be absorbed into Hindustan. The concept of East Bengal was unacceptable to many local Moslems. The relationship between Jinnah and the present Moslem Premier of Bengal, Suhrawardy, was far from cordial. Suhrawardy is frightened of partition and is ready to play with the Hindus. Jenkins, too, spoke of the possible growth of anti-Pakistan opinion in the Punjab and Bengal. The local Moslems would be satisfied to run Bengal as a Moslem-controlled Province.

The Governor of Bihar drew attention to the concentration of wealth, mineral and iron. The industrial development of Chota Nagpur was part of Suhrawardy's concept for the building up of an independent Bengal. Provincial devolution would, he felt, in the case of Bihar have wide repercussions. In the general discussion it was felt that a Sind– Punjab Pakistan was economically feasible. Mountbatten considered, however, that East Bengal might contract out and that also the North-west Frontier was a liability.

VICEROY'S HOUSE, NEW DELHI, *Wednesday, 16th April, 1947*

At the resumed Governors' Conference to-day Jenkins spoke about the need for an " Operation Solomon " for the Punjab and put forward the possibility of a statistical boundary commission. There was a big discussion on the whole draft Partition Plan, which Mountbatten had put together in time for the Conference. It is clear, from what the Governors have to say, that by far the greater part of the sub-continent is calm and quiet and ready to accept any reasonable solution.

I had lunch at the Imperial with Panikkar, who stressed that the Constitution of the Moslem League had been weighted heavily in favour of Moslems living in minority areas. This simple fact, he claimed, had enabled Jinnah to bring extra pressure on Moslem members living in majority areas. Bengali loyalties, he said, were increasingly cutting across those of Hindustan, and would require careful handling. He also argued strongly the need for an Indian equivalent to the British Privy Council to which unpredictable political and judicial problems could be referred.

Mountbatten has had a talk with Baldev Singh, the Defence Minister, who, in the presence of Jenkins, the Governor of the Punjab, denied being the treasurer of the Sikhs' appeal fund, which is undoubtedly being subscribed for warlike and unconstitutional purposes.

Baldev sought advice on the Army nationalisation scheme. What chance was there of British Services remaining on after June 1948? Mountbatten replied that it all depended on whether India wants to be in the Commonwealth. A face-saving formula is needed to cover the Congress resolution passed prior to 20th February to set up a sovereign independent Republic. Baldev's general attitude goes to confirm that partition is now the only solution acceptable to all parties.

VICEROY'S HOUSE, NEW DELHI, *Friday, 18th April, 1947*

Mountbatten was in buoyant mood at to-day's Staff Meeting. He had an interesting talk with Krishna Menon, who took upon himself part of the original responsibility for the Independent Sovereign Republic formula. The search, however, for another formula which will ensure a close link with Britain is being actively pursued by him and some of the Congress leaders. Menon has explained how initiative on Congress's part is impossible; even the semblance of it would lose them their position; it must come in some way from us. In the course of the discussion I said I felt that, at the military level, the analogy and advantages of the Combined Chiefs of Staff procedure in the war should not be overlooked, and Mountbatten agrees that this should certainly be kept in mind.

Ismay, Ronnie, George Nicholls and myself were out at Palam this afternoon to greet our families, who completed the last leg of their journey in Mountbatten's York making its return flight after taking Colville back to Bombay from the Governors' Conference. The York has for so long been the carrier of many V.I.P.'s and much gold braid that it was a refreshing contrast to see it in the guise of a flying *crèche*. Three Brockman daughters, one Nicholls son, and my Virginia and Keith issued forth into the broiling heat. Among the grown-ups were Ismay's two daughters, Susan and Sarah. My wife, Fay, is taking Miss Carey, our nurse, and the children on up to Simla to escape Delhi's intolerable summer heat, but will herself be returning shortly to join me, and I hope lend a hand in my office, where the daily round has begun to assume gargantuan proportions.

VICEROY'S HOUSE, NEW DELHI, *Saturday, 19th April, 1947*

Mountbatten gave us an alarming but none the less amusing account of his interview with the Sikh leaders. He found himself confronted by some very scruffy old gentlemen with long beards and large *kirpans* who put on their glasses, looking just like benign professors full of peaceful intentions, but telling a few fibs in the process. They all insisted that he must partition the Punjab, and said the Sikhs were the principal victims in the Rawalpindi riots.

Mountbatten mentioned the interview he had yesterday with Dr. Matthai, who had stressed that although responsible Indian leaders were now generally making dispassionate and temperate speeches, the Press was causing much trouble and was in his view an irresponsible and inflammatory element in the situation. Matthai suggested that the Viceroy should call together all editors and appeal to them to tone down their comment and implement in their own way the Gandhi–Jinnah Appeal. Dr. Matthai thought that this would have a tremendous effect. Mountbatten asked for my comment. I said that I doubted whether this approach was either feasible or even desirable. It would be physically very difficult to bring in all the editors concerned from distant parts, and when they had arrived at Viceregal request they would expect to be told news of some firm decision. They would, to say the least, be deflated at receiving only an exhortation. Moreover, I suggested the desirability of taking the matter up with Patel in the first instance in his capacity as Minister of Information.

At his meeting yesterday with Dr. Khan Sahib the suggestion was mooted that Mountbatten should pay an early visit to the North-west Frontier Province. The idea hitherto had been to postpone tours until the major Plan had been completed and approved, but the Frontier situation seems to call for special treatment beforehand. In our general policy discussion the Dominion Status issue was further thrashed out. Mountbatten pointed out that Nazimuddin, the Moslem League leader in East Bengal, was just as adamant as Jinnah about Pakistan. Ismay stressed that we were engaged in creating two Pakistans, which drew from Mountbatten the comment that whatever its implications he was beginning to think Pakistan was inevitable.

In the evening the Mountbattens gave a small dance in the walled garden by the swimming-pool for Pamela's eighteenth birthday. The fall of fountains and the glimmer of fairy-lights, the air soft and fresh, the dark-green cypress trees, red roses climbing on white walls, and the red and gold of the Viceregal servants—here was all one could ask of an enchanted garden.

VICEROY'S HOUSE, NEW DELHI, *Sunday, 20th April, 1947*

We dined at the Imperial with G. S. Bozman, Secretary of the Information Department of the Government of India, with whom I have been in very close touch over the Gandhi–Jinnah Appeal. Afterwards we sat out in the garden. The early summer evenings are cool and pleasant in New Delhi. The lawns of the Imperial are lit by floodlights, and the guests sit in basket chairs drinking long drinks. Every now and then a jackal will leave the shadows and run across the grass, and in the middle distance there is the pleasant tinkling of tonga bells. Bozman said that from his day-to-day experience of his chief, Vallabhbhai Patel, he was convinced that he was the strong man among the Indian leaders. Any discussions which failed to recognise this fact were likely to be unfruitful. He was essentially a practical man with whom business could be done, but if he was left out he was in a position to invoke a veto just as crippling as anything known at U.N.O.

Colin Reid of the *Daily Telegraph* joined us. Colin is a considerable expert on Middle Eastern affairs. As well as having spent quite a time here, he has made a special study of Moslem culture and politics in Egypt and the Levant. I put some questions in an effort to get a little beneath the immediate surface developments. So I asked Colin how real he felt the division between Hindu and Moslem to be? Surely there must be some margin of mutual interest? Colin's reply was that during the course of the past ten years the communal tension had risen to such a pitch that he doubted whether they would now give adequate consideration to their common interest. I then asked how much the division was religious and how much political? Colin felt there was no easy answer to that question. He had made a close study of the Koran in Arabic and he had tested out Jinnah on various occasions, but it seemed to him that he, Colin Reid, was better versed in the Holy Koran than Mohammed Ali Jinnah himself.

How close, I asked, was the bond between the Moslem League and the Moslems of the Middle East? Colin replied that the Mission from the Middle East which had recently come to visit the Indian Government had shown little interest in or sympathy with Jinnah or the Moslem League. But, I suggested, in the eyes of the world there surely existed a genuine identity between the Moslems of India and other countries. Colin insisted, however, that up to the present there was in actual fact no such thing as a united Islam of the spirit.

VICEROY'S HOUSE, NEW DELHI, *Monday, 21st April, 1947*

Mountbatten rehearsed his afternoon meeting with Liaquat, indicating that his final decision as to whether there should be a fresh election in the North-west Frontier Province would depend upon his estimate of the Moslem League's ability to form a responsible Ministry. He said he would make it abundantly clear that in spite of appearances he would not in fact yield to force or to the threat of force.

I have been asked to prepare a Press note announcing the forthcoming Frontier tour.

The Mountbattens gave a small dinner at the House for the Brockmans, Nicholls and ourselves, which was directly preceded by a garden-party to the Viceregal establishment. Mountbatten told us that he had been much shaken to learn that the three hundred and seventy-five guests were all of the officer cadre, and that there were in all some seven thousand persons on the Viceregal estate. He said he had told some of them that they ought to have a Mayor and had then added that he supposed he was their Mayor! This seemed to go down well with the guests and showed, he felt, that the Indian had a sense of humour, or at least the good manners to laugh at the right time.

While we were in the drawing-room before dinner Lady Mountbatten confessed that she found herself continually trying to move the heavy teak-framed chairs and sofas, only to be no less continually discovered by the servants in this undignified attempt! In this connection she quoted the experience of Lady Linlithgow, whose dog had had an unfortunate accident on the Viceregal carpet shortly before the guests were due to arrive. It took so long to find a servant of sufficiently low caste to clear up the mess that she was finally obliged to deal with it herself, and was caught by her guests and servants in the act!

Mountbatten incidentally called for a composite photograph of the various types of servants showing their uniforms, occupations and ranks. To hold it all in one's head is quite a memory test.

During dinner Mountbatten was full of quips and jokes. I particularly enjoyed his story of his butler in Malta who gave away Masonic secrets while in his cups. Mountbatten repeated the alleged secret words, and on seeing the expression on George Nicholls' face, asked whether he was a Mason. On George admitting that he was, he relentlessly asked if the words were correct. But George was not to be drawn, telling us instead that the only woman who ever knew the words was an Englishwoman who hid herself in a grandfather clock before the Masons arrived. When she was discovered, she was duly initiated. " I thought you were going to say eliminated," Mountbatten countered, " and every hour the clock struck they said, ' Where is she? ' "

An officer's name was mentioned, and Lady Mountbatten exclaimed, " Let us see him by all means, but don't let him arrange any more tours for us." She then told a story of a trip in the Arakan when the said hapless officer forgot that the river was tidal and she and Elizabeth Ward had to leave their jeep and swim for it to keep their engagement!

After dinner Mountbatten told me that the interview with Liaquat had been very interesting. Liaquat had spoken with much frankness about Wavell, saying they all knew that he was a very great soldier, but he had undoubtedly made his political position impossible for himself with the Indian leaders when they all went to London last December. On that occasion he had apparently taken an apologetic line, by asserting that he was merely a soldier and that he had made mistakes. After such a confession it became obvious, Liaquat said, that he could no longer carry on, and it was immediately after this that the idea of a successor began to come into the picture.

Mountbatten told us he felt it was a very great pity that, if he had to have this job, he could not have taken it on eighteen months ago. He might then have been able to influence events, but now with the time at our disposal this was almost impossible. There had been a catastrophic deterioration in the situation during the past few months, and political solutions must be found within the time limit, and therefore before one could really hope to influence events.

In a general talk about the Press I used the occasion to stress the importance of hard news ahead of time which enabled us to control speculation, and mentioned in this connection our success with the Governors' Conference. I also underlined my conviction of the importance of Patel in the situation. Altogether Mountbatten was in very good form throughout the evening.

VICEROY'S HOUSE, NEW DELHI, *Tuesday, 22nd April, 1947*

Mountbatten said to-day that representatives of approximately half of the inhabitants of India had already asked to be allowed to remain within the Commonwealth. They included the Moslem League, the Scheduled Castes and the Indian States—although all the States' subjects might not be of the same opinion as their Rulers. All these applicants, he added, seemed to think they were doing Great Britain a favour by asking to stay in. Mountbatten went on to inquire whether it was considered that there was any possibility of granting some form of Dominion Status to India as a whole, or more probably to the separate parts of India, in the near future. He envisaged the setting up of a Defence Council and a Governor-General as chairman with a casting vote. Ismay thought we should not rule out unilateral application by Pakistan for Commonwealth membership. Mountbatten directed that planning for the grant of Dominion Status to India, whether united or divided, before June, and possibly by January 1948, should continue concurrently with the Plan for the main decision.

He has come round to the view to-day that the Cabinet Mission Plan can somehow be resurrected in a new form and name. As originally presented, it was psychologically wrong. If the principle of two sovereign States could be accepted, union might be achieved through sovereignty. We had to recognise that the Moslem League were prepared to give up the B and C Groups (full Pakistan area) and to accept a truncated Pakistan if a real free centre went with it.

VICEROY'S HOUSE, NEW DELHI, *Wednesday, 23rd April, 1947*

This morning Mountbatten has had a three-hour session with Jinnah. I had lunch with George Abell, who told me that Jinnah had been friendly. Sometimes he is deliberately rude, but to-day his mood was to be accommodating. He seemed to be resigned to the partition of the Punjab and Bengal. He did not ask what the boundaries would be, and Mountbatten did not tell him. He is putting out " an appeal to reason " on the North-west Frontier Province and is clearly relieved at not being asked to call off Direct Action. He told Mountbatten, " Frankly, Your Excellency, the Hindus are impossible. They always want seventeen annas for the rupee." George's comment was, " I have a feeling this is true. By and large the Hindus' case is probably better than the Moslems', but they always spoil it by over-bidding."

Maulana Azad, the leading Congress Moslem, has put forward a new formula. It is that Mountbatten's personal interpretation of the British Government's statement following the London meeting with the Indian Leaders and Wavell last December on the right of Provinces to opt out of Groups, would be acceptable. He bases this on a dictum of Gandhi's. " The sole referee of what is or is not in the interests of India as a whole will be Mountbatten in his personal capacity."

VICEROY'S HOUSE, NEW DELHI, *Thursday, 24th April, 1947*

We held long drafting meetings with Ismay to-day hammering out the Plan to transfer power. It is typical of Mountbatten that he has already prepared a first draft of what he would like to say over All India Radio, and has asked his staff to consider and comment.

Jinnah's statement about the North-west Frontier Province has been released. Mountbatten is pleased with it, and on the whole it is what he wanted from him.

VICEROY'S HOUSE, NEW DELHI, *Friday, 25th April, 1947*

At to-day's Staff Meeting the first draft of the Plan was considered, but no clear concept for its final projection on the Parties and the public emerged. Ian Scott raised an important debating point, favouring the widest publicity for it prior to its submission to the Working Committees of the two Parties, who would then have the searchlight of world attention focused upon them. This technique might have the effect of drawing the more moderate elements in both Congress and Moslem League together again to preserve the bare essentials of unity.

Mountbatten agreed that it was most important that with the issue of the announcement the impression should not be created that partition was a foregone conclusion, but that the question had been referred for decision to the will of the people. To improve the chances of a return to a united India, he felt that an escape clause should be included in the announcement, and he would consider as counting as a form of union any plan in which the centre dealt with the same subjects as in the Cabinet Mission Plan—namely, External Affairs, Defence and Communications. The crux of the matter seemed to him to be that in the Cabinet Mission Plan the Hindu majority at the centre would be able permanently to outvote the Moslem minority and use the reserved subjects to subdue them. The alternative was that the representatives of Pakistan and Hindustan should come together on the basis of parity. If this form of a united India could be obtained it might be possible for the Punjab, Bengal and Assam to remain united. Abell pointed out that it would not be real parity, which depended on the relative strength of the two sovereign States. Mountbatten replied that he realised this point. " My object is to create the effect of two sovereign States or separate blocks negotiating at the centre rather than having a system of majority voting."

Among the various points raised by Mountbatten, whose mind ranged over the whole problem with much vigour and originality, were forebodings about the future of Calcutta. He felt that the Moslems would be bound to demand a plebiscite for it and that its fate would become a major issue. It would, however, be most undesirable to lay down the procedure of self-determination here, which might well give the wrong answer.

He reports that Patel has been complaining, "You won't govern yourself and you won't let us govern." But in fact we are aiming at a date as early as 19th May for the decisive meeting with the Leaders.

VICEROY'S HOUSE, NEW DELHI, *Saturday, 26th April, 1947*

At to-day's Staff Meeting I received various Press directives. An anxious telegram has been received from Olaf Caroe asking for guidance on the policy to be followed in dealing with the Press during Mountbatten's forthcoming tour of the North-west Frontier; in particular what was to be done about correspondents accompanying Mountbatten's party to the Khyber Pass. I am to reply that there are to be no restrictions and no impression of restrictions upon the Press. On the other hand, there will be no Press conference. I am to deal with all inquiries as they arise.

Mountbatten has decided to send Ismay and George Abell back to London with the first draft of the Plan, to hammer it out clause by clause with the Government and officials concerned. In giving background guidance about this trip, I am to explain that one of Mountbatten's principal objects in having Ismay and Miéville on his staff is in order to improve liaison with Whitehall and to enable them to visit London alternately at approximately two-monthly intervals. It is understood that the first to return will be Lord Ismay.

The Commonwealth issue is looming large. There has been a fair indication of Patel's policy on this subject in the leading article of to-day's *Hindustan Times*. Ismay drew attention to the relevant extract, which runs as follows :—

" If there is a settlement between the Congress and the League as a result of which the Muslim majority areas are allowed to constitute themselves into separate sovereign States, we have no doubt that the Union will not stand in the way of Britain establishing contacts with those States. It must be clearly understood, however, that the Indian Union will consider it a hostile act if there is any attempt by Britain to conclude any treaty or alliance involving military or political clauses."

Mountbatten's line on this is that he has received no instructions as to the attitude he should adopt in the event of one or more parts of India expressing a desire to remain within the Commonwealth. But His Majesty's Government had clearly enjoined him not to enter into any discussions on this matter which might imperil the chances of Indian unity; to attain which had always been and would remain his first ambition and determination.

Bob Stimson, the B.B.C.'s special correspondent in India, has shown me his latest script relayed throughout the day on all the B.B.C. news bulletins. " One most important fact," he said, " in the Indian situation, which tends to be overlooked in the rush of day-to-day news, is that India's attitude towards Britain has undergone a fundamental change in the last two months. The good-will established by Britain's ' Quit India ' statement has been consolidated by the new Viceroy in five industrious weeks."

VICEROY'S HOUSE, NEW DELHI, *Sunday, 27th April, 1947*

George Abell is back from his trip to Lahore, where he reports a serious situation. Jenkins, probably the ablest administrator in India, considers there is a grave danger of civil war. When asked by George whether there was anything else we could do but leave in June 1948, Jenkins admitted that there was no alternative, but there was a real peril that we would be handing over to chaos.

From Calcutta comes the news that John Christie, Joint Private Secretary to the Viceroy, has failed to sell the Bengal section of the Plan to Burrows, who was standing out for the doctrine of a free city of Calcutta. He describes its installation after June 1948 as mandatory. This seems to be a strange word to apply to a situation over which we shall have no control whatever at that time.

Miéville is very worried over an indiscretion and apparent leakage about our intentions, but not so Mountbatten, who thinks that the more the papers speculate about partition, the more they are preparing public opinion for its arrival. I am not so sanguine, and think that unchecked Press speculation could lead to serious trouble which could endanger our whole mission.

CHAPTER SIX

FRONTIER VISIT

GOVERNMENT HOUSE, PESHAWAR, *Monday, 28th April, 1947*

EARLY THIS MORNING I set off by air with the Viceregal party for Peshawar. The Mountbattens have taken Pamela with them, and the retinue includes Ian Scott, most of whose I.C.S. career has been in the Frontier regions, Muriel Watson, Lady Mountbatten's personal assistant, and Martin Gilliat. It was a bumpy journey, and Pamela and myself in particular were both feeling somewhat green on arrival. The most impressive spectacle on the way up was the mighty Nanga Parbat, which we could see from the air over a hundred miles away to the north, rising in perfect symmetry to some twenty-five thousand feet, overtopping by at least ten thousand feet the surrounding peaks. We touched down just after midday.

On arrival at Government House, where we were anticipating a nice quiet lunch prior to an afternoon of steady conference, we found ourselves confronting a situation of crisis bordering on panic. Sir Olaf Caroe, the Governor, in a state of some agitation, advised us that there was an immense Moslem League demonstration less than a mile away, which was to place its grievance before the Viceroy and was ready to risk breaking the law by forming a procession and marching on Government House. The only alternative, according to Caroe, was for the Viceroy to forestall this plan by marching on them and showing himself to the multitude. The demonstrators were estimated at well over seventy thousand, and had been gathering from the most remote parts of the Province, many of them having been on the march for several days. Mountbatten had a brief " council of war " with Caroe and the Premier, Dr. Khan Sahib, and it was agreed that the Viceroy should show himself without delay.

Mountbatten thereupon drove off to the demonstration, Lady Mountbatten, with great courage, insisting on going with him. The crowd confronting us was certainly formidable. We climbed up the railway embankment close to the historic Fort Bala Hissar, and looked down upon a vast concourse gathered at Cunningham Park and stretching away into distant fields. There was much gesticulation and the waving of innumerable but illegal green flags with the white crescent of Pakistan, accompanied by a steady chant of " Pakistan Zindabad ".

Within a few minutes of our arrival, however, the brooding tension lifted. The slogan changed; " Mountbatten Zindabad ", could be heard and cheers were raised. Sullen faces smiled. For nearly half an hour Mountbatten, in his khaki bush shirt, and Lady Mountbatten, also in a bush shirt, stood waving to the crowd, which had a surprisingly large number of women and children in its midst. Any sort of speech was out of the question. But the impact of their friendly, confident personalities on that fanatical assembly had to be seen to be believed.

As we swarmed down the embankment and drove back to a well-earned lunch, the relief of the Governor and local officials could not be concealed. They told us that it would have been quite beyond the resources of the local police and military to have deflected the crowd peaceably if they had made up their collective mind to invade Government House. As it was, after seeing the Mountbattens they struck camp and returned to their homes.

After lunch Mountbatten began a series of exacting interviews. I was present for two of them, one with Khan Sahib and his Cabinet of four Ministers, and the other with a deputation of local Hindu residents. He also met the local Moslem League leaders, for whom a special dispensation was made to leave gaol in order to see him. Superimposed upon this conflict, which was in itself sufficiently serious to become the focal point of the wider struggle between Congress and the Moslem League, was the very difficult relationship between the Governor and his Congress Prime Minister. This friction also had wider implications at the national level.

Mountbatten's diplomatic resilience was shown to good advantage in his encounter with Khan Sahib and his colleagues, at which the Governor was also present. He began by saying how grateful he was for the opportunity of meeting them in person. He would ask them and they could ask him questions. He appreciated Khan Sahib's public-spirited advice that he should go to meet the demonstrators. He had in fact done nothing but stand on the embankment. He had previously refused Jinnah permission to organise a procession to Government House. Khan Sahib, on his side, was at pains to confirm that he had called off a procession of Red Shirts—the Congress mass movement in the Province and counterpart of the Moslem League's Green Shirt organisation.

Mountbatten added that he had come to turn over India to Indians; to transfer power in accordance with the will of the people. He was already devising machinery for dealing with the Punjab and Bengal, but, he added, " The Frontier position involves particular difficulty for me. I shall be telling the Moslem League that I will not yield to violence. I tell you privately that I think elections are necessary, but I can make no firm guarantee to the Moslems that there will be any. Jinnah's promise is that if there is any election there will be no violence. You must trust my integrity. Jinnah accepts the position, and is asking his followers to call off civil disobedience." Mountbatten asked about the general control exercised by the Moslem League High Command. The reply was that the local Moslem League had run riot and taken charge. At the last election the Moslem League had definitely been defeated on the Pakistan issue, and even Rab Nishtar, a Moslem League leader of the first rank at the national level, was not returned. Then the Congress policy of " Quit India " had won, but that cry no longer held the people together, and many who had originally supported Congress were now looking ahead and wondering whether they would come under Hindu control.

When Khan Sahib turned to the question of Pathanistan the discussion became somewhat disjointed and explosive. Gandhi has for some time been actively interested in this concept, and has lately been stressing its virtues with renewed vigour. If it were to prevail it would create a new frontier nationalism cutting across the Province's communal and political solidarity with Pakistan. "If you destroy the Pathan nation," warned Khan Sahib, "terrible things will happen."

Mountbatten went on to ask why there was no coalition government in the North-west Frontier Province. Khan Sahib replied heatedly, "If Congress want a coalition, I shall not remain in." Mountbatten hastened to add, "I was asking for information only." "Our people are very poor," Khan Sahib continued. "The Moslem League here represent only self-interest and a very privileged class of Khans." Caroe pointed out, "There are some very wealthy Congress supporters as well."

Mountbatten inquired about the state of communal feeling in the Province. Caroe replied, "The Moslem masses are protecting Hindus and Sikhs, except, of course, in Hazara. The hearts and minds of the Moslems are sound." Khan Sahib alleged that Moslems had been allowed by officials to break the law. Caroe replied firmly that he knew of no single instance where officials were not trying to do their duty, but they were always blamed.

Following a discussion on constitutional procedure, with complaints from the Governor of unjustifiable executive pressure on the part of the Prime Minister, and from the Prime Minister of interference in the Government on the part of the Governor, Mountbatten intervened to say, "I am out here to do a job with no axe to grind. I want to transfer power in terms of the will of the people. Ideally I would have a plebiscite here, but there is no time." He then discussed the implications of demission to the Provinces, partition generally and in relation to the North-west Frontier Province and the solemn duty placed upon him. "My problem", he added, "is whether to hold an election before we go, or whether law and order are sufficient for the Government to hold on." He suggested a joint committee of the two High Commands to advise on elections. The British, he said, always carried the rap, but he reiterated that his mandate was impartiality. Altogether it was a tense and taut session, which tested Mountbatten's resources to the full.

No sooner was this meeting with the Ministers over than we entered into a session with local Hindu representatives. They explained that their deputation was more communal than political or anti-Moslem League, and they made it clear that they were not concerned with the fate of the Ministry, but with the life and security of innocent Hindus and Sikhs. Mountbatten: "I am trying to get at the facts. Do you support the Government?" The Hindus: "We are prepared to live at peace under any Government." Mountbatten: "I am glad of this sensible attitude. I am trying to act constitutionally." There were complaints about the lack of police, who were stretched to the utmost. Four Brigades were at hand, but there were murders in Peshawar and lack of any effective police action. Mountbatten stressed the danger of using soldiers in place of police. The two had different functions. He added that there were at this moment more troops in the North-west Frontier Province than anywhere else in India, and Caroe added that more use was being made of them than at any time in his twenty-five years' experience, even including 1930–31. Mountbatten said that he was out to get the larger solution and end the uncertainty, but it would have to be a solution acceptable to all.

I was not able to stay on for the third meeting, this time with the Moslem League leaders specially released from gaol for the occasion. Among the delegation were the young and fanatical Pir of Manki Sharif and Khan Abdul Quayyum Khan. I understand from Ian Scott that they spoke at great length and with the utmost vehemence. Mount-batten has wisely given instructions that they should all be lodged in one gaol, so that they can meet and consult each other. He also agreed with their proposal that they should be allowed to go to Delhi on parole for consultation with Jinnah.

I was for some time heavily engaged in drafting and securing approval for Press notes covering the day's exciting but exacting activities, and was only able to come in at the tail end of a reception given by Dr. Khan Sahib. Later in the evening there was a dinner-party at Government House attended by all members of the Government and leading civil and military officials. Paying his tribute as one of the guests at this last bout of Viceregal splendour that Peshawar will see, was Brigadier Sir Hissa-muddin Khan, a famous local landowner and personality almost more Anglophile than the British. Mustering all his medals, and dressed in archaic regimental uniform, he made a brave showing, and recalled past glories. He told me that the first Viceroy he had served was Curzon, and that his first assignment was as a very junior officer of the guard outside the great man's bedroom. It was not an easy job, for Curzon was such a light sleeper that the officers of the guard and the sentries had to put felt over their boots to avoid disturbing him.

GOVERNMENT HOUSE, PESHAWAR AND RAWALPINDI,
Tuesday, 29th April, 1947

After an early breakfast, we set off for a tour of the Khyber and for the *Jirga* (tribal meeting) at Jamrud. We made the journey in a procession of half a dozen cars. Muriel Watson and I were well attended by the Governor's Secretary, Mr. R. H. D. Lowis, who gave us an invaluable commentary as we moved up into the barren and forbidding hills. We passed the famous Islamia College, where a few years ago Ian Scott had been the Principal. On the way back we were regaled by cries of " Pakistan Zindabad " from a number of the students who were perhaps alive to the important role their college could play in the training of much-needed officials for the new State they were so fervently hailing.

We passed the fort where the Guru Hari Singh is buried, and were told how on his death his body had been propped up in Jamrud for all to see. We then came to the great Jamrud Fort hewn out of the rocks—the garrison of the Khyber Rifles.

All the way on our twelve-mile journey the *khassidars* were spaced out guarding both sides of the road from nearby hillocks. They were a tribal police force, about one thousand six hundred strong, who were encouraged to keep order among their warlike brothers through sharing in Government benefits. The Afridis have apparently squatted on the Pass ever since the days of classical Greece. Their system of rule was described as being one of heredity based on character, which, if it is accepted, is as stable a system as any. Mr. Lowis explained that we were moving up into the heart of the Pathan kingdom, which had two ethnic boundaries—the Hindu Kush and the Indus. We reached the top of the Pass at Charbagh, and from there we looked out into Afghanistan. Lady Mountbatten told me she first came to the Khyber as a girl of nineteen, and was very much of a pioneer in doing so. Each detail of the rugged route had remained vivid in her memory.

We then turned back to Landi Kotal, where Mountbatten met the tribal *Jirga* of *Maliks* (elders) representing all eight clans of the Afridis as well as the Shinwari, Mullagori and Shilmani tribes. The scene provided an extraordinary contrast with the bleak, austere grandeur of the Pass itself. Landi Kotal camp, indeed, was just like a leafy Sussex village in summer time. The *Jirga* itself was a colourful assembly. Many of the tribesmen squatting in the shade of the trees looked very old and benign, and it was difficult to imagine that they were some of the toughest warriors in the world.

Their spokesman, one Khan Abdul Latif Khan, who spoke in Pushtu translated by Caroe, put forward at some length, and with occasional supporting interjections from his fellow leaders, the various demands. Several of these were of a local character, but on the wider front he pleaded that, in the event of the British Government vacating India, the Khyber should be returned to them. Moreover, he made it clear that while they belonged to no particular party, their sympathies were with their Moslem brethren. Indeed, he indulged in a considerable anti-Nehru and anti-Hindu diatribe. Nehru, who was actually stoned when he visited the Frontier last year, had warned Mountbatten to expect a hand-picked *Jirga*, but I must say that this one seemed to be genuinely representative.

Mountbatten's reply dealt with all the specific points raised, advising that it was up to them to negotiate their agreements with the successor authority. He added a characteristic personal point, " As I expect you know," he said, " I am a sailor, and had the honour of fighting in a battle in the North Sea in company with H.M.S. *Afridi*, called after your tribe because of its famous warlike qualities. Although we have had to fight you Afridis in the past on occasions, we respect and like each other. Your *Jirga* has a reputation for wisdom and foresight. For the last sixteen years you have behaved and stuck to your agreements. In this critical time, when power is to be handed over, do not lose that reputation."

As tokens of good-will Khan Abdul Latif Khan then presented the Viceroy with a number of gifts, including a haversack, Pathan dagger and *chappals*, and a rifle of splendid craftsmanship made somewhere in the Khyber caves. After a short break for coffee, which only helped to heighten the home-from-home feeling, we again set off in our single file of cars down the hills back to Peshawar.

On our return, a second but smaller *Jirga*, this time of Wazir and Mahsud tribesmen, was awaiting us in the grounds of Government House. They, too, were very outspoken in their attitude to a Hindu raj. Mountbatten assured them, " I have taken note of what you have said about Pakistan, and I have taken action about the release of prisoners from gaols. Arrangements are being made among themselves as to when they will come out. The sooner the present tension can be relieved the better for all concerned." There followed short talks with Hindu and Sikh minority delegations, who, not unnaturally, spoke with much more moderation.

Immediately after lunch we left by air for Rawalpindi, arriving there an hour later. We had hardly touched down and set foot in Command House before the Governor, Sir Evan Jenkins, whisked us off to Kahuta, scene of some recent severe communal rioting. Dusty, and with parched throats after a twenty-five-mile car drive, we arrived to find that the havoc in the small town was very great. Picking our way through the rubble, we could see that the devastation was as thorough as any produced by fire-bomb raids in the war. This particular communal orgy involved the destruction of Sikhs and their livelihood by Moslems who were proving difficult to track down. The Moslems in the area seemed to be quite pleased with themselves, and to be unable to appreciate that the local Sikh traders were one of the principal sources of their own prosperity. Economically the ruin which the two communities inflict upon each other is complete and horrifying both in its immediate and long-term implications.

After a thorough tour—and on such occasions no detail escapes their eagle eyes—the Mountbattens sat at a small table and listened to various local leaders and representatives explaining the situation and putting forward their grievances. One Dewan Pindi Das Sabharwal regaled us with a highly coloured address some five pages in length which was not on the agenda. Jenkins was not unnaturally annoyed, as the remarks were full of gross accusations against himself as Governor and gave various strange statistics, including a reference to three thousand one hundred and ninety-nine forcible conversions.

On our return to Rawalpindi I met some Indian and British Press friends at the local hotel and went into some of the difficulties they are having in filing stories from here. I got back only just in time for the dinner at Command House, where I sat next to Colonel Still, an intelligent man who engaged me in an interesting talk on Parliamentary democracy and the need for the " cunning good man " to run it. He gave a definition of barbarism as " an absence of values to which appeal can be made ". Propaganda was thus to be seen as a concession to, if not an actual by-product of, barbarism.

VICEROY'S HOUSE, NEW DELHI, *Wednesday, 30th April, 1947*

Our party split up—Mountbatten returning direct to Delhi, and Lady Mountbatten carrying on with her tour of the riot areas. I found myself busily engaged with correspondents who were anxious to receive background guidance on the result of the visit. It was necessary to tread warily. The full force of Congress and Moslem League interest was temporarily focused on the Province, and the air was full of speculation.

My first job was to deal firmly with Altaf Hussain, the Editor of *Dawn*, who published a shockingly inaccurate story from his Peshawar correspondent under the following banner headlines: " Mountbatten Confers with Frontier Leaders—Manki and Quayyum Refuse to be Released on Parole—Huge Demonstration by Pathan Men and Women—Viceroy Flying to Jamrud." In so far as Mountbatten had spent over two hours with Manki and Quayyum, who had both been the chief spokesmen of the Moslem delegation, his first reaction was to make a personal protest to Jinnah, but I dissuaded him from doing this on Hussain's assurance that the story would be corrected to-morrow. This particular correspondent's imaginative powers reach their peak with the reference to the Viceroy's flight to Jamrud, where there is no airfield !

Clearly there were few tangible results to report, but in bringing the local Moslem leaders into touch with Jinnah, and thereby the wider context of events, Mountbatten certainly helped to take the edge off the immediate crisis. The only chance of calling off the civil disobedience campaign rests with Jinnah himself. The Frontier leaders are wild men who, if left to their own devices, have neither the will nor resource to achieve a reasonable settlement. The whole visit has brought home to us the need for achieving the wider agreement on India's future as quickly as possible. If we do not, there will be a complete disintegration of what remains of law and order both in the Frontier and the Punjab, not to speak of the other northern Provinces. It is certainly a great dispensation that south and central India should be remaining so calm.

Doon Campbell, of Reuters, telephoned at midnight to tell me of two very strongly worded statements just put out by Jinnah and Dr. Rajendra Prasad. Jinnah, he said, was in effect launching his irredentist campaign against a " truncated, or mutilated, moth-eaten Pakistan " and demanding a " national home " of more ambitious dimensions, in fact of all Provinces included in Groups B and C of the Cabinet Mission Plan, regardless of their communal majorities (i.e., Sind, the Punjab, North-west Frontier Province, Baluchistan, Bengal and Assam). Prasad's statement, it seems, draws attention to the historic Moslem League resolution at Lahore in 1940 which launched the concept of Pakistan, but which spoke of it as comprising areas where Moslems were numerically in the majority. In the third session of the Constituent Assembly which opened earlier this week, Prasad, speaking as its new President, had already prepared the minds of members for the partition of India, but, as a part of the process, for the division of some of the Provinces as well.

Prasad is one of the most influential of the Congress high command, and has been holding the key Ministry of Food and Agriculture in the

Interim Government. When I had tea with him at his home the other day I was impressed by his serenity and undoubted depth of mind and strength of character. He is essentially a moderate and a conciliator, a man of the people whose good reputation has little to do with the demagogic arts, but is the outcome of long and loyal service to the Nationalist cause. He will undoubtedly have a key role to play in the new regime, whether in a united or divided India.*

VICEROY'S HOUSE, NEW DELHI, *Thursday, 1st May, 1947*

I was present at the lunch-party to-day, and sat next to Mr. Bardoloi, Prime Minister of Assam, quiet-spoken and unassuming, as are so many of the front-rank Congressmen.

At to-day's Staff Meeting we had a further discussion on the problem of the retention of India within the Commonwealth. We have received a reminder from London that in any consideration of the granting of Dominion Status the Indian States are not at present British territory at all, and could hardly be incorporated as part of the British Commonwealth.

As far as British India was concerned, Mountbatten came down heavily against the concept of allowing only a part to remain in, with the consequent risk of Britain being involved in the support of one Indian sovereign State against another. He personally favoured the formula that only British India as a whole should be permitted to remain in the Commonwealth. In the meanwhile a completely non-committal attitude on the question should be maintained. Ismay's personal view, however, was that it would be virtually impossible, both on moral and material grounds, to eject from the Commonwealth any part of India that asks to remain in. If Pakistan were involved, relations with the entire Moslem bloc extending from the Middle East had to be considered. British backing, if not of the whole, then of a part of India, might be the one way to avoid a civil war. Ian Scott subscribed to Ismay's argument.

George Abell, while agreeing that the British would have a continuing moral responsibility, felt that the worst way of fulfilling this might be the unilateral support of Pakistan. I said that I agreed with George, and felt that support by Great Britain of one part of India only would result in the sub-continent becoming the centre of international tension and intrigue. Miéville raised the important question whether under the Statute of Westminster all members of the British Commonwealth would have to be consulted about the inclusion or ejection of the whole or parts of India. He added that V. P. Menon, Reforms Commissioner and, as such, an *ex officio* member of his Staff, had advised him that Patel might be ready to accept an offer of Dominion Status for the time being.

We are turning our attention to the Bengal situation, and Sir Frederick Burrows, who was unable to be present for the Governors' Conference owing to illness, arrived yesterday for a twenty-four-hour visit. Mount-

* He was, in fact, to become the first President of the Indian Republic following the adoption of the Indian Constitution in January 1950.

batten has enjoyed meeting him again, and found him congenial company. Burrows made his reputation as a member of the Soulbury Commission, which duly recommended Dominion Status for Ceylon and was taking its evidence in Colombo a few months after Mountbatten had established his S.E.A.C. Headquarters in Kandy.* He certainly provides an interesting contrast to most of his predecessors at Government House, Calcutta. For he is very proud of his years of service as a railwayman, and on one occasion is said to have startled Calcutta society by declaring that the main difference between himself and previous Governors of Bengal was that while they were accustomed to "huntin' and shootin'", he was accustomed to "shuntin' and hootin'"! He delighted in exchanging military memories with Mountbatten, strictly as between sergeant-major and Admiral.

VICEROY'S HOUSE, NEW DELHI, *Friday, 2nd May, 1947*

I have put out the announcement that the Mountbattens will be leaving for a short visit to Simla. Mountbatten is anxious to make it clear that no interruption of business is involved, and the statement explains that he has now come to the end of preliminary meetings with representative Indian leaders, and will be leaving after the weekly Cabinet meeting on the 6th, returning in time to preside over the next one.

I have also released an account of Lady Mountbatten's adventurous three-day tour, during which she covered nearly one thousand five hundred miles by plane, besides considerable distances by car and on foot. She left Lahore at seven this morning in the Viceroy's Dakota, arriving over Mooltan, the last place on her long itinerary, just before 8.30. She was unable to land, as there was a dust-storm over an area of about twenty miles radius, and visibility was very poor. The plane circled left and right at varying heights down to about three hundred feet, but failed to sight the airfield. Muriel Watson had the utmost difficulty in inducing her to call off the search, and she only agreed to do so after she had sent a message to the Mooltan Commissioner expressing her regrets and her resolve to return at the earliest possible date.

I set off to-night by the Delhi Mail for a quiet long week-end with my family at Mashobra, prior to the arrival of the main Viceregal party in Simla on Tuesday.

* In fact, it was on the advice of Lord Mountbatten, after he had called a meeting with Their Excellencies, the Governor and Commander-in-Chief, Ceylon, in May 1944, that a Commission was sent out.

CHAPTER SEVEN

CRISIS AT SIMLA

"THE RETREAT", MASHOBRA, SIMLA, *Saturday, 3rd May, 1947*

THE TWO-HUNDRED-MILE journey from Delhi to Simla takes some twelve hours to complete by rail. The train left the chaos, noise, smell and heat of Delhi Main at 10.30 last night, and I slept fitfully in the ice-cooled heat of the carriage. Just before 7 a.m. I arrived at Kalka, which links the plains with the foothills, to be greeted already with a cooler and fresher air. Here I changed into the famous white rail-motor and started on the three-hour and five-thousand-feet climb to Simla, successive bends and loops opening up ever more splendid vistas.

None-the-less the Himalayas do not reveal themselves with the shattering impact of the Andes, which strike down from some fifteen thousand feet sheer into the Pacific Ocean. They dominate the senses with a slower crescendo. Save for small terraced farmsteads striving to extract life from the parched earth, the first foothills reflect only the barrenness of the plains from which they rise. Only at about four thousand feet is there the fertility of a more temperate zone and the sense that one is moving into a world of mountains. While at this level one is reminded of the Ceylon monsoon-bathed scenery one thousand six hundred miles to the south. After the cloudless skies of Delhi it was a strange and exhilarating experience to feel mist and rain beat against one's face.

On arrival at Simla I had the somewhat embarrassing experience of being driven through the Mall. The privilege is reserved only for the Viceroy's, Governor's and Commander-in-Chief's vehicles. Simla is built upon a razor's edge, and its life is centred on the main street, and without strict limitation of motor traffic the congestion would be complete. The road is given over to pedestrians and rickshaws. Accordingly to appear in a Viceregal car is to move at a snail's pace and to invite stares of startled curiosity. Once clear of Simla itself, I was driven another seven miles up the road that leads to Tibet. A milestone on the way reads, "Tibet 191 Miles". I have a yearning to follow that road to the end. Our house can be reached only by a rickshaw path which overlooks the large Viceregal orchards. A sentry guards the gate of this remote "Retreat". It is an idyllic place, for long the week-end house of Viceroys withdrawing from cares of State when Simla was the summer seat of Government.

"THE RETREAT", MASHOBRA, SIMLA, *Monday, 5th May, 1947*

For the past forty-eight hours I have been able to relax and from our mountain aerie drink in the splendour and solitude of the Himalayan landscape. For days on end mists and cloud act like a vast backcloth, allowing one a vista of no more than the valley below and the neighbouring peak of Shali, a mere twelve thousand feet high, and snowless in the spring. Then suddenly the curtain rises, and stretching before one in an uninterrupted arc of over ninety degrees is the eternal snowline, range after range, sixteen thousand feet and more. No doubt there are many other vistas of the main Himalayan range as impressive as this, for the "roof of the world" covers over two hundred and fifty thousand square miles and includes at least forty peaks of over twenty-four thousand feet. But the splendid and awesome vision from Simla serves as a symbol of this immensity.

During my brief respite here in Mashobra the pace of political events in Delhi quickened. Ismay and George Abell left for London on the 2nd May, taking with them the draft Plan for the British Government's consideration.

On Saturday there was the first major Indian Press attack upon Mountbatten, significantly enough from the *Hindustan Times*, to which some weight has always to be given, in so far as it is edited by the Mahatma's son, Devadas Gandhi, and owned by his wealthiest supporter, G. D. Birla. At any given time it is the mouthpiece of Nehru or Patel or of the Mahatma himself.

The article began by saying, "For the first time since Lord Mountbatten assumed the Viceroyalty the feeling that he may not be playing fair has come among Congressmen and Sikh leaders." There then followed revelations of the Viceroy's main conclusions which were sufficiently accurate as to indicate inside knowledge, and some no less well informed but somewhat threatening Congress reactions. These included a demand for special terms for the Sikhs in the Punjab. There was also an ominous unwillingness to concede a fresh election on the Frontier. "The Congress Working Committee", according to the writer, "has made the Frontier question a test case. It has made clear to the Viceroy that any proposal to dismiss the Frontier Ministry and hold fresh elections will make the Congress change its entire attitude towards the British Government."

I understand that yesterday Mountbatten had two important interviews with Gandhi and Jinnah, the net effect of which made Mountbatten wonder whether Ismay's departure had not been premature. By a freak of chance the interviews overlapped, and Mountbatten had the political insight and social finesse to bring the two leaders together for their first meeting in three years. But once the formalities of greeting were over the encounter baffled Mountbatten's calculations. For Gandhi and Jinnah, with their chairs far apart, were quite unable to raise their voices sufficiently, so that they seemed to be like two old conspirators engaged in long-distance dumbshow. Although Mountbatten strained his ears, much of their conversation escaped him. However, his primary purpose was amply achieved, for they agreed to have a full discussion with each other at Jinnah's house.

Before leaving for Simla, Mountbatten has been gathering in the views of the Governors of the Punjab, Bengal and North-west Frontier

Province on the desirability or otherwise of referenda for their Provinces. Briefly Caroe is in favour for the North-west Frontier Province, Burrows non-committal for Bengal, although on balance against, and Jenkins took an extremely gloomy view of the situation, casting doubt upon its acceptability either to Jinnah or the Sikhs. Mountbatten, however, held firmly to the view that in the last analysis Jinnah would acquiesce, and that the only way the Sikhs could improve their position was through negotiation.

"THE RETREAT", MASHOBRA, SIMLA, *Tuesday, 6th May, 1947*

Jinnah and Gandhi met for three hours at Jinnah's home in Aurangzeb Road. An agreed statement was issued, which read as follows:—

" We discussed two matters; One was the question of division of India into Pakistan and Hindustan, and Mr. Gandhi does not accept the principle of division. He thinks that division is not inevitable, whereas in my opinion not only is Pakistan inevitable, but is the only practical solution of India's political problem.

" The second matter which we discussed was the letter which we both have signed jointly appealing to the people to maintain peace; we have both come to the conclusion that we must do our best in our respective spheres to see that that appeal of ours is carried out and we will make every effort for this purpose."

Although the meeting in itself was clearly abortive, the balance of tactical advantage—as the smoothly worded text suggests—undoubtedly lies with Jinnah: one more nail has been driven into the coffin of the Cabinet Mission Plan. The unresolved question is just how far Gandhi can or will resist the tidal flow of events towards partition.

"THE RETREAT", MASHOBRA, SIMLA, *Wednesday, 7th May, 1947*

My brief respite came to an end to-day, when I was summoned to Viceregal Lodge. Mountbatten has brought up with him V. P. Menon, who was closely involved in all the 1945 Simla and the 1946 Cabinet Mission Plan negotiations. Although he has suffered a period of eclipse, he is still the trusted confidant of Vallabhbhai Patel. It must be confessed that Viceregal Lodge is an ideal venue for quiet, calm deliberation, and the Viceroy's workroom here in refreshing contrast to his air-cooled and sombre teak-lined study in Delhi. The pale green of the former has decided him to have a similar colour scheme in the latter. He believes that the darkness of his Delhi room itself induces an atmosphere of depression. He could not understand how past Viceroys could have endured it, and thought it was monstrous that he should be needing electric light throughout the day during an Indian summer.

On arrival I was plunged into two successive Staff Meetings, the first without Mountbatten and the second with him. At both we considered fully the desirability of an alternative plan based on the assumption, which V. P. held was more than possible, that Jinnah would not accept the Plan in the draft announcement. Mountbatten said he had always borne in mind the possibility of rejection by Jinnah, and in all the interviews he had had both with him and Liaquat he had watched carefully for any sign pointing to such an intention, but none had been given. Every test he had applied led him to the belief that they intended to accept, and he could see only two possible suppositions for Jinnah not doing so—the first, if his real aim was to keep the British in India, and by prolonging the bargaining to make it more difficult for the British to leave, in the hope of obtaining thereby a more favourable award; the second, if he had reached the conclusion that Pakistan was not practicable.

But he seriously doubted whether either of these considerations was in Jinnah's mind. None-the-less he agreed with V. P.'s thesis on the advisability of having available a clear alternative in his dealings with Jinnah. The second-line plan would involve demission of power under the present constitution. It would not in the last resort require the agreement of the Indian leaders. Provincial subjects would be demitted to existing Provincial Governments, and Central subjects to the existing Central Government; but it would put the Moslems under the Hindu majority.

A telegram has been drafted for dispatch to London, giving them the background and asking for approval to hold such a plan in reserve. We also went further into the possibilities of retaining India in the Commonwealth, and V. P. confirmed both Patel's and Nehru's positive approach to the subject and the need for dropping the terms " King-Emperor " and " Empire ", to which so many Indians objected. V. P. was finally asked to prepare a paper setting out clearly the procedure whereby a form of Dominion Status could be granted to India under the alternative Plans of Partition and Demission.

"THE RETREAT", MASHOBRA, SIMLA, *Thursday, 8th May, 1947*

At to-day's meeting a problem of some moment affecting our relations with the Indian and world Press was on our agenda. Ever since our arrival, the Foreign correspondents have been seeking an off-the-record interview either with Mountbatten or with Ismay on his behalf. The political negotiations have been so intensive that it has been necessary to protect Mountbatten from any commitments other than those directly concerned with the formulation of the Plan itself, and now Ismay is away for at least another fortnight. On top of this, the *Hindustan Times* article last week only confirms that the leading Delhi editors and their correspondents know far more than would be available to them through normal channels. The clamour for some sort of access to the Viceroy, for background guidance, is more insistent than ever.

My feeling is that while an interview with Mountbatten himself remains out of the question at this time and would involve discrimination against the Indian Press, it would be wise and equitable if Miéville were to stand in for Ismay. I am convinced that the effect of such contact will be to damp down speculation, particularly in the editorial offices of London and New York, during the critical ten-day hiatus between now and Mountbatten's proposed presentation of the Plan to the Leaders. Whether it is "yea" or "nay" to the Foreign correspondents' request, it will in either case involve a calculated risk. No decision was taken to-day. Most of the staff would, I think, like Mountbatten to say "no" out of hand, but while he is rightly adamant that he personally should not take any part, he shares my view that Miéville should fill the breach.

"THE RETREAT", MASHOBRA, SIMLA, *Friday, 9th May, 1947*

The Dominion Status question was discussed at great length this morning. Mountbatten began by saying he thought it most desirable that if Dominion Status was to be granted to India before June 1948 the grant should in fact take place during 1947. He went so far as to say that he would like to see Dominion Status by 31st December, 1947—giving as his reason the startlingly apt precedent of a plenary session of the Quebec Conference during the war. The meeting had been asked to approve a directive that war with Japan must be ended by 1948. To this President Roosevelt had said he would never agree. Hopkins intervened, " Well, make it 31st December, 1947."—President Roosevelt, " Agreed."

Nehru and Krishna Menon have arrived, and much will depend on Mountbatten's powers of persuasion with them if the Dominion Status concept is to come to light. Already Krishna indicates resistance to any splitting of the Army if early Dominion Status is accepted. Miéville was inclined to think that there would be more advantage to India than to the Commonwealth from India remaining in, but Mountbatten considered that the value to the United Kingdom both in terms of world prestige and strategy would be enormous; for India as a whole the immense asset of constitutional continuity. He appreciated the many administrative difficulties, particularly those facing Pakistan, but these were inherent in the situation anyhow. " What are we doing? " he asked. " Administratively it is the difference between putting up a permanent building, a nissen hut or a tent. As far as Pakistan is concerned we are putting up a tent. We can do no more."

He told us that in the rush of business yesterday he had missed his thirty-fourth anniversary of joining the Navy as a twelve-years-old cadet.

This afternoon there was a brief respite from the intensive discussions. The Mountbattens brought Nehru out to tea at " The Retreat ". But for the mountains surrounding us, it might have been a typical English garden tea-party. To begin with there was a certain tension which stifled small talk. Fay, sitting next to Nehru, managed to elicit from him his views on the sugar shortage (they had actually brought their own sugar with them) and his antipathy to Simla. This characteristically was derived from his aversion to the spectacle of the rickshaw coolies, whose labours he thought were an affront to human dignity.

Mountbatten asked Nehru if his responsibilities as Minister for External Affairs covered communications with Burma, and if so, what had become of the great road and airfield projects which had been built during his S.E.A.C. days at immense cost. There had been clamour for years for a land link with Burma—were these being kept up? Nehru showed some interest, but felt that the cost of maintenance would be very heavy.

After tea Nehru said he would like to see our children. Mountbatten introduced our son Keith as his godchild, exclaiming, " He stands up so straight he will fall over backwards! " We then went on a grand tour of the house and Viceregal orchards.

The Mountbattens fell in love with the place, and are quite determined to come back again. During our walk up and down the orchard terraces Nehru was very agile, and confessed to a liking for hill-climbing. He gave us a demonstration of a new technique by walking uphill backwards. This, he said, made breathing easier at high altitudes, and rested the calf-muscles.

"THE RETREAT", MASHOBRA, SIMLA, *Saturday, 10th May, 1947*

At our Staff Meeting to-day Mountbatten reported on a breakfast conversation he had had with Krishna, while V. P. spoke of contact he had made with Patel. The impression grows that the Dominion Status formula increasingly appeals to both the Congress leaders. Krishna Menon takes credit as the first to have suggested an early transfer of power to India on this basis. He thinks Nehru is attracted to the concept, if only because it may give Mountbatten opportunity to bring his influence to bear on the more recalcitrant Princes. V. P. suspects that likely delay in completing the Indian constitution may also encourage Nehru to look towards Dominion Status as an interim device to fill up the time. The main difficulty on the Congress side seems to be the fear of the left wing exploiting Dominion Status as a " sell out " to Britain.

To-day I put out the momentous communiqué announcing that the Viceroy had invited the five Leaders to meet him at 10.30 a.m., and the Indian States' Representatives in the afternoon, next Saturday 17th May, the purpose being " to present to them the Plan which His Majesty's Government has now made for the transfer of power to Indian hands ".

At six o'clock this evening, after a preliminary run through with Mountbatten, Miéville met the Foreign correspondents for the long-delayed background talk, in his own house. He brought out the important points very well—the need for a quick political solution, but a democratic one also; how, in a matter of such magnitude, the onus of choice must fall upon the people themselves or their elected representatives; how the Leaders were being brought step by step towards agreement. This was diplomacy by discussion, and not by *diktat*.

I gather from Eric Britter, who is staying with us, that the talk has had a very steadying effect, and in particular provided enlightenment for the American Press.

"THE RETREAT", MASHOBRA, SIMLA, *Sunday, 11th May, 1947*

Mountbatten has had a shattering day. He rang me up at Mashobra just before we were due to entertain a party of Press correspondents, most of whom had been at yesterday's talk with Miéville, to tell me just this—that it would be necessary to postpone the meeting with the Leaders announced last night in our communiqué as due to take place on 17th May. Would I prepare a second communiqué? This is certainly the stiffest request in political Public Relations I have ever received, and having done my best to conceal my anxiety and mental turmoil from our tea-party, I arrived at Viceregal Lodge at 6.30 in the evening to find despondency, not to say alarm.

It seems that last night Mountbatten gave Nehru the chance of reading the draft Plan as revised and approved by London, and that Nehru, having read it, has vehemently turned it down. He is convinced that it involves a major departure in principle from the original draft prepared by Mountbatten and his staff which Ismay and George Abell took back with them to London at the beginning of the month.

Nehru was satisfied that both in the Cabinet Mission Plan, which he was at pains to stress is still not dead, and in the Mountbatten draft, his concept of India as a continuing entity had been preserved. In the London draft, however, the breakdown seems to him to amount to little less than connivance at Balkanisation. He really wants it to be fully established that India and the Constituent Assembly are the successors to, and Pakistan and the Moslem League the seceders from, British India. Many of the detailed objections he raises are trivial, and could in themselves be easily disposed of. He will have nothing to do, for instance, with the proposed procedure for Baluchistan. This is, no doubt, an over-estimate, but the changes have aroused in him all the old suspicions of London as the home of an alien Civil Service whose hearts are hard, and understanding strictly limited when it comes to handling India to-day.

The one immediate result of his attitude is to make it necessary for Mountbatten and his staff, depleted by the absence of Ismay and Abell, to push ahead at once with a second revised draft at the highest speed for transmission to Ismay, who by the time Mountbatten's telegrams warning him of this *volte-face* reach him will be a somewhat confused and frustrated Viceregal envoy.

Having scratched my head over the second communiqué, I went up with Miéville to see Mountbatten in his study to discuss the publicity difficulties and dangers before us. His hair was somewhat dishevelled, but he was still marvellously resilient. He told us that only a hunch on his part had saved him from disaster. Without that hunch, " Dickie Mountbatten ", he said, " would have been finished and could have packed his bag. We would have looked complete fools with the Government at home, having led them up the garden to believe that Nehru would accept the Plan." He said that most of his staff, with natural caution, had been against his running over the Plan with Nehru, but by following his hunch rather than their advice he had probably saved the day.

I stressed that it was out of the question for us to put out any post-ponement announcement without ensuring full clearance and con-sistency with London. After some urgent exchanges it was agreed that the announcement should read as follows : " Owing to the imminence of the Parliamentary recess in London, it has been found necessary to postpone H.E. the Viceroy's meeting with the Indian Leaders announced to begin on Saturday 17th May, until Monday 2nd June."

The wording of this communiqué, coming so closely upon our Press party and within twenty-four hours of our firm announcement to the world of the earlier date, has caused me more anxiety than any Press statement I have issued in the past or am likely to issue in the future. I have visions of the whole structure of confidence and good-will we have so carefully built up falling to the ground and an unrivalled feast being provided for the hungry Press speculators.

The weakness of our position is that at a moment of crisis we have told the truth, but it is not the whole truth and nothing but the truth. No one in Delhi is likely to believe that London was the source of the postponement, and if they do, that in itself will only help to evoke old suspicions. Everyone knows that Nehru has been staying with the Viceroy, and from the strictly Public Relations point of view I believe it would have been preferable to base the postponement on the grounds of drafting detail. However, there was certainly no time to argue out the publicity refinements of the dilemma we are in. The essence of the matter is that we have put out with the utmost speed a firm decision no less firmly postponed, and have secured London's approval for it. Textual adornments involving delay are unacceptable.

"THE RETREAT", MASHOBRA, SIMLA, *Monday, 12th May, 1947*

Mountbatten, who has now had a chance to sleep on yesterday's developments, said that although he seems to have been able to establish his own integrity with the Indian Leaders, undoubtedly a phobia persists against any document or proposal issuing from London. Clearly any re-drafts will have to be made by his own staff in India. He has decided that one revision must be to take away any option for independence either for Bengal or for any other Province. He felt that it would always be possible to reconsider this decision if there was at any time a request from both parties for Provincial independence. Nehru has his own plan similar to ours proposing an early demission of power to the Interim Government on a Dominion Status basis.

After the meeting Fay and I were guests at a small "family" lunch-party which took place under a cedar tree in the garden. Krishna Menon, who has stayed on to patch up some of the rents in the Plan caused by Nehru's visit, was there. Most of our discussion was taken up with the Indian Boy Scout movement, in which Krishna is interested. Here again politics and intrigue seem to dominate the scene. After lunch Mountbatten held forth on the strategic problems facing India, whether united or partitioned. It is interesting to note what a revelation such discussions are to the Congress leaders, whose whole lives have hitherto centred round purely political considerations.

CHAPTER EIGHT

THE PLAN REDRAFTED

VICEROY'S HOUSE, NEW DELHI, *Wednesday, 14th May, 1947*

THE COURT CIRCULAR announces that Their Excellencies have left Simla and have arrived in Delhi. This simple formula covers a virtual migration. Douglas Currie * estimates that including servants the move by road and rail involves three hundred and thirty-three people. The Viceroy's own party made the spiral descent down the mountains in a procession of twelve cars, the Mountbattens leading in their open Buick.

I took morbid pleasure in counting the number of bends between Simla and Kalka—over a distance of fifty-two miles there are more than eight hundred. Between Kalka and Ambala the turnings are normal, perhaps one to every two miles or so. Then for the one hundred and twelve miles between Ambala and Delhi, as if to compensate for having been such a circuitous wanderer, the road becomes a straight line stretching as if to infinity. At regular intervals mud-built villages simmer in the deadening heat. Bullock-carts taking days on the trek to and from the Delhi mart move almost imperceptibly, and draw slowly aside to let the cars rush past to incomprehensible objectives at baffling speeds, defying the natural order of things. Wherever a group of people are gathered there are friendly looks and greetings for the cars with the Viceregal crowns upon them. Down the road are place-names that recall India's long embattled history. At Panipat the Emperor Babar won his crowning victory which ensured the predominance of the Moghul conquerors. Little trace of these historic events is to be seen to-day. Not until the same road approaches Agra, about one hundred and twenty miles to the south of Delhi, do the monuments of Moghul power and magnificence assert themselves.

On arrival it was soon evident that the postponement of the Leaders' meeting and the reason given for it had been sceptically received. We are sweltering in very great heat—113 degrees in the shade; and the shade gives but very little relief. I shall clearly have a difficult job to hold down speculation. The Indian Press are somewhat annoyed by Miéville's Press party, while the Foreign Press who attended it are mystified by the developments which so quickly followed in its wake and of which, of course, no sign was given.

VICEROY'S HOUSE, NEW DELHI, *Thursday, 15th May, 1947*

Mountbatten has had a courteous but firm summons to return to London for consultation. At first he reacted strongly against the

---

* Colonel D. H. Currie, C.I.E., C.B.E., Military Secretary to the Viceroy and Governor-General throughout Lord Mountbatten's term of office.

proposal, saying that there was nothing for him to go home for, but the alternative proposal from the Prime Minister that a member or members of the Cabinet should come out was even more unacceptable to him.

This morning's meeting was largely taken up with preparation of urgent signals to Ismay and with the mechanics of the trip home. The Prime Minister has sent a proposed text for a communiqué to cover the visit, which seemed to me to be very well phrased and not to let us down unduly after the somewhat rash decision to attribute the postponement of the Leaders' meeting solely to the impending Whitsun recess. Mount-batten is naturally anxious to make it clear that he is returning of his own volition, and not simply by urgent summons. He plans now to present the revised Plan first to Jinnah and then to Nehru. He is also seeing the two key seconds in command, Patel and Liaquat, to-day. V. P. stressed that Nehru's moodiness at Simla was very largely due to his absence from his colleagues; with Patel to strengthen his arm his fit of depression will soon pass.

I spent a very busy day with the Press which culminated at 7 p.m. with the issue of the communiqué announcing the Viceroy's return to London. By this time I had Walt Mason, Preston Grover—both of Associated Press of America—Norman Cliff, of the *News Chronicle*, and Sidney Smith, of the *Daily Express*, all in the room at the same time, and the telephone ringing continuously.

I must say that I agree with V. P. that the decision to leave for London should have a steadying effect on the general situation and help to dam the rising flood of speculation.

VICEROY'S HOUSE, NEW DELHI, *Friday, 16th May, 1947*

Nehru and Patel have asked Mountbatten to add Kripalani, Congress President, to the invitation list for the Leaders' meeting. They feel that his presence would help them in carrying Congress as against purely ministerial opinion. Moreover, they point out that Kripalani's status as President is the same as Jinnah's *vis-à-vis* the Moslem League. Mount-batten has decided to write and say that while he recognises Kripalani's importance, he cannot agree to having him at the meeting itself, but would be ready to see him privately either just before or just after it. This is a typical teasing problem, which is deceptively trivial at first sight, but which can so easily develop into a major crisis. If Kripalani is not asked, Congress nurse the sense of grievance that they have had to make yet one more capitulation to Jinnah. If he is asked, Jinnah is duly offended.

V. P. has drafted very brief but cogent Heads of Agreement. There are eight in all. It is a bold effort to get round the difficulty of the Leaders refusing to take the full burden of unpopular decisions and hiding behind their inability to decide on behalf of their respective Party machines. The Heads of Agreement press for early Dominion Status as an interim arrangement based upon the Government of India Act of 1935 with modifications, and envisaging one or two sovereign States. If one only, power should be transferred to the existing central Government. The sixth Head asserts that the Governor-General should be common to both the States. Finally it attempts to cover the problem of dividing the Armed Forces. It proposes that units should be allocated according to the territorial basis of recruitment and placed under the control of the respective Governments. It makes a special provision for the distribution of mixed units.

Mountbatten has failed in his efforts to get Jinnah and Liaquat to sign the document or even a letter agreeing to it. According to him they appeared absolutely to accept its general principles, but were not willing to state their agreement in writing. V. P. said that Patel's and Nehru's main concern was that Jinnah should accept the Plan in such a way as to make it clear that it really was his last territorial demand, and not just an interim arrangement. He felt it would satisfy Congress if Jinnah made it clear that he himself accepted the announcement and would use his good offices to put it into effect.

Mountbatten said that he had cautiously tested Jinnah's reaction to the threat, failing agreement, of demitting power to the Interim Government on a Dominion Status basis. Jinnah had apparently been very calm, and had said simply that he could not stop such a step in any event. In some respects this may well turn out to be the most delicate and decisive moment for Mountbatten's and Jinnah's diplomacy. Mountbatten felt that Jinnah's reaction was both abnormal and disturbing. It was certainly shrewd. The *ballon d'essai* has gone up and come down again, providing only the evidence that Jinnah has a very steady nerve. Mountbatten feels that Jinnah is well aware of his potency as a martyr butchered by the British on the Congress altar.

Lady Mountbatten has carried out her promise and returned to Mooltan. By starting from Delhi at five o'clock in the morning, her aircraft succeeded in defeating the dust which blotted out all visibility when she made her first attempt to get there ten days ago, and a successful landing was made two hours afterwards. She was able to visit hospitals and refugee centres and see the riot areas, talking to a large number of the victims. She said that her heart ached for them, that many families had been wiped out, their homes and property completely destroyed, whilst those who had survived lived in permanent fear of further attacks.

It is very difficult, in advance of a political settlement and of concrete plans for rehabilitation and compensation, to do more than give them what help is possible with food, clothes and supplies, but her presence has undoubtedly done much to raise morale among these suffering people. Mooltan itself has a forty per cent Hindu community. Lady Mountbatten was greatly encouraged to note that during the riots the Moslem police and Hindu troops had worked in such complete co-operation that after order had been restored they had actually had a dinner to " cement relations ". " This ", Lady Mountbatten said, " in the midst of all the sorrow and suffering, gave me hope and faith that peace and order would come before too long."

VICEROY'S HOUSE, NEW DELHI, *Sunday, 18th May, 1947*

The Mountbattens left Palam this morning at 8.30 for London. A large party was at the airfield to see them off, including Colville, who, as senior Governor, is temporary acting Viceroy for the fourth time. Mountbatten is taking V. P. and Vernon back with him. V. P., after all his efforts at Simla, is now in the ascendant and enjoys Mountbatten's complete confidence. He combines to a remarkable degree administrative and drafting skill of the first order with political flair. His position as a member of the Viceroy's staff is one of considerable delicacy, but his skill as a *rapporteur* and mediator is outstanding. It argues much for Mountbatten's judgement of men that he should have sensed V. P.'s capabilities so early on.

Mountbatten has been at great pains to make this one of the fastest India-to-England flights. He is travelling in his war-time York *MW 102*, which has special long-range tanks, and is using double crews. They will touch down only twice, at Mauripur (Karachi) and Fayid (Egypt), before reaching Northolt to-morrow at 10.30 in the morning, in a little more than twenty-four flying hours.

VICEROY'S HOUSE, NEW DELHI, *Thursday, 22nd May, 1947*

Jinnah has dropped a carefully timed and placed bombshell. He demands an eight-hundred-mile " Corridor " to link West and East Pakistan. The technique of releasing it seems to have been copied from Stalin. Doon Campbell, of Reuters, to whom the story was given, told me that it was in answer to a questionnaire which he had lodged with Jinnah some days previously. No one was more surprised than he to find himself with such a scoop on his hands. In a telegram to Erskine Crum in London I reported, " Jinnah's answers were not verbal, but written out ". As soon as Reuters released the story, Jinnah's secretary specially rang up Foreign correspondents drawing their attention to it. Correspondents informed me privately that Jinnah offered this interview to several of them. They considered he was determined to make the statement anyhow, and merely used Reuters' request as a peg to hang it on. Reuters was, of course, a well-chosen instrument for Jinnah to exert the maximum pressure on London at this critical stage in the Viceroy's deliberations with the Government, for through the exclusive use of this source he was ensuring for himself the greatest possible coverage in the British Press.

In spite of a lot of inspired speculation to the contrary by the London correspondents of the Indian papers, Mountbatten's negotiations are proceeding smoothly. His presence in London has already done much to restore the confidence of the Cabinet and officials and given coherence to their proceedings. He has already had valuable meetings with the Opposition leaders, without whose support the timing of the whole operation, based as it is upon the quick passage of the Independence Bill through Parliament, would be frustrated. In the present delicate situation

Mountbatten's personal authority and guidance were needed to secure their vital co-operation and to set their legitimate doubts at rest.

Mr. Attlee, who throughout has assumed full personal control of the Government's India policy and any action arising from it, has successfully injected a sense of the utmost urgency into his colleagues. The strain falls particularly on the Lord Chancellor's and India Offices. To meet Mountbatten's vital timing problem, the Lord Chancellor promised to have the necessary Bill ready for presentation to the House by the first week in July, which will involve surely the fastest drafting of a major Parliamentary Bill in our history. Indeed, its scope is without parallel or precedent in the proceedings of any Parliamentary Government. There was, of course, considerable concern on the defence aspect of Partition, but otherwise Ismay was able to send us optimistic and encouraging news. Dominion Status as elaborated by Mountbatten and V. P. Menon had been warmly welcomed, and only a few editorial amendments and clarifications were required.

VICEROY'S HOUSE, NEW DELHI, *Friday, 23rd May, 1947*

I reported again to Vernon in London :—

"Jinnah interview—*Hindustan Times* the only leader comment this morning. It takes a firm line but is not unduly provocative. With regard to the ' Corridor ' it states categorically, ' If the existence of Pakistan is dependent on the " Corridor " it will never come into being '. . . . I consider that political and Press reactions at this end are not as strong as might have been expected. . . . The interview has been aimed primarily at London."

VICEROY'S HOUSE, NEW DELHI, *Monday, 26th May, 1947*

I have written to Vernon in London :—

" Indian papers are containing an increasing number of reports indicating dissentient voices in the Cabinet over the Plan. Bevin is cited most frequently as objecting on the defence issue, and Cripps and Alexander are also mentioned. The Cabinet's displeasure at Viceroy's handling of situation is also widely suggested, the *Indian News Chronicle* going so far as to carry the report, ' Viceroy threatens to resign? ' All this is obviously speculative, but I suggest it might be helpful if Joyce from London could give authoritative guidance on the unity of the Cabinet and how close agreement is to being reached inside ten weeks of the Viceroy's arrival here."

Jinnah's " Corridor " demand has produced delayed, but none the less definite, reaction. The flames of controversy are being fanned, and this whole affair is characteristic of the mounting tension, which will be relaxed only with a quick political decision. The reserves of good-will which Mountbatten has so assiduously built up over the past two months are rapidly running out during his absence in London. I have advised Vernon :—

" Prasad and Deo (Congress Secretary) have made forceful statements—Prasad says, ' Jinnah's demands will not merit a moment's scrutiny ', and Deo considers that they ' are increasing under the illusion that the British can still help him '. The country, however, cannot be intimidated with such bullying tactics, and the demand for a ' Corridor ' cannot be granted.

" *Dawn* has, of course, hit back at Prasad and Deo with a provocative leader under the heading ' Cranks All ', the key passage of which runs as follows : ' The demand for a corridor is not a new one. Quaid-e-Azam Jinnah has many times in the past raised that point which is so vital in the context of Pakistan. If Pakistan is to be real, solid and strong the creation of a corridor linking up its eastern and northern areas is an indispensable adjunct. Be that as it may, we have no doubt, however, that if Muslims can win Pakistan—as indeed they have already won it—they can just as well build a corridor somewhere for the linking up of the two segments of Pakistan. Mr. Deo knows that too well '.

" On Saturday Nehru gave an interview to the United Press of America which contains his first public reference to the extra-territorial issue. ' Mr. Jinnah's recent statement ', he said, ' is completely un-realistic and indicates that he desires no settlement of any kind. The demand for a corridor is fantastic and absurd. We stand for a union of India with the right to particular areas to opt out. We envisage no compulsion. If there is no proper settlement on this basis without further claims being advanced, then we shall proceed with making and implementing the constitution for the union of India '."

Nehru confirmed that his attitude was hardening by intimating to Miéville that he was falling back on the alternative Demission Plan, in view of Jinnah's rejection of the main proposals of the draft announcement. He would like the Interim Government to be treated immediately by convention as a Dominion Government. Jinnah will never commit himself. Nehru alleged that he accepts what he gets and goes on asking for more. There could be no one-sided commitments.

VICEROY'S HOUSE, NEW DELHI, *Tuesday, 27th May, 1947*

Reports from Burrows showed that he is seriously worried about the unsettled state of Calcutta, and in the last day or two he has realised that the tension is even graver than he had suspected. He therefore wants Mountbatten's approval to talk on the wireless in an effort to calm everyone down. He refers to a report in the *Amrita Bazar Patrika* which quotes Nehru as having said that a new phase of the struggle begins on the 2nd June, and that he is not optimistic about a peaceful settlement.

I have been checking the authenticity of this alleged statement, and can find no trace of confirmation. The incident is further evidence of the prevailing jitters and uncertainty. Eric Britter has told me that in

Calcutta Moslems and Hindus have already taken up their battle-posts. Houses and whole streets have become prepared positions, providing strong points and fields of fire.

VICEROY'S HOUSE, NEW DELHI, *Saturday, 31st May, 1947*

Mountbatten is back in Delhi. He at once summoned his staff for discussions. There is only this week-end between us and the fateful conference which will decide the future of India.

We have had two long Staff Meetings to-day, at the first of which Colville was present. Mountbatten's physical and mental strength are astounding. He seems in no way tired by his journey or the protracted high-level discussions in London; on the contrary, he is more resilient and energetic than ever, and pours out directives to his staff.

Mountbatten is anxious to deal adequately with recent utterances by Gandhi at his Prayer Meetings in favour of a united India which seemed to suggest the forcible imposition of the Cabinet Mission Plan. Both Colville and Menon expressed their belief that Gandhi would not press opposition to Partition to the point of actively sabotaging the Plan.

Mountbatten is now quite clear in his mind that he will treat Jinnah more in sorrow than in anger, stressing the personal embarrassment caused by the " Corridor " demand. He has returned armed with a vital message, which he can use at his discretion, from Mr. Churchill to Jinnah, which states that it was nothing less than a matter of life and death for Jinnah to accept the Plan.

My Press task is complicated by Mountbatten having to hold a Burma Star party on the same evening as the first meeting with the Leaders. The publicity mechanics for this are elaborate and tiresome, and include an exchange of messages with a mass rally of Burma campaigners in the Albert Hall in London arranged some time before there was any indication that it would coincide with these critical meetings in India.

I have been engaged all the past week in long conferences with the Ministry of Information and All India Radio, and we have produced a publicity blue-print which I hope and pray will work. Over and above the issue of the text of His Majesty's Government's announcement—to be synchronised with London—there will have to be communiqués on the two meetings with the Leaders, as well as on the meeting of the Indian States Representatives on the afternoon of the 3rd June.

The text of Mountbatten's broadcast will also have to be released, and his voice will be heard over a world-wide network. Provision is being made, on Mountbatten's instruction, for broadcasts at short notice by Nehru, Jinnah and Baldev Singh, and possibly by Auchinleck as well. I hold myself in readiness to cover success or failure, or the more likely contingency of a provisional and indecisive answer.

VICEROY'S HOUSE, NEW DELHI, *Sunday, 1st June, 1947*

I wrote to my mother :—

" We are on the eve of great events here, and I am up to my eyes in the last-minute details of planning the publicity for Mountbatten's momentous announcement on the transfer of power which is due to be made on Tuesday. The atmosphere is very tense, and if the verdict is for Partition—as it almost certainly will be—considerable communal unrest can be expected, but any decision will be preferable to the present uncertainty. It should be noted, though, that the fury is internal and fratricidal and that the British are probably more popular with both Hindus and Moslems than at any time in living memory.

"The main effect of the Government's 20th February Announcement has been to bring the Congress High Command round to the acceptance of the partition of India as inevitable. Gandhi refuses to align himself with this concept, and is putting up a fierce rear-guard action against it. How far he will carry this opposition is one of the big imponderables.

"Nehru and Vallabhbhai Patel, the two big Congressmen in the Interim Government, accept Partition on the understanding that by conceding Pakistan to Jinnah they will hear no more of him and eliminate his nuisance value, or, as Nehru put it privately, that by ' cutting off the head we will get rid of the headache '. In this they are being rather sanguine, for Jinnah's appetite shows signs of growing with what it feeds on, and his latest demand for an eight-hundred-mile corridor to join West and East Pakistan is a good example of his irredentist tactics. Agreement therefore is being approached from both sides with the worst possible grace. Partition is undoubtedly a tragedy, but a worse tragedy would be to try to impose a unity unacceptable to the great majority of the hundred million Moslems."

CHAPTER NINE

THE GREAT ACCEPTANCE

VICEROY'S HOUSE, NEW DELHI, *Monday, 2nd June, 1947*

THE GREAT MOMENT has arrived. The Leaders drive into the North Court in their large American cars. I was in the Viceroy's study, which is now duly transformed, its dark panels painted a pale green. It is quite a small study, with an informal almost intimate atmosphere, compared with the Council Chamber and even the adjoining reception-rooms. The painting of Clive in the entrance hall looks down upon this apotheosis of the Raj. Jinnah was the last to come, a few minutes late. Mountbatten did his best to promote some friendly small talk, but it was clear that the atmosphere was electric. The problem of including Kripalani has been solved by conceding to Jinnah, Rab Nishtar; so the Big Five have become the Big Seven.

Mountbatten was anxious not to have any hold-up of proceedings for this initial meeting. Photographic coverage was confined to the Government of India man. This caused immense indignation among Indian and Foreign photographers, who, headed by Max Desfor, "walked out" in high dudgeon and submitted a signed protest to me. I fully appreciate their grievance, and hope to be able to remedy it to-morrow, but the vital thing is for Mountbatten to get proceedings off to a good start without any extra neural distraction.

The conference lasted for just on two hours. Vernon reported that Mountbatten did most of the talking, and was in masterly form, giving a closely reasoned analysis of developments. His opening remarks were a challenge to them to rise to the level of the events they were creating. He said that during the past five years he had taken part in a number of momentous meetings at which the fate of the war had been decided, but he could frankly remember no decisions reached likely to have such an important influence on world history as those which were to be taken at this meeting. He made it clear that he was not forcing the pace against their will. A terrific sense of urgency had been pressed upon him by everybody to whom he had spoken. They had wanted the present state of uncertainty to cease; therefore the sooner power was transferred the better for all.

Having made his last formal attempt to resuscitate the Cabinet Mission Plan, and Jinnah having for the last time formally rejected it, Mountbatten then turned to the dilemma presented by Partition. Congress, he said, did not agree to the principle of the partition of India, but, if this were unavoidable, insisted on the partition of Provinces to avoid the coercion of Moslem or Hindu majority areas, while on the other hand Jinnah resisted the partition of Provinces but demanded the division of India.

Mountbatten was at pains to stress the backing of the British Conservative Opposition. The Plan, he said, was not a Party issue in London. He spoke of his distress about the position of the Sikhs, and disposed firmly and finally of the suggestion of a referendum whether Calcutta should become a Free Port.

With characteristic finesse, he introduced the new Paragraph 20 of the Plan under its heading " Immediate transfer of power ", and defended the resulting Dominion Status not from the imputation of Britain's desire to retain a foothold beyond her time but from the possible charge of quitting on her obligations. Therefore, he said, it was abundantly clear that British assistance should not be withdrawn prematurely if it was still required.

Jinnah in one of the earlier interviews had startled Mountbatten by making a distinction between his agreement with and acceptance of a certain proposal. Mountbatten invoked this particular piece of pedantry to his own advantage to-day.

After copies of the Plan had been handed round, he said he felt it would be asking the Indian Leaders to go against their consciences if he requested their full agreement. He was merely asking them to accept the Plan in a peaceful spirit. When Nehru asked for a further definition of the difference between agreement and acceptance, Mountbatten at once replied that agreement would imply belief that the right principles were being employed, but he had to violate the principles of both sides, so could not ask for complete agreement. What he asked for was acceptance denoting belief that the Plan was a fair and sincere solution for the good of the country. Nehru then said that while there could never be complete approval of the Plan by Congress, on balance they accepted it. Nishtar rounded off these devious dialectics by pointing out that acceptance of the Plan really implied agreement to make it work. Mountbatten cordially agreed, and from that moment knew that the essential battle was won.

Jinnah then embarked upon an elaborate explanation as to why he, the all-powerful Quaid-e-Azam, could not take any decision himself. He entered into the spirit of the proposals, he said, but both he and his Working Committee would have to go before their masters, the people, prior to a final decision. Mountbatten observed that there were times when leaders had to make vital decisions without consulting their followers and trust to carrying them with them at a later stage. A decision taken at the top and afterwards confirmed by the people would be in accordance with democratic procedure.

Jinnah then went as near to the brink of affirmative decision as could reasonably be expected from one who had got so far by saying " no " so often. He emphasised that he would go to his masters, the people, with no intent of wrecking the Plan, but with the sincere desire to persuade them to accept it. He could only give his personal assurance that he would do his best. He would try in his own way to bring round his own people.

Mountbatten wanted the reactions of the Congress and Moslem League Working Committees and of the Sikhs by midnight. Kripalani and Baldev Singh agreed to send a letter that evening. Jinnah felt unable to report the opinions of his Working Committee in writing, but agreed to come and see the Viceroy and make a verbal report. This satisfied Mountbatten.

To crown his success he secured the agreement of Nehru, Jinnah and Baldev Singh to follow him with broadcasts to the people over All India Radio to-morrow evening. Mountbatten said he would let them see his script in the morning. Patel, who had said very little, pointed out with a wry smile that the general rule was for the scripts of broadcast speeches to be submitted to the Honourable Member for Information (i.e., himself) before they were used. Jinnah without a smile retorted he would say in his broadcast what came from his heart.

Never was Mountbatten's genius for informal chairmanship and exposition more signally displayed. His natural talent for this procedure had been enhanced by three years of almost daily discussion as Supreme Commander. Vernon told me he had never seen him more alert, keeping the discussion within his chosen terms of reference. The atmosphere at the outset was undoubtedly tense, but his opening speech soon brought with it the sense of sweet reasonableness and genuine good-will underlying his whole sponsorship of the Plan. Not even Mr. Jinnah's formality and stiffness could resist Mountbatten's urgent will to succeed.

As planned beforehand, Mountbatten asked Jinnah to stay behind partly to counterbalance any Moslem League criticism that he was about to see Gandhi, who never comes in company with Congress leaders, in a separate interview, and partly to apply more personal persuasion and form a clearer judgement of the ultimate attitude he is likely to take. But Jinnah made no comment. All will now turn on his midnight visitation.

Then at 12.30 the Mahatma arrived. In one sense he has been present throughout the whole proceedings, and uncertainty as to his ultimate reaction to the formal presentation of a Partition Plan undoubtedly had an inhibiting effect on the Congress leaders earlier in the morning. They were only too well aware of Gandhi's unpredictable response to the promptings of his inner voice. There have been wide-spread fears that he will at the bidding of his complex conscience go to extreme lengths to wreck the Plan in one final effort to prevent the vivisection of India. Mountbatten faced this interview with considerable trepidation. Imagine his amazement and relief when the Mahatma blandly indicated on the backs of various used envelopes and other scraps of paper that he was observing a day of silence.

When the interview was over Mountbatten picked up the various bits of paper, which he thinks will be among his more historic relics. On them the Mahatma had written: " I am sorry I can't speak; when I took the decision about the Monday silence I did make two exceptions, i.e., about speaking to high functionaries on urgent matters or attending upon sick people. But I know you don't want me to break my silence. Have I said one word against you during my speeches? If you admit that I have not, your warning is superfluous. There are one or two things I must talk about, but not to-day. But if we meet each other again I shall speak."

Behind this quaint procedure lay a great act of political renunciation, of self-effacement and of self-control. When I went in to have a few words with Mountbatten about the Press communiqué at the end of this momentous morning I, too, collected a trophy from the small round table—nothing other than a " doodle " by Mr. Jinnah extracted from his subconscious at the moment of his greatest political victory. I am no psychologist, but I think I can detect the symbols of power and glory here.*

At four o'clock we had a Staff Meeting, and had a complete run through of the paper on " The Administrative Consequences of Partition ". This is a masterly document of some thirty foolscap pages, largely prepared by John Christie, and it will certainly not be possible for posterity to say that we found a political answer at the expense of an administrative one. Here is the master plan which, under the umbrella of Dominion Status, should make possible essential continuity for the new régimes.

No sooner was the Staff Meeting over than I was engrossed in background talks with one correspondent after another. I endeavoured, as far as possible, to see them separately. I spoke with restrained optimism —the slip between cup and lip is the major occupational risk of Indian politics.

I broke off from these talks just in time to attend the Burma Star party. The Moghul gardens were thronged with uniforms, for the guests were limited to recipients of the Burma Star and former members of S.E.A.C. Mountbatten, in his bush shirt, spoke to his guests both on the microphone and privately as though nothing was on his mind save S.E.A.C. reminiscences. The Press arrangements for this party vexed body and spirit at such a moment.

VICEROY'S HOUSE, NEW DELHI, *Tuesday, 3rd June, 1947*

Mountbatten began the day with an early morning Staff Meeting, at which he told us of his dramatic midnight encounter with Jinnah. As Jinnah had categorically refused to give any answer to the Plan in writing, Ismay joined Mountbatten as a second witness of what he was ready to say. He began by reiterating at great length the remarks he had made round the conference table in the morning, and no amount of pressure from Mountbatten would make him agree to a firm acceptance from the Moslem League Council when they met. All he would undertake was that he would use his best endeavours to persuade them in a constitutional manner to accept and that his Working Committee would support him.

Mountbatten then reminded Jinnah that the Congress Party were terribly suspicious of this particular tactic, which he always used, whereby he waited until the Congress Party had made a firm decision about some plan, and then left himself the right to make whatever decision suited the Moslem League several days later. Mountbatten warned him that Nehru, Kripalani and Patel had made an absolute point that they would reject the Plan unless the Moslem League accepted it simultaneously with themselves; and furthermore accepted it as a final settlement.

* See reproduction opposite page 97.

Nothing Mountbatten could say would move him; he once more took refuge behind the excuse that he was not constitutionally authorised to make a decision without the concurrence of the full Moslem League Council, and pointed out that he could not in any case call this Council Meeting for several days. Mountbatten then said, " If that is your attitude, then the leaders of the Congress Party and Sikhs will refuse final acceptance at the meeting in the morning; chaos will follow, and you will lose your Pakistan, probably for good." " What must be, must be," was his only reaction, as he shrugged his shoulders.

Mountbatten then said, " Mr. Jinnah! I do not intend to let you wreck all the work that has gone into this settlement. Since you will not accept for the Moslem League, I will speak for them myself. I will take the risk of saying that I am satisfied with the assurances you have given me, and if your Council fails to ratify the agreement, you can place the blame on me. I have only one condition, and that is that when I say at the meeting in the morning, ' Mr. Jinnah has given me assurances which I have accepted and which satisfy me,' you will in no circumstances contradict that, and that when I look towards you, you will nod your head in acquiescence."

Jinnah's reply to the proposition itself was to nod his head without any verbal undertaking. Mountbatten's final question was : Did Jinnah consider that he (Mountbatten) would be justified in advising Attlee to go ahead and make his announcement to-morrow? To this he replied, " Yes ". On this last assurance Mountbatten and Ismay both felt that the maximum possible measure of acceptance had been wrung out of him prior to his meeting with the Moslem League Council in a week's time.

Shortly after Jinnah left, Kripalani's letter arrived. It makes certain reservations of detail, but constitutes a firm general acceptance of the Plan on behalf of the whole Congress Working Committee.

Mountbatten agreed that yesterday's protesting and frustrated camera-men should be allowed to swarm over the study and photograph the Leaders at the round table before their second meeting began. He made the most of it to create an atmosphere of good humour, which was in noticeable contrast to yesterday morning's strained silence. He explained that while the Leaders had all been hard at work, one group—the photo-graphers—had staged a sit-down strike. He was sure the Leaders would not like to be the cause of them going through that ordeal a second time. Even Jinnah could scarce forbear a smile.

Mountbatten resumed by duly reporting on Jinnah's visit to him last night and his acceptance of Jinnah's assurances and proposed action. Jinnah confirmed this by the appropriate silence and nod of the head. He then referred to the three Parties' grave objections to different specific parts in the Plan, and was grateful that these had been aired. But since he knew enough of the situation to realise that not one of the suggestions would be accepted by either of the other Parties, he did not propose to raise them at this meeting. He accordingly asked all the Leaders to signify their consent to this course, which they did; thus voluntarily but almost unwittingly disposing of every substantial point of controversy.

After Mountbatten had pronounced that the Plan seemed to represent as near to a hundred per cent agreement as it was possible to get, Jinnah, Kripalani and Baldev Singh all added that they considered that the Viceroy had correctly interpreted and recorded their views. Mountbatten said the Plan would now be announced officially, and none of the Leaders raised any objection.

It looked, therefore, as though all would be plain sailing, but when Mountbatten appealed for restraint on the part of subordinate leaders and the burial of the past in order to open up the prospect of building a fine future, Liaquat could not resist the temptation to suggest that restraint was needed not so much from subordinate as from super leaders, for example, Mr. Gandhi at his Prayer Meetings. This touched off all the old bitterness of feeling.

Jinnah and Liaquat insinuated that Gandhi was inciting the people to do as they liked and look to other authorities than the Leaders at this conference, while Kripalani retorted that all Gandhi's actions were devoted to non-violence, and Patel considered that Gandhi would abide loyally by any decision taken. Mountbatten was obliged to bring this dangerous discussion to a halt by saying he thought the subject had been ventilated sufficiently. He accepted Mr. Gandhi's special position on the one hand, and on the other was sure the Congress Leaders would appreciate the point of what had been said.

Mountbatten then with a dramatic gesture, lifting it above his head and banging it down on the table, presented " The Administrative Consequences of Partition " to the startled Leaders. This high-powered Staff paper, which Mountbatten has had made ready for this day, contains thirty-four closely typed pages of foolscap, and is already a masterpiece of compression. This brings the Leaders within the hour right up against the hard executive realities of their political decision. As Mountbatten said afterwards, the severe shock that its appearance gave to everyone present would have been amusing if the general atmosphere of administrative indifference were not so serious.

Here again a slip of the tongue, the merest molehill, was built up characteristically, if unwittingly, to mountainous proportions. Mountbatten suggested that there might be preliminary consideration of the paper before it was submitted to a " Cabinet meeting ". Liaquat and Jinnah at once raised elaborate objections to the " Cabinet in the United Kingdom " being the deciding authority. Several minutes had passed before it became clear that Jinnah had understood Mountbatten to be referring to the British, and not the Indian Cabinet or Interim Government. He then complained that he had been misled. " You mean the Viceroy's Executive Council. A spade should be called a spade." His mind, he said, worked in constitutional terms.

Liaquat then asked whether majority votes would decide the issue in the inter-Party Partition Committee which it was proposed in the paper to set up. Mountbatten said no, negotiations would be on the basis of what was fair. He relied on a new spirit entering into the discussions, now that the issue of Partition had been finally settled. Liaquat replied sharply that it was not a matter of a new spirit, there was difference of opinion on the critical issue of the division of the Armed Forces.

The discussion, surprisingly perhaps, moved into calmer waters. It was quickly agreed that division should be made on the basis of citizenship, which in its turn would be based on considerations of geography. Jinnah declared stoutly that it would be his intention in Pakistan to observe no communal differences, and those who lived there, regardless of creed, would be fully fledged citizens.

At four o'clock the members of the States Negotiating Committee assembled in the Council chamber to be given in advance of to-night's official announcements and speeches the background to the decisions reached by Mountbatten and the Leaders. It was a difficult meeting. Once again a photographic circus provided light relief and enabled Mountbatten to get off to a friendly and informal start.

Round the big oval table were seated the cream of the Princely counsellors. Their Highnesses of Bhopal, Patiala, Dungapur, Nawanagar and Bilaspur. Sir Mirza Ismail, Dewan of Hyderabad, Sir B. L. Mitter of Baroda, Sir Ramaswami Mudaliar of Mysore, Kak of Kashmir, Srinivasan of Gwalior, Sir C. P. Ramaswami Aiyer of Travancore, Sir V. T. Krishnamachari of Jaipur, Panikkar of Bikaner, Sir Sultan Ahmed, and D. K. Sen representing the Chamber of Princes.

It is interesting to note how many of the finest Indian minds from British India are Prime Ministers of the States. Many of them are front-rank lawyers, which aids them in their approach to such constitutional conundrums as the lapse of Paramountcy. Their relationship to the Princes they serve is very much that of a barrister with a valuable brief.

After another very skilful and persuasive explanation of the origin and purpose of the Plan, Mountbatten was subjected to some acute cross-examination on its application to the Indian States. They were all particularly anxious to know whether it would be possible to arrange for Paramountcy to lapse before the actual transfer of power in British India—the assumption being, of course, that the States would then be in a better position to bargain with the successor governments.

Mountbatten did his best to inject a sense of reality into the meeting. The creation of two new States would inevitably mean two strong central governments which could not afford to delegate their powers instead of one weak one for the whole sub-continent which could. On the other hand, he felt that the acceptance of Dominion Status by them both offered a measure of protection as well as compensation to those Princes who had stood so loyally by their alliances and friendship with Britain. Whatever decisions they reached, he advised them to cast their minds forward ten years and to consider what the situation in India and the world was likely to be by then.

While this meeting was going on I was immersed in preparing releases, working out various deadlines and planning with All India Radio world-wide transmissions which include Britain and America. I imagine that the concentration of Press and Radio interest in to-day's events is heavier than for any single development in Asia since the surrender of Japan. By this morning the Dominion Status secret had leaked out into the Indian Press. Mountbatten was not unduly disturbed, and felt that the information might, indeed, serve to act as a shock-absorber. However, one had to be on guard to meet the obvious risk of premature release of the Announcement's actual text—a danger which in its turn had to be set against the likely dilemma arising from the complete clogging of the entire Delhi cabling system.

To cope with this situation simultaneous releases of the Announcement were arranged through India's diplomatic representatives in Western and Eastern hemispheres, while I took the calculated risk of making the text of Mountbatten's broadcast available to the Press on an embargo basis three hours before it was delivered. This last move became doubly necessary, as the texts of the broadcasts by Nehru, Jinnah and Baldev Singh were not made available until shortly before they were to go on the air. If Mountbatten's speech had been held back as well, the jam on the lines would, I think, have been beyond control.

I accompanied Mountbatten in the Viceregal Rolls to All India Radio, where officials were leaning out of all the windows and cramming the balconies. A small crowd had also gathered round the entrance to the building. Fay, who was on a balcony, told me afterwards that a small group of *Sadhus*, distinctive in their bright caps of holy orange, began shouting out slogans just as we were entering the building. No sooner had they started to demonstrate than they were scooped into our following police car. The neatness of the operation made the assembled Indians, otherwise passively polite, scream with laughter. These *Sadhus* have come from various parts of the country, and have pitched their tents on the banks of the Jumna, there to protest against the betrayal of Hindu life and custom which they are convinced any form of Partition must involve.

After a brief voice test, Mountbatten spoke with a slow and deliberate diction, in contrast to the quick-fire delivery of his private conversation. It was a well-balanced oration without hyperbole, relying for its impact if anything on under-statement. This was undoubtedly the right note for Mountbatten to strike. His message was subdued and objective at the moment of personal triumph.

As soon as the reading was completed Mountbatten went into an adjoining studio to be photographed by newsreel camera-men as if engaged on the actual broadcast. This was a somewhat exacting operation, because the camera-men lacked recording apparatus and it became necessary to synchronise the movement of Mountbatten's lips with the All India Radio recording. The task was not made easier by Mountbatten's unwillingness to accept that anybody but himself knew how to handle this problem. I would have wished to spare him this performance, as it was clear that the unparalleled strain of the past sixty hours was beginning to tell upon him.

We were fiddling with lights and voice timings throughout Nehru's moving address, which was compelling alike in its mood and expression. Here was neither arrogance nor apology, but a true reflection of the sadness which accompanies all success—the frustration in victory. Perhaps Nehru's greatest strength is that although he has reached the heights as a partisan campaigner he retains detachment of spirit. The artist and the scholar in him are always near the surface. So at this climactic moment he was able to say, " We are little men serving great causes, but because the cause is great something of that greatness falls upon us also."

Then followed Jinnah. The experts in Moslem League dialectic assured me that his speech was a masterpiece. As one of them put it to me immediately afterwards, " This is the language that will be understood in the bazaars, and it means peace." By objective standards I could not detect the magic. He seemed to me on this occasion to be well below the level of events which he had done so much to create.

His opening sentence was devoted to a thinly disguised criticism of the authorities for not having previously afforded him—as a non-official—facilities for broadcast. " I hope that in the future I shall have greater facilities to enable me to voice my views and opinions, which will reach directly to you live and warm rather than in the cold print of the newspapers." But I could find no liveliness nor warmth in what he had to say. Perhaps the nearest he approached to both these qualities was in the tribute he paid to Mountbatten. " I must say that I feel that the Viceroy has battled against various forces very bravely—and the impression that he has left on my mind is that he was actuated by the highest sense of fairness and impartiality. And it is up to us to make his task less difficult, and help him, as far as lies in our power, in order that he may fulfil his mission of the transfer of power to the peoples of India in a peaceful and orderly manner."

With great skill he avoided a final declaration of intention while leaving an impression of acceptance. Perhaps the smoothest riddle was set in his words, " It is for us to consider whether the Plan as presented to us by His Majesty's Government should be accepted by us as a compromise or a settlement. On this point I do not wish to prejudge." Nehru's last words had been " Jai Hind ", Jinnah closed with " Pakistan Zindabad ". This he said in such a clipped voice that some startled listeners thought at first that the Quaid-e-Azam had thrown dignity to the winds and pronounced " Pakistan's in the bag "!

Baldev Singh spoke last, and in view of the unmitigated loss which Partition meant for the Sikhs and the intense bitterness it was likely to engender among his co-religionists, his words were eloquent and courageous. He gave a clear call to India's Defence Forces to uphold their high standards of discipline, particularly against the pressures of unpleasant internal security duties. In contrast to Jinnah, he saw the Plan not as a compromise, " I prefer to call it a settlement."

While the tremendous news of India's Partition and the Leaders' potential agreement was being flashed across the world, Mountbatten returned quietly to Viceroy's House, and after dinner he called me in to consider the details of to-morrow's Press Conference. This will be his first exposure to the Indian and Foreign Press, and upon his ability to carry this most critical audience with him much will depend. The great virtue of this conference is that it gives him the chance of retaining the initiative which with to-day's historic Announcement he has undoubtedly seized. He proposes to adopt the method which makes him feel most at ease, namely, to speak without notes—but in view of the maze of detail and the various problems of emphasis he has wisely decided to have a rehearsal with his staff.

Over well-earned whiskeys-and-sodas we shot various likely questions at him. The impression he gave me of neural overstrain at All India Radio has entirely vanished, and I go to bed confident that he is already master of to-morrow's meeting, which is the culminating point of all the operations in my special field of responsibility.

VICEROY'S HOUSE, NEW DELHI, *Wednesday, 4th June, 1947*

This morning to an audience of some three hundred representatives of the Indian and world's Press in the Legislative Assembly, Mountbatten has given the most brilliant performance I have ever witnessed at a major Press conference. He began without note or loss of word, expounding for some three-quarters of an hour a political Plan of the utmost complexity both in its detail and implication. It was a speech which must have cleared many lurking doubts among that audience of professional sceptics about the Plan's substance and purpose.

There then followed nearly a hundred questions, the great majority of which came from Indian correspondents, and were directed at him not so much for purposes of information as for political propaganda. Seated directly below him were Ismay, Miéville, George Abell, Ian Scott, V. P., Vernon and myself, but only twice was it necessary to call upon any member of his staff for guidance.

Quite a number of the questions were hypothetical and were dealt with accordingly. Thus, almost at the outset he was asked, " Profiting by our past experience, we would like to know, in the event of the Moslem League Council rejecting the Plan, what would be the fate of Pakistan? " Mountbatten: " That is a hypothetical question. If it ever arises come and see me, and I will tell you what I will do." Questioner: " But we have had past experience of this." Mountbatten: " You may have, but not of me. Honestly, come along to me if it happens."

He was very closely cross-examined on the proposed referendum for the North-west Frontier Province, which is still the focus of Congress attention, and there was also a prolonged inquisition about the status of the Indian Princes. Here again Mountbatten scored heavily, for with every answer he was able to bring home more clearly the constitutional propriety of the Plan.

"May I draw your attention," asked a correspondent in a voice registering self-satisfaction at the production of a teaser, " to the Raja of Sarawak's example where he claimed to have the popular support and yet he was dethroned? Are you following two different principles in this instance? "

Back came the reply in a flash, " Exactly the opposite is the case. He was not dethroned. He claimed that he had popular support to dethrone himself. In other words, he meant, ' I have got the support of the people to take such action as I believe to be in their interests '. Not only did he consult the legislative machinery, which was pretty primitive, but members of Parliament were sent out to decide whether the wishes of the people of Sarawak were that the Raja should abdicate in favour of a Governor, and they decided that that was the wish of the people, and so he abdicated : He was not dethroned." Questioner : " Is it not a fact that His Majesty's Government brought out the Raja of Sarawak and refused to countenance his re-installation?" Mountbatten : " Most emphatically not. I personally took him back when I was in S.E.A.C. and put him on his throne."

When a correspondent tried to draw him on the Moslem League's demand for a " Corridor "—and thus, on a point never discussed in the Plan—he replied, " Which paragraph in the Plan are you referring to? " He was questioned about the Sikhs—their prospects and attitude—and he made it clear that the whole Sikh problem under the Plan had given him probably more concern than any other single issue. He was pressed in particular about the terms of reference of the Boundary Commission which is to work out the actual lines of demarcation in the Punjab and Bengal and the Moslem majority district of Sylhet, in Assam. When a Sikh correspondent asked whether a property qualification would be a factor, Mountbatten smilingly replied, " His Majesty's Government could hardly be expected to subscribe to a Partition on the basis of landed property—least of all the present Government."

During the Conference he gave the first informal indication that 15th August would be the likely date for the actual transfer of power to the two new Dominions. Actually it was on this issue of Dominion Status that he was subjected to the most searching scrutiny of all, and was involved in an encounter with Devadas Gandhi, who has a most disarming manner, and who by the persistence of his inquiries gave a possible clue, I felt, to his father's state of mind.

Mountbatten did not at first quite follow the drift of what Devadas was asking; but it was, in effect, that the British should reject any offer on the part of any single individual State to become a Dominion, and should insist on India as a whole reaching a decision on the question of membership of the Commonwealth. He said he felt there was " a great potential for mischief " in allowing the respective Constituent Assemblies the ultimate decision on this matter. Behind the inquiry was the old suspicion that Dominion Status was something less than independence, together with the new one that if Pakistan opted to remain in and India to go out, Pakistan might become a base for British imperialism.

Mountbatten's last words on the subject were, " From all the questions that have been asked there is one thing which I sincerely believe is not yet clear to the people. Somehow people seemed to have some doubts about this word ' Dominion Status '. It is absolute independence in every possible way, with the sole exception that the Member States of the Commonwealth are linked together voluntarily. In fact they look for support, mutual trust and in due course affection."

Whether or not Devadas was wholly satisfied with the answers to his particular points, the enthusiasm of the correspondents as a whole, judging from the spontaneous applause when Vallabhbhai Patel, who was in the chair, called the proceedings to a close, was remarkable from such a case-hardened body. I spoke to some of them afterwards. Andy Mellor of the *Daily Herald* described himself to me as stunned by the performance, saying that he had never heard anything like it and did not expect to do so again; Eric Britter called it a *tour de force*; while Bob Stimson drew attention to its impact on the Americans, who had been deeply impressed by the argument—which was for them a revelation—that Dominion Status provided the best constitutional means for transfer of power, and spelt genuine freedom for India, and was not just a device for enabling the British to hold on.

Mountbatten on his return to Viceroy's House soon had indications that there was more underlying Devadas' doubts than had appeared at the Conference, and all was not well with the Mahatma, who was proposing to make highly critical comment on the Plan at his Prayer Meeting this evening. Indeed, last night, just before the Leaders were due to broadcast, he had indicated that they were not above or beyond criticism, and had even gone so far as to single out Nehru for a double-edged comment. After referring to him as " our King ", he added, " We should not be impressed by everything the King does or does not do. If he has devised something good for us, we should praise him. If he has not, then we shall say so."

Mountbatten wisely decided that the time had come to clear the air with Gandhi and to prevent his apparent misgivings taking firmer and more dangerous shape. So just before the Prayer Meeting he invited him to come round to Viceroy's House. Gandhi was clearly in a state of some distress, feeling under the first impact of the Plan that his lifelong efforts for the unity of Hindus and Moslems had fallen about him. But Mountbatten, summoning all his powers of persuasion, urged him to consider the Announcement not as a Mountbatten but as a Gandhi Plan; in all sincerity he had tried to incorporate Gandhi's major concepts of non-coercion, self-determination, the earliest possible date of British departure, and even his sympathetic views about Dominion Status.

Once again Mountbatten carried the day; just how decisively can be seen by what Gandhi said to-night. " The British Government is not responsible for Partition," he told the Prayer Meeting. " The Viceroy has no hand in it. In fact he is as opposed to division as Congress itself, but if both of us—Hindus and Moslems—cannot agree on anything else, then the Viceroy is left with no choice." The Viceroy had worked very hard and had tried his utmost to bring about a compromise. This Plan was the only basis on which agreement could be reached. The Viceroy did not want to leave the country in chaos; hence all his efforts. Never surely had a Viceroy achieved such swift and decisive conquest over Gandhi's heart and mind.

I had a personal telegram of yesterday's date from Joyce reporting, " A packed House of Commons listened with intense interest to Prime Minister's announcement this afternoon. Proposals and first reaction from India undoubtedly created profound gratification among all Parties. Sense of unity and recognition of tremendous issues and possibilities involved were comparable only with most historic moments during war." After referring to the splendid B.B.C. reception and coverage he ended, " This has been a great day for us all ".

Mountbatten held a Staff Meeting at 7.30 this evening. Having broken the deadlock of a generation, there is still to be no respite for him or indeed any of us.

Already I detect the first sign of a storm over the States. Bhopal has resigned his position as Chancellor of the Chamber of Princes, and cannot be deflected from a course of personal isolation and independence which runs counter to all the current developments.

Nehru is not reacting favourably to the Paper on the " Administrative Consequences of Partition ", and there will clearly now be much more acute difficulty in maintaining the structure and existence of the Interim Government.

VICEROY'S HOUSE, NEW DELHI, *Thursday, 5th June, 1947*

George Jones, the *New York Times* correspondent, who has been very ill and is due to leave India in the next few days, came round to see me this morning to ask for my personal impressions of Mountbatten in about three hundred words, as he wants his last feature to be an appreciation of the Viceroy. Mountbatten in three hundred words? It is not easy at close range. But I have dictated this note :—

" Perhaps the most abiding impression is his tremendous creative energy, by which I mean not only the energy which is in himself, but which he injects into all about him.

" In the three biggest jobs of his life to date—Chief of Combined Operations, Supreme Commander and Viceroy—his capacity as a morale-raiser was given the fullest scope, for he took on all three jobs when the respective situations were at lowest ebb and morale accordingly depressed.

" By upbringing and temperament he is at home with high politics. There is his renowned charm of manner, and sensitivity to the personal nuances on which so many great political events depend.

" His position as Supreme Allied Commander was good training for this job. It involved semi-political responsibility on behalf of more than one nation; it was something new in war, and Mountbatten and Eisenhower were probably the only two military leaders who really had the chance of a full ' work out ' in this capacity. During the nine months after the collapse of Japan, as the virtual military Governor of a vast area comprising half a dozen countries and some one hundred and twenty million people, he was wholly absorbed in tremendous problems affecting simultaneously the status of Indonesia and French Indo-China, peace with Siam, the rehabilitation of Burma and the maintenance of law and order in Malaya. Together they comprised the most intensive training-ground possible for him in the psychology of Eastern nationalism prior to becoming Viceroy.

" He is essentially an extrovert character, who does not relish silence or solitude, but is at his very best in public.

" With his staff, he thinks aloud. He carries less prejudices than any man I have ever known, and although he can be relied upon for a clear and decisive point of view, he always requires of himself and his staff good reason for holding it. His objectivity and disinterestedness, which spring from a number of factors—scientific training, interest in things mechanical, Royal birth which removes a great many of the normal temptations of personal ambition—are tremendous sources of strength to him.

" It would be wrong to suggest a faultless image, and perhaps the most serious defect is a tendency to get caught up in trivial detail without realising that it is trivial. Allied to this trait is anxiety over secondary problems and vanity over minor achievements. It must be confessed, however, that in the present assignment he has remained firmly at his own level, and throughout the five years I have been with him I have always found him giving those who serve him the fullest measure of responsibility and support. All in all a rare and refreshing spirit, and whether on the quarter deck or in Viceroy's House, a democratic leader of the first magnitude."

Indian Press comment on Mountbatten's Conference is generally very cordial and appreciative, although a critical note is occasionally struck. I have advised Joyce accordingly :—

" *The Statesman* in its account of the Conference reports, ' It was a remarkable performance, physical, rhetorical as well as logical, and a great majority of the journalists must have come away deeply impressed by the Viceroy's evidently profound understanding of the Indian problem'. Its leader comment called it, ' An extraordinary achievement of intellect and personality, and by it many lurking misconceptions should be removed from the public mind.'

" The criticisms so far are from the *Hindustan Times*, which reflects Devadas Gandhi's persistent inquiry at the Conference, and states, ' We still hope that it will be made quite clear in due course that membership of the Commonwealth would be open only to India as a whole', and from the *Indian News Chronicle*, which argues that if there is no independence option for the North-west Frontier Province on grounds of the danger of Balkanisation, what about the States? His Excellency is asked to throw the whole weight of his influence ' on the side of progress and fair play, and prevent the States Rulers playing an anti-national role.' "

This morning Mountbatten held his third meeting with the Leaders, at which the paper on " Administrative Consequences of Partition " was fully discussed. It was very hard going, with both sides anxious above all to avoid administrative decisions and largely unaware of their meaning. Jinnah was at great pains to explain that both States would be independent and equal in every way, while Nehru was equally insistent that India was carrying on in every way as before, and that Pakistan was the outcome of permission to dissident Provinces to secede, which must not be allowed to interrupt the work of the Government of India or the continuity of its foreign policy. In this atmosphere of recrimination

Mountbatten made it clear that he would not accept the continued requests of both sides to act as arbitrator on all outstanding matters in dispute. They have agreed to try to find a mutually acceptable judge for this thankless task.

The Plan, now forty-eight hours old, has undoubtedly led to a *détente* throughout the country as a whole, but among the Leaders in Delhi it has induced no brotherly love. The situation here is still very tense, and it is such that the most trivial incident could touch off a major crisis.

CHAPTER TEN

ADMINISTRATIVE CONSEQUENCES

VICEROY'S HOUSE, NEW DELHI, *Sunday, 8th June, 1947*

THE CORE OF Mountbatten's problem remains political, and the most immediate danger is of the dissolution of the Interim Government caused by the resignation of one or other of its component parts. It was always a feeble instrument. Now that the principle of Partition is effectively accepted, there is not even the pretence of inner loyalty and purpose to hold it together. Mountbatten realises only too clearly, however, that if one or other of the Parties were to resign from it before Partition is ratified by Act of Parliament in Westminster, the prospects of the 3rd June Plan would be gravely imperilled and his own position hopelessly compromised.

To-day it seemed that this very peril was upon us, for the Cabinet meeting was only just saved by a desperate diversion on Mountbatten's part from breaking up in complete disorder. In an effort to narrow the controversy by limiting its duties, he suggested a moratorium on all policy decisions and high-grade appointments.

A formula was found for submitting these matters to Mountbatten direct, to avoid contentious issues being decided by the inevitable Congress majority vote in the Cabinet. At this point Nehru sought Mountbatten's approval for certain diplomatic appointments which he asked him to agree were not the concern of Pakistan. Liaquat at once objected, saying that he did not, for instance, wish to see an Ambassador appointed to Moscow. Unfortunately, just such an appointment was envisaged, and the nominee was none other than Nehru's sister, Mrs. Pandit.

The ensuing scene was babel, with everyone talking furiously at once. Nehru asserted that rather than tolerate Moslem League interference in the Government's affairs he would insist on a majority vote being taken, and that if the Government was to be turned over to the League he would immediately resign. Mountbatten had finally to call each member of the Cabinet individually to order, deferring further discussion of the particular issue and adding, " We are not going on with the next item until there is a row of smiling faces in front of me." This had the intended effect. Everyone laughed; the tension was broken. But the incident shows by how thin a thread the success of the Plan hangs. Critical days and decisions lie ahead of us.

Encouraging evidence, however, of the world's approbation is to be found in the hundreds of Press reports coming in to my office. The American reaction has been especially enthusiastic. Walter Lippmann's comment in yesterday's *Washington Post* is perhaps the most heartening, coming as it does from such an experienced judge of the significance of world events.

" Perhaps Britain's finest hour," he writes, " is not in the past. Certainly this performance is not the work of a decadent people. This on the contrary is the work of political genius requiring the ripest wisdom and the freshest vigour, and it is done with an elegance and a style that will compel and will receive an instinctive respect throughout the civilised world. Attlee and Mountbatten have done a service to all mankind by showing what statesmen can do not with force and money but with lucidity, resolution and sincerity."

Robert Neville, the Delhi correspondent of *Time and Life*, told me that Mountbatten's performance at his Press Conference could be compared only with Roosevelt in his prime.

VICEROY'S HOUSE, NEW DELHI, *Monday, 9th June, 1947*

At our Staff Meeting to-day there was a prolonged discussion on the implications of Dominion Status, and in particular of Mountbatten remaining on after the transfer of power to serve for a limited period as joint Governor-General of both Dominions. This concept has been encouraged on the one hand by Congress's willingness to propose him without condition either in this capacity or as Governor-General of India alone, and on the other by Jinnah urging that he should definitely stay on to see the Interim phase through in the capacity of a unifying head of the two States.

Mountbatten's first assumption was that Jinnah also had in mind a common Governor-General, but only when he was in London did it become apparent that Jinnah wanted three Governors-General, one of India, one of Pakistan and one, Mountbatten himself, in an overall position as Supreme Arbitrator for the division of assets, most of which, of course, are in India. This was quickly ruled out by the British Government as impracticable. Mountbatten also told him frankly that it would be quite impossible for himself to assume this supra-national role; but at the same time has been pressing the advantages from Pakistan's point of view of a joint Governor-Generalship as the best guarantee of a fair physical transfer. He has frankly advised us, however, that he is most averse to staying should the invitation come from only one side. Jinnah so far has been careful to conceal his final intention. If it is in favour of a joint Governor-Generalship, some special provision will be needed, however, in the Independence Act, and a decision from him within the next three weeks is essential.

The All India Moslem League Council met to-day in the ballroom on the first floor of the Imperial Hotel. Towards the end of its deliberations there was a sudden but apparently carefully planned eruption of *Khaksars*, who came in through the garden at the side of the hotel and startled peaceful residents during tea by rushing through the lounge brandishing *belchas*, or sharpened spades. With these formidable weapons they wrought the maximum of havoc in the minimum of time and, shouting " Get Jinnah ! ", were half-way up the staircase leading to the ballroom where Jinnah and the Council were still in session before Moslem League

National Guards could grapple with them and turn them back.   It took police with tear-gas to bring the disturbance to an end.

The Imperial, which is New Delhi's leading hotel, houses the majority of the Foreign correspondents.   Here was a reversal of nature—the news seeking them out.   But only a few were there at the time to benefit from this providential sensation.   Preston Grover and Walt Mason of Associated Press of America found themselves in the midst of the fray, and, being two of the swiftest operators on the typewriter I have ever seen, they had helped in the restoration of law and order and had filed their story before most of their colleagues knew that anything was amiss.

Jinnah behaved with great composure.   Sidney Smith of the *Daily Express* saw him afterwards, and told me that Jinnah had no doubt but that the assault was an attempt on his life.   The only previous attempt to assassinate him—in Bombay in 1943—was made by a *Khaksar*.

The *Khaksars*, or "Servants of the Dust", are a group of militant Moslem fanatics with much the same storm-trooper ideology as the far more formidable Rashtrya Swam Sevak Sangh, offshoot of the Hindu Mahasabha.   Led by Inayatullah Mashriqi, they have been engaged on terrorist activities ever since their foundation in 1931.   Their demand is for an undivided Pakistan stretching from Karachi to Calcutta, and to them Jinnah is as much the betrayer of Moslem interests as Gandhi is in the eyes of Hindu extremists of Hinduism.

A party from Viceroy's House going along later in the evening for dinner found the place in the utmost disorder.   The large grill-room was a shambles.   Its air-coolers were smashed and its furniture broken up. The forces of fanaticism and revolution are on the move, and this incident confirms that the crust upholding order from the depths of chaos is dangerously thin.   Under the present tense conditions all the leaders provide far too easy targets for far too many would-be assassins.

VICEROY'S HOUSE, NEW DELHI, *Tuesday, 10th June, 1947*

The Moslem League Council has passed a resolution in phraseology designed to infuriate the Congress, but in terms which mark the nearest approach Jinnah is likely to make to a substantial acceptance of the Plan.   After expressing satisfaction at the abandonment of the Cabinet Mission Plan, it qualifies its refusal to agree or give consent to the partition of Bengal and the Punjab by deciding that it had to consider the 3rd June Plan for the transfer of power as a whole, and by giving full authority to Jinnah to accept the Plan's fundamental principles as a compromise.

Dominion Status and the joint Governor-Generalship was again the main theme at our Staff Meeting to-day.   Jinnah makes no move and gives no sign.   In the course of our discussion, which became somewhat discursive and hypothetical, Mountbatten said he believed there was considerable confusion in Nehru's mind about the magic date of June 1948.   Nehru was apparently working at immense pressure to complete the new Constitution before that date, and had emphasised so strongly that this was his objective that Congress prestige might seriously suffer if they did not succeed.   Mountbatten pointed out that the date of June

1948 now had no significance whatever, and he was anxious that I should stress this in all the background information I gave to the Press.

I have—I hope—given temporary quietus to the Press speculators by announcing :—

(1) The Mountbattens are going up to Simla for a genuine forty-eight hours' rest.

(2) That they are visiting Kashmir on the 19th at the genuine invitation of the Maharaja.

(3) That a genuine V.I.P. is visiting us in the person of Montgomery, who is on an Eastern Grand Tour.

"THE RETREAT", MASHOBRA, SIMLA, *Saturday, 14th June, 1947*

George Nicholls, Fay and I left yesterday for Simla shortly after 5 a.m. to cover as many miles of the parched plain as we could before the full heat of the sun beat down upon us. In these early hours there is a life-giving freshness in the air and it is easy to understand why many Indians— Sardar Patel among them—are up by 4.30 in the morning, completing nearly half a day's work before breakfast.

We reached " The Retreat " by tea-time—the beginning for me of a week's withdrawal from the Delhi ferment. Our Simla visit last month was no respite, but, on the contrary, the most critical and exacting phase of all the negotiations leading to the 3rd June.

In the Himalayan stillness, where no 'phone rings, it is possible now to pause and take stock of the progress to date and the task ahead. I wrote in this vein to my mother to-day :—

" Mountbatten's diplomacy has succeeded for several reasons, but primarily because of his own personality. He is a wonderful talker, and able to put across his own essential sincerity. The outward expression of the man is his weaving energy. He never lets up, and never allows a situation to harden against himself. When towards the end of April the situation looked more than usually dark and uncertain, Ismay roused my spirits by saying, ' I like working for lucky men.' No reflection, of course, was intended by him on Mountbatten's ability. On the contrary, it is borne in on all of us that he induces success and outflanks failure by the range and variety of his initiative.

" He is very sensitive to the different temperaments of those with whom he is negotiating, and has, as a result, won the complete confidence of Gandhi, Jinnah, Nehru and Patel, who, in spite of their close identification with the struggle for independence, are as diverse a quartet as it is possible to imagine. He is, in short, my idea of a political thoroughbred.

" I must stress the importance of Patel in the agreements so far reached. He has a rough exterior and uncompromising manner. His achievements tend to remain below the surface, but he was probably the first of the Congress High Command to realise that the 20th February statement implied Partition if a political settlement by June 1948 or before was to be achieved. Having absorbed that vital implication, he has never wavered, and has stood firm against the inner voices and neural indecisions that have sometimes afflicted his colleagues.

"Patel's realism has also been a big factor in the acceptance of the Dominion Status formula for which Mountbatten has worked so hard. This is inevitably a delicate plant. Personally I wish we could evolve an even looser Commonwealth concept which did not so directly involve the King's Sovereignty but could take in a Republic. This needs close consideration, because I believe the present symbolic ties of the British Commonwealth are not really applicable to a Congress-controlled Indian Union, and should be modified to include for the first time on equal terms peoples of different races.

"We are in the heart of Sikh country here, and the prevailing atmosphere is one of tension and foreboding. Since the beginning of June sentries have been on all-round-the-clock guard at ' The Retreat ' for the protection of our families and Moslem servants. Undoubtedly both Nehru's and Jinnah's speeches on the 3rd June helped to calm Hindu and Moslem fears and to avert the immediate outbreak of a major communal conflict, and taking the sub-continent as a whole, the popular reaction has in fact been remarkably calm. Nevertheless, Sikh unrest in the Punjab is growing hourly. The implications of the 3rd June are now all too clear to the Sikh people. They see that the Partition of India means substantially and irrevocably the partition of the Sikhs, and they feel themselves to be sacrificed on the altars of Moslem ambition and Hindu opportunism.

"Lying along the perimeter of Hindu and Moslem power, the Sikhs number some six million—no more than twenty per cent of the total Punjab population—but they succeeded in achieving influence out of all proportion to their numbers by maintaining their own unity and holding an effective balance of power within a United Punjab. With Partition, however, they are trapped, and no juggling of a Boundary Commission can prevent their bisection. They react accordingly, and their leaders, hopelessly out-manoeuvred in the political struggle, begin to invoke more primitive remedies.

"Sikhism, which is based on a most complex religious and social structure, does not encourage, or at the present moment enjoy, leadership of high quality. Baldev Singh, Defence Minister in Nehru's Government, is, as his speech on 3rd June showed, a man of high character and wide vision, but he is a voice in the wilderness. Nor does Patiala, the leading Sikh Prince and Chancellor of the Chamber of Princes in succession to Bhopal, have a decisive influence. Power is passing to the wilder men, such as Master Tara Singh and some of the younger I.N.A. officers. Rough weather lies ahead of us; in spite of all that has been already achieved, the outlook is still stormy and unsettled."

"THE RETREAT", MASHOBRA, SIMLA, *Wednesday, 18th June, 1947*

Gordon Mosley, the B.B.C.'s Representative in Delhi, is staying with us. A cable has been received from Sir William Haley proposing most ambitious B.B.C. coverage of the transfer of power, to include a team of three top-line news observers—Wynford Vaughan Thomas, Edward Ward and Richard Sharp—two feature-writers—Francis Dillon and Louis MacNeice—and three mobile recording units. He described one of the most important objectives of this visitation as being to provide material for programmes describing the British record of achievement in India.

I have stressed Mountbatten's as well as my own deep conviction that it would be far wiser for this high-powered team, when it arrives, to concentrate on present trends and future prospects rather than on invocations of the past.

VICEROY'S HOUSE, NEW DELHI, *Monday, 23rd June, 1947*

I have returned refreshed for a further spell in the Delhi furnace.

During the past ten days Mountbatten and the staff have been engaged in intensive operations over a wide front which may be said to add up to general progress in the campaign to clinch acceptance of the Plan. The principal development has been the All India Congress Committee's clear endorsement of Partition. In spite of verbal cross-fire and an abortive effort to achieve a Concordat signed jointly by Kripalani and Jinnah, the main political decision of the two Parties can no longer be said to be seriously in doubt.

At the decisive moment Gandhi came down in favour of acceptance, and the latent opposition among the more communally minded members of the Congress High Command could not take shape against the frail little man's massive authority.

As for the Provinces directly affected by the Plan, the Referendum for the North-west Frontier Province has, after much heart-searching and some evasive action, been accepted by Congress. At first Dr. Khan Sahib threatened to boycott it, but on Gandhi's advice the local Red-Shirt movement is to put its passive-resistance principles into practice and peacefully abstain. Caroe is retiring on leave while the referendum is being held. The letters exchanged between Mountbatten and Caroe were duly released just before I left for Simla. Mountbatten wisely decided to entrust the Province to a military régime and Lieutenant-General Sir Rob Lockhart, G.O.C.-in-C., Southern Command, India, who knows the Frontier well, is to take Caroe's place as Governor to supervise this very delicate operation. Nevertheless, I think we can say that as far as politics at the centre are concerned the peak of the Frontier crisis has already passed.

Over Bengal, Jinnah is being particularly difficult. While demanding portfolios in the Interim Government at the centre for his own Moslem League as a continuing right, he refuses them in the Interim Administration for the West Bengal Congressmen.

The Punjab Legislative Assembly has to-day formally opted for Partition, following on a similar decision in Bengal three days ago, where Suhrawardy's move to achieve an autonomous and united Province finally died away before the disfavour of the two great Parties. So the wheel turns full circle, and Congress, which in an earlier generation had bitterly opposed Curzon's partition of Bengal, now, forty years later, sponsors the self-same policy.

The Leaders have taken a basic decision about their policy towards the States in agreeing to the establishment of a States Department in Delhi which will deal with all matters of common concern and with the formulation of their final relationship. In the meanwhile it was agreed that the new Department should take over everything short of Paramountcy from the existing Crown Representative's Political Department.

That Paramountcy after the transfer of power is a problem bristling with political and legal difficulties has been brought home to Mountbatten from various discussions which he has had during the past ten days with the Leaders, with his old friend Sir Walter Monckton, constitutional adviser to the Nizam, and with Bhopal and his adviser Sir Zaffrullah Khan.* They have been stressing that what was good enough under the Cabinet Mission Plan is far from satisfactory under Partition, which is essentially a communal solution substituting two strong central Governments for one weak one. So they were pressing the claims of Dominion Status for some of the States.

Mountbatten has also seen for himself the paralysis of Princely uncertainty during his visit to Kashmir, from which he has only just returned to-day. Both Nehru and Gandhi have been very anxious that the Maharaja of Kashmir should make no declaration of independence. And Nehru, himself descended from Kashmiri Brahmins, has been pressing to visit the State himself to seek the release from prison of his friend Sheikh Abdullah, now President of the States Congress. Last year when Nehru visited the State he was himself placed under arrest by the Kashmir Government. Gandhi's view was that he himself ought to prepare the way for Nehru. The Maharaja has made it very clear that he does not welcome a visit from either. Mountbatten succeeded in deferring both visits by saying he himself had a long-standing invitation from the Maharaja and would like to see him first.

When he got there he found the Maharaja politically very elusive, and the only conversations that took place were during their various car drives together. Mountbatten on these occasions urged him and his Prime Minister, Pandit Kak, not to make any declaration of independence, but to find out in one way or another the will of the people of Kashmir as soon as possible, and to announce their intention by 14th August to send representatives accordingly to one Constituent Assembly or the other. He told them that the newly created States Department was prepared to give an assurance that if Kashmir went to Pakistan this would not be regarded as an unfriendly act by the Government of India. He went on to stress the dangerous situation in which Kashmir would find itself if it lacked the support of one of the two Dominions by the date of the transfer of power. His intention was to give this advice privately to the Maharaja alone, and then to repeat it in the presence of his Prime Minister with George Abell and the Resident, Colonel Webb, in attendance, at a small meeting where minutes could be kept.

* Subsequently the Foreign Minister of Pakistan.

The Maharaja suggested that the meeting should take place on the last day of the visit, to which Mountbatten agreed, feeling that this would allow him the maximum chance to make up his mind, but when the time came the Maharaja sent a message that he was in bed with colic and would be unable to attend the meeting. It seems that this is his usual illness when he wishes to avoid difficult discussions.

Needless to say, Mountbatten is very disappointed at this turn of events.

To-day's Staff Meeting had no fewer than eleven items on its agenda, including " Reconstitution of the Executive Council ", and " Governors-General ". Jinnah treats both subjects with oracular reserve, and, with an exasperating skill, conceals his intentions, leaving Congress and Mountbatten open to make the false move. Neither Congress nor the Moslem League are showing any real awareness of the administrative magnitude and urgency of the problems facing them.

Nearly three weeks have passed since the Leaders received the memorandum on the " Administrative Consequences of Partition " and accepted in principle the procedure it laid down by appointing the necessary Partition Committees. Vernon has worked out a long list of outstanding items calling for action or decision on their part if full progress is to be made, to which they have so far failed to provide any semblance of an answer.

The real weight is falling upon a Steering Committee of two men appointed after the Partition Committee's first meeting on 13th June. Nominated by the Congress and Moslem League representatives respectively, they are H. M. Patel, the Cabinet Secretary, and Mohammed Ali, Financial Adviser in the Military Finance Department. Both are Civil Servants in mid-career and of outstanding ability. I met H. M. Patel when I was in Delhi in 1943. He was then serving under Akbar Hydari in the important Civil Supplies Department. This was certainly a good apprenticeship, but he has advanced far since then, and as Cabinet Secretary to the Interim Government is one of about half a dozen administrators upon whom the new India will have to lean heavily as soon as it is exposed to the full administrative rigours of Independence.

Mohammed Ali is perhaps even more indispensable to Pakistan, which will be desperately short of home-grown officials of the front rank. But a great future could be safely predicted for Mohammed Ali in the Civil Service hierarchies of any country, and Jinnah, who is usually indifferent to the administrative implications of political life, has been quick to appreciate his vital value to the embryo State. It is a fortunate chance that both Patel and Mohammed Ali have worked together closely in the past and are on excellent terms with each other. In appearance they are alike but in personality they are contrasting figures, Patel always smiling and of sunny disposition, Mohammed Ali of ascetic outlook and high seriousness. With the assistance of expert sub-committees, which it has been wisely agreed should consist of officials only, both Patel and Mohammed Ali are optimistic that the administrative principles of Partition can be settled quickly and most of the actual separation effected by the deadline of the 15th August. In the meanwhile they need rather more dynamic political support than has so far been forthcoming.

VICEROY'S HOUSE, NEW DELHI, *Tuesday, 24th June, 1947*

In spite of Gandhi's courageous and decisive intervention at the All India Congress Committee in favour of the 3rd June Plan, one can never be quite sure when this volcano of non-violence will erupt.

I spoke to Devadas Gandhi on the telephone this morning, asking when he was proposing to call the next meeting of the All India Editors' Conference, of which he is the Chairman. In the course of the conversation he drew my attention to a Reuters report from London describing the forthcoming Parliamentary procedure for the enactment of Indian Independence. This was nothing more than an account of the traditional ceremonial in both Houses covering the passage of all Bills into law, the introductory paragraphs of which were worded as follows: "The British Parliament in thirty minutes of solemn ceremony will next month give Dominion Status to nearly four hundred million people of Hindustan and Pakistan. The Bill creating the two new nations, inscribed on vellum and parchment, will be drawn from a magnificent wallet embellished with the Royal Arms in colours and gold thread and read to both the Houses of Parliament."

Devadas said the reference to the creation of two new nations had very much distressed his father, whose view was that such a report emanating from Reuters must have Government authority behind it, and that this "two-nation" theory was wholly repugnant to the Congress outlook. In fact it had provoked the Mahatma into issuing a special message at his Prayer Meeting on Monday in which he had said, "The papers to-day talk of a grand ceremonial to take place in London over the division of India into 'two nations' which were only the other day one nation. What is there to gloat over in the tragedy? We have hugged the belief that though we part, we do so as friends and brothers belonging to one family. Now, if the newspaper report is correct, the British will make of us two nations, and that with a flourish of trumpets. Is that to be the parting shot? I hope not."

Devadas urged me to take the earliest opportunity to draw the Viceroy's attention to all this, and expressed the hope that Mountbatten might see his way to make some private disavowal of it, and, further, that I might be authorised to make a disclaimer that would be published. He added that his father felt so strongly about the matter that it could be taken for granted that he would raise it at his meeting with the Viceroy to-morrow. I spoke, I hope, with sufficient suavity, for I was frankly amazed that such a great man could see fit to make so much of so inoffensive a story. I told him that I was sure much more was being read into it than it could possibly carry.

I have reported on the whole thing to Mountbatten, whose reaction to this kind of psychological pressure is very healthy. It may perhaps be best summed up as the application of the guiding slogan of Ismay, who told me the other day that "each morning when I get up I say to myself 'Patience and proportion'."

To-night a big dinner-party was given in honour of Field-Marshal Montgomery, who arrived yesterday at Viceroy's House. He has been caught up in a strenuous round of interviews and discussions, and, in his usual incisive manner, has completed a lot of business.

The visit, planned some time ahead and without regard to political developments, has in fact turned out to be very well-timed. Montgomery has been able to form his own impression of the progress so far made over the partition of the Indian Army and to help decisively in solving the problem of the withdrawal of British forces from India. With regard to British troops a compromise agreement has been reached, largely conditioned by the shipping available, that their withdrawal from India should be phased over a period of six months from the date of transfer of power. Mountbatten has had Monty's support in resisting any suggestion that they should during this time be used in any operational role. He appreciates that it is not possible to hedge a political transfer of power with military reservations.

When Monty arrived yesterday I was at once called in to discuss arrangements for a photograph of the Viceroy and the Chief of the Imperial General Staff. While I was doing so there appeared just outside the window of the Viceroy's study a somewhat unusual visitant— a bullock temporarily off duty from mowing the lawns of the Moghul gardens. Monty at once noticed it, saying he was very glad it had turned up, and presumed that it must have known he was coming, for when he was last photographed here, with Wavell and Auchinleck, the most prominent member of their group had been a bullock! While waiting in the garden for the camera-men to come to the ready, Montgomery, detecting with his observant eye that one or two of the cameras were of German make, commented, " They're good. Better than most of ours."

At the dinner this evening Mountbatten paid Monty an unexpected compliment. On the front of their scarlet-and-gold uniforms Viceregal servants wear the Viceroy's personal insignia. In Mountbatten's case it takes the form of " M of B " set within the Garter. Mountbatten seized the opportunity provided by the form of Montgomery's title and membership of the Order of the Garter to make a variation in the monogram worn by the servant attached to him who waited upon him at dinner. He simply substituted the Garter enclosing " M of A " for the Garter enclosing " M of B ". This obviously delighted Monty.

VICEROY'S HOUSE, NEW DELHI, *Wednesday, 25th June, 1947*

There was a " family " dinner-party to-night to celebrate Mountbatten's forty-seventh birthday. Some forty members of the staff were asked, including wives and secretaries. Miéville spoke to me in very strong terms about the delay over any decision on the Governor-General issue and considers it to be, apart from anything else, rank discourtesy on the part of Jinnah, who continues to play the role of Delphic oracle and deal in riddles.

Jossleyn Hennessy, correspondent of the *Sunday Times* and Kemsley Press, told me this morning that Jinnah's Secretary, Kurshid, had given him for publication the story that Pakistan does not want the same

Governor-General as Hindustan, but that it will be impossible for Mountbatten to leave during the next few months, as there is so much for him to do. Bob Stimson also came round to tell me that Kurshid had said much the same to him, but with the decorative addition that Pakistan's Governor-General must be of Royal blood.

VICEROY'S HOUSE, NEW DELHI, *Friday, 27th June, 1947*

Now that the Punjab and Bengal have declared in favour of their own partition and, as a result, half of each will be taking their share in the formation of a new and separate Constituent Assembly, the full machinery for administering Partition is set in motion. The Partition Committee, which was limited to Congress and Moslem League members of the Interim Government, now gives way to a Partition Council of wider authority which includes Jinnah and can take final policy decisions.

The new Council met for the first time to-day, with Mountbatten once again in the chair and once again refusing arbitral status. But there is now no need for him to do so, as it accepted with surprising speed and unanimity Jinnah's proposal that Sir Cyril Radcliffe should be invited to serve as chairman of the Punjab and Bengal Boundary Commissions, with the casting vote on both.

Nehru, on his side, secured agreement for the Boundary Commission to work to very simple terms of reference, which are, to demarcate the boundaries of the new parts of either Province on the basis of ascertaining the contiguous majority areas of Moslems and non-Moslems, and in so doing to "take account of other factors". This was a compromise which met the desire of both parties—the Moslem League hoping that wide terms of reference in Bengal would improve their chances of securing Calcutta, and the Congress and Sikhs calling for the inclusion of property and other qualifications to give them a better chance in the Punjab.

The original intention was to put the vexed problem of boundary demarcation in the hands of the United Nations, but Nehru objected, on the grounds that this would involve cumbersome procedure and unacceptable delay. Radcliffe's colleagues will be four High Court Judges on each Commission, two each nominated by Congress and two each by the Moslem League. It calls for no special prophetic gifts, however, to suggest that the onus of unpopular decision will almost certainly fall on Radcliffe himself. I am sure Mountbatten has been absolutely right not to involve his present or future functions in these Awards.

VICEROY'S HOUSE, NEW DELHI, *Saturday, 28th June, 1947*

At our Staff Meeting to-day Mountbatten's attention was drawn to a leading article in *Dawn* casting doubt upon the Viceroy's methods and impartiality in the handling of the Referendum under the 3rd June Plan to be conducted in Sylhet. The complaint is that he has not arranged for military supervision similar to that provided in the North-west Frontier Province Referendum. Mountbatten was at first taken aback on this point of fact, saying, "My God, the fellow is right!"

and adding that in the general rush of business he had not fully appreciated that the Referendum was under his ægis in the same way as in the Northwest Frontier Province. The implications of the attack in *Dawn* were wholly misleading, for no irregularity had occurred or was intended.

I was given the somewhat delicate task of explaining to Altaf Hussain that the matter was being suitably dealt with. Hussain, whose gifts of self-expression are primarily in terms of invective, had closed his leading article with the threat that " If no satisfactory announcement is made within the next forty-eight hours we shall be compelled to return to the subject and indulge in some plain speaking". This was my opportunity to do the same with him at once. I then took him in a more reasonable frame of mind to see George Abell, and on the understanding that we would not be subjected to further threats and time-limits, we assured him that we would keep him posted with the steps the Viceroy proposed to take.

We parted good friends. It must be confessed, however, that Hussain is doing little more than reflect the current hauteur and touchiness of his Leader. Only to-day Mountbatten received a letter from Jinnah which provoked the strongest reaction I have ever heard from the usually bland and urbane Ismay. " It was a letter", he said, " which I would not take from my King or send to a coolie."

VICEROY'S HOUSE, NEW DELHI, *Monday, 30th June, 1947*

The Partition Council, largely as a result of Mountbatten's inspiration, has most surprisingly agreed without delay or dispute to the procedure for the division of the Indian Armed Forces.

Great praise is due both to Auchinleck and Ismay for providing the framework in which " reconstitution "—as Auchinleck has shrewdly termed it—can take place. But Mountbatten himself at the critical moment had the good sense to inject into the discussions Trivedi, the Governor of Orissa, who, as Secretary of the Defence Department during the war, is the only Indian civil servant with any experience of high-level defence organisation. He succeeded in quickly winning the confidence of Nehru and Sardar Patel, as well as enjoying the advantage of a long-standing friendship with Liaquat Ali Khan. Trivedi by intensive personal negotiation over the past week has succeeded in smoothing the way to concessions by both sides resulting in genuine compromise.

The basic principle adopted is that India and Pakistan shall each have in their own territories Armed Forces, predominantly non-Moslem and Moslem respectively, which as from 15th August are to be under their own operational control. Both sides have vehemently insisted on complete military independence as a condition of settlement, Jinnah and Liaquat Ali Khan openly asserting that they are not prepared to take over the reins of Government without their own Armed Forces in being.

Both sides, too, have raised strong objection to any form of centralised administrative control after the 15th August, but here Mountbatten has once again intervened decisively by insisting that the administration of the Armed Forces should continue under Auchinleck until the Partition of personnel and physical assets is complete. Briefly he is to remain in India in administrative control of Indian Armed Forces for the time being under a Joint Defence Council, to consist, besides himself, of the combined Governor-General or separate Governors-General and the two Defence Ministers.

To avoid confusion with the new Commanders-in-Chief of both Dominions, Auchinleck will be called Supreme Commander from 15th August until his task is completed. The target date is 1st April, 1948, but in the meanwhile he is to have no responsibility for law and order or any operational control over any units save those in transit from one Dominion to another.

It has never been possible to isolate the partition of the Indian Army from its wider political context. In all the circumstances of suspicion, ill-will and communal clash it is doubtful whether human ingenuity could have avoided this tragic necessity or achieved a more workman-like formula.

VICEROY'S HOUSE, NEW DELHI, *Tuesday, 1st July, 1947*

The tension in the Punjab grows as 15th August approaches. A straw in the wind is a letter which Auchinleck has received and forwarded from a Sikh refugee in Delhi. He complains that the Seventh Sikhs are still in the Basra area protecting the Persian oil-zone, but that " during these twelve months tragic events have occurred in their home-land which have upset the minds of our brave Sikh brothers abroad. When India is being divided our men should be home with their kinsfolk. I trust you will issue orders for their speedy return to their home before the August drama unfolds itself."

Jenkins reports that the situation in Lahore and Amritsar gives ground for grave concern. The violence takes the form of scattered but wide-spread arson and stabbing carried out by cloak-and-dagger techniques which are very difficult to suppress by normal police or military action. Having discovered how easy it is to burn down an Indian city, the incendiaries are particularly dangerous. Throwing fireballs through windows and skylights and making full use of roof-tops and narrow city lanes, they are almost impossible to catch in the act.

CHAPTER ELEVEN

TO STAY OR NOT TO STAY

VICEROY'S HOUSE, NEW DELHI, *Wednesday, 2nd July, 1947*

CONGRESS AND MOSLEM League leaders have been sitting in separate rooms at Viceroy's House poring over the terms of the Draft Dominions Bill, the title of which, incidentally, has been strengthened to that of " Indian Independence Bill ". Jinnah had been excusing himself from taking any formal view about the Governor-Generalship until he had had a chance to scrutinise the Bill, and delayed his decision for a few more hours under cover of a desire to consult with certain close colleagues who were engaged on the Referenda.

He has at long last " come clean ", and Jinnah's verdict goes in favour of Jinnah. He still professes to nurse the illusion that it would be possible for Mountbatten to supervise a fair Partition by remaining in some stratospheric capacity above the two new Heads of State. Jinnah indicated that he had taken the decision somewhat against his will on the insistence of his close friends, but it would be interesting to know who those friends are, as it would seem that his senior colleagues and well-wishers have been advising him strongly to the contrary, feeling he would have more power in his hands as Prime Minister. They were only too well aware that in the division of assets India starts with the initial advantage of having the overwhelming percentage of them in her physical possession, and that accordingly an eight-month spell with Mountbatten as joint Governor-General must be of primary advantage to Pakistan.

When Mountbatten asked him frankly whether he realised what his decision would cost the new State of his creation, Jinnah candidly admitted that it would possibly cost several crores of rupees in assets, but that he was unable to accept any position other than that of Governor-General of Pakistan on the 15th August. None-the-less he added that he particularly hoped Mountbatten would stay on as Governor-General of India, as he felt that this would help relations between the two Dominions.

An emergency meeting of Mountbatten's staff was held at Ismay's house at 9.30 this morning. The purpose was to consider various possible courses open to the Viceroy, who is placed in a most invidious and delicate position. Ismay thought it advisable for the staff to examine the facts of the situation and clarify our own views in order to provide Mountbatten with objective advice before we exposed ourselves to his own inevitably subjective reactions.

Jinnah has certainly maintained the element of suspense and surprise on this issue to the last moment. We all assumed that he would be bound to prefer the status and powers of Prime Minister to those of a constitutional Governor-General, and on the basis of this first assumption we went farther, and guessed that he would want to take advantage of Mountbatten as common Governor-General. Farthest from our thoughts was what has in fact happened—Jinnah's self-selection and Mountbatten's invitation from Congress alone.

After a careful consideration the general consensus of opinion was that in these unforeseen circumstances Mountbatten should be strongly advised to accept the unconditional Congress offer to him and remain on as Governor-General of the Dominion of India. The possible courses of action reduced themselves to three :—

(1) To agree to Jinnah becoming Governor-General of Pakistan, and for Mountbatten to stay on as Governor-General of India alone.

(2) To agree to Jinnah becoming Governor-General of Pakistan, and to ask Congress to nominate someone other than Mountbatten as Governor-General of India.

(3) To devise a formula whereby Mountbatten would be enabled to remain as Governor-General of both Dominions while at the same time substantially satisfying Jinnah's wishes to control Pakistan.

We shall not be meeting Mountbatten until to-morrow afternoon, which gives everyone time to develop their ideas. In making difficult decisions he is always very sensitive to the trends of public opinion, and may well be receptive to the views and arguments from my side of the house, so I am trying to compose my initial thoughts in writing.

In the meanwhile I have sent a wire to London suggesting that the Editor of the *Evening Standard* be invited to send a representative out to India to study a few of the elementary facts of the situation here. This proposal has been prompted by an unusually reckless piece of " Beaverbrookese ". The proposition put before the *Evening Standard* readers in a leading article is, " If it was possible to set up two Dominions in India, then plainly, had the requisite statesmanship been available, it would have been possible to convert India into a single Dominion owing an undivided allegiance to the Crown ". There are also some slap-happy references to " Balkanisation " and " an utterly reactionary step ", and the whole of our efforts are denounced as " political auction ".

What a pity that Beaverbrook, who genuinely believes in a liberal Empire in the Western and Southern Hemispheres, does not seem to understand what men of goodwill, who also seek a similar dispensation, are trying to do here in the East.

VICEROY'S HOUSE, NEW DELHI, *Thursday, 3rd July, 1947*

We had our Staff Meeting with Mountbatten this afternoon, and he asked for our views on the Governor-Generalship round the table one by one. All but one of us urged upon him that, in the interests of India, Pakistan and Britain, it was his clear duty to accept the Congress invitation. Our virtual unanimity and the obvious strength and sincerity of our collective opinion took him by surprise, for previously, before being confronted by the firm reality of Jinnah's decision, we had taken the view, informally and as individuals, that it would be undesirable for

Mountbatten to lose his objective and almost judicial status. But now it is clear to us that Jinnah, by identifying the Pakistan Governor-Generalship with himself, has created a wholly new situation.

When my turn came to speak I read out the note I had prepared. I was careful to confine myself to the publicity implications of the three courses considered. " It has been a political commonplace ", I wrote, " that with the transfer of power Pakistan would become the last outpost of British Imperialism and that the anti-British bias of Congress would quickly prevail. Congress invitations to His Excellency, Colville and Nye * knock that criticism on the head. From the view-point of British prestige it is a tremendous thing that Congress at the moment of victory in its seventy years' struggle with the British should spontaneously invite Englishmen to stay on in this way.

" Such an invitation gets our relations with the new India off to a start good beyond all expectations. At the same time the suggestion that H.E. † has sold out to the Congress is met by obvious evidence that Pakistan and Jinnah have got exactly what they asked for. In fact H.E.'s presence at the head of the new Indian State would naturally be interpreted the best guarantee that its relations with Pakistan would be carried on in a friendly and constructive manner, and as a buffer against excessive Congress claims.

" The argument that with Jinnah in his present mood and enjoying full powers, and with H.E. simply as a constitutional Governor-General, H.E. would not be able to exercise any substantial influence on Indo-Pakistan relations is a major consideration, but not directly a publicity problem. While no doubt it would be a limiting factor to H.E.'s usefulness, I think it would be widely realised that no one else would be able to do more, and, in view of his close association with Jinnah at this critical time, no other Governor-General would be likely to be in a position to do as much. The argument that a climb down is involved from Viceroy of all India to Governor-General of India less Pakistan cannot, I submit, be sustained nor should it be strongly stressed—climb down from what? The whole emphasis of H.E.'s mission here has been on the future—on the beginning of a new chapter in our relations with Indians, and not on ' the last Viceroy '.

" If H.E. were to hand over to a successor on 15th August, he would obviously be leaving on the crest of the wave, but once it was appreciated that H.E. had been invited by Congress unconditionally and had turned down their invitation, I believe there would be a considerable volume of criticism, both immediate and long term, that he was leaving the job half done and making ' a quick get-away '."

My conclusion, therefore, was that while a formula to satisfy Jinnah and retain a joint Governor-Generalship was theoretically desirable from every point of view, for Mountbatten to stay on in India alone would be

* Sir John Colville (later Lord Clydesmuir) and Sir Archibald Nye were invited to remain on after the transfer of power as Governors of Bombay and Madras respectively.
† Staff term for His Excellency the Viceroy and Governor-General.

favourably received in the British and World Press, while for him to leave on 15th August could not fail to provoke serious and justifiable criticism.

I may say that Jinnah's self-appointment is only one of a host of dilemmas crowding in upon the Viceroy and calling for urgent personal decision. The Congress and Moslem League comments on the Draft Bill are now in, and these, with Mountbatten's comments on the comments, are to be cabled to London. The objections are greater in length than in depth, and if the British Government decide to stand firm—as no doubt they will—on all the major points, I do not consider that there will be any last-minute retractions at this end. But it is always an outside possibility, and makes the next few days prior to the introduction and passage of the Bill in London a particularly anxious period.

In high politics, however, there is perhaps one compensation—when the burden becomes too heavy it seems that you just cease to feel the weight. This morning, reporting the latest developments on the future of the Interim Government, Mountbatten said, " Krishna Menon came in to see me last evening all tense and exclaiming triumphantly, ' I think I have prevailed on Congress not to resign.' All I could summon up by way of acknowledgement was to say, ' Really.' My mental process was to dismiss the whole matter as being only yesterday's crisis."

Among the miscellaneous items, we considered whether a partitioned India meant also a partitioned Kennel Club. This was only a test case, for the Military Secretary's office is being inundated with queries from various " All India " bodies as to what they should do next.

VICEROY'S HOUSE, NEW DELHI, *Friday, 4th July, 1947*

Mountbatten has to-day diverted the crisis over the future of the Interim Government by calling on all the members—Congress and Moslem League alike—to resign, and then inviting them to carry on until the actual passing of the Indian Independence Bill at Westminster. Behind this action, which plays for time and is not of course a final solution of the problem, lies a complicated and dangerous wrangle. Briefly, ever since the acceptance of the 3rd June Plan Mountbatten has been subjected to two conflicting pressures. On the Congress side it is largely a repetition with greater insistence of Patel's complaint, " You won't govern yourself, at least let us govern ". To this Jinnah's reaction is that if any Moslem League Ministers are removed they will resign en bloc, making it clear that they are withdrawing from all co-operation and washing their hands of the whole Partition scheme. Mountbatten is well aware that any such action on their part would once again wreck the prospects of peace and of Pakistan.

Nehru, tired and overwrought and subject to these increasing Congress demands to become master forthwith in his own house, has been on the verge of resignation on this issue over the past week. Jinnah first of all rejected outright any formula which involves the actual handing in of portfolios by the Moslem League members as being an insult to the League. When Mountbatten evolved a scheme and actually drafted a Press announcement to meet his susceptibilities under this heading, Jinnah changed his ground, saying that he would resist the scheme as illegal under the 1935 Act. This gave Mountbatten an unexpected opening, for on inquiry in London he found that there was sufficient foundation in Jinnah's legal complaint to make it impossible for him to proceed with reconstitution of the Government in advance of the passing of the Act.

At the Staff Meeting to-day we argued out at great length the possibility and consequences of Mountbatten staying on beyond 15th August as Governor-General of the Dominion of India only. We have not as yet succeeded in removing his grave misgivings. He fears the loss of objective status will be a crippling handicap to his usefulness and may well dissipate the good-will he has won from Hindu and Moslem alike.

Mountbatten now wants to have authoritative advice from London from the King and Prime Minister downwards before reaching a final decision. He also suspects that the Government may feel—not unjustifiably—that he has misled them and put them in a false position by over-selling the likelihood of a joint Governor-Generalship.

So he has decided that Ismay should leave for London at once, officially to be available to the Government while the Independence Bill passes through Parliament, but in addition to secure confidential guidance at the highest level as to whether he should stay on or come home. I am to go as well, and I will use the opportunity to make a parallel check on Press and other informed reactions to the new situation.

LONDON, *Monday, 7th July, 1947*

We left Palam in the Viceregal York on Saturday afternoon, touching down at Northolt by tea-time today. My whole vision of Indo-British travel has been foreshortened by my sequence of high speed and even higher priority flights over the past three years. England has never looked lovelier than when we flew low over Beachy Head. The cliffs of Dover and Calais stood out so clearly and close together that from ten thousand feet they seemed to be part of the same mainland, the straits appearing as the entrance to some mighty river or grand harbour. The green of English fields from the air has a soft, civilised quality not to be found in the vivid dark hues of lands washed by monsoons.

Ismay was in splendid form on this flight. He has the Roman virtue of *aequinimitas*. His bland *bonhomie* is a perfect foil to Mountbatten, with his more intense and uneven moods. Ismay had taken great pains over our itinerary, and so arranged that at our various landing-points— Karachi, Habbaniya, Malta—we landed in good time for dinner and left at a comfortable hour in the morning. He said the journey back to India with the Mountbattens in May had been an ordeal he would never undergo again. In an effort to beat the clock, all they had succeeded in doing was playing havoc with everyone's digestion!

By six o'clock this evening Ismay was in close conference with the Prime Minister at 10 Downing Street. The Prime Minister did not take long to reach the conclusion that the new and difficult situation in no way lessened, but rather enhanced, the need for Mountbatten to stay on in India.

LONDON, *Tuesday, 8th July, 1947*

After dinner yesterday Ismay attended a meeting at 10 Downing Street which lasted beyond midnight. Although there were some doubts expressed about Mountbatten's personal position arising from the change from an arbitral to a partisan status, particularly in the event of disputes between the two Dominions, Ministers were generally in favour of Mountbatten accepting the Indian offer. Attlee, it seems, went so far as to say that Mountbatten could see this thing through, and no one else could do so. The Government were deeply impressed by the Moslem League's support for the proposition which Ismay was able to convey to them in writing from Liaquat. The position is, in fact, that both sides have now requested Mountbatten to remain on with one side.

This morning the Prime Minister called in the following Opposition leaders: Salisbury, Macmillan, Butler, Samuel and Clem Davies. Ismay put the problem before them. Lord Samuel was rather anxious to revive the idea which he had originally expressed to Mountbatten in my flat, of a Viceroy presiding over the two Governors-General. But the general sense of the meeting was that such a suggestion was now too late to put into practice, and in any case likely to be unacceptable to the Congress. The Liberals were whole-heartedly in favour of Mountbatten remaining as Governor-General of India. But while the Conservative leaders were personally in full accord with the proposal, they felt that they could not commit themselves officially until they had had a chance to consult Churchill, who was down at Chartwell convalescing from a recent illness, and Eden, who was also unable to be present at the meeting.

Attlee accordingly suggested to Ismay that he should go down to Chartwell himself, which he did forthwith. Any expectations Ismay may have had of a difficult interview with the great man were quickly dispelled. He did not think the position had been in any way altered by Jinnah's action, and dictated a message for Ismay to send by cable to the Viceroy, the substance of which was that a constitutional Governor-General retained an unlimited right to receive information and to give advice, and that on this basis Mountbatten could give the new Government aid which he should not withhold. While leaving it with Mountbatten's conscience and judgement to decide when his usefulness was exhausted, Churchill stressed in particular the political value of his role in mitigating the communal tension, preserving the interests of the Princes and strengthening the ties of sentiment between India and the rest of the Commonwealth.

Ismay, much relieved, came back to London post-haste and told Churchill's Conservative colleagues of the interview and message which was relayed to Delhi immediately. This decisive expression of opinion, combining as it did the great man's breadth of view and immediate grasp of essentials with his ability to relate his exact ideas to perfect logic, set everybody's mind at rest.

With every day that passes the virtues of diplomacy by informal discussion are increasingly borne in on me.   It has certainly been possible for Ismay to dispel doubts both from the view-point of Mountbatten in Delhi and of the Government and Opposition in London with a speed and certainty which no amount of long-distance letters, *aides-memoire* or telegrams could have done.

LONDON, *Friday, 11th July, 1947*

A summons to Buckingham Palace and a further visit to 10 Downing Street have enabled Ismay to complete the first and most important phase of his mission and to provide Mountbatten with a conclusive answer to the reaction of opinion here.

I have also been busily engaged in collecting opinions, and have written to-day to Mountbatten giving him a *résumé* of my many editorial interviews.

" I have briefed everyone fully," I wrote, " on the situation that has arisen, but without in the first instance putting forward any views of my own.   I can report complete unanimity in urging the need for you to stay on and in stressing that the British Press reaction to your doing so will be favourable and sympathetic.   Frank Owen said that if your prestige stood at ninety when you left in March, it had now risen to one hundred and ninety, and that any decision you take, simply on the grounds that you had taken it, would be regarded as good and sufficient by the British public.   Lord Layton said that in his view Jinnah's decision would be widely regarded as a selfish and ambitious act, and that it would involve a marking down here with the British Press of his reputation, which was at its peak during his visit to England in December last. Then he had made a very considerable impression.

" I attended the Debate on the second reading of the Indian Independence Bill yesterday.   It was a bad House, and the attendance was nothing like as big as it should have been.   The speeches by the Prime Minister, Harold Macmillan for the Conservative Opposition and Hopkin Morris for the Liberals, were of a very high quality, and the tributes paid to your work from both sides of the House were inspiring to hear.   I am sure if you could come back for a few moments and get the feel of the atmosphere you would realise that you have a body of support in this country which very few Englishmen can hope to achieve for themselves and which will I am sure stand by you and Lady Louis in the coming months."

LONDON, *Tuesday, 15th July, 1947*

Prior to the Debates in both Houses I had long talks with Clement Davies and Lord Samuel, explaining how quickly events had moved since March and stressing the overwhelming difficulties in the way of creating the super-Viceroy Lord Samuel had in mind.   When the Bill was read a second time in the Lords to-day, having passed through the Commons in under a week without a division or any fireworks, it was Samuel's speech which I thought was the best of the star-studded bunch.

In the informal and almost intimate atmosphere of the Robing Room which the Lords are now using as their Chamber I heard him make an outstanding contribution to what was in any case a great proconsular occasion. Names that had upheld the authority and splendour of the Raj now gave themselves to the task of liquidating their former glory. Samuel was at pains to say that this was not an hour of defeat but of fulfilment, and as the senior Liberal spokesman he recalled how Mr. Gladstone had opposed the title and concept of " Empress of India ". He summed up by describing the Bill in a memorable phrase. " It is," he said, " an event unique in history—a treaty of peace without a war."

Lord Halifax, as in his decisive contribution to the Debate in March, did not hesitate to go beyond the Party line and give credit where he thought it was due. " I think it has meant much," he said, " for the long-term hopes which we may all cherish that the approach of His Majesty's Government to this tangled problem should have been inspired, as I think it has been, with courage and imagination, supported, as it has been, by the indomitable vigour and unrivalled resource of His Majesty's Government's representative in India to-day."

Samuel told me that Halifax was yet another powerful advocate of Mountbatten remaining on after 15th August. Considering the vigorous and often bitter Party spirit which had characterised Parliamentary proceedings during the two years since the Labour victory, the speed and unanimity with which the Indian Independence Bill has passed through both Houses was an inspiring spectacle.

Mountbatten had not only succeeded in reconciling the Parties in India, he had also managed to bring them together at home. The tributes paid to him went far beyond formal politeness. Perhaps the most significant and surprising tribute of all came from Lord Winterton, the Father of the House, for years a leader of the Conservative diehards in Indian affairs. He went so far as to assert that " No man since Wellington has been given such twin gifts of leadership in the military and constitutional fields ". He doubted, moreover, whether any member of the Government or Opposition front bench, including Churchill and Attlee themselves, had ever been given a greater task than that given to Lord Mountbatten, " who has solved it to the satisfaction of all men of good-will of both countries ".

Not the least interesting feature of the House of Commons Debate was the realistic acceptance of Partition by the Labour back-benchers, who in some cases actually welcomed it in principle.

LONDON, *Thursday, 17th July, 1947*

One of my last calls before our return flight to India was upon Mountbatten's mother in her apartments at Kensington Palace to-day. To meet the Dowager Marchioness of Milford Haven is to sense at once the presence of a personality of great moral authority and mental power. Although she was well satisfied with her son's achievements to date, she had no illusions about the dangers lying ahead, and felt he should set himself another time limit. He should not allow himself to become the victim of the politicians. "You could", she added, "stay on until you were Methuselahs in the hope of changing the Indian character." It was refreshing to talk with this great Victorian lady—grand-daughter of the Queen herself—and find her sufficiently emancipated from the past as to enjoy smoking through a cigarette-holder. She showed herself equally free of the tyranny of the present when she described the Americans to me as being "too old-fashioned to be snobs".

During Ismay's talks with the Ministers I understand that Listowel, the new Secretary of State for India, expressed some concern about the possible reactions of Indian Left-wing leaders, and in particular the Socialists, to Mountbatten staying on, saying that it seemed to provide an obvious stick with which to beat the Congress.

This evening I was introduced by Woodrow Wyatt at the House of Commons to Patwardan, who is a confidant of Jai Prakash Narain, the Socialist leader, and has been in London to watch the passing of the Act. He said he considered the invitation to Mountbatten a very astute move on the part of Congress. The Socialists hoped that Mountbatten's presence would mitigate the intransigence of the Princes and leave the door open to subsequent reunion. I asked him quite frankly what his attitude was to Mountbatten remaining on as Governor-General in view of Congress's Republican resolution? Speaking personally, he said he felt the Socialists would be quite satisfied to abide by whatever view Nehru might take of the matter when the time came. I told him that he could be sure Mountbatten would not over-stay his welcome by one hour.

I came away with the impression that the Socialists would not make an issue of Mountbatten or Dominion Status, but would concentrate primarily on the Princes where a sizeable Congress–Socialist vote was to be found. Patwardan was very anxious that the Viceroy should recognise the need for clinching democratic rights in the States. I said I noticed a tendency among some Left-wing thinkers to look for revolutionary action for its own sake, but Patwardan stressed that revolution was not in itself desirable. He preferred change by constitutional methods, and advocated revolutionary action only in the last resort.

LONDON, *Friday, 18th July, 1947*

On the Press liaison side of my work this London visit has, I think, been timely. I have been able to advise a number of editors on the problems that will be facing their correspondents after the transfer of power, and in particular to stress the reality of Partition in terms of news coverage. It would be idle, I said, to hope for balanced treatment of the news by writing about Pakistan affairs from Delhi and Indian developments from Karachi. Although the editors were vaguely aware that the problem existed, not many of them had specifically planned to double their representation on the Indian sub-continent. But I think the effect of my visit has been to give them a greater sense of urgency.

The B.B.C., on the other hand, were all set to launch one of the most ambitious feature and news programmes in their history, and I have had a useful interview with Sir William Haley, in which I delivered, as tactfully as possible (for Haley is clearly very much the maker of his own decisions and the holder of his own views), Mountbatten's request that the emphasis of the visit should be upon contemporary developments. Finally, I have been able to secure the concurrence of the highly competitive news-reel companies to send out one of their best men under a twelve-months rota agreement, which will considerably step up the presentation of Indian news through this powerful medium of publicity in time to cover the transfer-of-power ceremonies.

I have had a long talk with Francis Williams, for whom I have a high esteem. He has a deep insight into Public Relations problems, but I came away feeling very doubtful whether the Government as a whole have any such awareness or would dream of allowing their Public Relations advisers to be on the inside of the big decisions before they are taken in the way that Mountbatten has always insisted that I should be.

I had a number of interesting talks with Woodrow Wyatt, one of the Labour conquerors of Birmingham in the 1945 Election, and almost the only younger M.P. on either side of the House to make India his special subject. He went out as personal assistant to Cripps on the Cabinet Mission, and was also one of the M.P.'s on the Parliamentary delegation to the Far East.

Arising from that Grand Tour, he told me a charming story of his colleague Mrs. Nichol, a forthright Labour M.P. During the delegation's interview with Gandhi she thought that, as the only woman in the party, she ought to give a domestic twist to the conversation, so asked the Mahatma about his children. Had he any daughters? "I have a million daughters," said the Mahatma. "Are you satisfied?" "I am satisfied, Mr. Gandhi," she retorted, "but are you?"

HABBANIYA, *Sunday, 20th July, 1947*

On our journey back we are taking with us Major Billy Short, who has a very great influence with the Sikhs. He was attached to the Cabinet Mission, and was at Baldev Singh's right hand last December. He will not be a member of the Viceroy's staff as such, but will be seconded to advise Ismay, who has deep and well-founded forebodings about Sikh reactions in the Punjab. Short is a delightful companion, a man of wide human sympathies and of creative if slightly eccentric originality, for whom India seems to act both as a lure and as a release.

During the flight, once again carefully timed to avoid all unnecessary inconvenience, Ismay has dictated to his indefatigable secretary, Betty Green, a personal progress report of admirable lucidity and judgement. While the first to admit Mountbatten's great personal triumph in securing the Leaders' endorsement of the 3rd June Plan and the sense of momentary elation it produced, he confessed he felt that we were "over Becher's Brook first time round", and not more than that. He referred to the confidence and courage of ignorance which enabled the Leaders to dismiss from their minds the immense administrative problems they were creating.

" The biggest crime and the biggest headache ", he felt, was the partition of the Armed Forces. But he can take most of the credit for the master plan which has been evolved to achieve a smooth transition. I doubt whether anyone else could have begun to unscramble this egg. He can say with truth, " It is just possible that two really good armies will emerge from the process. It is true that they will not in sum total be equal to the single army out of which they have been fashioned." Provided the Joint Defence Council can be kept in being to ensure that the training, equipment and administration of the two armies are on uniform lines and that they act in accordance with unified policy, he felt that the damage of dissection would be substantially reduced.

He was able to report favourably on the present progress achieved by various sub-committees dealing with the Partition of the manifold assets and liabilities. This had meant that the prospects of both the new Governments being able to function at least on a minimum subsistence scale on the 14th August " are now not nearly so bad as we expected ".

In his concluding paragraphs, however, he sees all the signs of danger ahead. " I was worried when I was in London," he writes, " at the prevalence of the idea that everything was over bar the shouting. Personally I feel that we are nothing like out of the wood yet. There is so much explosive material lying about, and it remains to be seen whether it can be prevented from going off. I am for example extremely worried about the Sikhs. They imagine that they are going to get a far more favourable boundary than, so far as I can judge, the Commission can possibly award them. All possible precautions have been taken by dispatch to the areas of potential trouble of a joint India–Pakistan force under single command, but, even so, it may be a very unpleasant business. The truth of the matter is that both sides are in a panic, and people do sillier things when they are frightened than they do under the stress of any other emotion."

We are returning to a major problem, in some ways bigger than the problem of getting agreement between the political parties, and that is how to fit the Indian States into the new picture. It is not generally realised that the 300 millions in British India are governed by the Governor-General in Council, whereas the 110 millions in the Indian States are governed by their own rulers, but in conformity with the overall directions of the King-Emperor expressed through his Crown Representative, the Political Department and the Residents in each group of States. Co-ordination of the Government of these vast parts of India is achieved by the dodge of appointing one and the same man to be the Governor-General of India and the Crown Representative of the Indian States—and that man is known as the Viceroy. After 15th August there will be no Viceroy, Paramountcy will be retroceded and each Indian Prince will become an autocratic independent sovereign. Unless Mountbatten can get a workable solution accepted by all before 15th August I tremble to think of the chaos that will supervene throughout the sub-continent.

CHAPTER TWELVE

INSTRUMENT OF ACCESSION

VICEROY'S HOUSE, NEW DELHI, *Tuesday, 22nd July, 1947*

W E ARRIVED BACK at Palam this afternoon after a smooth but none-the-less exhausting flight. No one has yet succeeded in making six thousand miles by air a refreshing experience, and after the hectic tempo of events in London we emerged fairly limp to take our part in the vital last lap of the political transfer.

In our absence one crisis—and from the reports we received from Mountbatten when we were in London the severest of all so far in its onset and immediate implications—has been officially disposed of, although tension is still acute. Mountbatten has reconstituted the Interim Government so that it now amounts in effect to two Provisional Administrations, one for India and one for Pakistan, each dealing with its own business and consulting the other only on matters of common concern. The advantage of the plan was that it did not involve any resignation of the Moslem League members.

The order issued last Saturday, some twenty-four hours after the Royal Assent to the Indian Independence Act, spoke of the Governor-General approving "the redistribution of portfolios". Nehru and Patel were with great difficulty reconciled to the new formula. As for Jinnah, when Mountbatten presented the proposals to him he said, yet again, that he would give them his careful attention. But this time Mountbatten was for once in a position to tell him that his views and advice were not required, as he intended on his own initiative and responsibility to issue an order bringing the new arrangements into force forthwith.

With characteristic ingenuity, Mountbatten has prepared for his Staff and all the Ministers and officials concerned in the partition arrangements a small tear-off calendar giving the day of the month, and under it in bold type " X Days left to prepare for the Transfer of Power " until D Day itself is reached. The Partition Council, however, has already taken the hint, functioning smoothly and keeping up to schedule. This is largely due to the excellent briefing it has received from the Steering Committee. H. M. Patel and Mohammed Ali have been putting through a prodigious amount of preliminary work. The result is that at the meeting on the 15th July, for instance, no fewer than seven items which Mountbatten had anticipated would be highly controversial and difficult were disposed of in less than twenty-five minutes. The Partition Council itself has been meeting regularly three times a week.

I saw Mountbatten at 7.15 this evening, and having arrived ahead of my latest letter, unloaded on him many messages and impressions. He was in a most cheerful mood, and full of praise of our efforts in

London. I went on talking to him while he was dressing for dinner, and told him of the various offers, including the British Embassy in Washington, which it was rumoured in London would be made to him. He said once again that he was not in the market, and that his decision remained to keep His Majesty's Government to their promise to let him go back to the Navy, because, for one reason, he was tired out. He asked, incidentally, whether I had seen the latest offer in the Press. It was nothing less than the throne of Germany !

Mountbatten is now in the thick of the States problem. As with his diplomacy prior to the 3rd June Plan, he took the calculated risk, and is personally sponsoring the Instrument of Accession and undertaking to get all the Princes into this particular bag, while V. P. sold the project to Congress. He embarked with the assurance of Patel's decisive support given in a most statesman-like speech inaugurating the new States Department the day we left for London. The most intractable problem, however, is Hyderabad, which will undoubtedly call for special action. Mountbatten says he is ready to go there at short notice, and feels that the only chance of securing a reasonable settlement is to see the Nizam personally.

VICEROY'S HOUSE, NEW DELHI, *Thursday, 24th July, 1947*

I spent most of the day dealing with the release of the important Partition Council statement, which announces the setting up of a Boundary Force in the Punjab Partition areas. This special military command will cover twelve of the fourteen districts which one or other party claims to be " disputed " and will be led by Major-General " Pete " Rees, who until now has been in command of the 4th Indian Division.

The nucleus of the new force will in fact be provided by this Division, and altogether it will consist of some fifty thousand officers and men, mainly composed of mixed units not yet partitioned and containing a high proportion of British officers. It is probably the largest military force ever collected in any one area of a country for the maintenance of law and order in peace-time. It is certainly the greatest physical preparation that can be made from available resources against a danger of unknown dimensions, and it represents a considerable gamble on communal harmony prevailing over the rest of the sub-continent. Rees is to have two high-ranking military advisers—a Sikh and a Moslem—from the Indian and Pakistan Armies. After 15th August he will have operational control of the forces of both Dominions in the area, and, through the Supreme Commander and Joint Defence Council, will be responsible to both Governments.

Mountbatten, who at last week's Partition Council was given *carte blanche* to draft the whole statement, has also succeeded in injecting into it a solemn guarantee of civil rights for minorities and former political opponents in both the future Dominions and a clear declaration that violence will not be tolerated on either side, particularly in the areas affected by the Boundary Commission Awards. He is greatly excited over this coup, but frankly does not believe that either Party really knew what it was signing. He feels, however, that this part of the statement is potentially more important than the Gandhi–Jinnah Appeal last April, and may well become a " charter of liberty " for all communities.

Perhaps the most substantial phrase of all is the joint pledge to abide by the Boundary Commission's award, whatever form it may take. Taken as a whole, the statement is a blue-print on the grand scale, and a considerable moral victory for Mountbatten's diplomacy.

VICEROY'S HOUSE, NEW DELHI, *Friday, 25th July, 1947*

To-day Mountbatten had his first and last meeting with the Princes. For never again will they be addressed in full session by a Viceroy and Crown Representative. This was no formal hail and farewell, but a political occasion of the first order. The Princes are divided and uncertain, baffled by the pace of events. Mountbatten for his part had no detailed directives from London to support him. The brief references to the States both in the 3rd June and Cabinet Mission Plans only serve to underline that the essential transfer of power is between Britain and British India.

At the Council House the red carpet had been duly laid out for His Excellency and Their Highnesses and the Chancellor of the Chamber of Princes, the formidable bearded Maharaja of Patiala, with V. P. Menon looking like a dwarf beside this six-foot-four giant of a man, waited to greet Mountbatten at the entrance. V. P. is here in his capacity as Secretary designate to the Ministry of States, having been specially selected by Patel, with Mountbatten's warm approval, to be his right-hand man in what may well be the key administrative post in the new regime.

Some forty of the greater Princes and their representatives were lined up in the small ante-chamber for special introduction, while a half-dozen accredited photographers jostled unceremoniously for vantage points among them. It was stiflingly hot, and the portly Jam Sahib of Nawanagar stood directly under the one fan, complaining that it moved round far too slowly. Altogether twenty-five of the major ruling Princes and seventy-four States representatives were present in the semi-circular Chamber of Princes.

When Mountbatten rose from his rostrum to address this august assembly, a brief interval was allowed for the camera-men to photograph the historic scene. Mountbatten, as usual, was very patient while the battery of flash-bulbs burst around him. On this occasion some of the photographers were a trifle over-zealous and, running up and down the aisles, threatened to convert the proceedings into one of the more zany episodes of a Marx Brothers film. In so far as the speech was strictly confidential, Mountbatten could not begin to speak until they had left the Chamber, and I had to get up from my place beside V. P. just under the rostrum and virtually chase them out.

Mountbatten was in full uniform, with an array of orders and decorations calculated to astonish even these practitioners in Princely pomp. Once again he spoke without any notes, and was never at a loss for word or phrase. The speech was a perfect blend of the formal and the conversational, and caused me to think yet again how well adapted his oratorical style was to the British House of Commons and what a formidable Parliamentarian he would have made. His fluency was matched only by his extraordinary frankness.

He used every weapon in his armoury of persuasion, making it clear at the outset that in the proposed Instrument of Accession, which V. P. Menon had devised, they were being provided with a political offer from the Congress which was not likely to be repeated. Indeed, it was not even a firm offer as yet, and the main chance of it being one rested on his capacity to provide Patel with " a full basket " of acceptance. He reminded them that after the 15th August he would no longer be in a position to mediate on their behalf as Crown Representative, and warned those Princes who were hoping to build up their own store of arms that the weapons they would be likely to get would in any case be obsolete. One point in particular, made with perfect timing and emphasis, did not fail to find its mark with Their Highnesses. If, he said, the Instrument of Accession was accepted, he had good reason to think that Patel and the Congress would not interfere with their receiving honours and titles from the King under Dominion Status, which he knew meant much to them as exponents of the monarchical order.* In this connection it has undoubtedly been a source of strength in his relations with the Princes that Mountbatten has been able to speak not simply as Crown Representative, but as a cousin of the King. For these hereditary rulers the blood Royal carries its own authority. The core of his message this afternoon was contained in the cogent phrase, " You cannot run away from the Dominion Government which is your neighbour any more than you can run away from the subjects for whose welfare you are responsible ".

I cannot imagine, however, a more difficult assembly for any man to have to address than this one. Here was, in fact, an audience of hereditary shepherds in the unenviable position of lost sheep. Once again Mountbatten's morale-raising talent was seen to full advantage. For he somehow managed to infect them with his own spontaneous enthusiasm and powers of decision. In the process what began as an occasion of high seriousness soon developed into one of flippancy and banter, as Mountbatten began to deal with the mass of questions cogent and obtuse which were thrown at him.

Thus a certain Maharaja, absent from his State and from India at this critical moment, did not seem to appreciate the importance either of coming himself to the meeting or even of briefing his Dewan. For the Dewan had been sent no instructions whatever. " Surely ", Mountbatten asked, " you must know your Ruler's mind, and can take a decision on his behalf? " " I do not know my Ruler's mind," the hapless Dewan replied, " and I cannot get a reply by cable." Mountbatten thereupon picked up a large round glass paper-weight which happened to be on the rostrum in front of him. " I will look into my crystal," he said, " and give you an answer." There followed ten seconds of dramatic pause when you could have heard a princely pin drop. " His Highness,"

---

* Lord Mountbatten himself invested the Maharajas of Jaipur and Bikaner with the Grand Cross of the Star of India (G.C.S.I.) after the transfer of power.

Mountbatten solemnly announced, " asks you to sign the Instrument of Accession."

So accurately had he gauged the sentiment of this particular audience that everyone broke out into delighted laughter at this sally, which was clearly regarded as neatly combining the rebuke courteous with the advice timely. For on the whole it was probably wise to strike the humorous note as being the best method of penetrating what seemed to be quite a high proportion of thick skulls.

I returned to Viceroy's House and had a chat with Mountbatten, who had changed with remarkable speed from his " Number Tens " into a lounge suit. I was able to report that his whole performance, which was technically and tactically hardly less remarkable than the Press Conference, had made a very deep impression on all sides. I said it was clear that we would have to produce for the Press a sub-edited edition of the full confidential speech, and I proposed to go straight round and work on this with V. P. Whatever V. P. and I produced, he said, would satisfy him, and he did not want to see the text again. He felt that the questions had been incredibly unrealistic, and that very few of the Princes or their representatives seemed to have any idea of what was going on around them. Unless they accepted the Instrument they would be finished.

He then paid a very high tribute to V. P., saying that he had really come to love him, and that he had one of the most statesman-like minds he had ever encountered. He then recalled the element of chance which had brought V. P. and his ideas to the fore. The turning-point had undoubtedly been our visit to Simla in May and Mountbatten's " hunch " decision to show the Plan to Nehru. This had given V. P. his chance to submit the alternative draft with its Dominion Status formula. V. P. had confessed to him that when he first put up the idea at Staff level, only to have it turned down, he almost burst into tears. George Abell has been the first to admit that Mountbatten's vision and good sense in bringing V. P. right into the policy-making fold has been perhaps the biggest single personal factor in our success to date.

I duly went over to V. P.'s office, and we had no less than a three-hour session on the speech. It was a hard slog. But by 9.30 p.m. we had produced an authorised version which we felt had clearly separated off the publishable from the private without distorting the sense of the argument or the structure of the phrases. I must say there were still one or two sentences left in that worried me a little, and I was particularly anxious about the possible reaction in London.

None-the-less Mountbatten can regard the whole occasion as yet another personal *tour de force*. The Princes, leaderless, riven with dynastic and political dissensions, tried desperately to hide behind opportunism and indecision, but events were moving much too fast and on too large a scale to allow of any such halting tactics. Whatever the merits of earlier policies, the situation which Mountbatten as the last Crown Representative has to meet is such that only through some comprehensive and substantial act of mediatisation can the Princely order in India hope to avoid being swept away as a feudal anachronism. By a far-seeing act of statesmanship he has offered them the chance of survival, admittedly out of the main stream of Indian power politics, but with their basic personal prerogatives and succession rights secured. The times are out of joint for the Princes. This is all now that any of them can expect or, indeed, that most of them want.

VICEROY'S HOUSE, NEW DELHI, *Saturday, 26th July, 1947*

I had an interesting talk with George Abell about the dinner-party Their Excellencies gave last night to the Jinnahs. It was quite a small and informal affair, comprising only House guests and some of Mountbatten's staff. Jinnah completely monopolised the conversation by cracking a series of very lengthy and generally unfunny jokes. When Mountbatten tried to even out the conversation by talking to the guests next to him and leaving Jinnah to tell one of his stories to Lady Mountbatten, Jinnah broke off and interrupted across the table with, " I think Mountbatten would like to hear this one." It is customary for the Viceroy, representing the King, to precede his guests to and from the dining-room, but immediately this dinner was over the Jinnahs got up at the same time as Their Excellencies and walked out with them.

After dinner George said that in the spirit of a man who would in any case be leaving on the 15th August he attacked Jinnah for his handling of the Sikhs and on the grounds that men were being appointed in the West Punjab boundary areas whom he (George) knew to be inefficient. Jinnah apparently took it well, confining himself to the observation that he knew his people best. He only warmed up slightly when George observed that the trouble was that a statesman of Jinnah's calibre could not be everywhere at once, and that he had no doubt not been to see the particular men under criticism. Jinnah's attitude to the Sikh situation is, George feels, perilously unsound.

VICEROY'S HOUSE, NEW DELHI, *Sunday, 27th July, 1947*

Once again Mountbatten sent for me while he was immersed in a cold bath. He told me what is now an amusing but easily could have been a very different story. He was thrashing out with Lord Killearn, whom he had invited up from Singapore, the possibility of him accepting the Governorship of East Bengal, as Jinnah is very anxious to have a high-calibre British administrator acting for him in this outpost of Pakistan. They were discussing terms of service, and Killearn asked whether there was any possibility of Darjeeling being included in the Province, and if not whether some special arrangements could be made for him to stay at one of the Assam hill stations, such as Shillong, in the very hot weather. He said he was now sixty-six, had some young children and would not be able to survive the heat of Dacca the capital. Moreover, he understood the proposed residence of the Governor in Dacca was in a quite derelict condition. Mountbatten promised to look into the whole matter.

It so happened that his next interview was with Bardoloi, Prime Minister of Assam. After dealing with a number of routine questions on Assam which he was able to dispatch in a few minutes, he asked about Dacca. Was there any high ground there? Bardoloi said there was nothing higher than eleven hundred feet in the whole area. Mountbatten then asked about Darjeeling and which way the Award was likely to send it—into Pakistan or India? Bardoloi replied that it was almost certain to remain in India. Mountbatten then raised questions about Shillong and the Hill Tracts.

The purpose of these inquiries was completely misunderstood by Bardoloi, who rushed over to Gandhi in a state of great alarm, complaining that there was some major intrigue afoot to incorporate Darjeeling, Shillong and the Hill Tracts into Pakistan. Gandhi for his part said that while he did not put it past the British to organise a double-cross of this nature, he could not believe that Mountbatten himself would be a party to it. Bardoloi then saw Patel, who worked himself up into a state of great distress about it all. The result was that V. P. rushed up to Mountbatten's bedroom this morning full of alarm.

Mountbatten was of course able to explain the whole thing, and hopes in the next day or so to be able to laugh it off with the Congress leaders, but he regards the incident as revealing, and points out that if he had not established close relations with V. P. and if V. P. had not felt himself able to go straight to his bedroom this morning, this petty misunderstanding could easily have developed into a major crisis, and may still involve a considerable expenditure of time and effort to explain away to the satisfaction of all.

VICEROY'S HOUSE, NEW DELHI, *Monday, 28th July, 1947*

There was a colourful reception at Viceroy's House to-night in honour of over fifty Ruling Princes and a hundred of the States Representatives. The splendour of it only seemed to strengthen the sense of unreality and pathos surrounding the Princeely order at this time. When unity of purpose was of overwhelming importance for them, they were to be seen uneasy and obsessed with their own problems of precedence, each anxiously watching what the other was doing—and, as a Dewan remarked of one of them, " wandering about like a letter without a stamp ".

Those of Their Highnesses who had not already signified their intention of signing the Instrument of Accession were duly shepherded by the A.D.C.'s one by one for a friendly talk with Mountbatten. He in his turn passed them on in the full view of the company to V. P., who conducted them across the room to see Patel. There were Maharajas three deep in a semi-circle watching this process.

One veteran Prince was heard to remark, " Who's H.E. getting to work on now?" Craning forward to see, he added with relish, " There's no need for him to work on me. I'm signing to-morrow! " Fay overheard the following exchange between an old Prince and a young one. The old Prince asked, " How are things in your State?" The young Prince replied, " We have been having trouble in one place (which he named), but we have reached a settlement now." "We have trouble everywhere," the old Prince exclaimed, "but I don't let it reach the stage of a settlement."

VICEROY'S HOUSE, NEW DELHI, *Wednesday, 30th July, 1947*

Mountbatten left at first light this morning for Calcutta, where he is to make a rapid last-minute survey of the critical situation there. He rang up late last night asking me to deal with a number of minor Press problems as though the whole transfer of power depended on their solution. I have rarely found him difficult on the big things. It is the minutiæ that wear him down and tease his staff. To be of real value to him and survive as a member of his entourage, it is advisable to keep him at arm's length from these small problems, but occasionally he tracks one down when you are not looking.

During the brief lull provided by his absence I have to-day had my long-promised interview with Gandhi, arriving at midday for an appointment at his home among the Untouchables in the Bhangi Colony. Rajkumari Amrit Kaur has been trying to arrange this meeting for me ever since I first met her at Simla in May.

Gandhi's choice of the Bhangi Colony for his home in Delhi was, of course, one of his great symbolic acts. But even asceticism has its administrative problems, and it was, I believe, the famous Mrs. Sarojini Naidu who was once moved to exclaim about Bhangi, "If only Bapu knew the cost of setting him up in poverty!" Yet the poverty surrounding him here is real enough. The Colony stands on the verge of the wasteland that encircles Delhi, and is set against a background of barren boulders and dusty earth.

Two rather shabby sentries asked for my name, and passed me on to a secretary, who gave me such casual direction that I did not know quite where to go until a second secretary appeared on the scene. He conducted me to a bare little room where, I was told afterwards, Gandhi both works and sleeps. I found him on a platform raised a few inches off the ground and reposing on some cushions with a very large bolster at his back. During our conversation two secretaries came in silently, and behaved as well-trained acolytes are expected to do.

As I entered Gandhi said smilingly, "You will not expect me to get up." I was offered a chair, but I chose—almost subconsciously—to sit down cross-legged in front of him. I began by recalling that the last time I had the privilege of meeting him was seventeen years ago, when I was a boy at Westminster School. He had come very unexpectedly to speak to us, and we had all been deeply impressed by the event. He said he half-remembered the occasion, and added that he had been invited by some very kind Canon. I recalled that two days afterwards Lord Halifax had also come to the School to address us, and that in that year of the Irwin–Gandhi Pact the abiding memory was of the cordial terms in which each had spoken of the other. Both had left on our schoolboy minds the impression that here was the essential human good-will from which a genuine agreement could spring. "I was very close to Lord

Halifax in those days," Gandhi said almost wistfully; "not that I am not so now."

I said that I had just come back from London, where I had witnessed the Indian Independence Bill pass through both Houses of Parliament. I took the occasion to present Gandhi with three copies of the Hansards of those Debates—a gesture that seemed to please him—and drew particular attention to Lord Samuel's tribute to him in the Lords. He said he had noticed it, and that it was very kind of him to have made these remarks. He had once had some correspondence with Lord Samuel, and in the argument Lord Samuel had been magnanimous enough to admit himself in the wrong. That, Gandhi observed, was a very good sign in a man.

Turning to the general situation arising from the Act, he said that with the casting off of British domination the most tremendous responsibility had been thrown upon the Congress leaders, who had been brought up on only a few lakhs of rupees, and now had the vast resources of a State at their disposal. Both Governments needed time, a breathing space in which to establish themselves. He regarded Partition as an evil, but was ready to admit that out of evil could come good, if only the two Governments would play fair with each other. I said that it was not simply the future of India that was at stake, but that of the whole of Asia. The countries of South-east Asia in particular were looking to India, and the Chinese civil war only enhanced India's potential influence. He agreed emphatically. "The whole world", he said, "is looking to us. India is under the microscope."

When I turned to my particular business and interest here—the Press—I mentioned the need for Indian papers to begin taking a world view, and for Indian journalists to gain new experience in overseas assignments. He agreed that the need existed, but this particular contention inspired him to take up a favourite theme of his. "There is", he said, "a dangerous tendency for Indians to look to others for salvation. We must keep our self-respect and help ourselves. Look at the case of medicine and doctors. I do not know of a single Englishman who has come to India for treatment, but one is always hearing of Indians going abroad to be treated by this or that famous European surgeon. It is not right that India should only be a place for Indians to die in. There are many splendid surgeons, including Dr. Ansari. Admittedly", he added mischievously, "Dr. Ansari is concerned primarily with rejuvenation and offering one the chance of becoming thirty again and having a harem!"

The core of his argument was that with India now having won her political freedom it was the duty of Indians to show their faith and pride in their country not only by words but also by deeds. They had to realise that the amenities and assets which they had assumed were the monopolies of the outside world were not inevitably so at all. This was the real challenge of Indian Independence.

I was with him for just on three-quarters of an hour. Two girl secretaries steadily took notes of the Mahatma's words. Other followers of his came and went almost imperceptibly. Rajkumari sat at his right hand throughout the talk, but said very little. The sense of awe among the acolytes exceeded anything I had witnessed since attending an audience of Pope Pius XI; and as for the charm and magnetism of Gandhiji himself, the only similar experience I could recall was a long talk with Lloyd George in 1936. The contrasts in pomp and circumstance, between the Vatican and the Bhangi Colony, the Mahatma and the Wizard from Wales, are sufficiently obvious to be misleading. The points of religious and political comparison are perhaps the deeper reality.

VICEROY'S HOUSE, NEW DELHI, *Friday, 1st August, 1947*

I was given an account of to-day's luncheon at Viceroy's House to several of the leading Princes. After paying their bread-and-butter respects to Their Excellencies, they ran the gauntlet of A.D.C.'s, who helped to form virtual " Aye " and " No " lobbies on their attitude to Accession. Patiala and Bikaner entered into the spirit of the thing by passing through the " No " lobby and then roaring with laughter.

Apart from Hyderabad and Kashmir, which present special problems, Mountbatten's advice is having a decisive effect, and only two or three of the senior Princes seem to consider there is any advantage or merit in holding out against Accession. Unfortunately, Mountbatten's friend Bhopal is the leader of this group, which includes his close and important neighbour, the Maharaja of Indore. As the ablest Moslem Prince, I would guess he is not averse to playing an important role in the higher politics of Pakistan. He has for some time been one of Jinnah's closest advisers. Unhappily for him, his State is predominantly Hindu and in the heart of Indian territory.

VICEROY'S HOUSE, NEW DELHI, *Sunday, 3rd August, 1947*

Mountbatten is anxious to do all in his power to be available personally to those Princes for whom the act of Accession presents special difficulties; but as D Day approaches the volume of duties and decisions grows to fantastic proportions. So it is that he has asked me to keep in close touch with the Maharaj Rana of Dholpur and act in a personal and wholly unofficial liaison capacity between himself and His Highness, who is another old friend of his from the days of the Prince of Wales' tour in 1921, when they were A.D.C.'s together.

From the long talk I have had with him I find that he is a man of scholarly, almost pedantic, tastes and of an ascetic disposition. He is a fervent believer in the theory and practice of the Divine Right of Kings. He did not hesitate to quote with approval the example and doctrines of the Stuarts. He had, in fact, an almost mystical concept both of his status with the Raj and of his relationship with his subjects. In spite of these lofty views about his prerogatives, he is most unpretentious in his appearance and manner—a little man not much taller than Gandhiji, who under a pink turban wears a wistful expression.

He speaks slowly and with deep emotion at the ending of his treaty relationship with Britain. The tone is not one of anger, but of resignation. He has about him the peculiar melancholy of the fatalist. It is not sufficient to argue with such a man in terms of tactical self-interest. Essentially he is in search of sympathy and of the assurance that whatever course he takes Dholpur can do no wrong. Deep down he has no belief in the survival value of the new Indian Dominion, and contrasts unfavourably its recent and revolutionary origins with the long loyalist traditions of his own dynasty—his Paramountcy Treaty with Britain going back as far as 1765. It is tragic to see so sensitive and sincere a man confronted with such a dilemma. The landslide of Independence moves too quickly for him. If he were less conscientious he would find it easier to step aside.

The burden of work falling upon Mountbatten and his staff seems, if anything, to increase as each day brings us nearer to the transfer of power. I have enough Public Relations and Press problems calling for immediate decision and implementation to keep a whole Central Office of Information busy. Very careful thought has to be given to the planning of the elaborate ceremonial in Karachi and Delhi. Jinnah has raised difficulties about the degree of precedence to be accorded to Mountbatten in Karachi on 13th August. It has been politely but none-the-less firmly made clear to him that His Excellency's visit will be in his capacity as Viceroy, and any proposal that he should sit below Jinnah at the special meeting of the Legislative Assembly is therefore out of the question.

My tasks include submission of drafts for the King's messages to the two new Dominions, and assistance in polishing the texts of Mountbatten's formal Addresses to the two Legislative Assemblies, which all involve delicate problems of emphasis. Mountbatten would prefer to speak without any notes, but we have all prevailed upon him to admit, somewhat grudgingly, that this would be inappropriate on such historic and formal occasions, with the world's Press and radio picking up every word.

VICEROY'S HOUSE, NEW DELHI, *Monday, 4th August, 1947*

Having seen the draft schedule of arrangements for Independence Day in Delhi, I have come to the conclusion that they have too much British pomp and circumstance about them and lack some imaginative and informal act of identification with the Indian people. Accordingly, I have been round to see Mr. Kurshid, Commissioner for Delhi, and discovered that the municipality is proposing to give a party to some five thousand children in the gardens of the Roshanara Club in old Delhi. This seemed to me to be a perfect occasion for the Mountbattens to be present without ceremony. For at moments of great rejoicing Indians traditionally express themselves through celebrations for the children.

In spite of the misgivings of the unfortunate Douglas Currie, who had to organise perhaps the most exacting agenda that has ever fallen to the lot of any Military Secretary, Mountbatten agreed that the good-will value of such a visit outweighed administrative difficulties and security risk.

VICEROY'S HOUSE, NEW DELHI, *Tuesday, 5th August, 1947*

Following to-day's Partition Council and Joint Defence Council meetings, Mountbatten was in secret conclave with Patel, Jinnah and

Liaquat, having decided to introduce them to an officer of the now depleted Punjab Criminal Investigation Department sent down by Jenkins to give him a verbal report. This officer told of various statements made by instigators of disturbances arrested after incidents. These interrogations and intelligence from other sources implicated the Sikh leaders in a number of sabotage plans, including a plot to assassinate Jinnah during the State drive at the Independence celebrations in Karachi next week. Jinnah and Liaquat immediately demanded the arrest of Tara Singh and other Sikh leaders. Patel, however, was strongly opposed to this course, arguing that it would only precipitate a crisis already beyond control.

Mountbatten said he was prepared to support the arrests, but only if the authorities on the spot felt that this would be a wise step. He has therefore written off to Jenkins to consider with Trivedi and Mudie,★ the Governors designate of the East and West Punjabs, as a matter of urgency the desirability of arresting Tara Singh and his more hot-headed colleagues shortly before the 15th August.

Mountbatten has a very high opinion of Jenkins, who has held the fort in the Punjab under conditions of intolerable strain and slander. No man could have done more to preserve the last vestiges of order in the distracted Province. He deserves, but is far from receiving, the gratitude of both sides for his unremitting labours.

VICEROY'S HOUSE, NEW DELHI, *Thursday, 7th August, 1947*

We have our lighter moments. The Minutes of the sixty-eighth Viceroy's Staff Meeting held this evening begin as follows: Item 1. Astrology. The Viceroy said that he had just seen Mr. Mangaldas Pakwasa, the Governor Designate of the Central Provinces, and suggested that he should go down on the 13th rather than the 14th August to start taking over from Sir Frederick Bourne, thus enabling Bourne to leave to become Governor of East Bengal by the 15th. Mr. Mangaldas Pakwasa had said that this was out of the question on astrological grounds. The Viceroy pointed out that there was a complete lack on his staff of high-level advisers on astrology. This would be remedied forthwith. "H.E. the Viceroy appointed Press Attaché to the additional and honorary post of Astrologer to the Governor-General."

Following the Staff Meeting I met the cause of my astrological "appointment", Mangaldas Pakwasa, at a small lunch-party given by Vallabhbhai Patel, to which Fay and I were invited. The occasion was informal. In addition to Pakwasa and ourselves, there was only one other guest, an American visitor, Mr. Dall. Shankar, Patel's Private Secretary, who was a contemporary of mine at Oxford, and Maniben, the Sardar's devoted, one might almost say, dedicated, daughter, brought the lunch-party up to seven. Patel's home is nearly next door to

★ Sir Francis Mudie, Governor of Sind until the transfer of power, subsequently accepted an invitation from Mr. Jinnah to serve as the first Governor of West Punjab.

Nehru's and is, if anything, smaller and even less pretentious than the Prime Minister's residence.

It is a commonplace to draw the political contrast between Nehru and Patel, who after the transfer of power are likely to provide India with a virtual duumvirate; but the variations in personality and appearance are hardly less striking. Dressed in his *dhoti*, Patel conjures up the vision of a Roman Emperor in his toga. There are, in fact, Roman qualities about this man—administrative talent, the capacity to take and sustain strong decisions, and a certain serenity which invariably accompanies real strength of character.

He lacks Nehru's world reputation and world outlook, and he has deliberately confined himself to the tasks that involve surveillance of domestic politics. Here his powers and responsibilities are as wide as they well can be; they include control over all Government Information, Internal Security, the Police and, last but not least, the vital problem·of relations with the Indian States. The completion of his Accession policy should bring into the Indian Dominion more citizens than will be lost to it through the creation of Pakistan, for (excluding the twenty millions in Hyderabad and Kashmir) there are some ninety million States' subjects involved, which is considerably more than the population of Pakistan: he also holds in his hands nearly all Congress patronage. This is a formidable concentration of personal power under any régime. In spite of all these preoccupations, Patel has a shrewd grasp of India's strategic position in the world at large.

Off duty, as he was to-day, he is indeed the embodiment of the gentle Hindu, full of benevolence and smiles. He was interested to hear my first-hand account of the passing of the Independence Bill in London, and in the course of conversation the general subject of speech-making cropped up. He and Maniben laughed when I asked whether he enjoyed making speeches, Maniben reminding me that her father was a great orator in Gujerati.

Throughout most of the meal Maniben, who is on the inside of all the Sardar's official and top-secret activities, remained the silent acolyte. Dressed in the austere simplicity of her Khadi *sari*, and wearing at her waist a giant bunch of keys, she gave the impression of an efficient and wholly absorbed comptroller of the domestic household.

Nearly all the Indian leaders are surrounded by women members of their family, whether as wives, sisters or daughters, who exercise an extremely powerful influence on their careers. I had come out to India under the naïve impression that Indian women were completely submerged and had no say or interest in matters of State. This is certainly not the case at the summit of affairs. Miss Fatima Jinnah, Mrs. Vijay-lakshmi Pandit, Begum Liaquat Ali Khan and Mrs. Kripalani are formidable personalities whose ambitions and interests measure up to those of their respective menfolk. Not all of them would be content to remain so quietly in the background as Maniben, but it is doubtful whether the influence of any of them in their respective households exceeds hers with her father.

Moreover, Lady Mountbatten has, I know, been deeply impressed by her contacts with Indian women in the whole field of social service. Not only are their capabilities outstanding, but they are casting off the shackles of subordinate status.   An important facet of Indian Independence is the emancipation of Indian women.   Lady Mountbatten's leadership at this time is giving a great fillip to this liberating process.

VICEROY'S HOUSE, NEW DELHI, *Friday, 8th August, 1947*

Mountbatten has had several requests to broadcast to America, and even one proposal that he should hold everything to visit the U.S.A. as the star guest at a big Press-sponsored convention! In view of the tremendous pressure upon his time and energies, it has been necessary automatically to turn down all requests, but on my advice he has agreed to speak in a special programme which is being broadcast throughout the United States to celebrate the second anniversary of V.J. day, and will include the recorded voices of the leaders of nearly all the United Nations. Although he will be on the air for only three minutes, I feel this presents a splendid opportunity to drive home the double meaning of the 15th August.   He asked me to prepare him a draft, which he has substantially accepted.

After approving the elaborate arrangements for him to broadcast a recording of his message from his study, his words were beamed from All India Radio via the B.B.C. to America for actual transmission on the 15th.   "Two years ago to-day", he declared, "I had just returned from the Potsdam Conference, and was in the Prime Minister's room in 10 Downing Street, when the news of the Japanese surrender came through.   Here, as I speak to you to-night in Delhi, we are celebrating an event no less momentous for the future of the world—India's Independence Day.   In the Atlantic Charter, we, the British and Americans, dedicated ourselves to champion the self-determination of peoples and the independence of nations.   Bitter experience has taught us that it is often easier to win a war than to achieve a war aim; so let us remember August 15th—V.J. Day—not only as the celebration of a victory, but also as the fulfilment of a pledge."

VICEROY'S HOUSE, NEW DELHI, *Saturday, 9th August, 1947*

At our Staff Meeting to-day we had a full discussion on the Punjab crisis.   Over and above reports from Jenkins of a most serious situation in the boundary area, and urgent requests from him for more army, air and police reinforcements, Mountbatten was confronted with a Public Relations problem of some magnitude which had a direct bearing on the maintenance of morale and order.

It is rumoured that Radcliffe will be ready by this evening to hand over the Award of the Punjab Boundary Commission to the Viceroy. Following the expected but none-the-less complete failure of his Hindu and Moslem colleagues to reach any semblance of agreement, Radcliffe, under the terms of reference, has had only to consult himself.   Responsibility for publication, however, rests with the Viceroy.   Mountbatten from the outset had given his staff the most explicit directions that they were to have no contact whatever with Radcliffe while he was engaged on his difficult and delicate arbitral task and has himself kept clear of him after the first welcome. We had accordingly no firm knowledge how far or by what route he had proceeded.

Various points of view about publication were put forward. On administrative grounds it was argued that earliest possible announcement would be of help to Jenkins and would enable last-minute troop movements to be made into the affected areas in advance of the transfer of power. Alternatively, it was suggested that in so far as the Award would in any case be bound to touch off trouble, the best date to release it would be on the 14th August. Mountbatten said that if he could exercise some discretion in the matter he would much prefer to postpone its appearance until after the Independence Day celebrations, feeling that the problem of its timing was really one of psychology, and that the controversy and grief that it was bound to arouse on both sides should not be allowed to mar Independence Day itself.

With this view I wholly concur, and would go further, and say that for the Radcliffe Award to precede or coincide with Independence Day would be to risk destroying at one stroke the whole symbolic significance of freedom to Hindu, Moslem and Sikh alike. The Indian's facility for friendship can be so easily frustrated, his expectations and environment alike make the margin between happiness and mourning dangerously narrow. The condition of his joy is that it should be unconfined, and that he should have a temporary reprieve from his eternal fears.

No final decision was taken at our meeting to-day, and Abell was instructed further to discuss the timing problem with Jenkins. To underline the independent status of the commission, Mountbatten decided that the announcement when it was made should not be in the form of a communiqué from Viceroy's House, but should be published as a Gazette Extraordinary.

Jenkins has firmly rejected any suggestion that the Sikh leaders should be arrested before 15th August. He has advised Mountbatten that he thoroughly discussed the suggestion with Mudie and Trivedi, and they were all unanimous in recommending that such arrests would be more likely to endanger than improve the present precarious situation. All three had therefore decided that no arrests should be made. Mountbatten feels that as he has arranged to drive with Jinnah in the State procession, which is the occasion mentioned for the possible attempt on Jinnah's life, he can accept their decision without personal reproach.

VICEROY'S HOUSE, NEW DELHI, *Monday, 11th August, 1947*

To-night was one of family farewells. It began with Mountbatten conferring a knighthood on George Abell, and never was the sword laid on more deserving shoulder. He also decorated Ian Scott and Peter Scott with the C.I.E. and O.B.E. respectively. The I.C.S. members and Sir Eric Miéville, who is far from well, will all be leaving us on the 15th. They, together with V. P., helped to make the Staff party serving Mountbatten the finest team it has been my privilege to work with. George Abell was the pivotal figure. He had to adapt himself not only to a new Viceroy but to an administrative régime which involved his own subordination to Ismay and Miéville, both senior to himself and with long Indian experience behind them. The loyalty and grace with which he has met this situation have been admirable to behold.

Abell is one of those fabulous Olympians of double First and treble Blue vintage with the capacity for taking every form of work or play in his stride. But, for all his overwhelming talents, he himself does not overwhelm and has unusual charm. It has been tragic to find him the target of so much grotesque and self-defeating Congress propaganda.

I have been very gratified by his appreciation of my particular function in the team. He told me quite frankly that he had no idea of the potentialities of a full-time Press Attaché in the Viceregal hierarchy, and seriously regrets that there was no such post during Wavell's Simla negotiations. He said that the contrast between Wavell and Mountbatten was striking. Each had what the other one lacked, and each was a great man—embody them in one human being, and he was sure you would have one of the greatest statesmen that had ever lived!

VICEROY'S HOUSE, NEW DELHI, *Tuesday, 12th August, 1947*

Three days have passed since the first warning, and the Award is still not ready. At this afternoon's Staff Meeting—our seventieth and probably the last—Mountbatten agreed, in view of the uncertainty and our impending departure for Karachi, that John Christie and I should call on Radcliffe immediately to find out when we might expect the Awards to be in the Viceroy's hands.

For the duration of his stay in Delhi Radcliffe was given the Comptroller's House on the Viceregal estate, where he could work in isolation. Christie and I, hurrying round at very short notice, arrived to find that he was changing for dinner. When he appeared on the scene it was clear that our interview would not be an easy one, and that he was just as much alive to the proprieties of the situation as we were. He explained that both the Punjab and Bengal Awards were complete and ready, but that the Sylhet Award was not.

It seemed, therefore, that unless Mountbatten was to make a major issue of the matter, it would be physically very difficult for all three Awards to come into his possession before his return to Delhi on the evening of 14th August, or for the texts to be printed and available before the 16th—Independence Day itself being a national holiday. We returned at once to Viceroy's House and advised Mountbatten of the position, who was greatly relieved to have this ready-made solution at his disposal.

CHAPTER THIRTEEN

INDEPENDENCE DAYS

GOVERNMENT HOUSE, KARACHI, *Wednesday, 13th August, 1947*

MOUNTBATTEN LEFT FOR Karachi this morning to perform his last official duty as Viceroy of a united British India. This is, appropriately enough, to convey His Majesty's and his own greetings to the new Dominion of Pakistan on the eve of its inception. As we stepped off the aircraft, Their Excellencies were greeted by Hidiyatullah, the benign Governor-elect of Sind. There was also the usual bevy of photographers. As they drove off to Government House, Colonel Birnie, Jinnah's Military Secretary, told Mountbatten that he had been given information of a plot to throw a bomb at Jinnah during to-morrow's State procession, and that there had been discussions as to whether to cancel the drive or alter the route. Jinnah, however, had taken the view that if Mountbatten was ready to go through with the drive, then so was he. Mountbatten at once agreed that there should be no change of arrangements.

Jinnah and Miss Jinnah were awaiting the Mountbattens in the entrance hall, which had been decked up to look just like a Hollywood film-set, and all four were subjected to takings and re-takings under the dazzling light and sizzling heat of the arc-lamps. I made contact with Colonel Malik, the Government Information officer, at the Palace Hotel, and met some of the Foreign correspondents, who were rather critical of the Karachi proceedings to date. Some argued that Mountbatten had been insulted by Jinnah not being at the airfield to meet him, but I at once explained that I was sure Mountbatten did not consider that there had been any lack of courtesy or breach of etiquette involved. At yesterday's Constituent Assembly there had been, they said, an atmosphere of complete subservience, with everyone vying to outdo everyone else in verbal prostration before the Quaid-e-Azam.

In answer to my explicit inquiries, Malik gave me clearly to understand that Jinnah was not proposing to make any set speech for publication at to-night's banquet, and I advised Mountbatten accordingly. Imagine my surprise when, towards the end of the banquet, before all the assembled notabilities, comprising not only the Pakistan élite but a far from negligible nucleus of a Diplomatic Corps, Jinnah arose, adjusted his monocle and began reading with deliberate and somewhat laboured emphasis from a set script. The speech turned out to be one of considerable political significance, in particular for its cordial references to the new Dominion's future relationship with Britain and to Mountbatten's contribution to the creation of Pakistan.

If Mountbatten felt any dismay at being caught in this oratorical ambush he certainly did not show it, and by a fine feat of improvisation gave the impression of being even more word perfect than the Quaid-e-

Azam with his notes. For ten minutes the appropriate phrases and thoughts flowed from him in smooth sequence. He is a born raconteur, and his informal but quick-firing eloquence is ideally adapted to after-dinner speech-making.

This was not the only hazard triumphantly surmounted to-night. About a quarter of an hour before we were all due to take our places at dinner, young Lieutenant Ahsan, whose first day it was as A.D.C. to Jinnah, following his transfer from Viceroy's House, discovered that three distinguished guests high up on the table plan had failed to arrive. Bill Birnie and the wretched A.D.C.'s were thus left with the decision whether to leave gaps in high places or undertake the revision of the seating plan throughout. With stout resolve, they chose the latter course. Mountbatten and Jinnah were at once advised of the dilemma, and played their part in the operation by maintaining preprandial small talk for over half an hour, while the staff made feverish rearrangements.

After dinner we were merged in a larger reception, and to an accompaniment of soft drinks and sweet music played by a band of bearded warriors in kilts, the party ran its appointed course. Considering what lay behind all the arrangements—the hurried last-minute arrival of so many officials, the creation of a Government and a régime almost overnight—the reception was an administrative triumph. Jinnah himself as the host and hero of the occasion was an aloof, almost lonely figure, which may have helped to create a somewhat subdued atmosphere at this historic moment. He was to be seen, with his silver hair and immaculate white *ashkan*, towering above most of his guests, and talking to very few of them. They, for their part, did not presume to button-hole him. Here, indeed, was the apotheosis of leadership by remote control.

I had never dreamt that the creator of a nation at the moment of reaching the promised land could, when surrounded by his devoted followers, be at such a distance from them. Finding him standing alone, I spoke with him for a few moments. I tried to find suitable words of congratulation, but they died away before his mood of preoccupation, almost of reverie.

GOVERNMENT HOUSE, KARACHI AND GOVERNMENT HOUSE
NEW DELHI, *Thursday–Friday, 14th–15th August, 1947*

Accommodation at Government House, Karachi, is strictly limited. The number of V.I.P.'s here for to-day's ceremonies has taxed Bill Birnie's resources to the utmost. Housing and hotel shortage is acute; but by dint of dispersing and doubling up we were all successfully accommodated.

We were up early this morning for the ceremonies at the Legislative Assembly. I arrived about half an hour before Jinnah and the Mountbattens, passing along part of the official route. Neither the scale nor the enthusiasm of the crowds was anything like as great as I had expected. It did not seem to be on a higher pitch than some annual opening of Parliament. In the grounds facing the Assembly, however, with its small, semi-circular, shell-shaped chamber, every available inch was occupied. The Mountbattens as they drove up were given the same cordial reception as the Jinnahs, who had arrived a few minutes ahead of them. Cordiality, too, was the key-note of both Mountbatten's and Jinnah's speeches and of the reaction of the assembled Members. The precedence problem died a natural death. Lady Mountbatten pressed Miss Jinnah's hand affectionately as Jinnah sat down after giving his address.

If Jinnah's personality is cold and remote, it also has a magnetic quality —the sense of leadership is almost overpowering. He makes only the most superficial attempt to disguise himself as a constitutional Governor-General, and one of his first acts after putting his name forward was to apply for powers under the 9th Schedule rather than Part II of the 1935 Act which gave him at once dictatorial powers unknown to any constitutional Governor-General representing the King. Here indeed is Pakistan's King Emperor, Archbishop of Canterbury, Speaker and Prime Minister concentrated into one formidable Quaid-e-Azam.

The proceedings were over within the hour, and Jinnah and Mountbatten drove back in State together. Once again the greetings of the crowd, apart from some lorry-loads of hilarious sailors of the Pakistan Navy and the usual excitement of children, were decorous rather than ecstatic. As they turned in at the gates of Government House, Jinnah put his hand on Mountbatten's knee and said with evident emotion, " Thank God I have brought you back alive." By midday the Mountbattens had paid their last farewells—Miss Jinnah embracing Lady Mountbatten, and Jinnah, still emotional, declaring his eternal gratitude and friendship. They were flying back to the tremendous ceremonial round confronting them in Delhi.

As we passed over the Boundary area of the Punjab we could see several large fires, beacons of ill-omen dominating the landscape for miles around.

No sooner had we touched down than I was caught in a whirl of last-minute publicity arrangements. Tight and complex time schedules are involved, rehearsals with photographers and camera-men, discussions with the Information Ministry, distribution of hand-outs, invitations and inquiries from Delhi's hundred and twenty Indian and Foreign correspondents. Right up to the closing minutes of the day Mountbatten and his staff were busy at their respective desks. The Viceregal machine in the task of dismantling itself was at full pitch to the end.

As the midnight hour drew near and the last telegrams from Viceroy to Secretary of State were being drafted and dispatched, I found myself alone with Mountbatten in his study. To enable it to assume its sovereignty at the exact moment when the new order came into being the Legislative Assembly was convened late on the night of the 14th. After the passing of the resolution proclaiming Independence and inviting Mountbatten to become the first constitutional Governor-General, Prasad and Nehru were to call on Mountbatten and convey the invitation formally. It was expected that they would arrive at about 12.45 a.m.

As midnight struck Mountbatten was sitting quietly at his desk. I have known him in most moods; to-night there was an air about him of serenity, almost detachment. The scale of his personal achievement was too great for elation, rather his sense of history and the fitness of things at this dramatic moment, when the old and the new order were reconciled in himself, called forth composure.

Quite deliberately he took off his reading-glasses, turned the keys on his dispatch boxes and summoned me to help tidy the room and stow away these outward and visible signs of Viceregal activity. Although there was a whole army of servants outside, it never occurred to either of us to call them. Only when all the papers had been put away and his desk cleared were they called in to move some of the furniture and provide room for members of the Press who had been invited to witness the event.

Correspondents who had been at the solemn ceremony at the Legislative Assembly began to dribble in. They reported that immense crowds had gathered on the route and that we could expect Prasad and Nehru to be somewhat delayed. The proceedings in the Assembly had apparently been most impressive. With moving eloquence Nehru had said, " Long years ago we made a tryst with destiny, and now the time comes when we shall redeem our pledge, not wholly or in full measure, but substantially. At the stroke of the midnight hour, when the world sleeps, India will awake to life and freedom."

Weary but happy, having escaped from the greetings of tremendous throngs, Prasad and Nehru finally arrived. In the little scene that ensued, friendship completely burst the bounds of formality. The Press correspondents flanked the room, photographers stood on the circular table. Although Nehru had given approval that the Press should be there, I think he must have forgotten that he had done so. Whether it was the presence of an audience, or just the normal reaction after the great scenes in the Assembly, neither of them seemed to know quite what to do.

Finally Mountbatten and Prasad stood facing each other, with Nehru half sitting on Mountbatten's desk between them. Prasad began murmuring a formal invitation. However, he forgot his lines, and Nehru played the role of benign prompter. Between them they explained that the Constituent Assembly had just taken over and had endorsed the request of the leaders that Mountbatten should become the first Governor-General. To this message he smilingly replied, " I am proud of the honour, and I will do my best to carry out your advice in a constitutional manner ".

Thereupon Nehru, handing over a large and carefully addressed envelope, said in ceremonious terms, " May I submit to you the portfolios of the new Cabinet? " The ceremony was all over in less than ten minutes, but there was more humanity and hope in this unrehearsed encounter than in most of our Te Deums and victory parades.

I was once more alone with Mountbatten. Just to satisfy his curiosity and remind himself of the exact names of the Government to which he had previously agreed and which he would be swearing-in in a few hours' time, he opened the large envelope, but he was not to see his Prime Minister's submission that night, for by sublime oversight Nehru's envelope was empty.

GOVERNMENT HOUSE, NEW DELHI, *Friday, 15th August, 1947*

I doubt whether it will be given to me to live through a more crowded or memorable day than this.

At 8.30 the trumpets and the scarlet-and-gold which had heralded in twenty Viceroys summoned the State entrance of the newly created Earl Mountbatten of Burma into the Durbar Hall, the first Governor-General of the free India. The strangeness of this great occasion lay not in its points of contrast with Mountbatten's earlier Viceregal installation, but in its essential similarity to the March ceremony. Now, of course, it was the function of an Indian Chief Justice, Dr. Kania, to administer the Oath to the Governor-General, and for an Indian Secretary of the Home Department to officiate in swearing in the Ministers of the new Dominion. Once again the rich red-velvet canopies were lit with hidden lights above the golden thrones. The carpets were a veritable field of the cloth of gold. Lady Mountbatten in gold lamé herself adorned the splendid scene.

The Mountbattens had only just taken their seats on the throne when the whole Durbar Hall resounded with the explosion of one of the photographers' flash-bulbs. There was a momentary ripple of anxiety at this realistic portrayal of a bomb. The Mountbattens, with the full force of the floodlights upon them, gave no outward sign that they had either seen the flash or heard the report. At the end of the ceremony the great bronze doors of the Durbar Hall were opened and the link between the old order and the new was proclaimed with the playing of " God Save the King " followed by the Jana Gana Mana.

A few moments later and the whole distinguished company had dissolved, to be lost in the vast concourse massing round the Council House. No sooner had the Mountbattens on their State drive passed out of the main gates of Viceroy's—from now on Government—House and down the slope between the Government Secretariat buildings, than they were themselves engulfed and their landau almost lifted off the ground by the dense laughing throng.

I had moved quickly by a side route from Government House and had managed to slip into the Council House before the pressure became too heavy; but as the minutes went by it became increasingly difficult to admit the various official guests through the great doors without also letting in a flood of citizens who were generating their own frenzied enthusiasm with rhythmic chants of " Jai Hind ". Before long the great circular Council House was like a besieged fortress, and nobody knew how a way would be made for the Mountbattens, on reaching the entrance, to leave their carriage and actually get inside.

For a short while the situation looked ugly. The crowd, estimated at over a quarter of a million, began making formidable rushes to break into the building, and Nehru and other Government leaders had to be summoned from the Chamber to try to calm them down. At first their appearance only fanned the flames of excitement, but somehow, with Indians of all descriptions on every side pressing to shake them by the hand, the Mountbattens—their decorations and regalia miraculously intact—were safely shepherded into the main building.

Within the Chamber itself the enthusiasm and expectancy, though not less genuine, were sufficiently restrained to allow the formal ceremonies to come into their own again. Prasad began by reading out a whole series of congratulatory messages from all over the world, but by a technical hitch, comparable no doubt with last night's missing letter, he forgot to read out President Truman's message—a lapse which was remedied only after Dr. Grady, the American Ambassador, had expostulated in a loud whisper.

To the usual accompaniment of photographic barrage, Mountbatten then rose to address the Assembly. He began by reading out the King's message, which was cordially received, and then proceeded to speak with far more emphasis and spirit than he usually does when he has to keep to a script. Although the words had been carefully chosen, their underlying sincerity quickly drew the sympathy and applause of the packed Assembly. References to the success of the Accession policy, to his request to be regarded " as one of yourselves " and to the leadership of Nehru and Patel were all acclaimed. But his solicitude for Gandhi drew the most prolonged cheers, and it was some time before he could proceed.

In appearance he looked magnificent but approachable. As one Indian put it, " His gift for friendship has triumphed over everything ". It was psychologically sound for him to stress that he would definitely go when his work was completed in April. He also succeeded in convincing his audience that no pressure would be put upon them to stay within the Commonwealth. They were entirely free to make their own choice. Many told me afterwards how delighted they were that his speech had been so substantial. That it was in effect a policy declaration undoubtedly came as a welcome surprise.

Prasad followed with a long address which he spoke first in Hindi and then in English. In both languages he was almost inaudible. Of the Congress elder statesmen Prasad is a moderate by conviction and temperament. Where some of his colleagues may be lured into the pursuit of dialectical points beyond the bounds of good sense or self-interest, Prasad rarely indulges himself in outbursts or over-statements. To-day he spoke from the heart. " Let us gratefully acknowledge ", he said, " while our achievement is in no small measure due to our own sufferings and sacrifices, it is also the result of world forces and events, and last though not least it is the consummation and fulfilment of the historic tradition and democratic ideals of the British race." After tributes to the Mountbattens as representatives of that race he added, " The period of domination of Britain over India ends to-day, and our relationship with Britain is henceforward going to rest on a basis of equality, of mutual good-will and mutual profit."

After the speeches the National flag was unfurled on the Council House and a salvo of thirty-one guns was fired. The Mountbattens' drive home was only the second of several tumultuous rides during the day, and all the way back to Government House the cries of " Jai Hind " were mixed with " Mountbatten Ki Jai ", and even " Pandit Mountbatten " !

After lunch our procession of cars sped out to the Roshanara Gardens, where the Mountbattens in the blazing heat mingled with five thousand school-children. Here was an abundance of Indian side-shows to amuse, amaze and even horrify. The spectacle of a fakir apparently biting the head off a snake, when added to the prevailing heat and clamour, nearly caused poor Pamela to pass out on the spot. But she and her parents stood up to this symbolically significant visit with the utmost verve and good-will.

In accordance with long-established Indian custom at times of rejoicing, the Mountbattens' last act before leaving was to hand out gifts of sweets to the children. I do not deny that in pressing them to add this engagement to their already overcrowded list I have had its Public Relations value in mind, feeling that it was likely to make a deep impression on Indian sentiment because it was a genuine gesture of good-will and could readily be seen to be such.

On their return to Government House the Mountbattens only just had time to change for the culminating public ceremony, the unfurling of the flag near the war memorial in Princes Park. When we reached the specially constructed arena we showed our tickets to cheerful officials, who waved us on through numbered lanes. The planning for the whole ceremony had been based upon the assumption that a crowd of some thirty thousand people would be there, but unfortunately for the planners the numbers were nearer three hundred thousand. The result was that the first impression of everything under control gave way to one of incomparable confusion when we emerged into what were supposed to be the parade-ground and reserved stands. We were surrounded by the happiest of human hubbubs. The crowds had taken complete possession of all the chairs, standing on the backs, arms and seats, approximately six Indians to a chair.

In this maelstrom of rank and race, sex and caste were all lost in one vast unison—the desire of myriad human beings to reach the central dais with its flag-pole. In fact, the crowd became like some gigantic ocean remorselessly converging on a tiny island and liable at any moment to engulf it. Nehru himself only managed to reach the central platform by some desperate providence, and when he saw Pamela Mountbatten struggling to get through the good-natured crowd he rushed at them kicking out at random and snatching the topee off the head of one Indian in order to crash it down on the head of another. A distraught A.D.C. thought a riot might start at any moment, but he had missed the mood of this mighty assembly. On all sides there was laughter and good humour.

Near where I was standing one hero was trying to ride a bicycle. I got the impression that somehow the crowd had caught up with him before he had reached his destination, with the result that he could neither get on with his journey nor get off his machine. Fay, Marjorie Brockman and Pamela Nicholls were all trapped between the stands and the dais, but cheerful people shouted, " Make way for the memsahibs ! " Fay finally reached the B.B.C. recording van, where Wynford Vaughan Thomas was frantically engaged on one of his most vivid and spectacular outside broadcasts. He told me afterwards that it was the greatest crowd scene he had ever witnessed.

Suddenly the cheering swelled into a roar, and from where I stood I could just catch a glimpse of the A.D.C.'s in white followed by the fluttering lance pennants of the Governor-General's Body Guard, then the Governor-General's carriage and more Body Guard. The carriage and escort, moving fitfully, at last reached a point about twenty-five yards from the flagstaff. I could see the Mountbattens standing up, waving to the crowd, which was cheering and waving back at them. Nehru made some last frantic efforts to call for order and clear a little space, but his pleas were in vain, so there was no alternative but for Mountbatten to stay in his carriage, and, while the flag was being hoisted, take the salute from there.

Just as the flag was unfurled light rain began to fall, and a rainbow appeared in the sky, matching the saffron, white and green of the flag. If Hollywood had added this last touch, we would all have complained that once again they were overdoing it; as it was, it would seem to provide a dramatic omen to refute the gloomier astrologers. I must confess it would have taken a man of iron scepticism to be unimpressed by such an augury at such a moment.

Mountbatten's return journey to Government House was the final triumph of friendly informality. Nehru was unable to get back to his car, so Mountbatten pulled him into the State carriage, where he sat on the hood. En route four women, a child and a Press photographer, in grave danger of being crushed under the wheels, were duly rescued by Mountbatten and joined the party, helping to swell the numbers in the carriage to twelve—shades of Curzon and his Durbar!

Then, as grand finale to this historic day, we repaired to the State banquet at Government House, which was attended by most of the Cabinet, Diplomatic Corps, and military and civilian leaders. One or two of the Princes who felt uneasy about their degree of precedence when in the company of members of the new Government were the only notable absentees. The climax was reached when Nehru rose to propose the health of the King, and Mountbatten replied with the toast of the Dominion Government. Both speeches, delivered without notes, were for the benefit of the assembled guests alone. There were thus none of the restraints imposed by the demands of world publicity.

All present, said Nehru, would have seen how enthusiastic the crowds in Delhi had been in celebrating this great day. Similar scenes were undoubtedly being enacted all over India. Politics and economics had an important place in the relations between nations; but he wanted to stress the importance of the psychological and emotional factors in dealing with the people of India. Those who merely sat in their offices in Delhi handling political problems and economic planning—important as those issues were—were not in real touch with the nation. Different views might be taken of the benefits India might or might not have derived from her past connection with Britain, but it was altogether wrong that rule should be exercised by a Great Power over a people striving to be free. Now that India had attained her independence, the people not only showed their joy, but also made plain a remarkable change in their attitude towards the British.

In paying a special tribute to Mountbatten, he said he had seen so clearly from the outset how vital it was to act quickly and to make the correct psychological approach to India in giving effect to the policy of His Majesty's Government. Whatever shape the relations between Britain and India might take in the future, a new start had been made, and he hoped and believed that the friendship between them would endure.

Mountbatten in his reply said that his predecessors had been unfortunate in having to sit on a stationary bicycle, which was a very difficult balancing feat. He had, however, been given the " Go ahead " to start pedalling. It had been his function to pedal faster and faster, until a point was now reached when he was handing over the bicycle to his Government, who had gripped the handle-bars firmly.

I sat next to Feroze Gandhi, Nehru's son-in-law, Managing Director of the influential Lucknow *National Herald*. I stressed what was in my heart to say that whether India stayed in or went out of the Commonwealth the consolidation of friendship between our peoples was all that mattered.

At 9.15 p.m. three thousand guests filed upstairs and were individually presented to the Mountbattens—their final social *tour de force* on this day of days. All the State rooms and drawing-rooms were thrown open, and the floodlit Moghul gardens, festooned with fairy lights, were lovely to look upon. It was by now cool and the air soft and scented. The party went on in an atmosphere of cordial good cheer into the early hours of the morning. Gone was the sense of strain and stiffness which was so evident among the Indian guests at the first garden-party in March. Here was the social ease which only the underlying sense of equality recognised on all sides can bring.

So many appropriate words have been written in the many souvenir editions of the newspapers, but I liked best K. M. Munshi's comment on Mountbatten's appointment as Governor-General :—

" No power in history ", he writes, " but Great Britain would have conceded independence with such grace, and no power but India would have so gracefully acknowledged the debt."

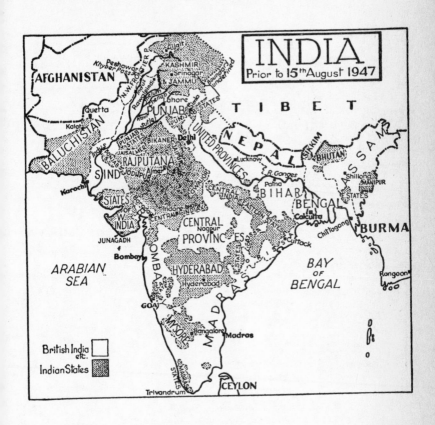

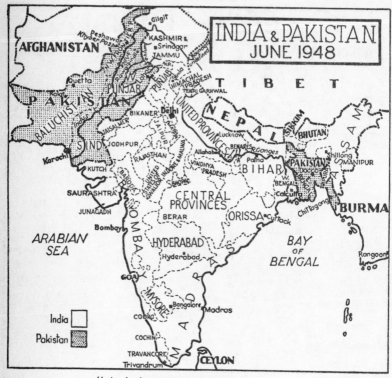

Hyderabad - *Standstill agreement with India*
Kashmir & Jammu - *Acceded to India (Oct. 1947)*
Referred to U.N.O. (Jan. 1948)

Part II

THE FIRST GOVERNOR-GENERAL

CHAPTER FOURTEEN

WAR OF SUCCESSION

GOVERNMENT HOUSE, NEW DELHI, *Saturday, 16th August, 1947*

VERY EARLY THIS morning the National flag was hoisted over the Red Fort in Old Delhi, and Nehru addressed a crowd estimated at some half a million, stretching, I am told, all the way to that other monument of Moghul splendour, the mighty Mosque of the Jama Masjid. But the rejoicings of the morning were all too soon tempered by the depression of the leaders this afternoon, when Mountbatten handed over to them the Radcliffe Award. He allowed them two hours in which to digest its terms before summoning a formal meeting in the Council Chamber of Government House. Liaquat was there, and not the least of Mountbatten's achievements in Karachi this week was in securing Jinnah's reluctant agreement for Liaquat to make this visit at all, coming as it did within twenty-four hours of his assumption of the Premiership of Pakistan. I was present at this sombre and sullen gathering, where the only unanimity was in denunciation of this or that communal " injustice ". The field was thus left clear for Mountbatten to point with well-timed emphasis the moral that in so far as it was impossible for all the parties to be equally satisfied with Radcliffe's verdict, the best evidence of its fairness seemed to rest in the undoubted equality of their displeasure.

We were given the first shots of what will undoubtedly be a prolonged and passionate controversy. Liaquat's dismay at the inclusion of the Gurdaspur District in East Punjab was offset by Patel's anger over the Chittagong Hill Tracts passing to Eastern Pakistan, while the resentment of both was blanketed by Baldev's dumb depression. None of the Leaders, however, saw fit to carry their criticism to the point of repudiating their unconditional pledge made in advance to accept the Award whatever its terms might be.

Even as we met, momentous news was coming in from both the partitioned Provinces which provided at once a warning and an example of the need for bold leadership. In the Punjab the people are taking the situation into their own hands. What Jenkins has aptly termed the war of succession has broken out in full fury in the land of the five rivers. This afternoon Auchinleck gave a terse and terrifying situation report to the Leaders which has caused them to decide on an immediate reinforcement of the Boundary Force.

In Calcutta, on the other hand, where the danger of a similar succession struggle was deemed to be no less acute, all is comparatively quiet, with only sporadic acts of violence. Gandhi has made his healing presence felt. With his sense of the fitness of things, he left Delhi before the Independence celebrations, no doubt feeling that it would be difficult for him to play an appropriate role in these official rejoicings and that more

urgent duties awaited him in the East.   On the 13th he invited the last
Moslem Prime Minister of a United Bengal, Shaheed Suhrawardy—a
man of fairly luxurious tastes—to take up his abode with him in a small
home in the Moslem quarter and to share in his acts of dedication.
That night Hindu youths stoned the place.   Gandhi's response was to
mark yesterday's Independence celebrations as a day of fasting.

In view of the grave Punjab developments, Nehru and Liaquat have
decided to go together at once to Ambala, and thence to Amritsar, where
they can make an appreciation and take the highest-level decisions on the
spot.

To-night I ran into the photographer whose life was saved and fortune
enhanced by yesterday's free ride on Mountbatten's carriage.   He
represents a paper of extreme left-wing persuasions, but this did not
prevent him from shaking me by the hand and exclaiming, " At last, after
two hundred years, Britain has conquered India."

GOVERNMENT HOUSE, BOMBAY, *Sunday, 17th August, 1947*

I was up by 4.30 a.m. to join the Governor-General's party for Bombay,
where he was due to say farewell to the first contingent of British troops
to leave India after the transfer of power—detachments of the Norfolks
returning home by the troopship *Georgic*.   By the time we reached
Bombay the weather had broken, and rain fell throughout the parade
and speech-making on the quay-side.   Mountbatten was in his khaki
drill, and was soon converting the occasion into a S.E.A.C. reunion,
adopting the procedure he had made famous throughout the length and
breadth of the Burma front.   Troops were asked to break ranks and
cluster round him while he addressed them from a small soap-box.
There was no lingering over sad farewells to all our former greatness.
The all-pervading drizzle did not damp down his accustomed fire and
fun.   It was all part of his pledge that when we hauled down the flag
we would do so with honour, dignity and good-will.   He secured for
this occasion a cordial farewell message from Nehru.   While it was
being read out by General Cariappa, I could not help thinking what a
revolution in sentiment the message embodied.

We returned to a lunch-party at Government House confident that the
main part of the day's public proceedings was already over.   The only
other event on our calendar was a tea-time reception at the Taj Hotel
given by the Governor and the Corporation of Bombay.   There had
been no particular publicity accorded to this engagement, and the procession of cars driving to the hotel attracted no more than a casual
curiosity.   But while we were inside, " bush telegraph " began to work
with potent effect.

By the time we were ready to leave about one and a half hours later a
crowd of some fifty thousand people had gathered round the hotel to
greet their new Governor-General.   They were but the advance patrols
of the greatest single assembly of rejoicing citizens which it has ever
been my lot to see.   So closely packed were they along the whole five
miles from the Taj to Government House that it took our procession

of cars well over an hour to complete the distance. The Bombay police estimated that the crowd, which was particularly dense on the sea-front towards Malabar Hill, cannot have numbered much less than three-quarters of a million.

I was in the fifth car with Muriel Watson and Symington, the Governor's Secretary. We could see the Mountbattens standing up in their open Rolls and the police helplessly trying to stop swarms of excited Indians climbing on the dash-boards to shake them by the hand or just to touch them. The Colvilles in the next car, and indeed all of us down the line, were hardly less warmly greeted. It was sufficient at this amazing moment to be acknowledged as an Englishman in order to be idolised. They wanted us to shout " Jai Hind " to them, and in return they roared " England Ki Jai ".

This drive was an indelible experience for every one of us who took part in it. Crowds are notoriously fickle, and the general desire to congregate in public places comes easily to the Indian, but all of us, I think, recognised in the up-surge of this tremendous demonstration some deeper stirring of the spirit. A whole era of anti-British agitation, of self-abasement and self-assertion arising from the sense of unequal status was swept away before our eyes. The people, without any prompting from their leaders, had shown themselves aware of the new relationship and Mountbatten's whole-hearted effort to bring it about. His genius for friendship had evoked an overwhelming popular response.

By the time we had reached Government House, dishevelled and dazed, all of us were conscious that we had witnessed something far beyond the range of individual effort or the scope of personal success. I wrote to my mother: " We saw with the passing of power the end of estrangement. We had believed that this might happen, but we had no idea that the transformation would be so sudden and so overwhelming. It was a very great moment. There was no sense of regret, only one of pride that such friendship could be shown with such spontaneous enthusiasm by so many thousands who had nothing else to give."

To-night there was a big farewell dinner and dance, the House guests including a number of ex-Governors who were leaving the next day by the *Empress of Scotland*. Government House, standing on a promontory with the waves of the Arabian Sea lapping the beaches, looked under the light of the full moon like some fairy palace of ivory and filigree.

GOVERNMENT HOUSE, BOMBAY, *Monday, 18th August, 1947*

Mountbatten left for Delhi this morning, but Lady Mountbatten, for whom an arduous programme has been arranged, is staying on. Her tour of the Bombay slums was characteristic of her thoroughness, and serves to explain the tremendous popularity she has gained for herself with the humbler Indian people. In heavy rain she inspected dozens of wretched dwellings, walking for hours on end through mud and filth. She did not hesitate to denounce what she saw as a disgrace to a great city, and appealed to the wealthier citizens to remove this blot from Bombay.

I also have stayed on for a party in my honour arranged at very short notice and with great gusto and generosity by Joachim Alva and his wife Violet. Alva, the energetic proprietor and editor of *Forum*, a news magazine for English-speaking Indian readers in the style of *Time* and *News Review*, was in one of his more lyrical moods. " From Tottenham's thorns ", he exclaimed, " to Mountbatten's roses is a far cry indeed." Sir Richard Tottenham had been Additional Secretary of the Home Department responsible for carrying out Lord Linlithgow's repression of the Congress's Civil Disobedience in 1942 following the failure of the Cripps mission.

I had no answer to that one. All I could say when my turn came for a brief impromptu speech was that my purpose was to be the instrument of Lord Mountbatten's policy of providing the maximum possible information at all times. For it was Mountbatten's profound conviction that most speculation and inaccurate reports in the Press spring from the lack of reliable information and not from malice.

GOVERNMENT HOUSE, NEW DELHI, *Wednesday, 20th August, 1947*

Lady Mountbatten has completed her remarkable non-stop tour of Bombay's Health, Education and Welfare institutions and units in addition to her inspection of the slums. Altogether she covered in just under three days seven hospitals, clinics and dispensaries, four social welfare committees, three colleges, one remand home and a young women's hospital—a formidable performance even by her own standards of thoroughness and energy. Her journeys through the city were a triumphal progress, crowds staging spontaneous demonstrations of greeting everywhere she went. It was a wonderful tribute to the impact of her personality on the people of Bombay.

Owing to heavy monsoon weather, our flight from Bombay yesterday had to be delayed for some hours, and we did not get back until late in the afternoon. We have returned to a grim situation at the centre. Nehru and Liaquat moved on from Ambala to Amritsar, there issuing an urgent appeal for peace. Nehru has also broadcast underlining the resolve of the two Punjab Governments, in co-operation with the Governments of India and Pakistan, to end the " terrible orgy "; " India," he pledged, " is not a communal State, but a democratic State in which every citizen has equal rights. The Government is determined to protect those rights." The refugee problem is already assuming monstrous proportions. It is estimated that already some two hundred thousand people are huddled in the improvised refugee camps, living under conditions which invite an outbreak of cholera on a prodigious scale.

We were guests to-night at the Chinese Embassy at a dinner-party given by Dr. Loh to some members of Government House, including Pamela Mountbatten. The meal was full of rich and rare Chinese delicacies cooked by His Excellency himself, so rich that they were clearly beyond the dietetic range of some of our party. There were splendid wines to wash away all fear and uncertainty. Digestion was not made easier by the sudden appearance about half-way through the meal of photographers perched on the window-sills, living embodiments of forked lightning. This dramatic interruption was not an outside Press scoop, but merely for the Ambassador's album.

GOVERNMENT HOUSE, NEW DELHI, *Friday, 22nd August, 1947*

I attended to-day's lunch-party. There were five guests, including the new Pakistan High Commissioner, Zahid Hussein, a nervous, diffident man made more so by his doubts as to his physical safety here in Delhi; and Mr. Kher, Prime Minister of Bombay, who from the talk I had with him to-day and during our Bombay visit made me feel that he may well turn out to be one of the strong men in the new régime.

I sat next to Shanmukham Chetty, the new Finance Minister, who is said to represent Nehru's concession to capitalist big business and the need for foreign investment. He speaks with the confidence of an expert, but does not give Kher's impression of political strength. I have heard the hope expressed that along with Matthai and C. H. Bhabha he will help to form the Cabinet's brains trust independent of Congress pressures, but I think it is doubtful whether any of them will be able to enjoy much more than a secondary status in the politics of the new order.

The conversation turned to the taking of oaths. Chetty said swearing was a very serious matter in India, and what he called the doctrine of the double check had firmly established itself. " It is based ", he said, " on the principle that in heaven they may not have all the files." He said that the swearing of oaths took three forms : on cows' tails, over camphor flame and on children's heads. There were, he added, heartless men who used *chupattis* (biscuits) under children's hats. There was considerable discussion on the economic situation and sterling balances. Chetty was at pains to stress that the Sterling Agreement between Britain and India is not affected by Independence.

Mountbatten has written a long letter to Nehru and Patel urging the need for economic planning. He is afraid these stern economic realities may be swamped by political considerations and by attempts to apply some of the more eccentric of Gandhi's theories, including the rigid enforcement of prohibition of all alcoholic drink, upon which a large proportion of provincial revenues depends, and the wholesale abolition of food and cotton controls, without which the general price structure may collapse, enabling speculators to seize the helm.

GOVERNMENT HOUSE, NEW DELHI, *Saturday, 23rd August, 1947*

Bob Stimson and I have been working closely with Lady Mountbatten on her B.B.C. broadcast. It provides a chance to get behind and beyond all the communal propaganda. Lady Mountbatten made the most of this opportunity. She has a beautiful broadcasting voice and read her script with great feeling. She spoke of the unknown heroes of India and mentioned the little Moslem doctor who abandoned his Delhi practice to set up an improvised dispensary at Gurgaon in the Punjab, the scene of some of the bitterest communal conflict. " There in the dust and heat he toiled ceaselessly for weeks on end to save the lives of Hindu and Moslem alike."

I am glad to say she agreed to end her broadcast by quoting the inscription from the Jaipur column which stands sentinel in the courtyard of Government House.   I have always admired the strength and scope of its message since I first came upon it in one of Lord Halifax's speeches as Viceroy.   Carved into stone are the words: "In Thought, Faith; In Word, Wisdom; In Deed, Courage; In Life, Service; So may India be Great."

GOVERNMENT HOUSE, NEW DELHI, *Monday, 25th August, 1947*

In the morning Mountbatten had a difficult session with the Joint Defence Council, the point of controversy being the future of the Punjab Boundary Force.   The two Governments would like to see the Force broken up and reconstituted on national lines with Indian and Pakistan Commanders-in-Chief.   Mountbatten went into the meeting aware that this idea would be completely unacceptable to Auchinleck and Rees, and that in any case it ran counter to his own views.   He managed so to steer the discussions that the matter was not formally raised, but could not divert Chundrigar, the Pakistan Finance Minister and representative at the meeting, from making some highly critical comment about the Force's conduct.

This was too much for Mountbatten, who had just urged that a word of appreciation from the Leaders to the officers and men of the Force was urgently needed to maintain their sorely tried morale.   If the Force did not receive proper support, the only thing would be to remove it, and then the responsibility for the resulting bloodshed would rest squarely on those who had caused it to be taken away.   Indeed, at one moment Mountbatten raised a ripple of amusement when he turned on Chundrigar with the fatherly reproof, "I hate to think what your Governor-General would say if he heard you talking like this."

The meeting authorised the publication of a communiqué about the Boundary Force.   Vernon and I were entrusted with the preparation of a draft for everyone's approval, with the result that we spent the afternoon running between the Pakistan High Commissioner's house in Hardinge Avenue, where Chundrigar is staying, and Nehru's office in the Secretariat.   Chundrigar was most insistent that a clause should be inserted indicating that severe action would be taken against the Boundary Force in the future if it failed in its duty.   We were ourselves already trying to tone down another sentence which indicated that the Boundary Force "with a few exceptions" was doing a good job.

We emerged from the discussions with the offending words deleted. The whole episode makes it abundantly clear that both Governments will have to change their attitudes to military forces doing difficult jobs on their behalf if they are not to have mutinies on their hands.   The days of glory from sniping at the upholders of law and order are over.

While waiting in the ante-room to Nehru's office, we reflected on the function of a minor official who spent the time spinning a paper-weight, answering the odd telephone call, glancing at the odd envelope and generally letting things take their course. It was hard to believe that one was sitting in a Prime Minister's office.

On our return to Government House, Mountbatten showed me a telegram from Monckton saying that he had been compelled to resign his position as constitutional adviser to the Nizam although he still had His Exalted Highness' confidence. He added that he felt that he ought not now to stay at Government House, as this action might be misconstrued. The news came as a great blow to Mountbatten. " We're sunk!" he exclaimed.

Ever since July the difficult negotiations between Hyderabad and the Government of India as to their relations after the transfer of power have largely turned upon the influence and availability of Monckton as a member of the Nizam's delegation.

As late as the 12th August, Mountbatten, with no settlement in sight, advised the Nizam that he had secured a special extension of two months beyond Independence Day during which the Government's offer to receive Hyderabad's accession would remain open. He also explained that although he would no longer be Crown Representative, he had been authorised to continue negotiations on India's behalf, and in the meanwhile had secured Indian recognition of the *status quo* in Berar, which was legally a part of the Nizam's dominion, but hitherto administered by the Governor of the Central Provinces. Finally he was able to give the vital assurances to the Nizam, after consultation with V. P., that the new Dominion would not regard Hyderabad's decision not to accede in present circumstances as a hostile act, and to add that he was satisfied that the leaders had no intention of applying diplomatic pressure by means of economic blockade.

The negotiations with the Hyderabad delegation were due to be resumed to-day. On receipt of Monckton's telegram Mountbatten called for V. P., and was discussing the new position with him when Vernon and I left to deal with the Boundary Force communiqué. On our return the situation seemed to have improved. A telegram from the Nizam had arrived asking Mountbatten to see Monckton on his behalf and encourage him to stay on in his service. The Nizam confessed that if Monckton returned at this juncture he would have great difficulty in appointing someone else in his place.

Monckton came round at once, and explained that he had resigned because of a most violent attack against him in the Hyderabad Press organised by an extremist Moslem organisation in the State, the Ittehad-ul-Muslimeen. He said that the Prime Minister (the Nawab of Chhatari) and the Minister for Constitutional Affairs, both fellow-members of the delegation, had also resigned for the same reason. The Nizam had refused to accept Chhatari's resignation. Monckton said he was prepared to withdraw his own only if there was a previous public withdrawal of the Ittehad's statement.

Monckton advised Mountbatten that he had brought the Nizam up to the point of offering a treaty which would cover the three central subjects of Defence, External Affairs and Communications, and was confident that he could persuade him to accept the equivalent of accession provided the term " Instrument of Accession " was given some such sugar-coating as " Article of Association ". Mountbatten pointed out that this was the precise issue over which Patel was most adamant, in so far as he was afraid of being accused of breach of faith with all the other Princely signatories to Accession Instruments. But Mountbatten promised to do his utmost to get his Government's support for the substance of accession if Monckton on his side could secure the Nizam's assent to it.

The news has also come through to-day that Bhopal has at last acceded —he was allowed ten days grace before his Instrument of Accession was actually published. " It is almost as hectic as it was before the 15th August," was Mountbatten's comment.

GOVERNMENT HOUSE, NEW DELHI, *Wednesday, 27th August, 1947*

V. P. and I had an important talk with Mountbatten in his bedroom early this morning on the subject of the Punjab Boundary Force and the Press attacks being made upon it both in the *Hindustan Times* and the *Indian News Chronicle*. V. P. said there was a growing feeling on both sides that the new Governments should have more direct military control over their respective areas. Mountbatten agreed that although the Boundary Force was undoubtedly the best military answer to the problem, he was ready to concede that in this instance psychological reasons might outweigh purely military ones. His mind was moving in favour of retrocession of the Boundary Force's area.

We then discussed the Press situation. V. P. thought we should not take the Delhi Press too seriously, as the big Provincial papers were all very steady on the issue. The *Hindustan Times* this morning carried a direct attack on Rees and a most objectionable cartoon implying that the Supreme Command's Headquarters were deliberately depriving the Dominion Armies of good officers in order to retain big jobs for themselves. As a result of our talk, Mountbatten has decided that he will see Devadas Gandhi and Sahni, the *Hindustan Times'* and the *Indian News Chronicle's* editors, this afternoon, and has instructed me to arrange the meeting.

Devadas and Sahni duly arrived at four o'clock, anticipating, I suspect, a chilly reception, but Mountbatten was in his best form, delivering his disapproval from behind a smoke-screen of engaging frankness. He has the rare knack of combining vehemence with *bonhomie*. He started the session with a general homily on the need to avoid attacking the military, who cannot answer for themselves. If soldiers begin answering back you get a situation, he said, as in Mexico, where they throw out the editors. As against this dangerous example he stressed the recent case of General Barker in Palestine, where Press criticism of the General's conduct was levelled not at the General himself, but at Bellenger, the Secretary of State for War and the Minister answerable to Parliament for the General's actions.

Mountbatten then turned to a general account of what was happening in the Punjab. The Sikhs, he said, had launched an attack just as Giani

Kartar Singh and Tara Singh before the 3rd June had told him they would. Mountbatten had expostulated with them at the time, stressing that the British would have gone. It would be Indian fighting Indian. But they were adamant, and had in fact observed that they were waiting for us to go. The situation was now out of their control. In an area less than two hundred by one hundred and fifty miles containing some seventeen thousand inhabited localities and only about the size of Wales, some ten million people were on the move. At this moment, through the withdrawal of all the Moslems, the police in the East Punjab were suddenly and catastrophically seven thousand under strength.

Mountbatten then explained in detail the military virtues of the Boundary Force and the capabilities of Pete Rees, whom he described as perhaps his ablest divisional commander in the Burma campaign. It was Rees—" the pocket General "—who had led the famous " Dagger " Division in its successful dash to liberate Mandalay. He had explained to the Defence Council that the limiting factor now was that Rees was under civilian control. It was only fair to add that Nehru had indicated that he was very impressed with Rees.

Mountbatten next explained the military alternatives by pressing one hand against the seam of his trousers and taking the seam as the Boundary Force command headquarters with its subordinate commands radiating out on both sides of the seam from his fingers. The national commands he described merely by turning the finger-tips of both hands in upon each other and placing them at right angles to the seam.

Sahni said at great length that he felt very bitter, as he came from the Boundary area. Devadas made no effort to defend the cartoon or the attack on Rees. Some constructive ideas arose during the talk, which lasted nearly two hours. These included sponsored Press visits and dissemination of neutral news by leaflet, the setting up of strongholds guarded by mixed forces to give immediate succour to refugees, and the appointment of custodians for refugee property to cover movable as well as immovable belongings.

GOVERNMENT HOUSE, NEW DELHI, *Thursday, 28th August, 1947*

Lady Mountbatten and Rajkumari Amrit Kaur, the new Minister of Health, have just come back from the heartland of the communal frenzy, visiting no fewer than twelve refugee centres and camps, as well as seven hospitals and a number of other medical units, engaging in numerous conferences with officials, from the Governors of the East and West Punjab downwards. It has been a heroic errand of mercy to the point of danger at the hour of trouble.

Rajkumari, by birth a member of the Kapurthala family, is a Christian and a close disciple of the Mahatma. She is a sensitive woman, whose air of resignation and sadness of expression serve to mask an indomitable will. Within twenty-four hours of becoming India's first woman Cabinet Minister she was confronted with one of the most gigantic tasks of human salvage even for this era of concentration camps and displaced persons. I first met her during our stay in Simla last May, and it was through her good offices that I had my talk with Gandhi.

I have just been looking through Lady Mountbatten's itinerary and speaking to Muriel Watson, who is worn out and deeply affected by the experience. On Tuesday 26th they were in Jullundur and Amritsar, which was, says Muriel, like a place of the dead. At the end of an exhausting day, having visited in all seven hospitals and refugee centres, where appalling conditions prevailed, news came through of a savage attack on a lorry of non-Moslem refugees from Sialkot. Lady Mountbatten at once returned to the Victoria Memorial Hospital to see the victims, many of them horribly mutilated. At 10.30 p.m. she was in close session with Tara Singh, who is at last beginning to tremble at the wrath he has so readily invoked. Lady Mountbatten left for Lahore at 6.30 the next morning, and visited a Moslem refugee camp and training-school before breakfast. There followed inspections of two more camps and two more hospitals before a sandwich luncheon and departure for Rawalpindi, where another thorough round of tours and conferences began. This morning they repeated the same proceedings in Sialkot and Gujranwalla, before returning to Delhi.

There could be no more compelling catalogue to testify to Lady Mountbatten's devotion to duty. Her report on the situation on both sides of the Boundary is disquieting enough. The refugees are now in a state of mass hysteria. Neither side has any trust in the intentions, assurances or actions of the other Dominion. She reports also that there is a complete lack of confidence in the Punjab Boundary Force.

"THE RETREAT", MASHOBRA, SIMLA, *Saturday, 30th August, 1947*

Mountbatten was in Lahore yesterday to take the chair at the Joint Defence Council, which Jinnah, to everyone's surprise, attended as a member. After prolonged discussion the decision was taken to disband the Boundary Force. Pete Rees received very few thanks from either side for his efforts to carry out a task of unparalleled difficulty. Without the whole-hearted backing of the Governments and Press on both sides, the position of the Boundary Force and its Commander became rapidly untenable, and otherwise steady and experienced troops began to feel the tug of communal loyalties deeper even than their military discipline.

Now that the Punjab Boundary Force and the Joint Defence Council's authority over it are at an end, Mountbatten's last executive responsibility lapses. He considers that as a matter of policy he should confirm his new constitutional status by freeing himself from day-to-day contact with the executive or from any direct administrative interference in the Government's action to restore the immediate situation. He has accordingly decided to go ahead with earlier arrangements and visit Simla for ten days of well-earned and badly needed rest.

Once again the retinue climbed the hill. This time the Mountbattens used the famous rail-car from Kalka, while the rest of us continued on by road. There was much amusement when, by a progression of fits and starts, we would streak ahead, only to be held up to allow the "Royal

Train " to pass at the points where the railway crosses the road.   Mount-batten waved at us with ever-increasing good cheer each time he received our loyal greetings! Considering that the whole journey was in an area of tension, the size of the crowds and the spontaneity of their welcome were most heartening.

Meanwhile Ismay has gone for his much-needed rest to Kashmir and has been asked by Mountbatten to do his best to get the Maharaja to make up his vacillating mind and accede without further delay to which-ever Dominion he and his people desire, thus ending the uncertain and dangerously unstable position in Kashmir.

GOVERNOR-GENERAL'S LODGE, SIMLA, *Thursday, 4th September, 1947*

Our respite has been little more than a long week-end.   Even during that time I have been kept busy with disquieting reports of a serious dispute brewing between the Government of India and its officials on the one hand and the Foreign correspondents on the other.   The trouble was apparently heightened by one of Nehru's many impromptu utter-ances, which on this occasion took the form of a general threat to the Press based upon a particular report by an individual correspondent unnamed. This approach, of course, immediately aroused fears of censorship among the correspondents, while touching off latent xenophobia among the minor officials.   Various correspondents complained that they were facing not just recrimination but actual intimidation.

Mountbatten told us late this afternoon that V. P. had rung up to pass on an urgent plea from Patel for him to return to Delhi immediately. V. P. said that the view of Nehru, Patel and all the responsible Ministers was that the situation was now so serious that his presence alone could save it.

George Nicholls and I, having made arrangements for the security of our families, whom we are having to leave behind at Mashobra, set off after dinner with our bearers and supporting servants.   Escorted by Sepoys with lanterns, we made our way along the winding rickshaw path to our cars waiting to take us down to Governor-General's Lodge.   We are spending the night here prior to setting out in the caravanserai at first dawn to-morrow.

CHAPTER FIFTEEN

RESPONSE TO EMERGENCY

GOVERNMENT HOUSE, NEW DELHI, *Saturday, 6th September, 1947*

WE WERE ON the road early yesterday morning, arriving at Government House during the afternoon, where we found V. P. awaiting Mountbatten with a message from Patel hoping that he will grip the situation firmly without delay. Nehru came round immediately to enlist his active and overriding authority to deal with the emergency, followed by Patel.

The decision of the Prime Minister and Deputy Prime Minister of the new India, taken only three weeks after the exhilaration of Independence, to recall Mountbatten in this way, is a great tribute to the quality of their character and leadership. For by this act they have shown themselves big enough to recognise that Mountbatten's experience in high-level administration is something which they have not yet acquired.

After Mountbatten had had two or three hours to acquaint himself fully of the scale of the crisis, he proposed that an Emergency Committee should be set up. This was at once agreed to by Nehru and Patel, and at their insistence Mountbatten accepted the chairmanship. Nothing less will meet the case, for we are in fact confronted with the deadly perils of war emergency without having available the normal instruments or priorities of war to counteract it. With the spread of communal fears and frenzies which we are witnessing in the Punjab, the scale of the killings and the movement of refugees become even more extensive than those caused by the more formal conflicts of opposing armies. As with nearly all the great migrations of history, the people themselves hold sway and create conditions which many can exploit but none can command.

The fact that Delhi itself is in the epicentre of this earthquake automatically converts a provincial into a national crisis. In this respect the Punjab catastrophe is perhaps even more deadly for India than for Pakistan, whose capital, Karachi, is at a safe distance from the disturbances. None-the-less Jinnah on his side has already made an urgent broadcast appeal to his people to help in restoring peace and in building up the new State. Even if the Boundary Award was " unjust, incomprehensible and even perverse," Moslems had agreed to abide by it. The new nation should see to it that what had been won by the pen was not lost by the sword.

It is easy to forget how far to the north Delhi lies—north even of Mount Everest. There are those who argue that it has always been too far removed from the hub of Indian life, and that with Partition this objection is reinforced; but a voluntary change of capital is one thing, a compulsory evacuation by the new Government within a month of attaining Independence quite another. And this is undoubtedly the issue, for nearly half a million refugees are moving towards the city, already overcrowded, bringing in their train disorders and disease wholly beyond Delhi's administrative resources to control.

Mountbatten had an exhaustive discussion with his own staff in advance of the first meeting of the Emergency Committee of the Cabinet over which he was to preside later in the afternoon. We were all asked to make recommendations, and we are all to be at the disposal of the Committee. Ismay is being recalled from Kashmir.

My own suggestions to help meet the Press and Public Relations side of the problem included proposals to secure the earliest possible publicity link-up with Pakistan; the re-naming and regrading of the Committee to Council of State; the appointment of a Public Relations sub-Committee to consist if possible of a representative from the Ministry of Information, the Commander-in-Chief's staff and myself; the firm avoidance of censorship which the Government may be tempted to impose, and finally the importance of playing down Mountbatten's role as chairman. With this last concept Mountbatten whole-heartedly concurred, as also with my views on the dangers of censorship. The Council of State concept was not seriously discussed and, owing to the tempo of the day's events, can be said to have been still-born. The Public Relations sub-Committee was no sooner mentioned than it was approved, and I was commissioned to promote it at once with the Ministry of Information and the Commander-in-Chief.

Mountbatten's reaction to the crisis was to set in motion procedure already tried and proved both at C.O.H.Q. and in S.E.A.C. He said his objective was to convert the Emergency Committee into a daily staff meeting at which spokesmen from every department of the " command " (in this instance Government Departments) could raise and answer questions. Out of these meetings priorities as between departments would be established. Once again Mountbatten showed himself a firm believer in the " sovereignty of discussion ". Only by this means does he consider that the snags can quickly be uncovered and the solutions found.

He also resolved to resume his old war and map-room procedure to provide the Cabinet and himself with the maximum factual information by visual aid both with regard to the number of disturbances and the movement of refugees. To this end he has decided to call in Pete Rees, whose Boundary Force Command closed down last week, to become head of a small Military Emergency Staff operating inside Government House. Pamela, who, with her medical and welfare work * and her Presidency of the Caravan Club (an Indian youth movement), has already done her full share to keep the Mountbatten flag flying, is to be his personal assistant.

* She worked regularly at an improvised free dispensary which has been functioning in tents where poor people from the towns and villages round Delhi who could not afford proper medical treatment or were unable to go into hospitals could receive full medical service. During eight months, without the regular or full-time service of any one doctor, the dispensary treated over five thousand cases, which was more than those handled in the out-patient departments of the Delhi hospitals.

The first Emergency Committee met in the Council Chamber of Government House at five o'clock, and sat for over two hours. Nehru opened the proceedings by turning to Mountbatten and saying, " I will only take your advice on one condition—that you will take the chair ". And Mountbatten accepted under another condition : that the fact is not to be published. Complete secrecy will be difficult, but, as I stressed at an earlier Staff Meeting, there could be no keener advocate of Press and Radio silence on this assignment than myself, and I am determined to do all in my power to maintain it.

It has been agreed that the Committee should consist only of essential Cabinet Ministers and other vital people, such as the Commander-in-Chief, the Supreme Commander's representative, the Chief Commissioner of Delhi, the Chief of Police, the Director-General of Civil Aviation, Medical and Railway representatives. Everyone else is to be co-opted as required. The Ministers who are to join Nehru and Patel as permanent members are Baldev Singh (Defence), Matthai (Railways) and Neogy (in the newly created post of Refugees). Altogether fifteen of us were there for this initial meeting.

The general mood at the outset was of dazed bewilderment and aimlessness before the unknown. Nehru, for whom all the horrors of the first month of Independence seemed to come as the crucifixion of his life-work, looked inexpressibly sad and resigned. Patel was clearly disturbed with deep anger and frustration. But for Mountbatten, weighed down by none of these inner misgivings, the occasion called forth all his powers of objective and dynamic decision, and he at once radiated confidence and a sense of purpose where none had existed before.

As soon as the actual constitution of the Committee had been decided we were promptly plunged into a number of " most immediate " items. The Ministry of Refugees had still to be set up. The Committee wanted to know by the next morning the name of the person appointed to be secretary to the Ministry. It then proceeded to tackle the difficult but urgent problem of accommodating this wholly new Department. Ismay was given the task of acting in a liaison capacity between the Emergency Committee and the Pakistan Government.

In the general zeal to get going, our newly fledged Public Relations Committee has been directed to " attempt to improve the standard of reporting of the Delhi newspapers on the communal situation, and to report "! On this occasion I think the result will be limited to our " reporting ", but it made everyone feel good, and that is the crux of the matter.

There was an exhaustive discussion on the imposition of martial law. Mountbatten considers there is a strong case for it in the Punjab, but only if all four Governments concerned are ready to back it. As this seemed on the whole unlikely, the Committee called for urgent examination of ways and means to stiffen existing acts in force in the East Punjab. Altogether some twelve items were cleared, from the setting up of a relief committee under Lady Mountbatten to the control of R.A.F. transport and the dropping of leaflets, from the freezing of assets to the disposal of jeeps. Everyone left the session somewhat breathless.

To-morrow Trivedi, the East Punjab Governor, with his Prime Minister, Gopi Chand Bhargava, and Home Minister, Swaran Singh, are to attend the Committee.

From Calcutta comes news of Gandhi's "miracle". His initial partnership with Suhrawardy did not achieve all that he had hoped; isolated stabbings and acts of violence continued. So on Monday he began a fast to end only if sanity returned to the city. On Thursday he was able to call it off after leaders of the various communities had given guarantees that the masses had already responded to the Mahatma's appeal through soul resistance for a change of heart.

After one of his Prayer Meetings, Hindus and Moslems by their thousands mingled and embraced in the Maidan. Hardened Press correspondents report that they have seen nothing comparable with this demonstration of mass influence. Mountbatten's estimate is that he has achieved by moral persuasion what four Divisions would have been hard pressed to have accomplished by force.

GOVERNMENT HOUSE, NEW DELHI, *Sunday, 7th September, 1947*

Our meeting began at eleven, but Trivedi and the East Punjab Ministers failed to arrive on time. Mountbatten started off by reporting that the situation in Delhi had worsened very considerably during the previous twenty-four hours. There had been a large number of incidents, including the stabbing of employees on the Government House estate, and far too many refugees were coming through before there was any organisation to receive them.

He turned at once to the question of banning the carrying of all weapons, which of course raised in its turn the problem of the *kirpans* or swords worn by the Sikhs. Patel felt that any suggestion of banning *kirpans* would raise great difficulties, as they had been recognised by the Government as religious weapons for many years. Mountbatten argued that the unqualified right of Sikhs to carry *kirpans* at this time stood in the way of precautions for law and order taken by every city in the world, but he agreed that the basic question was, which decision would lead to fewer people being killed—the banning of the *kirpan* or the safeguarding of Sikh religious feeling?

" If we go down in Delhi ", Mountbatten warned, " we are finished." Ismay suggested reinforcing the police with a cadre of special constables. Patel was doubtful, but Nehru in favour. Trivedi finally arrived at ten to one, starting off with an impassioned speech which was clearly based on the mistaken assumption that the Emergency Committee was nothing other than a Grand Inquisition on himself and his Government. In answer to Mountbatten's inquiry about the East Punjab's capacity to preserve law and order, and suggestion that this was the problem of top priority, Trivedi replied that the most urgent issue confronting him was the evacuation of refugees.

In view of the late arrival of the East Punjab contingent, it was decided to meet again later in the day, and we resumed at 6 p.m. It was a rather better meeting this time. Nehru and Patel stood firm about the Sikhs, and there is to be a ban on all weapons. " I will not tolerate Delhi becoming another Lahore ", Patel declared, and Nehru added, " I am certain in my mind *kirpans* may have to be taken away." Jeeps also are to be stopped from plying the streets—Nehru speaking of them as " a source of much mischief ".

The reports coming in which show the Delhi situation to be rapidly deteriorating call for coolness and strength. There has been a massacre at Willingdon airfield, and the Sikhs have delivered threats to the Australian High Commissioner and to the United States Ambassador. Mountbatten warned the meeting that the whole reputation of India is involved in providing complete physical security for its diplomatic representatives.

As token of his resolve to back his words with action, Mountbatten has put his Body Guard at the disposal of the Garrison Commander. Normally the Delhi Garrison is of brigade strength. But it has been pushed out battalion by battalion into the riot-torn Gurgaon district to try to keep the trouble out of the city itself. When, therefore, the trouble came in, there was simply no Garrison available. The Body Guard is certainly a *corps d'élite*, and in order to proclaim the perfect non-communal discipline, they have been patrolling the streets in sections of armoured cars, each consisting of one manned by Punjabi Mussulmans and one by Sikhs operating in concert.

GOVERNMENT HOUSE, NEW DELHI, *Monday, 8th September, 1947*

Less than forty-eight hours after our return Mountbatten's " Map Room " is in action. Situated in the ante-room next to the Council Chamber, it is designed to provide members of the Emergency Committee before their morning meetings with intelligence appreciations—supported by visual aids—of the disturbances and refugee movements on both sides of the Punjab Boundary. Much midnight oil has been burned to get the maps and flags in the correct position in time for this morning's meeting. There was a somewhat inauspicious start to the proceedings, as the unfortunate Lieutenant-Colonel detailed to give the situation report to the assembled notables fainted while doing so—undoubtedly from overwork.

My afternoon was given over to the first meeting of the United Council for Relief and Welfare—a title arrived at, incidentally, only after prolonged discussion—which is designed to co-ordinate the growing volume of voluntary relief. Lady Mountbatten was in the chair, and handled this body of volunteers and individualists with a perfect blend of charm and strength. They emerged from the session a potential team with a central purpose. No fewer than fifteen different organisations were represented at Government House to-day, and it is safe to say that only a dire emergency, together with Lady Mountbatten's administrative and diplomatic skill, would have brought them under one roof to pool their experience and effort.

Peter Howes tells me, incidentally, that among the many emergency duties falling on Mountbatten's British and Indian A.D.C.'s, attendance on Lady Mountbatten is hardly the most popular. For in the course of her tours of hospitals it usually involves assisting her to bring in to the local infirmaries any bodies they may see in the streets. She is not deterred from carrying out these errands of mercy, even when passing through areas where sniping is going on.

In the evening I had a long talk with the Nawab of Chhatari, the Nizam's Prime Minister. While anxious to be loyal to His Exalted Highness, he is finding it hard to interpret the diverse instructions he receives. Clearly his period of office and influence has not long to run. He and Monckton, who are both staying at Government House, had a meeting with Mountbatten to-day.

In the present emergency here in Delhi Hyderabad appears a less pressing problem, which makes Mountbatten think that this may be the psychological opportunity to promote the verbal variant to accession. At the Hyderabad end, the Nizam, in token of his desire to retain Monckton's services, issued a week ago a strongly worded *firman* (or official statement) condemning the attacks made on the members of his delegation as damaging the interests of the State. This he followed up with letters to Mountbatten confirming his confidence in Monckton and repudiating in picturesque terms the activities of the Ittehad, and in particular of its fanatical president, Kasim Razvi.

But while the Nizam himself may be moving haltingly towards an accommodation, Congress intelligence (which is remarkably well informed on States' affairs) has been picking up disquieting data about the efforts of the Nizam's Government to place orders for armaments in Czechoslovakia and in general to build up its separate sovereignty. Chhatari, however, is well aware that any such course would be disastrous for Hyderabad and India alike, and the mood of to-day's meeting was one of genuine desire on both sides to break through the deadlock. It has been conceded that the principals in the negotiations may not be able to agree on a formula at the first attempt, and on this understanding it was decided that Monckton and Chhatari should return to Hyderabad in a fresh effort to narrow the gap.

Just before turning in I looked out from my bedroom window towards the old city. I could see several big fires raging, and half expected to hear the wail of air-raid sirens and the drone of aircraft, or at least the shouting of mobs, but whatever horrors and sufferings were being endured at that moment, no sound of them reached out to me to break the sultry and sinister silence of the night. In pursuit of " feature epics " there is a British Press report of half a million people fighting in the blazing streets of Delhi, but this is manifestly gross exaggeration, and gives a wholly misleading picture of the furtive hit-and-run character of so much of this arson and murder. I want to try to see for myself what is really happening.

GOVERNMENT HOUSE, NEW DELHI, *Tuesday, 9th September, 1947*

To-day Mountbatten has seen Gandhi, who has just arrived in Delhi from his " miracles " in Calcutta, about which he is characteristically shy and self-deprecating. He confessed to Mountbatten that he had changed his mind about Government House, which hitherto he had denounced as the symbol of alien and false power. Now he was glad to find that it had been kept " a secure island in a sea of insecurity ". He was convinced that the emergency staff and the Committee working and deliberating far removed from public clamour may well have saved the Central Government.

This morning's Emergency Committee meeting had before it reports of a serious situation developing in Peshawar and other parts of the North-west Frontier Province, now in Pakistan. The immediate ministerial reaction is to believe the worst. There are moments when one feels that these two new nations are obsessed with some overwhelming death-wish and that there is no real awareness that to pursue the communal feud to its end must mean self-slaughter.

After dinner I repaired to the private cinema in Government House—almost the only source of relaxation left to Mountbatten now—and saw Joan Fontaine miscast in a lurid melodrama called *Ivy*. Release for her and the audience comes when she falls down a lift-shaft. Martin Gilliat invited me afterwards to get some fresh air and join him on his routine tour of inspection of the Delhi hospitals. The Governor-General's Body Guard—now reinforced, to the benefit of everyone's morale, by the 5/6th Gurkhas—has been detailed, at Lady Mountbatten's urgent request, to add to its tour of duty hospital protection. Perhaps the most horrifying feature of the current communal insanity is the lust of the strong to seek out the weak for massacre. Hospitals and refugee trains are thus the special targets of these crazed assassins.

Our particular mission was to see about the sentry-guard arrangements at the Victoria Zenana Hospital in Old Delhi. We were in a Government House hired car, a rather shabby Buick Eight. The crowns attached to the back and front bumpers were the only—and as it happened far from adequate—means of identifying its special status. A Sikh chauffeur drove us. Beside him on his right was Inspector Elder, Mountbatten's personal security officer. After being reassured by the nurse in charge at the Victoria Zenana that there had been no incidents during the day, and that the presence of the Gurkhas would do much to restore the confidence of the patients during the night, we decided to make a detour on our journey home and take a look at the Pahargunj area, one of the worst trouble-spots.

All was as quiet as the grave, the streets utterly deserted. We had reached the reverse slope of the large over-bridge near New Delhi station, and were cruising at about thirty miles an hour along the wide roadway, when, without any apparent warning and at point-blank range, we were fired upon. There was some shouting, then more bursts of fire. With a lively instinct for survival, Martin and I found ourselves crouching for cover on the floor, but not before Martin had been hit. Blood was pouring from behind his right ear. My immediate reaction was that he was very severely wounded. I heard Elder roar out in vain, " Stop shooting ! "

The car slewed round, and in a matter of split seconds I was conscious of the bigger danger of our piling up against the bridge and no doubt dropping over it. The next thing I knew was that the car had been straightened and was being brought to a stop. It was then that I became aware that this feat had been achieved by Elder, and that the Sikh driver, sitting very still at the wheel, was stone dead, killed by a volley which must have passed through my own head if my reflex actions had been a fraction slower.

In such an emergency one's senses are stimulated to give one almost a double vision of time and space. Everything seemed to happen at once and yet separately, now and for ever. Conflicting emotions crowded in on me. If I felt elation at my providential escape, this was largely offset by obsession with the driver's silent and uncomplaining death. I was deeply anxious for Martin, whom I thought to be a dying man, and felt no small concern for all of us, in case the picket turned on us again as we pulled ourselves out of our punctured and derelict car. But there was no sign of them or, indeed, of anyone. It was certainly an incongruous experience to find oneself in bow tie and white dinner-jacket deposited in the heart of Delhi's riot area at one o'clock in the morning and wholly stranded.

While we were trying to take stock of our position, an army lorry from the direction of the New Delhi station came out of the night towards us. Before we knew where we were we found it contained another picket, whose response to our signals was to come to the ready and train their rifles on us. It took all Elder's persuasive powers in the appropriate language to stop them shooting us first and finding out about us afterwards. Eventually, after much argument, they agreed to take us back to Government House by way of the Willingdon Hospital. There we handed over Martin, by now very weak from loss of blood, to Andy Taylor, Mountbatten's surgeon, by lucky chance on duty at the time.

After the good news that his head-wounds were only superficial, I reached Government House in need of a double whisky, and somewhat doubtful in my mind whether Mountbatten would deem the journey really necessary. I had asked no one's authority to go, and in retrospect it seemed arguable that I was taking an unwarranted risk not simply for myself but—as a member of his staff—for the Governor-General as well, in going at all. When I saw him in his bedroom at about two in the morning and was able to report favourably on Martin's condition, he gave no sign of " divine wrath ", but congratulated me on my escape in a way which made me feel that I had scored some marks for showing some enterprise.

I told him my bomb story—my closest escape until to-night's—when a five-hundred-pounder dropped on the pavement just outside our ground-floor flat in Westminster; the point of the story being that the bomb dropped just before 1 a.m. on the night of September 9th, 1940. Mount-batten set the seal on this evening's adventure with his comment, " Remind me to keep away from you on the night of 9th September, 1954."

GOVERNMENT HOUSE, NEW DELHI, *Thursday, 11th September, 1947*

V. P. told me before the Emergency Committee meeting that the Delhi situation was undoubtedly improving and that the Sikhs were answering Patel's appeal. But at the meeting itself I got the impression that Patel was changing his mind on the *kirpan* issue. There was quite a brisk exchange between the two strong men of the Government. " Murder ", said Nehru, " is not to be justified in the name of religion." " This is not fair," Patel retorted. " There is no question of doing so, but the Government must respect all religions."

A Delhi Emergency Committee has now been set up to deal specifically with the crisis in the capital and to leave the Cabinet Emergency Committee, from which it derives its authority, free to deal with the wider problems. One of the most dynamic members of the Cabinet, C. H. Bhabha, the Commerce Minister, is to be chairman, and H. M. Patel, the Cabinet Secretary, has been seconded to him. It will substantially take over the Municipal Administration, and meet on the same day-to-day basis as the parent body, which was in danger of becoming lost in a jungle of local detail.

In order to bring the emergency home to us, Lady Mountbatten has very justly imposed austerity on Government House kitchens. At a dinner-party for our distinguished visitors, Lord Listowel * and Sir Gilbert Laithwaite, Their Excellencies and guests, with customary ceremonial, were regaled with a three-course repast consisting of some cabbage-water masquerading as soup, one piece of spam and potato, a biscuit and a small portion of cheese. Listowel was impressed, but not quite as it was perhaps intended he should be, for he asked one of us afterwards whether this dinner had been specially laid on for his benefit!

GOVERNMENT HOUSE, NEW DELHI, *Friday, 12th September, 1947*

I had an interesting talk with Listowel over breakfast, and was able to explain fully to him the difficult Press situation that has developed here. Many factors are involved, personal and political. There is a sense of grievance as between the Indian Government and the Foreign Press, the former persuading themselves that the Foreign correspondents are as a body opposed to the new régime and always on the alert to exploit its difficulties, and the latter resentful at what they regard as the threat, and in some instances of the actual substance, of censorship. They are working in very difficult conditions, and, they allege, getting precious little official help.

Our Public Relations Committee consists, in addition to myself, of B. L. Sharma, a level-headed and technically accomplished Deputy Principal Information Officer, serving as the Ministry's own nominee, and Unni Nayar, *The Statesman's* Delhi correspondent, generously released by Ian Stephens, the Editor, to become the Commander-in-

---

* The Earl of Listowel succeeded Lord Pethick-Lawrence as the last Secretary of State for India in April, and Sir Gilbert Laithwaite was then his Departmental chief.

Chief's representative as a Lieutenant-Colonel, and to don once again his paratrooper's beret and wings. He is a forthright, attractive personality with a fine record as a war-time Public Relations Officer.

The three of us have been working very happily together serving in a supporting role to the Ministry of Information at the Emergency Committee and to the Press at Map Room conferences, where, to begin with, Pete Rees himself acted as the "military spokesman". Unfortunately, in his first attempt he strayed from the script and ventured on to the quicksands of personal opinion on a point of communal controversy, duly incensing the assembled Indian correspondents, some of whom are in a highly emotional condition. In the circumstances Rees agreed with Mountbatten that both on psychological and technical grounds it would be wiser to let Unni Nayar do the talking at the conferences, while he himself and his staff vet the accuracy of the many unreliable reports coming in to us. The quality of much of the Intelligence information is very low, and considerable discretion and checking are needed before putting it out under official authority.

This morning's Emergency Committee was a bad meeting, one Minister defeating its purpose by raising a whole series of low-level departmental problems, and another simply grinning at his Ministry's lack of office accommodation. No sense of grip was conveyed. It has, for instance, taken all day to get a loud-speaker for the Purana Qila Fort, which Moslem evacuees in their thousands have converted into a veritable ghetto. From the account given at the meeting, the Purana Qila situation is clearly very grave. Nearly eighty per cent of the refugees there have been inoculated, but there is hardly any food coming in to them, and without loud-speakers it is impossible to impose order upon the confusion or create confidence from the prevailing panic.

This evening at six o'clock Nehru addressed the Diplomatic Corps in the Map Room. This was his first contact with them since the onset of the crisis. He spoke with telling simplicity and frankness, and made no attempt to score debating points or hide behind apologies. With the scholar's eye, he related the immediate incidents of the tragedy to the deeper trends. "The history of India", he said, "has been one of assimilation and synthesis of the various elements that have come in. . . . It is perhaps because we tried to go against the trend of the country's history that we are faced with this. . . . It is for our common good that the situation must be controlled as soon as possible. Otherwise tremendous injury will be done to both Dominions. This is why we have had meetings at Ambala, Lahore, etc. Of course it is easier to come to conclusions at the conference table than to put them into effect, but still it is extremely helpful that we have a more or less common policy."

The assembled Diplomats afterwards expressed their appreciation of his objective and moderate approach. Hitherto they have been without reliable guidance, and this should do much to restore their confidence in the régime. Sir Terence Shone, the United Kingdom High Commissioner, gave me the name of the first British casualty in the troubles—a bank manager who had been shot. I remarked that the correspondents, Foreign and Indian, did not yet seem to have woken up to the new order or to have realised that the High Commissioner and his staff are now the primary source for all information about the British in India.

After the Diplomatic Corps had left I was called in for a talk with Nehru and Mountbatten on the subject of an alleged statement by Tara Singh which was being given currency in Pakistan. He is described as using words to the effect that " This is war ". General Thimayya, Area Commander, is to make a report on what really happened. Nehru is not unduly disturbed, but Mountbatten stressed the peril of letting inflammatory phrases or reports of phrases in the present crisis pass unchecked.

Nehru then said he proposed to give another Map Room talk, this time to the Press, and asked me for guidance on the points I thought he should make. I said that he should stress the scale of the administrative burden carried by both the central and East Punjab Governments; and that in urging on the Press the need to look at the problem in perspective he should himself help them to do so by providing as much authoritative data as possible.

While we were talking, a telephone call came through from Liaquat asking him to come to Lahore for a meeting on the convoy problem. It is assuming serious proportions in view of uncertainty about the Sikh attitude to a very large Moslem convoy passing through Amritsar. Nehru at first was unwilling to go to Lahore, saying he could see no use in the visit, but Mountbatten pleaded with him that it was vital for regular contact between the two Prime Ministers to be maintained, and declared that the whole reputation of the Government was at stake on the successful clearance of this major refugee convoy. Nehru, convinced by the force of Mountbatten's argument, finally agreed to go, and, on my suggestion, to say so at the Press conference. It was also agreed that Unni Nayar should go up with him to handle any publicity problems that may arise there.

Nehru went out of his way to assure me that I was doing good work here in Delhi, and these kind words, together with his request for guidance almost as a matter of routine, were gratifying signs of his confidence at a crucial moment, for it has been a week of heavy strain and hazard for us all. While it is still too soon to assess the full scale of the crisis confronting us on our return from Simla, my own belief is that Mountbatten's presence and example may well have saved both the capital and the Government from complete disintegration.

Already, at the end of the first week of its existence, the Emergency Committee has launched a formidable administrative counter-offensive against the prevailing chaos. It has requisitioned civilian transport, dispatched to Provinces and States ready to receive them tens of thousands of non-Moslem refugees who had come to Delhi, arranged for special trains for Moslems to go to Pakistan, provided guards, called for volunteer constables, arranged for the saving and harvesting of crops from deserted lands, given orders for the searching of passengers for arms on trains and for the stiffening of punishments for delinquent military and police guards of trains.

It has cancelled public holidays, including Sundays, helped to keep

22nd March, 1947. Lord Mountbatten on arrival at Palam Airfield being greeted by Pandit Jawaharlal Nehru, and Mr Liaquat Ali Khan

The Earl and Countess Mountbatten of Burma. Lord Mountbatten is wearing the mantle of Grand Master of the Order of the Star of India

2nd April, 1947. Mahatma Gandhi takes his morning meal at Viceroy's House for the first time in his life

5th April, 1947. Mr Jinnah meeting the Mountbattens for the first time at Viceroy's House

28th April, 1947. The Mountbattens returning from confronting the Moslem League demonstration at Peshawar

Off duty, Mashobra, Simla, 9th May, 1947. From left to right: Lord and Lady Mountbatten, the author, Pandit Nehru, the author's wife, Mrs Nicholls, the Hon. Pamela Mountbatten, Mr Britter and Colonel Douglas Currie

Mashobra, 9th May 1947. The author and his daughter, Virginia, with Lady Mountbatten and the Chinese Ambassador. Lady Mountbatten's dog Mizzen is in the foreground

High speed diplomacy, Palam Airfield, 18th May, 1947. Lord Mountbatten having a last-minute word with the author before departing for London

Meeting with the Leaders, Viceroy's House, 2nd June, 1947. From Lord Mountbatten's left, Mr Jinnah, Mr Liaquat Ali Khan, Sardar Rab Nishtar, Sardar Baldev Singh, Acharya Kripalani, Sardar Patel and Pandit Nehru. At the back, Sir Eric Miéville and Lord Ismay

Lord Mountbatten addressing the Princes, New Delhi, 25th July, 1947

Lord Mountbatten is here presiding, as the special calendar shows, over one of the last of his Staff Meetings. On his right and left are Lord Ismay and Sir George Abell; in the foreground, Lieut-Colonel Vernon Erskine Crum, Conference Secretary (left), and the author

Karachi Celebrations, 14th August, 1947. Lord Mountbatten is shown taking the salute of the Armed Forces of Pakistan outside the Legislative Assembly — Mr Jinnah and Miss Fatima Jinnah to his right and Lady Mountbatten to his left

15 August, 1947. Lord Mountbatten returning to Government House from the Durbar Hall after being sworn in as the first Governor-General of the Free India

Gandhi's last journey, 31st January, 1948

Hyderabad Mission, 15th May, 1948. The Nizam of Hyderabad photographed at the Hyderabad City Mosque

Homecoming, Northolt, 23rd June, 1948. Left to right: the Duke of Edinburgh, Lord Mountbatten, Mr Chetty, Finance Minister of the Government of India, Mr Attlee, Lady Mountbatten, and the author in the background

going two newspapers as well as All India Radio, arranged for Government servants to be brought to their work and for the telephone system to be maintained, provided guards for hospitals, arranged for the collecting and burying of corpses found in the streets, for the movement of food, for the broadcasting of daily official bulletins to the Provinces and for large-scale cholera injections.   This is but a random selection showing the variety and scale of its actions.

GOVERNMENT HOUSE, NEW DELHI, *Saturday, 13th September, 1947*

Nehru's Press conference was fairly successful, but he spoke a little too long and was not quite so convincing as to the Diplomats yesterday. He included most of the points I was anxious for him to make, but he did not punch them home quite hard enough, and gave the impression of being—as indeed he is—a very tired man.

None-the-less to see Nehru at close range during this ordeal is an inspiring experience.   He vindicates one's faith in the humanist and the civilised intellect.   Almost alone in the turmoil of communalism, with all its variations, from individual intrigue to mass madness, he speaks with the voice of reason and charity.

The negotiations for the transfer of power between March and August did not seem to me to evoke his full powers.   A certain moodiness and outbursts of exasperation were the visible signs of overstrain; but now somehow he has renewed himself, and in this deeper crisis he is shown at his full stature—passionate and courageous, yet objective and serene : one of the enlightened elect of our time.

A feature of the Emergency Committee set-up, which has greatly impressed all the Indians, has been the work of the Governor-General's Conference Secretariat.   Vernon makes long-hand notes on each item and records the decision of the Committee in each case, as summarised by Mountbatten.   He then dictates the minutes and decisions in lucid and unequivocal language to a relay of three stenographers who type their portion straight on to stencils.   Copies reach all concerned by a team of Despatch Riders within a couple of hours of the end of each meeting. At the following morning's meeting those concerned have to report progress publicly on each item in turn.   The result is that the Government of India is now working at racing-car speed instead of at the pace of the proverbial Indian bullock cart.

CHAPTER SIXTEEN

SHADOW OF JUNAGADH

GOVERNMENT HOUSE, NEW DELHI, *Sunday, 14th September, 1947*

MOUNTBATTEN HELD A Staff Meeting which was largely taken up with the discussion of the Purana Qila situation. Patel is apparently on the verge of deciding to send in a battalion in order to round up Moslem arms. Mountbatten argues that any such action would be disastrous and the surest way to provoke a massacre, and he is at a loss to understand how any such order could be seriously considered.

At the ten o'clock meeting of the Emergency Council Patel mentioned prolonged gunfire from some Delhi houses and pressed for action to clear up resistance pockets. General Lockhart, since 15th August the Commander-in-Chief, said that he could clear up the whole of Delhi in three days if he could concentrate troops on this particular job.

I had a good talk with Mountbatten, and found him in his usual buoyant mood. He has been seeing British troops awaiting repatriation, who told him they hate to sit around and watch all this misery, powerless to do anything about it. So he suggested that N.C.O.'s and men should offer their help to organise the camps.* He adds that he hopes to phase himself out of the Emergency Committee in about three weeks, first having the meetings every other day, and then handing over the chairmanship to Nehru. He confessed that he is now thankful that he took everyone's advice, and did not leave India on 15th August.

Ismay is back from Karachi. I saw him just before he went in to report to Mountbatten on his visit. He told me it was lucky he went when he did. He found Jinnah claiming to have lost all faith in the Government of India and on the point of breaking off diplomatic relations with it. Of the forty-eight hours Ismay was there he was closeted with Jinnah for no less than eleven. He was, incidentally, the first guest at Government House since the 15th August. He feels that he must have won the confidence of Jinnah, who called him to his face " a good fellow ", and issued him a cordial invitation to come and see him whenever he wanted to.

Apparently Jinnah was full of wrath against Congress, saying that he could never understand these men's hatreds and was now beginning to feel that there was no alternative but to fight it out. Ismay said he grappled with him, asserting that he was not given to overstatement but was ready to stake his life that the Government of India were determined to put down the troubles to the best of their ability. They were sincere men, and at the full stretch in their efforts. Ismay thinks that he has caused Jinnah to pause on the brink of precipitate action, but that his visit was only just in time.

* Their help proved invaluable and enhanced British prestige all round.

This evening a heavy storm broke over Delhi to cause a temporary truce to disturbances of the peace but to add to the miseries of the over-crowded refugee camps. Sheet lightning on a tremendous scale rent the sky.

GOVERNMENT HOUSE, NEW DELHI, *Monday, 15th September, 1947*

At this morning's Staff Meeting there was a round-up on the general situation arising from Ismay's Karachi visit. Mountbatten's analysis is that the Moslems and Hindus are at least under the control of their respective Governments in approximately equal ratios, but that the Sikhs are uncontrollable and even their leaders afraid of them. V. P.'s view was that there was no immediate prospect of harmony between Pakistan and India. Whereupon Mountbatten visualised the worst case as war between the two Dominions. If harmony is impossible, at least we should try to keep as far away from war as possible. V. P. felt that even this hope was dissipated, with Jinnah in his present frame of mind.

Mountbatten asked about Sikh motives. Was the objective to set up a Sikh State? V. P. replied no. Politically they had lost out, and had not even gained the Jullundur division. Their motive was almost entirely revenge. V. P.'s son was operating with three Sikhs who had lost their families. Their only objective was two Moslem lives for every one of their relatives'. Tara Singh, he felt, was essentially a frightened man.

The Emergency Committee meeting was a little better than yesterday's, but still far too much time was taken up on small miscellaneous items. Trivedi and the East Punjab representatives failed to arrive because of bad weather. Nehru reported on his visit to Lahore yesterday, and referred to the important decision he and Liaquat had taken to stop the hold-ups due to the policy of searching refugees for arms before crossing the boundary. But no sooner was the meeting over than Liaquat made a speech alleging that the Government of India was not carrying out arrangements agreed upon, and asserting, " To-day we in Pakistan are surrounded on all sides by forces which are out to destroy us ".

For the past ten days we have been completely absorbed in the Punjab cataclysm and the salvage of Delhi. Now a new crisis is building up from a wholly unexpected quarter. It has come to our notice that Junagadh, one of the two hundred and eighty Kathiawar States, failed to accede to either Dominion on 15th August, and is now proposing to do so to Pakistan, Jinnah concurring in the act. It is fair to say that in the welter of great events immediately before and after the transfer of power Junagadh was simply overlooked and, as a result, is now bracketed with the two major States of Hyderabad and Kashmir as being outside Patel's " full bag ".

Junagadh itself is a veritable patchwork quilt. Some three thousand three hundred square miles in area, with eighty-two per cent of its seven hundred thousand inhabitants Hindu and its Ruler and Government Moslem, it is completely surrounded by States which have acceded to India. Inside Junagadh are islands of territory from these States, and inside these States islands of Junagadh territory. Her railways, ports and telegraphs are an integral part of the Indian system. The Nawab is an eccentric of rare vintage whose preoccupation in life seems to be his pet dogs, of which he owns eight hundred, each with its own human attendant. On one occasion he organised a wedding for two of his dogs, costing three lakhs of rupees (twenty-one thousand pounds), and a State holiday was proclaimed in honour of the event.

How has all this confusion over Junagadh come about? At Mountbatten's meeting with the Princes on 25th July the then Dewan asked a series of questions, none of which gave any sign of an intention to accede to Pakistan. Indeed, he went so far as to advise Mountbatten that he proposed recommending to the Ruler to accede to India. The Junagadh Government had declared that Junagadh would make common cause with the other Kathiawar States, all of which have acceded to India. On the 10th August, however, just five days before the transfer of power, there was a *coup d'état*. A group of Sindi Moslems took over the Government. Shah Nawaz Bhutto became Dewan, and the Nawab a virtual prisoner in his own palace.

It has been freely recognised that the act of accession is the prerogative of the Prince. But India's readiness to recognise such acts was governed by a time limit of 15th August, which was, of course, the basis of Mountbatten's urgent appeal to the Princes on 25th July. Moreover, arising from that speech two other powerful factors have always been inherent in the choice of accession—first, in Mountbatten's own words, certain " geographical compulsions which cannot be evaded ", and secondly, the communal majorities of the Ruler's subjects.

Although Junagadh has a sea-board and a small port, Veraval, and thereby can claim direct access to Karachi, it is clear that any final decision by the Prince to accede to Pakistan would automatically be a direct challenge to the essential validity of the whole accession policy, with disastrous effects both upon the Kathiawar States and upon the Hyderabad negotiations, where the Moslem extremists would be greatly encouraged. Jinnah has clearly seen the wider possibilities presented by the Junagadh error of omission. No pressure has been put by the Government of India on Junagadh to accede, but when the likelihood of accession to Pakistan loomed large, two formal approaches were made by Delhi to Karachi for some declaration of Pakistan's intentions. No reply has so far been received.

Mountbatten called me in for meetings he is having with Ismay and V. P. on the Junagadh situation. V. P. is full of anxiety, and tried to persuade Mountbatten of the desirability of making a military and naval demonstration. He has prepared a paper based on the assumption that Pakistan is ready to help Junagadh with men and money.

I went round to see Ismay at his house in the evening, and found him perturbed by the somewhat feverish atmosphere induced by Junagadh. He considered that the Information Report, assessing Pakistan's likely intervention as a loan of eight crores rupees (some six million pounds) for the development of Junagadh's port and a garrison of twenty-five thousand troops, could only be regarded as childish in the light of her current resources and commitments.   The instructions given to me have been to advise on likely Press reactions and prepare a draft communiqué— neither of them easy tasks.

GOVERNMENT HOUSE, NEW DELHI, *Tuesday, 16th September, 1947*

We are advised that the Junagadh Accession has been sealed, signed and delivered to Karachi, but this is not yet an official certainty.   I was present at a further meeting which Mountbatten had with Ismay and V. P. Ismay spoke with great cogency about Jinnah's probable tactics and strategy over Junagadh.   Clearly on its face value the State is worthless to him.   It is an impossible military liability.   By no stretch of the imagination is it his policy to incorporate isolated pockets of Moslems, for there are already some forty million of them outside the Pakistan homeland.

Ismay sees the move essentially as one of traps and teasings on Jinnah's part.   He hopes by luring India into a militant reaction to secure a verdict on legal points and to create a valuable precedent for any attitude he may care to adopt towards the far greater Princely objectives of Kashmir and Hyderabad.   For Junagadh is in some respects Hyderabad in miniature— a Moslem Prince and oligarchy ruling over a predominantly Hindu State in the middle of Indian territory.

I have prepared the draft communiqué on the Junagadh situation. The Indian case on paper is strong enough, but as for possible Press reaction, I have felt obliged to give this warning.   " Although the above arguments are cogent in themselves, I doubt whether they would out-weigh the damaging impression that would be created with the Foreign Press by joining issue to the point of military demonstration at this time. Any such action however justified would almost certainly be regarded as precipitate and aggressive.   The Foreign Press are very much on the *qui vive* for warlike policy on the part of the two new Dominions." I urged that from the Public Relations viewpoint the immediate step should be no more than a straightforward non-recognition statement, the Government reserving to itself its future freedom of action, but leaving open the possibility of full negotiation.

On the Punjab sector of Indo-Pakistan relations Nehru has replied with commendable moderation to Liaquat's stormy utterances in Lahore. The Indian leaders, he declared, had sought to avert Partition, but once it was decided upon the Government had tried to discharge faithfully all the obligations flowing from that decision.   He spoke of derelictions of duty on both sides of the frontier, which he and his colleagues condemned and were resolved to eliminate.

At the Emergency Committee to-day Mountbatten has gained his point, and the Committee is now to meet every other day.   There was an important discussion on the Delhi refugees.   Dr. Zakir Hussain, chair-man of the Moslem Refugees Committee, gave a disquieting report on the current situation, urging that the present influx of refugees into the camps must somehow be stopped.   Disease was breaking out ; there were some fifty thousand already in the Purana Qila; sixteen thousand had been moved from the Ridge to Humayun's Tomb, but ten thousand more had promptly turned up there.

Throughout this long meeting, Maulana Azad, the Moslem elder statesman in the Congress, sat silent and impassive, as he always does, looking, with his pointed beard, just like Cardinal Richelieu.

GOVERNMENT HOUSE, NEW DELHI, *Wednesday, 17th September, 1947*

Mountbatten had long talks with both Nehru and Patel prior to the crucial Cabinet meeting this afternoon on Junagadh. He summoned all his powers of persuasion to head them off any decision which the world could interpret as putting India in the wrong, or any commitment to an act of war against what was now Pakistan territory. He reiterated Ismay's thesis that the whole manœuvre was almost certainly a trap and part of a wider campaign which Jinnah might be expected to launch for the express purpose of presenting Pakistan to the world as the innocent weak State threatened by the ruthless aggressor. He urged them to stand by the principle of a referendum both to discover the people's will and to disavow any intention of annexing territory.

Mountbatten had no difficulty in carrying Nehru with him at once, but it took rather longer to persuade Patel, whose whole Accession policy, as well as his personal emotions, were more closely affected by Junagadh. However he, too, was duly convinced by Mountbatten's arguments, and in particular by the impressions Ismay had formed of Jinnah's mood and motives. They both went straight into the Cabinet to explain their new point of view and, although they must have taken their colleagues by surprise, I understand they soon gained the day for a cautious approach. The two decisions of substance taken at the meeting were that Indian and local troops of acceding States should be disposed round Junagadh but should not occupy it, and that V. P. should visit the State to explain to the Nawab and Dewan the implications of their accession to Pakistan.

GOVERNMENT HOUSE, NEW DELHI, *Thursday, 18th September, 1947*

I have just seen a most charming and well-deserved letter from the famous Sarojini Naidu to Lady Mountbatten. Before the transfer of power there had been some speculation as to what position Mrs. Naidu, one of the great Congress personalities, would hold in the new régime. When the time came she was offered, and accepted, to the surprise of many, the Governorship of the United Provinces. The post was quickly to become one of tremendous importance, as on the ability of the United Province Government to prevent the Punjab troubles spreading across its own borders largely depended the fate of the whole of northern India.

The letter reads as follows :—

" Government House,
Lucknow.
10.9.47.

" To
The Governor-General's Lady
from a mere Governor.

Greetings—I have been watching your work and am filled with deep admiration for your untiring and infinitely fruitful spirit of compassionate and effective service. No woman in your place has ever put herself before in touch with the people. You have not been aloof and condescending in your well-doing—you have been gracious and intimate and personal—the last of the Vicereines is creating her own immortality in the hearts of suffering India. The Governor-General is proving himself indeed a great statesman as well as a great human being with imagination, authority and determination. I sent him on the 7th of the month a floss-bracelet or RAKSHA-BANDAN which Hind women send from huts and palaces equally to men whom they honour and trust and rely on as friends. The Rajput Queens used to send these bracelets on the full moon night of the special month to Moghul Emperors, etc.— one occasion when communal labels did not count !

" I don't know how long I shall be in these provinces, but my one real gift has been having full scope and bearing real fruit. My gift of friendliness. Men and women who have not spoken to each other for years meet under my roof every day in a more cordial manner after an initial moment of uncertainty. . . . O yes—the lions and the lambs lie down very pleasantly together in my green pastures. Each of us can only do our best, but as Browning says, ' There shall never be one lost good ' What a comforting belief.

I send you my love and also my benediction.

Your affectionate friend,
Sarojini Naidu."

GOVERNMENT HOUSE, NEW DELHI, *Friday, 19th September, 1947*

Liaquat is here as guest of the Government of India. It has been agreed under the new dispensation that distinguished Government guests should stay with the Governor-General.

In the afternoon, B. L. Sharma, Unni Nayar and myself met Colonel Majid Malik to try to work out ways and means of improving Press facilities and liaison in the East and West Punjab. No hint was given to us at this meeting that Liaquat had invited a number of Foreign correspondents to meet him after dinner to-night in his suite at Government House. I may say that Lady Mountbatten, somewhat startled by a request for drinks for twenty in Liaquat's room after dinner, had asked me whether I had any clue as to the reason. I could throw no light on the mystery until a few minutes later—B. L Sharma rang me up in some agitation for details about Liaquat's " Press conference ".

The Mountbattens were on the point of going into dinner with their guests, who included both Nehru and Liaquat. I at once pushed through an urgent message. "Sharma, who is very worried, advises me that the meeting is to be confined to Foreign correspondents. He thinks it will be exploited by the Indian Press, who will say that the Prime Minister of Pakistan has made Government House a base for propaganda by inviting the Foreign Press and omitting them." I also drew attention to the difficulties involved in inviting and selecting representatives of the Indian Press at this last moment and in keeping the conference wholly off-the-record. In so far as I considered the situation to be most embarrassing and liable to cause much misunderstanding, I felt the best solution would be to invite Liaquat to call his party off on grounds of pressure of work.

This message brought the Mountbattens and Nehru straight out into the adjoining study, where, with the zest of a schoolboy, Mountbatten said he would tackle Liaquat over dinner if, and only if, Nehru would agree to play his part by converting the occasion into a joint off-the-record session, in which case he himself was prepared to take the chair. The meeting should be put back half an hour, and I was to gather in a limited last-minute list of Indian correspondents. Nehru, I think, derived almost æsthetic satisfaction from the beauty of this plan and his usually sad expression gave way to a smile and the hint of a wink. At all events he found Mountbatten's proposal irresistible, as Liaquat did over dinner!

The conference itself was a tremendous success, and although no word of it could be quoted, it brought fresh hope and faith at a decisive moment to correspondents many of whom were seriously beginning to wonder whether any will to peace was to be found at any level within the two Dominions.

Mountbatten got the proceedings off to a good start. The two Prime Ministers, he said, had come together because there was much common ground between them. "That is not to say that either wants to help the other Dominion for its own sake, but both know that unless they come to grips with the difficulties confronting them there is danger of anarchy that will be disastrous to both."

Nehru stressed that in spite of all the developments of the past few months, the main problem was economic. "The other trouble will pass, but this we must solve or it will solve or dissolve us." The talk of war that was going around was "completely wild and absurd. If war should come all our dreams of prosperity would collapse for a generation."

Liaquat was no less explicit. "I agree that talk of war is absurd," he said; "if war should come it would be ruinous to both India and Pakistan; even more, it would mean another world war. None can contemplate that with equanimity. Pakistan wants peace for all nations but especially with India. We are, after all, two parts of the sub-continent. We could never dream of waging war against India."

Bob Trumbull, of the *New York Times*, asked Nehru how the immediate psychological problem was to be solved? "The first thing," Nehru replied, "is to reduce fear, the most enervating of emotions.

Once we have done that we can get on with other things, and the normal factors of life will resume operation." Nehru was asked if he was satisfied that he had complete control of his Government for the implementation of his policy, and if the British were doing all they could to help? Were both the Prime Ministers satisfied that the other Government was doing all in its power to remedy the situation?

Nehru responded with a brief dissertation on London School of Economics lines. " I am not satisfied with anything in India, and have not been for thirty years. Of course we must meet the situation in every way we can, partly by psychology and partly by force. If I may draw on my Socialist background, what is happening now is to a large extent an upheaval in the lower middle classes—the classes that first supported Hitler. When society is upset, strange elements come to the surface. Sometimes these are fascist or fascist-inclined. These groups take advantage of the situation. Undoubtedly there has been a communal trend in what has happened, but the trend now is away from killings and towards increased looting. There are instances of Sikhs looting Sikh shops, Hindus looting Hindu property and Moslems looting Moslems. In a sense this is worse, but in another way it is a hopeful sign. It is something we can deal with by persuasion or force, and that is the way we must deal with it."

Liaquat showed himself to be in general agreement with this thesis. The only qualification he made was in reply to a question to them both as to how these " brown-shirt " elements were to be combatted and the initiative taken back from them. " I don't agree," Liaquat said, " that the young elements in the Moslem League have the initiative. Besides, we are taking steps to restore discipline in the League. That is the important point." Asked if the two Dominions would welcome foreign capital and technical assistance in the task of recovery from this disruption, Nehru replied, " Of course we shall welcome foreign capital and technical assistance for our development but not foreign vested interest ". To which Liaquat added, " Same for us ".

Everyone went away feeling that the two Prime Ministers had risen above prevailing hatreds and shown themselves to be men of constructive outlook and compatible temperament. In the last analysis they were both moderates who had drunk deep of Western thought, and who were more effectively inoculated than some of their colleagues against the communal virus.

GOVERNMENT HOUSE, NEW DELHI, *Saturday, 20th September, 1947*

A court of inquiry set up to consider the Pahargunj shooting incident has taken its evidence and reported. Apparently we were fired on by a Madrassi picket which had only just arrived from the South of India earlier in the day, and was acting on general instructions given to troops to infuse more zeal into the enforcement of law and order in Delhi. We were the first victims of this mandate, but the court of inquiry, in the welter of conflicting evidence about warning signals or the lack of them, wisely decided that no one was culpably to blame. Examination of the car showed that we had been hit no fewer than six times from a range of about twenty yards, and suggested that we had been fired on from the front, side and rear.

In the circumstances the escape of any of us can only be described as violation of all the laws of probability. Publicity, of course, could not be avoided, and we have heard from Peter Scott * in London, who had an interview with the Prime Minister, that Mr. Attlee was disturbed by the incident, in case it meant that the troubles might now be assuming an anti-white character.

Constitutional Governor-Generalship brings no respite, and Mountbatten seems fated to have to juggle with three or four crises at once. In the midst of all the preoccupations with the Punjab and Junagadh, Walter Monckton has just arrived at Government House with the rest of the Hyderabad delegation—spokesmen of the Nizam's strange statecraft—for a further meeting with Mountbatten. The Ittehad-ul-Muslimeen—the extremist Moslem organisation in the State, which has been playing an increasingly powerful role in the formation of Hyderabad's policy since the transfer of power—got to work again on the Nizam while he was in a recalcitrant mood in a further effort to secure Monckton's removal. Monckton was in Delhi at the time, but after he had returned to warn the Council of the perils of a breakdown and of his own intention of leaving immediately for England, the Ittehad at the last minute seems to have been somewhat frightened by its own handiwork, and to have pleaded with him in forcible terms that if he were to leave them now it would be a disaster. Mountbatten is still hopeful that all will be well, even though little more than three weeks is left of the two months extension.

At to-day's meeting, which V. P. attended, the delegation stressed the importance attached by the Nizam to the distinction between accession and association. Accession, they felt, would lead to bloodshed. They were also frightened of interference from outside. Both Mountbatten and V. P. gave assurances that their fears were without substance, that the Indian Government had behaved correctly, and that its resources were at the Ruler's disposal if required to deal with disturbances. Mountbatten warned that unless agreement could be reached by the 15th October, breakdown must be envisaged, which would, he thought, be serious enough for India, but even more so for Hyderabad. The delegation has deposited some Heads of Agreement which are designed more to keep the ball in play than to decide the match.

Monckton said afterwards that he felt there was no fundamental difference of approach between Mountbatten and himself. He would continue to look for the formula which would allow statutory independence for Hyderabad, and which, while containing no direct reference to the word " accession ", would incorporate it on a *de facto* basis. Hyderabad, he added, was in no position to play the role of the fully fledged sovereign State. Provided the negotiations do not break down completely, he thinks that the Nizam will press him to stay on a little longer, but his decision to do so or not depends upon whether he can see

* Assistant Private Secretary to the Viceroy until 15th August.

a reasonable hope of achieving a compromise. If there is any such prospect he feels he ought to stay, if only because peace and order in the State may largely depend on his availability. But if not, it would be useless for him to remain. Both the Nizam and his Government are very volatile statesmen, pursuing a very inconsistent and wavering line of policy.

CHAPTER SEVENTEEN

MIGRATION OF PEOPLES

GOVERNMENT HOUSE, NEW DELHI, *Sunday, 21st September, 1947*

THIS MORNING AT 7.15 a party of sixteen left Palam airfield by the Governor-General's Dakota to make a round tour of some four hundred miles over the routes of the great refugee migrations between the East and West Punjab. The Government House party included the Mountbattens, Ismay, Vernon and myself. The Government witnesses were Nehru, Patel, Neogy, Rajkumari Amrit Kaur, General Lockhart, H. M. Patel and Shankar. Pandit Kunzru, the prominent Liberal who had just made some long-range criticisms of the Government's refugee policy, was also invited to come and see things for himself, but unfortunately he did not arrive on time, and we had to leave without him. At all the key points we came down to about two hundred feet.

We flew first in a north-westerly direction towards Ferozepur and Kusur, upon which columns of Moslems from Jullundur and Ludhiana in the East, and of non-Moslems from the bottle-neck of the Balloki Head bridge across the River Ravi, were converging. We passed first over Kallanur, which was supposed to be surrounded by non-Moslems, but there was no sign of any such activity, only a few people on the outskirts waving at us, and then on to Hissar, junction of road and rail, where again nothing seemed to be disturbing the peace of this quiet Sunday morning.

Only when we reached Bhatinda, an important railway junction, did we come across the first signs of major upheaval. Two trains, crammed with their human cargoes, were in the station. We could see the refugees clambering on to the tops of the carriages, bursting out of the sides, in occupation of the engine and tender itself. On arrival at Ferozepur we saw another such refugee train and more rolling-stock. As we approached the Ravi we had our first aerial vision of the scale of this desperate exodus. We were looking down on one of the greatest movements of population in recorded history, and then only on a small segment of it.

Hindus, Sikhs and Moslems have before now, in response to some crisis, gathered up their wordly goods and moved away, but these earlier treks were usually limited to one community, and there was always the expectation that the wanderers would ultimately come back to their home-land. To-day, however, there is this difference : the numbers on the move are incomparably greater than ever before, and this time there will be no return.

We struck the first great caravanserai between Ferozepur and Balloki Head, and pursued it far across the Ravi. We flew, in fact, for over fifty miles against this stream of refugees without reaching its source. Every now and then the density of bullock-carts and families on foot keeping to the thin life-line of the road would tail away, only to fill out again in close columns without end.

At Balloki Head, the actual boundary, the refugees waiting to cross the bridge overflowed and took on the appearance of a squatters' township. Here they had been brought to a standstill, but the general movement was very slow, and we could see men on horseback passing up and down who seemed to be giving some coherence, if not command, to the closely packed mass. At the roadside some families were flanked by their cattle, in many cases their only worldly asset, but few, if any, would be able to pass their livestock across the bridge. Already the flow of human traffic across it was beyond any conceivable capacity for which it had been built.

As we flew back into India we came down low over the northernmost of the Moslem refugee convoys making its slow and painful way along the main Lyallpur–Lahore road. Their exodus brought them across the Beas River, and involved an elaborate detour to save them from passing through Amritsar. We estimated that it took us just over a quarter of an hour to fly from one end to the other of this particular column at a flying speed of about a hundred and eighty miles per hour. This column therefore must have been at least forty-five miles long.

At the conference on Sunday, Nehru and Liaquat had told us how, to begin with, they had set their faces against any wholesale transfer of populations, but how events had rapidly become too large for them and had dictated the course of their policy.

To-day we saw for ourselves something of the stupendous scale of the Punjab upheaval. Even our brief bird's-eye view must have revealed nearly half a million refugees on the roads. At one point during our flight Sikh and Moslem refugees were moving almost side by side in opposite directions. There was no sign of clash. As though impelled by some deeper instinct, they pushed forward obsessed only with the objective beyond the boundary.

GOVERNMENT HOUSE, NEW DELHI, *Monday, 22nd September, 1947*

At this morning's Emergency Committee, Cabinet Ministers took a rather firmer and more urgent view than hitherto of the need to defend refugee trains. In the past few hours reports have come in of no fewer than four serious attacks on refugee trains, two on Moslems in Jullundur and at the Beas bridge and two on non-Moslems in the Lahore area. There was anxious discussion on the measures needed to tackle these bestial outrages.

During his visit Liaquat had referred to one train starting off with two thousand passengers, of whom only seven hundred had arrived at the other end, and of another completely lacking in any water supplies for a three-day journey. As in all these train horror stories, there is the usual factual confusion and difficulty in securing reliable data. In the meanwhile rumours fan hatreds.

One encouraging factor is that both the Governments of the United Provinces and East Punjab are showing strength in their resolve to tackle the disorders. Collective fines on villages which are known to be involved in these attacks are being imposed and levied within twenty-four hours. Should night trains be abandoned? In the effort to provide protection for passengers at night, sizeable Army contingents were involved. During one of the incidents several officers and sixty-four men had been engaged in a desperate hand-to-hand struggle.

As the debate continued, Mountbatten raised the wider issues—the need for establishing the proper priorities between the general maintenance of law and order and the rapid movement of refugees. He went further, and asked what was to be done after the refugee movement was over. More troubles might easily flow from failure to tackle these questions with the utmost urgency and on an all-India basis. We must know now what the plans for them are, and planning meant what is being done not only for to-day, but for next week and far beyond. Where will they go? Will it be an orderly settlement? Will it be dominated by black market, corruption and squeeze? This raised one of the greatest administrative problems in history. In a few days the head of the great fifty-mile column would have crossed the border. They were leaving the rich colony district of the Punjab. They were not going to a Promised Land. Their new home was superior only in that it provided physical safety.

Matthai said that the first two phases of the refugee problem—where to move them on arrival and how to feed them for the next six months—were the most difficult. The longer-term planning, he felt, was relatively easier. What arrangements, he asked, had been made for getting in the next harvest? Neogy said that many refugees had been attracted by the standing crops, and were spreading out to gather them. Some fifty thousand had already done so. He added that he was drawing up a scheme for collective farming. But, Mountbatten warned, there are at least two hundred thousand refugees in the convoy we saw yesterday, and immediate feeding arrangements will be needed for them. Patel remarked that there was three months' food in the East Punjab, but that the distribution of it was the real problem.

During this prolonged discussion Ismay whispered to me that all this really should be thrashed out in Cabinet committee under the Prime Minister's chairmanship; but I must say that I am inclined to think that it still needs Mountbatten's presence to provide the sense of urgency and establish the correct priorities.

Ian Morison, who has been acting as *The Times* Indian Correspondent during the past momentous months and reporting back his first brief experience of this seething sub-continent with outstanding lucidity and insight, and Eric Britter, who has now returned from leave, lunched at Government House to-day. Chhatari and Monckton were there too. Mountbatten gave us a dissertation on the need for anticipating public opinion, and quoted the example of his father in 1911, who was responsible then for instituting a system of lower-deck promotions which has ruled out the need for any major change since that date. He feels that the offer just made by the French Government to French Indo-China is a classic example of doing the right thing too late.

Incidentally I have just been reading Ian's brilliant article on the Punjab tragedy in last Friday's *Times*, which is the most perceptive diagnosis I have so far come across. He felt that war was the wrong word to use in describing an extraordinary phenomenon which had no exact parallel in European history and which is not easy to explain to people who do not know India. " In its recent manifestations ", he writes, " it has appeared rather as a sort of infectious hysteria or mental derangement. The carriers are the refugees. The incubation period is the time it takes a large number of refugees to move from one part of the country to another. It requires a suitable climate in the shape of a latent cleavage, usually economic, between the two communities. Auxiliary irritants which accelerate an outbreak are irresponsible politicians and journalists and those gangster elements who profit from anarchy. The outbreak is correspondingly severe if the resistance offered to it by the body politic—namely, the normal machinery of maintaining law and order—is reduced in strength. The initial symptoms vary, depending upon whether the two communities are evenly balanced or one greatly preponderates. In the first case each suffers from a psychosis of fear, a terror that it is about to be attacked; and in the second case the majority suffers from a psychosis of revenge, often both fear and revenge are mixed, and they are soon absorbed in wild and undiscriminatory hostility. . . .

" What causes this disease, this infectious hysteria? Western Parliamentary democracy requires certain basic conditions for its success, none of which obtains in India. In all those countries of Asia where populations are not homogeneous and where Parliamentary institutions have been introduced from outside, divisions have been formed on racial and religious lines, not on the lines of programmes and policies, and these divisions have been steadily intensified. . . .

" One of the symptoms of this disease ", he concludes, " is that each side passionately believes the other to be solely responsible. The outside observer studying this gigantic and terrible phenomenon wonders whether questions of ' responsibility ' and ' blame ' are not irrelevant. Either all parties concerned are responsible, officials who have sanctioned communal solutions, and politicians who have made inflammatory speeches equally with illiterate peasants who have speared women and children, or else there are certain cataclysms in human affairs in which men do not retain control over their destinies."

GOVERNMENT HOUSE, NEW DELHI, *Tuesday, 23rd September, 1947*

To-day's biggest development has been Jinnah's appeal to the Commonwealth to intervene in Pakistan's disputes with India. Nehru has apparently written a moderate and statesman-like reply. As with all Jinnah's major policy decisions, it would seem to be carefully timed and to coincide significantly with reports that have been reaching me from Foreign correspondents of an upsurge of anti-British feeling and comment in Pakistan. These include newspaper attacks on British officers on much the same lines as in India, assertions that the present troubles are mainly due to a British–Banya alliance, and criticism of Mountbatten himself, who is alleged to be disgruntled at not having achieved the double Governor-Generalship. It is noted that these themes are not discouraged in high places, and that the formation of public opinion on such matters is in the hands of very few. I get the impression that with his approach to the Commonwealth, which can only be a source of embarrassment in all the Dominion capitals, Jinnah may well be over-playing his hand. India, however, is in danger of doing just the same thing over Junagadh. The Jam Sahib of Nawanagar has just indulged in a bellicose Press conference calling for " coats off" and "no non-resist-ance ", etc.

The Amritsar situation is still very grave. Cholera has broken out, and the train attacks continue. Yesterday's decision to cancel all trains passing by Amritsar has been discussed to-day at the highest level, and Nehru, after consultations with Mountbatten, has confirmed that the decision is still in force. Telephonic communication with Amritsar is very difficult, but I succeeded on behalf of the Associated Press of India, who had been completely baffled in their attempts to get through, in securing from their local correspondent the text of a joint Peace Appeal from the two Sikh leaders, Tara Singh and Oodham Singh. Without Government House priorities, the " Appeal " might have been in-definitely delayed, but high importance was placed both by Mountbatten and Government circles on its rapid publication. The tone of their language had, in keeping with their patriarchal appearance, much more of an Old than New Testament ring about it. After boldly denouncing shameful attacks upon women and children, they added fiercely, " We do not desire friendship of the Moslems, and we may never befriend them. We may have to fight again, but we shall fight a clean fight, man killing man."

What effect this crude appeal will have on their followers it is difficult for anyone who has not made a close study of Sikh psychology to say. Both are undoubtedly big men in the complicated hierarchy of Sikh religious politics. The trouble is that the situation, as at other moments of supreme crisis in Sikh history, seems to have passed out of control of the leaders. Billy Short explained to me how the essence of the teaching of Guru Nanak, the founder of Sikhism, was " Where five of you are gathered together, there am I." The Sikh tradition, accordingly, is one of cell formation and spontaneous local leadership. Here is the source at once of Sikh strength and weakness. In the higher reaches of command the prevailing atmosphere is one of indiscipline and intrigue, and Short considers that authority is passing from the older leaders, such as Tara, Oodham and Giani Kartar Singh, to a number of younger men, chiefly ex-Indian National Army officers.

The Sikh leaders are at great pains to describe the Hindus as their brothers, but there are not many outward signs of brotherly love, and Tara Singh has been almost equally vehement in his dissatisfaction with the East as with the West Punjab Government. If Partition has meant immense economic sacrifice for the Sikhs, it also entails political concentration. Lying within easy reach of Delhi, they may comprise after the mass migration some fifty per cent of the total population of the new East Punjab Province.

Informed observers see in this situation all the ingredients of a Sikh nationalist movement, and consider that already the solution which has been mooted of creating a new Indian province of Sikhistan fails to measure up to Sikh demands. One complication, however, is the attitude and status of the Sikh Princes. Led by the Maharaja of Patiala, they can be expected to co-operate more willingly with the Government of India, and are far from enthusiastic about the aims of the Sikh party leaders. They may well hold the balance of power in this obscure struggle.

Billy Short has been working with the energy of a beaver to secure a Sikh–Moslem truce, and there is to be a meeting at Lahore to-morrow at which it is hoped Tara Singh will be present. Ismay is ready to play a mediating role should the occasion warrant it.

GOVERNMENT HOUSE, NEW DELHI, *Wednesday, 24th September, 1947*

At to-day's Emergency Committee there was another general discussion of policy on refugee movements. Chetty urged that top priority should be given to the clearing of Delhi, and went so far as to say that he wanted refugees to be stopped from coming into the city, and all non-Delhi refugees—Moslem and non-Moslem—already in to be encouraged to leave. Nehru turned to the need for the rapid creation of the new East Punjab capital city. He was convinced that there were many who would want to go to-day, a large proportion of them people of substance.

Patel, the administrative realist, argued that top priority should be given to keeping the trains going and to the evacuation of the refugee camps, which he said were "reservoirs of discontent". Mountbatten believed that an even more urgent problem than the resumption of the trains was the slowness of the progress of the refugee columns and the need to get them moving again. He went on to say that there was still far too high a premium on lawlessness. We must reassert the civic sense. As far as he knew, there was still no single instance of a trial either for murder or arson committed during the present troubles. There was also, he felt, the failure of the hitherto famous Intelligence system. What steps were being taken to remedy this?

Disquieting reports have been reaching Mountbatten about the morale and treatment of British officers. They have had to tackle overwhelming disturbances while lacking the military power or civil support from either side to suppress them. The feeling has grown that their effort is entirely unrecognised. They have had to serve without the basic amenities, particularly mail. Mountbatten and Ismay have both been pressing Nehru and Jinnah to issue statements paying tributes to their work. Jinnah replied frankly that he considered the reference he made in his speech at the banquet in Karachi on 13th August was sufficient.

The problem has now become acute as a result of a statement to-day made by the influential Liberal leader Pandit Kunzru, who is reported as saying that had British officers acted impartially, the situation would probably have been brought under control in the East Punjab. He also alleged that a British officer had been responsible for not preventing a large number of casualties in the Sheikhupura massacre at the end of August. Mountbatten rang Nehru at once about these grave allegations, pointing out that the statement as reported was both untrue and libellous, and that unless it was immediately refuted the position of British officers in the Indian Army would become unbearable. Nehru promised to make an early statement. Whereupon Gandhi intervened to suggest that perhaps a better way would be for Kunzru himself to make a public retraction. Ismay, however, is not satisfied with this solution, which in his view meets the demand of Indian but not of British opinion, and he has persuaded Nehru to issue a statement based on reliable evidence which categorically denies that the culprit at Sheikhupura was of British nationality. The whole incident shows that goodwill is still a delicate plant, but one which Nehru is always ready to nourish.

GOVERNMENT HOUSE, NEW DELHI, *Friday, 26th September, 1947*

The Emergency Committee is slowly phasing out according to Mountbatten's plan. It has now been decided that it should meet only twice a week, on Tuesdays and Fridays. The Committee has called for registration of all refugees in Delhi. Nehru said, " Advice as to how this is to be done is not to tell us you cannot do it ". There is still considerable tension in Delhi, and Mountbatten stressed the psychological aspect of the problem. It seemed that when a Hindu–Moslem brotherhood appeal was made, the loud-speaker vans were mobbed. What about seeking the advice of a psychologist? " I know the psychology of the Indian people ", Nehru replied, " and first priority should be given to the rounding up of leaders fomenting trouble." The Chief of the Delhi Police observed that they were not the usual *goonda* type, but clerks, doctors and officials. The citizens, it seemed, had decided to fight it out. Nehru commented, " We know well ahead that orders are being issued—who issues them? " And he repeated the query Mountbatten made yesterday, is the Intelligence organisation sufficient? The population, he said, must wake up to their responsibilities; the police alone cannot deal with this situation.

Unwittingly Gandhi seems to have added to the general tension, for during his Prayer Meeting this evening he made passing reference to the possibility of war with Pakistan in an address otherwise wholly devoted to his worship of God as truth and non-violence, but the phrase in question, " If Pakistan persistently refuses to see its proved error and continues to minimise it the Indian Government would have to go to war against it," has touched a raw nerve, and undoubtedly aroused intense and almost scared speculation among the Press, and will almost certainly find its way into the world's headlines to-morrow.

GOVERNMENT HOUSE, NEW DELHI, *Saturday, 27th September, 1947*

Mountbatten received a letter the other day from a Mr. Karda, pointing out the difficulties listeners to the All India Radio were experiencing in hearing the programmes and recordings of Mahatma Gandhi's words at his Prayer Meetings. This has led Mountbatten, who feels that these daily messages, with the exception of yesterday's, on which he immediately tackled Gandhi, are one of the great factors for the creation of confidence and sanity, to raise the matter with Gandhi personally, and to instruct me to follow it up in more detail. The outcome is that I have had a revealing and, I think, valuable talk with Gandhiji at Birla House this afternoon.

As I came into the room he was busy writing a note, and did not look up. When he did so he coughed rather heavily, " See—this is how I greet you!" I had been told during the morning that the interview would have to be postponed. But he now explained that the message that I should not come had been sent without his authority, and that he had it altered, as he was not so ill that he could not talk to me. He said that Mountbatten had not actually discussed with him the possibility of his making a studio broadcast, but had merely handed over the letter from Mr. Karda at the end of their last talk, suggesting that I should explain the position to him.

I began by pointing out that the broadcast reception of his Prayer Meetings was by no means satisfactory. The great listening audience eagerly awaiting his guidance were not always hearing very much of what he said. Often not more than one word in five came through. A number of special problems were involved in maintaining the audibility of outside broadcasts. There was the extraneous noise of the meeting itself. No doubt it was necessary at times for the Mahatma to turn his head away from the microphone. I did not add that his voice was very low and his tempo very fast. I pointed out that although wireless was a tremendously powerful medium for direct contact with the mass as individuals, very few of the world's leaders had fully exploited it. I considered that it would greatly help in pacifying public opinion if he could be prevailed upon to make a studio broadcast over All India Radio.

Gandhi's initial reaction was against the idea. " To make a set speech in a studio would be for me theatrical. I need to express myself through a living audience, whether it consists of five, or five lakhs." I explained that it was not necessary for him to go to a studio, and that the broadcast could be made just as well where he was sitting now in the form of a dialogue with his friends. He returned to his objection that the speech would have to be prepared in advance. This was contrary to his method of speaking spontaneously what was in his mind.

I replied that although a set script within a time limit was the normal procedure for radio talks, in his case, with his tremendous authority, the deepest impression would be conveyed if he spoke extempore for as long as he liked. He said he had often passed All India Radio, which he understood was one of the most up to date, even by European standards, but he had never been inside. He assumed that I had in mind only one special broadcast. I replied that I had not presumed to suggest more, but if he could be prevailed upon to speak periodically, I was sure that the impact on opinion would be even greater. " I have never really given full consideration to talking over the wireless," he said. " I would like two or three days to ponder over the arguments you have put forward. There are many hurdles to jump before I can make up my mind, but I think you have jumped over the first of them."

He then turned to wider themes. He said that what worried him most was that the trouble here in Delhi and the Punjab seemed to be deeper. He was unwilling to admit that his and Suhrawardy's influence had been decisive in Calcutta, and would not in fact feel confident about his own influence unless he achieved a measure of success here. He described in detail how he and Suhrawardy had started on their joint enterprise in Calcutta. Suhrawardy had shown great courage and endurance. His appearance in Gandhi's Ashram was a dramatic departure from the comfortable mode of life to which he was accustomed. By pledging himself on behalf of the Moslem minority, he had willingly accepted both discomfort and danger.

I suggested that the difference, perhaps, between Calcutta and Delhi was that he had been present in Calcutta to grip the crisis at the outset, whereas he had only arrived here when the troubles were in full flood. He said that this was not wholly true. There had already been quite a long sequence of disturbances before he and Suhrawardy set to work. The fact was that somehow the atmosphere in Calcutta was favourable to his influence; but here at present it was not. He spoke of the angry man who had asked him the day before how it was that if he really was a Mahatma and a miracle-worker he could not put matters right : " I dealt with him yesterday, as you no doubt saw." Gandhiji said he was profoundly anxious about the communal situation. Unless checked, the climax could only be that no Moslem could regard himself as safe living in India and no Sikh or Hindu in Pakistan.

During the latter part of our talk Rajkumari Amrit Kaur and the famous Miraben (Miss Slade) came in, and a young girl throughout took a full note of the conversation. Of his Calcutta adventure—one of the most dramatic achievements of his life—he had spoken with real zest. Clearly the incongruity of his association with Suhrawardy had appealed to his ever-present sense of humour. His eyes sparkled as he described the details of their joint bargain. One does not come away with the impression of a very old man in his dotage, or even anecdotage, but of one who lives with the intensity of youth and retains the boyish sense of fun which tragedy and the passing of time cannot wither.

GOVERNMENT HOUSE, NEW DELHI, *Sunday, 28th September, 1947*

Throughout my talk with Gandhi yesterday he showed himself to be wholly unperturbed by the stir which his Prayer-Meeting reference to war had produced. Speaking again last night, he was at great pains to put the phrase into perspective, as he had promised Mountbatten he would. Gandhian dialectic claimed that indication of when a cause for war could arise between the two States was designed not to promote war but to avoid it as far as possible. His final plea was simply, " India knows, and the world should know, that every ounce of my energy has been and is being directed to the definite avoidance of fratricide culminating in war ". This is undoubtedly the truth, but so great is his influence that his words assume a prophetic and almost mesmeric power. The concept of war is so repugnant to his nature that the use of the word at all by him was bound to be given special significance by the Press and public.

Sir Archibald Carter, the Permanent Under-Secretary of the Commonwealth Relations Office, is at Government House on the last lap of a big Eastern tour he has been making. The idea has been mooted that Ismay should return home with him to give a personal report on developments here since the transfer of power. Mountbatten considers that such a visit is urgently needed at this time, if London is to see the critical first six weeks of Independence in their proper perspective. Moreover, he called me in this afternoon to say that he thought I could once again usefully supplement Ismay's contribution to enlightenment by giving background guidance to my various contacts. Relations between the British correspondents in Delhi and the new Government have been far from happy, and some objective third-party view might well be of help to London editors. Indeed, it has already been necessary for me to invoke Mountbatten's help in promoting better understanding. He took the chair at a meeting at Government House on Friday between Nehru and Patel and representatives of the Foreign correspondents to discuss the growing list of outstanding grievances. After some plain speaking on both sides, an immediate breakdown was averted and dangerous suspicions largely dissipated.

Lady Mountbatten's welfare effort is prodigious, and the achievements of the United Council for Relief and Welfare which owe so much to her dynamic influence are already considerable. All the twenty-nine leading voluntary societies and agencies, as well as the representatives of the Government Departments of Health, and Relief and Rehabilitation, are represented on it. The Council has, through its members, already succeeded in rendering important help with the administration of refugee centres, Health and Welfare services in the camps and in the hospitals, first-aid posts, clinics and inoculation centres. Large quantities of clothing, food, linen, medical supplies and facilities for education and recreation have all been provided through the Council's initiative.

Lady Mountbatten's extensive tours have made a very deep impression on the refugees and welfare workers alike. They are no mere formality. With her unique Red Cross and St. John experience, she is providing the Government at the centre with detailed and expert guidance based on first-hand information on the most urgent of all its human problems.

GOVERNMENT HOUSE, NEW DELHI, *Monday, 29th September, 1947*

Mountbatten's day has been taken up with important policy conferences over Junagadh and the Punjab. The Junagadh crisis looks more and more like a highly explosive game of chess, with the State, its neighbours and satellites providing the chequer-board, and Karachi and Delhi moving the pieces. Ismay, from the conversations he had with Liaquat during his last visit to Delhi, is quite convinced that Pakistan's strategy is to use the whole Junagadh contest as a bargaining counter for Kashmir. This interpretation is borne out by a significant remark Liaquat made to Mountbatten on the same visit. " All right," he told him. " Let India go ahead and commit an act of war, and see what happens."

The first move was V. P.'s visit to the State ten days ago, which produced only limited results. He met the Dewan, who told him that the Nawab was indisposed, and therefore could not see him. However, the Sheikh of the small State of Mangrol, which up to the transfer of power had been under the suzerainty of Junagadh, used the occasion of V. P.'s presence in the neighbourhood to get away from his own State and voluntarily to accede to India, thus following Babariawad, which had already acceded. But the Sheikh, on his return to Mangrol, which coincided with V. P.'s to Delhi, found himself obliged to renounce his accession. On the 22nd the Government of India decided that the circumstances in which the letter of renunciation was written were such as to justify them ignoring it. Junagadh followed up this bloodless victory over Mangrol by sending troops into Babariawad.

These developments were near enough to a checkmate to infuriate Patel, who considers that an act of war has already been committed by Junagadh in sending troops to Babariawad, and that India should take all the necessary steps to oust them. Indeed, unless there is a show of strength and readiness in the last resort to use it, he is ready to resign. Just as Kashmir is close to Nehru's heart, so Junagadh is part of Patel's homeland. It is easy to dismiss this as mere provincialism, but it is necessary always to remind oneself that the concept of India as a nation is by European standards of geography and population considerably larger than life.

Mountbatten wrote to Nehru yesterday making the distinction between the planning of and preparation for military operations and their actual execution, stressing that a direct conflict between the two Dominions would not only undermine their moral reputation, but also put their physical survival in deadly peril. This advice is acceptable from Mountbatten. Unfortunately, the three Chiefs of Staff, who are all British, in their appreciation of the Junagadh situation, have quite independently underlined the Governor-General's estimate of the danger to a point where they have clearly overstepped the boundary between military and political advice. Thus further fuel has been added to Patel's indignation.

To avoid any further confusion of this nature, while at the same time to minimise the general risk of false decision and precipitate action by the Government, Mountbatten has recommended the establishment of a Defence Committee of the Cabinet. Within this context he has in mind ancillary committees such as the Chiefs of Staff Committee, Joint Intelligence and Joint Planning Committees; but he has at the same time propounded one vital modification of the British practice in which the Chief of the Imperial General Staff is wholly divorced from Operational Command. He has insisted that India would do better to adopt procedure whereby from each of the three Services one and the same officer should double the role of Commander-in-Chief and Chief of Staff. Nehru and Patel approved this idea, and Ismay has been asked to draft a paper elaborating its organisation in time for to-morrow's Cabinet.

As for Junagadh, Mountbatten has urged an intermediate course which allows for military reinforcement to continue, but only in undisputed territory around the State. He has also asked that Liaquat should be advised of the scope and nature of all impending troop movements to Kathiawar. Finally he wants a clear public statement that India will accept the verdict of the popular will in all States where accession is in dispute.

We have had a long meeting to-day with Trivedi, a forceful and flamboyant personality, and representatives of his Government. As soon as it was realised that the East Punjab would raise by far the most difficult administrative problems after the transfer of power, Trivedi was the automatic choice for Governor.

Dr. Bhargava, the Prime Minister, and Swaran Singh, the Home Minister, are the only two men of any standing in the East Punjab Government. Trivedi has from the outset, by everyone's tacit agreement, assumed special powers. This is not to say he has been able to get his Government to do all that he has wanted, but without his detailed guidance it is doubtful whether the Provincial administration could have survived the upheavals that overwhelmed it from the day of its birth.

He raised some big questions this morning. Translation from central to provincial spheres of duty may well have been behind his plaintive plea that " No paper plans work out ". He says covered accommodation for at least five lakhs (five hundred thousand) will be needed this winter, and he posed the problem whether this covered accommodation should have priority over the use of village schools and homes. Building resources do not allow of proceeding at full throttle with both. He wants the new East Punjab capital to be designed to hold a million people. He agrees that it should start from scratch. Mountbatten strongly advised that whatever land is selected should be frozen and no freeholds allowed, otherwise it would become a speculators' paradise.

Trivedi next turned to the security of the canals along the Indo-Pakistan boundary. The standstill agreement by which they have been controlled since 15th August is not working. Shots have been fired on workers. Who is responsible? Surely not the Pakistan Army? General Lockhart said the Pakistan Army was undoubtedly in a state of alert and expecting immediate invasion from the East Punjab. Trivedi replied that he had been expecting an identical attack from the West. Somehow confidence must be re-established. The proposal is that there should be a twice-weekly meeting with Mudie, the West Punjab Governor, the two Prime Ministers and the Area Commanders.

The train situation was discussed. The trouble-centre is now between Ludhiana and Amritsar, and there have been serious breakdowns along the main-line East route. Some of the Sikh Princes are adding to Trivedi's difficulties. Kapurthala pushed a column of refugees from his State into the main column without warning the East Punjab Government, and there were heavy casualties from starvation, while there has been a similar ruthless removal of Moslems from Faridkot.

At lunch to-day Trivedi told us that Sikhs and Moslems pass each other on the road and show fraternal unity in criticising their own

Governments! I sat next to Mr. Thapar, an East Punjab Government official, who has been making a close study of the whole casualty position. It is, of course, notorious that refugees, principal victims of atrocities, make very unreliable eye-witnesses. Whenever it has been possible to check the facts, the assessment of casualties by eye-witnesses has proved to be inflated more than a hundred-fold.

In Mr. Thapar's considered view it is most unlikely that the total casualties of killed and wounded will turn out to be more than one per cent of the total population in the area of disturbance. This is bad enough, but even if we were to double Mr. Thapar's percentage, and regard the whole of the Punjab as being equally affected—which is by no means the case—it would seem that Churchill's recent assertion that half a million are dead, wounded or missing since the troubles began six weeks ago is at least twice the likely figure, and thus more in accordance with his own forebodings than with the data before us here.

This evening after dinner Trivedi asked me up for a drink in his rooms, and I was with him until nearly midnight, while he gave his own impressions of the Punjab crisis. Considering the immense mental and physical strain he has undergone, I was much impressed by his general resilience. Like Churchill, he is a vigorous cigar-smoker and a man of expressive gestures. He made the following points:—

In the East Punjab there was, in fact, an administrative interregnum just when the first shock of the troubles had to be absorbed.

The troubles which had in fact started in Rawalpindi and Mooltan in March 1947, causing major migrations and continuing thereafter, came to a head with the transfer of power. Lahore was reported as out of control, with one per cent of the town on fire, by 14th August; by the 15th twelve per cent was reported to be in flames. The storm then passed to Amritsar.

Under prevailing conditions Simla was wholly impracticable as the administrative centre, so, in spite of the lack of physical facilities, he decided to move to Jullundur because the situation could be more easily controlled from there.

The first policy concept was to try to stop mass evacuation. His own tour between the 15th and 27th August had been devoted to that end. By the 28th he had the feeling that the situation was in hand. Then followed the massacre of Sheikhupura in the West Punjab. There were varying estimates of the casualties there. Mudie put them at three hundred, but the Army situation report gave the minimum figures as between seven hundred and eight hundred. There was a violent reaction in Amritsar. With this, Trivedi said, the realisation came to him that a major transfer of population was inevitable. From that day to this he has been trying to carry this policy through and to keep his Ministers up to the mark.

GOVERNMENT HOUSE, NEW DELHI, *Tuesday, 30th September, 1947*

A meeting has duly taken place of the Prime Minister, Deputy Prime Minister, Ministers of Defence and Finance and the Minister without Portfolio. It described itself as a Provisional Defence Committee, and then approved its own permanent composition and functions, receiving full Cabinet approval later in the day. The three Service Commanders-in-Chief, who are now automatically Chiefs of Staff of their own Services as well, are to attend all its meetings. Mountbatten has been invited to take the chair in a personal capacity " in view of his knowledge and experience of high military matters ".

Whatever the risks of misrepresentation across the border, this development is a notable victory for moderation and sane counsel. The Defence Committee instrument and Mountbatten's guidance freely invited and informally given cannot fail to serve as a restraining influence at a time of great stress, when passions are clouding judgement and the price of experience is high.

To-day's Emergency Committee was overcast with the news of an insensate attack on the Safdar Jung Hospital in Delhi. The outrage was committed by a gang from three local villages, and is in no way to be interpreted as a recrudescence of communal trouble in the city itself. Rajkumari Amrit Kaur, who as Minister of Health is carrying a tremendous administrative burden, was in great distress in giving the details. Mountbatten said that he was horrified and saw it as a severe psychological setback to all the work for peace put in by the Prime Minister.

On the wider front Nehru felt there was improvement. He said he had made a speech at Hauz Khas, and Moslems were mixed up in and moving freely among a crowd of some twenty-five thousand. This meeting had undoubtedly had a very good effect. Nehru's impression is that the trouble in Delhi is now confined to a hard core of agitators—perhaps not more than five hundred—who do not desire peace, and that, apart from them, there is a new atmosphere in the city, the majority of the people definitely wanting an end to the conflict.

For the past three weeks the Emergency Committee of the Cabinet serving as the chosen instrument for immediate high level decision has directed all the agencies of this new-born and stricken Government. It has been artificial respiration, and not wholly scientific in method, but the heart of India has continued to beat. The crisis, after reaching its peak in Delhi, the East Punjab, and Northern India as a whole, slowly but surely begins to ebb. Every morning we have anxiously watched the flags in the Map Room to see if the reported tension in the United Provinces, in such cities as Lucknow and Cawnpore, would burst out into a fresh orgy of killings, but the firm action of the Provincial Governments buttressed by support at the Centre has somehow held the movement of refugees along the Punjab–United Provinces border. There has, of course, been a wider dispensation—the frenzy having spent its first destructive force—disease and famine, which by all the laws of probability should have exacted the final penalty, by the deeper laws of providence have so far passed over without doing so. As far as human effort is concerned special credit is due to those responsible for health and food services on both sides of the border. A prodigious number of cholera injections, vaccinations and other inoculations have been carried out. India has flown large supplies of cholera vaccines to Pakistan. The works of mercy and healing shine out in the communal darkness.

CHAPTER EIGHTEEN

REPORT FROM LONDON

GOVERNMENT HOUSE, NEW DELHI, *Wednesday, 1st October, 1947*

W E ARE LEAVING for London in two days' time. In the meanwhile I am trying to gather in as much background information as possible to ensure that I am fully briefed on the latest facts and opinion trends.

This morning I had a most informative talk with Patel's private secretary, Shankar, at Aurangzeb Road. We began by discussing Press problems. In spite of the *modus vivendi* secured at last week's Government House meeting with the Foreign Press, it is clear that the Sardar and his circle are still full of resentment at British Press treatment of the Punjab troubles. He went so far as to ask me whether these were all the thanks Congress leaders were to get for the considerable political risk they had taken in accepting Dominion Status at all? I told Shankar that I thought history would accord to the Sardar great credit for his part in the transfer of power, and that his realistic attitude on the three major issues, Partition, Dominion Status and relations with the Indian Princes, was statesmanship of a high order.

I came away with the firm impression that the Sardar was well aware of the solid and immediate advantages Dominion Status conferred on India. In the wider context of the world conflict he clearly appreciates that if it comes to a show-down, India's interests are likely to be closely interwoven with those of the Western Powers. This being so, Dominion Status, or its equivalent, enables India to come within the orbit of Western good-will without incurring the formal liabilities of a treaty relationship. It must be stressed that Patel has never actually intervened in external affairs, and that this field is Nehru's unchallenged responsibility. Moreover, the prevailing view-point of Nehru places higher hopes on India's capacity to stand outside the struggle of rival World Powers, and, in the process, to build up a neutral bloc in Asia which could play a constructive mediating role through U.N.O. and by other means.

Shankar said that the Sardar had met with great success yesterday at Amritsar. He had made a big speech to what was perhaps the most representative gathering of Sikh leaders since the transfer of power. Nearly all the Jathadas had been present, and had responded favourably to his call for moderation.

Liaquat is back in Delhi for to-day's Joint Defence Council. I understand that this morning's meeting was a very difficult one. At the small lunch-party afterwards at which Nehru and Liaquat were the two guests and Vernon and myself were the staff members, the atmosphere was still somewhat strained. Liaquat, who was in a pea-green coat and looked far from well, got involved in an argument with Nehru over the movement of Moslems from Ambala. It was one of those occasions when we would all have liked to change the subject but seemed powerless to do so.

The background to all this tense talk is the action of the Pakistan Government in closing the Balloki Bridge across the Ravi, which is in the West Punjab. At the Council meeting Patel did his utmost to persuade Liaquat to open the Bridge, but in vain. Mountbatten, however, in a private talk with him afterwards, made a final appeal, and had the satisfaction of getting him to reverse his verdict before he left for Pakistan.

There has also been some plain speaking over Junagadh. Mountbatten at first had great difficulty in making either Prime Minister raise the subject at all—Liaquat's attitude being " Why should I? We have done nothing wrong. If India is worried, let India raise it ", and Nehru feeling that for himself to initiate discussion would only be interpreted as a sign of weakness, but Mountbatten finally prevailed on Liaquat to make the first mention. Mangrol and Babariawad were the points of contention. Mountbatten and Nehru underlined the clear right of both, with the lapse of Paramountcy, to accede to India. Nehru called on Liaquat to order the withdrawal of Junagadh troops from Babariawad. Just as he was doing this, a telegram was handed in indicating that Junagadh troops had now entered Mangrol as well. Nehru undertook not to allow Indian troops to enter either State until the legal position of both had been definitely established by higher authority, provided the Junagadh forces were immediately withdrawn.

Liaquat's attitude on this was reasonably conciliatory, but on the wider issue of Pakistan accepting Junagadh's accession in the first place he was adamant that they had been right in doing so. He takes his stand on the legal grounds that the ruler has the absolute right to accede without reference to the moral or ethnic aspects of accession.

GOVERNMENT HOUSE, NEW DELHI, *Thursday, 2nd October, 1947*

A few days ago the *Daily Telegraph* published a sensational report to the effect that Auchinleck during his recent visit to Karachi had stated, " Refugee traffic could be peaceably resumed in both directions if the Sikhs of the Punjab and the Sikh States could be effectively disarmed." Not unnaturally, Patel was greatly disturbed by the story, and has discussed its implications at some length with Mountbatten. In order to foreshorten surmise and correspondence, Mountbatten suggested, and Patel agreed, that I should take the earliest opportunity to see Auchinleck personally and check on the story's authenticity, and if possible secure his agreement to a disclaimer.

I went round to the Supreme Commander's house this afternoon. It seemed very quiet and deserted. The tremendous activities of the past six weeks have indissolubly linked Government House with the new order, but the tide of events has flowed past this residence of the C.'s in C., India, so that it now evokes only the memories of former greatness. Auchinleck glanced quickly through the report, and at once explained, in his usual measured but incisive manner, that he had no recollection

whatever of saying the words attributed to him either to Mr. Jinnah, with
whom he had prolonged confidential discussions about the future of the
Supreme Command, or to anyone else, least of all the *Daily Telegraph*
correspondent, whom he had not met and did not know. After a few
pithy remarks on the subject of Press sensationalism, he invited me over a
cup of tea in the garden to draft a disclaimer with him. This took only a
few minutes to compose, and within the hour I was able to report,
" Mission completed ".

Auchinleck's position as Supreme Commander is becoming daily more
difficult. His experience, prestige and integrity have been very valuable
assets in keeping the partition of the Indian Army clear of the great
political dispute from which Partition itself has sprung, but already there
are signs that the Supreme Command is being subjected to just the same
kind of pressures which made the already baffling task of the Punjab
Boundary Force finally impossible.

Keeping in mind the tension engendered by the Punjab, it is greatly
to the credit of Auchinleck and his staff that they have been able to make
such headway without so far attracting major controversy. From the
formation of the South-east Asia Command in the autumn of 1943
onwards I have watched Auchinleck play the role of self-denial. Now he
is called upon to preside over the most painful task of all—the partition
along communal lines of an Army the glory of which under British
command had been its capacity to embrace the loyalties of all Indian
races and religions in a common service.

KARACHI, *Friday, 3rd October, 1947*

Yesterday was Gandhi's seventy-eighth birthday. For the first time
the Court Circular, on Mountbatten's instructions, has referred to him as
" Mahatma Gandhi ". Hitherto it has always been the formal and
largely meaningless " Mr.". The actual occasion of this change is the
reference to Lady Mountbatten's birthday visit to him yesterday at Birla
House. I have written a note to Ian Stephens, Editor of *The Statesman*,
who has for so long been pleading for this particular courtesy.

We set out after lunch on the first leg of our trip to London. We
took with us as far as Karachi, Suhrawardy, who was in a very talkative
mood. Also with us is Ismay's eldest daughter, Susan, who is rejoining
her family in London. I am very sorry to say good-bye to her, as, in
addition to acting as hostess for her father, she has been working with
tremendous zeal as full-time secretary to me. She has been deeply
engrossed in my problems from the outset and has played her part to the
full in promoting good-will between Viceroy's House and the Press.

On touching down at Karachi, Ismay was at once driven off to stay
the night with Jinnah, the rest of us being billeted at the airfield. Accommodation is desperately short, but, for all that, Karachi is beginning to
assume the cosmopolitan atmosphere of a capital city. A growing
Diplomatic Corps throngs the Palace Hotel, where this evening I was
given one of the best dinners I have had in all Asia.

AIRBORNE KARACHI—HABBANIYA, *Saturday, 4th October, 1947*

Sir Archibald Carter joined us, and we set off after an early breakfast for Habbaniya. Once again we are over the wastes of Persia, which are lost to all life under merciless heat-haze. It is easy to imagine oneself to be looking down on the surface of some other planet.

Apparently Jinnah was in an angry and difficult mood. He is utterly convinced that the Indian leaders' real aim is to strangle Pakistan at birth, that Gandhi has never accepted Partition and under the guise of religious teaching is all the time spreading " Hindu poison ", and that Nehru, in spite of the appearance of moderation, is not really master in his own house. He regards Patel as the real dictator, who, he alleges, has entered into an unholy alliance with the Hindu Mahasabha and would be quite ready to overthrow the Congress if it failed to serve as an appropriate instrument for his anti-Moslem designs. It is clear that Jinnah, living in almost total isolation both from his followers and the outside world, is a far from happy man who is trying to exorcise his fears by nourishing his hatreds.

LONDON, *Wednesday, 8th October, 1947*

Ever since our arrival in London on Monday after a smooth, fast flight home, I have been caught up in a whirl of engagements, if anything, even more hectic than during our July visit. It has not taken long to discover that there is the deepest concern over the developments in the two Dominions since the transfer of power. The riot reports have not so far been placed in wider perspective, and there is as yet but little appreciation of the scale of positive achievement. I have just given an interview to the *World's Press News*, in which I describe how " a situation to try men's souls " is being steadily surmounted, explain the technical problems with which Press correspondents have been contending and put forward diplomatically some personal suggestions for improving coverage.

I have also prepared a report on the Press situation in India for Francis Williams in which I have drawn attention to all the difficulties as I see them. This is a malleable and desperately important phase in Indo-British relations, and it is vital to smooth out all unnecessary prejudices before they harden. In this context much hangs on quickly establishing better understanding between the Indian Government and the British Press—far more is involved than the alleged grievance or malice of any one correspondent or Government official.

" The core of the Indian Government's complaint [I wrote] is that the world is being presented with a completely unbalanced impression in so far as some ninety per cent of all the Foreign correspondents nominally responsible for covering news both in India and Pakistan are based on Delhi and some ninety per cent of their stories are accordingly taken up with the troubles either in Delhi itself or in the East Punjab. On the other side, the Foreign correspondents feel that their presence is resented, and that their problems are not understood. They argue that since

15th August there has been no adequate liaison provided by the Government, and that the Government despite its protestations does not genuinely believe in the freedom of the Press, or rather has not taken adequate steps to counteract the disbelief of its subordinates."

LONDON, *Saturday, 11th October, 1947*

I have to-day sent off my first personal progress report to Mountbatten, beginning with congratulations to him on the birth of his first grandson and to the baby on starting life in the best Mountbatten style by its attention to punctuality!

" I have had lunch [I continued] with Clement Davies, who described the political settlement of 15th August as a miraculous achievement which had enhanced our prestige throughout the world and was in no wise offset by subsequent developments in the Punjab. In his view both the Russian and American case against our ' imperialism ' in India were for ever destroyed, and no amount of special pleading from either quarter could reinstate it. The present disturbances only brought home the full extent of our past achievement, but Churchill's ' I told you so ' line was reprehensible and in any case fallacious. We could only have stayed on against world and British opinion; moreover, the communal explosion would inevitably have engulfed us if we had tried to stay.

" Frank Owen, when I saw him, agreed substantially with this view. The Churchillian attitude was, he said, wholly unrealistic. In his opinion for us to have stayed it would have needed an occupation force of half a million men and Russian methods of shooting all the nationalist leaders out of hand. He said he was not inclined to make political capital out of the disturbances in his editorial columns and viewed with sympathy the efforts of the new Governments to get things going.

" Among my general impressions at the end of the first week are, that our black-out of your part in the Emergency Committee has been completely effective—almost too much so, in as far as the efforts of the new Government to control the situation have not been fully appreciated and the strain on the Central administrative machine has been somewhat overlooked; that there is no tendency as yet to follow Mr. Churchill's line, but that both Governments are being closely watched for evidence of responsibility or irresponsibility on their part. The importance of Junagadh and Hyderabad in this context will be obvious."

LONDON, *Saturday, 18th October, 1947*

In just under a fortnight I have had in all some fifty interviews, two full-scale Press conferences—one at India House with the Indian correspondents in London, and the other with Francis Williams in the chair to the Lobby Correspondents in the House of Commons—a short talk with Sir Stafford Cripps and two meetings each with Noel-Baker, and Patrick Gordon-Walker, the new Secretary, and Under-Secretary of State for Commonwealth Relations.

Cripps, his power and prestige in the Government enhanced by the recent Cabinet reshuffle, has become co-ordinator-in-chief of the nation's entire economic effort, his mission being to pull the country back from the precipice confronting it during the convertibility crisis in the summer. No one talking to Cripps can fail to be impressed by his lucidity of mind and serenity of manner. If he is somewhat didactic, it is because he is in a position to be. None-the-less it is possible to appreciate that this element of certitude in his make-up, while of service to him in reaching decisions of high policy, may well have been a source of weakness during his momentous negotiations with the Indian leaders in 1942 and 1946. If intellect could have scaled the problem, his success would have been assured.

Noel-Baker and Gordon-Walker are clearly determined to bring fresh ideas to this new Department, which is a somewhat uneasy amalgamation of the old India and Dominions Offices. Both start from scratch as far as India is concerned, but that should not be a disadvantage in their case, for Noel-Baker's special knowledge of international relations and Gordon-Walker's of history give them the right background.

LONDON, *Wednesday, 22nd October, 1947*

I have sent off my final progress report to Mountbatten before we leave for Delhi on Saturday.

" Fleet Street [I wrote] finds genuine difficulty in adjusting itself to the transition of Congress from an anti-British movement into a Dominion Government, and there is a tendency to assume that Pakistan will inevitably have closer connection with Britain than India. On the other hand, there is considerable suspicion of Jinnah's aims and motives, Nehru's stock is rising, and he is most highly thought of in Government circles. Patel is still almost completely unknown.

" In the interviews I have had with Cripps, Noel-Baker and Gordon-Walker I was questioned about the High Commission's organisation both generally and from the Press viewpoint. I gave it as my personal opinion that its scope was inevitably restricted by your special status and influence, but that with your departure it would become one of the most important missions in the world. The objective should be to try to maintain through the High Commission the good personal relationships that you have been able to establish with the Indian leaders. Cripps said that if action was to be taken on this it would need to be done fairly quickly and he hoped you would put forward your own views on this important matter when you return to London for the Royal Wedding.

" Noel-Baker wondered whether India was giving consideration to the possibility of a new capital city. He realised that for the present Delhi had all the administrative facilities, but from what he had seen and read it would seem to be physically and politically vulnerable and too far removed from the heart of the Indian Dominion. Discussing Partition, he argued that from the viewpoint of international relations there was a *prima facie* case to be made out for it. A Central Government covering four hundred and ten million people was too large a unit for effective action or treatment through international agencies, and it was by means of such agencies, incidentally, that he believed British help and influence both in India and elsewhere might be most effectively brought to bear.

" He wanted to know about the progress and prospects of the Left in India, and I said that I thought they had suffered a temporary setback from taking such a direct anti-communal line.   The price of Jinnah's victory had, of course, been a big boost for the Hindu Mahasabha.   He asked how Government spokesmen could express appropriately their good-will towards the new régime.   I replied that I felt that an apprecia- tion by His Majesty's Government of the administrative load carried by the new Governments and reasoned recognition of their difficulties in any public statements would be well received, and that a balance should be held between over-emphasis on the ' sister Dominions ' theme and the appearance of neutral indifference to their problems.

" I was asked more than once about the prospects of Dominion Status, and, on the basis of my talk with Shankar, I said that I had the impression that the matter was still being weighed in the balance.   I was also asked about the position of Patel.   After stressing his important role in Con- gress's three great decisions over Partition, Dominion Status and the Accession of the Princes, I said I felt that, as the effective controller of the Congress Party, his first loyalty was likely to be to that Party and to its future.   It was obviously in some danger of breaking up, as it could no longer be held together solely by the anti-British appeal.   He had already largely deprived himself of the Princes as an alternative issue, and he must be under some pressure to substitute the Moslems, if only to avoid being trumped by the Mahasabha and the Rashtriya Swayam Sevak Sangh (R.S.S.S.).   Cripps suggested that the relationship of Nehru and Patel was a normal one as between the statesman-leader and the party second-in- command.

" Finally Noel-Baker was anxious to hear about your intentions and the likelihood of your being asked to stay on.   I said that I could not believe that you would easily reverse your publicly declared intention of leaving in the spring, but that here again the Indian Government had not reached a decision, but were, it seemed, shelving the matter for as long as possible."

LONDON, *Thursday, 23rd October, 1947*

Ismay asked me to invite John Beavan, the London Editor of the *Manchester Guardian*, to see him on the subject of a controversial leading article published nearly a fortnight ago, entitled " Retrospect "; it was the most sweeping attack on the whole of Mountbatten's policy that I have seen in a newspaper of this calibre.   The article spoke of the hustle with which the withdrawal was carried out and the tossing away of responsibility.   " The British departure turned into cut and run."   It was alleged that no effective machinery for joint action between the successor Governments of India and Pakistan was set up following the Partition announcement of 3rd June.   Why was no offer made to stiffen the Punjab Boundary Force with British troops?

" In fact all seems to have been staked on the gamble that if Partition was carried through at break-neck speed the turbulent and malignant would be too much out of breath to stir, and the gamble failed."

Ismay was in eloquent form, and in his answers to each point of criticism certainly succeeded in exposing the limitations of *ex post facto* arguments and assertions. He explained that no amount of advance planning—and there had been plenty—could have wholly provided against the force of the Punjab explosion and the particular form it took. He recalled the Punjabi, saying, " If one counts up to eleven one does not strike the man ", but the people were simply not prepared to do just that. Civilised peoples tended to cling to false concepts in their attitude to acts of savagery. He recalled Winston Churchill's definition of fanaticism as applied to the 1880 war against the Mahdi. Fanaticism, wrote Churchill, is not in itself a cause of war, but is something that can be exploited when war has begun. It is the outcome of oppression by the strong of the weak.

So, when the *Manchester Guardian* complained of lack of foresight in setting up administrative machinery, it had to be remembered that not everything could be solved by Chiefs of Staff papers. Improvisation was necessary, and the Chiefs of Staff themselves had to be ready to deal with just such emergencies as they arose. With, for instance, Dunkirk, we had no idea where we would reach the sea. We might have gone back along our lines of communication.

" India in March 1947 ", he said, " was a ship on fire in mid-ocean with ammunition in the hold. By then it was a question of putting the fire out before it actually reached the ammunition. There was in fact no option before us but to do what we did." He would be frank and say that he had just spent the unhappiest six months in a long official life, so he hoped he would not be accused of false complacency in saying that if he had had the time over again he would have given the same advice.

KARACHI—NEW DELHI, *Monday, 27th October, 1947*

We left Northolt on Saturday in a Lancaster, as the Governor-General's York was unserviceable and in process of a complete overhaul to be ready in time for the Mountbattens' return for the Royal Wedding. We reached Habbaniya yesterday evening, and were airborne at early light this morning, flying the long, weary journey over the wastes of Persia and Baluchistan to Karachi, eleven hours in all. The Lancaster is nothing like as comfortable as the York, the seating accommodation being in single line facing starboard. Bill Birnie, Jinnah's Military Secretary, came along to meet us, but we did not stay longer than for snacks and a drink at the airfield, as Ismay decided that we had better press on to Delhi at once.

According to Birnie, Jinnah keeps on stressing that the situation is different since 15th August, and he provides very few amenities and courtesies for his Military Secretary and A.D.C.'s, who are mucking in as best they may with house-painters, electricians, etc. Birnie spoke also of an apparent attempt on Jinnah's life the other day. Two men with the lower parts of their faces masked and wearing moon and crescent hats tried to get through the outer cordon at Government House. When challenged by the police they whipped out revolvers, saying, " Mind your own business ". They wounded a policemen, who succeeded, however, in blowing his whistle before he was himself knocked out.

CHAPTER NINETEEN

KASHMIR IMBROGLIO

GOVERNMENT HOUSE, NEW DELHI, *Tuesday, 28th October, 1947*

AT KARACHI WE had no hint of the drama awaiting us in Delhi. We arrived at Palam, very tired, at one o'clock in the morning. Vernon was there to greet us with the news that since dawn Monday Indian troops have been marching, or rather flying, into Kashmir. I was just about to get into bed at a quarter to three when Pete Rees called me and said that Mountbatten wanted to brief me at once on the latest Kashmir developments.

Events, Mountbatten said, had taken a serious turn, and three hundred and thirty men of the First Sikh Battalion were flown in to block a major invasion by North-west Frontier tribesmen, who are moving rapidly on Srinagar, the summer capital. He was very anxious that I should begin making my Press contacts early in the morning, but realised that it was essential that I should first be acquainted fully with the salient facts of a crisis which came to a head while we were on our journey from London. I was aware only that early in September there had been a hitch in the newly established relations between Kashmir and Pakistan— the Kashmir Government accusing Pakistan of failure to provide supplies of several essential commodities and protesting about a number of small border raids, and Pakistan making counter-complaint.

Three days before the transfer of power and the Accession time limit the Kashmir Government announced its intention of signing standstill agreements with both India and Pakistan. Subsequently the Indian Government's policy has been to refrain from inducing Kashmir to accede. Indeed, the States Ministry, under Patel's direction, went out of its way to take no action which could be interpreted as forcing Kashmir's hand and to give assurances that accession to Pakistan would not be taken amiss by India. The Maharaja's chronic indecision must be accounted a big factor in the present crisis. Almost any course of action taken quickly would have saved his State from this turmoil. Procrastination alone was fatal, but in combating major crises it would seem that, as with the Nizam, this is the only weapon in his diplomatic armoury.

The military and political implications of to-day's move are grave, and Mountbatten is, of course, under no illusion about that. Although his role can only now in the last resort be advisory, I get the firm impression that his presence may already have helped to save his Government, overburdened and distracted with the problems of the Punjab and Junagadh, from the most dangerous pitfalls. It was a sudden emergency, calling at once for restraint and quick decision. Mountbatten's extraordinary vitality and canniness were well adapted to the demands of the hour.

I gather from him that it was last Friday night (24th October), at a buffet dinner in honour of the Siamese Foreign Minister, that Nehru first spoke of bad news and reported that tribesmen were being taken in military transport up the Rawalpindi road. State forces, it seems, were absent, and altogether a most critical situation was developing. Mountbatten attended the Defence Committee on Saturday 25th, at which General Lockhart read out a telegram from the Headquarters of the Pakistan Army stating that some five thousand tribesmen had attacked and captured Muzaffarabad and Domel and that considerable tribal reinforcements could be expected. Reports showed that they were already little more than thirty-five miles from Srinagar.

The Defence Committee considered the most immediate necessity was to rush in arms and ammunition already requested by the Kashmir Government, which would enable the local populace in Srinagar to put up some defence against the raiders. The problem of troop reinforcements was considered, and Mountbatten urged that it would be dangerous to send in any troops unless Kashmir had first offered to accede. Moreover, accession should only be temporary, prior to a plebiscite. No final decision was taken on these vital questions on the 25th, but it was agreed that V. P. should fly to Srinagar at once to find out the true position there.

The information which V. P. brought back to the Defence Committee the next day was certainly disturbing. He reported that he had found the Maharaja unnerved by the rush of events and the sense of his lone helplessness. Impressed at last with the urgency of the situation, he had felt that unless India could help immediately all would be lost. Later in the day, on the strong advice of V. P., the Maharaja left Srinagar with his wife and son. V. P. had impressed upon him that as the raiders had already reached Baramula it would be foolhardy for His Highness to stay on in the capital. The Maharaja also signed a letter of accession which V. P. was able to present to the Defence Committee.

As for the military outlook, V. P. advised that the troops left in Srinagar had no prospect whatever of holding the invaders, for they consisted merely of one squadron of cavalry. In the light of this depressing data the Cabinet decided that the Maharaja's accession should be accepted and that a battalion of infantry should be flown in at dawn the next day.

Mountbatten then explained to me in more detail the reason for the line he had taken on accession at the Defence Committee and the modification it involved to his previous approach to the problem. He said that while urging the Maharaja to make up his mind about accession before the transfer of power, he had all along, from his visit in June onwards, exerted his whole influence to prevent him from acceding to one Dominion or the other without first taking steps to ascertain the will of his people by referendum, plebiscite, election, or even, if these methods were impracticable, by representative public meetings. When during the past forty-eight hours it became clear that the Government were determined, against the military advice both of their own Chiefs of Staff and of himself, to send in troops in response to a request from Kashmir for aid, he returned to the charge about accession.

He considered that it would be the height of folly to send troops into a neutral State, where we had no right to send them, since Pakistan could do exactly the same thing, which could only result in a clash of armed forces and in war. He therefore argued that if indeed they were determined to send in troops, the essential prerequisite was accession, and unless it was made clear that this accession was not just an act of acquisition, this in itself might touch off a war. He therefore urged that in the reply his Government asked him to send on their behalf to the Maharaja accepting his accession offer he should be allowed to add that this was conditional on the will of the people being ascertained as soon as law and order were restored. This principle was at once freely accepted and unilaterally proposed by Nehru.

As a first step towards popular Government after his accession, the Maharaja has released Sheikh Abdullah, leader of the National Conference, the strongest political party in the State, and is appointing him head of a Provisional Administration. The legality of the accession is beyond doubt. On this particular issue Jinnah has been hoist with his own petard, as it was he who chose, over Junagadh, to take his stand on the overriding validity of the ruler's personal decision.

Just before 4 a.m. Mountbatten mercifully dismissed us, otherwise I think I would have dozed off in front of him.

During this incredible day everything happened at once. Over and above a long list of Press interviews I was called in for a talk with Mountbatten and Nehru to consider a Government statement about its administrative achievements to date—a somewhat academic exercise at this particular moment. I was shocked to see how haggard and ill Nehru looked.

Mountbatten is disturbed by the editorial attitude of *The Statesman*, which in its anxiety over the decline in Indo-Pakistan relations has denounced the injection of Indian troops into Kashmir, and he asked me to arrange for Ian Stephens, the editor, to come and see him. About an hour later Stephens was with us, and Mountbatten began by saying, " You can't build a nation on tricks ". Jinnah at Abbotabad, he continued, had been expecting to ride in triumph into Kashmir. He had been frustrated. First there was Junagadh, then yesterday's fantastic hold-up of the Hyderabad delegation.* India's move on Kashmir was an event of a different order. Her readiness to accept a plebiscite had been declared from the outset. A large-scale massacre, including a couple of hundred British residents in Srinagar, by tribesmen would have been inevitable if no military move had been made. The Maharaja's accession gave complete legality to the action so far taken.

He wound up by telling Stephens that as a result of Auchinleck's intervention Jinnah has been prevailed on to invite Mountbatten and Nehru to Lahore to-morrow to discuss the Kashmir crisis. This is certainly a remarkable development, and, in answer to inquiries from Doon Campbell, Andrew Mellor and others, I duly stressed its hopeful significance. I was not able to tell them, however, what lay behind this invitation or just how vital Auchinleck's role has been during the past twenty-four hours.

* See pp. 227, 232-3.

In the middle of to-day's Defence Committee, Auchinleck rang up Mountbatten from Lahore to say that he had succeeded in persuading Jinnah to cancel orders given the previous night for Pakistan troops to be moved into Kashmir. The order had reached General Gracey, the acting Pakistan Commander-in-Chief in the temporary absence of General Messervy, through the Military Secretary of the Governor of the West Punjab, with whom Jinnah was staying. Gracey replied that he was not prepared to issue any such instruction without the approval of the Supreme Commander. At Gracey's urgent request, Auchinleck flew to Lahore this morning and explained to Jinnah that an act of invasion would involve automatically and immediately the withdrawal of every British Officer serving with the newly formed Pakistan Army.

Before Auchinleck left him he had not only called off the order, but also invited Mountbatten and Nehru to come to Lahore. Vernon, however, arriving late for dinner after some harassing hours on the telephone, announced, " It is the end ". The whole plan, he said, had broken down, as Nehru could not go to Lahore because of illness.

After the film-show to-night Mountbatten called in Ronnie, Vernon and myself for a chat on the day's events. Mountbatten said he had pressed strongly for the Lahore visit at this morning's Defence Committee, and they had all been sufficiently in awe of him not to raise a voice to say him nay, but he understands that at the Cabinet this afternoon, although his presence was still felt, the pressure on Nehru not to go was very heavy, and that on reaching his house he practically collapsed and had to be put to bed. Mountbatten is sure that his illness is genuine. Nehru has incidentally agreed to Mountbatten forwarding a message to Jinnah to say that he is ill and to ask for a postponement. Mountbatten has decided to telephone Jinnah in the morning in order to give him a personal account of Nehru's state of health, and to try to bring him down to Delhi.

The Government are undoubtedly jibbing at Lahore, and there is criticism not merely of place but of the timing as well. A comparison has even been drawn with Chamberlain's visit to Godesberg. There is an appreciable danger of Kashmir causing the growth of a mock heroic psychology here which it is the duty of our party at Government House to try to mitigate, but, as Ronnie rightly says, we have to get inside the problem or we will have no influence at all.

GOVERNMENT HOUSE, NEW DELHI, *Wednesday, 29th October, 1947*

Mountbatten went round to see Nehru in his room this morning. Patel joined them, and there was a frank talk about the general desirability of the Lahore visit. Mountbatten asked about going himself alone, saying he had no feelings of personal pride when the question of saving the two countries from disaster was at stake. Patel replied that he and the rest of the Cabinet were strongly opposed to either of them making the visit. Mountbatten then pointed out that Liaquat was also ill, and another meeting of the Joint Defence Council was in any case due to be held this week. It would be a friendly gesture for Nehru and himself to go to Lahore for that purpose. Nehru agreed, and Mountbatten returned to Government House, where he at once made his telephone call to Jinnah, who expressed pleasure at this proposal. Five minutes afterwards Doon Campbell rang me up to ask whether there was any truth in the rumour that Mountbatten had been speaking to Jinnah on the telephone!

Mountbatten had a ninety-minute talk with Gandhi to-day. At yesterday's Prayer Meeting the Mahatma struck an almost Churchillian note over Kashmir. His line was: the result was in the hands of God; men could but do or die. He would not shed a tear if the little Union force was wiped out like the Spartans bravely defending Thermopylae, nor would he mind Sheikh Abdullah and his Moslem, Hindu and Sikh comrades dying at their posts in the defence of Kashmir. That would be a glorious example to the rest of India; such heroic defence would affect the whole sub-continent, and everyone would forget that Hindus, Moslems and Sikhs were ever enemies.

The immediate military situation is serious. The Commanding Officer of the battalion flown in on Monday has been killed, and there has been a withdrawal, and fairly heavy fighting is going on four and a half miles west of Srinagar.

It is noteworthy that the situation in Hyderabad has reacted sharply to the Kashmir crisis. Only twenty-four hours after the Indian acceptance of Kashmir's accession and the fly-in comes the report of a dramatic hold-up of the Nizam's delegation by an Ittehad-inspired mob on the eve of its departure for Delhi to sign a Standstill Agreement. We are still awaiting the full details of this extraordinary development, but it is clear that the Nizam, in his efforts to cling to his prerogatives, is allowing himself to come increasingly under the influence of the Ittehad extremists.

Unfortunately a head cold which I brought back with me from London has taken complete charge of me, and I have had to spend the day in bed, feeling far more ill than I really am, and steadily losing interest in affairs of State.

GOVERNMENT HOUSE, NEW DELHI, *Thursday, 30th October, 1947*

I spent another day in bed. Pete Rees kindly called in to see me after dinner to keep me posted with news. The situation in Kashmir, he said, was very obscure, and there was no proper intelligence. He was convinced that if the tribesmen had followed their own looting instincts they would have been in Srinagar by now; but under the leadership of ex-I.N.A. officers they seemed, fortunately, to be more cautious.

After a difficult Defence Committee, Nehru's attendance at the Joint Defence Council in Lahore was formally confirmed and announced, but he has since had to send a message to Mountbatten that the doctor had decided that he is still not well enough, and so after all Mountbatten will go alone. Nehru is also greatly distressed by a Pakistan Government statement, issued with a sense of timing which seems to be Jinnah's stock-in-trade technique of applying diplomatic pressure. It is, in fact, a method which makes diplomacy almost impossible. In the statement the Kashmir accession is described as being " based on fraud and violence, and as such cannot be recognised ". There was, it added, conclusive evidence that Kashmiri troops were used first to attack Moslems in the State and even to attack Moslem villages in Pakistan near the border. All this had provoked the Pathan raiders—and so on, in terms which make it probably as well that Mountbatten cannot take Nehru with him.

Junagadh not unnaturally has fallen into the background of the news, but it still adds to the sum of everyone's worries. The Government propose to take over control of Mangrol and Babariawad to-morrow. During our London visit Mountbatten bent every effort to bring about a settlement by diplomatic means. Junagadh now assumes relation to the wider context of events in Kashmir. The consistency of Pakistan's case against the Kashmir accession is ill-served by the Junagadh precedent. The " fraud and violence " of accession when it involves India and Kashmir is strict legality when Junagadh accedes to Pakistan. The immediate propaganda value of Junagadh to India is greater than the physical possession of it, but on this issue Patel gives higher priority to himself as Minister of States than as Minister of Information.

It must be admitted that the Indian Government has been amply provoked. Following the meeting with Liaquat on the 1st October, Nehru had to send no fewer than three requests for the immediate withdrawl of Junagadh troops from Mangrol and Babariawad. Altogether some three weeks passed before a reply was received from Liaquat referring to a missing letter of an earlier date and indicating that he had asked for the withdrawal to take place. But even then nothing happened.

At a Joint Defence Council at Lahore on the 16th October, Liaquat indicated that he was prepared to entertain the principle of a plebiscite in Junagadh. Nehru proposed that V. P. should fly to Lahore for a general discussion, but this was turned down by Liaquat, who suggested that he should visit Karachi instead. On the 21st the Defence Council accepted the principle that Mangrol and Babariawad would have to be occupied. Two days later a plan was made ready, and two days after that—but only thirty-six hours before the Kashmir explosion—it was finally approved.

As a last resort Mountbatten suggested yesterday that the occupation should be entrusted to the Central Reserve Police, a cadre especially retained under the Crown Representative before the transfer of power, and still available for the purposes of upholding and enforcing law and order in the States, but at to-day's Defence Committee Patel was adamant that the operation should be handled by Indian armed forces.

GOVERNMENT HOUSE, NEW DELHI, *Sunday, 2nd November, 1947*

Since the troubles began I have been cut off from my family. I took the chance of a lightning visit by Peter Howes to Simla to see them for a few hours. They have now moved down from Mashobra to Observatory House, which is attached to the Governor-General's Lodge. We left on the return trip to Delhi first thing this morning. Peter Howes' grey Rolls was almost too large and high-powered for the twisting climb up and down the hills, but it ate up the miles across the plains.

All was quiet save for signs of recent communal troubles at Karnal. We saw lorries bringing out Moslems from the walled township. Moslem women were cowering against the wall.   As we rushed past, the car radio was thundering out Bach's Prelude and Fugue in F minor.   The incongruity of sound and scene and circumstance stirred thoughts in me which went deeper than words.   What are the bounds of human experience?   It was as if by one strange apocalyptic flash all the grandeur and misery of the world had been revealed.

On our arrival at Government House I found I was due to dine with the Mountbattens.   The Maharaja of Bikaner was among the guests. After dinner Bikaner gave a running commentary on a film describing his State's part in the movement and welfare of refugees.   By means of some fine colour photography the film told the story of how more than five lakhs of refugees had been phased through Bikaner.   They passed in their thousands over largely barren land, imposing almost overnight an immense strain on the State's resources and limited lines of communication.   Yet throughout the whole operation only one hundred and fifty Moslems died on the way.

Mountbatten, who was in good heart, told me he was very pleased with his three-and-a-half-hour talk with Jinnah at Lahore.   They were able to exchange views with rather more freedom than if their respective Prime Ministers had actually been with them.   Jinnah began by complaining that the Indian Government had failed to give timely warning to his Government of its intentions.   Mountbatten replied that Nehru's first action after leaving the meeting at which the decision to fly in the troops was taken was to telegraph to Liaquat.   Jinnah then reiterated the published statement that the accession was not bona fide, since it rested on violence and fraud, and would thus never be accepted by Pakistan.

The argument then got into a vicious circle.   Mountbatten agreed that the accession had indeed been brought about by violence, but the violence came from the tribes, for whom Pakistan, and not India, was responsible.   To this Jinnah would retort that in his opinion it was India who had committed the violence by sending in the troops, and Mountbatten would continue to stand his ground that where the tribesmen were was where the violence lay.   Thus it went on until Jinnah could no longer conceal his anger at what he called Mountbatten's obtuseness.

Mountbatten advised Jinnah of the strength of the Indian forces in Srinagar and of their likely build-up in the next few days.   He told him that he considered the prospect of the tribesmen entering Srinagar in any force was now remote.   This led Jinnah to make his first general proposal, which was that both sides should withdraw at once and simultaneously. When Mountbatten asked him to explain how the tribesmen could be induced to remove themselves, his reply was, " If you do this I will call the whole thing off ", which at least suggests that the public propaganda line that the tribal invasion was wholly beyond Pakistan's control will not be pursued too far in private discussion.

On inquiry Mountbatten found that Jinnah's attitude to a plebiscite was conditioned by his belief that the combination of Indian troops in occupation and Sheikh Abdullah in power meant that the average Moslem would be far too frightened to vote for Pakistan. Mountbatten proposed a plebiscite under United Nations Organisation auspices, whereupon Jinnah asserted that only the two Governors-General could organise it. Mountbatten at once rejected this suggestion, stressing that whatever Jinnah's prerogatives might be, his own constitutional position allowed him only to act on his Government's advice.

Jinnah's mood was one of depression, almost fatalism. He kept harping on the masochistic theme that India was out to destroy the nation of his making, and his attitude to every personality and act of policy across the border was coloured by that general assumption. Mountbatten with Ismay, who was present for most of the conversation, did his utmost to reassure him. It is doubtful whether he made any headway, but at least they left good friends on the surface. Mountbatten says that as a military operation the speed of the fly-in on 27th October left our S.E.A.C. efforts standing. It certainly seems to have left Jinnah standing as well and to have been a performance wholly outside his calculations.

In spite of Mountbatten's optimism and frankness, the events of the past few days have inevitably caused a widening of the breach between himself and Jinnah, which this latest meeting has by no means narrowed. For Jinnah would seem to have judged Mountbatten by himself and assumed that he retains almost Viceregal powers. This might well lead him to the further assumption that Mountbatten was the real author of the letter accepting Kashmir's accession, the directing hand responsible for the daring and dash of the fly-in and in general the moving spirit in causing this serious setback to Pakistan's interests and aspirations.

If this is so, it is a tragic misreading of the facts. Ever since the acceptance of the 3rd June Plan, Mountbatten has regarded as the central feature of his mission the promotion of good-will between the two successor States. Jinnah is not insensitive to issues of personal reputation, and it is strange that he cannot see that disappointment here would be likely to be regarded by Mountbatten as a measure of personal failure.

Apart from his vexation over Kashmir, it may well be that Jinnah does not consider that on wider grounds Mountbatten now enjoys the powers to serve as a restraining or mediating influence in India. As we have seen, Jinnah's concept of the proper functions of a Governor-General were made plain enough when he at once invoked the special powers allowed under the Independence Act.

Last but not least, although the two men have a considerable personal respect for each other, Jinnah is now wholly dedicated to the aims of his statecraft.* Deeper fears and colder calculations which are beyond Mountbatten's means to penetrate seem to possess Jinnah at this time.

* Just how deep was this regard of Mr. Jinnah for Lord Mountbatten was revealed to me recently by a personal friend of Mr. Jinnah's. He told me that just before his death Mr. Jinnah went so far as to say, " The only man I have ever been impressed with in all my life was Lord Mountbatten. When I met him for the first time I felt he had ' nur ' " (" nur " approximates in English to a " divine radiance "). He said that Mr. Jinnah added that he had never doubted Lord Mountbatten's integrity the whole time he was in India.

GOVERNMENT HOUSE, NEW DELHI, *Monday, 3rd November, 1947*

With the Kashmir crisis holding all the limelight, Hyderabad has escaped attention, yet only yesterday—some two and a half months after Independence Day—Mountbatten found himself receiving an entirely new Hyderabadi delegation of three led by Moin Nawaz Jung, one of the strong men of the Ittehad, and, it would seem, several stages further away from settlement than on the 15th August. Indeed, after developments which most significantly came to a head the night after Kashmir's accession and the fly-in, and which can only be described as of Ruritanian improbability, it is remarkable that the negotiations should be continuing at all. But for Mountbatten's and Monckton's persistence and will-power they would have broken down completely by now. As it is, the Nizam has succeeded only in completely forfeiting whatever reserve of confidence the Government of India—and Patel in particular—had in him, and I doubt whether their relations can ever be the same again.

During Ismay's and my visit to London, Mountbatten used all his resources as a conciliator to find the formula that would close the gap between accession and association. He even went so far as to recommend a lavish document—a hand-written vellum scroll, perhaps—with a heading confined to some such archaism as " Know all men by these presents ". It could then be accepted by both parties as an "Instrument", without suffix or prefix, but meaning accession to the Sardar and association to His Exalted Highness!

In the belief that the Nizam was susceptible to moderate influences only so long as Monckton was at his side, Mountbatten worked hard to secure agreement for a visit from V. P. Menon to the State so that negotiations could be continued in Hyderabad. The day before V. P. was due to leave—all the necessary clearance having been secured at both ends—the Nizam turned the visit down, on the grounds that V. P.'s presence would give rise to demonstrations and counter-demonstrations. The tone of this refusal and of Patel's reply to it were sufficiently offensive to the susceptibilities of both parties to have brought the negotiations to a final halt.

At this stage Mountbatten asked Monckton to come to Delhi as his personal guest, and Monckton proposed on the 10th October a year's Standstill Agreement which would give India most of the substantial advantages of accession while preserving the Nizam's symbolic status. Mountbatten succeeded in securing an extension beyond the two months for conducting the discussions on this basis. There followed some intense and bitter bargaining, when once again the complete collapse of the negotiations seemed imminent, but on the 22nd October a draft Standstill Agreement was prepared with various revisions which was acceptable both to V. P. and to the Nizam's delegation.

The delegation at once returned to Hyderabad to clinch the matter, and on the same evening showed the draft to the Nizam, who did not like the look of it and decided to refer the whole text to his Executive Council. The Executive Council, with the delegation present to explain points of detail, spent the next three days in discussing the draft, and on

Saturday the 25th October, with a formal vote of six in favour and three against, advised the Nizam to accept and sign the Standstill Agreement without further revision or delay. The delegation duly reported the result of the vote that evening to the Nizam, who indicated his approval of the decision. The Nizam, it seems, spent most of the next day preparing two collateral letters which involved an undertaking on his part not to accede to Pakistan and covered his position in the event of India leaving the Commonwealth or war breaking out between India and Pakistan. During the evening the delegation called for all the documents, as they were due to leave for Delhi early the next morning. But the Nizam, without explanation, excused himself from adding his signature that night.

At three o'clock in the morning a crowd estimated at about twenty thousand swarmed round the three adjacent houses occupied by Chhatari, Monckton and Sir Sultan Ahmed. There were loud-speakers in the crowd telling them to remain orderly and to create no disturbance beyond preventing the delegation from leaving. No Hyderabad police were seen at any time, and the Ittehad publicly took credit for this militant challenge. At about five o'clock in the morning Chhatari ultimately managed to make contact with the Army authorities, and the delegates and Lady Monckton were then safely evacuated to the house of an officer of the Hyderabad State Forces.

At 8 a.m. the Nizam sent a message to the delegates that they should not leave for a few days. He also advised Mountbatten by telegram that owing to " unforeseen circumstances " they could not return forthwith, and trusted that the Governor-General would not mind if they came on Thursday or Friday at the latest. Mountbatten at once agreed. When the Nizam actually saw the delegation in the afternoon of the 27th he said he wanted them to stay while he took final stock of the situation, but he expressed complete agreement with his Council's decision. He roundly denounced the Ittehad and Razvi, who, it seems, was personally responsible for organising the opposition, and asserted that he would force Razvi to accept the decision.

The next morning, at a second interview with the delegation, the Nizam called Razvi in, but far from converting him, it was Razvi who dominated the Nizam, spoke of the agreement as meaning the death of Hyderabad and pleaded for a chance to reopen negotiations in what he regarded as more favourable circumstances arising from the Indian Government's preoccupations with troubles elsewhere. He proposed a new delegation, preferably of three dissenting voters in the Executive Council. Monckton, Chhatari and Ahmed all explained that any such course of action would be illusory and disastrous, and thereupon tendered their resignations.

On Thursday the 30th the Nizam had a last interview with Monckton and Ahmed before the former left for London and the latter for Delhi. Ahmed, who at once reported the whole of the above bizarre episode to Mountbatten, fired a parting shot at his former master by saying in effect, " This will be the end of you, and your money ".

At the same time a telegram from the Nizam advised Mountbatten that owing to "the changed political situation" the old delegation had been dissolved and a new one created from the ranks of the dissenting voters within the Council. Moin Nawaz Jung, the new chairman, is also a brother-in-law of Mir Laik Ali, who has succeeded Chhatari as Premier, and who up to September was Representative of Pakistan in United Nations.

The possibility that all this manœuvring may be the prelude to some attempt by Hyderabad to align herself with Pakistan cannot be over-looked, and was very frankly dealt with by Mountbatten at his Lahore meeting with Jinnah. There has been general contact between Karachi and Hyderabad both before and after the transfer of power, but Jinnah was at pains to stress that he has had nothing whatever to do with the Nizam's reversed decision and has never discussed any form of agreement with him.

Moin on his arrival began by taking a lofty line that the Nizam wanted Hyderabad to be an independent sovereign State in close associa-tion with the two Dominions and with a foreign policy in general con-formity with India's. But Mountbatten has been extremely tough with him and his delegation, which he met for the first time yesterday. He told them that he had never in the course of his experience in international negotiations over some years come across so naïve and extraordinary a procedure as Hyderabad was now trying to adopt by reverting to a draft which had already, after days of patient examination, been rejected by the other party. He has made it clear beyond all equivocation that the Government still abide by the final version of the Standstill Agreement as worded when the previous delegation left Delhi, as accepted by the Nizam's Council and, until his sudden *volte-face*, by the Nizam himself. If the Nizam continued to repudiate his own decision, the responsibility for breaking off the negotiations would be his alone, and the Indian Government would make it clear to the world that this was so.

Nehru has made a big broadcast offering a United Nations controlled plebiscite for Kashmir, which Mountbatten raised with Jinnah on Saturday. It is altogether a moderate and well-argued statement. But Jinnah's objection, which he made quite clear at the Lahore meeting, is not to the idea of a plebiscite as such, but to the presence of Indian troops in Kashmir while it is being held, which he claims likely to prejudice any chance of it being impartial. Both Nehru and Patel seemed to think that a referendum could not be held during the winter months, and would in any case take time to organise. Mountbatten is concerned about the complacent assumptions in much of the thinking about Kash-mir, and has pressed for a military appreciation of just what a long-term commitment over a wide front would mean.

I dined à *deux* with His Highness of Bikaner—my first visit to Bikaner House since the days when it was an officers' mess for S.E.A.C. After an excellent dinner, rounded off by an eighty-year-old brandy which he told me his father had kept for fifty years, he gave me the story of his part in the Accession policy. The decisive meetings, he said, took place here in Bikaner House on the 7th, 8th and 9th February of this year with Nehru. Bhopal adopted a secretive attitude. Previously he had been very progressive and active in the States' interest. Bikaner told me that he was wholly convinced that without Accession there could have been no stability for the new Dominion, and that all the Princes must reconcile themselves to becoming constitutional rulers. He thought one of the key problems would be the small States with less than a million inhabitants and how to keep them up to the mark under the new dispensation.

He said that Mountbatten was a friend of his childhood, but that his admiration of him had been tremendously enhanced during the past few months. He was particularly impressed by his reasonableness combined with his power to take decisions. Mountbatten, he said, had saved the day by his personality. He also said that great credit was due to the far-seeing statesmanship of his Dewan, K. M. Panikkar.

I must say that Panikkar's brilliance of intellect and the Maharaja's steady common sense make a good partnership. At the moment when the whole Princely system seemed likely to be destroyed by indecision and discord, their initiative helped to provide a possible life-line between the old order and the new. Just before I left he said he hoped that my wife and I would be joining the Governor-General's party during their visit to Bikaner in January. Altogether a mellow evening.

GOVERNMENT HOUSE, NEW DELHI, *Tuesday, 4th November, 1947*

I had a chat this morning with Lady Mountbatten, who is rather concerned about the construction that might be put upon their departure for London for the Royal Wedding, and is wondering whether, in view of the dangerous and troubled situation, the Governor-General's and her trip should not be cancelled. Moreover, she is also, not unnaturally, loathe to interrupt the prodigious efforts she is making in the cause of refugee welfare on both sides of the boundary.

I urged strongly against cancellation, which could only serve to confirm the sense of crisis in the public mind. Their position, I added, was now strictly constitutional, so that it could not and should not be argued that the Governor-General's presence was now essential for the day-to-day conduct of affairs. It would be particularly appropriate for them to be present on this great Royal occasion not only as relatives of bride and bridegroom, but also as the chosen representatives of free India. I also believed that the visit would be well worth while, if only to enable Lady Mountbatten to give a first-hand account from her unique experience of the scale of the welfare problem here.

None-the-less her anxiety is well founded, for Liaquat has to-day launched another of his public diatribes in advance of the next Joint Defence Council. This time from his sick-bed he talked about the immoral and illegal ownership of Kashmir resulting from the infamous Amritsar Treaty*; about the dishonest rewriting of history which called the active sympathy of some outsiders a tribal invasion; about fraud perpetrated on the Kashmir people by its cowardly ruler with the aggres-

* The Treaty whereby Jammu and Kashmir were granted by Lord Hardinge after the First Punjab War in 1846 to Gholat Singh, the founder of the present Ruling House.

sive help of the Indian Government; as tail-piece he cast doubt on the genuineness of Nehru's indisposition. If this language is designed to clear the air, it is certainly an indirect approach to friendship.

In addition, the Defence Committee has heard a very gloomy report from Patel and Baldev Singh, who have just returned from the front. The Committee have accordingly ordered the Army to give top priority to the recapture of Baramula, which had been quickly seized by the tribesmen in their first onrush. Baramula commands the entrance to the Vale of Kashmir, and it is felt that its recapture would greatly reduce the chance of further tribal incursion into the valley. There have been a number of European casualties here, and some British citizens, including Sidney Smith of the *Daily Express*, are still cut off.

I attended the Mountbattens' lunch-party to-day. This is the first time that it has been cool enough to hold it out of doors since our lunch with the Wavells on the day of our arrival.

At dinner to-night in honour of the Asian Labour Conference, Vernon told me the latest news on the Hyderabad negotiations, which I must say verge on comic opera. In face of Mountbatten's inevitable firmness— what else could they have expected?—the new Ittehad-sponsored delegation is completely tongue-tied.

GOVERNMENT HOUSE, NEW DELHI, *Wednesday, 5th November, 1947*

I discussed a number of Press problems this morning with B. L. Sharma. We decided that the time had come to recommend to our principals (the Governor-General and Minister of Information) that our Public Relations triumvirate should be dissolved. Unni Nayar is at present in Srinagar, now wholly taken up with the Indian Army's Press problems in Kashmir, and B. L. is re-absorbed in his daily tasks at the Ministry of Information. It has been a pleasant experience working with them, and our little committee has served a useful purpose, if only because it has brought them to the fore.

I have had a talk with Choudhuri, Director-General of All India Radio, who told me of troubles in the State of Orissa. The primitive aboriginals there seem to have been infected by the upheavals in the north and to be bringing out their blow-pipes, bows and arrows.

GOVERNMENT HOUSE, NEW DELHI, *Thursday, 6th November, 1947*

I called round to see Alan Moorehead at the Imperial this morning. David Astor, the editor of *The Observer*, asked him to undertake a series of special feature articles on India and Pakistan since Independence. This is his first visit to India, and already the vast canvas excites his imagination. Even a short conversation shows him to be a most gifted impressionist, with a particular forte for descriptive analysis.

" What," I asked, " is your first reaction to India? " " It is rather like Spain," he replied—" men sit hating each other like the wrath of God— then, because the sun is too hot, shrug their shoulders and say ' what is the use? ' " He thought the phrase " India's pathetic contentment " was the complete reverse of the truth. On the contrary, he felt their mood was one of " apathetic discontent ".

GOVERNMENT HOUSE, NEW DELHI, *Friday, 7th November, 1947*

At the Emergency Committee to-day the powers and capacity of the East Punjab Government came under fire. Gopalaswami Ayyengar, who has joined the Nehru Government without portfolio but with special responsibility for East Punjab affairs, and Neogy were both critical. Nehru and Patel provided the postscript to the discussion. Nehru: " The Press says 'J'accuse'." Patel: " They have to defend themselves ! " One item before the meeting was the proportion of cattle refugees should be allowed to take with them from the Gurgaon district. The suggestion was that the ration of cattle to refugees should be ten per cent. " So if there are only five in a family," Mountbatten observed, " they can take half a cow."

I dined to-night with Ismay. It was a farewell occasion for Captain Yaqub Khan, second-in-command of the Governor-General's Body Guard, who under Partition is about to take down to Karachi the Moslem half of the contingent which will serve at Government House. There were just four of us, Pete Rees being the other guest. Ismay delighted us with numerous anecdotes and impressions of his war experiences with Churchill. It is difficult to know which to admire more, Ismay's talents as a writer or his skill as a raconteur. He combines economy of phrase and sharpness of observation, with mature judgement and a unique knowledge of great men at great moments.

Ismay said that when the Indian leaders talked of going to Lahore in terms of Chamberlain going to Godesberg he felt bound to remind them of Roosevelt going to Yalta. Discussing the late flowering of Jinnah's career, he recalled that in his own time with Willingdon, Jinnah was certainly not regarded as a figure of the first importance nor could his ultimate eminence have been foreseen. This brought to mind the vivid verbal snapshot of Jinnah a decade earlier given me by Lady Reading during our London visit. " Mr. Jinnah ", she had said, " was prowling around like a leopard in my days."

GOVERNMENT HOUSE, NEW DELHI, *Saturday, 8th November, 1947*

The Joint Defence Council met this morning after prolonged and vain efforts by Mountbatten to secure the presence of Liaquat and Jinnah. The Pakistan representatives were Nishtar, the Communications Minister, and Mohammed Ali, who as Secretary-General to the Government is already one of the most influential figures in the new régime. Mountbatten invited Nehru and V. P. to join Nishtar and Mohammed Ali at lunch. Afterwards he steered the conversation into two separate rooms, Nehru and Nishtar talking politically, and V. P. and Mohammed Ali considering the problem at the official level.

For the first time, the technique of broadcast invective and controversy has been temporarily set aside, and a serious effort has been made to seek a detailed working formula for a settlement of the dispute. There was a rather larger area of common ground than had been expected, but diametrically opposed views were held about the withdrawal of forces. Pakistan wanted the withdrawal to be simultaneous by both sides, while India was adamant that withdrawal could be effected only after Kashmir had been cleared of the raiders. To encourage the Indians that they are negotiating from increasing strength comes the news that the offensive ordered on Tuesday has succeeded and that Baramula has been re-captured. Altogether the Mountbattens can leave for London to-morrow with easier minds about Kashmir than had seemed possible forty-eight hours ago.

On the other hand, the Junagadh problem causes renewed worry. At last Monday's Defence Committee it was reported as little more than a routine item that Indian forces had duly entered Mangrol and Babaria-wad on the 1st November and that the occupation had been carried through peacefully. It was reasonable to hope that Patel would be satisfied for a decision on the occupation of Junagadh itself to lie in the pending tray until greater problems were safely resolved.

But to-day at about one in the morning the Dewan formally invited the Indian Government to take over the administration of Junagadh in order to save the State from complete breakdown pending an honour-able settlement of the several issues involved in Junagadh's accession. The Dewan advised Liaquat that he was acting with the support of public opinion, the authority of the State Council and of the Nawab himself, who had a short while before flown to Karachi. The Govern-ment at once accepted the request authorising their Regional Com-missioner in Rajkot to implement it.

All these developments were only brought to Mountbatten's notice late this evening. It is the first time since the transfer of power that the Government have carried out a major act of policy without fully con-sulting or notifying him in advance of the event. He feels this may be due to Patel's and V. P.'s desire to spare him embarrassment.

Finally, to complete the day's anxieties, the Nizam, recklessly drawing on the last reserves of good-will towards himself in Delhi, seeks to buy yet more time before signing the Standstill Agreement. His delegation, which left Delhi yesterday, has been brought by dint of four days sustained effort to the point where it was ready to advise the Nizam to accept the Standstill Agreement without amendment. The Nizam, on the strength of Mountbatten's forthcoming London visit, has now asked for a post-ponement until the 25th November. Mountbatten, after consultation with the Government, has replied agreeing to this, provided a settlement is reached by the end of the month.

GOVERNMENT HOUSE, NEW DELHI, *Sunday, 9th November, 1947*

We set out very early for Palam to see the Mountbattens off on the first leg of their flight to London. Right up to the last moment Mount-batten was far from happy about going at all, but, quite apart from Princess Elizabeth being a cousin, the bridegroom, Lieutenant Philip

Mountbatten, is not only his nephew, but has made his home with him in England for the past eighteen years.

At 10 a.m. I attended the Swearing-In of Rajagopalachari, who in Mountbatten's absence will be acting as Governor-General. Since the transfer of power this famous elder statesman of the Congress Party has been serving with distinction as Governor of West Bengal. The ceremony took place in the Council Chamber in the presence of the Cabinet. "C. R.", as he is generally called, dressed in his white *dhoti* and smiling benignly through his large dark glasses, gave the Hindu salutation. Everyone stood while Bannerjee, the Secretary of the Home Department, read out the words of the Royal Commission—"To our trusty and well beloved Chakravarti Rajagopalachari greeting". The Chief Justice, Kania, administered the oath to which only one alteration was made, the substitution of the words " affirm " for " swear ".

The ceremony was all over within five minutes, but this was quite long enough to convey the full sense of its historic significance. There were both fulfilment and dramatic irony in the spectacle of this Congress campaigner becoming the first Indian to act as head of State by means of the form and title of the Raj which it had been his life work to supersede.

I attended the acting Governor-General's first lunch-party which he gave to members of his staff. C. R.'s married daughter Srimati Namagiri, who is shy and retiring, is acting as hostess. The A.D.C.'s laid on the normal procedure for outside guests, our staff party being lined up for individual introduction. The ladies all curtsied, but C. R. pleaded, " Don't do that for me ! "

After the lunch he called for Vernon and myself. We expected little more than a few formal pleasantries, but our talk was far more prolonged and illuminating than that. We emerged from this encounter strongly impressed that when the time came here was the ideal successor to Mountbatten. There could, of course, be no greater contrast between the two men's minds and outlook. Mountbatten—dynamic, extrovert, tackling events at the surface with feverish activity : C. R.—introspective, essentially a scholar and thinker, anxious primarily about the underlying causes.

He asked about the scope of my work, and then proceeded to analyse the role of the Indian Press, which, he said, had a long way to go before it could achieve its full freedom. I asked him what influence it had on politics, and he said, " Very little ". The Congress had completely dominated the political scene, and the Press, instead of providing informed criticism, was nothing more than a body of political propagandists. If there were to be a change in the balance of power all the Press would do would be to follow suit, and one lot of propagandists would succeed another. He said he had just written to an old journalist friend of his in Madras, who was a critic of the Government, saying that the essential thing for the Indian Press to do was to concentrate first of all on administrative matters rather than on political formulæ. Once they began dealing with things which affected the daily lives of the people, they would begin to exert a genuine influence.

I told him I particularly admired *The Hindu* of Madras. He said that this was not surprising, in view of my British outlook and training, as here was a paper brought up on the best traditions of nineteenth-century British journalism. He agreed with the point Vernon made that Indian journalism was much nearer to American in its tendency to outspokenness and over-statement. C. R. drew attention to the excellence of the British magazine *Country Life*, which covered such a wide range of subjects and which had almost a religious quality about it. He felt that until India could produce papers of equal value to this, the British would continue to have the advantage over her!

He then turned to the general situation and said he was profoundly unhappy. Archibald Nye, who had " an almost missionary zeal ", had tried to console him, but the events of the last few weeks had largely shattered the dream of a lifetime. " I had always assumed that we were better than other people, that under the leadership of a man who had somehow found the secret of combining religion and politics without compromising his politics or contaminating his religion, we would, through our belief in non-violence, make rapid strides as soon as independence had been achieved." There was a sense of mission while fighting British rule, but that now seemed to be lost in the savagery and suffering that Indian people were inflicting upon themselves.

I remarked that the problem which distressed him as affecting the Indian people seemed to be common to everyone throughout the world; much the same dilemma was facing Europe; perhaps the problem and the solution were common to all people. There was really no consolation, he replied, in knowing that the evil was not confined to India. " I am not distressed at the usual struggles for power—the jealousies and intrigues; the trouble with India is that she has a solution to these problems through her religion and that she has now seemed temporarily to forget it."

He said he was hoping and praying for a revival of the Vedantic religious spirit. Their religion had something in common with Christianity, and indeed all other religions; but the Vedas were not based so much on the principles of Christian leadership, they were more closely related to the European pagan philosophies of Socrates and Marcus Aurelius. It was a code of conduct which had been known to the people over centuries and which helped to conquer their fears. Fear, he felt, was at the root of the trouble. Revenge was only fear at one remove. Nor was it genuine revenge that indulged in the indiscriminate massacre of women and children. Someone had said that if we could experience the full force of other people's suffering we should all die; that there was some form of compensation which prevented us from fully appreciating the horrors that surrounded us.

Turning to the Bengal situation, he said that it was wonderful to see that Bengal had been free of the communal disturbance; in fact the East and West Bengal Governments have been working to date on a closer understanding than East and West Pakistan. There had been common action from the outset between the two Prime Ministers.

There had admittedly been quite a considerable movement of middle-class Hindus from East Bengal, but this was not the outcome of persecution on the part of the East Bengal Government. These Hindus had moved because they did not think the prospects of security were very good, in much the same way as capitalist interests had moved out of the Dominion into the States. The only people who would come to any harm in the long run would be the Hindus themselves.

C. R. was pessimistic about the political prospects in England, and felt that developments in India had done the Labour Government a great deal of harm. I said I believed that Churchill had rather over-stated the case.

He said that the Indian Government were living literally from hand to mouth. A tremendous burden was resting on Nehru. The main ray of hope was the presence of Gandhiji. It was essential that his outlook should prevail.

Just as we were leaving, the A.D.C. came in to report that Mr. Bhabha would be ten minutes late for his appointment. " Thank goodness! I am most relieved to hear it," said C. R.—a reaction one would not expect to hear from Mountbatten!

GOVERNMENT HOUSE, NEW DELHI, *Monday, 10th November, 1947*

I have just prepared a Public Relations appreciation which recapitulates all the major developments since my return here from London. These are the principal points I have made :—

" Guidance on the tangled Kashmir, Hyderabad and Junagadh situation is not easy to give, and reliable information on the military situation in Kashmir is particularly difficult to extract. It should be noted that when Mountbatten visited Kashmir in June he did everything possible to impress upon the Maharaja the urgent necessity of acceding to one or other of the successor Dominions before the 15th August and of basing his decision upon some expression of the popular will.

" Moreover, Mountbatten was empowered to advise him on the authority of Patel that if his decision was to throw in his lot with Pakistan and join their Constituent Assembly in advance of the transfer of power, it would not be regarded as an unfriendly act by India. ' There is,' Mountbatten warned him, ' only one way for you to bring disaster to your country, and that is to do nothing.' His hesitation, followed by the inability or unwillingness of Pakistan to prevent tribal incursion into the State, have undoubtedly been the primary causes of the present crisis. It is probable that nothing short of a full-scale tribal invasion to the gates of his capital would have induced the hesitating Maharaja to accede at all.

" I am convinced that the Government of India were absolutely right to accept his Accession before offering to give him military aid, and to regard it unilaterally as an interim measure until the destiny of the State can be finally decided by a confirming plebiscite. It should be stressed that the accession has complete legal validity both in terms of the British Government's and Jinnah's expressed policy statements. But just how narrow the escape has been from irreparable disaster is to be seen from

Jinnah's dramatic invasion order given at midnight on the 27th October to his Commander-in-Chief, General Gracey, and cancelled solely as a result of Gracey seeing fit to refer the order to Auchinleck. Auchinleck's immediate intervention caused Jinnah to pause just long enough for second thoughts. Only thus were the two Dominions saved from being forthwith in a state of open war with each other.

" The Nizam of Hyderabad is undoubtedly playing for time to see how Kashmir develops before taking a final decision in favour of the Standstill Agreement. In the attempt he has carried on what can only be described as Ruritanian negotiations. The Ittehad which he originally encouraged has now become a veritable Frankenstein, and the whole issue now turns on whether the Nizam has the political and moral strength to resist the opposition to any form of agreement with India. If the Hyderabad problem can be solved I am confident that we shall be able to surmount the hump of the crisis.

" At his meeting with Mountbatten in Lahore on 1st November, Jinnah asked him to believe that he had at first been against accepting the accession of Junagadh and had demurred for some time only to give way finally to the insistent appeals of the Nawab and Dewan. But this was not the line taken a month earlier in Delhi by Liaquat, who gave no indications of any such misgivings. But whatever the motive or explanation, by accepting Junagadh's accession in the first place Jinnah was inevitably inviting a sharp reaction.

" Patel has responded to the challenge in a way which, if it raises domestic morale, is hardly calculated to win over world opinion. But although the Government's action in occupying the State will provide material for the suspicious and ill-disposed to summon up analogies with recent European history, it can still be claimed that there has strictly been no violation of law. It is perhaps worth noting that the invitation from the Junagadh Premier to administer the territory in the Ruler's absence does not in the Indian Government's view prejudice the Accession issue. Nehru has offered early discussion of the whole problem, but Pakistan demands what it calls the restoration of the Nawab's administration before such discussions can begin. India points out that it was the Nawab's administration and nobody else who decided to call in their troops. All this, however, leads into a labyrinth of detail and a web of propaganda, and it is important not to get lost in the one or entangled in the other.

" Taking the larger view of developments to date, Kashmir, Hyderabad and Junagadh are essentially one situation and react on each other. A move towards agreement in any one of these three States would ease the situation in the other two. Accession has been amply vindicated. All the acceding States have held firm, and in the three cases where there has been trouble the Ruler has each time been of a different community from the overwhelming majority of his subjects. If the Accession policy had not been duly sponsored and pressed home by Mountbatten and Patel there would undoubtedly have been complete chaos. As it is, the scale of the consolidation is indeed impressive. In so far as the Princely States before the transfer of power formed no part of British India, their accession now means the incorporation into the Indian Union of larger territories and populations than have been lost to it by the creation of Pakistan.

" Mr. Churchill's recent speeches in Parliament during the Debate on the Address on Burmese Independence and on the Punjab troubles have aroused old phobias. In two respects I feel that what he said should not be allowed to pass unchallenged. First, although we are admittedly wallowing here in a statistical morass, all the data available to us suggest that his round figures of the number of people who have lost their lives in the recent disturbances are an inflated estimate. Secondly, the implication of his speech on Burma, that Dominion Status is something less than Independence, should surely be taken up at once by the British Government as being false in political fact and legal theory and in any case completely contrary to its declared policy.

" My own impression, which has been confirmed since my return, is that the Government of India will not force the pace on withdrawal from the Commonwealth, and if they can find a suitable excuse for letting the matter remain in the pending-tray they will do so. I have for some time felt that one of the major objectives of Jinnah's policy has been to keep this issue at the boil and if possible to tease India out of the Commonwealth, leaving Pakistan as the ' Northern Ireland ' of the sub-continent. Mountbatten, as a cousin of the King, by his continued presence in Delhi as Governor-General of India, inadvertently makes it difficult for Jinnah to promote this concept.

" Be that as it may, evidence is accumulating that Mountbatten is to be made the target of a fairly heavy propaganda barrage from Karachi. The first salvo was an article in the *Pakistan Times* to-day accusing him of being in active command of the Kashmir operations. His return to London for the Royal Wedding should be the best refutation of this fantastic charge. But the depressing truism remains—the bolder the lie the wider the credence; from which it often follows that to deny an untruth is simply to spread a suspicion."

CHAPTER TWENTY

PROGRESS AND RELAPSE

GOVERNMENT HOUSE, NEW DELHI, *Tuesday, 11th November, 1947*

TO-DAY IS THE great Hindu celebration of Deepawali. As with our Christmas, the emphasis is placed on the family, and particularly on the children. All the houses are bedecked with lanterns, for it is the festival of the lights. C. R. called me in this morning saying he had composed a short Deepawali greetings which he thought might appropriately be his first message as Governor-General. The message addressed to the people of India had a peculiar rhythmic beauty, for, like Nehru, C. R. is a master of English prose.

"We may not," he wrote, "have the mind to indulge in festive rejoicings when we are surrounded by difficulties, and so deeply immersed in anxieties as we are to-day, but Deepawali is a great national day associated with hope and joy from time immemorial in India. The lights that are lighted on that day also represent the hope for more and more enlightenment, and the holy anointing done on the morrow of the festival is associated with the cleansing of the spirit symbolically called the Ganga Shan. May this Deepawali serve to purify the hearts and enlighten the minds of people everywhere in India irrespective of caste or creed or so-called race."

OBSERVATORY HOUSE, GOVERNOR-GENERAL'S LODGE, SIMLA, *Thursday, 20th November, 1947*

With C. R.'s agreement, I have been able during Mountbatten's absence in London to rejoin my family up in Simla. I am remaining on here until such time as the Comptroller's House on the Governor-General's estate is ready for us. My cheerful and efficient secretary, Maggie Sutherland, is sending up Government House papers by bag and is keeping in regular touch with me by telephone. Fortunately it is proving to be a period of relative quiescence for Mountbatten's staff.

I also see the newspapers, if somewhat belatedly. *Dawn* of 12th November has provided a significant postscript to what it terms "the rape of Junagadh". Nothing the Dewan or the Indian Government have done, it claims, "alters in the slightest the constitutional position of Junagadh whose accession to Pakistan stands and is sacrosanct according to law which in the present case is the Indian Independence Act of 1947 enacted by the British Parliament". What price the sacrosanctity of Kashmir's accession? Once again *Dawn* comes up like thunder—this time in advance of the event. For as early as the 24th August I see from my notes it asserted, "The time has come to tell the Maharaja of Kashmir that he must make his choice and choose Pakistan ". Should Kashmir fail to join Pakistan, " the gravest possible trouble will inevitably ensue ".

The military situation in the Kashmir Valley has been further stabilised with the capture of the tactically important town of Uri, but farther afield in Jammu and Poonch, where Moslem solidarity is greater, the position for both the Indian and State forces, thin on the ground and stretched out along difficult lines of communication, is not so secure. With the onset of winter, however, and with the Passes blocked with snow, the campaign is likely to be largely immobilised. It is hoped that those tribesmen who were more interested in quick loot than holy wars may soon begin to lose enthusiasm and trickle back to their homes ; but undoubtedly the Moslem population in Kashmir has been deeply stirred.

After having had time to digest last week's draft of a possible agreement, Liaquat has made his latest contribution to a settlement by denouncing Sheikh Abdullah as " this Quisling ", " an agent of the Congress for many years ", who " struts about the stage bartering the life, honour and freedom of the people for the sake of personal profit and power "— in so far as Nehru and Abdullah have ties of long personal friendship it is difficult to imagine a more wounding phrase. Secondly, he has seen fit to reveal while Mountbatten is still in London what he now calls " the terms " offered by Jinnah at his Lahore meeting with Mountbatten on 1st November—namely, a cease-fire administered by the two Governments ; simultaneous withdrawal of the Indian troops and invading tribesmen ; joint administration by the Governors-General and a plebiscite under their joint control and supervision. I may say that these proposals were at the time immediately transmitted by Mountbatten to his Government for their consideration : and I understand their reply had already been sent to Karachi in advance of Liaquat's " revelation ".

OBSERVATORY HOUSE, GOVERNOR-GENERAL'S LODGE, SIMLA,
Wednesday, 26th November, 1947

On all sides there are signs of a *détente* giving rise to the hope that the storms which have threatened to overwhelm the sub-continent following the transfer of power may at last be subsiding. All India Radio provided perhaps the most promising series of news items to be heard in any one evening since the transfer of power. First there is the Standstill Agreement with Hyderabad. Mountbatten on his return from London has— as Patel announced in the Legislative Assembly yesterday—seen the Hyderabad delegation " for the last time ", and precisely the same Agreement is being taken back for the Nizam's signature as a month ago.

Secondly, Nehru has made an important statement on Kashmir, which, while it once more accuses Pakistan of conniving at invasion, indirectly repudiates the recent dangerous suggestion of Sheikh Abdullah that there might now be no need for a referendum. If Nehru had not done this promptly, Mountbatten's own position would have been very difficult. Nehru has simply repeated the terms on which Accession had been accepted—that is, an Interim Government followed by reference to the popular will under an impartial tribunal. He rejects the doctrine of a simultaneous withdrawal of troops as providing in itself mere confirmation of Pakistan's connivance.

The third item of good news is a Joint Defence Council meeting, with Liaquat coming to Delhi to-morrow for it. This will be the first personal encounter between the two Prime Ministers since the Kashmir invasion.

Finally from Karachi comes the official announcement of the intention to disband the All India Moslem League and to confine the operations of the League to Pakistan. This is an enlightened decision which will help to free many of the forty million Moslems living in India from a difficult double allegiance. As such, it is a powerful and timely contribution to peace in the sub-continent.

OBSERVATORY HOUSE, GOVERNOR-GENERAL'S LODGE, SIMLA,
Saturday, 29th November, 1947

The Nizam has signed at last, and Patel has made a good statement paying tribute to Mountbatten for his decisive role in the negotiations. Certainly patience has been called for in dealing with the old Nizam, who adheres stubbornly to the methods of traditional oriental diplomacy. Wholly divorced from the developments of the outside world, he seems incapable of taking any decision until he has enmeshed himself in the webs of his own intrigues.

It has been a niggling operation until the last. When the delegation had their final meeting with Mountbatten on Tuesday they began pleading for very minor amendments such as the substitution of " will " for " shall ", and finally even a semi-colon for a comma, in a desperate effort to justify their existence and make good the assertion that the Government of India had agreed to changes in the text approved by their predecessors. It was for this reason that Mountbatten was at pains to stress that he would not agree to the change of even a comma. Some small amendments in the collateral letter were accepted, but here India stood firm in refusing to allow Hyderabad to have its own diplomatic representation.

The Ittehad and its extremist leader, Kasim Razvi—who was incidentally in Delhi during the last bout of negotiation—can claim no more than that the Standstill Agreement has been brought about by a purely Hyderabadi delegation. But this face-saving device has been effected only at the expense of Patel's confidence in the Nizam and his intentions. For all that, the Standstill Agreement allows a breathing space of a year for heads to cool and hearts to soften.

There has been another admirable speech by Nehru, this time on the refugee situation, in which he has made a strong plea against retaliation and revenge and put the whole vast problem into better perspective. Gopalaswami Ayyengar announces that Indo-Pakistan consultations to deal with all outstanding problems between the two Dominions are to take place first at secretarial and afterwards at ministerial level, which suggests that a serious effort is to be made to put relations on a working basis. Patel has described the talks with Liaquat Ali Khan as " cordial ", and Liaquat has now left for consultations with Jinnah. The Joint Defence Council is to be kept in being, and the next meeting will be in Lahore on the 6th December.

OBSERVATORY HOUSE, GOVERNOR-GENERAL'S LODGE, SIMLA,
Monday, 1st December, 1947

Kashmir may well have the effect of shifting the bias of Indian politics. It is beginning to dawn on the leaders that if the State is to be maintained within the Indian Union some three million Kashmiri Moslems have to be absorbed and appeased. Sheikh Abdullah is accordingly veering round in favour of the referendum to which India is pledged. There are the symptoms of a Gandhi–Nehru–Abdullah line-up against the Hindu Mahasabha on this issue, and of an open clash between communal and nationalist aspirations inside the Congress. Those in the Congress who want a Hindu State do not want Kashmir, but the Government's action in Kashmir has temporarily silenced them.

This profound but subtle discord is not confined to the Kashmir question; it breaks out on a wider front. The Hindu Mahasabha have just passed a resolution condemning an All India Congress Committee resolution on refugee policy which had laid down that the Congress did not intend to encourage Moslems to leave who wished to stay, and had boldly advocated the ultimate return of refugees to their original homes. Here are the makings of a major conflict between the Mahasabha and Congress, and the strong terms of both resolutions would indicate the possibility of an early show-down.

The London Press is beginning to comment on the recent signs of an Indo-Pakistan *détente*. First fruit of the Standstill Agreement with Hyderabad is the Nizam's decision to release the local Congress political prisoners. Most of the key men, including Swami Ramanand Tirth, the President of the State Congress, have been under arrest during the negotiations.

OBSERVATORY HOUSE, GOVERNOR-GENERAL'S LODGE, SIMLA,
Saturday, 6th December, 1947

Nehru has made a major statement on Foreign policy to the Legislative Assembly. This is the field in which his mind can spread itself, and I suspect that he gets the deepest satisfaction from being the Foreign Minister in his own Government. He is making a determined bid to keep India out of the scramble of power politics. He hotly denies that his aim is neutrality, but its broad effect will be something very like it. He calls for co-operation with both the United States of America and Russia, and makes no reference to Britain or the Commonwealth, beyond saying that he hopes to improve India's relations with *some* Commonwealth members, which would seem to imply a flank attack on South Africa.

In a reference to the decision taken by the United Nations over the partition of Palestine, Nehru commended the Indian proposal for two autonomous States within a federation. This, he asserted, is regarded in United Nations circles as wiser than partition, which had already led to so much trouble and would lead to more. India, he added, would gain in prestige by taking an independent line in this way on major issues of world policy. He made the point that politically Foreign policy depended on economic trends within a country. India's economic policies were not yet fixed, but had been diverted by the pressing needs of the immediate internal crisis.

At the same time, Asaf Ali, Nehru's first Ambassador to the United States, bids in Washington for American financial backing, urging that India was solvent and a good market. Asked about Indo-Pakistan relations, he replied he expected they would be close—at any rate at the economic level.

OBSERVATORY HOUSE, GOVERNOR-GENERAL'S LODGE, SIMLA,
Tuesday, 9th December, 1947

Our stay in Simla has been a quiet one. The place has a special stillness and unreality of its own, which to the newcomer give rise to a certain sense of foreboding as the sharp autumnal air heralds the onset of winter and the Himalayan snow-line creeps steadily nearer. The transfer of power, the troubles and now the approaching cold weather have completed the great exodus of Europeans.

Michael Hadow, formally Indian Civil Service and now of the High Commissioner's staff, who has come to see about the repatriation of British subjects stranded in the Simla area, is staying with us. He has been up to the St. Lawrence College, Kasauli, where he has found signs of an anti-British attitude among the Sikhs. He used to serve in the Political Department, which administered relations between the Indian States and the Viceroy in his capacity as Crown Representative. He told us a story of an inquiry by the Political Department into the affairs of a very small and jungly Indian State. The object of the exercise was to inspect Government papers. After prolonged negotiation the local " prime minister " led the way through a passage to the vaults, where he duly unlocked a big chest. Inside was disclosed one solitary file marked simply " Ladies' File ".

Archie John Wavell has also been staying with us for a couple of days. He had a lot of interesting things to say about his father's Middle East campaigns, with particular reference to the controversy over the operations in Greece. Clearly his father has suffered much injustice from his virtue of reticence.

GOVERNMENT HOUSE, NEW DELHI, *Wednesday, 10th December, 1947*

Our children, with Miss Carey, their nurse, have at last come down the hill with us. Ever since their arrival in April they have been up in Simla. Miss Cary was born in India, and knew it well in the days of Lord Halifax's Viceroyalty. Her knowledge of Indian conditions has been a great source of strength to us in our domestic life, and certainly relieved me of much anxiety when we were separated during the troubles.

We were part of a small convoy covered by a most reassuring Gurkha contingent. But there was no incident of any kind on the way down. The great refugee camps at Ambala and Panipat seemed to be in a more orderly condition than when I saw them last month. We take up our abode at the Comptroller's House. The present Comptroller, Ronald Daubeny, is a bachelor, and is living on top of his exacting duties in Government House itself. The Comptroller's House has a glorious garden, full of English flowers, in which for the next two months or so the children can revel until the inhuman heat of the sun drives them indoors from dawn to dusk. It was here that Radcliffe stayed when preparing his Award, and it was also allocated to Chiang Kai Shek and Madame when they visited Delhi in 1942.

During the time I have been in Simla both Ismay and Auchinleck have returned home. Ismay stayed on until Mountbatten was back from London. There had always been a gentleman's agreement between them that he should in any case leave by the end of the year. In the knowledge that his " Grand Design " for ensuring the effective administration of Partition both before and after the transfer of power had achieved its primary purpose, he felt that he could justifiably take his leave now. The temporary improvement in the political weather also encouraged him to advance the date of his departure.

After some bitter argument between the two Dominions about an appropriate closing date—set just before the transfer of power for April 1948—Auchinleck's Supreme Command was finally wound up on 30th November. During the three weeks of October when we were in London Mountbatten was engaged in difficult negotiations on the whole of this problem.

The outcome of the closure of the Supreme Command was the termination of its responsibility for British soldiers in India, who if they wished to stay on further in the service of the Indian or Pakistan Governments would require fresh contracts. Some four thousand officers and men who had initially volunteered were involved. Negotiations with London on the terms of their future service were instituted towards the end of September, and Auchinleck's original proposal was that the Supreme Command should be liquidated on 31st December, subject to three months' notice being given to all the British volunteers on the 1st October.

This notice was duly given, but Patel at once began putting on pressure for an earlier closing down of the Supreme Command. He complained to Mountbatten that by its continued presence in Delhi it was throttling the initiative of the Indian Army and acting as an advance outpost of Pakistan. Mountbatten protested in the strongest terms at any such attack on the Command's impartiality, stressing that Auchinleck's integrity was beyond dispute or doubt. Patel, however, was not to be deflected from his demand.

The Pakistan Government were equally outspoken, but in reverse. In their view it was the Indian Army which was sitting on top of the

Supreme Commander's Headquarters and actually influencing the decisions of the Supreme Commander. When Auchinleck himself suggested the 30th November as the closing date at a Joint Defence Council meeting in Lahore in the middle of October, Liaquat vehemently refused to accept the proposal. Afterwards Mountbatten had the matter out with him, and discovered that he was under the impression that a British Supreme Commander was in a position to assure the dispatch of stores to Pakistan more effectively than a committee consisting of the Commanders-in-Chief of the two Dominions. Mountbatten was at pains to explain that Auchinleck was only responsible for making administrative arrangements and that the execution of these arrangements had always been the responsibility of the Indian Government.

This did not cause Liaquat to change his attitude, and so the opposing views of the two Governments were referred to London. On the 7th November the British Government replied that they had reluctantly come to the conclusion that they had no option but to close down the Supreme Command Headquarters on 30th November.

With this particular cause of controversy removed from the agenda, it was found that the next Joint Defence Council meeting on the 26th November had a far more friendly give-and-take atmosphere about it than any meeting since 15th August. This session went on for some three hours, and dispatched no fewer than forty-four items of business. The most encouraging decision of all was that the Council itself should continue to operate, in spite of the termination of the Supreme Command. Mountbatten asked at this point to be allowed to give up the chairmanship because he had been told that Pakistan considered him to be biased in favour of India, but both the Pakistan and Indian representatives urged him in the strongest terms to stay on in the chair, which, somewhat reluctantly, he has agreed to do. It is no small achievement to have completed these delicate negotiations and to have maintained this measure of high-level military liaison against the tense background of the Kashmir crisis.

Many of the duties Ismay and Auchinleck were called upon to perform were very painful to them on personal grounds, but this did not deter them from bending all their energies and experience to mitigate the tragedy of partitioning the Indian Army. Their presence throughout this transaction ensured that Mountbatten received the best possible military advice at every stage.

The Emergency Committee of the Cabinet, too, has met for the last time, handing back to the Government for solution perhaps the deepest problem of all—the rehabilitation of the refugees from Pakistan. There are two possible solutions: that they should all remain in the East Punjab, or that a given proportion of them should be sent to other Provinces. The East Punjab Government has been standing for this second solution, claiming that the holdings from which these refugees came were large and rich and that they should be compensated by the allotment of at least ten acres to each family; any families remaining over from this allocation should, in their submission, be given land elsewhere in India.

The Central Government, however, stands firmly for the first solution, on the principle that the number of non-Moslems who have come into the East Punjab is smaller than that of the Moslems who have gone out, that the average family holding in India was two acres or even less, and that the spread of refugees throughout India will only spread the communal tension.   Therefore the Government of India is insisting that the East Punjab accommodates the lot.   They are aware that this will mean the concentration of a large number of discontented people, including a high proportion of Sikhs.

GOVERNMENT HOUSE, NEW DELHI, *Thursday, 11th December, 1947*

I have been acquainting myself fully from the records, and from a long talk I have had with Mountbatten on the varying and often dramatic developments in the Kashmir situation over the past fortnight, during which time there seems to have been almost a year of diplomatic effort. Mountbatten has struggled with what I can only describe as heroic zeal to close this breach and prevent the whole sub-continent falling apart from a mono-maniac obsession over the political future of a single Indian State, important enough in itself, but containing only four million out of its four hundred million inhabitants.

One of Ismay's most important contributions to peace was the part he played both early in November and during the " cordial " talks between Liaquat and Nehru in Delhi only last week.   Yet again Mountbatten had great difficulty in bringing the leaders together, as yet again Liaquat prefaced the meeting with a telegram designed to infuriate Nehru, to whom it was this time directly addressed.   He has once more described Abdullah as a " Quisling ", has accused the Indian Government of attempting to eliminate the whole Moslem population of the State, and repeated his demand for setting up an impartial independent administration immediately.

Nehru fortunately is not the man to let his justifiable indignation degenerate into false pride, and Mountbatten duly prevailed on the two Prime Ministers to have their first man-to-man talk on Kashmir since its accession.   After a long preliminary presentation of his case by Nehru, Liaquat, who was obviously very tired and weak after his recent illness, managed to ask a number of pertinent questions and to put forward proposals which Nehru promised to consider.   Ismay, with his own outstanding skill and experience in the drafting of high-level formulæ and with the support of V. P. and Mohammed Ali on behalf of the two Governments, at once put these proposals into more formal shape, and they provided the basis for four further meetings during the next two days.

Briefly the proposals were : that Pakistan should use all her influence to persuade the rebel " Azad Kashmir " forces to cease fighting and the tribesmen and other " invaders " to withdraw from Kashmir territory as quickly as possible and to prevent further incursions.   India should withdraw the bulk of her forces, leaving only small detachments of minimum strength to deal with disturbances.   The United Nations Organisation should be asked to send a commission to hold a plebiscite in Kashmir and to recommend to India, Pakistan and Kashmir, before it was held, steps which should be taken to ensure that it was fair and unfettered. Certain steps which it was intended to take towards this object, such as the release of political prisoners and the return of refugees, should be published right away.

With Ismay's help the position reached at the end of the talks was that, while there was no definite agreement, Nehru's criticisms were confined to detail. Liaquat, for his part, who came to Delhi insisting on the complete withdrawal by both sides, an impartial administration before a plebiscite, and an impartial plebiscite, only fully gained the last and partially gained the first of these conditions. He thus showed himself ready to make a concession of principle. Ismay left quite convinced that the formula was both on political and administrative grounds a workable solution and the only one that has so far been propounded. The atmosphere when Ismay left was promising. It seemed that the foundations had been well and truly laid; but conciliation is heartbreaking work.

Two days ago, and only two hours after Mohammed Ali, who had stayed on, was airborne for Karachi, Mountbatten was present at what he has described to me as one of the most depressing meetings it has ever been his lot to preside over. For the second time Patel and Baldev Singh appeared before the Defence Committee as messengers of woe. They had just returned from the front, and the reports they brought back, together with independent information reaching Nehru, hardened the Cabinet's heart against agreeing to the immediate plebiscite, or even, for the present, to continuing negotiations. The grievance was three-fold. First, reports of large concentrations of invaders, including tribesmen in the West Punjab; secondly, the allegation that Liaquat had no sooner left Delhi than he had done all in his power to encourage new raiders to invade the State; and thirdly, and perhaps more emotionally disturbing, continuing stories of ghastly atrocities, including the wholesale murder of non-Moslems and the selling of Kashmir girls.

Contact was only resumed as a result of Mountbatten planting a discreet suggestion with Liaquat that he should telegraph Nehru confirming the date for a resumption of negotiations. Liaquat did this, urging that the only way for bloodshed to be stopped was for the representatives of the two Governments to continue to meet together. Nehru at once responded to the spirit of this message and accompanied Mountbatten to Lahore for last Monday's Joint Defence Council.

The discussion on Kashmir lasted, with a break for a dinner-party, from three in the afternoon until midnight—seven hours in all. This meeting took place in a generally friendly atmosphere, with only occasional outbursts. None-the-less it convinced Mountbatten, who tried every means he knew of reconciling the divergent views, that the deadlock was so complete, and the political pressures both internal and external so intense, that only the introduction of a third party with international authority acting in an agreed capacity could now break it.

At this point, therefore, Mountbatten injected the suggestion that the United Nations Organisation might be called upon to fill the third-party role. Liaquat welcomed the proposal as strengthening his hand in any action needed to call a halt to the raiders. He did not, incidentally, confirm Jinnah's assertion that they could be called off by command simply from Karachi. Nehru wanted to know under what section of the Charter any reference to U.N.O. could be made. As it was now midnight, Mountbatten suggested that a further study should be made of this point. Nehru nodded his head wearily, and the meeting ended with the project left open.

Since returning to Delhi, Mountbatten has seen Gandhi and V. P., who are both favourably inclined to the invocation of U.N.O., and to-day he has had a further talk with Nehru, whose attitude to the idea is now less negative than it was at Lahore.

To-night there was a dinner for the Diplomatic Corps, followed by a showing at Government House cinema of the film of the Royal Wedding. There was also shown an Indian Government film on Kashmir of doubtful quality or propaganda value. There was a glorious shot of various sub-human types described as " captured tribesmen ", in the midst of whom could be discerned the mild features and modest figure of Eric Britter of *The Times*!

Nehru spoke to me about my copy of Trevor-Roper's " Last Days of Hitler ", which he borrowed after hearing about it from Mountbatten—who, incidentally, stayed awake the whole of one night reading it. Nehru told me he was greatly interested in the narrative, but added that he found it rather too concentrated for his personal taste.

GOVERNMENT HOUSE, NEW DELHI, *Thursday, 18th December, 1947*

Once again dark clouds appear over the horizon, and, as is so often the case with tropical climates, the storm looms over our heads almost before the sun has gone in. All the information reaching us at Government House suggests that events are moving fast in the Kashmir crisis and that the drift towards war has accelerated. Patel, it seems, has given the drastic instruction that none of the financial agreements with Pakistan are to be implemented unless Pakistan ceases support for the raiders. Some fifty-five crores of rupees (about forty million pounds) are involved, and the financial implications of this step for Pakistan, apart from wider political and moral aspects, are very serious. Pakistan has only about two crores in reserve and numerous urgent debts. The plea that will be made is simply, " Why should we give them the money to buy the arms to shoot our soldiers? ", and is not likely to be resisted when it comes before the Cabinet.

The Indian leaders have been receiving a growing volume of evidence from their own sources of information of Pakistan's connivance at the raiders' operations. This is the primary cause of the hardening of their attitude. Some of them see the whole Kashmir operation as a mere episode or diversion in a wider plot. Pakistan, having tied down Indian troops in Kashmir, they argue, will next sponsor trouble in Hyderabad, and finally march across the Punjab boundary against Delhi itself.

A less hysterical but hardly less dangerous view is that if Pakistan cannot stop the raiders coming in, India herself will have to, but this, of course, can only be done by sending Indian troops through Pakistan territory. If Pakistan resists—well, open war is preferable to phoney war, and as for timing, they support Macbeth's principle, " If it were done when 'tis done, then 'twere well it were done quickly." There is also a growing sense of alarm in Government circles at the impact of Kashmir upon the Sikh problem. They feel that the longer there is tension and fighting in Kashmir the more difficult it will be for the Indian Government to keep the Sikhs in check. It seems that unless Liaquat can be persuaded to come forward with political proposals which it will be extremely difficult for his country and his colleagues to swallow, the position is likely to deteriorate rapidly and dangerously.

While Kashmir dominates public attention, Patel has just returned from an important mission to Orissa and the Central Provinces. Aided by the indefatigable V. P., he has succeeded in persuading the so-called Eastern States of Orissa and Chhattisgarh—thirty-nine of them in all, covering some fifty-six thousand square miles, with a population of seven million—to take their Acts of Accession a stage farther and to merge themselves with their two neighbouring Provinces. The new terms, while providing for a complete cession of authority to the new Dominion for the governance of their States, at the same time allow these Princes to retain their civil lists, personal property, titles and succession rights.

An important precedent has now been set for all the Princes, large and small, who can henceforth expect to feel an ever-increasing gravitational pull towards the Central Government. Incidentally, it is interesting to recall that the first expression of view that the Orissa States should be brought into a close administrative relationship with the Province of Orissa came some twenty years ago from a sub-committee of the Simon Commission presided over by one of Simon's junior and comparatively unknown colleagues, Mr. C. R. Attlee.

The Mountbattens have returned to-day from their tour of Bombay and Jaipur. They hope before they leave in the summer to have visited all the Provinces and principal States, and so to have completed an itinerary which in the more leisurely days Viceroys undertook over the whole of their five-year term. Ronnie tells me that the Jaipur visit was magnificent. The occasion was the Maharaja's Silver Jubilee. He came to the *gadi* when he was ten years old. " Jai " is a very popular and progressive Ruler, and is the only member of the Princely order to hold a commission in the Guards, a distinction of which he is very proud. He is highly westernised, and it must have been strange to see him against the traditional pomp and circumstance of his State—the dazzling jewels and caparisoned elephants. I first came across him when I accompanied Mountbatten on his visit to Hong Kong in January, 1946. His State's troops were serving on garrison duty there at the time, and after Mountbatten had inspected them we had tea with the officers. They were a splendid body of men, a credit to the State and Ruler alike.

To-day also John and Patricia Brabourne have arrived to stay for about three months. John's father was the much-beloved Governor successively of Bombay and Bengal, as well as acting Viceroy for six months. His early death, due largely to overwork, cut short a career which many thought would culminate with the Viceroyalty. He was particularly popular with Indian Nationalist opinion, and the Mountbattens have found that the marriage of his son to their elder daughter is regarded as auspicious and appropriate here in India. The romance of the East has a personal meaning for the Mountbattens, for John and Patricia met each other in 1945, when both serving in South-east Asia Command, while Patricia's parents became engaged in India in 1922.

The Brabournes reached Government House just in time for the arrival of Admiral Palliser, Commander-in-Chief, East Indies Fleet, who is on a short official visit while his flagship is at Bombay. He was greeted in the grand manner. The Gurkhas each morning now have a full ceremonial changing of the Guard, and a variation of this ceremony to the sound of bagpipes and the tempo of the Gurkhas' quick march was specially laid on for the Admiral.

GOVERNMENT HOUSE, NEW DELHI, *Sunday, 21st December, 1947*

I had an interesting talk with Sri Krishna, one of the best informed of the Delhi political correspondents. His reports are syndicated to a large number of English and vernacular newspapers. The line he took is symptomatic of the new spirit of self-analysis which has come with Independence. Frank criticisms which were reserved exclusively by the Nationalist Press for the British Raj are now directed towards fresh targets.

He referred to reports of a split in the Cabinet, and claimed that the immediate cause of tension between Nehru and Patel was the action of Maulana Azad, the Minister of Education in the Cabinet. Patel has recently set up a sub-committee consisting of H. M. Patel, V. P., and Bannerjee to vet the appointment of all higher-grade civil servants. Azad has just appointed the well-known scientist Bhatnagar, who is not a career man, as the Principal Secretary to his Ministry, without reference to this sub-committee. There is also a dispute over the status and function of the famous Moslem seminary, Aligarh University, which remains on the Indian side of the border.

Maulana Azad, a great scholar and a man of retiring disposition, has during the past ten years been a central figure of controversy. As the leading Moslem Congressman and as President of the Congress throughout the war, he was titular head of the movement during the vital negotiations with both the Cripps and Cabinet Missions. He embodied in his position and person perhaps the most important symbol of the Congress aspiration to be a nationalist as against a communal party. His status was thus the focal point of Gandhi's clash with Jinnah, who always maintained that politically no one but a member of the Moslem League could represent Moslem interests.

GOVERNMENT HOUSE, NEW DELHI, *Monday, 22nd December, 1947*

I had a most revealing talk to-day with Robert Stimson of the B.B.C., who has just returned from a fortnight's coverage based on Karachi.

During his stay he had an important interview with Jinnah, who covered the theme of Pakistan's staying in the Commonwealth and duly complained of " British neglect ". From what Stimson tells me, there can be little doubt but that Jinnah himself is the spearhead and inspirer of the anti-Mountbatten campaign which is now being developed in Pakistan. The attack is not concentrated on any single grievance or criticism, but is designed to exploit over a wide front Mountbatten's vulnerable position as Governor-General of only one Dominion and to create the general impression of a man who is anti-Moslem and pro-Hindu.

Although it is privately recognised in responsible circles there that Mountbatten is a moderating influence, Jinnah seems to have reached the firm conclusion that Mountbatten's continued presence as Governor-General is operating against Pakistan's interest, particularly in terms of her relations with the rest of the Commonwealth. Stimson agrees that Jinnah's attacks on Mountbatten are the corollary to his reproaches about British neglect. The criticisms are being duly reflected at lower levels and among European " old koi hais ". Complaints were directed in particular against Mountbatten's reference in a speech during his recent London visit to only three per cent of the Indian sub-continent being affected by the recent disturbances. This is not surprising, for perspective is rarely acceptable either to the purveyors or consumers of prejudice.

Stimson's general impression was that, subject to four great queries, Pakistan was perhaps a stronger entity than some of the critics recognised. Those queries were : whether she could avoid war ; whether Jinnah had long to live (in Stimson's opinion he looked fitter than in August, and he was himself at pains to say that he hoped to be operating for at least twelve years) ; whether she could secure economic support, and whether she could retain any of her Hindus.

He thought that the Sindi Moslems were not so bitter as those in the West Punjab, and although Karachi was safer for Hindus than Delhi was for Moslems, the Hindus there were under a constant cloud of threat and petty persecution. A good deal of the rice crop had not been gathered in. There had been a wholesale exodus of bank staffs and a complete breakdown of the Hindu economy, on which so much of the State depended.

Stimson was astounded at what he called the fantastic optimism of the old guard, but there was as well a core of young, efficient and incorruptible Moslem leaders imbued with a sense of mission who were determined to make the new State work. Everything depended on whether they could succeed.

On Saturday the Indian Cabinet finally decided to appeal to the United Nations accusing Pakistan of helping the raiders. Liaquat and Mohammed Ali have been in Delhi since last evening, but nothing has emerged from yesterday's or to-day's discussions which makes it possible to cancel or postpone this sombre decision. Most of the time has been taken up by the usual atrocity claim and counter-claim. Nehru to-day handed in the official letter of complaint which is a necessary preliminary to a reference to the United Nations. Liaquat promised a reply in due course. So ends the first phase of the political and diplomatic struggle over Kashmir.

GOVERNMENT HOUSE, NEW DELHI, *Friday, 26th December, 1947*

Following the failure of the Delhi talks with Liaquat earlier in the week, a very critical situation has developed both over Kashmir and the payment of the cash balances. Mountbatten's warnings about the dangers and limitations of Kashmir as a battle-ground are being all too quickly borne out. Indian troops in Kashmir suffer a similar handicap to the Russian forces in Finland during 1939, when Russian superiority in man- and weapon-power was largely offset by the nature of the terrain.

The full weight of Mountbatten's military authority is against any extension of already vulnerable and tenuous lines of communication. Already the outpost garrisons are in trouble. The garrison at Poonch is completely cut off, save for air supply. Two infantry companies at Jhangar, attacked by a force of some six thousand invaders, have suffered heavy casualties, and a relieving force has had to turn back.

But perhaps the most serious news is of a concentration of another formidable enemy force, estimated at six thousand, in the Uri area. Uri is the farthest point so far reached in the advance towards Domel. Withdrawal from Uri would renew the threat to Baramula, Srinagar and the Vale all over again. In Mountbatten's view the fall of Uri might well give overwhelming impetus to the argument, stressed with ever-increasing insistence in Government circles, that the only way to deal effectively with the raiders is to occupy their bases or " nerve-centres " inside West Punjab—and this would mean war.

Mountbatten had a private staff meeting at 11.30 this morning with Ronnie, Vernon and myself—V. P. joining us. It was quite like old times. We discussed the draft of a letter he has prepared over Christmas Day to Nehru urging the overwhelming need for caution and restraint. I suggested a new paragraph to stress how embroilment in war with Pakistan would undermine the whole of Nehru's independent Foreign policy and progressive social aspirations. V. P. thought the revision an improvement, and Mountbatten agreed to its inclusion.

I honestly believe that this letter as finally dispatched will stand the scrutiny of history and should serve to steady and strengthen Nehru in handling a problem of peculiar personal intensity. His origins as a descendant of Kashmiri Brahmins, his friendship and political association with Sheikh Abdullah make it difficult for him to stand above this problem at the moment of decision.

Towards the end of September in a letter to my mother I wrote :—

" I should say that Nehru has never shown to better advantage than during the past months. He has moral and spiritual reserves which seem to enable him to stand above the day-to-day administrative crisis and to resist the psychological pressures."

Over Kashmir the sense of strain is more apparent. Mountbatten remarked to-day that his concern over Nehru was that he might find himself slipping unwittingly, by sheer force of circumstance, into a state of mind when he could be actually influenced by adulation and flattery. Mountbatten added that he himself knew what this danger was—it was one of the reasons why he wished to revert to a subordinate position and to go to sea again.

He was also most sensible on the subject of his departure. He felt it would be a great mistake for him to stay the extra year, as had been strongly hinted to him by Patel, until the coming into force of the new constitution. To do this would be to dramatise the change-over from a British Governor-General to an Indian President, and to make it that much more difficult psychologically for India to pursue what he is firmly convinced is the course of enlightened self-interest for her, and remain within the Commonwealth. If, on the other hand, he left as originally scheduled, the transition would be smoother and the change-over from one Indian head of State to another in 1949 more in the gradual nature of things.

On the ultimately decisive economic front the Government has added to its own burdens by its blind and bland acceptance of Gandhi's policy towards decontrol. The Mahatma's approach to economics is un-ashamedly pre-feudal, and he has converted the doctrine of *laissez-faire* beyond the dreams of Adam Smith into what is little less than a branch of metaphysics. We now have the spectacle of a Government trying to create a modern State and depriving itself of the power to tackle food-hoarders and price-ring profiteers save through appeals to their social conscience, the one commodity in which they are totally lacking. The decontrol policy has been opposed by Mountbatten as well as by every non-Congress member of the Cabinet and by all responsible Civil Service advisers without exception. It is the outcome solely of the Government's awe of Gandhi. It is causing almost at once a vicious spiral of inflation, and will involve an extra eight crores of rupees on Civil Service salaries alone to meet the rise in prices. Altogether it is estimated that some one hundred and ten crores of rupees will need to be pumped in to meet the cost of Gandhi's economic ideas. Sugar and salt have both rocketed up to one rupee eight annas a seer—the rise in the price of salt being no less than five hundred per cent.

GOVERNMENT HOUSE, NEW DELHI, *Saturday, 27th December, 1947*

Just before midday Nehru's reply to Mountbatten's letter arrived. It cannot really be regarded as a considered answer, and was apparently dictated late at night. He duly apologises for repetitions and failure to say what he means, but the general meaning is only too clear : he is still in a cold fever over Kashmir, and seized only of the immediate problem. However, he seems ready to go ahead with the appeal to the United Nations without waiting upon Liaquat's reply to the proposal.

That such action should be necessary is, of course, to be deplored, but tension over the Christmas week has become so acute that Mount-batten regards any procedure which automatically buys time and defers decision as perhaps the only escape route left from catastrophe. He has gone so far—with Nehru's knowledge and concurrence—as to telegraph Attlee and suggest that he should fly out immediately to meet the two Prime Ministers. He has no serious expectation that he will agree to come, but believes the suggestion should be made, if only to register on all sides his own sense of urgency. He has also advised Nehru himself to make direct contact with Attlee and give him a full account as he sees it. We had a hurried conference with Mountbatten just before he left for Gwalior, although conference is hardly the word for it. He was flying off in all directions at once and desperately signing Christmas cards in reply to hundreds received, trying to sort out those which needed Lady Mountbatten's signature as well as his own from those which did not.

GOVERNMENT HOUSE, NEW DELHI, *Tuesday, 30th December, 1947*

I have just read in *The Spectator* an interesting appreciation of Wavell's and Mountbatten's handling of the Indian situation by Brigadier Desmond Young, who was for some time in charge of Public Relations at G.H.Q. India when Lord Wavell was Commander-in-Chief.

" The impact ", he writes, " of Lord Mountbatten's forceful personality and astonishing energy produced electrifying results. He swept the Indian Leaders along at such a speed that they had no time to draw breath to quibble. In this highly charged atmosphere Partition was rushed through before the Hindu hatred of the idea had time to gather weight." He then turns, however, to what he calls Mountbatten's " two mistakes ". " First," he asserts, " he was not only to consent to splitting the Indian Army but also to insist on accelerating the process. The ideal would have been to retain the Army intact under Field Marshal Auchinleck for two years from Independence Day to assist the two Governments impartially in the maintenance of order. His second mistake was to accept the Governor-Generalship of the Indian Union when Pakistan refused a Joint Governor-General. His acceptance, perhaps under pressure from His Majesty's Government, inevitably put him in a false position in the eyes of Moslems when the trouble started."

In view of the source and possible currency of these two particular criticisms I have written to Joyce in London as follows :—

" I need hardly stress that Mountbatten and Ismay would have fervently welcomed any practicable arrangement for Auchinleck to stay on, but it was Jinnah who was most insistent of all in refusing to have anything to do with the retention of a joint military system after the transfer of power and in demanding the immediate creation of the Pakistan Army. The break-up of the Supreme Command was expedited not only at the request of the Government of India, without whose good-will Pakistan's interest in the matter would not have been served, but also at Auchinleck's own recommendation. In any case, Pakistan's objection as stated by Liaquat to Mountbatten was based on a completely inflated concept of the Command's real powers."

As for the second " mistake ", after referring to the highly embarrassing implications of Jinnah's last-minute rejection of the Joint Governor-Generalship I have pointed out :—

" The Congress offer to Mountbatten was made without any strings attached to it, and quite apart from possible Moslem reactions, it is certain that Congress opinion would, with far more justice, have objected to his refusing their offer simply because the Moslem League had not invited him as well.   But the true position about the Moslem attitude is that a dominant factor in Mountbatten's decision to accept the Indian invitation was the pressing plea of both Jinnah and Liaquat made on their own and Pakistan's behalf that he should do so.   There is no reason to doubt but that their request was made in anticipation of trouble ahead. So if Mountbatten is now placed in a false position with Moslem opinion, the remedy rests with those responsible for guiding it in Pakistan."

GOVERNMENT HOUSE, NEW DELHI, *Wednesday, 31st December, 1947*

1947 ends in foreboding over the future of Indo-Pakistan relations generally and Kashmir in particular.   It is difficult to stand back and assess the credit and debit balance of our last nine prodigious months in India.   The immediate situation seems always to overwhelm our thoughts and attention.   The occupational risk is to be preoccupied with the daily task.

Over Kashmir at least we go forward into 1948 with some clarification of the crisis.   Attlee has, as Mountbatten anticipated, turned down the proposal of a lightning personal intervention, feeling that there is no specific role which he would be able to play save that of conciliator in general terms, and he prefers to rely on the " proper channels " of the United Nations.   He has, however, sent an excellently worded message to Nehru urging caution.

On receipt of his reply the Government have decided to proceed with their appeal to the United Nations without waiting any longer for Liaquat's reply.   The wording of the complaint, which has been drafted while Mountbatten is still in Gwalior, is moderate in tone save for one disquieting phrase which reserves freedom of military action to the Government if the situation requires it.   Mountbatten has pointed out that the Security Council Committee cannot be expected to react favourably to a threat or even the hint of one.

Mountbatten has done everything in his power to urge on Nehru what an invasion of Pakistan territory would mean, particularly as the whole problem at India's request is *sub judice*.   Quite apart from the catastrophic effect on world opinion, it would involve the automatic departure of British officers serving with both Dominions.   This in itself might well, I suppose, work more immediately against Pakistan's interest than India's, but in any case I think Nehru is well aware that any such move would mean that Mountbatten's mission would be at an end.

Liaquat's reply to Nehru's formal letter of complaint came in just after the dispatch of the Indian reference to the United Nations.   It is a lengthy catalogue of counter-charge deliberately not confined to Kashmir, but ranging over the general theme of India's refusal to accept Partition and resolve to destroy Pakistan.   He wants the intervention of the United Nations to extend from Junagadh to genocide, " so that all pending differences may be possibly resolved ".

As a footnote to these international developments it is encouraging to learn from the situation reports that no attack has developed on Uri, and that the Indian troops there have made no contact with hostile forces, for Mountbatten continues to feel that this would be the event which might well touch off the wider conflict. My new year motto is Ismay's "Patience and proportion". Clearly we shall need more than our ration of both in the coming year.

GOVERNMENT HOUSE, NEW DELHI, *Saturday, 3rd January, 1948*

Mountbatten held a private investiture here this evening which was in effect a family party for sixteen of us, from Lady Mountbatten downwards, whose names are in the New Year's Honours List. As cousin of the King, from whom all honours are derived, Mountbatten is quite an authority on the subject. Over cocktails afterwards he told me that my own position as the recipient of an O.B.E. and C.I.E. within eighteen months of each other was exceptional. The prevailing rule, it seems, is that honours in two different orders cannot normally be conferred under a period of three years. Vernon and I take our place in the final list of C.I.E.'s. Our citation is dated 14th August and marks, I suppose, one of the last symbolic acts of His Majesty as King Emperor.

A feature of our little ceremony was the award of a certificate specially prepared by Mountbatten for V. P. in lieu of the K.C.S.I., which, as the servant of the new Government, he felt it was not possible for him to accept. Mountbatten was saying again to-night that he regards V. P. as one of the finest colleagues with whom he has ever had to deal, and that his presence as Reforms Commissioner and *ex officio* member of his Staff between March and August was a great dispensation.

To-night Ronnie Brockman was the recipient of his third "C" (C.S.I.), for he gained the C.B.E. for his services as secretary to the First Sea Lord (Dudley Pound) and the C.I.E. for his outstanding administration of Mountbatten's secretariat in South-east Asia Command. During these three years I had learnt to respect his remarkable skill in handling the flow of high-level business. But he has certainly excelled himself in this unique mission, quickly absorbing I.C.S. systems and relating them to Mountbatten's particular methods. Since the transfer of power he has ceased to be Personal Secretary to the Viceroy and become instead Private Secretary to the Governor-General, thus succeeding within the new constitutional framework to many of the formal functions of the old Private Secretary to the Viceroy (P.S.V.). But whatever the form and title, he remains, as ever, indispensable. He is very tall and robust, encouraging in all who work with him a sense of confidence and purpose.

CHAPTER TWENTY-ONE

CALL TO REPENTANCE

THE DAY HAS been largely given over to the celebration of Burmese Independence. The Governor-General and all his staff went to an attractive flag-raising ceremony at the house of the Burmese Ambassador, U. Win. Apart from two brief speeches by Mountbatten and the Ambassador, most of the time was given over to Burmese music and Sidaw dancing.

We then repaired to the Durbar Hall, where Mountbatten and the Ambassador took part in an elaborate presentation of credentials. Normally these occasions are held in the ballroom, and only the Military Secretary and those members of the Governor-General's staff concerned, together with the Ambassador and his staff, are present. After the presentations of the Chinese and American Ambassadors, even the making of speeches was dispensed with, but in honour of Burma's Independence there was almost as much pomp and circumstance as on March 22nd and August 15th. In addition to the actual presentation of credentials and the making of two more speeches, Mountbatten formally presented an historic Burmese *taktaposh* and carpet to the Ambassador. He also announced that he would be paying an official visit to Burma in March, when he would hand over the immense throne of King Theebaw, the last King of Burma before the British régime.

Mountbatten, as his title suggests, is very proud of his connection with Burma. His agreement with Aung San in March 1945 and his appointment of General Rance to take charge of Civil Affairs were two historic decisions which have had a vital bearing on Burma's attainment of Independence.

In spite of the catastrophic assassination of Aung San and nearly the whole of his Cabinet last July—a severe enough blow to have destroyed the régime at birth—the force of nationalism has brooked no denial, and has insisted on breaking the last cables of connection with the British Commonwealth. I suspect that the Burmese leaders were encouraged to force the pace under the impression that the Indian Congress Republican resolution of 1946 would become immediately operative with the transfer of power in India. They could not have foreseen that the historically anti-British Congress at the hour of victory would opt for Dominion Status. Here in Delhi I sensed among the Burmese, assembled to rejoice over their liberation, a certain wistfulness at this irony of history which takes them outside the Commonwealth just when its status is likely to be modified and its membership enlarged.

During lunch I sat next to the most famous of Burma's dancers, Po Sein. He is over seventy, and his admiring colleagues were at pains to tell me that he had acquired merit by building many pagodas. In the evening we saw him dance at a special performance at the Imperial Hotel, where the Mountbattens and most of the Diplomatic Corps were present. His rhythms and movements were executed with obvious mastery, but, like veteran stars the world over, he was ready to continue indefinitely, and the programme was only brought to a close by some gentle diplomacy on the part of the Ambassador.

GOVERNMENT HOUSE, NEW DELHI, *Monday, 5th January, 1948*

The Press is full of speculation about Mountbatten's attitude to Kashmir. This arises partly from the Indian Government's decision to refer the dispute to U.N.O., a course which Mountbatten is generally recognised to have advocated for some time. The *Daily Herald* was responsible for putting out a story—it should be noted that it did not emanate from Andrew Mellor, their conscientious and reliable Delhi correspondent— that Mountbatten was now pressing for the partition of Kashmir and that a difference of view between himself and Nehru had developed which had caused Mountbatten to threaten his resignation if there was a clash between India and Pakistan. I went round to see H. V. R. Iengar, Nehru's private secretary, and Nehru agreed at once to make a prompt denial describing the story with characteristic emphasis as " over one hundred per cent fiction ".

Then again Mountbatten is credited by the American newspaper *P.M.* with fathering " a still secret plan for changing the nature of the Common-wealth which would enable the Union of India to be associated with the British Commonwealth without remaining a Dominion ". This story emanates from London, bears a New York date-line, is printed in the *Hindustan Times Evening News* and is linked up with Krishna Menon's visit to Delhi. There is no case for confirming or denying a report of such complex origin. It is, of course, far firmer than the facts warrant. Mountbatten is naturally giving close thought to this problem, but is certainly not the " father " of any " secret plans " !

There is also a steady stream of rumours that he will be asked to stay as Governor-General beyond the time limit he set himself in his speech on 15th August. It is difficult for me to keep a rein on speculation which does not originate from Delhi itself and to make those who are not on the spot realise that Mountbatten is, for all his influence and prestige, a constitutional Governor-General. The Indian Government themselves are having their own Press worries. Nehru was seriously embarrassed by a premature leakage of the decision to refer the Kashmir dispute to the United Nations, which, it seems, could hardly have sprung from any other source than the Cabinet itself.

This evening, as a result of a suggestion made by Mountbatten to Nehru at their last meeting, Colonel Kaul came round to see me at my house. Colonel Kaul is to accompany Gopalaswami Ayyengar and Sheikh Abdullah, who are to represent India at Lake Success. My task was to brief Colonel Kaul on some of the Public Relations problems confronting them. I told him frankly that in my view Sheikh Abdullah's flamboyant personality might easily " swamp the boat ", and that on the other hand Ayyengar, who would undoubtedly bear the main brunt of presenting India's case, was largely unknown. The objective therefore should be to redress the balance and build up Ayyengar and play down Abdullah. The kind of Press conferences Abdullah has been giving in Srinagar would not be so suitable at Lake Success, and I warned him that nothing should be done to weaken the force of the case as it was to be presented to the Council, by premature Press conferences.

Finally I strongly urged that they should take out an additional member to their team to act nominally as an additional secretary, but in fact to handle all their Public Relations problems on the spot in a full-time capacity. For this task I strongly commended B. L. Sharma. Kaul knows him well and agrees with me that he is one of the most capable P.R.O.'s in Government service. He is going straight round to the Prime Minister to make this recommendation. Kaul has no illusions about the dangers ahead. My own view is that to let Sheikh Abdullah loose on the American Press without skilled guidance is to court disaster.

GOVERNMENT HOUSE, NEW DELHI, *Tuesday, 6th January, 1948*

At a Staff Meeting this morning we discussed a paper Mountbatten has prepared " On the case for the institution of a system of honours and awards for the Dominion of India ". It is a characteristic Mountbatten note—a demonstration of his particular dialectical jujitsu which leaves the would-be resister safely and happily pinned to the floor !

He has also put before us a most imaginative and closely reasoned case for developing the sapper strength of the Indian Army, especially through the Indian States forces, stressing the American method of using this arm of the Service on major peace-time projects to the immense saving of the Exchequer and advantage of the Army.

GOVERNMENT HOUSE, NEW DELHI, *Wednesday, 7th January, 1948*

With the willing concurrence of Patel, the Minister for States, Mountbatten is meeting the major and minor Princes in two separate conclaves at Government House this week, and once again is trying to provide them with the impetus which seems to be so sadly lacking from within their own ranks. He urged upon the major Princes to-day the desirability of forming a committee of privileges to regulate the conduct of their dynastic affairs.

During the general discussion Alwar alone saw fit to remonstrate. In a high-pitched and querulous voice, he observed, " If the people wish to live in hell, one should not compel them to live in paradise ". When Mountbatten was trying patiently to explain the advantages of the Princes and their families entering the Indian Union Diplomatic Service, Alwar interrupted him to say, " This should not be a favour. If Menon can be States Secretary, why not Bikaner? " " I am not here dispensing favours," Mountbatten replied sharply; " I am just trying to make common-sense of the situation." I noticed, incidentally, that at the morning meeting Bhopal gave V. P. a brotherly embrace, which is usually reserved for a salutation from one Prince to another.

GOVERNMENT HOUSE, NEW DELHI, *Friday, 9th January, 1948*

Patrick Maitland, editor of *The Fleet Street Letter*, whom I met on my last visit to London, has written asking me a number of questions for background guidance. Seeking my views on the prospects in Kashmir, he asks, " Is this conflict going to drag on for many months, and even for years, does the Indian Government honestly suppose it will gain anything by going to the Security Council, or are the Indian forces in such an unfavourable military position that the Indian Government has taken this course in desperation?"

I have replied, " The general perspective in which I see the conflict from here is that Kashmir is really the last major outstanding issue between the two Dominions. If one could achieve the basic solution here, everything else would fit into place. The battle-ground is not of India's choosing, is at the end of long and bad lines of communication and is one in which it will always be difficult for her to deploy her full strength. Therefore from the military point of view we could anticipate a protracted struggle. The problem, however, is essentially political, and centres round the will and capability of both sides to give effect to a cease-fire. In this respect it is somewhat similar to the Indonesian dispute.

" I think it would be quite wrong to indicate that India is appealing to the United Nations as the result of military desperation. On the contrary, India feels that she has a very strong case both morally and in law, and that the Security Council is the proper forum in which to present it. Perhaps the most dangerous feature of the situation is unwillingness to recognise what the cost of failure would be or to appreciate that a war on this issue between the two Dominions would surely bring the sub-continent into the vortex of the world power politics struggle.'

GOVERNMENT HOUSE, NEW DELHI, *Saturday, 10th January, 1948*

This afternoon Mountbatten completed Part Two of his exhortation to the Princes. This time he spoke to some fifty of the minor brethren or their representatives, arguing once more the wisdom and virtues of mediatisation and urging again as precedent the example of the German principalities and the settlement they made with Napoleon's Confederation of the Rhine. Many of the rulers whose knowledge of history and political theory had been severely taxed came away from the conference blinking as though having looked too long at a bright light. But I think it is fair to say that a few of the more discerning members are alive to the sense and value of his advice.

To-night the Mountbattens gave a dinner-party to the Princes. It is good to find His Highness of Dholpur at Government House in the thick of all the discussions, for when I last saw him in July he had given me the impression that he would retire to his State and never be seen in Delhi again. I had a talk with him after dinner, and he is worried about agitations which he feels the Congress are inspiring in his and neighbouring States.   When I asked him whether he had any details, the only instance he gave was a recent inflammatory speech by Dr. Lohia in Gwalior.   Dr. Lohia, however, is one of the leaders of Jai Prakash Narain's Socialist wing of the Congress, which may soon be splitting off altogether from the Congress movement.   They have, in fact, been opposed to Mountbatten's and Patel's Accession policy, and by no stretch of imagination can they be regarded as agents of Patel or the States Ministry.

Sheikh Abdullah just before his departure for Lake Success has fired off his first shots in a farewell Press conference at Bombay. He attacks *The Times* and the *Manchester Guardian* and accuses the B.B.C. of " panic-mongering ".   Clearly he is going to be hard to handle, and if this is a foretaste of the line he proposes to take in America, trouble lies ahead for the promotion of the Indian case.

GOVERNMENT HOUSE, NEW DELHI, *Monday, 12th January, 1948*

The first news that Gandhi is to begin another of his major fasts unto death came through to me at a Press party at the Delhi Gymkhana Club. The startling suddenness of the announcement at his Prayer Meeting made its intended impact on all of us. I was particularly surprised, as earlier in the evening, on returning from a game of squash with Vernon, I had passed the french windows of Mountbatten's study, and could see Gandhi there with him for an interview which I was aware had been arranged at short notice but did not understand to have any special significance.

He had, in fact, come round to see Mountbatten immediately after his Prayer Meeting, at which he had declared that the fast would end " if and when I am satisfied that there is a reunion of hearts of all communities brought about without any outside pressure but from an awakened sense of duty. . . . With God as my supreme and sole counsellor I felt that I must take the decision without any other adviser."   Indeed, prior to the Prayer Meeting he had been observing a day of silence, with the result that neither Nehru nor Patel was informed in advance of his proposed course of action.   He then went on to lay bare his profound unhappiness at the continuing bad communal atmosphere in Delhi, which seemed to prevail at all levels of life, and his resolve to meet this situation by his own chosen act of atonement.

During this talk with Mountbatten, Gandhi went out of his way to ask for a frank opinion about India's refusal to pay to Pakistan the fifty-five crores from the cash balances, which Mountbatten did not hesitate to give him, saying that he considered the step to be both unstatesmanlike and unwise.   Gandhi said that he proposed to take the matter up with Nehru and Patel, and added that he would make it clear to them it was he who had initiated the inquiry and sought Mountbatten's views.

As for the fast, Mountbatten at once realised that it would be impossible for him to challenge the dictates of Gandhi's conscience, and told him without hesitation that he welcomed his brave move, and earnestly hoped that it would serve to create the new spirit that was so badly needed. On this note of fellowship and understanding Gandhi left to give effect to his great decision. The fast is due to begin at eleven o'clock to-morrow morning.

At the Gymkhana Club the party fairly quickly dissolved, as various correspondents went back to file their reports and interpretations of the act. The general impression was that the fast was well-timed and that nothing less drastic would regain for the Mahatma the psychological ascendancy achieved in Calcutta. Much would turn upon the attitude of the Sikhs, over whom Gandhi had so far been unable to exercise the same measure of influence as over Hindus and Moslems. Throughout his stay in Delhi there had, of course, been the ever-increasing pressure of Sikh refugees from the East Punjab upon the capital.

There was also considerable speculation about the meaning and effect of Gandhi's move in terms both of his own and Nehru's relations with Patel. Gandhi's intervention over the unilateral proposal to impose a sanction against Pakistan by withholding the fifty-five crores under the partition of assets is likely to give edge to a Government crisis. For he has clearly reacted very strongly against this move, and seems to be prepared to face a head-on collision with Patel about it.

Nehru and Patel have undoubtedly been drifting apart, a process which has a cumulative effect as an ever-growing number of followers hitch their wagons to these two major stars in the political firmament. The rivalry is thus intensified by their respective satellites. Gandhi may well hope by a supreme effort to heal the breach between the two great men in the Indian Government, realising that he alone has the status to do it, and that if he fails not only the Congress Party but the entire régime would be placed in deadly peril.

You have to live in the vicinity of a Gandhi fast to understand its pulling power. The whole of Gandhi's life is a fascinating study in the art of influencing the masses, and judging by the success he has achieved in this mysterious domain, he must be accounted one of the greatest artists in leadership of all time. He has a genius for acting through symbols which all can understand. Fasting as a means of moral pressure and purification is part of the fabric of Hindu life. There is the unmistakable sense of everyone being drawn out of his preoccupations to share in a painful responsibility which no man can wholly ignore.

GAJNER, BIKANER, *Wednesday, 14th January, 1948*

In spite of Gandhi's fast, it has been decided not to cancel Mountbatten's long-awaited visit to Bikaner, but as a mark of respect for the Mahatma, there will be no State banquet.

Just before our departure Patel and Nehru came along separately to see Mountbatten. Their immediate reactions to Gandhi's decision are perhaps the best summary of the two men's divergence of opinion and outlook at this time. Patel complained that the timing of the fast was hopelessly wrong, and that it was likely to have the opposite effect to what the Mahatma hoped from it, whereas Nehru could not conceal his pleasure and admiration at Gandhi's action.

We left Palam at eleven, and arrived at the Nal airfield an hour and a half later, whence we were driven off to the Maharaja's shooting-estate at Gajner, some thirteen miles away. Here a great artificial oasis, with a lake nearly a mile long, has been built out of the Rajputana desert, which provides His Highness with a paradise for shooting—his great hobby in life. The Governor-General's party comprised twenty-eight of us—almost a full muster. Elaborate arrangements have been made for our comfort and pleasure, and a confidential memorandum of some sixty closely printed pages sets out the agenda to the last possible detail.

Thus when we arrived at the Lagoon Terrace the operation order read, " The Master of the Household will take the necessary steps to ensure that crows and other birds are not allowed to settle on the trees on the Lagoon Terrace for at least a week beforehand and special care must be taken about this on the day of the lunch."

During the afternoon a duck-shoot was staged on the Gajner lake. Duck flew by the thousand across the line of butts along the lakeside, and hundreds of birds were duly bagged.

We dined in a tent or *shamiana*, silk-lined and richly carpeted, and ended the day witnessing the Maharaja's sporting films. In pursuit of big game he has travelled all over the world. To enable him to emphasise some special feat, he would raise his stick, and the film would be stopped and the sequence reversed, the animal stumbling back to life only to be shot again!

LALLGARH PALACE, BIKANER, *Thursday, 15th January, 1948*

Having explained to His Highness that shooting was not one of my skills or pastimes, I was invited by him to make my début the hard way by joining in the famous Imperial Sand-grouse Shoot. I duly took my place at seven-thirty this morning at one of the butts with Bikaner's A.D.C. Altogether some thirty thousand birds flew over the area, making to and from the various tanks, and wheeling about in formations of anything from five to fifty at a time. They are regarded as very difficult birds to hit, flying very fast and swerving sharply. To the amazement of all—not least myself—I had a bag of twenty-four birds, bringing down one with my first shot. Most of the party brought down over fifty a-piece and some a hundred. When the " exploit " was brought to Mountbatten's and Bikaner's notice there was much amusement, the Maharaja pointing out that it took even King George V half an hour to bring down his first Imperial Sand-grouse. " Your performance ", Mountbatten said to me, " discourages all effort ! "

During the afternoon we left Gajner for a twenty-mile car drive to Bikaner itself and the great Lallgarh Palace, where we shall be staying until our return on Saturday. With spacious courtyard and quadrangle, it seemed in the quiet of the early evening to be like some university college.

At seven-thirty we repaired to the Karni Niwas Durbar Hall of the

Palace to witness the ceremony at which Mountbatten invested His Highness with the Insignia of the G.C.S.I.   We looked down from the gallery upon this assembly of leading nobles and officers of the State, garbed in their Durbar dress of rich red and yellow.   The Mountbattens, the Maharaja and his heir, all richly attired, took their places on a dais with golden chairs.   Both Mountbatten's and Bikaner's speeches, although carefully prepared, were not just formal utterances.   Both men spoke with the feeling that comes from long friendship and genuine identity of view.

After the ceremony was over we drove out in a convoy of cars to the Vallabh Gardens, where we were transported from the atmosphere of Bikaner to that of Beverly Hills.   For here was a country club with a cocktail bar shaped like a ship's cabin, and portholes looking out on an artificial lake with weeping willows.   We stayed on dancing, playing billiards or simply supporting the bar until just before midnight, when we returned to Lallgarh.   A heavy programme lies ahead of us to-morrow.

LALLGARH PALACE BIKANER, *Friday, 16th January, 1948*

It has been a full day of ceremony and sight-seeing, beginning with an impressive review of the Bikaner State Army.   Mountbatten and Bikaner arrived on the parade-ground sharp at 9.30, and after the Royal salute and inspection there was a steady crescendo of events from a march past of troops, followed by a trot past by the Ganga Risala and the famous Bikaner Camel Battery, to a gallop past by the Dunga Lancers; finally the review culminated in an advance of all the contingents in review order.   The quality of the riding was nothing short of superb, and Bikaner has every reason to be proud of the showing made by his State Forces.   The Bijey Battery on parade this morning served with great distinction under Mountbatten in the Burma campaign, taking part with the 25th Mountain Regiment of the 7th Indian Division in the battles of Kohima and Imphal, subsequently fighting its way down the Gangaw Valley and across the Irrawaddy.

Later in the morning we visited the Fort, the focal point of so much of Bikaner's history.   We were shown regalia conferred on Bikaner Rulers by Moghul Emperors and many other State treasures, including rich and rare illuminated Sanskrit and Urdu manuscripts.   After spending nearly an hour absorbing the intricate beauty of this place, we set out in a procession of cars again through the city streets, wet with recent rain. All along our route were gathered large crowds, who greeted the Maharaja and the Mountbattens with obvious signs of pleasure and esteem.

On our return to the Palace, while waiting to go into lunch I had an illuminating talk with Panikkar, who is still serving as the Maharaja's Dewan.   He was optimistic about the outcome of Gandhi's fast, which in his view was undoubtedly directed at Patel.   He added there was a definite clash between Patel and Gandhi when Gandhi arrived in Delhi three months ago.   Gandhi said then, " Vallabhbhai, I always thought you and I were one. I begin to see that we are two." Patel was in tears over his misunderstanding with Bapu.*

Panikkar interprets the relationship thus, Patel, although controlling the machine, is aware that Gandhi is still master of the masses, and that he could never hope, even if he so wished, to break the Mahatma's influence. Gandhi on his side is out to strengthen Nehru's hand, yet does not want to break Patel in the process, but only to bring him to heel.

This led Panikkar to pay tribute to Gandhi's political acumen. He said he had just had his first meeting with him after a gap of some twenty years, and had urged him to go slow in his campaign for constitutional development within the States. Gandhi protested, " You are asking me to crystallise reaction." " I had no answer to this," said Panikkar. " It was true." Gandhi's habit, he added, was to speak the language of his audience. Thus it was that such occasions as his Prayer Meetings were deceptive in their simplicity. In private conversation he was extremely acute. He also stressed that Gandhi is backed by what he called a remarkable intelligence system. Personal letters come pouring in to him from all parts of India reporting on the state of the nation.

We heard this afternoon that the Cabinet decided to transfer the fifty-five crores to Pakistan as a gesture of good-will. After the film-show to-night Mountbatten said this was the best news in three months. But Panikkar expressed concern to me about Patel's possible reaction to the decision.

Mountbatten spent a very useful one and a half hours in conversation with Panikkar this afternoon. This I believe is the first full-length meeting they have had for some time. The more I see of Panikkar the more impressed I am by his intellectual power and political shrewdness. He is the rare blend of the scholar and man of affairs who can bring his profound knowledge of history to the service of contemporary events. He is one of about half a dozen men who may well have a great influence in the shaping of Indian policy at home and abroad. He has his enemies, and there are some who assert that he is ambitious and untrustworthy, but I suspect that he suffers from the jealousy of those who resent being confronted with a superior intellect. It is the occupational risk of very clever men to be regarded as dangerous by their less gifted brethren.

Panikkar tells me that his advice was that Mountbatten should give top priority to the wider problem of Indo-British relations rather than to the specific Dominion Status issue. He stressed that Nehru was now more firmly persuaded of the need for Indo-British understanding. He hoped that Mountbatten would not be leaving until the broad principles had been settled. Mountbatten has suggested that Panikkar should accompany Nehru on his proposed visit to London in February, and should remain as a constitutional adviser to the Central Government rather than leave for China.† His instinct, however, is to leave India

---

* Bapu meaning Father—a term of endearment used to describe Mahatma Gandhi by many of his followers as well as in the Indian Press.

† Panikkar duly became the first Indian Ambassador to China, originally to the Nationalist Government of Chiang Kai Shek. After its overthrow on the Chinese mainland Panikkar's general prestige was such that Nehru was able to send him

for a couple of years, and not get too closely caught up in the political imbroglio.

After lunch the guests had a free afternoon, which some of us spent riding on camels brought round especially for our entertainment. Our general sense of insecurity seemed only to add to the camels' expression of indifference, not to say contempt!

In the evening we attended a Military Tournament at the King-Emperor George VI Stadium, at which the Body Guard and Camel battery gave an exhibition in the arts of the musical ride and drive with verve and precision sufficient to satisfy the most exacting patrons of Olympia or Aldershot. There was also a most impressive display of torch-light club swinging.

After the Tournament we were whisked back for the final dinner-party in the Durbar Hall, which takes the place of the abandoned State banquet, but is none-the-less a major social event in the life of Lallgarh. Afterwards Bikaner showed some more of his sporting films, this time in the dining-room, where many of the principal victims looked down balefully upon us from the walls.

GOVERNMENT HOUSE, NEW DELHI, *Saturday, 17th January, 1948*

We left for Delhi first thing in the morning, duly impressed by this example of Princely hospitality. Bikaner blends tradition with reform, and is setting a good example to his fellow-rulers in promoting his subjects' social solidarity among themselves and their political loyalty to the new dispensation.

Shortly after our return the Mountbattens called on Gandhi at Birla House. He is by now very weak. After he had greeted them with the words, " It takes a fast to bring you to me ", they had a brief discussion on the possibilities of breaking it. Gandhi said he had laid down seven conditions, all affecting the basic security and civil rights of Moslems both in Delhi and India as a whole, which would have to be implemented before he could be induced to call it off.

---

as first Ambassador to the Chinese Peoples Republic, where he presented his credentials to Mao Tse Tung. In this position he was destined to act as a vital link between East and West both before and during the Korean crisis.

CHAPTER TWENTY-TWO

MAHATMA'S MARTYRDOM

GOVERNMENT HOUSE, NEW DELHI, *Sunday, 18th January, 1948*

FOLLOWING THE CABINET's decision over the fifty-five crores, an inter-communal Peace Committee was set up under the direction of Prasad and Maulana Azad. It acted with commendable energy, and this morning succeeded in convincing the Mahatma that the necessary change of heart had taken place in Delhi to enable him to break his fast, which had lasted for a hundred and twenty-one and a half hours and had drawn deeply upon the frail little man's reserves of strength.

The fast has undoubtedly done much to raise Moslem morale; but there were signs of Sikh restiveness, and bands of Sikhs carrying black banners passed outside Birla House chanting "Let Gandhi die". Sikh representatives, however, duly took their part on the Peace Committee.

In a message he sent to his Prayer Meeting this evening he declared that if the pledge was fulfilled it would revive with redoubled force his "intense wish and prayer before God to be able to live the full span of life doing service to humanity to the last moment. That span, according to learned opinion, is at least one hundred and twenty-five years, some say one hundred and thirty-three."

GOVERNMENT HOUSE, NEW DELHI, *Monday, 19th January, 1948*

Vincent Sheean, who is on a special visit here for a number of American papers "in search of more history", and Bob Neville, the Delhi correspondent of *Time and Life*, had lunch with us to-day. Discussing the fast, Sheean, who clearly revels in original theories, thinks Gandhi gave it up—although he would never consciously admit it—because of the change in the weather. The sun did not shine, and Gandhi had been going out and sun-bathing. This would be God's way of telling his inner voice to relent and break fast. There has always been a close relationship between mys.ics and meteorology. He says he told Ed Snow about this before the fast was ended. Both agreed that Gandhi's fast is a phenomenal event which argues the vital power of religion. Neville stressed how Roosevelt always tried to bring religion into his politics.

They were both eye-witnesses of incidents which must surely place Nehru among the most informal and delightful of the world's great men. Neville told how Nehru disposed of a man who was lying down in the road in front of Birla House and stopping all the traffic from coming or going. The man described himself as "the voice of Krishna". After some fruitless argument Nehru picked him up by the feet and pulled him away, rubbed his hands and walked off as if nothing had happened!

Sheean in the course of an interview at the Prime Minister's house was taken into the dining-room by Nehru to see a Chinese painting. While groping about for the light, Nehru stumbled over the body of a man asleep on the floor. " Someone is asleep here," he said, and proceeded to carry on the rest of the conversation in whispers!

GOVERNMENT HOUSE, NEW DELHI, *Tuesday, 20th January, 1948*

Rejoicings over Gandhi's survival from his fasting ordeal were marred to-day by a bomb incident in the garden of Birla House. The bomb, a home-made affair, went off during the first Prayer Meeting which Gandhi has attended since the ending of his fast. The force of its explosion, however, was broken by a wall, which was slightly damaged. No one was hurt, and there was no panic, Gandhi continuing to conduct the meeting without showing any sign of awareness that anything untoward had happened. Indeed, Lady Mountbatten, who went straight round to visit him, found him wholly unperturbed. He told her he thought that "military manœuvres must have been taking place somewhere in the vicinity".

GOVERNMENT HOUSE, NEW DELHI, *Monday, 26th January, 1948*

I went round to see H. V. R. Iengar this morning, who advised me that rumours had reached the Prime Minister that I had given guidance at a recent party attended by Indian and Foreign journalists on the subject of the partition of Kashmir. It was alleged that I had advised the journalists to keep off the partition theme for the present, as it would be likely to come into prominence again later, probably as a result of British initiative at Lake Success. I was able to deny in the most emphatic terms having said any such thing. I pointed out that for the past fortnight I have been kept busy giving the lie without qualification to a report that Mountbatten had sponsored the idea when in London and was continuing to back it on his return here.

I was under the impression that I had been successful in killing this canard, but can only assume that there are one or two Press speculators who are not prepared to take no for an answer. It is encouraging that our staff relations with the Prime Minister's office are so close that this mischief can be strangled at birth.

The injection of the United Nations into the Kashmir crisis has slowed down the tempo of the political dispute almost as effectively as the weather has blanketed the military operations. The first session of the Security Council did not take place until the 15th January. After full-length statements of case and a series of private conferences, a preliminary resolution setting up a commission was passed on the 20th. It has always been Mountbatten's hope in supporting a reference to the United Nations that it would lead to the earliest possible dispatch of a commission—certainly by the end of January—to the scene of the conflict; but it now seems that the Security Council are settling down to seek an agreed resolution on the general issues of principle beforehand. If this proves to be the case then a big political opportunity may well have been missed and a serious psychological blunder committed.

The Indian and Pakistan " Heads of Proposals " bring out two main points of difference in their answers to the questions, what, if any, troops are to remain in Kashmir before the plebiscite is held, and should the existing administration be changed? India wants the present administration to be transformed into a Council of Ministers under Abdullah's leadership. This Council should then convene a National Assembly elected on Proportional Representation. This Assembly should then elect a new Government, which should hold a plebiscite under United Nations control. India insists on the complete removal of the tribesmen and the denial to them of Pakistan bases before being ready to consider the withdrawal of Indian troops.

Pakistan's position is quite simple. Her demand is for simultaneous and complete withdrawal of all forces and a neutral Administration. At Lake Success this thesis is the easier one of the two to present, and certainly for the delegates, several of whom until a few weeks ago had probably never heard of Kashmir save as a lush holiday resort, to understand. But unless India can establish some early formal recognition of her legal title and moral grievance as a plaintiff, we can anticipate an early disillusionment in Delhi with the processes of the new internationalism.

AGRA, *Tuesday, 27th January, 1948*

Kingsley Martin, editor of *The New Statesman and Nation* and a champion of the India League days, is paying his first visit to India as the guest of Nehru, who is a very old friend of his. At the moment Kingsley is staying with us at the Comptroller's House. During the lull provided by the Mountbattens' tour of Nagpur I had the idea of taking him on a sight-seeing tour of Agra and the Taj Mahal, but this was easier said than done, as nearly all the Government House transport was temporarily laid up. Nehru, on hearing of our dilemma, at once put a car at our disposal, and we drove off down the hot and dusty road on our pilgrimage to the shrines of Moghul greatness.

A journey with Kingsley is in itself an education. He has tucked away in his memory a whole library of significant facts and experiences to which he can refer at a moment's notice. But in spite of many years of hard editorial effort, he retains a wonderful boyish zest. I suspect that we started out with a certain prejudice against the Taj just for being as famous as it is. I had seen it once before from the air, when it looked like some miniature of itself in sugar icing, white on green.

On reaching Agra, after passing on the way the mighty tomb of Akbar, we were pleasurably surprised to find that the Taj was off the beaten tourist track, and that its actual environs were solitary and unsullied by commercial taint. Like all the great Moghul mausoleums, it is enclosed, and, like Humayun's tomb in the Lodi Gardens at Delhi, the tomb itself is completely invisible until you pass through the outer entrance. Then at the first sight the whole image is totally revealed. Critical judgment is suspended, and as one walks from shade into light along the formal line of cypress trees, the serene splendour of the place takes possession of the senses.

For me the contrast with the aerial vision was complete; from within it looms very large, and the dazzling whiteness is shot through with exquisite inlay, which includes words from the Koran engraved in black marble. We first saw the Taj in the glow of late afternoon, and then returned after dinner to see it under the full moon. We both felt that the romantic haze and the blurring of outline and detail meant some loss of the æsthetic magic of the daylight vision. There were no crowds of sight-seers to disturb the stillness, and only the lights of Agra and the bend of the River Jumna below recalled us to the world of life and movement.

AGRA, NEW DELHI, *Wednesday, 28th January, 1948*

We were up early to visit the historic Red Fort, where the great Akbar held court and where Shah Jehan, imprisoned by his turbulent son, could still, through marble lattice-work, see his wife's memorial—the crowning achievement of the master-builder of the Moghul Emperors. We passed through a maze of courtyards and vistas, the scale of conception and variety of design making one impatient to know more of the nature of the rulers who could aspire to live in such surroundings. The secular and religious motifs are perfectly intermingled, and, as if in the natural order of things, one comes at last to the Pearl Mosque, which sanctifies and adorns this fortress palace.

Afterwards we crossed the Jumna to see, at Nehru's special injunction, the tomb of Itmad-Ud-Daula. Although not on the same scale as the Taj, this tomb, with its exquisite traceries, is perhaps the most wonderful gem of all. It enshrines the father of Mumtaz Mahal, the Queen in whose memory the Taj Mahal was built. Fatehpur Sikri, the great capital which Akbar built only to abandon for lack of water, and many other memorials of the dead dynasty lay before us, but our time was running short, and we felt that we had already reached saturation point, beyond which we could not adequately absorb any more of these wonders.

GOVERNMENT HOUSE, NEW DELHI, *Friday, 30th January, 1948*

Mountbatten arrived back by air from Madras early this afternoon with his two daughters; Lady Mountbatten having stayed on to complete engagements. They have had another very arduous tour where, it seems, they once more received an overwhelming welcome from vast crowds that lined the streets wherever they went. At about ten to six I ran into George Nicholls, who told me that there had been an attempt on Gandhi's life, and that he had been hit in three places. Half an hour later I heard from Pearce, Mountbatten's driver, that Gandhi was dead. He had heard the news over the car radio, and told me that His Excellency was going round to Birla House immediately.

While I was standing by the car, Mountbatten came out and motioned me to come with him. He was very tense, and spoke in short, staccato sentences. He said that Rajagopalachari had rung through from

Calcutta impressing on him the need to take the utmost precautions about Nehru. Only two days ago while in Amritsar two men had been arrested carrying grenades while he was addressing a public meeting.

Mountbatten thought this was a most grave development, and that Nehru was now entirely alone and politically exposed. Everything depended upon his capacity to keep a grip on the situation in the next few hours. It was absolutely essential that he should speak to the nation at the earliest possible moment, but at the same time should give himself the chance to think out what he was going to say, because the nation would inevitably take its lead from him.

By the time we had reached Birla House the crowd had gathered and was peering into the windows of our car, only a few recognising Mountbatten in the dark. All was confusion. Young men were milling around in the grounds and pressing against the french windows. Inside, most of the members of the Government and leading Congressmen were standing with the listlessness of grief. We made our way to what I believe was Gandhi's bedroom. There was a smell of incense. Inside the room were about forty people, including Nehru and Patel. Everyone was in tears. Just outside were numerous sandals which people had taken off before entering the room.

In the far corner was the body of Gandhiji. At first I thought it was completely covered in a large blanket, but then I realised that his head was being held up by one of about a dozen women who were seated round him chanting prayers and sobbing in a plaintive rhythm. Gandhi's face was at peace, and looked rather pale in the bright light. Also they had taken away the steel-rimmed glasses which had become almost an integral part of his features. The smell of the incense, the sound of the women's voices, the frail little body, the sleeping face and the silent witnesses—this was perhaps the most emotionally charged moment I have ever experienced. As I stood there I felt fear for the future, bewilderment at the act, but also a sense of victory rather than defeat; that the strength of this little man's ideas and ideals, from the very force of the devotion he was commanding here and now, would prove too strong for the assassin's bullets and the ideas they represented.

After standing for some time in silent homage, we moved out into the main hall. As the evening drew on the crowds outside multiplied; one could see their faces pressed against the windows, and they banged insistently upon the glass. Members of the Cabinet were in one room, and Mountbatten went in to talk to them.

I heard Mountbatten saying that at their last interview Gandhi had said that his dearest wish was to bring about full reconciliation between Nehru and Patel. On hearing this, they dramatically embraced each other. He came out a few moments later, saying that he had succeeded in getting Patel to broadcast at the same time as Nehru to-night. This he felt—with justice—was a most important point to have gained. He reiterated that everything turned on Nehru's gripping the situation immediately.

The tension is such that one careless word and rumour will spread like a forest fire. Even on our arrival Mountbatten was greeted by a scaremonger who told him, " It was a Moslem who did it! " At that moment we still did not know the religion and name of the assassin, but Mountbatten, appreciating that if it was a Moslem we were lost anyhow and that nothing could then avert the most disastrous civil war, replied in a flash, " You fool, don't you know it was a Hindu."

I learnt from V. P. Menon a few minutes later that the assassin was apparently a Mahratta, who fired three times at point-blank range just as Gandhi was leaving to attend his Prayer Meeting. I also spoke with the Doctor, who was somewhat dishevelled and who had attended Gandhi in his last moments. He complained that there had been no medical stores in the house, but admitted that they would have done no good. Gandhi had just had time to sip a little water before losing consciousness, which he never regained.

There was a considerable discussion about the funeral arrangements. It seems that Gandhi has left the most explicit instructions through his Secretary, Pyarelal, and others that his body is not to be preserved or embalmed. On the contrary, in accordance with Hindu practice, it is to be cremated as quickly as possible. Gandhi was strongly opposed to any special worship of his remains.

Mountbatten had rather favoured allowing at any rate some twenty-four hours for the funeral to be properly arranged, but it is clear that it will have to take place to-morrow and will impose a very heavy strain on the Delhi administration. At Mountbatten's suggestion, Nehru agreed that the whole thing should be taken over by the Defence Ministry and that all available troops in Delhi should be on duty. Mountbatten has put his own Body Guard and the Government House Gurkhas at the disposal of the Area Commander.

As the moments went by with people standing or sitting about in various parts of the house—some, like Maulana Azad, in silent contemplation, others, like K. M. Munshi, acting as self-appointed organisers and trying to take charge of things—the crowd outside was steadily growing in numbers and in its insistence on seeing the Mahatma's body. Hundreds of eyes seemed to be peering into the house from all sides, and there was some anxiety whether the french windows could much longer take the strain of the throng pressing against them.

I warned Nehru of this danger of a mass invasion. He looked inexpressibly sad and careworn, but talked quite quietly and with amazing self-discipline, saying that all was arranged. The body would be taken outside and placed on a table to enable the crowds to-night to file past and pay their last respects. As the clamour of the crowd increased, he himself went out into their midst without any form of protection and spoke to them. H. V. R. Iengar, his secretary, told me that he is really worried about the Prime Minister's safety, and Mountbatten spoke earnestly with Indira and H. M. Patel, stressing the need for taking the utmost precautions.

We left at about twenty to eight, taking Maulana Azad and Devadas Gandhi back with us. When Devadas remarked that it must have been a madman, Mountbatten replied that if that was all to it, he for one would not be worrying, but that there were all too many signs of its being the outcome of a calculated conspiracy. Maulana, who does not allow himself to speak in English, though he can do so, nodded his head in agreement. Mountbatten thought it was a great catastrophe, and only hoped and prayed that by Gandhi becoming a martyr it would make everyone in India think seriously and, where necessary, mend their ways.

Back in the A.D.C. room I found Kingsley Martin, Gordon-Walker, who arrived yesterday, and V. P. Menon. V. P. said he was still too stunned to have any reaction, but believed that it could only have a good effect on all the best minds of India. While we were speaking, the Jam Sahib came in, told us that he had flown specially to Delhi to-day in order to meet Gandhiji at 6 p.m. Only this morning I myself had been in touch with Pyarelal and arranged for Gordon-Walker to see Gandhiji to-morrow evening.

GOVERNMENT HOUSE, NEW DELHI, *Saturday, 31st January, 1948*

Throughout the night the crowds filed past the body for the last *darshan,* or showing. His sons had undertaken the ceremonial washings. After breakfast the Mountbattens—Lady Mountbatten having flown back in the night—and most of his staff repaired to Birla House to be present for the departure of the funeral cortège on its six-mile journey through New and Old Delhi to the Raj Ghat, an immense open space by the banks of the Jumna. Military contingents of all three Services were moved briskly to take up positions on the route, and it was clear that both the military and civil authorities had done splendidly in meeting the almost impossible administrative demands made upon them.

Of one anxiety at least they were relieved. When the first news of Gandhi's assassination broke there was momentary if unexpressed dread that the assassin might have been a Moslem, and, if such had been the case, the communal consequences would indeed have been perilous. It was quickly announced that the assassin, Godse, was a Mahratta and a member of the Hindu Mahasabha. The effect of this news will be to cause deep stirring of the Hindu conscience.

On reaching Birla House we were all jammed into even a denser crowd than last night. The cortège consisted of a funeral carriage draped with the Congress flag, covered with flowers and drawn by a party of sailors. The Governor-General's Body Guard was there as escort. Ministers and Generals jostled for position by the funeral cortège with the humblest citizens, as Gandhi would have wished. The four-anna Congressmen, who had been soldiers in his many battles, were there in force. The body was brought down from the balcony and placed upon the bier.

Once again I was deeply impressed by the serenity of his face. The head was cushioned in flowers. Around the body sat Gandhiji's sons and granddaughters, the girls still weeping and gently stroking his head. Patel also sat immobile beside the body, pale and weary and looking straight ahead of him. He took no part in the strenuous efforts which both Nehru and Mountbatten were making to impose some order on the surrounding chaos and clear a way for the cortège to start upon its long, slow journey.

The speeches of both Nehru and Patel last night were very moving, and gained in strength from their lack of preparation. Apart from the personal loss, the blow smites Patel with particular severity. There were first of all the reports of differences between himself and Gandhi; then, as Home Minister in charge of internal security, he was officially responsible for Gandhi's safety. It is true that after the bomb incident ten days ago Gandhi specifically refused police protection, but there is clear evidence that the two attacks are part of one conspiracy, and the fact remains that the police were unable to track it down before the fatal shot was fired. Indeed, Gandhi's last interview had been with Patel, and it was in hurrying from this talk a few minutes late for his Prayer Meeting that the assassin crossed his path. Patel resolved to undergo the immense physical ordeal for a man of seventy-two of accompanying the body all the way to the burning-ghats.

At last the cortège began almost imperceptibly to move. It was now nearly eleven o'clock, and immense crowds had gathered all along the route. Indeed, they were far too great for either the police or military to hold in check. Their constant pressure kept the pace of the procession down to little more than a mile an hour. The slowness of the advance encouraged those spectators watching it pass by to try to accompany it; which meant that in due course the hosts following along behind were almost as overwhelming as those ahead.

On our return to Government House we climbed up to the dome of the Durbar Hall and looked down on the cortège, now some two miles away from us on the great open "Kingsway". We could detect no visible movement, and the crowd seemed to have settled round it like some vast swarm. The commentator's voice, over a portable radio we had brought up with us, told us that some headway was being made. Whether seeing it from the middle distance or hearing of its progress close at hand, the strange irony of this scene impressed itself upon me.

We were watching, I suppose, Gandhiji's first and last *darshan* along this Imperial avenue. Now the man who more than anyone else had helped to supersede the Raj was receiving in death homage beyond the dreams of any Viceroy. Gandhi dies one evening and is taken for cremation the following morning. Here is no long-heralded State funeral; all the same, the people have flocked within the hour and by the hundred thousand to have one last glimpse of him. Who, in the face of this overwhelming tribute, can honestly assert now that Gandhi had no genuine mass following?

The Mountbattens, their staff and guests, including most of the Governors who have arrived for a conference which it was too late to postpone, set out for the Raj Ghat. Great care had been taken to avoid the route of the funeral procession; but as we approached the banks of the Jumna our cars became swallowed up in the multitude, all pressing towards the cremation ground, and our speed was dictated by theirs.

As the Governor-General and his party, some twenty of us in all, made their way into the great barren arena, it was difficult at the first glance to appreciate the full immensity of the crowd, for the ground was too flat to give a real visual indication of the size. But as we walked out in lonely eminence towards the small brick platform and the piled logs, wherever we looked our horizon was closely packed humanity, and I became oppressed with much the same sense of claustrophobia as in Birla House last night. Here all that stood between us and a mass invasion of this reserved territory was a cordon of Indian Air Force men holding the line at intervals of three or four yards, who, it seemed, would be no more effective than the french windows of Birla House in holding back a determined onrush. As a precaution against the danger of all our party being pushed on to the flames, Mountbatten decided that we and the nearest section of the crowd should sit down on the dusty ground.

As the time passed and the tension mounted, close disciples of the Mahatma sat quietly round the funeral pyre, threading garlands of small white flowers; otherwise there was no sense of ceremonial preparation or sequence. There was *ghee* for kindling the fire, but it was still in a large tin which had been opened with a tin-opener; holy water was in a zinc bucket.

When the cortège at last reached the field, bringing with it yet another vast multitude, noise and confusion burst all bounds and, as we had feared, some seven hundred thousand people relentlessly converged upon the sacred spot. Everyone wished to carry out some last act of devotion. Statesmen and sweepers, Governors and peasant women mingled to throw flower-petals over the body before the logs were piled high. The priests read from the holy books. With pressure of the people threatening to crush us against the pyre, the ceremonial rites took a terrifyingly long time to complete.

When finally the fire was kindled, a great cry went up of " Gandhi is immortal ", and the crowd now took complete possession. The desperate attempts of some of us to make a small inner cordon having duly failed, Mountbatten got up and, scanning the crowds as though appraising a military situation, said quietly, " We must go now ". Linked together in a human chain, we did our best to follow him. His departure did much to save an ugly situation, for it started an exodus just where and when the pressure was most intense. The crowds quickly picked him out in his distinctive Naval uniform and did their best to make way. As we slowly extricated ourselves, the flames and smoke of the pyre billowed upwards.

It would be idle to say that the mood of this vast assembly was particularly mournful. It left much more the impression of a demonstration arising from the desire to witness a memorable spectacle. Judging by this afternoon, grief does not seem to be by any means the sole response of Hindus to a funeral, and their belief in immortality would seem to be rather more robust than ours when it comes to the test of ceremonial self-expression.

GOVERNMENT HOUSE, NEW DELHI, *Monday, 2nd February, 1948*

Bob Stimson called round to see me this afternoon. By his accidental presence at Birla House when the fatal shots were fired he was able twenty-five minutes afterwards to broadcast in the B.B.C.'s one o'clock news an eye-witness report which beat the entire world's Press.   There can surely be few precedents for such a scoop in the history of broadcasting.   Undoubtedly this first intimation of the event must have done much to enhance its dramatic impact on the British public.   Bob tells me he had no intention of going there for himself, but had at the last minute accompanied Vincent Sheean, who had particularly wanted to attend a Prayer Meeting.   Vincent Sheean, on witnessing the tragedy, was so deeply affected that he was unable to cable back any immediate account of it to America.

Bob tells me that an American Embassy official was the unsung hero of the occasion.   He was the first to realise what had happened and to leap forward and grip the assassin by the arms.   There was great discipline among the crowd, and no one ran away.   Everyone's first thought, he said, was for the old man's safety.   Bob tells me he has seen the assassin, the Mahratta, Vinayak Godse.   He is by no means uneducated and edits a small provincial newspaper.   His attitude was completely intransigent.   " Cut me into little pieces," he said, " and I will still maintain I did right."

Nehru has spoken with great frankness in the Assembly to-day.   The Government, he said, must bear responsibility for not ensuring the safety of Gandhi's life and of thousands of other lives.   Bob feels that the spirit of assassination may well have been encouraged rather than exorcised. He is off to see a mass memorial meeting, and is wondering whether there will be any further attempts on leaders' lives.   He described the situation as " Grand Guignol in the open air ".

Mountbatten's meetings with the Governors of the new India have, of course, been completely overshadowed by Gandhi's death, but it has been decided to proceed with them, and the Governors have been able to strengthen the administration in its resolve to put down communal violence.   C. R., in his capacity as Governor of Bengal, advocated immediately the suppression of all political organisations with communal objectives, naming in particular the Hindu Mahasabha and its militant wing the R.S.S.S.

GOVERNMENT HOUSE, NEW DELHI, *Tuesday, 3rd February, 1948*

The volume of the world reaction to Gandhi's death has frankly exceeded my expectation.   From every corner of the earth have come tributes and appreciations which show that his influence has reached out far beyond the boundaries of India.   The full meaning of his life may not be clear to many, but the importance of its mystery is recognised. As Kingsley Martin, who has been here with us for the whole drama, put it to me, the world is not doing so well with the techniques of materialism and power politics.   It recognised that Gandhi stood for something different, and, in view of his emphasis on spiritual values, probably better.   He has impinged upon the conscience of mankind.

In the words of the *New York Times*, " He strove for perfection as other men strive for power and possessions . . . the power of his benignity grew stronger as his political influence ebbed.   He tried, in the mood of the New Testament, to love his enemies, and do good to those who despitefully used him. Now he belongs to the ages.'

The *Christian Science Monitor* sees him "as the supreme individualist of our times". He thus became more than a leader of Indian nationalism. He was a world-wide symbol. The paper then makes a shrewd point which may be at the root of much of the misunderstanding about his aims and "dual" personality. "His faith", the article continues, "that the individual could move mountains through moral suasion lacked the great contribution of western thought, a sense of Law. Louis Fischer had said, ' to most people politics means government, to Gandhi it means men'. But without government man lacks the measure of his own ideals, and hence it is that the world found in Gandhi a blend of wily shifting politician with guileless unshakeable saint. He proved the moral force of a single man."

Attlee has broadcast to the nation. Truman has spoken of a great international tragedy and loss to the whole world. Smuts calls him a Prince among men. Jinnah for his part describes him as "one of the greatest men produced by the Hindu community and a leader who commanded their universal confidence and respect".

Yet, unhappily, it is just because the confidence and respect of the Hindu community were not universal that Gandhi's life has been taken. A tremendous sense of shame is evident in all the memorial numbers of the Indian papers. Many of their editions have been outstandingly well done. I was particularly impressed with the *Hindusthan Standard*, which, in addition to carrying three full-page portraits of the Mahatma, leaves its leader page completely blank save for this one paragraph in bold type. "Gandhiji has been killed by his own people for whose redemption he lived. This second crucifixion in the history of the world has been enacted on a Friday—the same day Jesus was done to death one thousand nine hundred and fifteen years ago. Father, forgive us."

CHAPTER TWENTY-THREE

CONFLICTS CONTINUED

GOVERNMENT HOUSE, NEW DELHI, *Wednesday, 4th February, 1948*

THE GOVERNMENT HAS sufficient evidence to show that Gandhi's assassination was not an isolated crime but part of a wider plot in which the assassination of Nehru and other Indian leaders was planned. Following upon an Assembly resolution hoping that early and strong action would be taken, the Government has announced that no organisations preaching violence and no private armies would henceforth be permitted.

At the same time the R.S.S.S.* has been declared illegal, and a large number of its followers are already under arrest. I have just seen an astonishing article from the R.S.S.S. paper, *The Organiser*, which proclaims doctrines that would have warmed the heart of Rosenberg. It speaks of a neo-culture which includes indoctrination of every age from under eight to over sixty; persons of the above ages are all eligible to take part in the activities of the R.S.S.S., their firm faith in their Hindu parentage, heritage and culture being the only requisites of membership. " No foreigner can make social inroads into this family. No alien can invade to subdue this spirit of corporate life. No enemy can fetter the progress of this neo-culture."

The writer claims that the R.S.S.S., founded in 1925, has grown into " oceanic expanses and Himalayan heights ", and that if no new branches were started it would take one person twenty to twenty-five years to go round every branch established in the country. This is, no doubt, wishful thinking, but banning the R.S.S.S. is a very different thing from breaking it.

I had an interesting talk this evening with Nye,† who wanted to see me on some publicity problems. He said he was very impressed with Patel, who was a real leader in the military sense. Once decisions had been taken there were no vain regrets and the objective was wholeheartedly pursued. He also had that second great gift of leadership, the power of delegation. V. P. had been given the job of organising the States, Patel was hardly aware of the details. In Nye's view this was the sign of a big man.

He spoke of Communist progress in Madras. They were cashing in on local divisions inside the Congress. There was a big feud going on between Brahmins and non-Brahmins, and the Prime Minister, a non-Brahmin, was currently " taking it out " of the Brahmins. The Com-

---

* Rashtriya Swayam Sevak Sangh, militant stormtrooper offshoot of the Hindu Mahasabha.

† Sir Archibald Nye, Governor of Madras and after Lord Mountbatten's departure United Kingdom High Commissioner in New Delhi.

munists, too, were exploiting the failure of the monsoon by urging the suspension of harvesting operations in order to secure new relations between landlord and tenant.   The Communists contained a great many young men with genuine idealism and sense of mission.   Their fundamental mistake, both here and elsewhere in the world, he feels, lies in their contempt for and breaking of the law.   If they operated more within the framework of legality, they would indeed be formidable.

GOVERNMENT HOUSE, NEW DELHI, *Thursday, 5th February, 1948*

I have been talking to Norbert Bogdan, Vice-President of Schroeders' Banking Group of New York, who is making a detailed survey of financial prospects and economic trends both in India and Pakistan. He is an experienced traveller and, I should say, a shrewd analyst, making his first visit to India.   For all the tragic convulsions following on Independence, he is deeply impressed with the achievements and potentialities of the two new States.

He is just back from Karachi, and had an interview with Jinnah yesterday.   He found him in a far more accommodating mood than he had been led to expect.   Jinnah was clearly disturbed about the implications of the Kashmir situation, and spoke of Gandhi in much more generous terms than he saw fit to use in his message, acknowledging to Bogdan how great was the loss for the Moslems.   Jinnah added that he was reputed to have said that certain men in responsible positions in India were plotting the economic and political destruction of Pakistan, but he was ready to give them the benefit of the doubt.   The real trouble was with the extremist groups, and he had been favourably impressed by the Indian Government's firm handling of these following on Gandhi's assassination.

There is one " extremist " who seems to have found the events of the last few days too great for him, and that is the Socialist leader, Jai Prakash Narain.   The Congress is now an elderly Party which has won its principal victory, and thus a democratic constitutional Socialist movement has the chance to build up a powerful following for itself in the next five years.   Gandhi's death left the Socialists with only two profitable choices—open opposition to the Congress or reconciliation with it and its capture from within.   Narain gave a Press conference which did neither of these things.   He urged the need for unity while at the same time denouncing Patel, thus rendering *rapprochement* with Nehru almost impossible.

Kingsley Martin tells me he had a long talk with him yesterday which he found rather disappointing.   Although he was still emotionally and mentally numbed by Gandhi's death, there was—Kingsley said—a certain lack of firmness in his pursuit of power which is the failing of so many social democrats of good-will.   He also detected a disquieting indifference to the interests of his followers or to the tactical question whether or not his aims should be to join the Government.

GOVERNMENT HOUSE, NEW DELHI, *Saturday, 7th February, 1948*

I have had the odd and almost eerie experience of returning to Birla House to have lunch with its fabulous owner, G. D. Birla. I had not been into the house since the night of the assassination. Now all that remained to recall to the visitor those hours of crowded confusion was the roping off of a small plot of ground in the back garden where the Mahatma had fallen, and where a commemorative stone is to be placed. Some of the turf in the vicinity had been taken away that night by those who even in the presence of death could not forego the hunt for souvenirs.

Birla in real life makes little effort to play the role of industrial magnate, newspaper proprietor, philanthropist and political patron. He is unassuming to the point of austerity. He has a hawk-like face, the features of an Indian Sherlock Holmes, and also, I would guess, that great detective's powers of observation. The other guests included Chetty, the Finance Minister, Krishnamachari, the very able Dewan of Jaipur, another business magnate named Mehta, and Norman Cliff, correspondent of the *News Chronicle*.

Throughout lunch the talk revolved round high finance and the prospects of barter agreements between Pakistan and India. For the sake of argument, cotton, jute or food were disposed of or withheld. All this accent on brokerage I found in strange contrast to the scenes and sentiments in these very rooms a week ago.

GOVERNMENT HOUSE, NEW DELHI, *Thursday, 12th February, 1948*

To-day crowds by the million paid their final homage to the Mahatma when his ashes were scattered upon India's sacred rivers and on the sea. The principal ceremony was the performance of the last rites at the point where the three rivers, Jumna, Ganges and the mythical Saraswati, meet.

In Delhi the Mountbattens and his staff attended this morning a moving memorial service at the Cathedral Church of the Redemption. Mountbatten and Matthai, who is an Indian Christian, read the lessons, and the hymns were those which Gandhi made his own at his Prayer Meetings, in particular " Lead Kindly Light ", " Abide With Me ", and " When I Survey the Wondrous Cross ". The congregation joined in with a fervour which would, I am sure, have carried the Mahatma's blessing.

As epilogue, Mountbatten broadcast to-night his final tribute to Gandhi, thus rounding off an ambitious series of panegyrics which began on the night of 30th January with Nehru's and Patel's strong calls to unity and repentance. Nearly every Congress leader has spoken, several with outstanding eloquence and with an astonishing mastery of the purest English prose. Among the phrases and thoughts that have remained in my mind was Sarojini Naidu's assertion, " It is therefore right and appropriate that he died in the City of Kings ", and her dramatic plea, " My Father do not rest. Do not allow us to rest. Keep us to our pledge."

" The real time for renunciation is now," said Prasad, " when you have got something to sacrifice." C. R. was also very telling with his contention, " Suppression and coercion cannot be avoided in this imperfect world, but let us clearly and once for all realise that good-will cannot be achieved except by good-will."

Some of the language, however, was turgid and the sentiment dross. There has been a dangerous tendency noticeable not only in these broadcasts but also in the Press and with articulate Hindu opinion to wallow in self-pity excusing inaction rather than to express a genuine and purifying sense of shame.

Mountbatten stressed the need for rallying under Nehru's leadership to give substance to the ideal of a progressive secular democracy. We have had considerable discussion on the appropriate line for him to take, and I was asked to put together a first draft. I soon found myself all too easily flying high. Mountbatten wisely shortened the text and played down the rhetoric.

He spoke first of Gandhi as his friend, and of his death coming with the shock of a personal bereavement to millions in every part of the civilised world. Then he called attention to him as the martyr in the struggle against fanaticism. The tragic manner of his death would, he hoped, shock everyone into sinking their differences, for thus, and only thus, would they be carrying out his ideal and enabling India to enter into her full inheritance.

GOVERNMENT HOUSE, NEW DELHI, *Saturday, 14th February, 1948*

Against the background of mourning for the Mahatma we celebrate another day of national Independence. This time it is in honour of Ceylon's assumption of full Dominion Status. The violence and civil disorders disfiguring many of the manifestations of rising Asian nationalism have been noticeably absent from Ceylon. The whole operation has been an accurate reflection of the people's sunny and happy-go-lucky temperament. Liberty has come smoothly because life, for all its grinding poverty, comes easily. To-day the Ceylon flag with its golden lion was unfurled on the flagstaff by Mr. de Silva, their Special Representative in Delhi, and got stuck on the way up. It would surely have remained permanently at half-mast but for the obvious concern of the Diplomatic Corps, some of whom were shaping to put the flag on top of the mast themselves. This encouraged the cheerful Mr. de Silva to make one final and successful tug at the rope.

Both Mountbatten and Nehru spoke—Nehru in the most informal and paternal mood, calling the island by its Indian name of Lanka and stressing the deep ties of religion, history and culture. After the flag-hoisting and the speeches there was tea—Ceylon tea. Nehru gave clear signs this afternoon that he is beginning to recover from the stunning impact of Gandhi's death and the pall of national mourning which has lain heavily upon him. He came up to us, and after we had made some remark about the excellent quality of the tea we were drinking, he waxed eloquent on the æsthetics of tea-making, commending the artistry of the

Chinese, who, he said, were reputed to infuse their tea with dew collected at dawn from the lotus leaf.

The subject of tea recalls a revealing comment made to us by Oleg Orestov the other day. He represents the Tass Agency here, and is due to return shortly to the Soviet Union. He has for some time been the Honorary Secretary of the Foreign Correspondents' Association, continuing to live with his family in the poorer part of Old Delhi throughout the troubles. During lunch with us he discussed the transfer of power quite frankly. In an appreciation of the persistent strength of British influence he cited in all seriousness and some dismay the Indian attitude to his tea-drinking habits. " How do you like your tea? " they would ask. " By itself," he would reply, at which the Indian would invariably exclaim, " But that is not the correct way to drink it. The British drink it with milk and sugar." Nearly all influential Indians with the attainment of Independence show themselves in his view to be quite unconsciously the exponents of the British way of life. This, he implied, was the ultimate victory of the Imperial system—to ensure the continuity of your own thought-processes and behaviour-patterns among an alien people to whom you have voluntarily liquidated formal power.

Narain, among others, has had his answer. Nehru, broadcasting to-night over All India Radio, declares himself distressed beyond measure by whisperings about differences between Patel and himself. " Of course," he said, " there have been for many years past differences between us, temperamental and other, in regard to many problems, but India at least should know that these differences have been overshadowed by the fundamental agreements about the most important aspects of our public life, and that we have co-operated together for a quarter of a century or more in great undertakings. Is it likely that at this crisis in our national destiny either of us should be petty minded and think of anything but the national good? "

So an end is put to speculation, and the lie direct is given to those who had doubted whether the two big men of the Government were big enough to hold together. On their solidarity at this time the future of the entire régime depends.

GOVERNMENT HOUSE, NEW DELHI, *Tuesday, 17th February, 1948*

At our Staff Meeting to-day Mountbatten reviewed the disquieting Kashmir situation. The reference of the dispute to the United Nations has at least offset the immediate risk of war, but a new danger is creeping up, the reality of which it is easier for us here in Delhi than for the Government in London or the delegates at Lake Success to discern. Various suspicions are seeping into the minds of the Indian Government and the politically conscious public which, taken together, could well develop into a major frontal attack on Indo-British good-will.

In the first place, there is bewilderment at the delay of the United Nations in accepting India's basic complaint that an act of aggression has taken place in Kashmir. This is regarded here as no mere formality, but as a basic point of grievance involving a threat to peace which the

United Nations was especially created to redress. Hence grows the suspicion that the United Nations is being made the forum for the promotion of international power politics. As evidence of this the published attitude of the American and British delegates, Warren Austin and Noel-Baker, are cited. Both are wildly accused of being unashamedly pro-Pakistan for a variety of unedifying reasons.

As a natural reaction from this disillusionment, which is genuinely and nationally felt, the belief is also spreading that India has most to hope, whether in terms of mediation or even of the veto, from Soviet Russia and her satellites. Some of this trouble has sprung from the failure of the Indian delegation to make its mark. A week ago Nehru ordered its recall for consultation and, it is to be hoped, reconstitution.

On the Public Relations side India fared even worse than I had feared she would. Even the Indian Press was obliged to print large indigestible chunks of Ayyengar's speeches three or four days after they had been delivered. The personality of Sheikh Abdullah and the procedure of Lake Success could not be reconciled, and the Indian case suffered accordingly. Moreover, the Pakistan delegate was their Foreign Minister, Zaffrullah Khan, an experienced and popular practitioner in United Nations dialectic, who was as suave and smooth as the Indian delegates were awkward and angular.

Mountbatten is worried because he feels that Attlee and Noel-Baker do not seem to be showing themselves sufficiently alive to the psychological influences of this dispute and that their attempt to deal out even-handed justice is producing heavy-handed diplomacy. The crux of the problem as seen in London is India's unwillingness to recognise that a plebiscite carried out under the auspices of Abdullah and with the sole support of Indian troops, even with Security Council backing, would not be regarded as fulfilling the condition of its fair conduct. In Mountbatten's opinion the United Kingdom delegate could with advantage take a less unfriendly line towards India by supporting the view that the first step should be for Pakistan to stop helping the raiders. The question of superintending the plebiscite without interfering with the legally constituted Government deserved, he felt, more sympathetic discussion and treatment than it has yet received.

In an appraisal of Attlee this morning, Mountbatten stressed first his absolute intellectual honesty—perhaps his greatest source of strength—secondly his status as a liberator and finally his profound personal affection for and interest in India. These were assets which must not be squandered. Mountbatten finds his present constitutional position of friendly adviser irksome at times. He can no longer step in between London and Delhi, and his only link now is with the King, who strictly separates his various sovereignties.

Nehru has just met a deputation of industrialists, and I understand he lost his patience with them. G. D. Birla, speaking in much the same terms as at our luncheon, said that Government policy was scaring off capital. Nehru replied that the Government were not scared, so why should capital be? None-the-less in the Legislative Assembly he has spoken in softer terms, saying that the Government's economic policy is being elaborated as the outcome of the meeting with the industrialists. Although academically an exponent of Socialism, Nehru is in fact upholding a mixed economy, in which he is trying to encourage a socially progressive capitalism to live alongside State enterprise.

GOVERNMENT HOUSE, NEW DELHI, *Sunday, 22nd February, 1948*

Walter Monckton has just arrived here following a week's stay in Hyderabad. We were aware that he was due to see the Nizam during the middle of February, and Mountbatten had accordingly written off to His Exalted Highness urging that he should seize the opportunity of Monckton's visit to come to a general settlement with India.

Rather to Mountbatten's surprise, the Nizam at once agreed with him. I say surprise, because some of the Nizam's privately expressed opinions of Mountbatten recently have been far from flattering. We are aware that he has been describing him as no friend of Hyderabad, as anyhow without power, and has been asserting that it was immaterial whether Mountbatten helped in future negotiations or not. But now he replies expressing the hope that Mountbatten, " as a member of the Royal Family of England, will give your invaluable help and support to Hyderabad in the long term agreement which may be in keeping with the high position Hyderabad occupies in the eyes of the world ". It is interesting to note that he always invokes Mountbatten's Royal connection, as if it endowed him with some special virtue and status in negotiating with Hyderabad.

For a month after the signing of the Standstill Agreement there was almost complete quiet, but shortly after the New Year there was an incident to show that the calm was deceptive. A trivial but none-the-less significant dispute arose over the allotment of accommodation in Hyderabad for K. M. Munshi, India's newly appointed Agent-General. The house already earmarked for him was not ready. So it was suggested that he should go into one of the vacant Residencies for the intervening eleven days. The Nizam at once protested against the proposal, seeing in it a sinister plot to revive Paramountcy. The Indian reply was simply that if Munshi was not to be allowed proper and adequate accommodation, neither he nor any other Agent-General would be sent at all. At this stage Mountbatten's good offices were invoked, and as a result of a brisk exchange of letters and telegrams the Nizam was induced to give way, and Munshi duly left on the 5th January to take up his post.

By the end of the month relations between Hyderabad and India had declined to the point where it could be said that the whole Standstill Agreement was liable to be denounced by both sides. There was a dangerous increase in the number of border incidents. The policy of pin-pricks was leading inevitably to wider irritation. The Hyderabad Government began by imposing some restrictions on the export of metals, and followed this up by withdrawing recognition of Indian Dominion currency in all normal transactions within the State.

More provocative than either of these moves, a loan of twenty crores of rupees (over fifteen million pounds) was understood to have been made available by Hyderabad to Pakistan. The circumstances of this deal were obscure and disquieting. Mountbatten has been very carefully into the matter, and from the evidence at his disposal it is difficult to avoid the conclusion that it was arranged by Moin Nawaz Jung, the present Minister for External Affairs and Finance, while he was actually a member of the delegation negotiating the Standstill Agreement. This provocative move was made, moreover, just when the Indian Government was considering withholding the fifty-five crores of assets from Pakistan. On the Hyderabad side come detailed complaints of economic blockade.

On the day of Gandhi's cremation Mountbatten had his first meeting with the new Ittehad-sponsored Prime Minister of Hyderabad, Mir Laik Ali, and advised him frankly that his Government should mend their ways and generally try to work in a spirit of friendship with India. Mountbatten doubts, however, whether he made any deep impression. Behind a suave outward manner he detected in Mir Laik Ali's outlook that blend of fanaticism and cunning which we have been reduced to regarding as the dominant characteristics of the Ittehad and its leaders. Much now depends on the ability of Monckton to persuade the Nizam and his Government to adopt more constructive policies, and on Mountbatten to prevent Patel and the Indian Government losing their patience before the resources of negotiation have been fully worked out.

GOVERNMENT HOUSE, NEW DELHI, *Monday, 23rd February, 1948*

Walter Monckton and V. P. were both guests at one of Mountbatten's informal Staff Meetings this morning. We burst the bounds of our agenda and indulged in reminiscence about Kashmir's accession and speculation about Commonwealth citizenship. On Kashmir, Monckton said that frankly the issues were not understood outside the sub-continent. V. P. stressed that Nishtar's * agreement to the accession policy on behalf of the future Pakistan Government was in fact secured before the transfer of power, and that Pakistan Ministers had subsequently admitted that the Junagadh accession was essentially a violation of the agreement. When Kak † came to Delhi in July he saw Patel, who told him that he did not want the accession of Kashmir against the people's will. Through Mountbatten's good offices he also saw Jinnah at this time.

Discussing problems of Commonwealth status, Monckton drew attention to the importance of the Nationality Bill in Britain, which was, it seems, in some measure the outcome of a letter he had written to Cripps. He explained that the position now is that one can be a subject of the King without owing allegiance in the citizenship sense. On the general issue of India and the Commonwealth, Mountbatten is preparing an *aide-memoire* which he wants to have ready in time for Gordon-Walker to see and to study. After his stay at Government House at the end of January,

* Sardar Rab Nishtar, Pakistan Cabinet Minister, whose portfolios included the Pakistan Ministry of States. He was a Moslem League representative along with Mr. Jinnah and Mr. Liaquat Ali Khan at the decisive meetings with Lord Mountbatten on the 2nd and 3rd June, 1947.

† Pandit Kak, the last Prime Minister under the old order in Kashmir, who had been responsible for the arrest of Nehru on his visit to Kashmir in 1946.

Gordon-Walker went down to Ceylon. He is now back in Delhi at a crucial moment in the Kashmir dispute. With a stalemate on the fighting front and a hiatus at Lake Success, the physical opportunity arises for renewing informal and indirect diplomacy.

My memory of Gordon-Walker goes back to my undergraduate days at Christ Church, when as a young History don there he guided me through the intricacies of seventeenth-century Europe. He seems to me to have all the qualifications for high office, the lucidity of the scholar's mind, a strong but attractive personality and administrative grip. He is one of the younger Labour intellectuals treading the Attleean way of Fabian moderation.

He sees the central issue between the two Dominions in the Kashmir dispute as being now the withdrawal of troops, and he feels it is easier to envisage the possibility of compromise both on the plebiscite and the Interim Government. He has, I think, been able to see for himself that Mountbatten is not exaggerating the bad impression caused here by the British attitude at the United Nations.

In the course of a long talk with Sir Girja Shankar Bajpai, Nehru's accomplished Secretary for External Affairs, he has, I understand, stressed quite firmly that friendship with Russia is obtainable only at the price of subservience, and that Russia in any case has no basic interest in India. I also hear, incidentally, that Bajpai has taken up the question of Korea with the American Ambassador, Grady. With the demarcation of Soviet and American influence along the 38th Parallel, the situation between North and South Korea is very similar to that between East and West Germany. Bajpai's argument is, if United States troops are not leaving Korea, why should Indian troops be called upon to leave Kashmir?

At this morning's meeting I urged that Gordon-Walker should be pressed to stay on until 29th February, the date of a possible visit from Liaquat. I feel strongly that a British Minister's presence during the next discussions between Liaquat and Nehru would serve as an inducement to moderation and compromise. No effective mediating influence has been available in the right place at the right time.

Mountbatten called for a post-mortem from me on the failure of the Indian case to establish itself with world opinion at the United Nations. I replied that quite apart from its actual merits it had been abominably presented, and that nearly every canon of Public Relations procedure had either been violated or neglected. Moreover, I felt that not enough attention had been paid to answering Pakistan's case against India, in particular the allegations of Congress "conspiracy" to secure the Maharaja's submission through Abdullah; just to ignore such charges was not wise.

GOVERNMENT HOUSE, NEW DELHI, *Wednesday, 25th February, 1948*

Mountbatten's *aide-memoire* on India and the Commonwealth, which sets out to make " certain tentative suggestions as to how the structure of the Commonwealth could perhaps be altered, particularly in nomenclature, to allow Asian countries to remain more easily associated with it," is now ready for Gordon-Walker. Although there has been a lot of staff discussion and thinking on the subject, it is very much Mountbatten's own document, characteristically bold, direct and original. It is also well-timed, for the Government of India is due to release the draft of the new Indian Constitution to the Press to-morrow. After circulation of the draft to Members of the Constituent Assembly, whose comments are required within a month, a revised draft will then be formally submitted to the Constituent Assembly for final approval.

Mountbatten says frankly that although individual Indian leaders are alive to the advantages of the continued Commonwealth connection, their political position has been weakened and the attitude of the Government adversely affected by the policy adopted towards Kashmir by the British delegation at the Security Council. This he puts forward as a political fact, and not as something over which he is trying to moralise. He said he would like to see the word " Republic " expunged from the Indian Constitution in favour of Commonwealth, but without promising to be successful in achieving this amendment, he adds, " I think there can be no doubt that there is room for a Republic within the Commonwealth."

He points out that the word Dominion is not in any case an easy one for India to swallow, after the Congress resolution in favour of a Republic. It still has a debased meaning here, whether of domination or of status short of full freedom. He also urges that the term " Commonwealth citizen " should be considered as a desirable alternative to British subject, although both terms could be used on occasion with advantage. His final point of substance is that in any arrangement made about the future structure of the Commonwealth it would be best if possible to leave the question of the formal link with the Crown unstated.

GOVERNMENT HOUSE, NEW DELHI, *Thursday, 26th February, 1948*

Vernon has asked me to comment on a draft memorandum he is preparing giving a brief survey of the Accession policy to date with particular reference to Junagadh and Kashmir. After covering some points of detail, I have made the following brief distinction between these two events. " Quite apart from the test of majority populations, the accession of Junagadh to Pakistan was in violation of the principle of geographical compulsion to which the Pakistan leaders had themselves subscribed. The accession of Kashmir was not. Moreover, from the strategic and economic points of view, while Pakistan had no interest in Junagadh, India had considerable interest in Kashmir. There were two further special factors involved in the case of Kashmir but absent from that of Junagadh—the use of force by tribal invasion to overthrow the Maharaja's régime before accession, and the presence (also before accession) of an important inter-communal political organisation in the State.

" Taking into account all these ' other factors ', the accession of Junagadh to Pakistan was wholly frivolous, while that of Kashmir to India was definitely arguable. It was just because of all the special circumstances attaching to both accessions that the Government of India accepted the principle of a confirming plebiscite for the action taken in both States. Finally, it should be noted that when India challenged the validity of the Junagadh accession, Pakistan asserted the doctrine of the Ruler's absolute and sacrosanct right to accede, but promptly challenged that right in the case of Kashmir."

I have to-day received two letters from Kingsley Martin, now in Karachi, full of interesting news and impressions, which serve to show, however, that the rights and wrongs of the Kashmir dispute cannot be finally reduced to any simple formula. He arrived in Karachi to find that All India Radio had broadcast a part of a recent article of his dealing with Kashmir explicitly from the Indian angle, without realising that it was an *ex parte* statement of case and that he had indicated that he was on his way to Pakistan to see how the matter looked from there. *Dawn* devoted a cartoon and a long leading article entitled " Appointment with Fiction ", castigating him " in rather amusing terms ". " I have just rattled off a cable," he adds, " giving points in Pakistan's favour but saying that my interest lies in settlement before the snow melts."

He has been to Lahore and Rawalpindi, and has spent a night with Sir George Cunningham, the famous Governor of the North-west Frontier Province, who returned to his former post at Jinnah's special request, backed, I may add, by Mountbatten and Ismay. Indian opinion has been inclined to suspect Cunningham of machiavellian designs and of secretly sponsoring the diversion of the tribes into Kashmir. But as token of her general desire to keep the tribes happy and stabilised, Pakistan is still paying the tribal subsidy which the British used to provide. Admittedly they are saving financially, and gambling politically by not keeping an Army there as well, but, as Cunningham pointed out—according to Kingsley—Army or no Army, once the holy war concept spread among the tribes, neither himself nor anyone else could have stopped them. It would have placed far too great a communal strain on the police or Army to have asked either to turn the tribal raiders back.

Most of the tribesmen have now returned home, but not all with much loot, and all ready to go in again at the call of a holy crusade. " As for the future he (Cunningham) confirms what I am told on all sides here, that the tribesmen can be controlled and carried off from Kashmir on one condition only, that they are assured that a settlement will be made that will be fair to the Moslems."

All this, Kingsley adds, " explains the strange remarks of Noel-Baker which so much upset Nehru about a plebiscite that seemed fair to the tribesmen. It sounded idiotic, but I now see what was meant. The figure given me from the Foreign Secretary to-day is that seven hundred and fifty thousand tribesmen are fully armed and willing to fight anyone who disappoints them, and also willing to settle down ! "

He says that the visit has now supplemented his opinion, if only because Pakistan is talking about completely different aspects of the situation. " They think here of tribesmen much as Indians think of Sikhs, as awkward, dangerous but indispensable and unavoidable allies." They urge that the rising in the Poonch area against the Maharaja began long

before his accession, which they regard simply as a trick to take the
" k " out of Pakistan, and that a great many Pakistani officers and men
come from Poonch.

He says he has met Mohammed Ibrahim, head of the Kashmir Azad
administration, which enjoys much the same measure of support from
Karachi as Abdullah does from Delhi. He spoke quite frankly of possible
compromises for a plebiscite after a cease-fire, with troops on both sides
occupying discreet strategic positions, tribes being pushed back, a plebiscite
organised by the United Nations and an Interim Government with a
neutral chairman.

Ideas of this nature are bound to be plausible and appealing to world
opinion, giving virtue to those that propound them. For India to sit
back relying solely on legal status and talk about a plebiscite which entails
Abdullah remaining in complete control both before and during it, will
be to fritter away their initial moral advantage.

GOVERNMENT HOUSE, NEW DELHI, *Thursday, 4th March, 1948*

The new Hyderabad delegation, consisting of Mir Laik Ali, Moin
Nawaz Jung (Mir Laik Ali's ambitious and powerful brother-in-law) and
Monckton, are in Delhi and have had two meetings with Mountbatten,
one on Tuesday and the other to-day, at both of which V. P. was also
present. Yesterday Mir Laik Ali visited Karachi, and at Mountbatten's
suggestion asked Liaquat to undertake not to cash the twenty crore
loan made by Hyderabad to Pakistan during the period of the Standstill
Agreement. He returned with this undertaking given to him verbally.

There has been a lengthy recitation of grievance on both sides, V. P.
quoting the loan to Pakistan and the ordinance making Indian currency
illegal, and Mir Laik Ali claiming the operation of a full-scale economic
blockade against Hyderabad. Mountbatten pointed out that all communal armies had recently been abolished in India and that Hyderabad
should by the same token disband the Razakars, the militant offshoot of
the Ittehad of whose depredations increasingly grave reports were being
received. He also urged upon the delegation the desirability of the early
introduction of responsible government in Hyderabad.

We have here the customary deadlock of timing and procedure con-
cealing the conflict for the ultimate power. Patel feels that it is useless
to negotiate for a long-term settlement until the Standstill Agreement is
working properly, and that the Standstill Agreement cannot be expected
to work without some measure of responsible government. As a first
step towards this, however, Patel was not ready to back the suggestion
that an Interim Government should be set up consisting of an equal
number of Hindus and Moslems. Mir Laik Ali for his part does not
think that he would be able to get beyond parity and admit a Hindu
majority Government until a long-term agreement is reached, although
he concedes that it might be possible for the two steps to be taken
simultaneously.

After the meeting a storm blew up over the issue of a communiqué,
and Patel refused to agree to the inclusion of any suggestion that India

had committed a breach of the Standstill Agreement. Here he is on firm ground as far as the Central Government is concerned. The trouble is at the provincial levels with local officials. In present conditions of administrative strain and inexperience it is easier to give instructions than to ensure that they will be carried out. Patel, however (perhaps from fear of implying the wider admission), was not even prepared to state in a communiqué that the goods due to Hyderabad, which it was claimed were held up, should be released. Monckton is extremely upset, and Mountbatten on his return from a dinner-party has spoken to him over the telephone promising to follow the matter up personally to-morrow.

GOVERNMENT HOUSE, NEW DELHI, *Friday, 5th March, 1948*

Monckton left for Hyderabad early this morning and Mountbatten pursued his inquiries about the communiqué in his absence. He talked with Nehru, who was very reasonable and sympathetic, but anxious that the question should be settled with Patel as the Minister responsible for handling the Hyderabad question. Mountbatten was due to see him this afternoon, but during lunch Patel had a heart attack and nearly died. He is completely laid up, and has been forbidden by his doctor to do any work whatever for an unspecified period, which may well cover the remainder of our term here.

I think he overtaxed his strength at the time of Gandhi's death by his determination to ride on the funeral carriage throughout the six-hour journey. When I saw him at the Raj Ghat he looked drawn and ill and seemed as if in a trance. The whole tragedy has hit him heavily, and he has undoubtedly carried more than his fair share of the burden of criticism as Home Minister for the failure to see that Gandhi was properly protected. His illness now is a serious blow for the Government at a critical time in its affairs at home and abroad, and it serves to underline how dependent the régime is upon its two key men.

In the immediate context of Hyderabad and the communiqué there is no one to be found who will assume responsibility for reversing his last decision. So Mountbatten has had to write off to Monckton that no Press statement should be issued for the present.

GOVERNMENT HOUSE, NEW DELHI, *Saturday, 6th March, 1948*

Mountbatten has seen K. M. Munshi, India's Agent-General in Hyderabad, who is active, purposeful and, I would guess, ambitious. He is moving up in the Congress hierarchy, although lacking the particular Congress badge of honour, prison service in resistance to the Raj. This not unnaturally only enhances the vigour of his nationalism to-day.

In his memorial broadcast on the Mahatma he presented himself as the student of *ahimsa*, or non-violence, who was ready to grapple with Gandhi on the failure of civil disobedience in 1942 because " it did not stand the scriptural test of *ahimsa*; as it evoked wrath in the enemy and not love ". From what he had to say to Mountbatten to-day, it is clear that he is not placing excessive reliance on *ahimsa* for dealing with

Hyderabad. If the activities of the Razakars are not quickly restrained he advocates sending in the Indian police to do so, which, by his own legal interpretation, he considers would come within the terms of the Standstill Agreement. He is already convinced that the Razakars cannot and will not be restrained by the present régime.

Mountbatten spoke firmly of India's need to adopt ethical and correct behaviour towards Hyderabad and to act in such a way as could be defended before the bar of world opinion. In the present state of negotiations Munshi's proposal for police action was absolutely wrong. Mir Laik Ali must be given a fair chance to deal with the Razakars, to implement the Standstill Agreement and introduce a measure of responsible government.

Mountbatten told me afterwards that while he has no doubt about Munshi's drive and ability, he is far from happy whether his temperament or political outlook fit him for this particularly delicate stage in the handling of the Nizam, which calls for unusual diplomatic patience and non-communal objectivity.

Monckton has now left Hyderabad for London, and we are afraid may well be ready to throw in his hand from the belief that further negotiations on the pattern of this week's performance are a waste of his time, and without Monckton the margin of Mountbatten's diplomatic initiative will be further narrowed down.

CHAPTER TWENTY-FOUR

BURMA REVISITED

GOVERNMENT HOUSE, CALCUTTA, *Monday, 8th March, 1948*

WE ARE OFF on the grand tour, nine days in all, to Calcutta, Orissa, Rangoon and Assam. The Mountbattens' schedule is fearsome even by their high-powered standards, and is set out in four slim booklets produced in four different colours by the Military Secretary's indefatigable staff. Travelling as light as possible, the party, including servants, still comprises over fifty persons, and is no small exercise in ceremonial logistics. I shall be staying on in Calcutta during the visits to Assam and Orissa, which will enable me to meet the Calcutta editors. We left Palam at 8.45 a.m., reaching Dum Dum airfield at one o'clock, where the venerable C. R., as Governor of West Bengal, had come to meet us. After presentations and inspections we started on the long motor drive through Calcutta's suburbs and slums.

I have travelled this way quite often over the past four years, but always with the same sense of foreboding, bordering on despair, at the sprawling squalor of the life it reveals—life lived below the margin of human rights and hopes. How can the slow processes of social reform prevail? Give us *this* day our daily bread, is their only plea. Emancipation is far away—from hunger and poverty, from industrial exploitation, from communal terror; and lying in wait to solve it all, the great Communist cheat.

We hurried past the citadels of the Clive Street area, out of Calcutta's bustle, noise and heat into the sudden stillness of Government House. There in the front lounge we found C. R. with the Mountbattens discussing the rest of the day's plans. He loves them dearly, and I think he is both amazed and amused at the tornado of official activity which threatens to overwhelm them and him over the next forty-eight hours.

Our first official function was the Mayor's tea-party, where the Mountbattens were regaled with a panegyric from the Mayor of deep and almost embarrassing purple. " Within your veins ", he declared, turning to Mountbatten, " courses in rich pulsation Royal blood." After declaring in a reference to partition that freedom for this ancient land " undivided and indivisible " had been achieved in violation of an axiom of history, he reached his peroration. " Your Excellency, by fingers that were deft and arms that were strong, you have laboured to raise a twin edifice. We look upon Your Excellency to unite your handicrafts by a bridge of Peace, a bridge of Delight." Whether it was this apocalyptic vision or the clatter of tea-cups, the denseness of the throng or the thickness of the air, Mountbatten was for once somewhat abashed, and read from his notes with heavy labour.

After the speeches were over and most of the guests had left, C. R.

came to my table and spoke about nearly everything with the devastating frankness of the really wise man. He said he was deeply worried about Kashmir. The country's resources were being squandered. It was like trying to mend a broken tea-cup at this party and forgetting all about the guests. He feared that Mountbatten might not be giving enough unpalatable advice. "Panditji", he said, "is capable of hearing profoundly unpleasant things." I replied that Mountbatten, with only an advisory role left to him, did not want to reach the stage where he could only irritate but not influence.

Turning to Patel and his illness, he gave us a short dissertation on the circulation of the blood. Patel's trouble was in the colon, where, he said, there is almost an autonomous circulatory system which only indirectly affects the heart. He stressed Patel's feminine characteristics, recalling Gandhi's comment that " there is something motherly about Sardar ". He said the adjectives he would apply to him—and most of us had our appropriate adjectives—were " loyal, affectionate, obstinate " ; and to be sure that I was aware of their gender, at once asked me with a smile, " Are you married? " But over and above these traits there was, of course, Patel's decisiveness, which C. R. is the first to recognise.

Before leaving us he had passed from personality to philosophy, bidding us reflect on the theory of the cycle which he described as " Life operating in a curve : if you proceed with sufficient vigour you end where you began, the bad disappearing with the good ".

After attending a garden-party given by Alec Symon, the British Deputy High Commissioner, we were whisked back in high-powered cars through the Calcutta night for the official dinner-party at Government House. Sixty-three guests sat down to table—forty-nine men and fourteen ladies. Royal etiquette was pursued with great thoroughness and detailed orders issued by the Military Secretary, which included special instructions for the fourteen ladies. " Ladies sitting on the opposite side of the table to His Excellency, the Governor-General, will not curtsey as they pass His Excellency but will curtsey at the throne room door." In spite of all this observance of the correct outward form —and his A.D.C.'s seemed to work to an even heavier duty roster than the Governor-General's—C. R. cannot for long sustain pomp and circumstance.

His speech to-night was wholly delightful in its studied artlessness, and contained some of the warmest tributes that can ever have been paid by an Indian Congress leader to a British ex-Viceroy. It was really most moving. He said he had started off in fear of Mountbatten because of his efficiency and rank, but he had soon been captivated by his charm. Mountbatten's charm, he added, " is a splendid quality because it comes from his heart. It means his heart is charming. Mountbatten has won us all by his charm. Even Patel ' fell for ' him—I think that is your phrase." He stressed again Patel's feminine streak beneath the rough exterior—" but don't tell him I said so ! "

Commenting on the turn of history's wheel which had brought the Mountbattens and himself to be dining together in this room in such auspicious circumstances, he said that Mountbatten during his recent

Delhi Convocation speech had referred to his engagement to Lady Mountbatten taking place in Room 13 of what was now Delhi University.* He had asked himself where he was at that particular time, and the answer was in Room 65—of the local jail.

Among the guests to-night was Sarat Chandra Bose, brother of Subhas, still the hero of Bengali nationalism. Sarat was at one time a member of the Viceroy's Executive Council. He is now a leading exponent of Socialist Opposition in Bengal's turbulent politics.

GOVERNMENT HOUSE, CALCUTTA, *Tuesday, 9th March, 1948*

The Mountbattens, after a full morning programme—Lady Mountbatten's first engagement being at 7.30 a.m.—lunched with the Bengal Press Advisory Committee at the Calcutta Club. The President of the Committee, Tushar Kanti Ghosh, who is also editor of the well-known Calcutta daily, *Amrita Bazar Patrika*, gave a short but highly polished chairman's introduction which was well above the average in expression and content for such occasions. Mountbatten took trouble over his reply, which he delivered with hardly a glance at his notes. It was an opportunity well taken to establish cordial relations with a very powerful section of the Indian Press, upon whom much depends for the creation of communal confidence in the partition of Bengal.

In addition to providing such important pro-Congress papers as the *Amrita Bazar Patrika*, Calcutta is the main headquarters of *The Statesman*. Ian Stephens has invited me to lunch with the editorial staff and to go over the office. As Mountbatten pointed out in his speech, it was from *The Statesman's* office that, with Stephens' generous co-operation, two newspapers were simultaneously produced—*The Statesman* itself, and "*SEAC*" under Frank Owen's dynamic editorship, which for nearly three years was one of Mountbatten's major morale-raising contributions to the Burma campaign, and post-war activities.

During the brief intervals between engagements I have, among other things, been discussing with Mountbatten a further outburst by Nehru on the Foreign Press. It is disquieting, and may well jeopardise the goodwill agreement achieved under Mountbatten's chairmanship in November.

Mountbatten tells me he had a most illuminating talk to-day with C. R., who had given his candid opinion that if Mountbatten had not transferred power when he did there might well have been no power to transfer. It might, in fact, have been impossible to produce any Plan at all, and then the British would have been left with the whole burden and odium, whether they stayed on or moved out.

In the process of preparing a first draft of a letter for Mountbatten on Nehru's speech, I missed the Sheriff's tea-party, but in the evening managed to get to a reception given by the officers of the Armed Forces in Calcutta at the Officers' Club, Fort William. The last time I had been

* At that time (February 1922) the temporary Viceregal Lodge at which Lord and Lady Mountbatten were staying.

inside this historic cantonment was in February 1945 for a major S.E.A.C. conference, at which Mountbatten hammered out plans for the recapture of Rangoon and for future strategy in the theatre.

Fort William, with its two square miles and six main gates, embodies the whole two centuries' history of the Raj, from Clive to Mountbatten. For Clive began the building of Fort William the year after Plassey. It took twenty-two years to complete, and cost two million pounds sterling —an enormous project by any standards of cash or construction. Originally designed to mount six hundred and twenty-nine guns, it has not known during its entire existence one shot fired in anger. Up to 15th August the title of the Bengal Government was " The Government of the Presidency of Fort William in Bengal ". Until the completion of the present Government House in 1802 the Governor with the Secretariat and High Court were all housed inside the Fort. Warren Hastings once lived here, and here was the residence of former Commanders-in-Chief, including Kitchener and Roberts.

We left afterwards for dinner at the Royal Tolley Gunge, which is, I believe, the oldest golf club in the East, founded in 1829. The British colony were here in full force, and once again the utmost cordiality prevailed. I had expected to find in Calcutta the last citadels of " old koi-haism ", but the wind, it seems, has blown them all away. After dinner the Mountbattens were at their phenomenal best during all the small talk, setting the conversational ball rolling with groups of a dozen people at a time, breaking down reserve and shyness without apparent effort, and all this after a back-breaking fifteen-hour day.

GOVERNMENT HOUSE, CALCUTTA, *Wednesday, 10th March, 1948*

The Governor-General's party, minus only myself, left for Orissa at crack of dawn. I spent the morning shopping, browsing in the *bouquiniste* section of Chowringhee. I am the sole House guest, and quiet reigns. C. R. called me in about the delivery of some of Gandhi's ashes to Burma. Rauf, the Indian Ambassador there, wants to bring them in himself, but C. R. docs not agree, and thinks it would be more appropriate for Mountbatten to deliver them. Mountbatten spoke to him from Cuttack on the telephone, and this was agreed between them.

In the afternoon C. R. invited me to join a tea-party he was giving to the Eastern Newspaper Society. Nine leading editors were there, and Shiva Rao, who, as well as being the chief correspondent of *The Hindu* in Delhi, and Delhi representative of the *Manchester Guardian*, is a member of the Constituent Assembly. He discussed with me the ethics of Nehru's use of a Foreign Correspondent's telegraphed message to criticise the Foreign Press, and felt that such action was valid only if the paper actually printed the message. It is a nice point.

In the evening I visited the big Industrial Exhibition, which is now in full swing here, feeling I would see very little in the inevitable crush when the Mountbattens make their tour of it on Saturday. The Exhibition had rather a fun fair atmosphere about it, but, for all that, was impressive in the scale and variety of its display. Some of the handicrafts from the Indian States were of very high quality. After an hour I was glad to escape from the noise and dust.

RANGOON, *Thursday, 11th March, 1948*

This morning I left in state for Rangoon, an A.D.C. accompanying me from Government House to Dum Dum, where I took off in the Governor-General's Dakota at ten o'clock, taking with me Max Desfor, John Turner of Gaumont British (representing all the News Reels under the Rota agreement) and Bill Stead of the *Christian Science Monitor*, who are all covering Mountbatten's Burma visit. As we circled over Mingaladon airfield the wonderful Shwe Dagon Pagoda stood out of the green earth, pointing its golden challenge to the sun.

We touched down shortly after lunch, about half an hour ahead of the Mountbattens' party, which was coming direct from Orissa. On stepping out of the aircraft, where all Burma's notabilities were already gathered, I was somewhat overwhelmed to have a note handed to me from the Director of Information of the Government of Burma stating that, as directed by the Ministry of Foreign Affairs, no fewer than three officials—U Pu Glay, U Chan Tun and U Hla Maung of the Government of Burma's Information Department—had been sent to meet me and obtain publicity material. They at once presented themselves in their national dress, which serves to conceal alike their sex and age. It must be confessed that the Burmese representatives on the airfield, from the Prime Minister, Thakin Nu, downwards, looked incredibly youthful, and probably are.

The Mountbattens duly arrived on schedule, but only after considerable confusion at the other end, as the whole party had overlooked the fact that there was an hour's difference between Burmese and Indian time, so that the latter stages of the Orissa itinerary had to be finished off at the double. After the customary greetings and inspections we drove away under formidable military guard to the ugly and pretentious Government House, rather like St. Pancras station without the saving grace of London soot, where the first President of the Independent Republic of Burma has been installed since January. On the occasion of my last visit to Government House, Sir Reginald Dorman-Smith had just resumed his tenure, after nearly four years of cold storage in Simla.

The President gave a tea-party in the grounds, which are laid out very much in English country-house style. I had a short talk with Thakin Nu, who has a friendly open face, and is, I understand, devoid of all the normal political ambitions, and desirous only of returning into the world of scholarship and contemplation. He told me that Burma's rice exports are only up to eight hundred thousand tons, whereas the pre-war export figure was three and a half million tons. During the tea itself I sat next to the President's little daughter, who was, I suppose, about ten years old. The whole place seemed to be alive with the laughter of small children; there are the two baby sons and daughters of the late

Aung San, while the Burmese President has four small children, who add sparkle and gaiety to this sombre setting.

Mountbatten had given us all instructions that we were not in any circumstances to throw our weight about, and was thereupon to be seen vigorously arranging the details of to-morrow's ceremony for the restoration of King Theebaw's throne! Superimposed upon this fuss there was a muddle (of which he was well aware) over the release of his speeches, followed by a muddle (not brought to his notice) over the official dinner. Mountbatten deliberately brought with him in this party as many as possible of his staff who served with him in S.E.A.C. Hence the presence of Ronnie Brockman, Elizabeth Ward, June Foster (Lady Mountbatten's and Ronnie Brockman's private secretaries) and myself. Elizabeth, June and I duly dressed for the great occasion, only to find we were not on the dinner list. In order to avoid an *embarras*, we arranged for some dinner to be brought up to one of our bedrooms, where we solemnly drank the toast of S.E.A.C. and "absent friends", amongst whom we included ourselves!

Afterwards there was an elaborate display, with full commentary, of Burmese dancing on the lawn, but the gestures and music still seem to convey no appreciable æsthetic meaning. They lacked for me the emotional and rhythmic qualities of Siamese dancing as I had seen it in the strange and exotic precincts of the great Boromphinam Palace in Bangkok.

RANGOON, *Friday, 12th March, 1948*

To-day's big round of official duties began at 8.30 with a tribute to the eight leaders assassinated in last July's mass killing. I remember the first impact of the news in Malta when I was returning with Ismay from London, and the sense it brought that the frail fabric of Burmese Independence must surely disintegrate under this overwhelming blow. Great credit is undoubtedly due to Sir Hubert Rance * for his steadfastness in this crisis, which in an instant deprived Burma of almost her entire Social Democratic leadership.

The eight bodies are still, six months afterwards, lying in State in their glass coffins, but to-day they were draped with flags. Hitherto they have been somewhat gruesomely in evidence, their mouths gaping wide. The Jubilee Hall, where they are to be seen, is very shabby, and the propaganda appeal outside is crude and naïve. Large canvas pictures of the eight men hang from the windows, and there is a terrible statue of Aung San in front of the entrance painted in real life colours.

At ten o'clock, in the ballroom of Government House, all was ready for the handing over of Theebaw's throne. Up to the last minute John Turner was desperately grappling with floodlights, awkward angles and even more awkward pillars.

"Behind me", said Mountbatten, "is the Mandalay Hlutdaw throne, which was last used by King Theebaw of Burma when he visited the

* As Major-General Rance he had formerly been Lord Mountbatten's Chief Civil Affairs Officer for Burma in S.E.A.C.

Hlutdaw in Mandalay, and which is a replica of the famous Lion throne of King·Theebaw, which used to stand in the great Hall of Audience in the Palace of Mandalay—now, alas, burnt to the ground.   I also bring with me another object of historical interest : a silver mat which, according to tradition, was woven by Queen Supayalat for King Theebaw." There-upon, with the assistance of most of his staff, he opened the curtains, and a huge wooden structure over thirty feet high, about the size of a two-storied house, was revealed.

It has been no mean task dismantling this throne in Calcutta, conveying and then installing it here in Rangoon in time for this visit.   It had to be broken up into as many as four hundred and fifty separate pieces, which were packed in sixty cases and sent off to Burma at the beginning of February.   The workmen engaged in this operation travelled with it, and just managed to complete the job of building it up again two days ago.

After this ceremony we drove straight to Rangoon University, a most impressive group of buildings.   We had arrived during examinations, and I was surprised to see the large number of Burmese girls among the examinees.   The students upon whom the new Burma will so largely depend for its future leadership were a most appreciative audience, and Mountbatten, who always reacts quickly to the mood of his listeners, spoke to-day with winning zest.

He recalled how these buildings of the University, now restored to the use for which they were intended, had been used first as a Japanese Army headquarters and then, with the liberation of Rangoon, as a hospital for Allied wounded and recovered prisoners of war.   He told how, as Supreme Commander, he had been startled by the news that his Air Forces had strafed the teachers' training-college, the reason for the attack being its use by the Japanese.   " I then gave instructions that so far as possible the buildings were to be spared, for I was certain that the Japanese were on the run, and I did not wish to see the whole University destroyed."

Afterwards I drove into the centre of the city, first to visit the well-established Indian Information Office there, and then to attend the State luncheon.   The streets had a tattered and unkempt appearance, and there was as yet no atmosphere of civic pride, or even control.   On the way to the lunch I ran into a big Communist demonstration of railway and dock workers.   A policeman whose allegiance to law and order seemed somewhat doubtful first tried to hold my car up, then waved it on, and then, as it slowly made its way through the throng, exerted his final authority by giving it a parting kick.

Mountbatten has spoken very frankly to the President, Thakin Nu, and U Tin Tut, the intelligent and highly westernised Foreign Minister, urging them to give higher priority to the primary task which Aung San had set himself of raising the living standards of the people.   In their present precarious condition, he urged that they should seriously consider whether an anti-Communist Government with a policy of the wholesale and immediate expropriation of all private enterprise at home might not defeat its object with regard both to Communism and private enterprise. Moreover, they were behaving in a very arbitrary manner in their external policy. Members of the British Commonwealth, originally exempted from the new law excluding foreigners from owning immobile property, had now been lumped in with the rest. Mountbatten said he could see no reason why a most-favoured-nation treatment clause could not have been applied, and advised them against passing any more discriminatory legislation of this nature without first consulting the Governments of India, Pakistan and the United Kingdom.

This evening he dined with the British Ambassador, Bowker, and the three members of the British Service Mission.* If the Government are afraid of telling the facts to the people, they are also, it seems, unwilling to hear the truth from their advisers. Mountbatten is worried lest the three British officers whose task it is to warn the Burmese Government of its true military position should themselves become the scapegoats if things, as they very probably will, go wrong. He is convinced that they must go on written record as having consistently given sound guidance, if Anglo-Burmese relations are not to be compromised from the outset.

RANGOON-CALCUTTA, *Saturday, 13th March, 1948*

At eight o'clock, in the cool of the morning, the Mountbattens and all their staff party visited the great Shwe Dagon, which dominates Rangoon with much the same physical and æsthetic authority as that of the Acropolis over Athens. We entered the precincts by the western approach, and all took off our shoes and socks before climbing what seemed to be an arcade of at least a thousand steps. At the top the great central pagoda stood like some vast memorial in the middle of a celestial market-place. A wide tiled pavement encircled it, and under its golden shadow sheltered numerous smaller pagodas, *tazaungs*, and shrines of precious Buddhist relics.

We saw two great bells: the Mahaganda bell, weighing some sixteen tons, and a mighty bronze bell more than double that weight, eight and a half feet high, seven and a half feet wide and a foot thick, presented by King Tharawaddy in 1841. There were Royal umbrellas—King Mindon's being thirty-three feet high and weighing one and a quarter tons; symbolic footprints of the Buddha; a Bo tree sprung from a seed brought from the holy land of India; a reclining Buddha, twenty-eight feet long, and finally the sacred spot where "King Okkalapa made an asseveration that he might be able to build a pagoda enshrining the relics of the fourth Buddha of this dispensation, and Gautama Buddha appeared in a vision, granting his wish".

As with the statues in Westminster Abbey, the quality of the relics is variable and the quantity excessive. I have now seèn the outward and visible signs of Buddhism, ranging from Kandy's Temple of the Tooth, commercialised, dark and dirty, to the coloured temples of Bangkok, strange and still and very clean, but have visited nothing to equal the solitary splendour of Rangoon's Shwe Dagon.

* The Army representative was Brigadier, later General, G. K. Bourne, one of Mountbatten's senior planners in the early days of S.E.A.C. He subsequently became the British military Commandant in West Berlin.

This was our last official function before saying our farewells. The tempo was too swift for us to form more than the most superficial impression. But one does not have to stay long or move slowly to realise that the upper crust of political authority and of civil order is dangerously thin. There are deep fissures between Burmans and Karens, between Aung San's Anti-Fascist People's Freedom League and the Communists, and between the Communists themselves. There are the symptoms here of complete political disintegration.

The Burmese authorities went to immense pains to assure the safety of our party, and I have no doubt were relieved to see us leave safe and sound from Mingaladon. The most anxious time for the police and military guards must have been yesterday afternoon's drive through the city, but there was no hint of hostile demonstration. On the contrary, groups of friendly citizens stood, stared and often smiled in cheerful recognition; for Mountbatten is probably better known to many of them than their new rulers—and he is known as a friend.

Back in Calcutta again the frenzied round was resumed. There was the visit to the Industrial Exhibition, which was the scrum I had anticipated it would be. Then, after some two hours allotted to Mountbatten for what the official engagement list describes as " homework ", we jostled our way through a reception given by the Calcutta Club. Between this function and dinner I was present at All India Radio for Lady Mountbatten to record a farewell broadcast to the people of West Bengal. Quite a lot of administrative detail had gone into the timing of this operation, but we had not taken sufficient account of Calcutta's weather.

At about tea-time a storm of incredible severity broke over the city. There was darkness and high wind, simultaneous thunder and lightning, and hailstones the size of shillings, which broke the glass of several windows in Government House. The servants were unable to close the shutters in the long corridors in time to keep the deluge from flooding the marble floors. Roads were soon like Venetian water-ways. We learnt afterwards that there had been a downpour of some two and a half inches in little more than half an hour. Lady Mountbatten's car reached All India Radio studios without flooding its engines, but some of the radio technicians were marooned in various parts of the city, and only by some rapid improvisation on the part of the Director was it possible for Lady Mountbatten to complete her broadcast, which she did with her accustomed flair. She has a most persuasive radio personality.

I just managed to get to the United Services Club in time for the annual dinner of the Mining, Geological and Metallurgical Institute of India, and sat on a very hard chair through very lengthy proceedings. There was one memorable moment, however, provided by an impromptu tribute to Mountbatten from C. R. As there was apparently no Press representative present to catch his words, I hurriedly noted them down on the back of my menu card.

He began by saying that he did not wish to emphasise Mountbatten's services to India, to which ample testimony had already been given, but to stress rather his services to Britain. Churchill might feel that what Hastings and Clive had won, Mountbatten had thrown away. But that was true only in a superficial sense. The deeper reality was that for the all-round suspicion, bitterness and ill-will that prevailed during the war years, Mountbatten had succeeded in substituting unqualified good-will between India and Britain. " Has not Lord Mountbatten then done greater service to Britain than Hastings and Clive? For this is the greatest service of all. In times to come it will not be Empires that count. It is good-will that counts. Therefore I say that he has done more for Britain than anyone else."

The example of brevity set by Mountbatten, who spoke for little more than three minutes, and by C. R. himself, was not, unfortunately, followed by all the other speakers. The West Bengal Minister of Commerce rattled through a tightly packed bundle of notes for nearly three-quarters of an hour. There seemed no reason why he should ever end, until suddenly, almost in the middle of a sentence, he made a dramatic pause and announced, " I have good news for you, I have finished "— at once sitting down, to the warmest applause of the evening !

GOVERNMENT HOUSE, CALCUTTA, *Sunday, 14th March, 1948*

Once more the Mountbattens leave by early light, this time for Assam. I would very much have liked to be with them and to have met the Hydaris again, by now well-established in Government House, Shillong, but I am staying behind for my talks with Calcutta editors. The only other Government House guest is Rauf, the Indian Ambassador to Burma. At dinner to-night we discussed the course of the trial in Rangoon of the Burmese leader, U Saw, who has been accused of plotting the murder of the eight leaders. The actual assassins have not been apprehended, but it appears that the circumstantial evidence against U Saw is quite strong. C. R. raised the question of the use of force in international affairs, and in particular of atomic power. With his gentle guile, he drew me on to express extremely rash personal opinions on world strategic problems. He felt that the atomic bomb was likely in the long run to defeat the very strategic purposes which it was intended by its users to serve.

I am deeply impressed by C. R. He has immense moral authority, which is exerted without any outward gesture. There is no raising of the voice or haughtiness of manner. He has the true strength of the humble in heart. He is, I suppose, one of the oldest of Gandhi's campaigning disciples, and there is also a family link, for Gandhi's son Devadas is married to a daughter of C. R. Only a man of C. R.'s powerful character and deep conviction could have dared to resist Gandhi's will in 1942 by advocating the acceptance of the Cripps Plan, and even promoting his own partition formula at that moment of inflated expectation. He retired, of course, into the wilderness, yet never wholly lost his influence.

It was Gandhi who performed the " miracle " of Calcutta last September, but it is C. R. who, as Governor, has consolidated the communal good-will which Gandhi engendered. The minorities here have looked on him for fairness and friendship, and he has not failed them. To place a

Madrassi Liberal to preside over Bengal's fanatical and factious politics was a calculated risk. His popularity to-day is good to see, and the communal quiet in this seething, over-populated, hunger-ridden and revolutionary city is in no small measure a reflection of his benign authority.

I went in to see him this morning, and said that as far as I could tell I alone had taken any record of his tribute to Mountbatten at last night's dinner. I told him I would like to release the text of what he had said to the Press. He agreed, adding in characteristic fashion that he hoped particularly that I would send the account to London, where he liked to think it would do Mountbatten good as coming from an Indian.

GOVERNMENT HOUSE, CALCUTTA, *Tuesday, 16th March, 1948*

I re-joined the Mountbattens' party at Dum Dum, where the switch was made from Governor-General's Dakota to Governor-General's York for the return flight to Delhi. The Assam visit was, it seems, a great success, with rather more " organised leisure " than in Orissa or Rangoon. Turner and Desfor have come back enthusiastic about the tribal dancing, which they found to be highly photogenic.

For myself the past two days in Calcutta have been wholly delightful. Before I left, C. R. presented me with signed copies of his translations for the lay reader of the great Hindu scriptures, the Bhagavad Gita and Upanishads, writing on the fly-leaf of the latter, " In spite of our obvious failings, I suppose our minds and morals bear some impress of the holy books held in reverence in India for some few millennia. No one can understand the people of India unless one goes through these scriptures sympathetically." All that I have seen of him on this visit only goes to confirm my belief that he would be the ideal, even if somewhat unwilling, successor to Mountbatten as India's first Indian Governor-General.

In this connection Patel for some while now has been urging Mountbatten with remarkable vehemence and insistence to extend his term beyond April in the interests of the people of India, and would like him to stay for the regulation five years. Mountbatten has regretfully refused to consider this; but when Nehru at the beginning of this month asked him, on behalf of his Government, to stay on for at least another year or even a few more months he finally decided to make the gesture of extending his time from April to June 1948, this having been the date announced in London for his departure when the original schedule for the transfer of power was set and published.

CHAPTER TWENTY-FIVE

DEFINITION AND DETECTION

GOVERNMENT HOUSE, NEW DELHI, *Friday, 19th March, 1948*

ONCE MORE WE are back in harness in Delhi. To-day there has been the first meeting between Liaquat and Nehru for two months. Mountbatten has had some difficulty in bringing them together under the ægis of the Joint Defence Council. They have decided that this should be its last formal session. It was in any case due to close down on the 1st April, but Mountbatten had in mind to continue it in its existing form (under his chairmanship until he left, and then successively under the Prime Minister of the Dominion in which it met) for a further year, with a view to the widening of its function in due course to cover financial and economic questions, communications and external affairs. Although this concept did not commend itself to either side, the two Prime Ministers recognised the value of the Joint Defence Council as a pretext and cover for regular personal contact, and Mountbatten had no difficulty in getting them to agree that they should continue to meet at approximately monthly intervals to discuss matters of common interest and concern.

Not the least remarkable feature of the past six months of bitterness and frustration has been the life-line of sanity thrown out and grasped by both Nehru and Liaquat. One always feels that if matters could be left to these two, and the pressures and stresses to which they are both subjected removed, a firm settlement of all outstanding differences would soon be signed, sealed and delivered.

During this particular discussion, while there was amicable agreement on a number of secondary problems, no mention whatever was made of Kashmir. This was not for lack of background developments. The Chinese delegate, Dr. Tsiang—the present chairman of the Security Council—has on his own initiative put forward proposals which are at last basically satisfactory to India. But unfortunately Dr. Tsiang has not waited to gain wider sponsorship in the Security Council for his plan, with the result that it is far more likely to provoke bitterness and narrow the already slender margin of negotiation and good-will. Something is seriously wrong with the procedures of Lake Success. Oh, for a return to some " sinister secret diplomacy " to counteract the effect of these " public disagreements publicly arrived at "!

The new Indian delegation has, I am glad to say, been reinforced by B. L. Sharma, who is to cover the sadly neglected Public Relations side of their efforts. He was only asked at the last minute, and hardly had time to pack his bag. I managed, however, to send him a number of personal introductions, and am confident that he will do well. Sheikh Abdullah has not rejoined the party. His particular brand of self-assertive oratory bludgeoned the United Nations delegates and the American public without persuading them. He generated more heat than light.

Perhaps the most disquieting, though far from unexpected development in the propaganda campaign over Kashmir at the United Nations, has been the attempt by Zaffrullah Khan to offset India's complaint by widening the area of grievance on Pakistan's behalf and in the process to indulge in what the Americans call "character assassination". He has now introduced Mountbatten's name at a moment when it is impossible on constitutional grounds for Mountbatten himself to make a public reply.

We have had full staff discussions of the problem, and Mountbatten has wisely decided to ensure that his answer to the allegations, together with the relevant facts, should be placed on the records of the Joint Defence Council before it is disbanded, so that it should be brought to the notice of both the Pakistan and Indian Governments, and that the British Government should be fully briefed, in so far as the attacks on himself as Viceroy would almost certainly implicate them as well.

Zaffrullah's two main charges were that, as Viceroy, Mountbatten knew of a Sikh plan from the beginning of July, and that knowing it, he failed to take effective action in the form of arresting the leaders and crushing the trouble makers despite previous assurances that he would.

Mountbatten's memorandum makes it clear that while no one in the higher spheres of Government was under any misapprehension about the scale of the Sikh problem and the urgency of solving it, neither he nor anyone else was aware of any specific Sikh master plan. There was, indeed, no hint of such a plan prior to the meeting with the British Intelligence officer on the 5th August, nor did the meeting itself provide conclusive proof of the plan's scale or "operational" significance.* Mountbatten takes his stand on a letter of admirable lucidity, dated 9th August from Jenkins, which forwarded the unanimous view of all three Punjab Governors—Jenkins himself and the two successor Governors-designate—that nothing more should be done before actual transfer of power than to make plans for the Sikh leader's arrest, which could be implemented quickly on either side of the boundary as required.

It is interesting to note from this source that Mudie, the Governor-elect of the West Punjab and as such the principal spokesman for Pakistan's interest, urged that unless the West Punjab could be quite certain of the ultimate attitude of the East Punjab on the matter, the confinement of the Sikh leaders not on criminal charges, but under Jenkins' emergency powers, might be most embarrassing. It was not clear, Mudie added, where the leaders could be confined without causing trouble—Jenkins could hardly send them to what would in a few days be a part of Pakistan; on the other hand, if they were left in the East Punjab they would be a centre of agitation.

A further Pakistani charge has been brought into the open with the allegation that the Boundary Commission award was changed to the

---

* See p. 152 for reference to Mountbatten's acceptance of the risk of driving in state with Jinnah on 14th August, following the threat of an attempt on Jinnah's life during this State drive.

disadvantage of Pakistan as a result of improper pressure from Viceroy's House just before publication. Here the evidence was a letter dated 8th August sent by Abell to Jenkins stating that the intention was for the Boundary Commission Award to be presented on the 11th, and containing an outline of the envisaged Award which showed the *tehsils* (sub-districts) of Ferozepore and Zira as going to Pakistan.

Abell was, in fact, shown a strictly provisional forecast by Radcliffe's secretary, which he sent to Jenkins, who sometime before had asked that if any sort of advance information could be given him, it should be provided so as to enable him to dispose police and troops to the best advantage. This forecast proved ultimately to be wrong to the extent of two *tehsils* and two days. There is, in fact, no more nor less to it than that.

The whole baseless proposition is, of course, rendered plausible by presenting the bald evidence of Abell's letter, but if there was any reason for Jenkins to have been secretive about its contents at the time, would he have been so crazy as to leave it for his successor at Lahore? Or, indeed, if Mudie had thought that his British colleagues had been playing a dishonourable game, is it conceivable that he would have let this letter leave his possession? Quite apart from the challenge to Mountbatten's honour, who would dare to accuse a man of Radcliffe's legal integrity and personal reputation of having submitted to external pressure from any quarter before reaching a judicial decision?

NEW DELHI, *Sunday, 21st March, 1948*

The Indian and Pakistan Press have reacted to the Chinese Plan along expected lines. The *Hindustan Times* regards it as "the first serious attempt to solve the dispute on a reasonable and practicable basis", adding that "the main provisions are such as can and should be accepted by self-respecting and peace-loving nations". *Dawn*, on the other hand, ventures to hope that "the Security Council will show the same sense of realism as it did before and in that light view the Chinese attempt at 'compromise' by granting one party almost everything and the other party nothing". The Pakistan argument is still that the status of the administration must be decided after, and not before, a free and unrestrained verdict of the Kashmir people.

The only new element in this depressing debate is a suggestion in the *Hindustan Times* yesterday—and in view of Devadas Gandhi's and G. D. Birla's connections it is always advisable to pay some attention to *ballons d'essai* released from this quarter. Discussing terms of reference open to the Kashmiris in a plebiscite, the paper states, "We think it would be wrong and unjust to call upon them to vote only for accession with either Dominion. They should be given a free choice to accede to either or to be independent."

I have just seen a draft report by Lady Mountbatten of the activities of the United Council of Relief and Welfare from its inception in August up to the end of February. It records an inspiring achievement built up in three distinct phases of effort. First there was the emergency life-saving of the refugees and the provision of safe transit camps. This led soon into the second phase of organising and equipping camps where an increasing number of refugees could recover their strength before re-settlement. The third phase, now in hand, finds the United Council tackling the long-term problem of vocational training and re-settlement. The vast welfare task of recovery of abducted women, children and orphans has also come under the United Council's wing. Forcible conversions are one of the ugliest manifestations of the communal madness. A regular search service has been set up. Lady Mountbatten has rightly stressed the scale of the challenge confronting the Council almost over-night. In a matter of a few weeks five to six million refugees have been moving from India to Pakistan, while some five and a quarter million have come from the reverse direction. Probably the only comparable cataclysm is that facing U.N.R.R.A. in Europe, but, as she justly points out, U.N.R.R.A. have been able to plan their operation over years in their struggle to meet the demands of the European refugee problem.

The best tribute to Lady Mountbatten's leadership of the United Council is through the bare statistics of her activities on its behalf. Since her visit to the Punjab at the end of August she had made ten more major tours up to the end of January, carrying out seventy inspections of individual refugee camps and fifty tours of hospitals. All this is on top of the Mountbattens' general tour schedule, in which they are still trying desperately to complete a five-year Viceregal progress in nine months. During a further ten tours to States and Provinces she has paid sixty-six visits to hospitals, social-welfare centres, colleges, training establishments, etc. It is a prodigious effort of body and spirit, and has captured the imagination of India as only the propaganda of deeds can do.

GOVERNMENT HOUSE, NEW DELHI, *Tuesday, 23rd March, 1948*

Mountbatten continues to take a close interest in the whole question of India's future relations with the Commonwealth, and has asked us to prepare a short situation report. There is not, of course, much initiative that he can take. His views are known both here and in London. Decision as to India's role and title now rests with those who frame and approve the Indian constitution. But clearly we are approaching a climactic moment in the history of Commonwealth relations when it becomes necessary to re-define a concept so largely indefinable. I recall from my school days the dictum of the wise historian that " to define the faith is to limit the faithful ". The Commonwealth has certainly prospered to date on an instinctive understanding of this principle.

I have just been reading a most interesting article in the January issue of *International Affairs* * on " The implications of Eire's relationship with the British Commonwealth of Nations ". It is by Nicholas Mansergh,†

* Quarterly publication of the Royal Institute of International Affairs.

† Abe Bailey Professor of Commonwealth Relations at the Royal Institute of International Affairs.

who, incidentally, visited India—and Viceroy's House—last summer. In this paper he advocates the doctrine of " external association " as being the most promising formula for the future development of the Commonwealth and as being applicable both to Eire and India.

External association involves no formal constitutional link, and, as envisaged by de Valera, under it Commonwealth citizenship would be discarded and citizenship of reciprocal rights substituted. Eire's position in the Commonwealth, Mansergh points out, has only been maintained so far because, while de Valera has steadily pursued the doctrine of external association, the rest of the Commonwealth has no less steadily refused to take cognisance of his actions. Now, with only one more link remaining to be broken, and Eire's declared intention being to break it, the agreement to differ can no longer be sustained.

In a note to Vernon about the Staff paper, I have written : " To my mind the key question is whether or not the concept of the Commonwealth is to be widened beyond the terms envisaged in the Statute of Westminster. My personal view is that the Indian decision, when it is reached, will probably be politically ambiguous, as the Irish one was, and that it will then be up to the other members to decide whether the terms of membership need to be altered to include India or are wide enough as they stand. Before preparing any paper on the subject I think we would be well advised to check up with B. N. Rau * whether there is any expectation that some new over-all concept of Commonwealth will be elaborated *pari passu* with India's own changed position. I saw Rau at the Nepalese party the other evening, and said we would appreciate an early talk with him.

" Given adjustments, it would not necessarily follow that the Indian Head of State would need to be nominated by the Crown for the Commonwealth link to be maintained. Some formula for confirming the appointment of an elected President might perhaps be evolved which would enable the draft constitution to go through unamended. Citizenship may well prove to be the key test, and the issue would be not the supersession of India's Commonwealth status by some form of citizenship, but common citizenship comprising Commonwealth status."

I have just received a letter from B. L. Sharma in New York which bears out my contention that India's failure at the United Nations has been in no small measure due to defective Public Relations. He writes, " There is little doubt that our case has not been understood in the States," and considers that one of the reasons for this lack of understanding is the very low measure of interest in Kashmir, which to the Americans is " not even a minor irritation, their interest being devoted almost exclusively to major international issues such as Palestine, Western Europe, Czechoslovakia, Russia and Korea ". But he has discovered also that there is much actual and potential good-will for India. He does not think there has been a deliberate attempt to misinterpret India's case.

★ Sir Benegal Rau, later the Chief Indian Delegate to the United Nations, was the Senior Civil Servant primarily responsible for the drafting and preparation of the Indian Constitution.

" From the talks I have had so far I gathered the impression that the basic facts about the Kashmir situation have not been explained."

Turning to the long-term Public Relations task, he makes what I believe is a vital point of policy which so many Government departments and large-scale institutions overlook, to their own and the general cost in the publicity field. " What has struck me most is the urgent need for meeting individual requirements rather than preparing omnibus services on the principle of take it or leave it. Partly because of financial limitations, and partly perhaps due to the irresistible fascination of an easy solution, our services have been framed with a view to meeting the general requirements of various countries of the world. I am convinced that this is a wrong policy." I too am convinced that this appreciation goes near to the heart of the Public Relations matter.

GOVERNMENT HOUSE, NEW DELHI, *Wednesday, 7th April, 1948*

The past fortnight has been comparatively serene at Government House. The Mountbattens have been most of the time on tour, having been away from Delhi on four occasions since the 20th March. They have visited Kapurthala; at last completed the twice-postponed tour of Travancore and Cochin in the far south; spent twenty-four hours at Udaipur, with its artificial lakes and island palace, and finally have just returned to-day from a week-end's rest at Mashobra.

There have been moments of light relief, it seems, on tour, as when the Maharaja of Kapurthala, now seventy-six years old—the last seventy-one of which he has been on the *gadi*—referred to the Mountbattens during his speech of welcome as " Lord and Lady Willingdon " !

Coherent conversation with the Maharaja of Cochin, who was in a very feeble condition, proved difficult, as the only political question he put to Mountbatten was to ask him whether he had ever met Stalin. Otherwise his sole topic of conversation was his family, which numbers in all four hundred and sixty-one members. In Travancore and Cochin the dynastic system is on a matriarchal basis, the sons of all the female members of the ruling family succeeding in strict rotation according to age. It is thus a matter of chance if the ruler of the day is the brother or third cousin twice removed of his predecessor. In a family the size of the Cochin dynasty the system inevitably means that a series of very old gentlemen follow each other on the throne in rapid succession.

Mountbatten has come back to meet an immediate crisis over Hyderabad. On our return from Burma there was a letter awaiting him from the Nizam. As he was due to leave Delhi again, and wished in any case to phase out of the controversy, acting in his constitutional capacity " on advice ", he asked the Ministry of States to reply on his behalf, and advised the Nizam accordingly. This States Ministry letter, drafted originally by V. P., heated up by Patel and cooled down by Nehru, was not seen by Mountbatten until after its dispatch, when it was still very stiff and threatening in tone. It openly accused the Nizam's Government of breaches of the Standstill Agreement, and called upon it to fulfil its obligations and ban the Ittehad and Razakars.

Monckton, who had previously indicated that he would be washing his hands of the whole matter, has now returned to the scene, reaching Hyderabad on the 28th March. The effect upon him of the States Ministry letter and the general situation which he has found in the State has been profound. Usually calm and affable, he arrived in Delhi last night in a mood to do battle with all comers, the Governor-General included. He brought back with him the Nizam's reply, a skilfully drafted document which scores several points off the Indian *démarche* and has all the hallmarks of his own inspiration. The opening paragraph of the letter speaks of information reaching the Nizam which has given him reason to regard the letter from the States Ministry as being in the nature of an ultimatum, and a prelude to an open breach of friendly relations. He therefore makes " a final appeal " to Mountbatten to exercise his good offices and prevent such a contingency.

As the result of a very frank talk to-day based upon their firm friendship and deep understanding of each other's mind and motive, Mountbatten has succeeded in reassuring Monckton that the Government of India envisage no ultimatum and that they are no party to blockade. Nehru came along shortly afterwards to confirm this in person.

Another large rock has been thrown into the pool, however, with the publication to-day in a number of Indian papers, including the *Hindustan Times*, of a bloodthirsty speech alleged to have been delivered on the 31st March by the fanatical Ittehad leader, Kasim Razvi, at the inauguration of " Hyderabad weapons week ". As reported, Razvi urges the Moslems of Hyderabad not to sheathe their swords until their objective of Islam's supremacy has been achieved. One of the most sinister phrases quoted is " our Moslem brothers in the Indian Union will be our fifth columnists ". Language of this nature, of course, is designed to induce communal strife throughout the whole of south India, which has so far, by a merciful dispensation, remained immune from the deadly passions of the north.

GOVERNMENT HOUSE, NEW DELHI, *Sunday, 11th April, 1948*

The Razvi plot thickens. Monckton left yesterday for Hyderabad not only convinced of the need for the Nizam to introduce responsible and representative government at an early date, but also firmly intending to proffer the advice that he should order the early arrest of Razvi. But to-day a telegram arrived from Monckton advising Mountbatten that the Hyderabad Government is satisfied that the alleged " Jehad " speech of 31st March was never in fact delivered, and that accordingly it looks like a calculated attempt to prevent the resumption of friendly relations.

Mountbatten called me in at once, asking me as a matter of urgency to find out the available facts. So I have in effect donned my deer-stalker hat, and am now absorbed in solving " the mystery of the Razvi oration ". It will need all Sherlock Holmes' powers of deduction if I am to sift my way through the contradictory but inconclusive evidence surrounding this episode; as it is, I share Dr. Watson's bewilderment. The first strange feature, of course, is the extraordinary delay of a week between the publication of the address in the Indian Press, much of it in direct speech, with references to the audience's enthusiastic interjections, and its alleged delivery on the 31st March.

Two days ago, in the Legislative Assembly, Nehru, in describing the speech as a direct incitement to violence and murder, spoke of it also as " one of the many inflammatory speeches of Mr. Razvi ". Yesterday, in confirmation of this, the *Hindustan Times* and other papers duly quoted from a carefully chosen list of similar utterances by Razvi, some of which I had not seen before, but all of which are accounted for as having been made from September onwards. Now, under an authoritative Associated Press of India dateline, Razvi seems to have perpetrated an even more grotesque verbal aggression than the one I am trying to track down. For now he is reported as demanding nothing less than the return of ceded territory in Madras and asserting, with the bravura of a Moghul Emperor, " The day is not far off when the waves of the Bay of Bengal will be washing the feet of our sovereign "

GOVERNMENT HOUSE, NEW DELHI, *Friday, 16th April, 1948*

Part of Mir Laik Ali's and Razvi's denial is that there was neither a rally nor a weapons week on the 31st March at which the alleged speech could have been made, but this is not correct. Eric Britter ★ was there, and I have now checked on the facts as far as he knows them. He tells me that he was present at a parade between eight and ten on the morning of the 31st, and that Razvi took the salute at a gathering of between four and five hundred Razakars, but that there was definitely no speech made while he was there. He heard the parade being dismissed, and stayed on for some twenty minutes afterwards, returning to a house with a veranda room, where about twenty or thirty other people were also present. Tea and cakes were handed round, and the conversation was confined to small talk. Britter adds that Razvi came to the door with him and saw him off, but he is naturally in no position to say whether Razvi held any meeting afterwards. So the element of mystery remains.

What information I have been able to collect from the various sources suggests that Razvi's meetings, public and private, are regularly attended by agents both of Munshi and the Nizam. No doubt, to complete the circle of hide and seek, the Nizam's and Munshi's sayings are being reported back by agents of Razvi. The reality of these shadowy figures is anyone's guess, but I am ready to believe that Razvi is providing them with ample source material and is engaged on a political campaign which, if it succeeds, can only end in the bloodshed it constantly invokes and in a final rupture between India and Hyderabad.

Britter, while certainly holding no brief for Razvi, considers that India is in danger of unduly forcing the pace in its Hyderabad policy. He believes that time is needed, by which he means freedom from Congress or Communist pressure for some five years, during which the transitions first to a Government of communal parity and then to one of Hindu majority rule can be effected. Under these conditions he considers

★ Delhi correspondent of *The Times*.

that the forces of moderation and reform would prevail, but that present impatience must induce the violent answer. The obverse to this image of peaceful change is that the record of the Nizam over the past quarter of a century encourages the belief that, if left to his own devices and in possession of a sovereignty which he never enjoyed under the paramount power, he will continue to reinforce the prerogatives of himself and of the communal oligarchies around him.

My sense of the situation is that he is playing for time, hoping thereby to avoid concessions, and that the dominant need is to bring home to him by all the resources of persuasion that the transfer of power is a reality, that the time for finesse is already over, and that his State's and his own highest interest lie in a quick settlement.

At the present moment Mountbatten is closely engaged in meetings to hammer out a formula which will break the dangerous deadlock. Monckton returned here on Wednesday, and Mir Laik Ali arrived yesterday. To-day, in the peaceful seclusion of the Government House swimming-pool grounds, Mir Laik Ali had lunch with Mountbatten alone. They were two hours together in all, and Mountbatten feels that he has at last begun to make some impression upon Mir Laik Ali's obstinate personality and devious attitude to the problem. He is still convinced, however, that he is by no means the appropriate Prime Minister for the difficult diplomacy ahead. His mulishness in negotiation cannot fail, if persisted in much longer, to cause a final breakdown.

This is perhaps the decisive moment. Patel is now sufficiently recovered to have a hand in official negotiations, which means that all the principals, apart from the Nizam himself, are now directly engaged—Mountbatten serving as a one-man " good offices commission ".

GOVERNMENT HOUSE, NEW DELHI, *Saturday, 17th April, 1948*

After three days of intense discussion, with Mountbatten seeing Nehru, V. P. and Monckton each morning to achieve an agreed line of action before the official meetings with Mir Laik Ali, a four-point programme has in principle been accepted. It was taken up by V. P. to Patel in Mussoori, where he is now recuperating, and, to Mountbatten's surprise and relief, Patel at last withdrew his veto on anything other than full accession, giving the plan his vital support.

The four points calling for the Nizam's agreement are :—

(1) Immediate steps to bring Razvi under control, beginning with a ban on Razakar processions, public demonstrations, meetings and speeches.

(2) The release of the imprisoned States Congress members, beginning at once with the leaders.

(3) Genuine and immediate reconstruction of the existing Government to make it representative of both Communities.

(4) The early introduction of responsible Government and the formation of a Constituent Assembly by the end of the year.

Monckton has told Mountbatten that he proposes to advise the Nizam to confirm his acceptance of these points by changing his Prime Minister. He appreciates that Mir Laik Ali is thoroughly distrusted here, and that no single move would create more confidence in the Nizam's intentions than the appointment of a man of the calibre of Zain Yar Jung, Hyderabad's urbane and able Agent-General in Delhi. His loyalty to the Nizam is not in doubt, but neither is his underlying realism. He has made a considerable impression on the Government, and in particular on V. P.

GOVERNMENT HOUSE, NEW DELHI, *Sunday, 18th April, 1948*

Monckton has left with Mir Laik Ali for Hyderabad. To-day's arriving guests at Government House are the Maharaja and Maharanee of Kashmir, for a stay of four days. We have been almost as closely engaged in finding a formula to cover his visit as in settling the Hyderabad dispute.

The original request to Mountbatten to invite the Maharaja came from Patel, but Mountbatten, feeling that such an invitation was liable to be widely misinterpreted, particularly outside India, replied that he felt Patel should send the necessary letter of invitation mentioning that the Governor-General would of course be glad to put him up as a Government guest. This was done, but the Maharaja said he would not come at all unless the Mountbattens personally invited him to stay. Mountbatten has conceded the point, but I have in reserve a communiqué which will make it clear that he is coming to see Patel. Personally I feel the visit will not cause much speculation and there will be no need to release it. The tide of events has already flowed far past the Maharaja.

GOVERNMENT HOUSE, NEW DELHI, *Monday, 19th April, 1948*

Last week a majority of the members of the Security Council, having exhausted the possibilities of producing any plan fully acceptable to both sides, tabled an agreed resolution making various recommendations—but nothing more—to the two Governments. Nehru's reaction was at first violently adverse. He wrote to Mountbatten yesterday calling the resolution something entirely different from the original Chinese resolution of Dr. Tsiang and arguing that it rejected every contention put forward by the Indian delegate. The only course now open to the Indian Government, he added ominously, was to oppose it completely. Mountbatten replied that in his opinion few if any of the amendments in the new resolution were fundamental. Vernon was instructed to write out the differences in the form of a table which was duly prepared in time for Mountbatten's meeting with Nehru to-day.

At the outset, it seems, Nehru was fully resolved to issue instructions of general condemnation to Ayyengar at Lake Success, but Mountbatten, with his overwhelming persistence and flair for argument in detail, finally prevailed on Nehru to break down and localise his objections under four specific headings, three of which on analysis can be seen as expressions of the Government of India's desire not to allow a whittling down of

Sheikh Abdullah's authority. Mountbatten has also been instrumental in securing Nehru's agreement that the proposed plebiscite commission should be allowed to come to India.

I saw Mountbatten immediately afterwards, and he was deeply satisfied with the outcome of the talk, which has clearly caused Nehru to act upon second thoughts and to avoid taking a dangerous decision from a pre-conceived position.

GOVERNMENT HOUSE, NEW DELHI, *Wednesday, 21st April, 1948*

Under the new dispensation Delhi's social life is reverting from sherry—six to eight, to tea—four to six. Patel gave this new fashion a boost by holding court over the tea-cups in the garden of his home at Aurangzeb Road. It was his first social appearance since his serious illness. The Diplomatic Corps, a galaxy of Princes, Cabinet Ministers, Congress leaders, business magnates and editors were there standing around in groups or taking their places at the small tea-tables. Many of them were lining up to say a few words of greeting to the Sardar, who, bolstered and blanketed, reclined on a sofa. He was looking very fragile, as indeed he still is, but the whole occasion served as a gentle reminder that executive authority still flows from him. The Mountbattens spent about a quarter of an hour with him, and he was obviously highly gratified to see them.

To-day's tea-party was at V. P.'s home to about a dozen journalists, Indian and European, to introduce them to His Highness of Kashmir, who looked very ill-at-ease and said very little. Indeed, when questions were asked about his departure from his capital, it was left to the Jam Sahib to give us a homily on his brother-Prince's courage and general devotion to duty. I came away feeling that the whitewash had perhaps been laid on too thickly. The Maharaja, who is a broken man and in a somewhat pathetic plight, has been complaining bitterly over the treatment meted out to him. His home has been commandeered, Cabinet action taken without his being given any advance intimation. He wants to know where the authority lies to protect him from these indignities. Mountbatten has brought the matter up with Patel, who in his turn has promised to discuss it with Nehru.

Mountbatten tells me he had a very interesting post-mortem with the Maharaja yesterday, upbraiding him for not taking the advice he had proffered to him in June to accede one way or the other by the 15th August. At first the Maharaja was inclined to defend his indecision by saying, " Look at the trouble that boiled up when I did accede, and think what would have happened if I had done so earlier." But Mountbatten pointed out that if he had acceded to India on time, Pakistan simply could not have moved, and if to Pakistan, India would not have done so. Patel's pledge on this had been categorical.

CHAPTER TWENTY-SIX

STALEMATE

GOVERNMENT HOUSE, NEW DELHI, *Saturday, 24th April, 1948*

MONCKTON LEFT FOR London on the 19th, and wrote to Mount-batten from Karachi reporting on the results of his conversations with the Nizam. He warned that of the four points agreed to in Delhi, the one most likely to cause trouble in Hyderabad and to stand in the way of a quick settlement was the problem of providing machinery for the introduction of responsible government. The formation of a Constituent Assembly on a simple population basis giving the Hindus the overwhelming majority within a week would simply not be feasible for the Nizam. Monckton stressed, however, the need for the Nizam to insist upon a reconstruction of his Government to make it more genuinely representative of all shades of communal opinion. The Nizam had wanted Monckton to stay, but he refused to do so, on the grounds that he was sure he could not remain on in the State without com-promising himself unless and until a new Government had taken over.

The expectation has been that the Nizam would implement the four-point programme through one of his decrees or *firmans*. The *firman* was duly issued yesterday, and the expectation duly disappointed. Nearly all the psychological value of its practical concessions to the need for implementing the four points has been wantonly thrown away in a phrase.

After an expression of hope that " those political parties which are not represented in the present Interim Government in Hyderabad will join and take a proper share in shouldering the responsibility of the Govern-ment ", the *firman*, with the dialectic of the death-wish, continues, " I have felt apprehensive that mere imitation of a form of Government elsewhere might poison the atmosphere of our country in the same way as it is doing in other places ". The readiness to lose so much in order to score so little, baffles the best mediating intentions.

GOVERNMENT HOUSE, NEW DELHI, *Wednesday, 28th April, 1948*

Much of the Indian political comment in the Press and elsewhere on Kashmir has accepted as a commonplace that the British delegation to the United Nations has sinister designs which include a permanent readiness to betray the Indian cause in the interest of power politics. It is therefore refreshing to find the ever-resourceful *Dawn* redressing the balance with the following *bon bouche*. " Panicky Britons thought India might become friendlier to Moscow. It is apparent that in these circumstances once again a deal was struck between Britain and India and once again Britain decided to betray justice and the Mussulmans. With such betrayals British Imperial history is too shamefully crowded already as Muslims all over the world know."

Mountbatten is then accused, in passing, of having " deliberately gerrymandered the partition to put every conceivable handicap in Pakistan's way and to leave her crippled from birth ", of having created the Kashmir problem by rigging the Punjab Boundary Award so that " India was provided with the argument as well as the advantages of an artificial contiguity with Kashmir ". This design was, of course, put into effect " with the help of Sir Cyril Radcliffe ", and so it goes on.

It is hard to conceive within the confines of a single paragraph false-hoods suggested or truth suppressed on such a lavish scale about Mount-batten's part in these matters. It is hate propaganda of ripe vintage. Dr. Goebbels himself would have nodded his head in approval. Mount-batten is inclined to dismiss attacks of this nature as representing no more than the small change of political controversy, the outpourings of those who have not yet succeeded in adapting their minds to the change from irresponsibility to power. I am not so sanguine, and would like to see the lie direct given at once to the makers of such myths. The more far-fetched and impudent the allegation the greater the following among the credulous and prejudiced who provide the cannon-fodder of fanaticism. Truth, if it is to prevail in public life, must be louder than the still small voice.

Fay and I dined to-night amid fairy-lights on the lawn of the Delhi Gymkhana Club. Our host was Shri Krishna,* who had collected an interesting party. The principal guest was Dr. Ambedkar, the Minister of Law, the leader of the Untouchables, and a colourful personality in Indian politics over the past twenty years. He is now one of the principal figures associated with the preparation of India's new Constitution, which finally removes the stigma of untouchability from the Statute book. As part of his emancipation, Ambedkar, himself an untouchable, has only recently married a lady doctor who is a Brahmin. The custom of centuries cannot be uprooted overnight, and the event has caused quite a stir. His wife was with him this evening, but, as is the custom with so many Indian ladies on social occasions, had little to say.

Ambedkar himself was in expansive vein, and gave us a revealing analysis of some of the features of the new Constitution. He pointed out, for instance, that the special powers reserved to the judiciary under its provisions were greater than those enjoyed by the United States Supreme Court. As evidence of the enduring quality of the 1935 Act, he said that some two hundred and fifty of its clauses had been embodied as they stood into the new Constitution.

We had a discussion on Cabinet government. Ambedkar referred to the complaint that the present system was working too slowly in India. He thought that where a matter of policy affecting two departments was involved the issue should at once be settled as between the Ministers concerned. He commended the Geddes proposals and the system of non-departmental Cabinet chiefs with groups of departmental deputies under them. He said he was very sorry Mountbatten was leaving before

* Shri Krishna, well-known Delhi political correspondent.

the Constitution was finally passed. The Commonwealth issue, he felt, was likely to be decided outside the Constituent Assembly.

GOVERNMENT HOUSE, NEW DELHI, *Friday, 30th April, 1948*

Tension over Hyderabad is steadily mounting. Border incidents abound, further to inflame the passion of those whose heads are already too hot.   The report of Nehru's Bombay speech to the All India Congress Committee last Saturday in which he was alleged to have said, " There are two courses now open to Hyderabad—war or accession ", raised the political temperature to boiling point.

Mountbatten, who was on tour when he first saw " Accession or War " headlines the next day, was horrified, and on his return to Delhi he was in touch with Nehru immediately.   Nehru was no less dismayed, and explained that he had been completely misreported, having made no reference either to war or accession.   The error had apparently crept in because his address spoken in Hindustani had been taken down by a Madrassi-speaking stenographer.

It is a sobering thought to realise that millions of Indians are as wholly unintelligible to millions of other Indians as they would be to Greeks or Italians, and that there are at least seven major languages and some two hundred and thirty dialects scattered throughout the sub-continent. The Babel of tongues is certainly no less confusing than among the Europeans themselves.

Nehru proposes to put the speech right at a Press Conference to-morrow, but a week has gone by, and it is an axiom of publicity that a denial or a correction made at once has at the best about one-tenth of the impact of the initial false report.   From the Hyderabad end Mir Laik Ali succeeded in delivering himself of a major oration in the Hyderabad Legislative Assembly without referring to any of the four points at all. This performance has merely had the effect of further whittling away Delhi's belief in the good faith underlying the Nizam's *firman*.

GOVERNMENT HOUSE, NEW DELHI, *Tuesday, 4th May, 1948*

The Hyderabad stalemate has been causing Mountbatten much anxiety. He is anxious both on personal and public grounds to bring the negotiations to a happy ending.   Properly exploited, he believes that the short time—now little more than six weeks—before he hands over the Governor-Generalship to C. R. should serve as an inducement to both sides to iron out their differences.   But it is no mean problem to decide just when and how his influence can be brought to bear with the maximum effect, particularly in Monckton's absence.

Mountbatten's proposal has been to send a last warning letter to the Nizam now, and a draft has been in active preparation, but I have weighed in heavily, urging him not to do this until all other remedies have been tried.   My case is that the letter as drafted in its present form is psychologically the wrong approach.

As I put it in a note to Ronnie, " No doubt it will read well on the record in ten years' time, but the judgement of history will be not only whether the advice was good but also whether it was so presented to the Nizam that in his present mood and situation he would be likely to accept it. A letter of this nature should only be released in the last resort after every other expedient has failed, when it should be lodged as the final friendly plea. H.E.'s greatest gift is undoubtedly direct diplomacy by personal contact. The objections to his visiting Hyderabad are very weighty and will be pressed by the Government without whose authority he cannot now go. My submission therefore is that the primary aim should be to get the Nizam to Delhi with no strings attached to the visit, but simply for the purpose of providing Mountbatten with an opportunity of talking to him as man to man.'

At a meeting at ten o'clock this morning at which V. P., Ronnie, Vernon and myself were present, Mountbatten agreed with my view. V. P. raised the point that the Nizam would probably reply by renewing the invitation for Mountbatten to go to Hyderabad, but he agreed that this difficulty could be overcome on the grounds of Mountbatten's limited time here.

A general talk followed on the Princely situation. The process of the States' integration, which began with the group in Orissa and Bihar and which has been driven forward on Patel's behalf with dynamic energy by V. P. himself, has for the time being at least reached saturation point.

The covenant for the largest union yet created was signed on the 22nd April. It is called the Malwa Union, and comprises the Gwalior-Indore–Malwa group of States, twenty in all, covering an area of forty-seven thousand square miles and involving a population of more than seven million. There has been some delicacy in naming the Rajpramukh or Constitutional head of the Union nominally elected by a Council of Rulers. Gwalior, who is a twenty-one-gun Prince, is to have the position. Even more difficult was the choice of a capital city. Here the compromise is Gwalior for the winter and Indore for the summer capital. Bhopal has reiterated his desire to remain out of the Malwa Union, but has gone quite a long way to make his peace with the Government, and has announced his intention to introduce responsible government in his State.

Only to-day another type of merger takes place. The State of Kutch is to be merged direct with the Government of India. This, I understand, is being done primarily because of Kutch's important strategic position. There are other variations of the pattern. The Rulers in the Deccan States and the Gujerat Rulers—over one hundred of them in all—have both merged under separate agreements with the Bombay province. East Punjab and Madras have entered into similar arrangements with adjoining States. One of the most comprehensive self-supporting mergers has been the formation of the Saurashtra Union of the two hundred and seventeen Kathiawar States. The Rajpramukh here is the Jam Sahib of Nawanagar, who has entered whole-heartedly into this new dispensation and promises to play an increasingly important part in Central politics. These Unions are to be governed through popular ministries.

To-morrow yet another covenant will be signed, this time for the union of the Sikh States. Negotiations here have hinged round the attitude of Patiala. He was entitled to remain out on his own, but without him the other Sikh States could not achieve a viable union. V. P. told us that he has now definitely decided to come in, on the understanding that he and his State are given a position in it commensurate with their relative importance, so he is to be Rajpramukh, and Kapurthala his deputy. This is certainly a great victory for V. P., and should undoubtedly turn the balance of power in Sikh affairs in favour of the Central Government and against the ambitious exponents of Sikhistan, a separate Sikh State carved out of the East Punjab.

Another remarkable development has been the formation of a Union of Rajputana Princes. It began as a merger of the smaller States, but then took more significant shape as a result of Udaipur's decision to join in. When Mountbatten visited Udaipur, His Highness told him that he had decided of his own free will to take this step, as being in the highest interests of his people. The Udaipur dynasty is one of the most august in India, and the Ruler's entry is likely to have a considerable effect on the other major Rajputana States, which, as viable units, have their individual representation in the Constituent Assembly. Of the nineteen States enjoying this initial right, seven have now joined one or other of the Unions.

It is high statesmanship that can cover a revolutionary act in the mantle of traditional form. V. P. was saying this morning that the sins of the father had indeed been visited upon the sons. It was the failure of the old Patiala and Bikaner to accept the 1935 Federal Plan that nearly broke up the whole structure of the Indian State. Only Mountbatten's last-minute sponsorship of accession saved the day, thus enabling the present Patiala and Bikaner to play a vital part in consolidating the new relationship.

Mountbatten freely confessed that he did not foresee, when he negotiated the Instrument of Accession last year, that the extension of subjects would be demanded or granted so soon; but he mentioned an interesting opinion expressed by Nye that the seriousness of the States problem had not been appreciated at all outside India, and was in fact graver in its implications than the problem of dealing with the Congress, Moslem League or Sikh leaders. Nye said that he had practically despaired of any friendly settlement with the Princes, and had visualised trouble of incalculable dimensions after the 15th August. He would not have been surprised if it had taken at least a generation to reach the position achieved by May 1948, and he felt that history would recall this as a most remarkable feat.

Just how much the climate has changed can be seen with the entry of His Highness of Dholpur into the scheme of things. Last August his mood was such that any concept of merger beyond accession would have been wholly unacceptable, but here he is to-day, his Princely status duly acknowledged, Rajpramukh of the United State of Matsya.

Mountbatten also raised at this morning's Staff Meeting the problem of the Defence Committee. Policy is still unrelated to military capability. Mountbatten reminded V. P. that he had agreed to the initial march into

Kashmir as an acceptable military risk, but now the situation was different. As a commander with some experience in logistical problems, he felt that Nehru and Patel were not fully facing up to the military implications of the position. Mountbatten said he was very disappointed that the Defence Committee procedure was not being properly adopted. He only hoped that when he phased out it would be kept up, and begged V. P. to back it.

Before the meeting broke up he recapitulated the revised approach to Hyderabad. He said that my proposal to try first of all to get the Nizam up to Delhi should be regarded as firing the " right barrel ". The " left barrel " of a final appeal and remonstrance he would charge to meet all eventualities, but not fire.

In the afternoon I went round to Hyderabad House, an impressive residence at the far end of Kingsway and the vista. I was shown into a large drawing-room, where most of the blinds were drawn. In the middle distance I could just see large photographs of the two handsome daughters-in-law of the Nizam, who are also the daughter and cousin of the last Caliph, and thus in themselves the symbols of His Exalted Highness's religious and dynastic aspirations. Zain Yar Jung duly appeared with his son, to whom he introduced me, and we all took tea together. He conveyed an impression of suavity and polish without any trace of the fanatical streak. I find it difficult to believe that he can have much in common with the Ittehad clique. Their trust in him and his influence over the Nizam are factors that must no doubt be assessed with some reserve at this time.

I broached the whole question of a possible visit from the Nizam. He felt that His Exalted Highness would only come up if transport was made very easy for him. It was a long journey, and a special air-cooled compartment would be needed. He hated flying, and even the idea of it was utterly repugnant to him. He still drives about Hyderabad in his 1910 Rolls. Bombay suggested itself to Zain as a possible compromise meeting-place. He also felt that Monckton would have to approve and come out again from England to hold the old man's hand. He said finally that he was not wholly unhopeful that the Nizam might agree.

I returned to Government House, where I at once reported the gist of the talk to Mountbatten. He was not in favour of the Bombay suggestion, and anticipated liaison difficulties with the Government of India. He wants a Staff appreciation giving alternative courses of action.

When I went into the study he was immersed in the details of the Mountbatten family tree, which he has been compiling for some years. I am told it is nearly finished, but I doubt whether it ever will be, for it is indeed a dynastic " Domesday-book ", and in so far as he is related to nearly every royal and ruling house in Europe, there would seem to be no end to the possible arrangement of the genealogy. As the time comes for him to phase out he is to be found taking an occasional hour off to pore over this vast labour of love. The project is a further example of his passion for the accurate, detailed and decorative presentation of fact which is an important ingredient in his intellectual make-up. His mind revels in the cross index and the visual aid.

GOVERNMENT HOUSE, NEW DELHI, *Sunday, 9th May, 1948*

After seeing a somewhat tiresome film at the Government House cinema, called *Copacabana*, Vernon told me of talks between Mountbatten, Zain and V. P., and subsequently with Zain and V. P. alone. Zain only got back this evening from Hyderabad. He had carried Mountbatten's letter of invitation and has brought back the Nizam's reply. It merely confirms the counter-invitation which Mountbatten was not wholly surprised to receive in the first instance by telegram on the 6th May. For the purposes of the record, Mountbatten's letter and the Nizam's telegram crossed. In the reply which Zain has just handed in, the Nizam gives as one of the reasons for saying " no " that any such move " is certain to give rise to grave misunderstanding both inside and outside Hyderabad which I am bound to avoid ". Vernon tells me, however, that Mountbatten was bubbling over with optimism, wholly unwilling to admit defeat, and confident that if he could meet the Nizam face to face he could yet pull off an accession agreement.

Zain warned that there is a marked deterioration in the local situation. Some Government supporters have swung over to the Razakars, indeed a " No confidence " vote in Mir Laik Ali was only just averted, and Zain says there are men about now who regard even Razvi as a moderate. V. P. was very calm and sensible, and ready to offer economic concessions as well as access to a port.

Vernon reports, however, that we are getting dangerously near to the point where there will only be two alternatives left—force or the threat of force. I said I felt that the crux of the matter now was to know where the real power lay. What was the exact status of the Nizam? Much would depend on the appreciation he had formed of his own position, both from within and from without. The Nizam himself must not be under-estimated. I went in to see Mountbatten, who thinks that the Nizam is at last really frightened. Apparently when Mir Laik Ali's position as Prime Minister was raised with him, he was not indignant, but at once asked, " Who do they want? "

GOVERNMENT HOUSE, NEW DELHI, *Monday, 10th May, 1948*

As a result of the difficulty experienced in hammering out a satisfactory Staff appreciation for Mountbatten, Vernon and I came to the conclusion that there was insufficient data, particularly as far as the Nizam's position was concerned, for us to put forward any adequate plan of action. Moreover, it seemed to us that the latest exchange of letters had brought us back to the stalemate. There was little likelihood of the Government agreeing to Mountbatten visiting Hyderabad now that the Nizam had shown himself so intransigent about coming to Delhi. The position was further bedevilled in so far as the Indian Press intelligence network was well aware of the attempt to bring him here and of its outcome. The whole episode is, in fact, public property. For Mountbatten to go now would therefore be regarded as wholly unacceptable appeasement.

On the other hand, it seemed to us that if one of his staff were to be sent as a kind of " King's messenger " with a brief and non-committal letter of introduction to the Nizam, it might be possible to establish at least some measure of personal liaison and confidence, and in general help to restore some momentum to this dangerously static situation. We went in to see Mountbatten and developed this thesis. He is warmly in favour of the concept and wishes me to play the role of " King's messenger "! He proposes to take the matter up with Nehru, V. P. and Zain. I am to be at the ready and prepare a draft of the introductory letter.

GOVERNMENT HOUSE, NEW DELHI, *Wednesday, 12th May, 1948*

It is generally agreed that I should visit Hyderabad as soon as possible, with the objects of meeting the Nizam face to face on Mountbatten's behalf, of forming a personal up-to-date impression of the situation and if possible inducing a sufficient sense of urgency in the Nizam and his advisers for them to reopen negotiations and in general make the best use of Mountbatten's last few weeks here. At a Staff Meeting this morning, V. P., who warmly approved my proposed visit, said there was now definite evidence that the Communists and the Razakars were actually combining together, and that this was not being sufficiently stressed. Mountbatten found it difficult to believe that such an alignment could be taking place, but V. P. was insistent, regarding it as indeed the central factor in the situation.

Mountbatten began the meeting by asking after Patel's health. V. P. replied that he was a bit worried about the irregularity of his pulse and lack of sleep. One of his entourage, a doctor, was constantly talking to him about his pulse, which only increased its irregularity.

GOVERNMENT HOUSE, NEW DELHI, *Thursday, 13th May, 1948*

Before the Defence Committee (which as a result of Mountbatten's initiative has at last been called) Mountbatten button-holed Nehru to get him to confirm in my presence what he had said to Mountbatten yesterday—namely, that he welcomed my going to Hyderabad, and that if the Nizam acceded, the Government of India would do all in its power to accord him full physical protection. In my briefing the possibility has not been overlooked that he is no longer master in his own house, and that some smooth and secret Palace revolution has been, or is about to be, put into effect.

After the Defence Committee I saw Nehru again and drove off with him to receive further guidance. He said he wished only to make some general observations with regard to my visit. His philosophy in the matter was that to try to avoid trouble was often the best way of inviting it. It was not possible to go on just watching shooting incidents and other disorders that were taking place daily on the Hyderabad border.

After leaving Nehru I returned at once to Government House, to find V. P. still with Mountbatten. They seemed quite pleased with the Defence Committee, which had been discursive, but had enabled the military and political leaders to form a more sympathetic understanding of each other's viewpoint. Mountbatten professes himself to be optimistic about my mission. It was agreed that I should go completely under the auspices of the Hyderabad Government. At five o'clock I went round to Hyderabad House for a further talk with Zain and his son, Ali Khan. Zain's plea was, " If only the Government of India would not press too hard all would be well ".

GOVERNMENT HOUSE, NEW DELHI, *Friday, 14th May, 1948*

I have had a final run through with Zain. I am to be the personal guest of Mir Laik Ali. No exact time-limit has been set for the trip. It is agreed that I should be free to decide on the spot, but Zain himself hopes to reach Hyderabad before I leave it.

The letter I am conveying to the Nizam expresses disappointment at His Exalted Highness's refusal of the invitation to visit Delhi, and doubt as to whether it will be physically possible, apart from other considerations, for Mountbatten to come to Hyderabad in the limited time now left to him. However, Mountbatten writes, " Before I leave I am most anxious to establish some form of contact with you over and above the formal negotiations and exchange of letters ".

I am then duly introduced as one who has by now served with Mountbatten longer than any other member of his personal staff and who has been throughout intimately acquainted with all the high level developments in his Commands, particularly during this present appointment. " He knows my mind completely and enjoys my fullest confidence." " I may say ", Mountbatten concludes, " that I have been extremely disturbed by reports which have been reaching Delhi with regard both to the Communist and to the communal situation in Hyderabad, and in particular to the effect that these may be having on Your Exalted Highness's own position. I trust therefore that you will not hesitate to let Mr. Campbell-Johnson have your frank estimate of the position from the general and personal point of view. I would not wish him to convey my personal message except to your Exalted Highness alone, for the presence of others would vitiate the personal contact between you and me which I hope he may be able to establish."

So there it is. To-morrow I leave on a mission of unknown dimensions and opportunity. All that is certain is that for the next forty-eight hours or so I shall be completely cut off from my base, as no contact with Mountbatten in Delhi, or rather in Simla, or with the Government of India, will be practicable. It is certainly by far the most difficult and delicate task I have ever been called upon to undertake during six years in Mountbatten's service. However, I have lived long enough in the vicinity of his influence to have caught something of his own buoyant disposition.

CHAPTER TWENTY-SEVEN

MISSION TO THE NIZAM

HYDERABAD, *Saturday, 15th May, 1948*

I LEFT WILLINGDON airfield by a charter line Dakota shortly after breakfast, and after a brief pause at Bhopal arrived at Hyderabad just before lunch. I was met on the airfield by Captain Baig on behalf of Mir Laik Ali, and by no less than three representatives of Munshi's staff. Their presence called for my first diplomatic decision within three minutes of arrival, for they conveyed a pressing invitation to me to call first on Munshi and to dine with him this evening. I indicated that I was the personal guest of Mir Laik Ali and until I knew what plans he had for me I could not make any engagements, although, of course, I would be calling on Mr. Munshi. Munshi, it seems, has returned specially from Bangalore in view of my visit, and has ensured that what began as a confidential anonymous mission will now be covered in a blaze of publicity, for he has advised all the Press of my arrival and his return.

With this initial hurdle cleared, we rode off on the ten-mile drive through Secunderabad and Hyderabad, which are linked cities. The first impression was of cleanliness and quiet. There were not many people to be seen, and those that were, whether in the streets or houses, seemed to be going at a leisurely pace about their lawful business.

On arrival at the Prime Minister's house, " Shah Munzil ", I was at once taken round to see Mir Laik Ali, who was slightly indisposed. He said that he was delighted that I should be his personal guest, and that he had made no special arrangements for dinner for me that evening; therefore he agreed that it would be the best thing for me to accept Munshi's invitation to dine, particularly in view of the fact that he was due to return the following morning to Bangalore. He said that he was arranging for me to meet the leaders of all shades of opinion, and that I was to regard myself as free to go anywhere and see anyone I liked. The main point he made was to stress that there was still no let-up in the economic blockade, and that they were still unable to get chlorine for the water-supply of Hyderabad City. They had ordered a number of buses for service in the city, but these were rotting away in Bombay—their spare parts removed and their upholstery ripped—and very large demurrage charges were mounting up. I said that I was sure that grievances of this nature should not be allowed to fester, and without knowing the full rights or the wrongs of the particular cases he mentioned, I was confident that such matters could be satisfactorily disposed of within the framework of a wider agreement.

After a late lunch I was told that His Exalted Highness would receive me in little over an hour's time—i.e., at 5 p.m. I was duly driven to his official residence, " King Kothi ", as it is called. The Prime Minister had preceded me by some ten minutes, and was there on my arrival. I was shown at once into a modest reception-room cluttered high with Victorian bric-à-brac. I could just discern in the dim light, hanging on the wall, a large portrait of King George V.

Mir Laik Ali stepped forward to introduce me to His Exalted Highness, who was sitting almost invisible on a large settee. I was staggered by his threadbare appearance, and for the instant failed to realise I was in his presence, but I pulled myself together in time to greet him with fitting courtesy. He was dressed most shabbily in what looked like a thin white cotton dressing-gown and white trousers, with caramel-coloured slippers and light brown cotton socks lying loosely about his ankles. He wore a brown fez, which was perched on the back of his head. He is a small man with a pronounced stoop; his mouth is loose and his teeth are in a deplorable condition. His hands shook, and while talking he fidgeted and knocked his knees together in such a way as to give the observer the impression of incipient palsy or St. Vitus' dance. But his whole personality is held together by the intensity of his expression and the vehemence of his high-pitched voice.

I could not ascertain whether the Prime Minister proposed to stay or leave for the interview, but on presenting Mountbatten's letter to the Nizam, which he opened and read slowly, an opportunity clearly presented itself for him to see me alone if he wanted to, but he quite deliberately refused to take it, and Mir Laik Ali stayed stolidly on. Having read the letter, the Nizam turned on me quite fiercely, and said that he was well aware of Lord Mountbatten's limited time and powers out here. " What could he hope to do in a month?" he asked. He said that he trusted that Lord Mountbatten had clearly understood that it was quite impossible for him, the Nizam, to leave Hyderabad, and if Lord Mountbatten was not free to come and see him, well, then (and he gave a gesture of farewell), he was sorry for it, and would say good-bye and God-speed to him.

The Nizam said that as far as his relations with the Government of India were concerned, they had his terms. He acted through his Prime Minister and his Constitutional Adviser, and he had nothing more he could say to any other party, even on a private basis. I said that Lord Mountbatten was naturally deeply concerned to do all in his power to achieve a settlement before he left, but time was short, and it was for His Exalted Highness to consider whether there was any way in which the Governor-General's good offices could be used. He was, I believed, aware of Lord Mountbatten's general approach to the problem, and if there were any points of detail or emphasis that I could fill in, I would be only too happy to do so.

I referred to the special status that Mountbatten had had in effecting the Standstill Agreement. " That is all over now," he replied. I tried tactfully to explain how Mountbatten believed accession or its equivalent was in the Nizam's best interests, but he dismissed the whole subject with a wave of the hand. Laik Ali intervened at this point to say that he would be quite ready to take a plebiscite on the issue if only it could be organised peacefully, but the law-and-order problem involved in carrying it out had compelled him to turn it down, to which the Nizam added, "Quite right, quite right."

I was unable to draw him out on the question of his reaction to the Communist threat in Hyderabad. It was, he said, "a matter of detail which you can discuss with my Prime Minister".

He said that the fate and policy of the other Princes in India were no concern of his, and that he regarded them merely as noblemen to whom some courtesies were due.

The remainder of the interview was largely devoted to the Nizam's giving me a lecture in forcible terms on the Moslem philosophy of life, the basis of which was that our ends are appointed. He remembered discussing this matter with Lothian, the British Resident, who at the time was an atheist, and who held some opinions to the effect that there was "a measure of chance in our lives, as on a race-course".

It was the Nizam's view that we either had a good or a bad fate. He said that the situation might improve in the next two or three days, or it might get better later on; he could not say. But he was prepared for whatever was appointed for him. He then asked me if I had heard of Mohurram in the Moslem Calendar, and I replied politely that I had. "Ah," he said, "but you do not know what it means. It is the commemoration of the death of the Prophet's grandson. And the acceptance of death and loss is an inherent part of our faith." (In this respect it should be noted that the Nizam visits and prays at the grave of his mother every evening at six o'clock.)

On returning to the subject of Mountbatten's interest in the survival of the Nizam's dynasty, I explained that Mountbatten was a firm believer in constitutional monarchy, at which the Nizam took me up and said vehemently, "That is where I join issue with him. Constitutional monarchy may be all very well in Europe and the west; it has no meaning in the East."

The conversation was steered by Mir Laik Ali to the Commonwealth issue. The Nizam was interested in knowing what chance there was of India's remaining within the Commonwealth. I said that this matter was very much under consideration at the moment, and that there were influential forces who considered that India should stay in. At this point I said I could perhaps make an observation which had no relation to my being a member of Lord Mountbatten's staff, which was that whether India remained within or went out, British opinion, as represented by the present Government, would be most averse to one part of the Indian sub-continent receiving more favourable treatment than another, simply as a result of Commonwealth membership. Any calculations made on this basis would, I was sure, be illusory. This point, I think, went home.

After a few general remarks on the troubled world situation, and the Nizam's expression of concern over the latest developments in Palestine, the conversation ended with him conveying his most cordial compliments and wishes to Mountbatten.

The interview, which lasted nearly an hour, was not a particularly easy one to handle, in view of the Nizam's somewhat disconcerting appearance and manner, but as providing an opportunity to study his personality and mind it was revealing. Although he may be physically decrepit, he is obviously mentally alert and in full command of his faculties. I was, in fact, left with the impression that I had been spoken to by an eccentric elderly Professor on his special subject. He is a Prince of the old school—arrogant and narrow, but on his home ground formidable. His mood throughout was one of aggressive fatalism.

I saw no evidence of the Nizam being a prisoner. There was quite a large number of police at the entrance and by the road, but there is nothing abnormal in this, bearing in mind the attempt on the Nizam's life in the autumn, and the lack of any real frontage to "King Kothi", which was not much farther off the main road than an ordinary house in Delhi. Mir Laik Ali incidentally stayed on after I left.

On my return to the Prime Minister's residence, Moin came round to see me. He was clearly anxious to know my reactions to the Nizam. I said merely that the discussion had been of a general nature, and that there was little encouragement to derive from it. Moin complained to me about the abortive Press communiqué last March,* the Indian attitude to which had made the Government feel that they did not know where they stood.

We discussed treaty or accession, and Moin indicated that what they really feared was that accession might be changed so that it meant in fact accession not on three but thirty-three subjects involving uniformity of laws and loss of internal autonomy which the Nizam would never give up. Moin also gave me to understand that the free movement of Indian Defence Forces through Hyderabad territory would be unacceptable.

I then left to dine with Munshi. I may say that travelling in a fast car it took me forty minutes to reach Munshi's house, which is at the far end of Secunderabad, fairly near the airfield. In this place he is, of course, completely out of touch with the life of the city, and can only see those who have the time, petrol or political inclination to visit him.

I found him somewhat baffled and depressed. He said that he had lost faith in Mir Laik Ali as the result of what he termed a completely bogus report the latter had given of an interview he had had with him. He told me that the position as between Moin and Laik Ali was somewhat ambiguous. Although they were brothers-in-law, they did not see eye to eye, but Laik was definitely on the crest of the wave as far as influence with the Nizam was concerned.

Munshi said that he did not think that anybody meant business either with regard to responsible government or to accession, but he agreed with the preliminary view I had formed that the Nizam was politically master of the situation. I reassured him that my trip was personal and informal and that I had come with the full knowledge and approval of the Prime Minister and V. P. He seemed quite happy to return to Bangalore to-morrow morning, saying that his wife no longer liked living in this place and that his relations with the Government were so strained that he had virtually lost all contact with them.

* See pages 293-4.

HYDERABAD, *Sunday, 16th May, 1948*

I have completed a crowded day, talking and being talked to in unending flow. I told Mir Laik Ali that it would certainly be interesting to meet Kasim Razvi privately, if there was no publicity for the meeting, and it was understood that I was only seeing people whom he himself particularly wanted me to see. He replied that he would definitely like me to meet Razvi and that the latter would be calling on him this morning prior to a tour he was making. I was advised to drop in.

I did so, and after a few minutes of small talk the Prime Minister left me alone with Razvi. In my opening remarks I said something about feeling depressed at the turn of events, to which he at once retorted that he was not a bit depressed; he was just desperate. He wished me to understand that his sole purpose was the defence of the Moslems; to them only did he owe loyalty. I asked him whether there was any truth in the report that the Communists had been approaching the Razakars with a view to common action. " When you say the Razakars ", Razvi replied very fiercely, " you mean me. I tell you the condition of the Moslems here is such that they are themselves rapidly becoming Communist. I have warned them [he did not indicate exactly who ' them ' referred to] that this was likely to happen."

He then categorically asserted that he was quite prepared to work with the Communists and had taken preliminary action to that end. To make doubly sure that I had not misunderstood him, I said that I presumed one difficulty in his way would be the direct challenge thrown down by the Communists to the Nizam himself—i.e., the Communists' warning that there was to be " no truck with the Nizam ". Razvi paused for a moment and said yes, that he appreciated that difficulty, but later, when I returned to the subject, he made it quite clear that both the dynasty and the Government were secondary considerations to him if the Communists proved to be the only allies he could use to save the Moslems from destruction. " If only India will leave us alone for two years, I promise that I will create something they will envy. Hindus already are joining the Razakars." I asked whether without a political settlement there might not be the same crisis at the end of two years, and all he could say was yes, but he added that, for one thing, he did not believe that the Indian Union would survive for more than two years.

He said that he had absolutely no expectation of a peaceable solution, and showed great intensity of racial hatred in discussing the Hindus. He thought that Gandhi's death was symbolic of their behaviour. Hindus always killed their Gods to make them into super-Gods. I asked him whether he did not consider that the Communists, as at present organised, were predominantly Hindu. He said that that was so, but that they were less communally minded than other parties.

I said that it was widely held that he was the real strong man in the State, and asked him what his views were on that. He said, " Don't believe all the slanderous reports about me as a wire-puller and maker of Governments. I am the least person here. I am simply the champion and servant of the Moslems' cause, on behalf of which I will stop at nothing. The Government call me in for my views on occasion, which I give to them with complete frankness." He told me that to save Moslems from death and Moslem women from being ravished he was ready to die. The Congress representatives in Hyderabad were men of straw. "Let me look after the Hindus," he said, smiling for the first time.

Razvi is the complete fanatic. He stares with eyes that bore holes into you and would strike terror into his friends and enemies, were it not for a streak of absurdity and charlatanism about him which even while he rants gives him away, making it difficult to take him completely seriously, and conveying the firm impression that his megalomania has far out-run his real power. In appearance he is slight and dapper, sporting a beard of Mack Sennett proportions beneath a fez worn at a rakish angle. As he walked briskly away he looked like a blend of Charlie Chaplin and a minor Prophet.

Having disposed of Razvi, my next appointment was with General El-Edroos, the Commander-in-Chief of the Hyderabad Army, a tall, handsome and, I can well believe, very able officer of Hashemite Arab stock. He served in the field in the Burma campaign under command of Mountbatten, for whom, incidentally, he has the highest respect. He said that there was some trouble in the Sholapur area, that Indian troops had been helping ruffians to make their way over the border, and that Indian aircraft had been making reconnaissances. He was writing to Bucher and Elmhirst * privately on this subject. He referred to the ordinance position. He said he had made a frank offer to Himmat-sinhji † (without, of course, conceding him any right of inspection) to see things for himself, which he had done, and he understood that he had been satisfied. He said that the Communists were very well armed and that the economic blockade was virtually complete.

He stressed the intensity of the political suspicions of both sides, and said that although he was a soldier, he could not help asking why the Central Government were pressing so hard. I said that he must appreciate that with the creation of Pakistan a strong Centre for the Indian Union was essential. "Cannot they see", he said, "that Pakistan was their own making, and that the pressure they are putting on here is causing a crisis and arousing Moslem fanaticism?" "Without this pressure", he went on (he clearly was referring to Munshi), "Hyderabad in my view would have fallen like a ripe plum." He said that now a serious position was growing up which was taking more and more the form of guerilla activity. I said I had just seen Razvi, and that he was physically smaller than I had expected. El-Edroos, who is something of a giant himself, replied with a laugh, "It's the little ones that are dangerous."

I went straight from my talk with General El-Edroos for a very long session with the Prime Minister. We had lunch together alone, and talked for almost two hours.

Mir Laik Ali began by explaining that he was putting forward proposals for representative government. He could not just get rid of the

* General Sir Roy Bucher and Air Marshal Sir Thomas Elmhirst, Commanders-in-Chief of the Indian Army and Air Force respectively.
† General Himmatsinhji, Indian Army, Adviser on States Forces.

Legislative Assembly, so he had in mind to set in motion electoral procedure for a Constituent Assembly to be elected in addition to it. (I assume ultimately to supersede it.) He said that he had discussed the matter with the leaders of all parties, and he left to them the choice of the electoral procedure they wished to adopt, which was either to use the existing vocational roll (clearly heavily weighted in favour of the Moslems) or to make a fresh electoral list, the preparation of which, together with the conduct of the election itself, could not, in his view, take less than eighteen months.

He said that his dilemma was that the Congress boycott of the now two-year-old Legislative Assembly meant that he had literally nothing but their own word to go on for the political basis of their popular support. They were not, he pointed out, like the Congress elsewhere, which was genuinely elected before it carried out its boycott policy. He said he was awaiting the reaction of the parties and hopes to make an announcement by the end of this month.

He then repeated Moin's views on the accession issue and said that his basic objection was that there were not just three subjects, but that under those headings there were ninety-one in all, as defined under the Indian Constitution. He said that the internal identity of Hyderabad would assuredly be blotted out. He therefore favoured a special treaty which would be exclusive to India, and which would include: a common Foreign policy; a defence agreement, Hyderabad having an army of twenty-five thousand, some ten thousand of which would be put at the disposal of the Indian Union; and a communications agreement in which he foresaw no special difficulty.

By forcing the pace Moslem fanaticism was being assuredly aroused. He was very critical of Munshi, who, he said, had openly spoken of Hyderabad as the site of an old Hindu State. He was mixing only with Congress friends, and had been putting out at regular intervals dates for the " D " day, first on the 10th March, then later on in March, then 23rd April, until even the Hindus had ceased to believe him.

I told him I was sorry to find the Nizam in a mood of such complete fatalism. I said frankly that I considered something more than that was required if a solution of any kind was to be possible. He told me that I must appreciate that the Nizam was literally ready to bare his chest and die rather than do anything which he would regard as a betrayal of the interests of his people. While not questioning His Exalted Highness's courage, I stressed that it was his people who stood to suffer most from a show-down.

I told him the form taken by my interview with Razvi, and asked him for his reactions. He told me that he thought Razvi must have meant that he would ally himself with the Communists only as a very last resort and after the collapse of the Nizam and Government. I replied that this was not clear from what Razvi had said to me, and told him that if Razvi were to go unchecked much longer, the Nizam and the Government might find themselves literally as the nut in the nut-cracker.

This conversation did not represent any major advance, so far as I know, on any of the previous views Laik Ali has held either on responsible government or accession.

After lunch I visited the famous Osmania University, which is the special pride of Zain, for he was its architect and, as such, responsible for its daring blend of Moslem and Hindu styles. It is still far from complete, but there is enough of it to realise that it is a great concept and a fine monument to Moslem cultural aspiration in the South.

Later in the afternoon I had my appointment with the Prince of Berar, the Nizam's heir. He lives in more sumptuous quarters than his father. There were also present General El-Edroos and Samader Yar Jung, the Private Secretary to the Prince, a most subservient individual with a very hoarse voice, who half bowed to His Highness every time His Highness spoke.

Perhaps the most amusing moment occurred when we were discussing Mountbatten's capabilities and were all agreed that he was a man of great determination and energy. Thereupon the Private Secretary, almost doubling over the Prince, observed, " In these respects he may be said to have the same characteristics as Your Highness"! Most of the conversation was small talk, but the Prince expressed the hope that Mountbatten would still be able to come down, and the bowing Secretary particularly emphasised their desire that Indo–Hyderabad relations would improve soon.

The only item of interest is that the Prince of Berar was apparently worried about his health, saying that either his throat was causing his teeth to go bad or that his teeth were affecting his throat, but in either case he wished to consult his doctor in London at the end of June. He said that he was having some difficulty in getting a passage (this may mean that the Nizam is objecting to his going). I did not get the impression that he has any political significance in the present situation. Laik Ali told me, " His Highness likes to live comfortably," and that they were both boon companions when they were young men, from which I gathered that Laik Ali's own position might not suffer unduly when the Prince succeeds to the throne.

At 6.30 I saw Mr. Claude Scott, who has been acting as Director of Information for the past five months. I met him last August in Bombay when he was assistant editor of the *Times of India*. He is a shrewd journalist, and is a definite acquisition to Hyderabad on the Press side of things. He said there was no doubt in his own mind that the Nizam was master of the State, and that Razvi would be quite unable to call Moslems into any conflict involving disloyalty to the Nizam. He also stressed the communal form that had been taken by Communist-inspired disorders in the South. Villages, he said, had been attacked, but Hindu houses were left untouched.

At 7.30 I went round to General El-Edroos' house for a second talk. He told me that one of the reasons why the Nizam had refused to come to Delhi was the fear that he would not be able to get back, and that I might well be advised to check on this. He pointed out Hyderabad's strategic importance. While recognising their military weakness, he said that should the worst happen, they could and would cut off India from the South. He believed an agreement was possible if the politicians allowed a Treaty giving India control in External Affairs, administration over Defence and Communications. What more could they want? he asked. If India pressed this matter too far, he went on, resistance was certain. Scott had said this as well.

I returned just in time for the buffet dinner given in my honour at "Shah Munzil". About eighty guests had been invited, of all political persuasions. I met too many people for too short a time to do more than gather some disconnected impressions. I had a few moments, however, with Deen Yar Jung, the Police Chief, a grey-haired, dignified and quiet-spoken man whom many regard as the real power behind the throne. Scott had told me that Deen saw the demonstrators coming on the 25th October, and undoubtedly could have diverted them, but chose to look the other way. I took the occasion to tell Deen, who sees the Nizam regularly, and who had just come from an audience, that I was disturbed at the line taken by His Exalted Highness, and was sure more emphasis on constructive thoughts would be needed quickly. I think Deen had been detailed to get my reactions. I also told him of the advantages which would have accrued if the Nizam could have seen his way to visit Delhi.

It was a glittering social occasion, Hindu and Moslem mixing freely, and even if the atmosphere was somewhat subdued there was—once again—no sense of imminent crisis. For all the feverish propaganda, I could not help feeling amid the shadows and soft voices on the lawns, which looked out on the still lake and the Golconda Ridge and fortress beyond, that these men lived at a slower tempo and were stirred with less passionate ferocity than their compatriots in the stern and stormy regions of the North.

HYDERABAD, *Monday, 17th May, 1948*

Mir Laik Ali had suggested that I should use the occasion to visit any part of Hyderabad I wished, and I decided that it might be most profitable to visit the south-east Area, where frequent Communist raids are reputed to be taking place from across the Madras border. General El-Edroos very kindly laid on an *Expediter* aircraft to cover the first hundred miles and take me down into the Khamam area. We left at 7 a.m., and on arrival at Khamam I was met by Brigadier Habbib Ahmed, in command of Khamam Area, and by local Army Divisional and Police officers. We travelled in all one hundred and eighty miles by car, in some of the hottest weather ever known in the area—118 degrees were recorded across the border.

The first journey was along the Khamam–Madeira Road leading into what is known locally as the Madeira Peninsula. It is in this area that there has been most trouble. It comprises some sixty villages, which join Hyderabad through a very narrow bottle-neck. We got as far as this bottle-neck, no more than a mile wide, when we ran into a road-block, which had been put down that morning. Brigadier Habbib was quite confident that we would not run into any trouble in the salient itself, but I insisted on turning back, as I pointed out that the amount of embarrassment that would be caused not only to Mountbatten, but also to the Hyderabad Government, if I were involved during this private visit in any incident would be out of all proportion to the advantages gained by seeing some of the villages there.

We then started on the second part of our trip along the main Khamam–Ashiwaraopett Road. The actual physical damage was not very great, but the effect of incursions and intimidations was to cause the wholesale movement of villagers across the border. I saw two or three " home-made " efforts to blow up bridges, and several tree road-blocks. Militarily speaking the situation was well under control, but it was clear that morale in the villages was low. The road was of very high quality and in excellent repair as, indeed, were all the roads I saw.

The attacks for the most part have been centred on Customs Offices, and I was given a report of forty-one such attacks, made between September 1947 and January 1948. Excise trees * have also been exten-sively burned, but the worst damage that I saw was at the village of Ashiwaraopett itself, which is as far east as one can go before reaching the Madras Presidency. This village was attacked early in January by as many as two to three thousand local tribesmen, known as Gonds, who inhabit the area on both sides of the border. They were, I am told, Communist-led, and burnt the place in a thorough fashion. Moslem and Hindu houses alike were attacked, burnt and looted. The local officer explained that only in the later stages of the raid had it taken a communal turn, with concentration on the Moslem houses.

Brigadier Habbib told me that he was quite happy about the general military position in the area and that the incursions were largely of a hit-and-run nature. It is clear, however, that these raids not only in the south-east but also from Bombay and Central Provinces are involving a wide dispersal of Hyderabad forces, and military patrolling is needed to maintain local confidence. A glance at General El-Edroos' map at H.Q. confirms this.

I asked the local Police Chief, who had just come from the Bombay area, what help he received from the Razakars, and he replied, smiling, that the Razakars, for what use they were, were mostly confined to parades in the cities. Another factor which makes it difficult to control the situation in the area is that whereas Hyderabad is responsible for the salient, India has an island of territory just inside the border. From the purely administrative point of view, it would undoubtedly be much easier if these two blocks of territory were swopped.

I dread to think what the sun temperature was in the cockpit of the *Expediter* at about 3.30 on this blazing afternoon. I merely know that I felt I was breathing in fire. Only when we dipped low to circle once round the Golconda massif did the first breath of cooling breeze strike us.

I had hardly touched down before I was plunged into an extraordinary and, for me, wholly unexpected tea-party, which was organised by Zahir Ahmed, the energetic young Secretary for External Affairs. He had brought together a group of about a dozen prominent Hindu and

* These trees, from which toddy is made, are sources of Revenue.

Moslem leaders—both from the Majlis and the States Congress—some of whom had not met for several years. Some very heated words were exchanged between Mr. Ganarival, an influential Congress worker, and Mr. Rais, the leading Moslem editor and member of the Hyderabad Legislative Assembly, and the most extreme opinions were fully developed. Mr. Rais argued that he would not have anything to do with the Congress spokesmen so long as their loyalties were divided. Mr. Ganarival retorted that he would, and indeed could, not have anything to do with the Government until popular representation was conceded.

Some of the Moslem spokesmen were unhappy about the linking of Foreign policy with India's, particularly if it means taking a line which is hostile to Pakistan's. There was agreement that Hyderabad's future had essentially to be solved internally. Congress spokesmen were not prepared to concede that their loyalty to the Nizam was at stake. Mr. Rais, in a moment of great frankness, advised us that Hyderabad was a Moslem State, and that what was involved was a crude issue of power which the Moslems were not prepared to give up.

At this point I decided that I needed some liquid refreshment, but I am glad to report that I was able to leave with all shaking each other warmly by the hand and agreeing to meet again, and with a general consensus of opinion that I was a reasonably fair-minded young man. Once again I was impressed by the contrast between the social affability and the political bitterness of the contending factions. After the meeting I was button-holed by the Associated Press of India reporter and obliged to make a brief non-committal statement, but to say anything, even to the point of "no comment," is, in the present highly charged atmosphere, bound to provoke some criticism. By and large, I think I have avoided opening myself to attack on a wide front, in any case the risk is acceptable.

At 8 p.m. I had a last talk with the Prime Minister. I told Laik Ali that I wanted to be sure that the Nizam's refusal to visit Delhi was not based on any fears as to his personal security. He said that there might have been some such doubt in the Nizam's mind, but that the dominating and compelling motive was that if he had come, his move would have been seriously misunderstood in the State. I told him that I had been frankly worried by the reliance that seemed to be placed on Opposition support in England. I said that I was sure that this was a most dangerous illusion. For Hyderabad to become a Party issue in the British House of Commons could not serve the real interests of the State. Laik Ali told me that he entirely agreed. He personally had the greatest admiration for Mr. Attlee, and he did not want Hyderabad to be bandied about in Party debate anywhere. He said that he was most pleased that I had made the visit, which he felt had been helpful in every way.

After I had had a quiet dinner with Zain's son and beautiful daughter-in-law, Zain himself, who had arrived that afternoon, asked to see me, and I went along to his house at 11 p.m. He said that he had seen the Nizam alone. He had again been very vehement. "But", added Zain, "he always is." He was very firm on the issue of his Legislative Sovereignty, but Zain had told him that it was quite essential for him to form a new Government on a much broader basis than the present one.

He gave me to understand that the Nizam and Laik Ali had at last agreed to do this. The Nizam then apparently raised the question of my interview, saying that he had spoken exactly what was in his mind to me without any reservations. The Nizam believed that there was a ten per cent chance that Mountbatten would even now come himself, and asked Zain what he felt. Zain said that it must to some extent depend on the kind of report I sent in. The Nizam then began to ask questions about me. Who exactly was I, what were my politics, etc.

Zain thinks that solution is possible if the Legislative reservation is made. He even went so far as to feel that the word accession might be brought about. He is proposing in his talks with the Nizam on Tuesday and Wednesday (the Nizam had asked him to stay and have an extra day for an extra talk) to see if this would be acceptable, provided it was strictly limited to three subjects. He said that he was proposing to speak frankly with El-Edroos, who was alleged to be giving military assistance to the Razakars. This was causing considerable disquiet in Delhi. Finally, Zain hoped that I would be able to postpone my visit to Simla until he got back on Thursday evening, when I could give Mountbatten the latest information.

HYDERABAD, NEW DELHI, *Tuesday, 18th May, 1948*

After an early breakfast and a final courtesy good-bye to Mir Laik Ali, I was accompanied by Captain Baig on the long drive to the airfield. Captain Baig's talents as an A.D.C. have been fully tested, and he has been to endless trouble in steering me from place to place on time throughout my fantastic schedule. I leave in the knowledge that everything possible has been done to throw open the gates to me. From the Nizam downwards I get the impression that everyone has spoken with the maximum frankness of which he is capable, and there have been surprisingly few evasions. If Deen Yar Jung was reticent, he was at least receptive. As for my own contribution, I hope and believe that I may have been instrumental in tempering the general "death-or-glory" attitude I found on my arrival.

The return flight in the aircraft was my first chance to compose my thoughts. My main impressions are :—

The Nizam is the key man in the situation. As regards the major issue of relations with the Indian Union, nothing is being done without his approval or connivance. Moreover, I consider that any agreement he finally enters into will be honoured, in the sense that his régime is strong enough to withstand internal opposition from any quarter.

He is in a mood of aggressive fatalism, and in my judgement is ready, and has the strength, to try to perform a "Samson Act" on the Government of India; in other words, if he goes under, full preparations have been made to ensure that the political and social structure of the State should go under with him. Razvi's role in this scheme of things is to ensure that this process of disintegration is completed, and that a mere military victory will not suffice to solve the problem.

On the other hand, the Nizam is searching furtively and anxiously for an honourable settlement. He is a ruler of the old school; he has no liking for the trappings of the Constitutional Monarch, and will put up the same kind of resistance to that status as Queen Victoria did. The tighter the corner, the more he will fall back on prerogatives. I do not believe that he will voluntarily accept an accession solution which makes him anything other than the official fountain-head of law and custom inside his own State.

Any appreciation of the Nizam's attitude must take into account that the prospects and policy of his fellow-Princes do not interest him at all— he regards them merely as impotent noblemen—and that he is obviously a deeply religious man. In times of trouble the Nizam is liable to lean heavily on his traditional Islamic beliefs, and I am sure he spoke to me with complete sincerity on this.

In this political bargaining no great advance has been made since Laik Ali's speech to the Hyderabad Legislative Assembly on 27th April. It seems likely, however, that the Nizam will take a final stand both on the accession and the representative Government issues by the 1st June.

With regard to Mountbatten's position, there is a very widespread feeling that the only chance of a settlement will be through his good offices and influence. But the Nizam is clearly sceptical whether either can turn the scales in time. A position, however, may conceivably be reached in the course of the next fortnight in which the differences of detail and interpretation are narrowed down sufficiently for Mountbatten to provide the final pressure. For the moment there is no more to be done with the Nizam; the differences need to be ironed out between Zain and V. P.

On arrival in Delhi I went straight round to see V. P., who, with his responsibilities for implementing the merger policy, on top of all these Hyderabad worries, is grotesquely overworked. He clearly feels that the trip has been useful, but was in no mood to discuss the issue of Hyderabad Legislative Sovereignty. I got the impression that his general attitude to Hyderabad has hardened while I have been away, but at least I succeeded in getting him to reserve his judgement on the progress made until Zain's return to-morrow. V. P. began speaking of "final terms", but I had reached that stage of physical and mental exhaustion when I began finding difficulty in following him point by point.

I spoke to Ronnie on the telephone in Simla and have promised—so help me—a full report to be dispatched to-morrow.

CHAPTER TWENTY-EIGHT

FAREWELL PHASE

GOVERNMENT HOUSE, NEW DELHI, *Thursday, 20th May, 1948*

I SPENT ALL yesterday cut off from the world in a stern effort to complete my report for Mountbatten to read a day in advance of my own arrival in Simla.

This afternoon I had an hour's interview with Nehru, and ran through my general conclusions with him. He considers that the Nizam may have been deliberately " giving me the works ", and in view of his refusal to enter into any discussion with additional parties, he would naturally rely on generalities. He agreed with me that Deen Yar Jung, who was the real founder of the Razakars, was strong enough to face up to the implications of disbanding them.

The Prime Minister said that the history of Hyderabad was not glorious and that they had nearly always given way to pressure, citing their collapse before the Mahrattas.

He realised that the Nizam was genuinely concerned about his treasures and personal prerogatives, and he was ready to give assurances on these. He said he had no intention of forcing accession in terms of the Indian Constitution on Hyderabad. Any further subjects would be a matter of separate negotiation. Nor had he any intention of swallowing up the Hyderabad Army.

He referred to the Nizam's religion, and said that his emphasis on Mohurram in his talk with me was significant, as it commemorated the event which marks the break between the Shia and Sunni Sects of the Moslem faith. The Hyderabadis were Sunni Moslems, and it was suspected that the Nizam himself was a crypto-Shia.

I said I hoped he had not been unduly disturbed about the publicity, and explained that it was primarily due to the zeal of Munshi's staff. I had done my best to keep it under control. (I understand there was some criticism from one or two members of the Cabinet, but it did not come from Nehru or Patel, who were not worried.) Nehru said again this afternoon that it did not matter or affect the value of the visit.

Nehru says he finds the Nizam's attitude hard to understand, as he does not believe that he is at all cut out for a heroic role.

After some initial uncertainty as to whether they were going to meet, Zain went round to V. P.'s house at 9 p.m., and I joined them shortly afterwards.

With the background of general border tension, V. P. was strongly of the opinion that the present uncertainty cannot be allowed to linger on, and after one or two tentative programmes had been considered and rejected, a complicated sequence of meetings was worked out involving an invitation to Mir Laik Ali to arrive in Delhi on the 22nd, a visit by

Nehru and V. P. to Patel in Mussoori, and Mountbatten's participation at a decisive point in the discussions, and in advance of any firm decision.

The conversation, although somewhat incoherent and protracted, was frank and cordial. The gravity of the situation was recognised in the light of border incidents and the Sardar's views. Zain himself gave no indication whatever of the Nizam's attitude on any of the main subjects under discussion, but V. P. reassured him on the limitation of accession to three subjects—anything more to be negotiated; the identity and integrity of the Hyderabad Army; and the Nizam's legislative powers. (This last is a most tricky constitutional and political issue on which we will need to brief ourselves carefully.) Laik's position and the reconstitution of the Government were considered. Zain stressed the difficulty of Laik dismissing the whole Cabinet except himself and re-forming it, but this matter will be frankly discussed at the forthcoming meeting. The possibility of Zain himself taking part in a new Government was considered. He said he would prefer to serve as Deputy to someone else, but was ready to co-operate provided his appointment came from the Nizam direct, and not as a result of pressure from the Government of India.

Zain seemed to feel that V. P.'s proposals on all these subjects were being made in a more palatable form than before, but so far as I know there was no change of ground on the Indian side. V. P., however, spoke in the most fervent and emotional terms of his esteem for Zain and of his wish for settlement, and the understanding that clearly exists between the two men is encouraging. The situation now largely revolves round the Mussoori meeting with Patel and the measure of discretion V. P. can get from that meeting. V. P. anticipates that it will be no easy encounter.

Both V. P. and Zain were good enough to say that my visit to Hyderabad had been helpful.

GOVERNOR-GENERAL'S LODGE, SIMLA, *Saturday, 22nd May, 1948*

To complete this crowded week, Fay and I set off on our last trek to Simla. The Mountbattens and nearly all the Staff have been here ever since the beginning of my Hyderabad trip. So much has happened since I left, and I have been so absorbed in my own activities, that it seems almost like a return from exile.

I have had two long talks with Mountbatten alone. He says he only wishes now that he had sent me down earlier, as the value of my report to him is in its objectivity. He has found it very hard, in view of his own friendship for Monckton and his personal desire to achieve a settlement before he leaves, to avoid a subjective approach to the problem. In this connexion I gave him my frank opinion that the Nizam may well be placing more reliance on C. R.—a Southern Indian and a Madrassi—than on himself as Governor-General. Mountbatten was not worried about the Nizam's negative attitude. The vital objective of stirring up a sense of urgency among the ruling group in Hyderabad and of causing a renewal of negotiations has, he feels, been secured. For, he says, until I went neither side seemed prepared to make a new move.

There has been quite a heavy Press reaction to my visit, which has touched the speculative nerve. Some of the comment is critical of Mountbatten for having any more dealings with the Nizam after his refusal to come to Delhi, and some, including *The Hindu*, of myself for touring the boundary regions, seeking information and going beyond my proper mandate. Mountbatten was not in the least disturbed by this. On the whole I have got off very lightly. The important thing is that I was not embarrassed with excessive Press inquiry during the visit itself, which I might well have been as a result of Munshi's zealous efforts to publicise my arrival.

A handsome garden-party was given by the Mountbattens for the East Punjab's notabilities this afternoon at Governor-General's Lodge. There was a fine showing of brocade and silk sarees. A band played, and Their Excellencies mingled with their guests on the terraced lawns.

GOVERNMENT HOUSE, NEW DELHI, *Tuesday, 25th May, 1948*

I left Simla on Sunday morning with Vernon after little more than thirty-six hours there. I am surfeited with travel. The logistics of my last week are a serious challenge to constructive or sustained thought. We returned to the furnace in Delhi as advance guards to Mountbatten, who has spent the last twenty-four hours in Patiala. We were able to advise him on arrival that Mir Laik Ali, who reached here on Sunday, has apparently come in completely the wrong spirit and is so out of touch with reality that he claims that the crisis is now past. Mountbatten therefore got to work on him to-day in what I believe is the longest interview he has had with anybody on the entire mission—five hours in all.

The background to this interview, as indeed to my own visit, has been a fairly large-scale concentration of Indian forces in the vicinity of Hyderabad's boundaries with India, their immediate function being to bring the constantly recurring border incidents under control. The latest and most serious of these has been the Gangapur train incident, which, involving two non-Moslem deaths and a number of wounded and missing, has done much to inflame Indian opinion. A Defence Committee meeting two days before I left for Hyderabad decided that military preparations must go on, but that ten days' notice would be required by the Army before it could undertake offensive action. The assurances Mountbatten has had from Nehru satisfy him that no invasion save in dire emergency, such as a large-scale Hindu massacre, is at present contemplated. He is now confident that there will be no such move before his own departure, or even before the advent of the monsoon.

There is thus still a small, but only a small, margin of time left for achieving an agreed pacification. Something drastic therefore had to be done to make Laik Ali see the imminence of the danger and to prove to him that to play canny was by now the rashest gamble for him and his State. I told Mountbatten in Simla that I was tempted to regard Mir

Laik Ali's attitude as that of the highly intelligent fool—one who can give all the right reasons for doing all the wrong things.

Mountbatten began by giving him with brutal frankness a picture of what would probably happen if no settlement was reached and Hindu blood began to flow in Hyderabad. If after his departure in a few weeks India were to decide upon armed intervention, what could be done by the Hyderabad army? Laik Ali said he fully appreciated the military position, but that he considered accession ten times worse than paramountcy. He explained that while he was personally in favour of democratic institutions, he was opposed to the introduction of responsible government in Hyderabad simply because it would without doubt lead to accession. When V. P. entered the room Laik Ali proposed a long-term agreement for five or even ten years covering the three central subjects.

GOVERNMENT HOUSE, NEW DELHI, *Wednesday, 26th May, 1948*

Discussion between V. P. and Laik Ali *à deux* went on far into the night, and V. P., with his prodigious powers of drafting and formula-finding, has produced comprehensive "Heads of Agreement". They are divided into two parts, and cover eleven principal items, Part I dealing with the basic relation between Hyderabad and India, and Part II with the interim measures to implement Part I. V. P.'s "Heads of Agreement" met Laik Ali's request to be able to present to the Nizam a third alternative to accession, which is ruled out anyhow, and a plebiscite.

Mountbatten himself is strongly of the opinion that a plebiscite would be the best solution, as the "Heads of Agreement" open up another depressing vista of protracted and niggling negotiation over detail. Laik Ali's personal view would seem to be in the same sense, for he said that he thought a plebiscite would " save the face of both sides ". At the Indian end the plebiscite finds favour, in particular with Patel, whose blessing is indispensable, even though there is recognition that it would not automatically lead to accession.

GOVERNMENT HOUSE, NEW DELHI, *Saturday, 29th May, 1948*

This is a most critical moment in the tantalising Hyderabad negotiations. V. P. has been to see Patel at Mussoori, and has returned from him with a constructive but strongly worded message. Patel comes down once more in favour of the plebiscite. As for the "Heads of Agreement", he accepts the basic relationship in Part I without amendment, but would tighten up the interim measures of Part II by shifting the balance of control more in favour of the non-Moslems. The final paragraph of Patel's message written in his own hand urges that if Laik Ali means business he should come up with plenipotentiary powers from the Nizam. " It is no use ", he writes, " discussing with a person who has to go back every time for instructions."

He wants a telegram with a twenty-four-hour time-limit to be sent, saying that if Laik Ali cannot return with authority and agreement on the fundamentals within that deadline, the Government of India would draw the conclusion that Hyderabad do not want to continue the negotiations and are merely playing for time. His last words are "finalise within a week". Nehru has expressed great distrust of Laik Ali. Intelligence about his activities confirms that we are dealing with a very sly procrastinator, but his—or the Nizam's—response cannot be delayed much longer.

On the credit side is Monckton's decision to come out again. Mountbatten has expressed his delight at the news, saying that he will try to hold the position until his arrival, but pointing out that powerful influences—growing stronger every day—are at work militating against the settlement which they both want.

Monckton, however, is not due in India until the 3rd June, which happens to be the day when I and my family are due to leave Bombay by sea for home. It is thus possible for Monckton's and my paths to cross in Bombay on the morning of the 3rd without undue administrative inconvenience, or danger of breach of confidence. As Monckton is arranging to fly straight on to Hyderabad and has not been fully in the picture on the developments during the period of my own visit onwards, Mountbatten sees in my presence a providential opportunity to brief him before he is called upon to give what may be the decisive advice to the Nizam. So there will be no fading away for me until I am finally aboard the ship.

This evening there was a farewell Staff party to Fay and myself in the Panelled Room. We do not actually leave until Tuesday morning, but this was the only time that the Mountbattens could come, and, characteristically, they wished to be there. It was a very pleasant family affair. I am very sorry to be leaving before the final curtain. I would have liked to have been present for the *dénouement* over Hyderabad, and to have witnessed the series of ceremonies of formal farewell, which I am sure will burst the bounds of formality. But there it is. The phase-out programme was arranged some time back, and it would be very difficult to amend our plans. During the party there was much amusement at my alleged likeness to a large portrait on the wall of the renowned Tippoo Sahib. The picture shows a man of dismal and almost morose countenance, and the comparison did little to raise my morale!

Afterwards Mountbatten presented me with a silver cigarette-box generously inscribed. We were much moved by these tokens of confidence, appreciation and friendship. For myself, my biggest reward has been the privilege of serving a great man on a great mission.

GOVERNMENT HOUSE, NEW DELHI, *Sunday, 30th May, 1948*

We have this evening been to a large reception given by V. P. at the Delhi Gymkhana Club, which attracted, so far as I could see, nearly every celebrity in Delhi. For the Mountbattens it is the first in a formidable sequence of farewell parties during the next three weeks. Through the middle of this milling throng a messenger brought in no fewer than three letters from the Nizam, which immediately absorbed the attention of host, principal guest and Prime Minister. Most of the Indian and Foreign Press were present, and it did not take these intelligence experts long to recognise that important and far from favourable information had come through, as Mountbatten, Nehru and V. P., moving into a corner, put their heads together and talked in anxious undertones.

At first sight it would seem that hopes of settlement under Mountbatten's auspices have received a severe set-back. In the first letter the Nizam's reaction to the "Heads of Agreement" was simply that he could do no more than await Monckton's arrival. In the second he returned a brusque "no" to the discreet suggestion that he might consider appointing a new and more acceptable Prime Minister—a suggestion which Laik Ali himself, with what degree of candour it is difficult to say, had expressed himself as ready to sponsor if it would serve the cause of good-will. The third is simply a renewed invitation to Mountbatten to visit him in Hyderabad. Here again the terms of the invitation are singularly lacking in warmth or even courtesy of expression.

Mountbatten decided—wisely, I think—to reply only to the first letter, expressing regret at further delay and the hope that when Laik Ali comes to Delhi the next time he would be allowed to bring with him plenipotentiary powers to reach a settlement.

In addition to these deplorable notes of negation from the Nizam, Laik Ali has weighed in denying the accuracy of Vernon's notes on his meeting with Mountbatten, Nehru and V. P. on the 26th and asserting that he had never agreed to India's declaration of right to overriding legislation in the three central subjects. Everyone in the room at the time, however, is quite certain that he did agree. This letter only seems to reinforce Nehru's warning that Laik Ali is not to be trusted, and that his sole objective is to delay matters. Monckton's intervention assumes hourly more decisive importance.

In spite of the current tension Zain Yar Jung creates calmness and confidence with dinner-parties at Hyderabad House. Almost our last engagement before leaving was to dine with him and his family and entourage. As we sat out in the gardens after dinner, one of the Hyderabadi ladies exchanging polite conversation put such small items as Standstill Agreements, Instruments of Accession and Paramountcy into their proper perspective. "Delhi", she sighed, "is not what it was. There are no Moghul Emperors now!"

M.V. CALEDONIA, *Thursday, 3rd June, 1948*

As I write, we are now comfortably installed in a State room (somewhat to the chagrin of a Maharaja who felt it should have been allotted to him) of the M.V. *Caledonia*, a twenty-thousand-ton ship of the Anchor Line on her maiden trip from India to the United Kingdom. We left the Comptroller's House at eight o'clock on Tuesday morning on the eight-hundred-mile and twenty-six-hour train journey to Bombay—even in the air-cooled compartment quite a marathon, with three of us and two small children.

This morning, after elaborate planning and the passing of many telegrams, I had my meeting at the Santa Cruz airfield with Monckton.

It could hardly have got off to a worse start. The Moncktons had arrived in a specially chartered aircraft, and had not unnaturally assumed that, as they were in transit and only staying for an hour or so, the normal procedure adopted by most countries of sealing it up would be observed. The customs authorities and police, however, who for some unknown reason did not seem to show any awareness of this particular V.I.P. flight, proposed holding up the party to search their baggage. Although there was apparently legal authority for such action, the Moncktons were furious, and quite prepared not to proceed with the Hyderabad visit at all. Only by revealing my identity—which I had hitherto been at pains to hide—was I able to assist the Moncktons over this hurdle.

As my last official duty before boarding the ship, I reported back to Mountbatten by telegram that Monckton at the outset was clearly in a state of doubt and despondency and unaware of the by now crucial importance of his advice in swaying events favourably. He felt the chances of the Nizam agreeing to anything were a hundred to seven against, and if he was over-pushed, he himself was ready to suggest that he should fight it out. I stressed the reality of the political tension and the urgency of the time-factor, and was able to say that I had left him in a much more constructive and hopeful frame of mind than I had found him.

Monckton urged that he must have time to handle the Nizam in his own way, for he was hardly ever susceptible to direct assault in one interview. However, if and when a point of decision was really reached, he would come to Delhi immediately. After advising him of Mountbatten's and Patel's support for a plebiscite, I was relieved to hear that he had already, of his own accord, arrived at a conclusion firmly in favour of this solution. He thinks that the Nizam's sharp reply about Laik Ali's possible replacement as touching his prerogatives might have been the outcome of some mishandling in the original transmission of the proposal. Monckton intends to tackle this problem himself, and considers Zain to be the only feasible alternative.

Apart from the customs interruption, I was well satisfied with this meeting. It helped to confirm my own belief that in politics much turns on the art of being available in the right place at the right time. Monckton, for his part, said he was most grateful for it, as he confessed that while it would not have been desirable for him to stop off at Delhi first on this visit, he would have been at a disadvantage in going straight into the Nizam wholly unbriefed on the situation from the Indian end.

As the ship cast off this afternoon I could not help feeling the ache of emptiness. It has certainly been a sharp transition from involvement to idleness. As we move out into the Arabian Sea, and the lights of Bombay flicker in the receding distance, all is calm, but we are warned that cyclonic storms lie ahead of us. So it seems that there is to be no escape from riding out rough weather.

LONDON, *Wednesday, 23rd June, 1948*

We reached Liverpool yesterday, after twenty days at sea. The cyclone duly met us one hundred and fifty miles out of Bombay, and remained to lash us all the way to Aden. I was back just in time to watch the Mountbattens and all the rest of the party touch down at Northolt, the same journey having taken them forty-eight hours by air.

Both the Duke of Edinburgh and Mr. Attlee were at the airfield to invest this homecoming with unique distinction, for I doubt whether a Royal Duke and a Prime Minister of the day have been present together before to greet a Viceroy or Governor-General on his return. There were other Ministers, high officials and senior officers, B.B.C., Newsreel and Press representatives, not to mention photographers in large numbers, and last but not least a Guard of Honour of a hundred Indian sailors from their new cruiser, the *Delhi*, which is still in Portsmouth.

Attlee's presence, too, was particularly appropriate, for the transfer of power in India may well be regarded as the most momentous policy decision of his Premiership. In its conception and implementation he has throughout carried a special responsibility, so that history will undoubtedly link Attlee and Mountbatten in much the same way as it has Morley and Minto, Montagu and Chelmsford.

While we were all in the ante-room having tea, Mountbatten, who was discussing the Hyderabad situation with the Prime Minister, called me over to say a few words about the impressions I had formed of the Nizam on my visit. Mr. Attlee listened carefully to the brief picture I drew; then said that he was quite satisfied that everything humanly possible had been done to secure an honourable settlement for the Nizam, and that we could all go away with clear consciences in this matter. I do not as yet know the details of the breakdown, having only heard over the intermittent ship's radio that attempts to reach an agreement had failed.

It is strange to think that the Mountbattens and their Staff party, who for the past fifteen months have worked in such close unison, are now dispersing for the last time. The more intensely you live in the vortex of great events, the harder it is to break away and accept normalcy as your lot. As we go off into this soft summer evening, most of us will be taking a spell of leave, if only to learn over again how to cope with the daily round at the routine pace.

LONDON, *Monday, 28th June, 1948*

In spite of the lures and distractions of Bradman's farewell Test Match at Lords, I have now had time to piece together the drama of Mountbatten's last three weeks in India. The ship's radio had reported only the briefest statement of the Hyderabad breakdown, together with short reports of Mountbatten's final broadcast, and some indication that the farewell scenes in Delhi had been no less heart-warming than those of the 15th August, and in many ways even more remarkable, in so far as they were now simply expressions of personal gratitude to the Mountbattens.

From long talks I have had with Ronnie and Vernon, and one or two with Mountbatten himself since their return, and from notes which were maintained right up to the day of their departure, it would seem that the course of events after my meeting with Monckton was briefly as follows.

Monckton stayed for three days in Hyderabad, returning with Laik Ali to Delhi. At first the discussions were stormy and the negotiations more than once on the verge of complete collapse. Nehru refused to see Laik Ali, Monckton threatened to leave for home. Mountbatten at one point saved the day by telephoning Nehru to say he was quite sure he could find a satisfactory solution, when in fact he had no idea how or where to seek it. But somehow a life-line was maintained. Nehru made a helpful speech on the 8th June, posing and answering the question for his critics as to why the Indian Army had not already marched in. He replied that whenever force was employed it created more problems than it solved. The storm subsided, and Mountbatten was left with effective control over the negotiations.

Monckton, for his part, recognised that something more than a long-term plebiscite was required to restore the situation. Patel, from his sick-bed, still wanted unqualified acceptance of accession. He now urged that no more formulæ should be provided from the Indian side. This was acceptable to Monckton, who put up two documents—a draft Firman to introduce responsible government, establish a Constituent Assembly early in 1949 and reconstitute immediately the existing Government. The second document was the first part of V. P.'s " Heads of Agreement " in full. Laik Ali once again played for time, saying he must return to the Nizam. On the 9th June rumours reached Delhi that a Pakistan representative was in Hyderabad, but Laik Ali denied this on oath, and agreement was reached that he should return to Hyderabad for consultation.

On the 12th June, Monckton reported getting the proposals past the Nizam and through the Executive Council, except for two points—the issue of overriding legislation, and the composition of the Constituent Assembly. This led to further difficult discussions, first between Mountbatten, Monckton and Nehru in Delhi, and then at a meeting with Patel and most of the Cabinet at which Mountbatten was present in Mussoori. But the proposals were agreed as modified by the Nizam subject to the deletion of any direct reference to parity in the composition of the Assembly, and the substitution, instead, of the words, " in consultation with the leaders of the major political parties " in Hyderabad.

On the 13th June, Monckton strongly urged Laik Ali to come up, with plenipotentiary powers this time, but once again he was limited in his discretion both by the Council and the Nizam himself. On the 14th June, Laik Ali asked for four new amendments to the " Heads of Agreement ". These were, first, that the Government of India would only request Hyderabad to pass legislation similar to that in force in India, and not peculiar to Hyderabad; secondly, that Hyderabad should be allowed to retain eight thousand irregulars; thirdly, that the Razakars should be disbanded gradually, and not all at once, and fourthly, that the state of emergency under which India might station troops in Hyderabad should be defined under the Government of India Act. Mountbatten felt there was little hope of getting these additional points past the Government of India, but, much to his pleasure and surprise, Nehru was ready to agree.

On the 15th June, Mountbatten saw the Hyderabad delegation and reported this unexpected success. Laik Ali at once raised two new points. He wanted declarations of economic and fiscal freedom to be included. Once again the Government of India agreed to give sympathetic consideration, and suggested that these could be stressed in a collateral letter. Mountbatten said that on this point Nehru went so far as to propose the inclusion in the collateral letter provision of facilities for joint collaboration in the economic development of Hyderabad. Laik Ali, apparently not realising what he meant, actually asked for this to be deleted. Only on Monckton protesting that it would be most unwise for Hyderabad to pass over this offer, and Mountbatten explaining that it had hitherto always been conditional upon full accession, and was thus a further example of good-will, did Laik Ali withdraw his request. But, as Mountbatten pointed out, the incident was typical of his exasperating obtuseness at this time.

Laik Ali left for Hyderabad with the final document and all the amendments, Monckton stressing upon him the need now for total acceptance, or total refusal. An answer was awaited at 7.30 that evening, but no message came through until 9.40, when the Nizam regretted his inability to give a final word without taking the opinion of his Council. This was physically not possible until the next day. The delay was accepted in Delhi.

On the 16th at noon, Mountbatten and Monckton were informed that the Nizam had been recommended not to accept the proposals on four new grounds which Mountbatten, and, I understood, even Monckton, considered so unjustifiable and ridiculous that it was decided that Monckton should fly down to Hyderabad during the night to read out and underline Mountbatten's reply.

His most serious objection was the deletion of the words " on a basis which I shall consider later " in a sub-paragraph of the Firman referring to the setting up of the Constituent Assembly. This deletion had already been agreed to by his delegation, and could by no stretch of the imagination be regarded as a major point of substance. Another objection was his unwillingness to allow the economic agreement (which in any case had only been offered by India at the last minute) to be settled by a collateral letter. He now wanted it in the body of the agreement.

By midday on the 17th there was a telephone message from Monckton with the one word " lost ". By the evening a completely new point had been raised by the Nizam, which he had never mentioned before, concerning India's right to station troops in the event of emergency. He asked for the negotiations to be continued. Nehru and V. P. waited for Monckton, and then held a Press conference releasing the terms that had been made available to the Nizam.

Even now Nehru promised to leave this present offer open for acceptance and impose no time-limit. Monckton told Mountbatten that he had been particularly disappointed to find that Laik Ali had spent three hours with Razvi before even seeing the Nizam. He also gave his view at an informal Press conference that the so-called blockade of Hyderabad had not been imposed by the central Government, and probably not by the Provincial administrations either, but rather by the individual action of low-level officials.

Mountbatten now withdrew officially from the negotiations, but made one last effort in a long, persuasive telegram, a revised "left barrel", which was supplemented by a message from Monckton. Both told him to have the courage of his convictions and not allow himself to sacrifice the interests of his State at the behest of the Ittehad clique. The Ittehad extremists made it quite clear that they were not prepared to enter into any concessions which would limit their control over the State, and when it came to the crisis, the Nizam lacked the will to assert himself against this group.

Mountbatten feels that the main reason for failure is that the principals on either side have never been able to get together throughout the entire eleven months of negotiation, and he is still confident that if the Nizam had come to Delhi and he could have acted as mediator, agreement could have been reached. Similarly, if the Hyderabad delegation had had more negotiating powers and ability to appreciate Monckton's magnificent negotiating skill and fundamental personal loyalty to his client, the Nizam, the outcome might well have been favourable.

The prolonged Hyderabad negotiations, with their crescendo in the last two weeks of his term of office, made it impossible for Mountbatten to effect any last-minute act of mediation over Kashmir. In March he had secured the agreement of the two Prime Ministers to meet each other at roughly monthly intervals. But two months had passed without any action on this, and Mountbatten suggested that Nehru should write to Liaquat to propose a meeting, preferably in Delhi, which would enable Liaquat to say good-bye to Mountbatten before he left. But the attempt had first to be postponed owing to Hyderabad, and then abandoned owing to Liaquat's illness.

The ground had been prepared for detailed discussion of various solutions. The Indian Cabinet, although very bitter about reports of the participation of large regular Pakistan Army units, were still in a comparatively receptive mood for settlement. When Nehru sent detailed evidence of the Pakistan Army's intervention, it was significant that Liaquat in his reply did not specifically deny the charge, but stressed realistically the danger to the security of Pakistan. "As the Indian Army approaches the North-west Frontier", he declared, "the tribesmen feel directly threatened." It is Mountbatten's opinion that here again the inability of the two principals to come together at this particular moment was politically and psychologically most unfortunate.

But frustrations with the Nizam and over Kashmir are but incidentals when set against the Mountbattens' decisive victory over the hearts of the Indian people. The Mountbattens' last day in India was, I hear from all sides, a triumph beyond contrivance or imagination. It was borne in upon them with overwhelming emphasis that India's people and Government had recognised the meaning of their mission and the sincerity of their endeavours, and were hailing them as liberators and friends.

There was first a farewell address by the Delhi Municipality. To receive this they drove through densely packed streets, along the Chandni Chowk, the great highway of Old Delhi, down which no Viceroy had passed since the assassination attempt on Hardinge in 1911. They were mobbed, cheered and garlanded all the way to the Gandhi grounds, where a crowd of a quarter of a million had gathered, and where a further quarter of a million were trying to gain entrance.

In the evening at the last of the great State banquets,* given this time by the Cabinet, Nehru spoke in memorable terms, paying heartfelt tributes to the Mountbattens, not forgetting Pamela, " who, coming straight from school, and possessing all the charm she does, did grown-up person's work in this troubled scene of India ". Of Mountbatten himself he declared, " You came here, sir, with a high reputation, but many a reputation has foundered in India. You lived here through a period of great difficulty and crisis, and yet your reputation has not foundered. That is a remarkable feat."

He next spoke of Lady Mountbatten as possessing " the healer's touch ". " Wherever you have gone, you have brought solace, you have brought hope and encouragement. Is it surprising therefore that the people of India should love you and look up to you as one of themselves and should grieve that you are going? "

Referring to the wonderful demonstration of friendship and affection by the common people of Delhi four hours before, " I do not know ", Nehru said, " how Lord and Lady Mountbatten felt on that occasion, but used as I am to these vast demonstrations here, I was much affected, and I wondered how it was that an Englishman and Englishwoman could become so popular in India during this brief period of time. . . . A period certainly of achievement and success in some measure, but also a period of sorrow and disaster. . . . Obviously this was not connected so much with what had happened, but rather with the good faith, the friendship and the love of India that these two possessed. . . . You may have many gifts and presents, but there is nothing more real or precious than the love and affection of the people. You have seen yourself, Sir and Madam, how that love and affection work."

Mountbatten and Lady Mountbatten, visibly moved, replied with the eloquence of the heart. At the end gifts were exchanged, the Government presenting the Mountbattens with an inscribed tray bearing the signatures of all the Governors of the Provinces, and Cabinet, and Mountbatten handing over on behalf of the King the gold plate presented originally by the Worshipful Company of Goldsmiths and Silversmiths to King George V for use in the State dining-room of his Viceroy in New Delhi. This he did at the King's express wish as " a symbol of the friendship of all English men and women, and indeed of all the people in the United Kingdom to the people of India ". After the dinner there was a glittering reception, which was attended by no fewer than six thousand guests.

Among Lady Mountbatten's last public acts was to visit the two great refugee camps of Kurukshetra and Panipat, where some three hundred

---

* It is interesting to note that the Mountbattens themselves throughout their fifteen months in India carried through, on top of all their other activities, a prodigious programme of entertainment at Government House, which played no small part in the promotion of good-will. Altogether they entertained 7,605 guests to luncheon, 8,313 to dinner and 25,287 to garden-parties, at homes and tea-parties.

thousand refugees still shelter. One of the Indian A.D.C.'s with her reported that he had never visited scenes like it in India. The refugees gathered round her in their thousands, in tears at saying good-bye to her. In many other camps refugees collected their pice and annas to buy a railway ticket for one of their members just to carry some small gift to her as token of gratitude.

It was at another unique gathering—a dinner given to the Mount-battens by the entire Diplomatic Corps in Delhi—that the Chinese Ambassador, doyen of the Corps, a scholar and a man of fine sensibilities, came nearest perhaps to catching the inner meaning and mood of this historic leave-taking. By way of bidding farewell to the Mountbattens he quoted the lines of a famous Chinese poet :—

> " Deep is the water in the Peach-blossom spring,
> Deeper still is our hearts' feeling
> When good friends are leaving."

CHAPTER TWENTY-NINE

EPILOGUE

On 9th November 1948 shortly after my return home I addressed The Royal Institute of International Affairs on the theme of "India in Transition". This obliged me to collect my thoughts and review all my notes on the subject while the whole experience was fresh in my mind. The speech provides a natural final entry to sum up and round off my daily record.

"It may be said of the British Raj, as Shakespeare said of the Thane of Cawdor, 'Nothing in his life became him like the leaving it'. . . . This Bill is a moral to all future generations; it is a Treaty of Peace without a War."

Such was Lord Samuel's considered tribute, paid during the House of Lords debate on the Indian Independence Act, to the creation by compromise and consent of two new nations involving one-fifth of the entire human race.

It was certainly the privilege of a life-time to be given the chance, as a member of Lord Mountbatten's staff, of playing some personal part in this unique transfer of power.

In announcing to Parliament on 20th February, 1947, Lord Mountbatten's appointment as Viceroy, Mr. Attlee stated that he would be "entrusted with the task of transferring to Indian hands the responsibility for the government of British India in a manner that will best ensure the future happiness and prosperity of India". But Mr. Attlee then added that there was to be a time limit for achieving agreement if possible and for transferring power in any case by June 1948—the principle no doubt being that a time limit would induce the necessary margin of agreement between the two great Indian political parties, the Congress and Moslem League, as nothing else had so far succeeded in doing.

In spite of the immediate controversy it provoked, this time limit, on which Lord Mountbatten had himself insisted before accepting the post, was in effect the logical conclusion of the policy decision of the British Government early in the war to cease recruitment for the Indian Civil Service. The normal complement of that Service was never much more than eleven hundred; by November 1946 it had fallen to five hundred and twenty British officers in senior positions, with the remainder Indians. In 1939 the Central Government Secretariat was run on the basis of, approximately, thirty senior administrative officers, but by the end of the war the number of officers of equivalent grade had risen to three hundred.

The same situation was developing in the Provinces. This tremendous bureaucratic growth of work coinciding with the decline in the number of British senior officials made it clear, quite apart from other considerations, that it was going to be virtually impossible to hold on to India administratively beyond 1949. It is doubtful whether the police establishment was strong enough by 1947 to enforce any policy opposed by both major parties, and it is fair to say that any large military commitments in India to maintain the Raj would have been wholly unacceptable to the British Government or people.

The original schedule Lord Mountbatten set himself was to produce a plan by October 1947, discuss it with the British Government and put it to the Indian Leaders by about January 1948. While he was still at home this approach was considered much too hurried, but he had hardly set foot in India when he reached the firm conclusion that it was, in fact, much too leisurely to meet the situation then confronting us. We were faced by rapidly rising Hindu–Moslem tensions; " Direct Action " had been launched by the Moslem League in August 1946; there were riots and reprisals for riots. This set off the spark, and disturbances of great intensity took place in Bengal and Bihar. The trouble spread to Lahore and the North-west Frontier Province. In his first talks with Lord Mountbatten the Moslem League leader, Mr. Jinnah, gave a frank warning that unless an acceptable political solution was reached very quickly he could not guarantee to control the situation from his side. A similar warning was given by Congress leaders.

Although it was still officially in being, the so-called Cabinet Mission Plan, negotiated throughout 1946, had already broken down. This was the last attempt to achieve a unitary system for India, and it was based on an elaborate three-tiered structure of Provinces and groups of Provinces. Group A comprised the present Dominion of India, while Groups B and C conceded the substance of West and East Pakistan respectively; but all three Groups were to support a weak central authority. This " Grand Design " broke down, as many had done before, on detail—vital detail, certainly—but a significant warning for Lord Mountbatten about the nature of the Indian deadlock and how to handle it. It seemed that the Indian approach was to start with an overall agreement and work steadily away from it; while the British approach was to tackle the difficulties first and hope to be left with some common ground at the end.

Unity had been our greatest legislative and administrative achievement in India, but by March 1947 the only alternatives were Pakistan or chaos. Lord Ismay likened the position to " taking charge of a ship in mid-ocean with a fire on the deck and ammunition in the hold ". Lord Mountbatten discovered from personal discussions with the Leaders of the Moslem League that they would insist on partition at all costs and fight a civil war rather than accept transfer of power to a Hindu majority union, while Congress showed themselves as champions of unity, but not at the price of coercion. By the same token they insisted that no non-Moslem majority community should go against its will into Pakistan. Provided that was not done, they would raise no fundamental objection to partition. After seventy-three days of diplomacy by discussion involving unparalleled concentration of will and intensity of effort on the part of Lord Mountbatten, the 3rd June Plan was in principle accepted.

The Plan had three main features. First, it was partition within partition. The Punjab and Bengal, the communal composition of which were almost equal, were given the right to decide on their own partition prior to option for India or Pakistan. Mr. Jinnah, while stressing the tragedy of this step, was also unable to resist its logic. For some time there was possibility of Bengal separatism expressing itself, but this died away as the transfer of power drew near. As a result of this partition, West and East Pakistan were divided by some eight hundred miles. Secondly, it involved the partition of the Sikhs; this was the outcome of the partition of the Punjab, upon which the Sikh leaders insisted. Lord Mountbatten was surprised at the vehemence of their attitude, in view of the price they would have to pay for it, but was given no practicable alternative by them.

The third main feature was Dominion Status. This was a masterstroke on many grounds, but in particular because it made possible the maximum administrative and constitutional continuity, on the basis of the great India Act of 1935. As Lord Mountbatten himself said shortly after his return to England, " I know of no other country in the world to-day in the fortunate position of having a constitution that is already a working constitution, but which can be amended by a stroke of the pen day by day to be made to work more agreeably to themselves."

So much for the Plan; let us turn now to some of the major consequences of the partition of British India.

First of all it meant in effect an administrative within a political transfer of power. Action was at once taken to meet the demand for the partition of the magnificent Indian Army. A Supreme Command gave higher direction until its disbandment in November to this complex and delicate task. A Joint Defence Council meeting alternately in India and Pakistan, with Lord Mountbatten acting as chairman on behalf of both Governments, enabled steady contact on major military problems to be maintained right up to Lord Mountbatten's departure. It also provided a safety-valve at more than one moment of crisis for private consideration of all outstanding inter-Dominion disputes. A Partition Council was formed to deal with all civil issues, including transfer of assets and endless technicalities involved in partition. Finally an Arbitration Tribunal was appointed to give awards when agreement by other means had failed. Considering the range of the controversy involved, these instruments of partition worked with remarkable speed and administrative smoothness.

Provision was made in the Act, on Mr. Jinnah's suggestion, for Lord Mountbatten to be Governor-General of both Dominions, and for some time it seemed as if this might be acceptable, but at the last moment Mr. Jinnah decided otherwise. No doubt he was in the best position to judge, but in so far as India held the majority of physical assets, it was arguable that an interim joint Governor-Generalship might have been in the best interests of Pakistan.

The second major consequence was, of course, the violent communal reaction in the Punjab. In terms of the geography and population of India as a whole, the troubles were concentrated into a limited but vital area for both countries. The people rose up against their leaders' acceptance of partition. In this communal irruption twelve million Hindus,

Sikhs and Moslems were involved, and migration of some nine million people began overnight in an area the size of Wales. A far greater catastrophe was avoided only by an almost miraculous absence of large-scale famine and disease. I flew over columns of refugees stretching for more than sixty miles, creeping along narrow roads, the families carrying all their worldly goods in bullock-carts. There had been many communal migrations before, but never of this magnitude. Moreover, this time there would be no return.

For Pakistan the immediate danger was to the key Province of the West Punjab. They were receiving impoverished Moslems in place of wealthy Sikhs. For India the decisive threat was to Delhi, which was right in the epicentre of this earthquake. Before long some four hundred thousand refugees were moving on the capital, bringing in their wake suffering and bitterness. It was by her heroic efforts in organising relief for the refugees that Lady Mountbatten made her name immortal in India. Her dynamic but human personality, combined with her unique Red Cross and St. John experience, helped greatly to build up the morale and improve the conditions of thousands in the crowded refugee camps.

Within three weeks of Independence Day the Prime Minister, Pandit Nehru, and Deputy Prime Minister Patel, with great political courage, invited Lord Mountbatten, now constitutional Governor-General, to come down from Simla and take over the chairmanship of the Emergency Committee of the Cabinet. It assumed full war powers, and Government House itself became an operational headquarters. The Cabinet would meet there each morning and go into a Map Room, where the movements of the refugees and outbreaks of disturbances were pin-pointed on wall charts. As the days went by, it became evident that the situation was being held along the boundary of the East Punjab and United Provinces through the firm action taken both by the Provincial and Central Governments to halt refugee movement there. If the Government had shown weakness at that point, the trouble might well have spread across the whole of Northern India.

It may be asked whether all possible precautions were taken to meet this crisis, or whether something was left undone. In trying to answer this question I would suggest that the following considerations should be borne in mind.

Once the Leaders had accepted Partition it became impossible to maintain for very long the Interim Congress–Moslem League Coalition Government in Delhi. It was only with the utmost difficulty that this Government had been set up in 1946 and held together subsequently. Ever since March the Punjab had been administered on an emergency basis under Section 93 of the Government of India Act; but it was quite out of the question for the Central Government to function under that regulation as well. After 3rd June the Interim Government fell apart; each side wanted to take control of their respective sovereign States, and they could have been deflected only at the cost of the overthrow of the Partition Plan. Transfer of power, in the last analysis, was an unconditional act.

As a precaution against trouble following upon the Award of Sir Cyril Radcliffe, who, with the agreement of both Governments, had been invited to draw the actual boundary lines for the Punjab, Bengal and Sylhet, there was the largest concentration of troops ever known in the Punjab. In fact, a special Boundary Force was set up in the area directly affected. The task was found, however, to be quite beyond its resources, and by October command had to be handed back to the two new Governments.

In the dispersal of forces before 15th August, Independence Day, provision had to be made to meet the hardly less tense situation in Bengal and Calcutta. But here a completely different " Third Force " was to succeed in keeping the peace. It would have been impossible to have foreseen the miracle of Gandhi's moral influence, and wanton to have relied upon it in advance of the event. I have heard an expert estimate that the situation in the Punjab could have been restored only with double the amount of troops in fact employed (which would have meant some four divisions), and even then only on the assumption that they were all communally reliable.

Then there was the form taken by the Sikh rising. The operations were mostly carried out by small groups with cleverly planned mobile attacks on trains and villages. It was, in fact, a rank-and-file revolt, and any action to arrest the wilder Sikh leaders—seriously considered at the time, but rejected—would have been more likely to have touched off or intensified the disorder than to have brought it under control. The Punjab troubles must be regarded as a cataclysm, but in the context of India as a whole the fierce fire of communal madness consumed itself and was by resolute action at provincial level prevented from spreading further afield. Finally it should be remembered that Partition did not cause the communal crisis, it was the communal crisis that served to induce Partition.

One of the major consequences of Partition was its effect on the position of the Indian Princely States. Five hundred and sixty-five of them in all, ranging from Princes of States as large as European nations to landlords controlling a few thousand acres, they ruled over a third of the Indian sub-continent in area, and a quarter of it in population. They stood outside British India being in treaty relationship with Britain the Paramount Power. Thus the term Viceroy was a composite term covering the dual status and function of Governor-General of British India and Crown Representative of the Indian States. United, they might well have been a formidable factor in the situation, but when we arrived in India in March 1947 we found the Princes distracted and fatally weakened by great internal dissensions. On 25th July, after prolonged efforts to achieve some unity of purpose among them, Lord Mountbatten spoke to them in the Chamber of Princes for the last time in his capacity as Crown Representative. He took the initiative in advising them all to accede to one or other of the two new Dominions as the effective successor Powers to the British Raj.

The basic principle of Accession was that it was vested in the personal discretion of the Ruler, since he was an autocrat. But it was recognised that this discretion should be qualified by the geographical contiguity of the State to the successor Dominion, the communal composition of the State, and a plebiscite if necessary to ascertain the will of the people. Lord Mountbatten met with a remarkable measure of success, and all but three of the five hundred and sixty-five States had acceded by 14th August. They had recognised the force of his argument that voluntary mediatisation was their greatest chance of survival in a rapidly changing world; that the protection of British paramountcy was no longer a practicable source of authority, but that, as constitutional rulers, they could make a vital contribution to the political and social solidarity of the two new nations.

The constructive statesmanship of Congress, and in particular of Sardar Patel, the Deputy Prime Minister, who became the first Minister in charge of relations with the States, must be acknowledged. For acceptance of the survival of the Princes at all meant on the part of Congress a major reversal of long-established policy and avoidance of the temptation provided by an easy target.

Accession was to be followed closely by the Merger policy. Several great Princely blocs were formed. Of special importance were the Unions of the States of Orissa, Malwa (which includes Gwalior and Indore), Gujerat (involving a mosaic of some two hundred Princelings under the leadership of the Jam Sahib of Nawanagar), and the Phulkian Union of the leading Sikh Princes. One consequence of the settlement with the States was an approach suggested strongly by Mountbatten by the new Indian Government to individual Princes to undertake political and diplomatic duties outside their State boundaries. A ruling Prince was appointed Governor of Madras, and another became one of India's delegates to the United Nations. It had been a bloodless revolution and a political achievement of the first magnitude, largely lost sight of abroad on account of more lurid and dramatic news, among which must be counted events in those three States who failed to accede by 15th August.

There was first of all the case of Junagadh. This was not of primary importance in itself, but significant for the precedents it set. Junagadh was a small State of some five thousand square miles, with a Moslem ruler who finally acceded to Pakistan. By his action the twin principles of geographical contiguity and communal majority inherent in Accession were both violated. After various complicated negotiations, India took over the State, and a plebiscite confirmed popular acceptance of this action.

Junagadh was a mere curtain-raiser to the complex problem posed by the delayed accession of Kashmir. Lord Mountbatten himself had visited Kashmir in June, and armed with an assurance from Sardar Patel on the Indian side, strongly advised that any decision taken prior to 15th August would be acceptable to both successor States. The Maharaja, however, chose to ignore this opportunity, and only acceded to India on 26th October, when confronted by large-scale tribal invasion coming largely from the North-west Frontier Province of Pakistan. Here was a Hindu ruler with a State geographically continguous to both Dominions and the majority of his subjects Moslem. Kashmir's accession was rendered more complicated still by further special factors.

There was a powerful Kashmir States Congress movement led by Sheikh Abdullah, a Moslem Congressman of forceful personality and national status in India. Moreover, Nehru, himself descended from Kashmiri Brahmins, and Sheikh Abdullah were not only political colleagues, but also close personal friends.

But from the military viewpoint Kashmir is an area of great strategic importance to both countries. Pakistan has inherited the burden of the North-west Frontier, and a major conflict of interest between the two Governments along this line could gravely undermine the security—already strained by the partition of the Indian Army—of the entire sub-continent. It was soon clear that the Kashmir commitment would involve a dangerous drain of man-power and money and a distraction of effort going beyond the margin of safety or the dictates of prudence. For India in particular it means the deployment of her military strength to the maximum disadvantage along tenuous lines of communication and on a front where superiority of numbers and armour can rarely be exploited.

Finally there was the appeal to the United Nations by India at the peak of the crisis in December 1947, which gave the dispute an international status. There is no easy solution to Kashmir. In one sense it symbolises the general clash of sentiment and interest which made Partition inevitable. It may well be that there was inherent in any settlement of the general Congress–Moslem League conflict one outstanding and insoluble dispute. When the formula was the Cabinet Mission Plan, it was Assam; in the spring of 1947, it seemed, from the emphasis placed upon it by both Gandhi and Jinnah, that it would be the North-west Frontier Province. A turn of the wheel, and the clash might well have centred round Bengal or Calcutta. Moreover, both sides were sustained by fervent and not unfounded belief in the strength of their cause—Pakistan relying more on natural justice and economic necessity, and India more on legal right and political morality.

The third and perhaps most important State of all to stand outside Accession was Hyderabad. This, too, was a special case, with a Moslem Prince (direct descendant of the Moghul Emperor's Viceroy) and a small Moslem oligarchy as the governing caste; the State geographically in the heart of India, and the subjects eighty-six per cent Hindu. In view of the Nizam's special status, Lord Mountbatten, although now a constitutional Governor-General, was empowered to carry on negotiations for a Standstill Agreement with him beyond 14th August. But perhaps because of developments in Junagadh and Kashmir, or of expectations of support from opinion abroad, or from some inner compulsion, the Nizam tried to stall and play for time.

At the end of October a duly accredited delegation, including his Prime Minister and his constitutional adviser, Sir Walter Monckton, accepted the substance of a Standstill Agreement and returned to Hyderabad to recommend the Nizam's signature. His Legislative Council formally approved. The Nizam then excused himself from signing for a few hours, during which time members of the delegation, due to return to Delhi, were surrounded at their homes and subjected to physical intimidation by the Moslem extremist party, the Ittehad-ul-Muslimeen. When they saw the Nizam in the morning, they found that he had changed his mind, and they duly resigned. The Nizam, in the knowledge that he had already secured the maximum concessions from the Government of India, then blandly appointed a new delegation consisting entirely of Ittehad members.

After this bizarre episode it argues much for Lord Mountbatten's diplomatic resource that he was able to keep the negotiations alive at all. But he prevailed upon the Government of India to receive the new delegation, making it clear that he would not support the change of a single comma, and in November it reported back to the Nizam with precisely the same terms as before. This time he signed. He had gained a month's repite, but lost much of the Government of India's essential confidence in the process.

There followed moral and physical violations of the Standstill Agreement, which was valid for a year pending a final settlement. Hyderabad sponsored various acts to display her status as an independent nation. A loan was offered to Pakistan, and State Congress leaders were imprisoned without trial. But most provocative was the activity of Kasim Razvi, head of the Ittehad-ul-Muslimeen Party and of the Razakars, embryo storm-troopers. I met Razvi when I visited the Nizam on Lord Mountbatten's behalf in May 1948. I can only describe him as expressing the most violent race hatred I had encountered in anyone since a meeting I had with Forster, the Danzig Nazi, just before the war.

On the Indian side there was an undoubted blockade of the State, which included the stopping even of medical supplies. Most of this obstruction seemed to be organised at Provincial levels; but while the Central Government did not authorise it, neither did they succeed in bringing it effectively to an end. Then there was Communist intervention, which was designed to embarrass and confuse both sides.

Britain never recognised Hyderabad's title to independence, and in a famous letter to the Nizam in 1926, Lord Reading laid down that Britain's relationship was one of undoubted Paramountcy. It was unreasonable to expect that the successor Power, consisting of Hyderabad's kith and kin, should now concede what the British Raj had so consistently refused. Right up to the eve of his departure it seemed that Lord Mountbatten might find a formula to cover Hyderabad's final relations with India, but unhappily it was not to be. Three months after he left, a military demonstration and occupation was provided to clinch the argument.

Some of the Indian diplomacy on the spot was undoubtedly clumsy, and the presentation of their case throughout was generally deplorable. India has been severely criticised for forcing the pace, but it has to be remembered that in giving the Nizam more time they would also have been allowing Razvi and his fanatical movement fresh scope. Indian intervention effectively checked the spread of communal violence and insured political consolidation throughout South India.

The Nizam, with his love of diplomatic finesse, left himself just enough margin to save his dynasty. As the leading Prince in India, his great mistake had been retirement into his State as a result of the clash with Lord Reading in 1926, and complete withdrawal from central affairs thereafter. From his isolation he failed in 1947 to recognise the meaning of Partition, which inevitably involved the setting up of two strong Central Governments instead of one weak one.

The shock of change was intensified by the deaths, so soon after the transfer of power, of the two great national leaders, Gandhi and Jinnah. I cannot presume to assess the full measure of Gandhi's moral and spiritual stature, but his political power and personal magnetism, judging by the devotion he aroused in millions from one end of the sub-continent to the other, can have few precedents in history. He had an amazing instinct for the mass propagation of ideas, reinforced by the direct contacts which he assiduously encouraged through his Prayer Meetings and vast correspondence with people in all walks of life.

Jinnah, on the other hand, derived his authority from remote control. He made no concessions to the masses and had no contact with them. He combined tactical suppleness and capacity to profit from his opponents' mistakes with an iron will and the maintenance of the single objective. He was an unique phenomenon, in that he conceived of Pakistan at the age of sixty and realised it at seventy. Like Gandhi, he was steeped in the idiom and outlook of British law, but had virtually no interest in or understanding of the administration of government.

Fortunately for both countries, Jawaharlal Nehru in India and Liaquat Ali Khan in Pakistan, statesmen of the first rank by any standards of comparison, whether in the eastern or western world, survived to lead middle-of-the-road and middle-aged Governments and to undertake fairly late in life a major re-orientation of ideas with the disappearance from the arena of the two basic opponents of the Congress and the Moslem League. For the British helped to keep the Congress together and the Congress the Moslem League.

Inside India the Congress was assailed both from the right and left. During Lord Mountbatten's time the Mahasabha—the Hindu communal counterpart of the Moslem League, with aspirations to emulate and counteract the Moslem League's political success—was always active, but was unable to canalise Hindu resentment at Partition sufficiently to thwart the 3rd June Plan. Subsequently the Mahasabha suffered a serious setback as the result of its suspected complicity in Gandhi's assassination; but, for all that, it remained a formidable force.

The Socialists, under the leadership of Jai Prakash Narain, lost valuable time and opportunity in making up their minds whether to bid for office as a ginger group within the Congress or to reinvigorate the Legislative Assembly by constructive Parliamentary Opposition. By wavering they simply provided fresh openings for the Communists, who under the war-time "Grand Alliance" had been léft free to co-operate with the British Raj, while the Congress High Command languished in gaol. The Partition decision, however, and in particular the force of communal sentiment in Bengal, came as a blow to the Communists, who had concentrated most of their effort in the industrial slums of Calcutta, and had directed their propaganda strongly against the division of India.

After the transfer of power, Communist effort seemed to move from Bengal to the South. There was a big conference of Communists from South-east Asia under Indian leadership early in 1948, in which there were signs of the usual deviationist troubles. Communism is likely to provide a potential threat to the Congress just so long as there is extensive misery to exploit.

While Pakistan derived its inspirations from providing a Moslem homeland, the Indian Union aimed at creating loyalty to a secular democracy. With some forty million Moslems left after Partition on the Indian side of the border, not to mention eight million Christians, six million Sikhs and other smaller communities, India is certainly something more than a Hindu state. Gandhi himself was to become a martyr in the cause of Hindu-Moslem solidarity.

The Indian constitution, which was under active preparation and discussion during Lord Mountbatten's term of office, is a synthesis of the great Western charters of liberty. The obvious hiatus between the vision of this document and the realities of Indian life does not destroy the validity of the vision. It represents a great tribute to the liberalising influence of British thought, and is a fundamental attack upon the aims and aspirations of communalism. The Indian constitution offers fresh hope for the eighty million Untouchables, who under purely Hindu dogma were pariahs polluting food with their shadow, but are now Indian citizens with equal rights before the law. One of the principal personalities in Nehru's Government, and as such a prominent personality in the preparation and sponsorship of the Constitution, was Dr. Ambedkar, the well-known leader of the Untouchables.

Economically, Pakistan, in spite of the initial disasters, quickly showed herself to be a viable State with the supreme asset of a solvent agricultural economy. There was a surplus of food and jute in the first Pakistan budget. India, however, was soon suffering from inflation, and, in response to the Gandhian ethic, rather than on grounds of strict economic justification, from the altogether too rapid removal of controls over basic commodities. The controls had to be clamped on again, but the operation was difficult and the damage had been done.

The transfer of power was an unique response to an essentially revolutionary situation. It is usual for revolutions to get out of control and defy the calculations of those who lead them. Perhaps Lord Mountbatten's greatest achievement lay in producing a solution which had about it sufficient substance and support to survive the storm of the immediate revolutionary crisis and to maintain in spite of Partition the vital links between the past and the future.

Independence through Partition was not the culmination of the long cherished aim, but it was none the less the response to a challenge as real as it was to many surprising. It is not sufficient to say that if the requisite statesmanship had been forthcoming unity could have been preserved. A wealth of British genius and eminence, talent and service had been thrown into the task of its nourishment. The conflict that had preceded Warren

Hastings was not to be liquidated with the departure of Mountbatten, but a *modus vivendi* was achieved based upon equity, compromise and acceptance if not agreement after discussion. It is in the controversies settled rather than in the communal traumas and tragedies immediately surrounding it that the long term historical significance of the transfer of power will be seen to lie. Constitutionally the British Commonwealth was transformed and its political theory enlarged. But it was perhaps in the psychological field that the greatest revolution of all occurred. In advance of any final definitions of Commonwealth membership Indo-British relations under Mountbatten's imaginative leadership had already improved be-yond all expectation. Subordinate status had become as hateful to impose as to bear. Cutting across the pretensions of the free world, sapping the strength of the whole democratic cause was a tragic discrepancy between theory and practice in racial relations and a widening gulf between the aspirations of East and West. It is my belief that the voluntary transfer of power from the British Raj to India and Pakistan served to reverse these two most dangerous trends in the history of the modern world. By bringing such a vast proportion of the white and coloured races together on terms of an equality unforced because mutually recognised it pointed the way to an integration of peoples which no amount of planning from above could on its own achieve.

The movements of mass opinion are still largely phenomena wrapped in mystery. But the extraordinary revolution in sentiment that undoubtedly took place in India in August 1947 was not just a single overwhelming demonstration of popular joy and goodwill. An enduring reconciliation occurred too strong for propaganda to create or destroy. For those of us wholly absorbed in the final phase and caught up in the celebrations of Independence it was easy to overlook that there lay behind the event traditions of honour and trust over two centuries which, when the time came to go, engendered neither bitterness nor taunts but generous thoughts and warm emotions. Both Britain and India, as Nehru pointed out, are essentially Mother civilisations. We emerged from the transfer of power as friends and equals and we would be worse than fools if we ever allowed estrangement to creep in again. For the implications of this upsurge of goodwill reach out beyond the reckonings of our own day and age.

PRINCIPAL PERSONALITIES

In the course of this narrative more than two hundred and fifty names of prominent personalities are mentioned. Many of the references are only incidental and most of them self-explanatory. Footnotes have been kept to a minimum. With the coming of Independence the functions and duties of many of the leaders and officials either changed or were terminated. The following are some of the principal *dramatis personæ*, with (where applicable) their official positions before and after 15th August, 1947 (Independence Day), within the period covered by this book. Cross-references are provided wherever Christian names or abbreviated titles have been used. It should be noted that C.O.H.Q. and S.E.A.C. refer to Combined Operations Headquarters and South-east Asia Command (Lord Mountbatten's two major War Commands).

ABDULLAH, Sheikh, Leader of the National Conference Party in Kashmir State. After accession to India was appointed Prime Minister by the Maharaja of Kashmir. Member of Indian delegation to United Nations, January 1948.

ABELL, G. E. B. (later Sir George), Private Secretary to the Viceroy (P.S.V.).

ALI, Mir Laik, President of the Nizam's Council from November 1947.

AMRIT KAUR, Rajkumari, Mahatma Gandhi's Secretary; Minister for Health in the Government of the Dominion of India.

AUCHINLECK, Field-Marshal Sir Claude, Commander-in-Chief in India until 15th August; Supreme Commander administering partition of Indian Army until 30th November, 1947.

AYYENGAR, Gopalaswami, Minister without Portfolio in the Government of the Dominion of India; Leader of Indian delegation to United Nations in January 1948.

BALDEV SINGH, Sardar, Sikh leader; Member for Defence in the Interim Government; Minister for Defence in the Government of the Dominion of India.

BHABHA, C. H., Member for Works, Mines and Power in the Interim Government; Minister for Commerce in the Government of the Dominion of India.

BHOPAL, The Nawab of, Ruler of Bhopal State; Chancellor of the Chamber of Princes until May 1947.

BIKANER, The Maharaja of, Ruler of Bikaner State.

BRABOURNE, Lord and Lady, son-in-law and elder daughter of Earl and Countess Mountbatten of Burma.

BROCKMAN, Captain (S.) R.V., R.N., Personal Secretary to the Viceroy; Private Secretary to the Governor-General of India from 15th August, 1947.

CURRIE, Colonel D. H., Military Secretary to the Viceroy and to the Governor-General of India.

CHHATARI, The Nawab of, President of the Nizam's Council from May 1947 to November 1947.

CHRISTIE, W. H. J., Joint Private Secretary to the Viceroy (J.P.S.V.).

C. R. refers to C. Rajagopalachari.

ERSKINE CRUM, Lieutenant-Colonel V. F., Conference Secretary to the Viceroy; and to the Governor-General of India.

GANDHI, Mahatma, "Father of the Nation".

GANDHI, Devadas, Managing Editor of the *Hindustan Times*, and son of the Mahatma.

GEORGE refers to Sir George Abell and to Commander Nicholls, according to context.

GILLIAT, Major M. J., Deputy Military Secretary to the Viceroy and to the Governor-General of India.

HOWES, Lieutenant Commander Peter, R.N., Senior ADC to the Viceroy and to the Governor-General of India.

HYDERABAD, The Nizam of, Ruler of Hyderabad State.

ISMAY, Lord, Chief of the Viceroy's Staff; and of the Governor-General of India's Staff until December 1947.

JENKINS, Sir Evan, Governor of the Punjab until 15th August, 1947.

JINNAH, Mohammed Ali (Quaid-e-Azam), President of the All India Moslem League; first Governor-General of the Dominion of Pakistan.

KASHMIR, The Maharaja of, Ruler of Jammu and Kashmir State.

KRIPALANI, Acharya J. B., President of Congress.

LIAQUAT ALI KHAN, General Secretary of the All India Moslem League; Member for Finance in the Interim Government; Prime Minister of the Government of the Dominion of Pakistan.

LOCKHART, Lieutenant-General Sir Rob, General Officer Commanding-in-Chief, Southern Command, India; Governor of the North-west Frontier Province from June to 15th August, 1947; Commander-in-Chief Indian Army, Dominion of India, 15th August, 1947, to January 1948.

MATTHAI, Dr. John, Member for Transport and Railways in the Interim Government; Minister for Transport and Railways in the Government of the Dominion of India.

MENON, V. K. Krishna, High Commissioner for India in the United Kingdom from August 1947.

MENON, V. P., Reforms Commissioner to the Viceroy; and from July 1947 Secretary of the States Department, Government of the Dominion of India.

MIÉVILLE, Sir Eric, Principal Secretary to the Viceroy.

MOHAMMED ALI, Financial Adviser in the Military Finance Department of the Government of India; Member of the Steering Committee of the Partition Council; Secretary-General of the Dominion of Pakistan.

MONCKTON, Sir Walter, Constitutional Adviser to the Nizam of Hyderabad.

MOUNTBATTEN OF BURMA, Rear-Admiral the Viscount (created Earl, August 1947), last Viceroy of India, 22nd March to 14th August, 1947. First Governor-General of the Dominion of India, 15th August, 1947, to 21st June, 1948.

MOUNTBATTEN OF BURMA, Countess, wife of the last Viceroy and first Governor-General of India.

MOUNTBATTEN, the Lady Pamela, younger daughter of Earl and Countess Mountbatten of Burma.

MUNSHI, K. M., Agent-General for India in Hyderabad from December 1947.

NEHRU, Pandit Jawaharlal, Member for External Affairs and Commonwealth Relations in the Interim Government; Vice-President of the Interim Government; Prime Minister of the Dominion of India.

NICHOLLS, Commander (S.) G.H., R.N., Deputy Personal Secretary to the Viceroy; Deputy Private Secretary to the Governor-General of India from 15th August, 1947.

NISHTAR, Sardar Abdur Rab, Member for Communications in the Interim Government; Minister for Communications and States in the Government of the Dominion of Pakistan.

PATEL, H. M., Secretary of the Indian Cabinet; Member of the Steering Committee of the Partition Council.

PATEL, Sardar Vallabhbhai, Member for Home Affairs and for Information and Broadcasting, and from July 1947 for States in the Interim Government; Deputy Prime Minister of the Dominion of India.

PATIALA, Maharaja of, Ruler of Patiala State, and from May to August 1947 last Chancellor of the Chamber of Princes.

PRASAD, Dr. Rajendra, Member for Food and Agriculture in the Interim Government and President of the Constituent Assembly.

RAJAGOPALACHARI, Chakravarti, Member for Industries and Supplies in the Interim Government; Governor of Bengal after 15th August, 1947, and first Indian Governor-General of the Dominion of India, 21st June, 1948.

REES, Major-General T. W., Commander Punjab Boundary Force July to September 1947; Head of Governor-General's (India) Military Emergency Staff September to December 1947.

RONNIE, refers to Captain (S.) R. V. Brockman, R.N.

SCOTT, C. P., Assistant Private Secretary to the Viceroy (A.P.S.V.).

SCOTT, I. D., Deputy Secretary to the Viceroy (D.P.S.V.).

TRIVEDI, Sir Chandulal, Governor of Orissa, Governor of East Punjab
    from 15th August, 1947.
VERNON, refers to Lieutenant-Colonel V. F. Erskine Crum.
V. P. refers to V. P. Menon.

INDEX

INDEX

to succeed Lord Wavell as Viceroy, 17; Naval career, 17, 19; agreement with Wavell's policy, 18; reply to Prime Minister's offer, 19; acceptance of Viceroyalty, 19; additional Vice-regal Staff, 20; Combined Operations, South-East Asia Command, 21, 43; Public Relations, 21; Chester Street, 17, 21, 34; Viceroy's House, 21, 38, 41, 49; a wide mandate and time limit, 22; Princely States, the, 22, 47, 48; Constituent Assembly, 22, 43, 48; temporary offices, 23; Press reactions to appointment, 23; debate on appointment, House of Lords, 25; debate, House of Commons, 26–9; previous visits to India, 29–30; first meeting with Nehru, 30; Governor-General's Instrument of Instructions, major points of, 31; Indian Civil and Military Services, compensation of, 33, 43; Indian Sterling, Balances, 33; Royal Automobile Club, party at, 35

Flight to India, 35; arrival at Delhi, 38; arrival at Viceroy's house, 39; letters to Gandhi and Jinnah, 41; Swearing-in Ceremony, 41–2; absence of Nawab of Bhopal and Maharaja of Bikaner, 43–4; meets Nehru and Liaquat on Budget, 43; Staff Meetings, 43, 45, 46, 51, 71, 102, 115, 116; meets Patel, 46; Asian Relations Conference garden party, 49; Indian National Army, liquidation of, 52; strives to keep Cabinet Mission Plan alive, 55, 56, 60, 70; Diplomacy of discussion, 56, 58; Armed Forces, alleged inadequate representation of Moslems in, 58; proposes truce in communal disturbances, 59; British Residents, dinner to, 60; Gandhi–Jinnah " Peace Appeal ", 61; Simla house-party, 62; his Plan, broad principles of, 62; Governors' conference, 64–6; Sikh Leaders, his interview with, 66; Liaquat on Wavell, 69; considers Dominion Status formula, 70; session with Jinnah, 70; The Plan, first draft considered; Partition not a foregone conclusion; Hindu majority's voting power; plebiscite for Calcutta, 71; Ismay and Abell take draft of Plan to London, 72

Visits North-West Frontier Province, 74; Moslem League demonstration, 74; interviews local Leaders and residents, 75–7; hears plea for return of the Khyber from tribal *Jirga*,

78; attitude of tribesmen, 79; arrival at Rawalpindi, visits Kahuta, inspects riot-torn area, 79; favours concept that only British India as a whole remains in Commonwealth, 81; visits Simla, 82–3; Press attack upon, 84; asks V.P. to prepare alternative Demission Plan, 86; Dominion Status, Nehru's and Krishna Menon's reactions, 87; Nehru's rejection of Draft Plan revised by London, postponement of meeting with the five Leaders and Indian States Representatives, 88; second revised draft Plan prepared by Staff to be presented to Nehru and Jinnah; fails to obtain signatures of Jinnah and Liaquat to V. P.'s Heads of Agreement, 93; departure for London, 94; good progress with British Cabinet, 95

Back in Delhi, 97; meeting with Leaders (2nd June), 99–100; distinction between agreement and acceptance, 100; meeting with Gandhi (Day of Silence), 101; Partition, administrative consequences of, 102, 104, 112, 121; Jinnah's midnight meeting, 103; second meeting with Leaders, 104; meets States' negotiating Committee, 105; broadcasts over All India Radio, 106; Press conference, 108; assumptions regarding Jinnah and Governors-General, 115; visits Kashmir, 120; Field-Marshal Montgomery, dinner, 122; forty-seventh birthday, 122; Sylhet referendum, 124; Armed Forces, division of, 125; as Governor-General of Dominion of India, 128; urged to accept Congress invitation (Campbell-Johnson's note), 128–30; calls on members of Interim Government to resign, 130; reconstruction as two Provisional Administrations, 138; sponsors Instrument of Accession, 139, 147; address to Princes, 140–2; Princes, reception of, 144; leaves for Calcutta, 145; alleged implication of Sikh leaders in sabotage plans, action in regard to arrests of, 149; broadcast celebration of V.J. day, 151; leaves for Karachi; last duty as Viceroy, 154; speech on creation of Pakistan, 155; last telegrams as Viceroy, 156; Constituent Assembly's invitation to become first Governor-General, 157

Created Earl, 158; inauguration as Governor-General, 158; address to Constituent Assembly—crowd scenes, 159; gifts to children, 160; at War

HAMISH HAMILTON PAPERBACKS

'Among the most collectable of paperback imprints . . .'
Christopher Hudson, *The Standard*

All books in the Hamish Hamilton Paperback series are available at your
local bookshop or can be ordered by post. A full list of titles and an order
form can be found at the end of this book.

QUEEN VICTORIA
Her Life and Times 1819–1861

Cecil Woodham-Smith

A new conception of Queen Victoria emerged from this biography. Mrs.
Woodham-Smith had access to previously unused information and her
book established once and for all the true character of the young Victoria.
Its publication was a landmark in historical research. Intensely readable
and sympathetic, this biography deals with the Queen's wretched
childhood, her passionate nature, her devotion to the Prince Consort and
her native shrewdness in politics. Sadly the author did not live to
complete the second volume of this life, but her word on the young
Queen is unrivalled.

'. . . unlikely ever to be surpassed.' Michael Ratcliffe, *The Times*

'. . . quite indispensable to any student of this peculiar sovereign.' Paul
Johnson, *Guardian*

ALBERT, PRINCE CONSORT

Robert Rhodes James

A man of outstanding ability, Albert, Queen Victoria's Consort and
husband, has had a lasting influence upon the history of his time and on
the development of the British Constitutional Monarchy. His
achievements were innumerable: the reformation of Cambridge
University, the organization of the Great Exhibition of 1851, the building
of Osborne and Balmoral, and his promotion of social reform and town
planning, to name but a few. In this extremely readable biography,
Robert Rhodes James does full justice to this talented, complex man.

'Prince Albert was a man of great character and of noble achievement. In
Robert Rhodes James's book he receives a worthy tribute. Indeed this is
one of the finest biographies I have ever read.' A. J. P. Taylor, *Observer*

ASQUITH

Stephen Koss

In this outstanding political biography, Stephen Koss traces with masterly insight the controversial career of H. H. Asquith, the man who has been regarded as both the victim and the agent of the Liberal decline.

'This is the best biography of Asquith yet to be written and a book indispensable to every lover of political history.' A. J. P. Taylor, *New Statesman*

'Professor Koss's style is easy, and agreeably astringent. . . . His assembling of the materials conceals the enormous trouble he has taken both to evaluate the latest sources and to slip these almost effortlessly into context.' Andrew Boyle, *Listener*

ANOTHER PART OF THE WOOD
A Self Portrait

Kenneth Clark

Kenneth Clark's sharp witty account of his eccentric Edwardian upbringing and his swift success in the world of art after leaving Oxford is a classic of its kind and a pleasure to read.

'An immensely entertaining memoir . . . rich in deliciously dry tales . . . all told with perfect brevity and wit.' Michael Ratcliffe, *The Times*

'A stylish, dazzling work flecked with touches of learning and imagination, wit and malice.' Kenneth Rose, *Sunday Telegraph*

THE LIFE OF ARTHUR RANSOME

Hugh Brogan

For a man who longed for a quiet existence, Arthur Ransome had an extraordinarily adventurous life comprising two stormy marriages, a melodramatic libel suit, and a ringside view of the Russian Revolution. In this absorbing book, Hugh Brogan writes with sympathy and affection of the author of some of the best loved books for children.

'The wonder is, from Mr Brogan's enthralling account, that Ransome ever got down to writing *Swallows and Amazons* at all.' A. N. Wilson, *Sunday Telegraph*

HUGH WALPOLE

Rupert Hart-Davis

'Rupert Hart-Davis's book is a remarkable feat of understanding and restraint. . . . He shows us the man himself, and the spectacle is delightful.' Edwin Muir

'Fully to appreciate how remarkable an achievement is Mr Hart-Davis's biography of Hugh Walpole, it is necessary to read the book. No summarised comment can convey the complexity of the task accomplished or the narrative skill, restraint and self-effacement with which it has been carried through.' Michael Sadleir

BEYOND FRONTIERS

Jasper Parrott with Vladimir Ashkenazy

Vladimir Ashkenazy is known throughout the world as one of the greatest pianists of our time. Despite his fame he is a very private man, but his experiences as a child prodigy under the Soviet system and his subsequent emigration to the West have affected so profoundly his views about music, politics and people that this book has grown out of his wish to share these thoughts with others—to communicate in a medium other than music.

' . . . a far cry from the usual collection of amiable anecdotes surrounding the life of a virtuoso. Instead, it is an examination of the thoughts, musical and political, of a great artist, written with intelligence, wit, and even wisdom.' André Previn

DIAGHILEV

Richard Buckle

This first full-length life of Diaghilev to appear for nearly forty years contains much new material about the great Russian creator of modern ballet. Boris Kochno has placed at the author's disposal Diaghilev's unpublished memoirs and supplied endless details about his work and life. The full story is told of Diaghilev's extraordinary undertakings. The evolution of the new Russian Ballet, its crises during the period of Fokine and Nijinsky, and the wartime years with Massine are described in fascinating detail. Richard Buckle's insight into Diaghilev's mind enables him to write with authority about the triumphs, disasters and outstanding vision of a creative genius.

'An epic, marvellously colourful, copiously detailed story—not only a life of the man himself but a chronicle of the artistic revolutions of which he was master-strategist.' Max Loppert, *Financial Times*

MRS. PAT
The Life of Mrs. Patrick Campbell

Margot Peters

Beautiful, witty, talented, Mrs. Patrick Campbell became a legend in her own lifetime. Her theatrical career encompassed tremendous triumphs and unmitigated failures. Her private life was controversial and tragic. In this superb biography Margot Peters captures the magnetism of an outstanding actress and extraordinary woman, who remains today as intriguing as ever.

'The book has been researched with exemplary care and accuracy. The famous bons mots—nearly always witty, sometimes cruel and personal, but usually devastatingly apt—are quoted with appropriate relish. There is a wealth of material, never before made public, to enthrall the reader.'
John Gielgud, *Observer*

TWO FLAMBOYANT FATHERS

Nicolette Devas

'A marvellous account of growing up in the artistic Bohemia of the 1920s with friends and mentors including the still-roaring Augustus John and the young Dylan Thomas, who was to marry her sister Caitlin. Candid, touching and engrossing: one of the finest autobiographies of our time.'—Philip Oakes

MARY BERENSON:
A Self Portrait from Her Letters and Diaries

eds. Barbara Strachey & Jayne Samuels

This superbly edited book of extracts from Mary Berenson's letters and diaries provides an absorbing picture of her extraordinary complex relationship with Bernard Berenson, and of their life and work together in Italy.

'Mary . . . writes with a startling, unsettling, often hilarious candour which makes it hard to put the book down.'—Hilary Spurling, *Observer*

A DURABLE FIRE:
The Letters of Duff and Diana Cooper 1913–1950

ed. Artemis Cooper

For long periods before and after their marriage in 1919 Duff and Diana Cooper were apart, but they wrote to each other constantly, witty, gossipy letters that have been admirably edited by their granddaughter to form this delightful collection.

'It is rare to find a correspondence duo in which both sides are of equivalent verve and strength . . . a unique, inside account of a charmed circle whose members governed England between the wars.'—Anthony Curtis, *Financial Times*

NANCY MITFORD	Harold Acton	£4.95 ☐
MEMOIRS OF AN AESTHETE	Harold Acton	£5.95 ☐
A CACK-HANDED WAR*	Edward Blishen	£3.95 ☐
UNCOMMON ENTRANCE*	Edward Blishen	£3.95 ☐
THE DREAM KING	Wilfrid Blunt	£4.95 ☐
THE LIFE OF ARTHUR RANSOME	Hugh Brogan	£4.95 ☐
DIAGHILEV	Richard Buckle	£6.95 ☐
MISSION WITH MOUNTBATTEN	Alan Campbell-Johnson	£5.95 ☐
AUTOBIOGRAPHY	Neville Cardus	£4.95 ☐
ANOTHER PART OF THE WOOD	Kenneth Clark	£4.95 ☐
A DURABLE FIRE	ed. Artemis Cooper	£4.95 ☐
TWO FLAMBOYANT FATHERS	Nicolette Devas	£4.95 ☐
PETER HALL'S DIARIES	ed. John Goodwin	£5.95 ☐
HUGH WALPOLE	Rupert Hart-Davis	£6.95 ☐
ASQUITH	Stephen Koss	£4.95 ☐
VOLTAIRE IN LOVE	Nancy Mitford	£4.95 ☐
A LIFE OF CONTRASTS	Diana Mosley	£4.95 ☐
BEYOND FRONTIERS		
	Jasper Parrott with Vladimir Ashkenazy	£4.95 ☐
MRS PAT	Margot Peters	£5.95 ☐
THE SECRET ORCHARD OF ROGER ACKERLEY	Diana Petre	£4.95 ☐
ALBERT PRINCE CONSORT	Robert Rhodes James	£4.95 ☐
MARY BERENSON		
	eds. Barbara Strachey and Jayne Samuels	£4.95 ☐
THE YEARS WITH ROSS*	James Thurber	£4.95 ☐
THE DRAGON EMPRESS	Marina Warner	£4.95 ☐
QUEEN VICTORIA	Cecil Woodham-Smith	£5.95 ☐

All titles 198 × 126mm, and all contain 8 pages of black and white illustrations except for those marked*.

All books in the Hamish Hamilton Paperback Series are available at your local bookshop, or can be ordered direct from Media Services. Just tick the titles you want and fill in the form below.

Name _____

Address _____

_____

Write to Media Services, PO Box 151, Camberley, Surrey GU15 3BE.

Please enclose cheque or postal order for the cover price plus postage:

UK: 55p for the first book, 24p for each additional book to a maximum of £1.75.

OVERSEAS: £1.05 for the first book, 35p for each additional book to a maximum of £2.80.

Hamish Hamilton Ltd reserve the right to show new retail prices on covers which may differ from those previously advertised in the text or elsewhere, and to increase postal rates in accordance with the PO.